SHADOW
OF A DOUBT

SHADOW OF A DOUBT

SKYLAR JAMES

INTERIOR ILLUSTRATIONS BY
KELLEY McMORRIS

 ADAPTIVE BOOKS

AN IMPRINT OF ADAPTIVE STUDIOS
CULVER CITY, CA

Copyright © 2015 Adaptive Studios Inc.
First paperback edition, 2017

Visit us on the web at
www.adaptivestudios.com

Library of Congress Cataloging-in-Publication Data
James, Skylar
Shadow of a Doubt / by Skylar James

B&N ISBN 978-1-945293-20-7 (paperback)
ISBN 978-0-9864484-4-7 (ebook)
[1. Horses—Fiction. 2. Friendship—Fiction. 3. Kentucky Derby—
Fiction. 4. Single Parent Families—Fiction. 5. Equestrian—Fiction.]

Printed in the United States of America.

Interior design by Neuwirth & Associates.

Adaptive Books
3578 Hayden Avenue, Suite 6
Culver City, CA 90232

10 9 8 7 6 5 4 3 2 1

For Dar.

SHADOW
OF A DOUBT

Prologue

I RECKON YOU'VE COME to hear the story of Shadow of a Doubt and how he came to be known as the finest horse in all of Jessamine County, the great state of Kentucky, and the world over. Mind you, I say this is the story of how that came to be *known*, not how it came to *be*, seeing as how Shadow had greatness inside of him from the moment he was born. And if there was one person who knew that better than anybody, it was Fyfe Flynn. Fyfe had what some might consider a peculiar childhood, in that she spent more time around horses than people, and as a result she had become a keen judge of equestrian character. She knew Shadow was something special right away. She felt it in her bones the first time she ever laid eyes on him.

Fyfe told anyone who would listen that Shadow was the finest horse that ever was, and she didn't say it lightly. She had seen pictures of those Arabian horses they've got out there in the desert. They were beauties all right. So were the Clydesdales, which could grow to be over six feet tall and nearly two thousand pounds. Once, she even saw an Appaloosa at a county fair that could write his name in the dirt with his hoof. No doubt about it, those were some mighty fine horses. But Shadow? Well, he was just plain something else. . . . He had heart.

But it's no use trying to understand what things were like with Shadow in the picture if you don't understand what they were like when he wasn't. That's why Shadow's story starts some years ago, long before his own humble beginning, back when Fyfe was barely even nine, and before heaven opened up and gave this world the best doggone horse it'd ever seen.

1

CHURCHILL DOWNS LOOMED grand in the foreground on a steamy May afternoon. The majesty of the place was inescapable. It hung thick in the air cut with buzzing mosquitos and the excited chatter of the well-heeled crowd. It was in the smell of horses and fresh cut grass. It was in the energy and optimism of the standing room only working class mobs, come to put borrowed money on a hunch. It was in the history beaten into that track by thoroughbred hooves, again and again every year since the illustrious Kentucky Derby was first run in 1875.

The twin spires of the landmark grandstand stretched high into the air: the Bluegrass answer to skyscrapers. The crowd would swell to more than 150,000 race fans that day.

Welcome to the Run for the Roses, known the world over as the most exciting two minutes in sports. Where heroes are tested, legends are born, and history is made. This here's the Kentucky Derby.

"Peanuts! Get your peanuts here!" Fyfe Flynn barked to the bustling crowd. A tray full of roasted peanuts hung from her neck by a worn leather strap. The low-slung brim of her cap shielded her eyes from the hot southern sun. "Hot, fresh, peanuts here. Get 'em before the horses do!"

Fyfe was nine years old, but you wouldn't know it by looking at her, on account of her being small and all. Small ran in her family. Her daddy was small his whole life and her granddaddy never grew to be more than five feet tall in all his days. But Fyfe didn't pay no mind to size. She was spirited and industrious and one look at her would tell you as much. She had a curious button nose dotted with freckles and a mess of light brown hair. She was rail thin, owing to a genetic predisposition and a complete inability to sit still. She was all hustle and gumption as she jostled her way through the crowd undeterred, fighting against the crush of race fans like a salmon swimming upstream.

"Hey there, mister." Fyfe shuffled across a full row

of seats, making her way toward a heavyset man with a push-broom mustache and his wife in her Sunday best. "Enjoying the races? See you brought the missus with you. Lovely hat, ma'am." The missus was tickled pink and the mustache was not amused.

"Well, aren't you sweet?" the woman replied and nudged her husband, "Frank, give her some money for the peanuts."

"I don't want peanuts," the mustache gruffly answered back, refusing to take his eyes from the daily racing form.

"That's beside the point."

"How many bags can I do you for?" Fyfe chirped.

"Just the one we don't want in the first place," the mustache grumbled. He begrudgingly dug in his pocket for some money and Fyfe shoveled a scoop of peanuts into a paper bag. The mustache held out the money but pulled it back as Fyfe reached for it. "You been back to the stables?"

"Sure I have!"

"Who do you like in the sixth?"

"Firestarter's favored to win."

"Says that right here." He gestured to the tip sheet. "But who do *you* like?"

"I've got my eye on Rocky Road."

The mustache laughed. "Alright, forget it then."

"Forget nothing. I'm telling you, it's Rocky Road in the sixth."

"The odds are thirteen to one."

"The bookmakers don't like him 'cause he finished bad in his last race, but that track was sloppy. This one's dry as a bone, and they laid new topsoil this morning."

"Is that so?"

"And he's posting in first position. Right up on the rail is his sweet spot."

"How old are you, kid?"

"Nine. But I've been told I'm an old soul."

Fyfe handed over the peanuts and the mustache paid her, then tossed her an additional coin. "Here's a little something extra. Penny for your thoughts, as they say." To the man's surprise, Fyfe tossed the coin back to him. "Put it on Rocky Road for me." She winked and turned on her heels. "Peanuts here! Hot and salty!"

"Hey Fyfe," The concession manager got her attention. "Run some peanuts up to first class."

"Right away, boss." She started up the long set of stairs that lead from the stands to the boxes.

"Oh, and Fyfe," the manager called after her, "careful not to breathe too heavy. The air gets awful thin up there."

The open-air boxes of first class were front row seats to the lap of luxury. Tall, frosty mint juleps and elaborate ladies' headwear (everything from bonnets to faux birds' nests) were dead giveaways for the Derby. It's a good thing, too, otherwise you might not have known you were at the races: Up here in the box seats, you needed opera glasses to actually see the horses.

Colonel Ansel Epsom had a bellowing laugh that let loose like a roar and filled the first class box. The Colonel always wore a white linen suit with a plaid bow tie and corresponding pocket square. The pocket square remained neatly and precisely folded in his breast pocket as long as all was going well. But if one of the Colonel's horses began to fall behind in the race (an event which rarely ever happened, and *never* happened twice), he would remove the square from its pocket and discreetly dab the flop sweat from his brow.

The Colonel was the patriarch of a prominent Southern family. Horse racing was in his blood. The Epsom lineage had trained generations of thoroughbreds, and had laid claim to a wealth of Derby prizes over the years. Unfortunately, their perennial winning streak had taken its toll on the Colonel's humility. His nose was so high he could drown in a rainstorm.

The Colonel's wife, on the other hand, was given to such silly trifles as kindness, humor, and on rare, special occasions, even small talk. This was the crux of an enduring disagreement between them. But Mrs. Epsom took full advantage of the Derby to exercise her right to whimsy and don an unmistakably smart and vibrant hat. Today she sported a tightly wound straw number in a clash of pastels, with a wide brim and a lace veil that drooped down in front of her eyes. It was the epitome of fancy and the antithesis of taste.

Fyfe made her way up to the box and tenuously stepped inside. She knew the concession manager had been joking about the air being thin up here, but she kept her breathing slow and measured anyway. "Afternoon, Colonel Epsom, Mrs. Epsom."

"Hello, Fyfe." Mrs. Epsom acknowledged her with a faint smile. "Look at you, shilling peanuts. Isn't that quaint?"

"Would you like to buy a bag, ma'am?"

"Oh, no you don't!" The Colonel's booming voice put an abrupt end to their pleasantries. "Save 'em for the clubhouse. Shells on the floor are bad luck for the race."

"Oh, pshaw, Ansel! You and your silly superstitions." Mrs. Epsom detested the very concept of superstitions. "Honestly, listening to you, one would think it was all luck that went into winning, and no hard work or actual talent at all."

"Luck never hurts. Besides, the trainer's in charge of the hard work, the horse is in charge of the talent, and I'm in charge of the hocus pocus. If it ain't broke—"

"Isn't."

"Huh?"

"If it *isn't* broke. Now, Fyfe has a job to do. Let her do it."

Tired of bickering with his better half, the Colonel turned to Fyfe and eyed the tray of peanuts. "How much for the lot of 'em?"

"Gee, Colonel, I dunno. Nobody's ever asked me that before."

The Colonel peeled some bills off a thick roll he kept in his pocket. "Does this cover it?"

It was more money than Fyfe had ever held in her hands before. "It sure does!"

"Good." The Colonel took the tray of peanuts from Fyfe and unceremoniously dumped them over the side of the box into the grandstand below. Then he handed the tray back to her. "Now you're all sold out. Run along."

As Fyfe hightailed it out of there, the Colonel called after her, "Don't go bothering your pa! He's got a Derby to win!"

2

THE STABLES JUST before the start of a race were a kind of controlled chaos. Jockeys dunked themselves in ice baths, nursed their injuries, and stretched their muscles while the trainers barked last minute pep talks into their ears. The horses were being brushed down and saddled up. It was all rituals and rigmarole in precious little time, a well-oiled machine.

Roscoe Flynn looked sharp in his bright blue jockey silks. The color matched his eyes, which sparkled like sapphires amid the dark tan of his complexion and ubiquitous five o'clock shadow. He fixed a saddle on to Gilda Cage, the most majestic palomino filly one could ever have the pleasure to lay eyes on.

"Aren't you Roscoe Flynn?"

"Who's asking?" Roscoe turned around, coming face-to-face with another jockey.

"LeRoy. I'm on the number nine horse."

Roscoe pulled off his glove to shake the man's hand.

"I saw you race that horse on short rest in Louisiana. How you pulled out that win, well, it's beyond me. What you do on a horse, it's plain artistry, Mr. Flynn. I'm a big fan."

"That's awful nice of you, Mr. LeRoy. Good luck out there today," Roscoe said. And he meant it.

"Pa! Hey, Pa!" Fyfe pushed through the crowded stable and found her way to Roscoe. A grin crept across Roscoe's face at the sound of her voice.

"Shouldn't you be selling peanuts, little lady?"

"I sold out." Roscoe raised a suspicious eyebrow. "I swear!" Fyfe had a natural love of horses and she stroked Gilda's muzzle with a kind and steady hand. "Am I too late to give her a carrot?"

"'Fraid so, kiddo. She's about to race." The corners of Fyfe's mouth drooped. "But there is one thing she does still need, if you're up to the task."

"What?"

"A great, big hug around the neck."

Fyfe lit up and Roscoe lifted his daughter high enough to wrap her arms around the horse. "Go get 'em, girl," Fyfe whispered in Gilda's ear. "We're all rootin' for ya." Gilda responded with a soft nicker and a warm nuzzle. She understood.

"Better go find yourself a spot in the stands," Roscoe said as he lowered Fyfe to the ground. "And let her hear you cheer for her as she goes by."

As Fyfe skittered off, Roscoe guided Gilda to her place in the procession. She fell in line next to a white horse named Cream of the Crop.

"Hey, Gilda," Cream of the Crop whispered.

(Of course, this sounded like nothing more than whinnies and neighs to Roscoe and the other jockeys. Animals have their own way of communicating that's entirely indecipherable to the human ear.)

Cream of the Crop nodded toward Fyfe. "Gives you something to run for, don't it?"

"That it does," Gilda answered.

"Every little girl ought to have a horse."

"Every horse ought to have a little girl."

The race was about to start and the crowd was already packed ten people deep against the fence in the grandstands. Fyfe tried to nudge her way to the front but no one was giving up any ground. She tried jumping in the hope that she might be able to catch a glimpse of the race over the heads in front of her, but she was too small. Then it hit her. She dropped to the ground and crawled on her hands and knees through the crowd, under their noses and between their legs. She popped up right at the rail, snagging herself a spot front and center.

"You again?" said a gruff, familiar voice. She had ended up right next to the mustache from the stands.

"Don't worry, I'm all out of peanuts."

"Here." He handed her a small wad of cash.

"What's this?"

"Turns out your thoughts are worth quite a few pennies after all. Rocky Road took the sixth by three lengths."

She grinned and stashed the money in her pocket.

"Come on, Gilda!" she cheered.

"Let's go, Gilda!" the mustache cheered too.

Twenty champion thoroughbreds, regal and dignified, were paraded onto the track with much pomp and circumstance, ceremoniously making their way to the starting gate while the Louisville Marching Band played "My Old Kentucky Home."

Fyfe figured herself a pretty tough character but she couldn't help but get a little misty-eyed as Gilda and her pa took to the track, looking like the pride of Kentucky. As the horses readied themselves at the starting gate, the crowd went quiet. The tension began to mount. The whole world seemed to stand still for just a moment.

Gilda eagerly scratched at the dirt beneath her hooves. Roscoe posted up on his saddle and steadied her with his reins. Fyfe white-knuckled the railing, full of anticipation. This was it. This was everything.

The Churchill Downs bugler raised the horn to his lips and blew.

And they're off!

The horses bobbed up and down with each long, graceful stride. They danced around the track in rhythm, like the wooden steeds of a carousel.

But Gilda raced like she was the only horse out there. Her powerful haunches propelled her out in front of the pack. Her jet black eyes squinted with determination. This race was hers for the taking.

The other horses surged and retreated, pulling ahead then falling behind in a flurry of hooves and clouds of dirt. No one could catch Gilda. She quickly broke away from the pack and lit out on her own. As she galloped along the backstretch, streaking across the horizon like a shooting star, Fyfe shut her eyes and made a wish. . . .

Just two minutes later, it was over, and Gilda and Roscoe had secured their place in history as champions.

The vision of them standing there in the winner's circle burned itself into Fyfe's brain. Gilda was blanketed in fifty-four perfect red roses, as her pa hoisted his trophy into the air, with Colonel Epsom right behind them, clutching his giant check. Fyfe pinched

her thigh through the wool of her pant leg to avoid her emotions getting the best of her and leaking out her eyes. It felt like an eruption of good fortune and glad tidings, and all seemed right and well with the world.

The newsmen clamored for a shot, the rapid-fire flashes of their cameras exploding in the afternoon sky like a lightning storm. But somehow the photographs could never do that moment justice. There was an aura the pictures couldn't capture. You couldn't see it, but you could feel it like a freight train. And it was the most special thing Fyfe had ever felt. It wasn't glory or victory. It was none of the things that come along with winning, exactly. It was making good on a promise you made to yourself. It was seeing things through to the end. It was believing in something, and the pride of knowing you were right to believe all along.

Greatness visits a man when he needs it the most. And in that instant, when greatness fills him up and bursts right out of him, that man *becomes* the moment. It's one split second of euphoria when, suddenly, this crazy mixed-up world makes a little bit of sense. And you just want to freeze time and live in that moment forever.

That moment belonged to her daddy, the great Roscoe Flynn. And as happy as she was just then, she couldn't help also feeling a little forlorn, knowing that a lifetime is made up of an infinite amount of moments, and wondering how any of them could ever be as great as this.

FLYNN FARM WAS dusty and modest. There was a small area where they grew fruits and vegetables, not because it was that kind of farm exactly, but because it had been done for as long as anyone could remember. Plus, Fyfe liked picking apples off the trees and eating them right there in the field. And the ones that fell to the ground would get soft and mushy and make a great treat for the animals.

The animals were the most important part of the farm. While the crops were fickle and unfruitful, the animals could always be relied on to get by. There was a cow for milk, a hen for eggs, a rooster to get things running in the morning, a strong workhorse to pull the plow, and a Shetland pony to . . . well, no one was quite sure what he was for.

The farm did a little of everything, and nothing particularly well. There was just enough milk and eggs and potatoes and parsnips to squeak by, but mostly it was the kind of farm that told the tale of a farmer who lacked a general interest in farming. Roscoe was always more for racing than he was for agriculture. And he came from a long line of Flynns of the same persuasion. There was history in that no-good patch of land; too much to turn his back on. So like his daddy before him, and his daddy before that, he drove the plow horse when he had to and rode a racehorse every chance he got. He was a jockey, after all. And a darn good one. Farming put food on the table, but racing kept the lights on.

Mother Flynn made use of the farm as a way to feed the family, and on rare occasions when the farm was flush, she sold what goods they could spare to the neighbors or at the local farmers market. That was until she up and left one day. She'd said she was fixin' to go to the movies, and Roscoe had just assumed she was off to catch the matinee. Turned out she wasn't off to *see* a movie, she was off to *be* in a movie, and she set out for the West Coast, chasing the silver screen and greener pastures. After she left, Roscoe and Fyfe went to the movie house every Sunday, wondering if she might turn up fifty feet tall. They never saw Mother Flynn in pictures, but she never came back, either, and just like that, the farm work fell to Fyfe.

It was hard labor with modest reward. Eventually, they took on a boy from down the road to help part-time. His name was Cletus Everett Pikeman the Third, but he was known simply as Pike. He was a kind boy, honest and hardworking. And unlike the Flynns, he had a knack for farming. He'd gotten the idea to plant hayseeds so they'd have something to take to market come spring. But the dirt was too dry and most of the crop withered and died before it was even knee-high. As it turned out, Flynn Farm (like the Flynns themselves) was mighty resistant to farming.

Pike was a few years older than Fyfe, but that didn't bother her one bit. She didn't hang around with other kids much since she did her schooling from home, early in the morning. She'd already had a full day's lessons and was ready to go to work with the chicken, cow, and horse by the time most other kids were just waking up. She sometimes fantasized about home-room chitchat and brown sack lunches, but all in all she figured she wasn't missing much.

Still, she was grateful for Pike's company and soon developed an avid interest in all the things that interested him, like comic books, bugs, and soapbox racing. Fyfe had always been something of a tomboy, more prone to fishing than fashion, and preferring roughhousing to playing house. That suited Roscoe just fine, especially after Mother Flynn up and left, since what he knew about the fairer sex could fill a thimble, with room to spare. But Fyfe and Roscoe were close as kin could be and their bond would be the envy of any father and daughter—or father and son for that matter.

Not more than a hundred yards across the way from Flynn Farm was the Epsom estate, where Colonel Epsom and Mrs. Epsom hung their expensive hats. It was an old plantation, overgrown with ivy. It's been said that one of the great many differences between a farm and an estate is how dirty your boots get walking to the front door. And the Colonel could eat off his boots. But he much preferred his fresh oysters and warm sweetbreads served on fine china, which is yet another difference between an estate and a farm.

The Epsom estate had an awful lot of property for just a few people. It was just the Colonel and his wife and their staff. Some estranged sons and daughters showed up every once in a while to indulge their morbid curiosities about the Colonel's sturdy constitution, but they never stayed long.

The staff turned over so often you'd think the place had one of those revolving doors like they've got at the department stores in the city. (Fyfe took a spin in one of those doors once when her pa took her to Spalding and Sons to get a dress for church. She didn't much like it on account of it being awfully itchy—the dress, that is, not the store.)

After her victory in the Kentucky Derby, Gilda Cage retired from racing. As the old adage says, always leave on a high note. The Colonel put Gilda to use as a breeding mare, hoping that her champion genetics might bless the next generation. After all, the Colonel's business was racing and his livelihood was winning, and as he himself admitted, his contribution to this delicate equation was merely the "hocus pocus."

In the springtime, Gilda was pregnant with her first foal. And as fate would have it, the Flynn Farm had an expectant mare of its own. Her name was Esther Mae, and though she was a thoroughbred by birth, you wouldn't know it at first glance. She lacked the majesty and classic beauty of the breed, but what she wanted for in size and stature she more than made up for in character. She was a hard worker who had readily given her life to thankless and tiring labor on the farm. She was by all accounts a good horse.

The fact that both Gilda and Esther Mae were expected to deliver around the same time was not exactly the Grand Canyon of coincidences. Horse breeders and farmers often bring new animals into this world, so the timing was bound to match up every now and again. But in this case there was something more to it. These two mothers-to-be were kindred, their fates intertwined.

It was April the eleventh the morning Gilda went into labor. It was unusually breezy despite the temperature being mild, and dark storm clouds gathered overhead.

Something was stirring in the air. Something wasn't right.

Gilda's labor was difficult from the start. She possessed tremendous strength, so it was unusual to hear her roar with pain. The Colonel didn't even recognize the sound until the attending veterinarian let him know with a dour expression and a stern shake of his head that the situation was indeed grave.

No one could say for sure whether it was fate, coincidence, or just dumb luck that sent Esther Mae into labor at nearly the exact same time as Gilda. Most likely, Esther Mae heard Gilda's squeal and it frightened her into a premature labor, one that was not without grave complications of its own.

Now here these two mares lay not more than a hundred yards from each other, both fighting for their lives after what should have been routine suddenly became fragile and dangerous.

Hours passed before a light could be seen at the end of the tunnel. Finally, Gilda delivered her foal. But soon as she did, that light at the end of the tunnel flickered out like a candle: Gilda's foal was stillborn. He left this world before he ever had the chance to join it. When Gilda looked upon her colt and realized that tragedy had taken the foal from her, she bucked and writhed, fighting against the terrible and unjust, though there was nothing she could do. The doctor and several stable boys held her down, whispering prayers under their breath for the grieving mother.

Across the way, Esther Mae was still battling death's grip. Fyfe knelt by her side, cradling her head, trying to soothe her. In a fit of pain, she neighed and reared her head back violently, accidentally knocking Fyfe over.

"Fyfe, get away from her! You could get hurt." Roscoe was trying to deliver Esther Mae's baby, but he was worried about his own baby, too.

"No! She needs me," Fyfe held on harder, fighting through the labor with Esther Mae. Her embrace helped the horse muster the strength she needed to push through.

All of a sudden a tiny, high-pitched whinny cried out. It was the foal! He stumbled about and Esther Mae let out a soft, fluttering snort, an expression of pure joy. Fyfe cheered and went to meet the new colt. But she quickly noticed Roscoe wasn't cheering. She looked to Esther Mae, who clumsily and helplessly dug at the grass with her front hooves, trying in vain to stand up.

"Pa, what's wrong with Esther Mae?" Fyfe went to her, trying to help her up.

"Let her alone, Fyfe."

"Why can't she stand up?

The horse's hindquarters hung limp, as both her back legs had been broken in childbirth. Roscoe had seen horses go lame before, but never like this. Never this bad.

"I said, leave her be. She needs to rest. Be a good girl and tend to her colt. Show Esther Mae he's cared for. All right?"

"Help her, Pa. You have to help her." Fyfe looked at her father, who didn't move a muscle. He knew what Fyfe didn't. "Please, Pa! Do something."

"Go inside and get a nice warm blanket." He looked to the dark clouds brewing up above. "Storm's coming."

Fyfe took off like lightning. She tore across the pasture to the farmhouse, threw open the front door, and bounded up the creaky steps. She pulled open a wooden chest and scooped up a thick fleece blanket. Then she heard it—the loud, echoed bang of her daddy's rifle. Fyfe went white as a sheet. No, it couldn't be. . . .

She came running out of the house, carrying the blanket, sprinting as fast as her legs could carry her. The first drops of rain began to fall, then suddenly the storm cloud broke and let loose a torrential downpour, soaking her to the bone. Still, she ran, and she ran, and she ran. All the while thinking, *Please, don't let it be true.*

When she reached Esther Mae, Roscoe stepped in front of her to shield her from the scene. He too was drenched from head to toe by the rain, so it took Fyfe a moment to realize he was crying. She'd never seen her father cry before. It had clearly pained him to put down poor Esther Mae, but there was no other way. He did with mercy what nature would have done in time. Her injuries were far too great for her to recover.

Roscoe took the blanket from Fyfe's arms and opened it up. "This will do fine. Well done, kiddo. Now see to that colt. He looks cold."

4

THE NEXT FEW days got worse, not better. Esther Mae's colt was barely bigger than a house cat and was born weak. Without a mother, the poor thing didn't know how to live. But he had a companion in Fyfe. She did not leave his side once, ever since she had first wrapped that fleece blanket around him. She spent the days talking to him, consoling him, and teaching him what she knew of the world. She slept in the stable next to him every night. She took her meals there, too. There was no separating that girl from that horse.

But the more time wore on, the weaker and weaker the colt became. Without a mother to take his milk from, he refused to drink. They tried getting him to take milk from a goat, but he wouldn't. They tried feeding him with a baby bottle, but he wouldn't take that either. It looked as though cruel fate would swallow him up just like it did his mother. It wasn't long before the colt stopped standing. Then he quit opening his eyes. Fyfe stayed by his side, watching his chest rise and fall over and over, terrified he might quit that, too.

Each morning, Roscoe would go across the way to check in on Gilda, who was also close to his heart. He'd report back to Fyfe that she, too, had lost her will to carry on, and was so grief-stricken that she was refusing to eat. Her health was waning and her bitter end seemed to be looming near.

Then, out of the blue, Fyfe had an inspired idea. "We need to give our colt to the Epsoms."

"How's that now?" Roscoe didn't quite follow.

"He needs a mama. And Gilda needs a baby."

"The Colonel don't want our colt."

"Both mama and baby are liable to pass if they don't get help soon. It's plain fact, and you know it as well as I do, Pa. Putting them together is the only chance we've got to make 'em both whole again."

"I'm afraid the Colonel wouldn't think our horse was up to snuff, Fyfe."

"Why not?"

"Cause he's not a racehorse."

"How do you know? He's just a little thing. He's not even grown yet!"

"That's precisely the point. He's little."

"What's wrong with little?" Fyfe looked indignant. "I'm little. You brought me up not to apologize for my size. You told me a person shouldn't take up more space than he needs, and the space I've got suits me just fine. I figure the same goes for a horse."

Roscoe looked at her with pride.

"Well? What are you waiting for?" Fyfe said. "Go tell all that to the Colonel."

"It's not as easy as that."

"Sure it is! You wait and see—he may just be a race-horse yet."

"No, Fyfe. He won't."

"Don't be that way, Pa. Can you look me in my eyes and tell me it's *impossible*?"

Roscoe thought it over. How could he keep his daughter's hope alive and be honest with her at the same time? "Can I say beyond a shadow of a doubt that he absolutely, under no circumstances, could never race . . . ?" He rubbed the back of his neck, then reluctantly said, "No, I guess not."

"Hooray!" Fyfe grinned ear to ear as she wrapped her

arms around her dear old dad. "Then that's what we'll call him—Shadow!" She released her hold on Roscoe. "What are you waiting for? Go tell the Colonel!"

Desperate not to lose his prize-winning breeding mare, the Colonel agreed to what he called Fyfe's "harebrained idea." He'd try anything to get Gilda nursed back to health.

Fyfe, Roscoe, and the Colonel waited with bated breath as Shadow was introduced to Gilda. Shadow was scared, distrustful of everyone except Fyfe, owing to the brutal and merciless way he came into this world. He wouldn't go near any of the other animals at Flynn Farm, and it looked like Gilda was no different. Until Gilda slowly approached him, that is, and let out a gentle snort to let him know it was safe. She'd do him no harm. He let her come closer and closer until she was so close they were nearly touching. He collapsed into her, feeling at home at last. They nuzzled each other, enveloped in each other's warmth, and it was clear how badly they needed each other. Gilda gave Shadow a loving lick and their bond was sealed.

That afternoon, Shadow began taking milk from Gilda. From that day forward, she was his mother and he was her son.

5

A WHITE PAINTED FENCE ran round the large horse-training pen on the Epsom estate, where Roscoe was breaking in a brand-new ink-black stallion for the Colonel. It was a process called round penning, whereby the horse learns to respond to its handler's voice. Roscoe called out "hee-yah!" and chased the stallion with an unfurled rope lariat as it trotted around the circle.

"Flynn!" Roscoe turned to see the Colonel standing on the veranda, watching him. "Come inside a minute."

Truth be told, Roscoe was the sort of man who felt more comfortable *out*side, but he didn't put up a fuss. Being in the Colonel's employ as his winningest jockey and sometimes trainer, Roscoe knew he had a good thing going and tried not to quarrel with the

Colonel whenever possible. Still, it had been his general observation over many years that troublesome things tended to be *in*side matters, so it was with vague trepidation that he followed the Colonel into his study, where he sank into an oversized leather chair across from the Colonel's oversized wooden desk.

"What is it you wanted to see me about, sir?" asked Roscoe.

"About your colt. Shadow," said the Colonel.

"What about him?"

"Take him back."

"But he's so happy here, Colonel. With his mama."

"Gilda is *not* his mama. She's got to move on. It's time he was weaned, anyway."

It was true that it had been some time since Shadow had come to know Gilda as his mother, and that Shadow's infancy had ended.

The Colonel continued. "Besides, at this stage he'll start to imprint. Can't have him getting used to the good life he can't maintain."

"Would that really be so bad?"

"I reckon it would, Roscoe. There's an upper class and a working class. I didn't make it that way, but that's the way it is. Shadow is working class. There's no use pretending he's anything else. Gilda's foal might have been a champion, we'll never know. But Shadow's not cut out for it. He doesn't have the genetics. He's a clumsy little runt, a born workhorse, and since you lost Esther Mae, I figure you're short one. So take him back to Flynn Farm and put him to work."

"With all due respect, Colonel, Flynn Farm doesn't need another mouth to feed."

"Just because my pockets are deep doesn't mean they're ripe for the picking. This isn't a charity."

"No, sir. I understand, but—"

"Shadow's got two choices: the Flynn Farm or the glue factory. Take your pick."

That was the end of the discussion. Roscoe *wanted* to tell the Colonel just how rotten and cruel he was, but knowing it'd cost him his job, he held his tongue. "I'll see to it Shadow leaves with me at the end of the work day," Roscoe said with a quiet sigh of resignation.

As quick as that, Shadow was returned home to the Flynns'. That evening, when Shadow left the Epsom property, no one told him he was leaving for good so it was a decidedly unceremonious departure. He didn't even have the chance to say a proper goodbye to Gilda, who he'd come to know as his mama. As the days and weeks went on, he missed her an awful lot. But he could see her from across the way, and from time to time, he even got to talk to her when no one was looking. After all, it wasn't but a fence between them. Though when looked at a certain way, that fence was mighty powerful.

No doubt about it, life on the Flynn side of the fence was harder than life on the Epsom side, for man and horse alike. Back at the Epsom estate it had seemed like the whole world revolved around racing. It was all Shadow had ever known, so naturally he assumed he would one day grow up to be a racehorse, too. But now that he was back at Flynn Farm, it was clear the road to his future was paved with dirt, not gold, and that he'd likely have to lay the dirt himself.

Being a workhorse was hard. There was no glory in it. No thrill to be had. But there was one sparkling silver lining to his new life: his old pal Fyfe.

It was like no time had passed at all for Fyfe and Shadow. Fyfe felt her prayers had been answered when Shadow came back, and the two of them were thick as thieves. Fyfe loved that horse and she told him so often, even if just with an extra carrot or some castor oil to shine up his coat.

A little more than a year and a half had gone by since Shadow returned to Flynn Farm, and he'd grown up some by now. He had settled comfortably into position as a plow horse, and today was the first day of plowing season. It was not even 7 a.m. and the red line of the thermometer had already crept past seventy degrees. It was going to be a scorcher.

Red, a scrawny, cockeyed rooster strutted along the fence to his regular morning perch. The first sliver of sun peeked over the horizon in the distance. He stretched his neck, opened his beak wide, and just as he was about to let loose a nice, loud crow, he saw something out of the corner of his eye. It was Shadow, wide awake, standing right there next to him.

"Morning!" said Shadow.

"Oh no, you don't," clucked Red. "I wake everyone up around here. You got no business being up and about 'til I say so. Go back in the barn and pretend you're asleep. Don't let no one see you."

"Alright, Red." Shadow turned and started back for the barn.

Red frowned and muttered under his breath, "Trying to put me out of a job . . . got my feathers all ruffled. . . ." He called after Shadow: "When you wake up, let 'em see you yawn a little bit. Really sell it!"

"Okay, Red," Shadow answered back.

Shadow snuck back into the barn past the other

animals, all fast asleep, and lay down in his stall and shut his eyes tight. Red crowed his morning wake-up call and sounded the official start of the day. Shadow made a big show of yawning and stretching, just as he had promised.

Gladys the cow took notice. "Goodness me, Shadow! Are you just waking now? You're usually up long before the sun, watching those racehorses train next door."

Fact of the matter was, Shadow had a habit of waking up early. He had something of a natural alarm clock. He'd go to bed dreaming of racing, and he'd dream about it all night long until his excitement could no longer be contained and roused him from sleep, just in time to watch the thoroughbreds across the way trample the early morning dew off the dirt. Most days, Shadow didn't move an inch or make a peep, watching all the action right from his stall. But on rare occasion, like today, he wandered outside the barn and it made Red's blood boil. If he didn't go along with the charade and pretend to wake up late, Red would henpeck him for the rest of the day.

"I guess I slept in today," said Shadow.

"Just as well. You'll need your rest. Today's a big day."

Scout, Roscoe's trusty mutt, nosed the barn door open. "What's so big about it?" he asked.

"Today is the first day of plowing season," answered Shadow, sounding uncharacteristically ho-hum. He knew he had a grueling day of work ahead of him.

"Want me to teach you how to play dead?" asked Scout.

"If only it were that easy," said Shadow.

"It is! Look, you just lie on your back like this"— Scout demonstrated—"and stick your paws in the air, like so." He jutted his furry white paws skyward.

"No," interrupted Shadow with a chuckle, "I meant if only it were that easy to get out of plowing."

"Oh." Scout scampered up off his back. "Why isn't it?"

"Well, because plowing's important. You can't sow seeds if you don't plow the dirt, and you can't grow nothing if you don't sow seeds."

"So if you don't plow, we don't eat?"

"Pretty much."

"Good luck out there," said Scout, only half joking.

"There is a silver lining though." Shadow had a way of always seeing the bright side of things. "I get to spend the whole day with Fyfe out in the field! There's nothing better than that in this whole wide world."

Oats, a Shetland pony standing no taller than waist-high, bristled at Shadow's relentless good nature. "For Pete's sake, Shadow. Do you really *wake up* this happy?"

"Let him be," snapped Gladys. "Ain't no crime to greet the day with a smile."

"Since when does a *smile* require so much flapping of the lips?" Oats buried his head in some hay.

"You're just cranky because you don't have a job to do today," said Gladys.

Oats hated whenever the matter of his utility came up. He was of no actual use to the farm and he figured it was just a matter of time until people caught on to that fact.

"Ahh, go get milked, why don't you?" he muttered.

"Did somebody say 'milk'?" Raelynn the hen blinked the sleep from her eyes. "Is it time for breakfast?"

"Who's hungry?" Fyfe's voice rang out right on cue as she made her way down from the farmhouse carrying a bucket of feed. Fyfe was sneaking up on eleven years old now, but despite what she considered her advanced age, she was still as small and spunky as ever. She nudged the barn door open and wasted no time doling out breakfast.

"Hello Gladys, you great big sweetheart," she said as she scooped feed into the cow's trough.

"Here you go, Red and Raelynn, you rascals." She scattered some grain in front of the rooster and the hen.

"Good morning, Oats." She gave the Shetland pony a scoop from the bucket and pretended to answer for him in a persnickety voice, *"What's so good about it?" That's not at all what I sound like*, he thought. She playfully tussled his mane.

She continued on down the line to Scout, his tongue hanging out and tail wagging. She was about to shovel out a serving of feed for him when she realized: "Scout, you dog! You already ate your breakfast in the house. Thought I wouldn't notice, did you? What a dirty trick!" Scout whimpered. "Alright," Fyfe said with a laugh, "half a scoop for resourcefulness."

She had saved the best for last.

"Hiya, Shadow! How'd you sleep, old friend?" Shadow fluttered air through his nostrils onto Fyfe's neck. She smiled. "Well, *I* didn't sleep a wink," Fyfe said, in response. "I was too excited to spend the whole day with you! After all, it's plow day!"

6

Plow day fell on a Saturday, which meant Pike would be by to help with the work. But while logic might have suggested Pike, being the bigger and stronger of the two, take up the plow, Fyfe reserved the plowing for herself while delegating other chores and busywork to him. That was her time to spend with Shadow and she didn't want to miss a minute of it. So while Pike went about collecting eggs from Rae-lynn's coop, Fyfe plowed the field with Shadow.

The midday sun burned hot overhead as Shadow dragged the heavy plow behind him, slow and steady. Fyfe followed a pace behind, minding the machinery. Their work was far from done and only getting harder as time went by.

Fyfe squinted into the distance. "Hey Shadow, you see that?" Shadow's ears pricked up, as if to answer, "see what?" Fyfe held a hand above her eyes as though she were trying to make out something far in the distance. "Way out there past the brush where the walnut trees are. I think that's . . . well, if I'm not mistaken . . . by golly, it is! It's a bugler!"

Shadow's ears pricked up and he gave an excited neigh.

Fyfe unhooked the plow. "We better hurry. We can't miss the starting horn." She jumped up on Shadow's back, grabbed hold of his mane, then leaned as far forward as she could, practically climbing up on Shadow's neck. She reached her mouth right up to the horse's ear and sounded the *da-da-da-dunh* of the bugle with her lips. Shadow took off, cantering across the field. "Rounding the bend, it's Shadow out in front," Fyfe called the imaginary race. "Ladies and gentlemen, have you ever seen such a beautiful horse? He's got stiff competition out there on the track today, but no one can hold a candle to Shadow. No siree Bob, there's no match for this pint-sized powerhouse, this tiny turbo, this miniscule magnifico." Shadow was in heaven: the wind blowing through his mane, his head in the clouds, and his best friend on his back. "Ladies and gents, it looks like he may just make Derby history. This is the home stretch—"

"Fyfe!" Roscoe stood in the doorway of the farmhouse, not at all pleased by what he saw. Fyfe quickly slowed Shadow to a halt. Then she turned him around and headed back.

"Sorry, Pa," she hollered as they got a little closer. "We were only playing."

"There's work to be done."

"Yes sir." Fyfe led Shadow back to the plow. But as they walked she leaned forward once more and whispered into Shadow's ear, "And the crowd goes wild! Haaaaah!"

The sun set at the end of a long day, retreating behind the dusty skyline and leaving a rose-colored palette in its wake. Shadow returned to the barn, his spirits high despite being completely spent.

"Shadow, you poor thing! You look exhausted," said Gladys.

"I am, but I really had the most wonderful day! Fyfe and I pretended we were racing in the Kentucky Derby."

"Now, why would you fill your head with silly notions like that? Don't you like it here?"

"More than anything, Gladys. I do. It's just terrific being here with you guys, and of course Fyfe is the best pal any horse could ever have. It's great . . . only . . ."

"Only what, Shadow?"

"Nothing."

But you could see it in his eyes. It was something.

Just then the barn door flew open and Scout the dog bounded in. "Hey everyone! Guess what? A trailer just pulled up in front of the Epsom estate with a new colt inside. A new horse has come to live next door!"

All the animals were excited over the news, even crotchety old Oats. "How did he seem? What did he look like?" asked the Shetland pony.

"I'd reckon he's about your age, Shadow," replied Scout. "But he's a might bit bigger. And he's a thoroughbred, too, with the most beautiful roan coat I ever saw."

"How exciting!" Gladys chimed in. "He must be a racehorse if the Colonel bought him. I bet he's glorious."

"And fast as all get out!" cooed Raelynn.

"Yeah, *get out of the way*!" joked Red. "Them race-horses will run you right over!"

The chitchatting and speculating about the mysterious new horse went on for quite a while, and in all the excitement, nobody noticed that poor Shadow was crestfallen. He couldn't help but feel a not-so-tiny pang of jealousy at his new neighbor, on the fast track to greatness, moving into the Epsom estate with *his* mama, no doubt living the life *he* was meant to live. "You know, Gladys, I am pretty tired after all. I think I'll head off to bed early."

"You go right ahead, dear."

Shadow retreated into his barn stall. It was cozy and warm, stacked high with fresh hay. A small window just big enough to hang his head through gave Shadow a clear view of the starry night sky. But he had no use for stars. Instead, he gazed out across the way toward the Epsom estate. His eyes drooped shut as he drifted off into a deep but restless slumber.

The next day was a Sunday. And Sunday being a day of rest, the farm animals were free to do whatever they pleased, so they found themselves a nice mud pit and had a proper romp. The animals loved to cover themselves in the soft, cool mud. It was the only way to beat that Kentucky heat. They loved to splash it, fling it, pack it, slip, and slide in it. On most occasions, Shadow was the ringleader for exactly this type of recreation.

But not today.

While Gladys, Raelynn, Red, and Oats cavorted in the wonderful stink and filth, Shadow stood alone, clean as a whistle. He stared across the way at the Epsom estate. "Does the grass look *greener* over there to you guys?"

"Come play with us, Shadow!" shouted Gladys.

"Nah, not today. I don't feel like it."

"You wanna play something else? We can play 'Guess That Smell'!" suggested Red.

"That game's awful." Oats said, sticking his head up from under the mud. "It's flatulence. It's always flatulence."

"Yes, but *whose* flatulence?" replied Raelynn.

"Thanks guys, but I'm okay. I don't want to play today." Shadow spent the whole rest of the day like that: withdrawn and forlorn, watching the pasture just across the way.

The next morning rolled around and Red raised the farm with a throaty crow. Shadow's eyelids fluttered open, but instead of greeting the day with his usual gusto, he simply sighed and got to it. Shadow was in a funk.

After breakfast, Fyfe and Shadow rode out to the far edge of the property, where it ran along the backwoods. Roscoe had noticed the fence back there needed mending. The bottom slat had been pushed out at the bottom and the wood had splintered and needed to be replaced.

Fyfe hopped off Shadow's back and knelt down to have a look at it.

"Get a load of this!" she said to Shadow as she ran her finger across a row of tiny indentations on the wood. "Teeth marks." She leaned in close to examine them. "Coyote, maybe. The Hicks lost two chickens and a house cat to coyotes just last week."

Fyfe got to her feet and went to pull the spare fence slat from Shadow's saddle when she realized his mind was someplace else entirely. He stared off into the distance aimlessly.

"What's wrong, boy?"

Shadow blew a puff of air through his nostrils. Fyfe knew his noises and could tell he was upset. She knew just what to do.

"Maybe we don't have to fix it right away. We can just push this slat back into place, then we'll check the rest of the fence and come back here later."

She wedged the wood back in place with a few good whacks. Then she hopped up into Shadow's saddle and they trotted along the fence under the guise of surveying its overall condition, but in reality they were headed to a very specific spot. On the far side of the property, the Flynn farm and the Epsom estate came together, with just a few feet of fence separating the two. When they got to that stretch, Fyfe nonchalantly announced this was as good a place as any to take a break. Fact was, this was the exact perfect spot to hear the radio that the stable boys next door had tuned to the broadcast of the race up at Saratoga. Prep season was already underway, and the circuit was heating up.

Fyfe plopped down in the grass and lay flat on her belly. She motioned to Shadow and whispered, "Get down!" Shadow knelt down next to her. Of course it was impossible for a horse to hide in the grass, regardless of how un-manicured it was, but knowing that those in the Epsom employ did not take kindly to stealing (even of free airwaves), and that Roscoe was not a fan of slacking on the job, it seemed right that they at least make the effort. Besides, Fyfe liked the way the cool grass felt against her back as she rolled over to stare up at the clouds.

A soft southern breeze stirred the air and the earthy smell of the grass filled their nostrils. Fyfe and Shadow were in heaven. As Shadow listened to the radio he was lost in the moment. He didn't pay much attention to the announcer calling the race. Those were just details. He listened to the rumble of the hooves and the deep rolling sound they made as the horses circled the track, loud at first, then faint on the backstretch, then coming back to life in a roar as they pounded toward the finish line. His heart beat in time to their rhythm. He wanted more than anything to be a part of it.

Fyfe looked up at Shadow and saw how happy he was. She ran her fingers through his mane.

"There's nothing in the world like a good race, is there, Shadow?"

Shadow nickered, blowing a breath of hot air onto her face, and she smiled.

"You belong out there on the track." Shadow laid his head down. "You've already got a racehorse name." She lowered her pitch, impersonating a man's voice. "*Who've you got to win, Bob? Shadow of a Doubt, without a doubt!*" She laughed. "I don't suppose it's likely . . ." she leaned in conspiratorially and gave Shadow a little wink—"but it's not impossible."

Little did Fyfe know, she had planted the seed in his head. But unlike most other seeds planted on Flynn Farm, this seed had sprouted roots. The rest of the afternoon dwindled away with their daydreaming, and they never did get back to mend that fence.

7

WHEN THE SUN came up the next morning, Shadow was already stirring, and itching to get out of that barn. So when Fyfe came to fetch him he nearly ran right out.

Fyfe went to work tacking up Shadow's saddle with the collar and hames harness, then she hitched the old rickety cart to its traces. She loaded up the cart with a spading fork, a shovel, a rake, and a big barrel of topsoil to till for new crops. Fyfe noticed Shadow was fidgety and she tried to soothe him with long strokes along his back. Then she mounted the saddle and started out toward the field.

But Shadow had ideas of his own. Next door at the Epsom estate, the new roan colt was in plain view. He looked glorious just lapping the training pen, trotting steady, breathing heavy and even. Between his natural athletic prowess and classic good looks, he was an embarrassment of genetic riches. Shadow couldn't take his eyes off the new horse and started veering off-path in the direction of the pen.

"Where you going, boy?" Fyfe asked. She looked ahead and saw the roan colt with the Epsoms' trainer. "Morning, Mr. Bertrand!" called Fyfe, as Shadow took them closer. Not taking kindly to the interruption of his work, the trainer responded only with a tip of his cap.

Fyfe tried to steer Shadow back on course with a tug on his bridle, but Shadow shook it off and continued on toward the pen.

"Better keep Shadow away from here, Fyfe," said Bertrand, with a watchful eye. "The Colonel's got high hopes for this one. Wouldn't want no fuss breaking him in. Ya hear?"

"Yes sir, Mr. Bertrand." Fyfe gave a hard yank on Shadow's reins. "Come on, Shadow. We don't want any trouble now." Shadow whinnied and started trotting straight for the pen. The rickety cart bobbed behind him then hit a stone and upended, breaking loose from the harness in the process. Shadow kept going, getting an extra burst of energy, having ditched the cart and lightened his load. Fyfe bounced in the saddle helplessly.

Shadow charged ahead, his eyes fixed on the white picket fence separating him from the roan colt. Shadow thought if he could just get over that fence, that better life would be his, too. He too could train and run, he too could experience that excitement, that *joy*. He too could be a racehorse, if not for that four-foot fence. He lowered his head, preparing to jump.

Fyfe caught on and warned him, "Shadow, don't you dare." But it was no use. Shadow had made up his mind and he wouldn't be deterred.

"No, Shadow." Fyfe's tone grew stern. She pulled back on the reins. Nothing. They were so close now and Shadow truly believed that everything he'd ever wanted was almost within reach.

"*Please!* Stop!" Fyfe cried out. She sounded scared.

Shadow dug his hooves into the dirt and careened to a clumsy halt, just inches from the fence, practically stumbling head-over-hooves in the process. He couldn't do it. He couldn't betray Fyfe like that. Not when she begged him not to.

Fyfe jumped down out of the saddle. Her chest heaved and her face was pale as a sheet. She was fully aware of how risky the maneuver Shadow had nearly pulled would have been, and how badly they both could have been hurt in the process.

Roscoe was working in the Epsom barn when he heard the commotion and came running out. "What in God's name is going on out here? Fyfe, are you hurt?"

"I'm fine, Pa."

"What happened?"

"I lost control of him. He must have gotten spooked or something. It was my fault."

"That's plumb fiction, Fyfe," the trainer, Bertrand, interjected. "Tell your daddy the truth, or I will."

Fyfe stared daggers at Bertrand. She wasn't talking.

"That horse got caught up with the new colt here. His eyes wandered and he lost his course. There was no stopping him," Bertrand told Roscoe. He looked hard at Shadow, sizing him up. "You better watch that runt of yours, Roscoe. He's liable to stir up trouble for ya if he interferes with the training and the Colonel gets wind of it."

"Much obliged for the advice, Bertrand. We'll let you get on with it then." Roscoe hopped the fence back to his property and grabbed hold of Shadow's reins. As he led him back toward the barn he called over his shoulder to Fyfe. "See about mending that cart. It's no use to us broke."

"Where are you taking Shadow?" Fyfe demanded to know.

Roscoe didn't answer. He led Shadow inside the barn, with Fyfe trailing behind. He sorted through a musty trunk filled with various horse tack and fished out a pair of blinders, then set to work fitting them to Shadow's bridle.

"Oh no, Pa. He didn't mean it," pleaded Fyfe.

"It's for his own good. These'll keep him from seeing anywhere but straight ahead. He won't get distracted."

"No. It was my fault. I should have made him stay the course. Don't punish him for my mistake."

"It's noble of you to bear the blame. But this is for the best." Roscoe's eyes were filled with sympathy, but he kept fiddling with the tack. "You could have gotten hurt, kiddo. You both could have."

Shadow wasn't used to the blinders. He bucked his head trying to get free, fighting the panic of his newly narrowed sight.

"Shhhhh," Roscoe calmed Shadow. "I know, I know."

Fyfe could barely stand it. She bit her lip, hard, nearly drawing blood. But Fyfe knew better than to argue with her father when he had set his mind to something such as this.

It took most of the afternoon for Fyfe to repair the busted wagon, so it was nearly evening by the time she and Shadow set out again for that firewood. The roan colt was training late into the day. Shadow couldn't see him around the leather cups of the blinders, but he could still hear the sound of the colt's hooves kicking up the dirt, and his ears twitched fiercely with every step.

That night, when the work was done and all the other animals were having a hearty dinner of potatoes, turnips, and leeks, Shadow snuck out alone. He made his way along the fence to the spot on the far edge of the property where it jutted up against the Epsom estate.

"Mama!" Shadow whispered, trying to get Gilda's attention. He could see the barn where he knew her stall was, just past the training pen. He hung his head over the fence, stretching his neck as far as it would reach, and tried again. "Psssssssst! Mama!"

Whap! One of the Epsom farmhands batted Shadow on the nose. Shadow was shocked. That had never happened before.

"Sorry, Shadow," the farmhand said. "But the Colonel says you can't be over here no more. This here's Epsom property on this side of the fence and you don't belong here. Now, go on. Back up." He put a hand on Shadow's shoulder and pushed him back a few feet.

Shadow's heart broke. He was so close to his mother, but there may as well have been a whole world between them. It was almost more than he could stand.

Feeling sad and alone, Shadow lay down next to the fence. He could hear his friends laughing and having a grand old time back at the barn, but sometimes you just need your mama and no one else will do.

After dinner Fyfe came down to check on Shadow out in the field. She brought him a soft, overripe apple and a handful of sugar cubes, but Shadow had no appetite and wasn't in the mood for sweets. Fyfe laid the food next to him in case he changed his mind, and she sat with him awhile, humming "My Old Kentucky Home" while Shadow drifted off to sleep, sad as could be.

8

"WAKE UP. SHADOW, wake up." Shadow's eyes blinked open to see Gilda Cage looking down on him. "Why are you out here, my beautiful boy?"

"Oh, Mama! Didn't you hear me calling you before?"

"I'm sorry, my son. I was in the grooming stable and didn't hear a thing."

"How did you know I was here, then?"

"A mother always knows." Gilda was warm and comforting.

Shadow hung his head. "I had the worst day, Mama. They made me wear these blinders and they were awful. And everyone was so mad at me. I don't blame them for being angry, but I'm tired and my back hurts from pulling the cart. I just wish . . . I wish I could be over there with you."

"There, there. Is it really so bad there, with all your friends?"

"No, it's not. And I should be grateful that I have a good home. I know I should. Only, I miss you, Mama."

"I miss you too, Shadow. More than you could ever know. But you're not so far away. And don't forget, a mother's love is a powerful thing. There is no fence tall enough or strong enough to keep it from you. Never you mind these silly pieces of wood. They don't mean you're loved any less."

"But they do mean something." Shadow tried with all his might to reconcile himself to the way things were, but he couldn't. "On that side of the fence there's a chance."

"A chance for what, my love?"

"To race." Shadow's eyes lit up at the mere mention of the word. "To race like you did, Mama. To be great like you."

Gilda nuzzled her sweet son.

"Why is that new roan colt a racehorse, and I'm never gonna be nothing but a workhorse? What makes him any better than me?"

"Ain't nobody better than you. Nobody. You're just different, that's all. And different is good. Different is what makes you special."

"Yes, Mama."

"Now go on up to the barn and go back to sleep."

Shadow started for the barn, but only got a few steps before he turned back. "Even though I'm not a racehorse, you reckon it'd be alright if I dreamed about the Derby?"

"I think that'd be real nice, Shadow."

"I love you, Mama."

"I love you too, Shadow. I love you more than fifty-four red roses."

Nothing in the world could have meant more to Shadow. To be loved more than a Derby prize, well that was something special indeed.

Shadow made sure not to wake the other animals as he crept back into the barn. He laid down and nestled against a cozy bale of hay.

"I heard what happened today, your going after that new colt," whispered Oats. Shadow was startled. He didn't realize anyone else was awake. "They have a name for what you've got. They call it a pipe dream."

"What's that?"

"It's when you want something so bad that the very idea of it's enough to keep you going, even though a part of you—the biggest part—knows it could never happen. You won't race any more than I'll tap dance or Gladys will swim the English Channel. And someday, there will come a moment when you figure out what everyone else already knows—that your dream is never going to come true."

Shadow looked bewildered, not sure what to make of what Oats was saying.

"What do you know about Shetland ponies, Shadow?" Oats persisted.

"Not much of anything, I guess."

"Well, back in the day, they used to call us 'pit ponies'. We worked underground in the mines hauling coal and saltpeter because the caves were too small to fit a regular horse. But then the mines began to close and all of a sudden, we became obsolete. Sure, the lucky ones found a farm somewhere to take them in.

"But there wasn't enough good luck to go around. The pit ponies were put out in droves without so much as a pat on the back. You don't think those poor helpless dopes had dreams? Every one of them had a head full of stars. I guarantee it. And where did it get them? Their heads were stuck so high up in the clouds they couldn't see the sky was falling right below them! I wasn't always the only one, Shadow. There were millions more just like me. They all had dreams—dreams so big they'd fill the Hoover Dam and spill out the sides. A bunch of damn fools."

"Maybe you're looking at it all wrong. Bad things happen no matter what. Having a dream is a nice distraction," Shadow said. "It's not too late for you to have a dream of your own, you know."

"Don't you get it, kid? Dreaming's for dummies."

"Suppose I don't care. Suppose I'd rather be a happy dummy than a miserable cynic. What's the harm in dreaming anyhow?"

"Sooner or later, you wake up. And all you're left with is tears on your pillow and heartache thumping in your chest."

"Then that's the way it'll be," Shadow said defiantly. "No matter how slim the chances, somewhere there's a razor's edge that says I got some kind of a shot. But a dream can never come true if you don't bother dreaming it in the first place."

"So that's it, huh? You close your eyes and float away until your old pal Oats tells you the sky is falling?"

"The sky is falling every single day. And every

morning it comes back up." Shadow lay down. "I'll see you in the winner's circle, Oats."

"That'll be the day, huh?" Oats lay down in his stall, disappearing behind the partition. "'See ya in the winner's circle. . . .'"

Shadow shut his eyes and thought of his game of make-believe with Fyfe as he drifted off to sleep. *"And the crowd goes wild! Haaaaaaah!"*

9

ANOTHER SIX MONTHS went by and Shadow was nearly two and a half years old by then. Horses have a different way of aging than humans do, so at this point, he was mostly grown. In fact, this was the age when a young colt typically hit his stride as a race-horse. So that racing itch had a mighty powerful hold over Shadow right about then.

While Shadow idled over at Flynn Farm, all those dreams of racing just pent up inside him, the horses across the way at the Epsom estate were getting ready to race for real. Things were heating up on the track with the official start of the season just around the corner.

Today was the first preliminary round and there

was a lot riding on it, so to speak. A strong start would set the tone for the whole season, and an early win would leave you sittin' pretty. Roscoe, wearing his jockey silks, was up before the sun, leaning against the stove sipping a hot cup of coffee.

Fyfe bounded down the stairs.

"Whoa there! What's got you all worked up?" Roscoe asked.

"It's race day!" cried Fyfe.

"Today's just a qualifying round."

"A race is a race, that's what I say!"

"Oh, it is, is it?"

Fyfe went about straightening her father's uniform, tucking and adjusting where it needed it. "Which horse does the Colonel have you riding today, Pa?"

"It's me and The Duke. What do you think of that?"

"You're a shoo-in! The Duke's stride has been looking good and long. He'll go the distance, alright."

"I think you're right, Fyfe." Roscoe noticed the time and tossed what was left of his coffee down the drain. "We best be heading next door to collect the horse."

"Better hurry! The Duke hates it when we're late."

"The Colonel's not so fond of it either."

Roscoe and Fyfe went hustling across the way.

"Morning, Bertrand," Roscoe said as he opened the gate to the training grounds. Bertrand responded with a quick nod. The Duke was warming up in the training pen. "Have you seen the tip sheet for the race yet? How's it look for The Duke?"

"His odds are good."

"Is he favored for the win?"

"Can't say that he is, Roscoe."

Roscoe furrowed his brow. "Who, then?"

"The Colonel entered a second horse at the last minute. The roan colt. *Bred Winner.*"

It was quite unusual for the Colonel to enter a second horse so close before the start of the race, and even more unusual for him not to mention it to Roscoe. Roscoe felt an almost imperceptible tremor run up his spine: a jockey's worst enemy—*nerves.*

"Why would he enter Bred Winner when our odds are already strong with The Duke?" wondered Roscoe.

"Don't know. Take it up with the Colonel if you'd like," said Bertrand, knowing full well that it wouldn't get Roscoe anywhere, since once the Colonel made up his mind to do something, there was pretty much no stopping him. Roscoe knew it, too. No use dwelling on the why; he'd been sold out and that's all there was to it.

"You know who's riding him?" Roscoe asked.

"He hired that Boone fella up from Texas."

"I thought Boone had a horse."

"Now he's got a new one. Job's a job, I suppose."

Roscoe scraped the dirt with his boot, letting the news sink in. Then he turned and started for the stables.

"Roscoe," Bertrand called after him. "If it's any consolation, I heard a couple of the local boys turned it down."

Back at the Flynn's barn, the animals crowded around a tiny window trying to get a view of the Epsom racing stable. Shadow craned his neck out as far as it would reach, hoping to catch a glimpse of the action.

"Can you see anything?" Oats asked, too short to reach the window himself.

"What's happening?" clucked Red the rooster as he flapped his wings. He could only stay aloft for a few seconds at a time.

"I don't see anything," cooed Raelynn the hen, no better at flying herself. "Where is he?"

"Looking for me?" The animals startled at the voice behind them. Shadow whipped around and saw the roan colt standing before them, right there in the barn.

"You're the roan colt," said Shadow.

"The name's Bred Winner."

"Hi! I'm Sh—"

"I know who you are. You're the one always staring over the fence like a chump, watching me train." This hurt Shadow's feelings. He didn't know what to say. "I just came by to see if you wanted an autograph before the race," taunted Bred Winner.

"Why don't you go back where you came from?" barked Scout. He wasn't going to let anyone talk to his friend that way.

"It's really all about a fence for you fools, isn't it? Here and there, us and them? But it's not that simple. There is no them. There's only *me*. And I'm going to prove it today. This race will change the course of history." Bred Winner glared at Shadow, looking menacing and unpredictable. Then he added, "Don't forget to tune in on the *radio*, chump."

"Go on! Get out of here!" Scout chased the thoroughbred out of the barn, barking after him. "Get!"

"What do you suppose he meant by all that?" Shadow asked.

"Oh, he's just blowing off steam," assured Gladys.

"Yeah, he's all talk," said Red, but he didn't sound too sure.

Oats, the wisest of the bunch, looked the most worried. "Only time will tell. . . ."

10

IT WAS A beautiful day for a race. Back in the stables, an undeniable energy crackled in the air. The beginning of racing season was electric. Everyone was still "0–and–0" and full of hope.

A young stable hand picked up The Duke's saddle, but before he could even set it on the horse's back Roscoe came running up.

"Whoa!" Roscoe snatched the saddle out of his hands with a smile. "I always take care of my own horse, son."

"I'm sorry, Mr. Flynn," the stable hand said nervously. "I didn't know. It's my first day."

"No need for sorry. I appreciate the help. Now, scram," joked Roscoe. He grinned and gave the kid a reassuring pat on the shoulder. Little did he know, the kid would save that shirt for the rest of his days: It had been touched by a real life legend.

Roscoe went to work saddling up The Duke. He'd just about got him fixed when he was interrupted.

"What are you doing with that mangy mutt?" said a familiar voice.

"Well if it isn't Ángel Arnaz." Roscoe turned to see his old friend standing behind him. "I'll have you know this horse is an original bloodline thoroughbred."

"I was *talking* to the horse," Arnaz said with a grin.

Roscoe embraced him and clapped him on the back.

"Who're you riding?" asked Roscoe.

"Abracadabra in the five spot."

"You like her chances?"

"I don't love 'em. The boss says he'll pull her from the circuit if we don't at least show. I tried to tell him, horses are like wine, you gotta let 'em breathe. But you know how it is—business." Arnaz shrugged. "I hear The Duke's looking real good this season."

"This might be our year."

"Every year's your year, Roscoe."

Roscoe's eyes wandered to Boone, the fly by night jockey getting a leg up onto Bred Winner's back.

"Let's hope so."

Roscoe did his best to put Bred Winner out of his mind and reassure The Duke that all their hard work and practice would certainly pay off. After all, The Duke was a champion horse at the very top of his game who was widely considered to be a front runner in this year's big races. But when the Colonel came back to the stable before the race, he devoted the lion's share of his time and attention to Bred Winner and Boone. It was a slap in the face and it stung, but this close to the race, Roscoe's mind was focused on one thing and one thing only: winning. And so, with his head down and eyes forward, he mounted The Duke and took his starting position at the gate. The Duke was the number one horse in this heat, Bred Winner the number nine.

The bell sounded, the gates flew open, and the horses were off! The Duke set out with an easy lead. His stride was long and light, just like Fyfe said it was, and that carried him far out front. He took the first corner a little loose, but Roscoe tucked his nose in and they picked up speed. Rounding the second corner, they were in the lead by at least three lengths.

The Duke may have been the most graceful horse on the track, but Bred Winner had more sheer power than any other horse out there. When his hooves connected with the ground, they made a thunderous clap as he barreled through the pack like a freight train. Bred Winner was closing in fast.

The Duke hugged the rail tight, and Bred Winner came in hot and heavy right on his tail. All of a sudden, it was clear: This wasn't a clean fight. Bred Winner was *trying* to make contact with The Duke. He was going to charge him!

"Let him breathe!" Roscoe yelled to Bred Winner's jockey, pleading for a shred of good sportsmanship. But it was no use.

Bred Winner would not relent. He surged forward. They were so close Roscoe could feel Bred Winner's hot breath on his ankle.

"What are you doing? You're bearing in!" Roscoe's eyes flashed with panic as the massive thoroughbred collided with The Duke, forcing him into the rail. The Duke went down. Hard. Ricocheting off the rail, The Duke rolled to the ground, throwing Roscoe off his saddle. Roscoe lay on the track, helpless. The other jockeys pulled back on their reins and tried to steer their horses clear of the accident as they barreled past him.

But The Duke was injured and as he scrambled to his feet he accidentally trampled Roscoe, all but crushing his knee under the tremendous weight.

Roscoe cried out in pain. The cheers from the crowd just a moment before now turned to gasps and screams. Grown men averted their eyes, but they couldn't escape the grotesque sound of bone crunching under hoof. It was sickening.

Fyfe watched helplessly from the stands. Time stood still. The wind stopped blowing. The salty smell of roasted peanuts disappeared. The tiny chunks of dirt kicked up by the horses' hooves hung suspended in mid-air. The whole world stopped. Her chest heaved and her stomach sunk. Roscoe was hurt—bad. Her hero had fallen.

11

THE ACCIDENT HURT Roscoe in more ways than
one. His body was badly injured, and the doctors
put a handful of metal screws in his knee to hold it
together, which left him with an unmistakable hitch
in his step. But worse than the physical beating he'd
taken was the mental one he put himself through. He
got it in his mind that what happened was no accident, that it was foul play. He knew it in his gut, where
it counted, and it ate him up inside.

Roscoe wanted nothing more to do with the Epsoms from that point forward. But he had no choice.
After a long physical recovery drained the Flynns' fi-
nances, and with their main source of income suddenly gone, Roscoe had to swallow his pride. As soon
as he was well enough to stand on his own, Roscoe

went straight to the Colonel to ask for a job. Jockeying was the only thing he knew how to do in this world. Now that he could no longer do that, he hoped to rely on the Colonel's kindness to find his way.

When he arrived, the Colonel was out for a ride and so he waited patiently on the front steps of the Epsom estate.

"How's the knee?" the Colonel asked Roscoe as he rode up.

"They've consulted with all the king's horses and all the king's men, there's no putting it back together again."

The Colonel dismounted his horse.

"That's a joke," Roscoe added, when the Colonel failed to acknowledge it with so much as a half smile.

"I'm glad you can find humor in your situation. A weaker man might pity himself." He handed his horse off to a stable hand and started up the steps. "Come inside."

They took a seat in the Colonel's office, where the Colonel poured himself a tall brandy and offered Roscoe none.

Roscoe spoke first. "The fact of the matter is, sir, they say I'll never ride again."

"Shame. You were good."

"Well, I was wondering if maybe I couldn't stay on as a trainer. You know I do a lot of the training myself anyway, unofficially of course. I've broken in thirty, forty horses for you over the years. Heck, I trained Gilda Cage from a young filly and I helped get Bred Winner into racing shape."

"Roscoe—"

"Hear me out. I know Bertrand's been your trainer for as long as anyone can remember, but I don't mind being second fiddle. I'll make a fine right-hand man. I'll prove it to you!"

"Bertrand's gone, Roscoe. I fired him this morning."

"You fired him?"

"I'm bringing in a new man. From Italy, by way of New York City. He's got a way of doing things all his own, with newfangled equipment and modern methods."

"What's wrong with the old methods?"

"They're outdated. If Bred Winner's gonna go all the way to the Derby he needs to get out of the dark ages. Which means Bertrand—and you—are out."

"Our training is tried and true. It's the same regimen Gilda came up on."

"It's antiquated. And you're a relic. And since I can't

very well mount you on the mantelpiece or put you in the curio cabinet like I would any other relic, I've got no place for you."

"Please, Colonel. Think of my daughter. What will we do for money?"

"Pull yourself together, Roscoe. A man's got every right to make his case, but what you're doing now sounds an awful lot like begging and I won't have it. Go home. And don't come back."

Roscoe stood to leave, but stopped at the door. He looked back at the Colonel, the paunchy fat cat with a tin heart. "You said before I was good." He put on his hat and tugged on the brim. "With all due respect, sir. I was great."

IT DIDN'T TAKE long before big changes started happening at the Epsom estate. The day after Roscoe's disappointing visit with the Colonel, the animals heard the rumbling of a truck across the way. There was a ton of clattering and carrying on and a strange voice with an exotic accent. Scout had snuck over there to investigate, but he hadn't reported back yet. The farm animals scurried from one barn window to another, trying to get a glimpse of what was happening.

"Do you think they're moving?" asked Red.

"They're taking stuff in, not out, birdbrain," squawked Raelynn.

"I'm worried about Scout," said Gladys, pacing the floor. "He's been over there an awful long time."

"Maybe they're bringing in a new horse," suggested Shadow.

"Not unless they're building one," said Oats. "Just listen to all that clanking around."

Finally Scout pawed his way back into the barn.

"Scout! Are you okay?" Gladys asked, relieved to see him.

"A stable boy spotted me and gave me a swat with the broom, but I'm fine."

"So what's going on over there?" asked Oats impatiently.

"The new horse trainer has arrived! Some foreign fella named Bianchi. He's got a whole truck full of fancy equipment and they're practically tearing down the whole barn to rig up all his contraptions. You've never seen anything like it! There're pulleys and scales and all kinds of gadgets you couldn't imagine."

"Well, what do they need with all those doohickeys and thingamajigs?" Red asked. "Don't you train racehorses by running 'em in a circle?"

"I think so," mumbled Shadow, unsure of himself.

"The new trainer's even got a doctor's bag!" Scout continued. "Like the kind Doc Crump carries when he has to make a house call. None of the horses seem sick, but I saw him give an injection to Bred Winner.

The needle must have been as long as my tail!"

"I can't believe they hired a new trainer," said Gladys. "So Bertrand's out and Bianchi's in."

"It doesn't seem right." Shadow shook his head. "Roscoe's the best horseman there is. He should be over there training Bred Winner and the lot of them. Not some stranger."

"I think that's the point. They brought in a stranger to do strange things," Red said. "They're up to something. I can feel it in my feathers."

"Do you suppose this is what Bred Winner meant when he said the course of history was going to change?" asked Shadow.

"Something happened in that race to set all this up," Oats agreed. "And no good can come of it."

The funny thing about time is that it's got a way of whipping by faster than a greased-up jackrabbit when times are good, and of practically standing still when times are bad. The clocks at Flynn Farm all but ticked backward nowadays because times were just about as bad as they got.

Roscoe was out of work. He had been for some time, and the bills were piling up. He had no way to pay the mortgage on Flynn Farm and the bank had begun nipping at his heels, threatening foreclosure. They'd put it to him plainly: "You've got three months to pay up or get out."

He had hoped he'd have profits from the farm to fall back on, but it had never been a particularly fruitful piece of land. He, Fyfe and Pike planted new crops, row after row of turnips and potatoes, working in the field from dawn 'til dusk. But even if by some miracle this new lot made it to harvest, crops needed time to grow—time they didn't have.

The animals tried hard to keep the Flynns afloat, too. Gladys and Raelynn figured they would contribute by producing extra milk and eggs, but as it turns out, that's not the sort of thing you can do simply by putting your mind to it. To make matters worse, not only was Raelynn unable to increase her egg output, she awoke one morning to find no eggs at all. She had gone to sleep on her roost and left a nice big egg in her nest. When she woke up, it was gone.

"Eggs don't just disappear!" she squawked. She kicked up the straw on the barn floor looking for it. "Help me find it. Where did it go?"

"Maybe the coyotes snatched it," suggested Scout. "I saw two of 'em slinking out of the henhouse down the way just the other night."

"Look!" Red nodded his head in the direction of the food trough. "Half the feed is missing from the trough, too."

Gladys *tsk*ed. "For shame! Helping themselves to what little we've got."

"If the Flynns think I'm not pulling my weight around here, they're liable to sell me off!" Raelynn was becoming hysterical.

But in the end, it wasn't Raelynn they got rid of.

"Pike, I'm going to have to let you go," Roscoe told the farmhand in a stern yet conciliatory tone of voice.

"Is this about the missing egg?" replied Pike. "I didn't take it."

"I know you didn't. The fact is, I can't afford to pay you anymore." Pike just stared at Roscoe, squinting the sun out of his eyes. "I understand if you're upset—"

"No, sir. It's just that—well, I'm worried, I guess."

"You'll be fine. There's plenty of work to be had for a strong young man like you."

"It's not me I'm worried about, sir." Pike craned his neck to look back at the field. "You and Fyfe are good people, but there ain't a farmer between you. I'm sorry, sir, but that's God's honest truth. I hate to think what might become of you two on your own."

Roscoe wanted to tell Pike he was every bit as worried as he was. He wanted to explain how sometimes life could make a grown man feel helpless and small. But he didn't. "You'll be sorely missed."

Pike nodded. "That row of cabbage I seeded needs mulch."

"I'll see to it."

Just then, Fyfe walked by, lugging a hose over her shoulder.

"Fyfe," Roscoe called to her stopping her in her tracks. "Say goodbye to Pike."

"You're not working today, Pike?" Fyfe asked.

Pike was old enough to understand pride, and kind enough to spare Roscoe his. "No. My folks want me home, so I won't be coming around no more," he said.

"Well maybe I'll see you around sometime," Fyfe said. "We could still be friends."

Pike nodded his head. "Sure. I'd like that."

Fyfe was truly sorry to see him go, not just because he was such a swell pal, but because it gave her the strong suspicion that once again her friend count would be whittled down to zero.

13

ROSCOE WAS DETERMINED to do whatever it took to keep a roof over his child's head. Trouble was, the Colonel had blacklisted him on the circuit so no other racehorse owner would hire him as a trainer. Even though the Colonel had no use for Roscoe himself, that didn't mean he wanted him taking his expertise elsewhere. And the Colonel was known to be a vengeful man, so no one dared cross him. Roscoe was damaged goods. Without jockeying or horse training, the only thing left for Roscoe to try was hard labor. And he looked everywhere for it.

He went, hat in hand, looking for work as a stable boy. At the first place he went, the prospective employer recognized him, and was shocked the Hall of Famer was looking for work shoveling dung. Roscoe explained how badly he needed the money, and how the bank was about to take the farm that had been in his family for three generations. The prospective employer couldn't help but relish how hard the mighty Roscoe Flynn had fallen, because that's just how people are, even though they ought not to be. But just the same, he showed Roscoe a kindness by offering him a conciliatory cold glass of lemonade before sending him on his way without a job, but having earned himself a good story to tell the cronies at the racing club. The same thing happened time after time, everywhere he went.

If something didn't change drastically, and soon, the Flynn family would lose everything.

Roscoe took to having terrible fits in his sleep, worrying about how he was going to provide for Fyfe, and how he was going to keep the animals from being put out. If the farm had to be sold off, he could only hope to find someone to sell the animals to, but times were hard all around. And the Flynns' animals weren't exactly the crème de la crème of livestock, so there was the off, and ugly, chance they could end up at the butcher.

The stress weighed heavily on Roscoe, and that weight was beginning to crush him. His were the kind of problems that had a way of changing a man from soft to hard, from good to bad, and they were taking their toll. Try as he might, he couldn't hide them from Fyfe any more.

Fyfe was giving Shadow a good scrubbing behind the barn. She poured a bucket of warm water down the horse's back and went about brushing his coat.

"I'm worried about Pa," she said to Shadow. He snorted to communicate his sympathy for his friend. "I know you are, too. It's not just the money. He's been let down and turned away all over town. His spirit's broke. He loved racing so bad, I'm not sure there's anything left of him without it. When a man loves something so much, it gets so that they're one and the same almost. It's like—well, I guess it's like you and me. Fyfe Flynn and Shadow of a Doubt, you can't have one without the other." The girl wrapped her arms around the horse's neck. "No matter what happens, you and me, we'll stick together. We'll run away if we have to." Shadow bucked his head, as if to nod in agreement.

"This is bad," said Scout as he slipped into the barn after eavesdropping on Fyfe and Shadow. "This is very, very bad."

"What are you going on about?" demanded Oats impatiently.

"Roscoe's got money troubles he can't shake, and there's no work in sight. If things continue like this, we could lose the farm."

"They can't take our home!" clucked Raelynn.

"What will happen to us?" crowed Red.

"This isn't my first farm. I know how this goes down." Oats' cautionary tale took on the aura of a campfire ghost story as all the other animals leaned in close and listened carefully. "Sure, they'll try and sell us off to other farms. But who knows? They could just as easily put us out to pasture."

"What does that mean?" asked Gladys, terrified.

"It means we'd be left to fend for ourselves! Let's face it, we're not exactly a prize-winning lot. Maybe nobody will want us. Then what? We'll be strays. No purpose, no family, no farm to call home."

Gladys went weak in the legs.

Raelynn piped up, "Stop it! You're scaring her." But she was scared, too.

"Do what you want," Oats said. "But I'm not waiting around for the hammer to fall." Oats started digging up the dirt. "I'm making a break for it. Anyone have a spoon?"

"Anyone have a thumb?" Red shot back.

"What do you have to worry about? You haven't had a job to do on the farm in years," said Raelynn.

"There's a worse fate in store for me: a life sentence at the petting zoo with a million sticky hands yanking at my tail. Or worse, doomed to a country fair as some sort of sideshow freak, roaming from town to town with the rest of the carnies. Trust me, we didn't know how good we had it."

Roscoe had gotten a day's work helping to mend a bridge that passed over Mud River out by Logan County. Fyfe had insisted on coming along, so the foreman agreed to let her pitch in for an additional twenty cents on the dollar for the extra set of hands.

Early that morning, Roscoe piled their tools into the back of the truck then he and Fyfe hopped in the front seats. But when Roscoe keyed the ignition, it wouldn't go. He tried again and it gurgled and sputtered but nothing happened. It was flooded. The old truck did this from time to time and Roscoe knew it'd cost him half a day and a pretty penny to have it fixed, so there was nothing he could do just now. Roscoe banged the steering wheel in frustration.

"What now?" asked Fyfe.

Roscoe and Fyfe hitched their cart to Shadow and chucked their tools on top. Having to ride a horse and cart to a job he was humbled to take in the first place didn't help his pride any. But the time for pride had long gone. He snapped the reins and they headed off.

Of course they arrived at the bridge late, and when they finally got there, they were met with snickers and sideways looks from the half dozen other men who had also been hired on the job.

"You fellas still get around by horse and buggy up there in Jessamine County?" teased one of the men, and they all belly laughed. Clearly, Roscoe's reputation had preceded him.

"I *heard* you were a horse man," joked another.

"Really?" Fyfe piped up. "Because I didn't hear nothing about *you* at all."

That was enough to get the bullies to back down. Roscoe stifled a guilty little grin, proud of how skillfully Fyfe had cut those big, tough loudmouths down to size.

Roscoe joined right in with the rest of the men, ripping up damaged wood and replacing it with new boards. It was backbreaking work. The splinters from the old wood ripped his hands raw and the new boards were heavy and hard to hold. Fyfe scurried around, delivering nails and tools to each worker as they were needed, and also doing a bit of quality control, discovering a bent nail here or a missing bolt there.

The job took the better part of the day and it was just about dark when they finished. But before they could go home there was one last thing that needed to be done. They had to shore up their work underneath the bridge. It was an easy enough job, just a few good whacks with a hammer and a bag of nails, but it required one of the men to shimmy into the suspension underneath the bridge. And while there were a handful of men on the job, Roscoe was the only one of shimmying size. The others were burly fellows, sturdy and solid.

Roscoe explained to the foreman that he might not be the best man for the job, on account of his knee being injured, but the foreman told him if he was fit enough for the job to begin with, he was fit enough for this particular task, and he should carry on with it or forfeit the day's pay. There was no point arguing further, so Roscoe removed his jacket, ready to hoist himself over the railing when Fyfe interrupted, "Let me do it, Pa!"

"No. It's too dangerous," Roscoe protested.

"You're injured. You've got no business going down there hurt."

"Well, I got no choice either."

Roscoe grabbed hold of the railing but just as he hoisted himself up, Fyfe tugged hard on his sleeve and pulled him back down.

"My footing is more solid. You know that's true."

That wasn't the point he was arguing. "What kind of father would I be if I let you fight my battles for me, Fyfe?"

"What kind of father would you be if you got hurt again? Maybe even worse this time. Where does that leave me, without you?"

"This ain't your responsibility, Fyfe."

"We don't have the luxury of principles right now, Pa."

There was a knot in Roscoe's stomach. Deep down, he knew he wasn't up to the job. It'd be far less risky for Fyfe to do it. She was right. But he'd die if anything happened to her.

"I'll be fine," she promised, somehow reading his thoughts.

Roscoe thought on it for another beat, then he nodded and laced his fingers together to give her a boost.

Fyfe placed her boot squarely in Roscoe's hands and raised herself up on the railing. She swung her leg over then carefully lowered herself down on the other side.

Roscoe held his breath in fear. "Careful now. Nice and slow. Easy does it. . . ."

Fyfe shimmied under the suspension of the bridge, and all the men breathed a deep sigh of relief when they heard the *tap-tap-tap* of the girl's hammer as she went to work. Finally they heard "All done! Coming up!" as Fyfe shouted out to them from underneath the bridge.

The men cheered and Fyfe was grinning ear to ear as she climbed out from under the bridge. She got one foot on the railing and—

She slipped!

She banged her chin on the railing as she fell, and the impact knocked her unconscious. Fyfe plummeted into the waters below and was swept away by Mud River's powerful current.

"Fyfe!" Roscoe called desperately.

The whole thing happened so fast that by the time Roscoe spotted Fyfe in the water, she was already a couple hundred yards down river.

He went to jump in after her, but the other men held him back, knowing he could never catch her and that if he dove in, father and daughter would both likely perish. They scrambled across the bridge and to the bank so they could follow the river, hoping they might have a chance of pulling her out downstream where the brush collected way down by the river bend.

But before they could even clear the bridge, Shadow took off after Fyfe. He was still hooked up to that same old rickety cart that had been broken once before, when Fyfe lost control of Shadow that day they went out to collect firewood. This time, the cart's wheel hit a rock and it busted right up again and came loose from Shadow's harness. Free of it, Shadow was able to really get some speed now.

He galloped over the wet, muddy, uneven ground, steadily gaining on Fyfe, her limp body floating downstream. Shadow soared over the stones and downed branches as though he were gliding on air.

Shadow, breathing hard, his whole body shaking, caught up to Fyfe. He tried to nip her shirt collar between his teeth, but it was impossible at this speed. He surged ahead to where he saw a large, heavy branch broken from the trunk of a tree. It took three or four big pushes for him to hoist it into the water's edge, just far enough out to snag Fyfe, whose body folded over it like a rag doll.

Roscoe and the men were about a minute behind Shadow. They caught up, and Roscoe waded into the water and pulled Fyfe out. He slapped her cheek to snap her back to life, and Fyfe coughed up a mouthful of river as she gasped for air. Roscoe hugged her tight and buried his face in her neck. "I'm sorry, Fyfe. I'm so sorry. It's all my fault." He kissed her head again and again. He was overcome with guilt and relief all at once.

Roscoe looked back to the other men standing on the shore, slack-jawed. Roscoe called out to them with tears of joy in his eyes, "What's everyone gaping at? She's okay! Fyfe is okay!"

Fyfe looked up at her father, who was still cradling her in his arms. "They're not lookin' at me, Pa. They're lookin' at Shadow."

It was true. The men were in awe of Shadow. It wasn't just that he was fast. His elegant stride was a thing of beauty, his unbridled power something to behold. He didn't just run fast. He ran like a thoroughbred. He ran like a *racehorse*.

14

FYFE WAS LAID up in bed, buried under overstuffed pillows and scratchy wool blankets. A thermometer tucked neatly under her tongue read one hundred and two. During the day she'd burn up like grease on a skillet and at night she was plagued by terrible fits of chills. Things had been this way for several days, ever since she had nearly been swept away by Mud River.

The doctor came and went, leaving behind cough medicine for a chest cold, sticky yellow drops for a bad ear infection, and a foul-tasting syrup for the worst case of pneumonia he could remember ever having seen. The doctor's orders were to take three spoonfuls of the stuff nightly, but Fyfe detested the noxious, sludgy soup, which she insisted smelled like a stray cat's business, and swore to recover swiftly, before the bottle was done.

Despite her health having been ravaged, Fyfe was of surprisingly high spirits—a fact that the doctor hoped would speed her recuperation, though she was not recovering as quickly as he'd like. In the days after the accident, it seemed all Fyfe could think about and talk about was her pal Shadow and what a tremendous feat he'd pulled off. She swore up and down and to anybody who would listen that she owed her life to that horse. And she was right. Each person who came to look in on her heard the story of Shadow's birth three years ago, how Fyfe had played some small role in saving Shadow's life that day, and how the horse had returned the favor in time. She praised Shadow, and though she wasn't well enough to get out of bed, she saw to it that Shadow got a hero's helping of carrots every night for a week.

Roscoe wasn't as cheery as his offspring. He worried about Fyfe something awful, and he couldn't shake that horrible feeling that everything that had happened was entirely his fault. He blamed himself and, what's more, most folks figured he should. After all, Fyfe had no business working on that bridge to begin with, and she most certainly had no business working *under* it. It was the money troubles that had clouded Roscoe's judgment on both accounts. It had filled him with fear, and he got so fearful that he couldn't think straight. Now, all those powerful emotions—the fear, the guilt, the remorse—all swirling around together, had made a permanent home in his gut. And they were darn near strong enough to tear a man apart.

A little more than a week had passed since the accident by now. It was after nine o'clock and Fyfe had drifted off to sleep in a feverish haze. Roscoe adjusted her blankets, tucking them squarely under Fyfe's chin, and swept her sweat-dampened hair off her forehead. He paused a moment to watch his sweet angel sleep. Then, careful not to make a sound, he quietly crept toward the door, silently turned the doorknob and, like a practiced magician, noiselessly opened the usually creaky old door.

"You know what we've got do, Pa." Fyfe was not sleeping at all, that trickster. "We've got to train him."

"I know nothing of the sort," Roscoe whispered. "Good night."

"But Pa! It's the only thing *to* do!"

"You need your rest, Fyfe. Now I said good night." And that's all there was to it. Or so he thought.

The next morning, bright and early, Roscoe brought

in a breakfast tray and Fyfe picked up right where she left off the night before.

"He deserves a chance. He earned it," she said buttering her stack of toast.

"That's not the way it works, Fyfe. Men don't always get a fair shake in this world and the same goes for horses," Roscoe explained.

"That's not the world I want to live in."

"There's just one world. We don't get to choose."

"Well, then you're wrong about it." Fyfe wouldn't take no for an answer, not from her old man and not even from the world itself. "Just think about it. Where would the world be if no one gave Picasso a paintbrush? Or if nobody gave Thomas Edison a lightbulb?"

"No one *gave* Edison the lightbulb. He came up with it all his own."

"Well, that's what Shadow did, didn't he? Pulling me out of the river like that, that was his lightbulb moment. He's shown us he's got what it takes. But he's taken it as far as a horse can on his own. Now he needs us to help him take it all the way."

"It's not as easy as all that, Fyfe." Roscoe's fuse was burning short. "Eat your breakfast." Roscoe went downstairs and put a kettle on the stove for coffee. He rubbed his bad knee and grimaced. It was as though the screws they put in his knee were a conductor for all the negative energy and frustration and hurt around him. It all just channeled right into those metal pins and sent a sharp pain shooting up his leg, into his back, and all the way through to his brain.

"Why not?" Roscoe turned to see an indignant Fyfe standing on the stairs, barefooted and in her long johns. This was the first time she'd been out of bed in a week. She was frail and sick, but also willful and defiant.

"What are you doing out of bed?" Roscoe said.

"You said it's not as easy as all that. Why isn't it?"

"Training horses takes time. And hard work. It's not a sure bet."

"There's no such thing as a sure bet. You taught me that yourself."

Roscoe sighed. "Horses are unpredictable. And they'll let you down, Fyfe."

"Shadow won't. He's got to race. And he's got to win."

"Why? Because you want him to?"

"Because we *need* him to." Fyfe crossed the room to where Roscoe stood. She reached up and put a comforting hand on his shoulder. "I know what's going on. Since your accident, things 'round here have been bad and they're only getting worse. I saw the notice the bank left on our door." Roscoe's eyes turned glassy with tears. He didn't dare blink, for fear of setting one loose. "If we don't do something—something real big and brave—we're going to lose the farm."

"You shouldn't concern yourself with that, Fyfe. Those are grown-up troubles. Don't you worry. I'll get work. Day and night if I have to. I'll work 'til I drop—"

"It's not going to be enough, Pa. We've got to think big. And Shadow, he's our only shot. We train him up good, you ride him—"

"I *can't* ride," Roscoe said with deep regret. "My knee's shot, kiddo. That's why we're in this mess in the first place."

"So what? You can do on one knee what other men can't do on two. Are you telling me you're not itching to get back up on the horse?"

"Sure I am, but my knee—"

"I'm not looking at your knee. I'm looking in your eyes. And I believe you've got another race in you. Maybe it won't be your best, but it'll be good enough. We get ourselves a shot at some nice fat race purses. And I know you'll say I'm plain crazy, but I believe

Shadow might even have a Derby prize in him."

"Go on!" Roscoe dismissed the idea with a wave of his hand.

"He's our *only* shot, Pa. You know it as well as I do."

Roscoe considered it for a long while, until finally his expression gave way and softened.

"Besides," Fyfe smiled, "it couldn't hurt to have something to believe in again."

"No, Fyfe," Roscoe smiled back. "I suppose it couldn't."

And so it was decided. Shadow was going to be a racehorse. Now the only question was: Would he be any good?

15

TRAINING BEGAN THE very next day. Shadow was nervous. He'd waited his entire life for a chance like this and he didn't want to blow it. It felt like the whole world was his to lose.

Roscoe came out to the barn to fetch him and right away started hooking the plow to his collar. Shadow was confused. Late last night, Fyfe, too excited to sleep despite the fact that her medicine made her quite drowsy, snuck into the barn after bedtime and broke the news to Shadow: His racehorse training would start first thing in the morning! So why, then, was he being hooked to the plow? He bucked his head, but Roscoe paid him no mind and carried on. With the plow in tow, Roscoe began to lead Shadow around the perimeter of the farm, as far to the edge of the property as the law would allow. With each beleaguered step, Shadow grew more and more frustrated. He wanted to run! Why were they plowing when they should be racing? By the time he'd gone half way around, his back hurt from dragging the heavy equipment. He'd never pulled the plow this far before. The sun glared overhead and sweat trickled into his eyes and burned. It took them more than three hours to go the whole way around.

Fyfe was waiting for them on the front step when they returned, still in her long johns with a blanket from her bed wrapped around her shoulders. Roscoe unhooked Shadow and gingerly removed his collar.

"Why do you have him on the plow?" Fyfe demanded.

"He's gonna be a racehorse, isn't he?"

"Yeah . . . ."

"Well, a racehorse needs a track."

Shadow didn't realize it, but he and Roscoe had cleared a great big circle all the way around the property. They'd been carving out a track this whole time. It wasn't much to look at, but it would get the job done sure enough.

Whenever Shadow had thought about training, he'd imagined galloping at top speed, unbridled and free, feeling the wind against his face. But speed was only a small part of training. Today had been a lesson in patience, endurance, and discipline, and it was only the first of many.

"Now what?" asked Fyfe.

"Now, we train," answered Roscoe.

Time was precious.

Fyfe stayed perched on the front step as Roscoe and Shadow set off. She wanted to be a part of it all. When it started to get dark out, Roscoe insisted she go inside. She put up a fight, but he couldn't allow her to stay out in the cold, not as sick as she was. She stomped inside and, a few seconds later, Roscoe heard an awful racket coming from inside the house. Then he saw the top edge of their living room sofa slide into place in the window. Fyfe kneeled backward on it, face glued to the windowpane, and watched from there.

Every time Shadow and Roscoe made a lap, Shadow would look for Fyfe in the window. He loved the way she looked at him. In her eyes, he was already a racehorse. He always had been.

By the time they called it quits it was after ten o'clock at night, and both Roscoe and Shadow were achy and tired. Roscoe rinsed Shadow with a bucket of cool water and brushed him down.

"You did good out there today." Roscoe looked at Shadow curiously. He may have been giddy from exhaustion, but he had a strange feeling that maybe—just maybe—they'd be able to pull this thing off. "Let's see if we can make dreams come true. What do you say? Huh, Shadow?"

Shadow snorted. Roscoe's lips curled into a weary smile and he turned off the light.

Roscoe made his way from the barn up to the house. He opened the front door, but it only opened a few inches, blocked by the edge of the sofa Fyfe had shoved there. He nudged the furniture aside and wiggled his way in. Fyfe had fallen asleep with her chin resting on the windowsill. She didn't want to miss a minute of Shadow's training, but she couldn't keep her eyes open one second longer. Roscoe gently laid her down on the sofa and covered her with a heavy blanket. He fetched a sugar cube from the kitchen and pressed it into the palm of her hand so as soon as she woke up, she would know that Shadow had done well in his training and deserved a reward. Then he sat down on the sofa beside her, kicked off his boots, and went to sleep.

The next morning, Shadow was awoken by the sound of Roscoe's boots scraping against the barn floor as he shuffled in. Shadow opened his eyes, still bleary with sleep, and saw a single sugar cube on the floor in front of his stall. He sniffed it. It smelled like Fyfe. She must have been in to see him while he was sleeping.

Shadow had gotten back to the barn last night after the other animals had already gone to sleep, and they were still asleep this morning. It felt a little lonely.

When Roscoe came to fetch him, Shadow was relieved to see he didn't have the hames harness, which meant he wouldn't be using the plow in today's training. Instead, they'd be focusing on the technical aspects of racing: the foundation. One of the first things a racehorse has to learn when he starts to train is how to listen to his trainer. The trainer communicates with a set of basic verbal commands, not so much words as sounds, combined with gentle taps of the jockey's heel, something like Morse code. It is a language unto its own, and like learning any language, some take to it quicker than others. Shadow was one of the *others*.

Roscoe would call out to him, but he would get confused. Was it one click for walk and two for run? He knew that "whoa" meant stop, but forgot what meant slow. And all the taps felt the same to him. He was trotting when he was supposed to be walking and slowing when he was supposed to be stopping. And the more mistakes he made, the more nervous he would get, which in turn caused him to make even more mistakes. Roscoe got frustrated, and that just made Shadow even more nervous, until he was something of a wreck.

Shadow was tenacious; he proved that yesterday when they carved out the track. But that wasn't enough. He needed skill, too. Did he have what it takes? Things were off to a rocky start and both Roscoe and Shadow were wondering if maybe this horse was just a workhorse, and not a racehorse after all.

At the end of a very, very long day, Shadow returned to the barn. He opened the barn door and was met with hoots and hollers and a rousing round of "For He's a Jolly Good Fellow." Shadow was embarrassed by the fanfare. He didn't think it was possible, but the barrage of undeserved kudos made him feel even worse about having failed so miserably at training.

"Oh, wow! A real live racehorse in our midst!" exclaimed Raelynn.

"Living the dream, boy-o!" said Red with an excited flap of his wings.

"Tell us all about it!" Scout yelped with a wag of his tail. "Did you learn loads of new things?"

"Did they teach you how to walk all over again?" inquired Gladys.

"Oh, I don't know, guys." Shadow hemmed and hawed. "It all happened so fast."

"Was it everything you imagined?" asked Red.

"I suppose so, sure."

"Must have been real fun out there," said Oats. "The kid doesn't want to stop."

"What do you mean?" asked Shadow.

"Well, you've been running around on that track all day, now here you are giving *us* the runaround."

Shadow looked down at the dirt. The jig was up.

"What's going on, kid?" Oats persisted.

"I might be having second thoughts about this whole racing thing," Shadow confessed.

A collective gasp emanated from the group. Shadow scrambled to think of something to say so as not to let them down. "Well, what about the farm work?" he suggested, his argument lacking even a trace of confidence. "If I'm off racing and gallivanting around and whatnot, who's going to pull the plow?"

"But what about the money?" pleaded Raelynn. "Didn't Fyfe say we need the winnings from the race to save the farm?"

"You *are* gonna save the farm, aren't you, Shadow?"

Gladys asked, looking up at him with all the faith in the world in her big cow eyes.

"I want to! Believe me, I do." Shadow looked around the room at their hopeful faces. "I just don't know if I can."

"Huh," Oats sniffed with a whiff of disappointment. "I didn't think you had any quit in you, kid. Guess I was wrong."

Shadow's nostrils flared and his breathing became heavy. "I'm not quitting!" He stepped toward Oats, coming face-to-face with him defiantly. "I'm trying to do the right thing for all of us. I've never wanted anything so bad in my life as to be a racehorse, and now that I've actually got a shot, do you think it's easy to walk away? But I might not win. I might not be any good at all! And then what? It's all for nothing and the farm goes to pieces while I'm out mucking it up on the track. That's reckless, arrogant, and cruel. And *that's* what I don't have in me."

His temper calmed a bit and he lowered his voice. "If I stay the course and pull the plow, then maybe we'll get enough crops to sell to have a shot at saving the farm. That's the safe bet."

"You remember what I told you about pipe dreams, Shadow?" reminded Oats. "That there would come a moment when you'd realize that it's not going to come true? This is that moment. Only, I was wrong. Now is when you need your dream more than ever. As crazy and foolish as that dream seems now, you can't give up on it. You have to keep reaching for that big, beautiful pipe dream, not just for you, but for all of us. Because it's *our* dream now, too."

The other animals nodded in agreement.

"Thanks, Oats," Shadow said. He was inspired by Oats' newfound faith in him. It gave him the courage he needed when his was all but spent.

"And don't worry," Oats continued, "we'll take care of the farm."

"Who's gonna pull the plow if I'm out racing?" wondered Shadow.

"I will," said Oats. "Or Gladys. Heck, any one of us can do it. But not you. You're meant for something better. You're destined for it. So go be a racehorse. And save this farm."

It felt good to know someone else believed in him. "*You're* gonna pull the plow?" Shadow joked.

"Hey, I guess we both got a promotion," Oats answered with a smile of his own.

16

SHADOW ROSE EARLY the next morning determined to do better at his training. But Roscoe had a hard day of work planned, and by midday Shadow was already exhausted. He had spent all morning walking the track, pulling a cart weighed down with logs. It was heavy and slow going, but he pressed on while Fyfe shouted words of encouragement from her spot on the fence. By his fifth lap, Roscoe was satisfied with his pace, and with a verbal cue he spurred Shadow into a trot. He was moving at a steady clip now, despite the heavy cart. Six more laps this way. Then, finally, Roscoe unhooked the cart.

"Let's try a few on your own," he said to Shadow.

"On his own?" Fyfe chirped in. "But you never train a horse without a rider."

"Shadow's a special case," Roscoe explained. "He's spent his whole life doing a *job*. But racing—racing's not a job; it's an art. I can train him. I can help, tell him what to do. But ultimately it's up to him out there. He's got to learn what that feels like." He looked Shadow dead in the eyes and spoke softly. "Don't give it everything all at once now. Pace yourself, boy."

With that, he gave Shadow a slap on the backside and sent him off. Shadow had gotten so used to trotting with the cart that when he was finally free of it, it was like he'd been shot out of a cannon. He liked to go fast, and it felt good not to be burdened by the cart.

Fyfe was excited by how Shadow whipped around the track lightning fast. "Way to go, Shadow!" she shouted after him. But Roscoe was concerned.

"Whoa!" Roscoe shouted. But Shadow ignored him. He wanted to burn it up. He had too much to prove. Roscoe could sense something was wrong. Shadow was too fast. He was out of control.

"Pace yourself," Roscoe urged. "Stop!"

But Shadow didn't want to stop. He was going so fast, he couldn't stop if he tried. But he couldn't keep going, either. Eventually, his legs gave out and his feet got tangled up and he went down. Hard. He careened into the dirt, head over hooves, a messy twisted pile of limbs.

Fyfe watched him take the fall and the color drained from her cheeks. She sprang into action, leaping off the fencepost where she was perched and running across the track as quickly as she could in her frail state to help him. Roscoe was already trying to get the horse on his feet by the time she reached them. Roscoe yanked Shadow up and he stumbled a few steps, but he was okay. Fyfe, Roscoe, and even Shadow himself were shocked that he had escaped unscathed.

"That's it," Roscoe declared breathlessly. "He's done."

"For today?" Fyfe asked.

"For good."

Roscoe grabbed Shadow by the reins and started to lead him back to the barn. Fyfe trailed behind.

"No, Pa! He'll get better."

"That's not it."

"Give him half a chance!"

"What if he breaks a leg? Then what? Are you gonna put him down? Because I can't. I had to show Esther Mae her way out of this world and I'll be damned if I'll take her colt too."

"He's not going to get hurt."

"That's exactly what I used to think about myself. Now look at me." Roscoe limped along toward the barn. "Horses aren't like people. He gets hurt, you gotta put him down."

"No!" Fyfe yanked on Shadow's other rein, pulling against Roscoe and stopping him in his tracks. "It's not over."

Roscoe went into the house and came back with the rifle. He forced it into Fyfe's hands. "See how your finger's shaking on that trigger? You telling me you could squeeze it if you had to?"

Fyfe shut her eyes.

"Look at him, Fyfe. Open your eyes." Roscoe grabbed the barrel of the gun and raised it up, aiming it at Shadow, point blank. "Could you do what needed to be done if the time came?"

Fyfe stared straight down the barrel of the gun and right into Shadow's eyes. They told her everything she needed to know. He wanted to race. He *needed* to race.

"If you're asking me, could I take his life if I had to, rather than take his chance to really live it in the first place?" Her finger steadied on the trigger. "Then, yes sir. I believe I could."

She was unflinching. No matter how many times she proved it, Roscoe could never believe how strong his little girl was. Stronger than he was a thousand times over. He gingerly pried the gun from her hands.

"Alright, then. Back at it tomorrow."

"He's ready now."

Shadow pushed himself hard as he could for the rest of the training session. But it wasn't enough for him. After Roscoe had brushed him down and fed him, and retired to the house to turn in, Shadow went back out. He snuck out onto the track to get in a few more laps on his own.

"You've got to hold back some, child."

Shadow stopped short. He thought he was out there alone, but was happily surprised to hear his mother's voice. Gilda stood on the other side of the fence, watching him.

"Mama! What are you doing out here so late?"

"Same thing I was doing in the barn. Same thing every mother is doing everywhere: Worrying about my son."

Shadow's chest heaved with each shallow breath. His heart was going a mile a minute.

"You're pushing too hard, Shadow," Gilda said tenderly.

"But I have so much catching up to do."

"Take it from someone who's been in a race or two. As many times as you run around that track, you're only chasing yourself."

"How can I be chasing myself and still be losing?"

"You've got a powerful talent raging inside you, child. But you have to learn to control it. Strength and stamina are every bit as important as speed."

Shadow's breath finally slowed down and, as his last bit of adrenaline dwindled away, he realized how very tired he was.

"And so is rest," Gilda said with a sweet smile. "Go back to the barn. Get some sleep."

"Yes, Mama." Shadow started toward the barn and Gilda watched him go. "By the way." Shadow turned back to face her. "It was thirty-nine."

"What was?" asked Gilda.

"The number of races you were in. It wasn't one or two, it was thirty-nine. You finished in the money in all but six. Eighteen wins. One Derby prize. You were the best there ever was." He idolized her. "You *had* to chase yourself, Mama. No one else could catch you." He started back for the barn and called over his shoulder, "Goodnight, Mama."

Now it was Gilda's heart that skipped a beat.

. . .

The next day was no better than the last. Shadow didn't just feel like he was failing, he felt like he was drowning. Like he was being swallowed up by a tidal wave of *not good enough*. He could sense Roscoe's frustration and feared Fyfe would become disappointed in him, too. That worry weighed him down every bit as much as those logs in the cart that he pulled around the track.

Afternoon rolled around and Shadow was relieved of the cart and allowed to run free. Roscoe was putting him through the paces, galloping him around the track.

"Tighten up those turns. Watch your corners," Roscoe urged. Shadow went into the next turn too early. Roscoe tried correcting him with a click, but Shadow didn't understand. He made the same mistake again. "Hug that rail! Stay on it!" shouted Roscoe, excited. No use. Shadow turned wide again.

Fyfe watched from her post on the fence. A raindrop came down and landed on her nose. She looked up at the storm clouds brewing overhead and felt another drop, then another, and another. "Starting to rain, Pa!" Fyfe hollered. "Better bring him in."

"Not yet," said Roscoe.

Fyfe held out her hand, counting the drops that splashed onto her palm. "It's about to break any second."

"Best get inside then."

"Track's liable to get slippery."

"Duly noted, Fyfe. Thank you."

"But, Pa—"

"We don't have time to lose." Roscoe turned his focus from Shadow to Fyfe. "He'll have to push through. Now get."

Just as Fyfe hurried inside, the rain started to come down in sheets. It slicked the track in all of fifteen seconds. But, to Roscoe's surprise, Shadow didn't miss a beat. A minute later and the whole thing had turned to mud, and that's when Shadow really hit his stride. Most horses get sloppy on a wet track. They lose their footing and the mud slows them down. But not Shadow. As it turned out, he did his best work in the slosh. He was light and his gait was short so his hooves didn't sink into the mud, which kept him moving nice and fast, like he was gliding right on top of it.

Roscoe couldn't believe his eyes. Shadow went into a turn like he was right up on that imaginary rail, exactly where he should have been. He picked up speed and went into the next turn hard and fast and

found the pocket. The raindrops just rolled off his back. A grin crept across Roscoe's face and he let out a loud holler, "Woohooo!"

He turned to Fyfe, to share this moment with her. She was in the house, jumping up and down on the sofa right in front of the window. Roscoe ran to the house and she flung the front door open and leapt into his arms on the front porch. He spun her around.

"Would you look at that, kiddo?" Roscoe exclaimed.

They gazed out at Shadow, still running circles around the track.

"It's a thing of beauty, Pa. You can't teach *that*." She yelled out to the field, "You hear that, Shadow? We found your ace in the hole!"

Shadow basked in the glory of their celebration as he let their approval wash over him. All it took was that one moment to break the streak and turn it all around. From there on out, things were looking up.

AFTER THAT, SHADOW got a little better each day. He felt a little more confident and a little surer that he might just be a racehorse after all. Shadow had raw talent, and it was that natural ability that allowed him to persevere even when the odds were against him. There was something special inside of Shadow. And out on that hodgepodge track, it shone each day a little brighter than the last.

Before too long, Fyfe recovered from her pneumonia. There had been a few moments when her condition took a turn for the worse and the doctor thought the illness might not let go of its grip on her, that perhaps Fyfe was too small and frail to overcome it. But she showed that old coot of a doctor what for when she bested that nasty pneumonia, emerging victorious from her long battle with the thing.

Roscoe thanked his lucky stars for the girl's health. Every night forever after, he remembered in his prayers the good doctor, all the kind people who had looked in on her when she was ill, and even McCallum & Foster, the drug makers of that miserable elixir she had hated so much. But the sickness Fyfe acquired that day in Mud River never truly left her. The ear infection she developed bobbing around in the chop left her with lasting damage: Some considerable hearing loss and an upset equilibrium that caused her to become unbalanced without warning. Both would go on to plague her for the rest of her days. She quit climbing trees after that, on account she had trouble finding her footing. And her hearing failed her on more than one occasion, though she never let on. Fyfe was determined not to allow her disability to get the better of her.

The combination of Pike's absence and Fyfe's illness, along with Roscoe's preoccupation with Shadow's training, left no one to tend to the farm, and it had gone from bad to worse. Of course, at this point no one on Flynn Farm had any illusion that this dusty acre would provide much in the way of income or sustenance. But a plot full of dried-up dirt and withered seedlings served as a terrifying reminder that it was race or bust.

Shadow's slow ascension to basic competency and decent middling achievement as a qualified racer was cheered on every step of the way by his number one fan, Fyfe. She never became impatient with his slow progress or frustrated by his failures. She never doubted Shadow's promise, not for one split second. And it was Fyfe's indelible high spirit and unwavering faith that pushed Shadow to keep trying and to get better. And when he finally got good enough that it was absolutely undeniable that they had a true-blue, red-blooded no-doubt-about-it racehorse on their hands, Fyfe turned to her father and said, "See! It's like you said, Pa. Training horses just takes time." (She had a precocious way about her, so that even when she was telling him that he was right, somehow it came out sounding like "I told you so.")

Of course time was a luxury that, like any other luxury, they didn't have. The Prep Season was already underway, and while Shadow was training, other horses were busy racing. All in all, racing season lasted about eight months from start to finish. If the Kentucky Derby was the big ol' cake with a cherry on top, there were plenty of other crumbs and morsels along the way. There were eighteen Prep Season races (those were the crumbs, where each win was worth just ten points), followed by sixteen Championship Series races jammed into a ten-week run (these were bigger, juicier morsels where a first place finish earned fifty points in the first leg, and one hundred points in the second). At the end of it all, the top twenty scorers earned a berth at the starting gate at the Kentucky Derby.

So while the scorebooks were already filling up with ticks as more and more horses racked up points in the preliminary rounds, so far Shadow had a great, big zero. But Roscoe kept a cool head. The way he figured it, Shadow's training was progressing well and, if they stayed the course, he'd be ready to race in another three weeks, just in time for the final two races of the Prep Season. That would get their foot in the door so they could get a feel for it, and maybe even earn a few points and graduate to the big leagues.

It seemed like Shadow hit his stride right on schedule. Once he got good, it was a short road to great. He had the basics down pat now, having mastered the commands and the language of clicks and kicks, and he had reached the point where he could really make each run his own, combining the best of his natural talent with Roscoe's expertise and experience on the track.

For Fyfe, watching Shadow gallop across the farm he used to plow was a thing of beauty. He looked every bit the thoroughbred; the horse he'd always been but could never truly embrace, until now.

But he couldn't have done it alone. He relied on the help of his friends, both human and animal alike. As Shadow ran laps, Oats, Scout, Red, Raelynn, and Gladys took to trailing behind him, cheering him on with whinnies, barks, moos, and cock-a-doodle-doos.

He didn't have all the fancy equipment the other trainers had, so Roscoe was forced to improvise. But what the Flynn Farm lacked in resources they more than made up for in ingenuity. For instance, the (not so) famous Flynn Apple Slalom was a jerry-rigged training technique, which put Shadow through the paces, bobbing and weaving between tightly spaced overripe apples. If he misstepped and trampled an apple, it would squish under his hoof, making it slippery and thus subsequent bobbing and weaving that much harder. (This was Scout's favorite training exercise, as he would gleefully run out to gobble up the collateral damage of Shadow's sloppy trotting.)

The improvised Apple Slalom was just one of many

shabby but effective training tools employed by the Flynns. There was the obstacle course made from old, broken farm equipment; Fat Tuesdays, when Roscoe would weigh the pockets of his jockey uniform with broken pieces of cement from the front drive to build up the horse's strength and resistance; and Shadow's least favorite, the Crusher, where Roscoe and Fyfe would hold gigantic bales of hay and use them to check Shadow into the picket fence as he ran by them. This would ready him for when other racehorses would box him in or crowd him against the rail on the track. Shadow hated this exercise most of all, because the hay was prickly and because nobody enjoys being shoved, even by non-prickly things. But it made him better. It made him *good*. He learned to absorb the impact and rebound off the fence, and eventually to brush past Roscoe and Fyfe entirely, letting the bales just roll off his back.

More than all the other animals, it was Oats who really dedicated himself to Shadow's training. Perhaps he was the first to see the true champion in Shadow, or maybe he just wanted the win more badly than the rest of them, but Oats took it upon himself to be Shadow's personal animal-trainer. Sure, Roscoe could handle the people stuff okay, but Oats figured he'd pick up where he left off (which was pretty much nightfall and Sundays). He had a whole mess of tips and techniques of his own to contribute to Shadow's training.

One night, Oats came to Shadow's stable with a tattered old race book he'd found in the trash, no doubt thrown away by one of the Epsom's stable hands. The book had an illustration of a horse on the cover, shown mid-race, his nostrils flaring, his eyes wide.

"It's come to my attention," Oats professed, studying the picture, "that if you want to be a racehorse, you've got to make the 'racehorse face'." He looked at Shadow's rather unaffected face with great disappointment. "Let me see your race face."

Shadow showed a little teeth. Oats sighed, discouraged.

"No, like this—" he curled up his lips, flared out his nostrils, and peeled back his eyelids. "Race face!"

Shadow tried to mimic Oats's expression, which looked something like a tortured Shetland pony in a wind tunnel. Still holding the expression, Oats managed to eke out two words without moving his lips: "Eyes . . . wider . . . ."

The next morning was Sunday, so they started early, so early it was still dark out. Oats and Shadow started the day off with a run, trotting to their very own marching song:

Oats called out the first line: *"I don't know but it's been said."*

And Shadow answered back: *"This old farm is in the red."*

" I don't know but it's a fact."

"The Derby purse will put us back in black!"

"Sound off!"

"One-two, three-four . . ."

Shadow stood at the start of a sloppy stretch of dirt wetted down into ankle-deep mud. "Welcome to the mud run!" Oats shouted like a drill sergeant. "A.K.A. the Slip 'n Slide. Don't bother crying for your mommy, but I *will* make a 'mudder' out of you!"

Shadow loved training with Roscoe, and with Oats. Every once in a while they'd hear dings, beeps, and boops coming from the barn on the other side of the fence as the Epsoms' new trainer's newfangled equipment clanged and sputtered its way along, but they paid the strange noises no mind and went on about their business.

The sun set on another long and glorious day of training. The last three weeks had come and gone in the blink of an eye. Shadow had run out of minds to change at Flynn Farm, having convinced Fyfe, the other farm animals, Oats, and even Roscoe that he had what it took to be a racehorse. Now he was ready to show the rest of the world, and just in time.

Roscoe led Shadow back behind the barn to remove his training gear. He talked to the horse as he went about his business, not because he believed the animal was listening, but rather as a way of purging his own mind and setting his thoughts free by letting them out in the open.

"Won't be long now before you're a genuine, bona fide racehorse, Shadow. Come Saturday you'll have your first race," said Roscoe. "Then we'll see what kind of giddy-up you've got in you after all."

Shadow snorted a puff of hot breath through his nostrils.

Roscoe found a short stick in the dirt and lifted one of Shadow's hooves, then dug at the mud caked thick in his horseshoe. "Do you have any idea what you're getting into?" A twinge of worry flashed across Roscoe's face and his hand jumped instinctively to his bad knee. "You could get hurt out there. You understand me, Shadow?"

The horse bucked his head.

"There's no foolin' out there on the track," Roscoe continued, determined to make his point. "The Colonel is hell-bent on winning, and he'll stop at nothing to see that his horse crosses that finish line first. He's ruthless and, what's worse, he's underhanded. Steer clear of Bred Winner if you know what's good for you. We're all counting on you and you're no use to us hurt."

Roscoe's thoughts wandered. He began to worry about his knee and how it would hold up in a race. Jockeys are taught to "train through the pain" and that's what he'd been doing. But training was different than racing. He hoped he had at least one more race left in the old knee, but he knew nothing was promised in this life.

If Roscoe was wary, Shadow was downright petrified. There was a deep well of fear down in Shadow's stomach. He took heed of Roscoe's warning and was afraid of getting hurt, but that was only part of it. His greatest fear was letting down Fyfe and the rest of the Flynn Farm family. He was prepared for a fair fight, but he'd come to realize that might not be what he was in for.

18

"*VELOCE! VELOCE!*" THE new trainer Bianchi bellowed through a megaphone. His voice was deep and his accent was thick even when he wasn't barking orders in his native Italian. They didn't have many strangers around these parts so the way the English language got twisted up by his foreign tongue fell unkindly onto local ears in most cases. But it was clear from the start that Bianchi had not come to town to make friends, or to ingratiate himself into the local culture. Indeed not. That foreign tongue of his would taste no Southern hospitality.

"*Veloce!*" Bianchi shouted once more, as Bred Winner ran round and round the track, faster and faster. But Bianchi wasn't satisfied. "Give him the stick," he instructed the jockey riding Bred Winner. The jockey responded with a tap of his whip.

"Let him feel it!" Bianchi commanded.

The jockey reluctantly obliged, whipping Bred Winner with a firmer wrist this time.

"Again. Harder."

The jockey hesitated. He knew what he was being asked to do was cruel, but he was afraid of the consequences if he disobeyed.

Bianchi's voice, laden with a dangerous mix of determination and ruthlessness, cracked through the megaphone. "Hit him again."

The jockey struck Bred Winner again and the horse shuddered in pain. But he welcomed it. He *needed* it. It wasn't possible for Bred Winner to push himself any harder. The sting of the whip made his muscles jump and spurred him on just a bit faster, and he was grateful for it. He panted hard. The veins in his neck throbbed. He was at his breaking point.

Satisfied Bred Winner had nothing left to give, Bianchi put an end to his torture. "Alright, horse. That's enough." Bred Winner slowed and nearly stumbled, unsure what to do with his hooves when they weren't galloping at lightning speed. "It's time to take your medicine."

The trainer opened his black doctor's bag and pulled

out a syringe. He plunged the long, thick needle into an opaque glass bottle and pulled the hammer back, slurping up a murky goo that bubbled into the syringe's chamber. The jockey walked Bred Winner over to Bianchi, but Bred Winner caught wind of what was coming his way and began to stir.

"Shh . . . there's a good boy," Bianchi said in an effort to soothe him. But Bred Winner could not be calmed.

Bianchi took the reins from the jockey and yanked hard, jerking the horse's head back, then stuck the long, steely needle into his backside. Bred Winner writhed in agony as the mystery fluid coursed through his body, sending his muscles twitching in a fit of spasms. He neighed loudly and angrily. "That's right," Bianchi taunted, "drink up."

"Bianchi!" The trainer turned to see the Colonel looming in the entryway of the training barn. "What business has any horse of mine got standing still?"

"We were just getting ready to go again, Colonel," Bianchi said, then he sent Bred Winner back to trotting.

"Hook him up to one of your fancy, newfangled machines, why don't ya? Show me what I'm paying for."

Bianchi complied once again, attaching the horse's bridle to a weighted contraption that provided resistance against his speed. As Bred Winner ran faster, he pulled against it harder, and the machine automatically counterbalanced, adding more weight to provide greater resistance. By this time the juice from the injection had the horse firmly in its grip. He chomped at the bit in his mouth wildly and powerfully, and snot flung from his nostrils as he whipped his head to and fro.

"How's the training progressing?" The Colonel asked.

"This horse is strong" is all Bianchi replied.

The Colonel was not one to mince words, so when he spoke, he spoke in no uncertain terms. "I expect Bred Winner to win on Saturday. If he doesn't, it's curtains for the horse and a one way ticket back to Spaghettiville for you."

"Do not worry. His performance in the preparatory races has been flawless. He is only nine points shy of securing his place at the Derby already. That is practically unheard of. It does not matter if he wins this one, Colonel."

The Colonel hitched his britches up. "There are many things about me my wife doesn't care for. Chief among them are my superstitions. She thinks they're foolish. But to me, they're sacred. There's no such thing as losing just one race. Losing is contagious. It spreads like a virus. So Bred Winner will win this one, the next one, and every one after that, right up to the Derby itself. The Epsom family has been on a winning streak for the better part of a century, and I'm not about to let it slip through our fingers. *Capisce?*"

"Yes, Colonel," replied Bianchi.

"There are two things that matter in this world: money and reputation. And both of 'em rely on winning. Do not let me down."

Nightfall had brought with it an unusual chill in the air that evening. Cold, wet dew settled onto the grass in the dark, and it was slick under Shadow's hooves as he snuck away from the barn and made his way along the fence at the far edge of the Flynn Farm property, where it butted up against the Epsom estate. To his surprise, Gilda was waiting for him at the other side of the fence.

"Mama! What are you doing here?" asked Shadow.

"Waiting for you, of course," she replied. Shadow could see her breath puff into a cloud and hang in the crisp air, and he felt guilty he had kept her waiting in the cold.

"But how did you know I was coming?"

"You've got your first qualifying race tomorrow, don't you?"

Shadow nodded.

"Are you scared?"

He nodded again.

"I thought you might be."

"What if I lose? Or get hurt? What if Bred Winner doesn't fight fair? What if I make a mistake? Or what if I'm just not good enough?"

"That's an awful lot to be afraid of. Sounds to me like maybe you're just scared of racing."

"What kind of a racehorse is scared of racing?"

"The best kind. I was a bundle of nerves every race I ever ran. *What if the track is sloppy? What if the jockey had a big lunch?* You stay up half the night worrying about all the what-ifs, then you spend the other half thinking about the what-if-nots. *What if I don't pull a good starting post? What if I forget to smile in the winner's circle?* Nerves are just a part of racing. They let you know you've got fire in your belly."

"If I have even a shred of the talent you had, Mama, well, I might just do okay," Shadow said.

"You can only be you, child. And tomorrow, on that track, that'll have to be enough. You're a racehorse, Shadow. I've known that from the day I first saw you. A mother always knows. Only question is: are you ready to let the rest of the world know it?"

A hint of courage glimmered in Shadow's eyes.

"I love you more than fifty-four red roses," said Gilda. "And someday soon, when you find yourself wearing that blanket of flowers at the end of the big race, you'll finally know how much that really is."

Shadow nuzzled his mother's neck and she whispered into his ear, "Brace yourself, child. It's more than you think."

19

"WHAT DO YOU say, race fans? Can you feel the electricity in the air?" The silver-tongued race commentator Skip Sullivan chattered into a handheld microphone as throngs of excited fans crowded into the stands. Skip, better known as "Skip the Quip"—so named for his alacrity of diction, witty observations, and wry remarks—was the go-to guy for race rundowns, the equestrian authority. "Yes siree Bob, it's a heck of a day for a horse race!"

Roscoe stood by Skip's side, his palms wet with perspiration. Roscoe was out of his element in the midst of the fast-talking, adjective-flinging, fancy-pants commentator. He had done plenty of interviews with Skip over the years but had enjoyed not a one. Roscoe had felt uneasy around guys like Skip his whole career. Somehow talking never seemed like the important part of racing to him.

"Have I got a treat for you today, race fans! I'm here with the one, the only, elusive Hall of Famer, Mister Roscoe Flynn." Skip tilted the microphone toward Roscoe.

Roscoe leaned in to the microphone deliberately and said quite curtly, "Much obliged."

"A man of few words. You prefer to let your horse do the talking, huh Flynn-ski?"

"Yep," Roscoe answered.

"You don't say," Skip prattled on sarcastically. "Well, this is going fine. I don't suppose I could sweet-talk you into stringing together a few syllables about your horse?"

"I can talk about horses all day. And in plain English too." Roscoe had his own brand of wit when it suited him.

"That's swell! Lay it on us, Flynn-flam. I saw your Shadow of a Doubt back there and he's no bigger than a common house cat. Are you telling me that pip-squeak has a shot at the purse?"

"If—no, *when*—Shadow wins it won't be in spite of his size, it'll be because of it. His smallness will give him the edge in needling through the pack. He's nimble, he's agile, and he's got more spirit than you could shake a stick at. Shadow's the biggest little racehorse in all of Kentucky."

"That's quite a vote of confidence for a pocket-sized pony. But let's get real. Today's race is the first qualifier in the long road leading up to the Kentucky Derby. Are you and Shadow hoping to move on in that circuit?"

"We're going all the way."

"You think you can take down Ansel Epsom in the big race? Swipe the purse right out from under the old boss man?"

Roscoe's eyes narrowed. "If the Colonel wants it, he's gonna have to come and take it from me."

"You heard it here first, race fans!"

"Can't we shut that racket off?" Colonel Epsom barked at one of the lackeys in the clubhouse, referring to Skip the Quip's voice booming over the loudspeaker. The lackey fussed about, trying in vain to shut off the noise. But everyone at the track had already heard Roscoe's challenge cut through the airwaves.

The Colonel unfurled his pocket square and dabbed vigorously at the pearls of sweat beading at his temple and at the back of his thick neck. He was not used to being challenged, and the flop sweat usually reserved for the final moments of an unsavory close call or, daresay, even a photo finish, had presented itself early today as a result. About this he was not happy. And it was a well-known fact that when the Colonel wasn't happy, nobody was happy.

"Where's my race form? Where's my wife? This whole operation's falling apart at the seams!" The clubhouse staff scattered and scurried to appease the Colonel.

"Come now, Ansel. What's all this fuss?" Mrs. Epsom floated into the clubhouse and gracefully slipped off her dainty lace gloves in an entirely unperturbed manner. It always propelled the Colonel into another stratosphere of frustration when Mrs. Epsom kept her cool under pressure. His complexion began to turn beet red.

"I feel it in my bones, Hedy," said the Colonel.

"What's that, dear?"

"Losing." His expression was grave and desperate. "The ache of impending defeat. I feel it deep down in my bones."

"Don't be silly. You couldn't possibly." She stifled a wry, guilty smile at taking pleasure in torturing her husband. "Perhaps it's gout."

. . .

The racing stables were abuzz with the raw energy of pent up animals itching to be unleashed. The horses were loud and boisterous, and the jockeys, groomers, and stable hands hustled to finish their final preparations, knowing it wasn't long before they were due at the starting line.

Fyfe used a coarse boar bristle brush to stroke Shadow's coat, getting it nice and shiny. She gently lowered Shadow's head by the reins and carefully arranged his mane into what she considered a winner's coif. Then she leaned back to admire her handiwork. "There he is." Fyfe beamed. "What a beaut."

Shadow playfully fluttered a breath of hot air at her and Fyfe returned the gesture in kind, flapping her lips like the horse.

They were on the precipice of finding out whether this whole crazy idea was going to work, whether Shadow really was a racehorse all this time, whether they had a shot at winning the purse, whether there was any hope of saving Flynn Farm after all. Yet there they were, horsing around, like they didn't have a care in the world. They had a way of putting each other at ease like that, Fyfe and Shadow. They believed in each other so doggone much it didn't matter what anyone else thought. Each other was all they needed. (Which was mighty convenient, because that's about all they had.)

The head stable hand called out the time. It was five minutes 'til the race. Fyfe ran off to collect her pa, leaving Shadow on his own. She wasn't gone long before Bred Winner started making trouble.

"Psst!" Bred Winner called to Shadow from his stall across the way. "Nervous for your first race?"

"I've got just as much right to be here as you do," Shadow answered back with courage.

"Sure you do," Bred Winner snorted. "As a matter of fact, I'm looking forward to racing against you. And leaving you in the dust! Then I can show everyone out there you're nothing but a joke."

"Just you watch. I'm gonna be a champ!"

Bred Winner scoffed, "More like a *chump*. Don't you get it? I'm destined to be a winner—born and *bred*, like the name says. My pedigree is impeccable: generation after generation of winning pureblood thoroughbreds. And you've got nothing but a bunch of ordinary plow-pullers doing belly flops in your gene pool. You're just a workhorse in a tired old hand-me-down saddlecloth. Like I said, a joke."

Just then, a groomer came to fetch Bred Winner

from his stall to brush him down one last time before the race. Shadow looked at the saddlecloth on his own back, slightly frayed at the edges, its once bright colors worn with wash and wear. He was so proud of it just a moment ago, and now he was ashamed.

"Two minutes 'til the starting gate!" bellowed the head stable hand.

Meanwhile, Roscoe was slowly making his way to the front of a very long line at the betting window. As he inched his way along, he jingled the coins in his pocket impatiently, knowing the race was about to start. Finally it was Roscoe's turn at the window. He emptied his pockets out onto the counter, shoving every last cent over to the man behind the window.

"Hey Sal," Roscoe greeted the familiar face.

"You're gonna get me fired one of these days," the man behind the window answered.

"Come on, you know they can't run this place without you."

Sal shrugged. "What do ya got?" He counted Roscoe's money.

"Let it ride. Put it all on Shadow of a Doubt."

"Win, place, or show?" asked the clerk.

"Friend, we'll be lucky just to get on the board."

Sal entered the bet to show and slid the ticket across the counter.

Just then: "Hey Pa!" Fyfe spotted him across the crowd. She was holding her father's racing silks balled up in her arms, wearing his helmet with the chin strap dangling loose. "Race is starting!"

Roscoe and Fyfe rushed back to the stables together. Roscoe hurried to put on his uniform as they walked. He handed Fyfe the ticket from his bet. "Hang onto this."

"I thought jockeys weren't allowed to bet?"

"Sal's been taking my bets ever since I started racing here. Besides, the track's always happy to take your money. It's not 'til you try to cash out that they start asking questions. That's why you're gonna cash it for me if we win."

"Me? I'm just a kid!" cried Fyfe.

"Well, then we'll find somebody. This is what they call champagne problems, kiddo."

"Where'd you get money for the bet anyhow?"

"I used the entry fee we put aside for Shadow's next race."

"Well, what'd you go and do a thing like that for?"

Roscoe buttoned his racing silk. "I reckon if we don't finish in the money this time, there ain't much use in entering him in another race. If he doesn't perform here, he'll never make it to the springboards."

"I guess so," Fyfe replied, clearly disappointed in her father's lack of faith. "But are you sure that's smart?"

"It's gambling. Ain't nothin' smart about it." He stuffed his shirttails into his britches. "W.C. Fields said it best: 'Horse sense is the thing a horse has which keeps it from betting on people.'"

Fyfe led Roscoe through the crowded stables in a whirlwind.

"Gimme a minute, eh kiddo?" Roscoe stalled. "Make sure Shadow's saddled up."

Fyfe busied herself with the saddle as Roscoe slipped away behind the paddock, just outside the frenzy of all the pre-race commotion. He was alone. He unbuckled his belt and pulled it from the loops of his pants. Then he folded the leather and placed it firmly between his teeth. Using both hands, he grabbed hold of his calf and pulled his leg up toward his chest. He bit down hard on the belt, squelching his cries of agony. Sweat beaded on his upper lip. Pain pulsed through his leg and ran up his spine to where it clanged like a bell ringing in his head. There was a loud snap and his knee gave way. He pulled it to his chest and the expression on his face relaxed. The knee would swell up like a balloon and hurt worse than ever by nightfall, but for now, he had bought himself some time. Of course, he knew this little party trick had a limited run. But he needed the momentary reprieve, no matter what the price.

As he was threading his belt back through his trousers he heard a loud thump. He spun around and there, at the other end of the paddock wall, was Bred Winner. This was the first time he'd seen that horse since that fateful day when Bred Winner took him and The Duke out in the race.

The *thump* sound had come from Bred Winner's hoof hitting the wall as he tried to back away from Bianchi. Roscoe looked on silently as Bianchi dug deep in his nefarious black doctor's bag and produced a syringe filled with the mysterious, cloudy goo that Bred Winner had come to fear and hate—and need. Bianchi administered the shot to Bred Winner and he instantly reared back with adrenaline and rage.

Bianchi was none the wiser that Roscoe had witnessed his dirty trick. Just like the foul play that brought Roscoe to his knees not so long ago, this would remain a bitterly kept secret between man and beast.

Roscoe tried to shake off what he'd witnessed as he made his way back to the stall where Fyfe and Shadow were waiting for him. He greeted Shadow with a strong, comforting pat on the back then hoisted himself up into the saddle. As he shifted his weight onto his bad knee, another twinge of pain shot through his leg and he grimaced. He picked up Shadow's reins, took his riding helmet from Fyfe, put it on, and fastened the chinstrap just as the head stable hand cried out for the racers to take their places.

20

SHADOW WAS A bundle of nerves as he entered the starting pen for the race. He was posting in the number three spot. Bred Winner had pulled number one. Shadow looked to the horses on either side of him, hoping for a friendly nod or maybe even a "good luck." But he found no such pleasantries as the serious horses steadied themselves for the starting horn.

Shadow peered through the slats of the gate at the track ahead of him. The dirt was red and had been raked through. He pricked up his ears, waiting for that horn to sound. This was it. Now or never. Shadow held his breath. It felt like an eternity. Like maybe in that split second, flowers had bloomed then withered, wars had been fought and won, a million trillion lives had been lived. The next second, the starting horn piped to life and the gate in front of him flung open.

He was off like a shot! Shadow was the first horse over the starting line and gained a nose-length lead right off the bat. The pack stayed thick at first, with Shadow, Bred Winner, Butterscotch Betty, and Thar She Blows at the front of it. The clamor of hooves trampling the dirt with powerful force created a rhythmic rumble that sounded like thunder clapping in every direction all around Shadow. He listened carefully for Roscoe's commands through the noise.

But going into the first turn, Shadow strayed from the rail and by the time he hit the back straight, he found himself smack dab in the middle of the pack. He went to work, weaving in and out of the fray, trying to make up lost ground. Roscoe helped him find the openings and then he slipped right through, just like threading a needle. As he maneuvered between the thoroughbreds, he was able to brush past them without slowing or losing his footing, despite their boxing him out. His endless training shunning haystacks was paying off.

Suddenly, he was out in front again. He was soaring. But Roscoe gave a little tug on the reins. "Ease off, boy," Roscoe warned. "Pace yourself." Shadow bucked his head like a pitcher shaking off a catcher's call. He sprinted dead ahead, fast as he could.

By the time they rounded the final bend, the horses were barreling down the track with full force. The air around them grew warm from the heat coming off the horses' bodies.

Shadow's legs were starting to give out. He could hear his own heartbeat pounding in his ears. His pace slowed by just a splinter of a second, but in a race this tight, a microsecond could make all the difference. *Click-click.* Roscoe signaled to Shadow to speed up with a click of his tongue. Shadow tried to go faster, but he didn't have it in him. He'd given everything he had right out of the gate and burned out too early. He was used up.

Bred Winner pulled ahead going into the homestretch. My Two Cents and Thar She Blows were right on his heels. Shadow was falling behind.

Skip called the race from the commentator's booth. "Shadow of a Doubt has got some speed on him, alright, but a rookie horse like him might not have what it takes to stay in it."

"Come on, boy!" Roscoe begged him.

Butterscotch Betty overtook Shadow, relegating

him to fifth position. Shadow was losing it on the straightaway! Bred Winner was out in front by several lengths. At this point, the race was his to lose.

Roscoe signaled Shadow again but couldn't get any more speed out of him. Running out of time, Roscoe posted up in the saddle and leaned forward to whisper into Shadow's ear. "Come on, boy. Do it like you did that day at Mud River. Do it for Fyfe."

This ignited a fire inside Shadow. His legs began to stretch just a little further, his hooves pushed against the ground just a little harder, and suddenly the wind was at his back. His muscles rippled, his legs burned, his breathing was heavy and labored, but he was gaining once again.

Shadow couldn't be sure if it was real or imagined, but just then, he could swear he heard Fyfe cheering for him all the way on the other side of the track, one of thousands shouting in the stands. "Go Shadow! You can do it!"

Whether he really could hear it or not, Fyfe screamed her lungs out for that horse. She screamed until she was red in the face, and then she kept on screaming. And so did every little guy, underdog, and downtrodden, beat-up old so-and-so. They stood up and they cheered and they stomped their feet for one of their own. "Let's go, Shadow!"

Butterscotch Betty, Thar She Blows, and My Two Cents all fell by the wayside.

"I can't believe it!" shouted Skip over the loudspeaker. "Here comes Shadow of a Doubt sprinting to the head of the pack. Make way for the comeback kid!"

It was the final stretch now: just Shadow, Bred Winner, and a white chalk line a hundred yards away. A few seconds to change the world.

One. Shadow's heart beat faster. *Two.* The crowd roared to a deafening frenzy. *Three.* Fyfe held her breath, too scared to breathe. *Four.* Bred Winner's eyes darted to the side and flickered with a glint of fear as he clocked Shadow at his flank. *Five . . .*

Five seconds and it was all over.

A single hoof came down in the dirt, breaking the pristine white chalk line, which was eviscerated seconds later by dozens upon dozens more hooves kicking up the powder into a cloud of dust.

The whole track went stone silent. The horses slowed to a stop. The peanut vendors stopped barking. You could hear a pin drop in the stands. "It's a photo finish, folks," said Skip. "This one's just too close to call."

Shadow panted, too exhausted and too anxious to catch his breath.

The door to the race office flew open and a young clerk bolted from it holding a single sheet of paper in his hands. His light footsteps clicked across what seemed like an interminable stretch of asphalt and up the long set of stairs reaching to the commentator's booth, where he handed the paper to Skip the Quip.

Skip read it, his expression registering a hint of disappointment, then leaned into the microphone and said, "Bred Winner takes it by a nose."

A loud whoop rang out from the ivory tower, otherwise known as the box seats, as the Colonel rejoiced in his victory. He latched on to one of the lackeys standing idly by and twirled him around. Mrs. Epsom looked away, appalled by his antics. "For Heaven's sake, Ansel," she said. "You look like a fool."

"Hedy, my daft little gimlet, are you so oblivious to the sport at hand that you don't realize that's *our* horse that just won?"

"I'm perfectly aware."

"And that by winning, he earned himself ten big, fat gorgeous points? Do you know what *that* means?"

She stared at him coldly.

"Of course you don't," he continued. He lifted the dainty robin's egg blue hat from her head and placed it crookedly on his own. "It means we're going to the Derby."

Roscoe led Shadow back through the paddock. Shadow felt like a failure for not having won, but to the rest of the world, he was a hero. He had burst out of virtual obscurity and catapulted himself into a dead heat with a heavyweight. Bred Winner was a sprinter unlike anything the sport had ever seen, and Shadow had held his own.

As Roscoe made his way to the stables, he felt the familiar claps on the back from other jockeys, a feeling he once knew so well. He got Shadow to his pen, removed his saddle and used a sponge to wash some water over his back to cool him down.

Out of nowhere came Fyfe, bolting straight for them. Without a word she wrapped her arms around that horse's neck and wouldn't let go, not for nothing. Shadow's head had been spinning up until this point, a million emotions coursing through him at once, adrenaline clashing with disappointment. But it all stopped the minute Fyfe held him tight. He was suddenly at home and all was right in the world. She was proud of him. He could feel it.

"Congratulations, boy," she whispered. "I knew you could do it." The horse nuzzled his head in the girl's shoulder.

Shadow earned four points for placing, and Roscoe made a pretty penny on the bet he placed. Of course it wasn't enough to line their pockets or anything like that, but it was a sufficient boost to morale to be that much closer (though still so very far) from making a payment to the bank on the farm, and they earned back the money they needed for Shadow's next race.

Roscoe allowed two small indulgences with the winnings: a new secondhand saddlecloth for Shadow, and a few pieces of the saltwater taffy Fyfe was so partial to. She favored the root beer and molasses flavored candies in particular, and could spend the better part of an afternoon working them over between her jaws.

Roscoe didn't dare spend one red cent on himself, but he did take considerable satisfaction and an overwhelming sense of pride in rewarding Fyfe and Shadow. It was nice to be living large for just a moment, even if the Flynns' interpretation of it was a used square of cloth and a dollop of sugar wrapped in wax paper.

Back at the farm, the animals had all crowded up against the fence to listen to the radio broadcast of the race blaring across the way at the Epsom estate. They cheered and wept in celebration of Shadow's success. Even cantankerous old Oats couldn't keep the corners of his mouth from turning skyward.

"Is that a smile I see, you gruff ol' son-of-a-gun?" Gladys teased.

Oats didn't have a snappy comeback or a clever

barb for once. He simply said it like it was: "We might just make it after all."

The animals stayed there all day, glued to that fence, trying to make the moment last forever. They didn't even notice it had gotten dark out until they heard the ambling motor of Roscoe's truck as it eased up the driveway. Roscoe and Fyfe retired to the main house for the evening, and Shadow couldn't wait to see his friends. He proudly showed off his shiny, (not-so-) new saddlecloth.

Raelynn regaled the group with a retelling of the afternoon. "I swear it on a stack of Bibles, Shadow. Oats had a tear in his eye! Crying like a newborn, he was!"

"Ah, I was not. I have allergies."

"To what?" she challenged him.

"Pollen."

"Now I know you're fibbing. Nothing's been pollinated on this farm for years!"

They all had a laugh at that.

Eventually, the animals tuckered themselves out, and they all settled in for a good night's rest. All except Shadow, that is. He was still so wound up from the race that sleep seemed entirely out of the question—possibly forever. It had been the most exciting day of his whole life and it wouldn't be complete until he could share it with his mama. So Shadow crept out to the fence and signaled to Gilda. She snuck out and joined him at the fence, but Shadow didn't let her get a word in edgewise.

"I have so much to tell you I think I'm gonna burst! I didn't win the race, and at first I was so upset with myself. I thought maybe I'd never get to race again because I didn't do well enough, and I was so afraid I let everyone down. But then everyone said I did good! What do *you* think, Mama? Did I do good?"

"Yes, my love. In fact, I believe the sky's lit up a little brighter tonight."

"Why's that, Mama?" Shadow looked up at the canopy of twinkling lights up above.

"Because it's got one more star."

Shadow realized she was talking about him, and it felt like the greatest accomplishment of all to be a star, even if only in his mama's eyes.

"I want to tell you all about it, right from the start—"

"I already heard the whole thing on the radio today, Shadow."

"Oh." Shadow looked down at the dirt. "Okay."

"Which means I'll know if you leave anything out, so you better make sure to tell me every little detail."

Shadow looked back at his mama, excited. He and Gilda lay down nose to nose on either side of the fence. "Well," he began, "we got there nice and early so it still smelled like fresh cut grass from the infield . . . ." Shadow talked on and on until eventually mama and son both drifted off to sleep.

21

"Hey, Shadow! You awake?" Fyfe's voice roused Shadow. He was still in the field, where he had fallen asleep out by the fence, only now the sun was up and Gilda was gone. Fyfe kneeled down across from him and unfolded a piece of paper, laying it out between them. "I did some tinkering last night and I think I got it figured out. Now, it was way past my bedtime when I did some of this math, so it might be a little wonky, but it still seems to hold in the light of day."

Shadow stared at the piece of paper in front of him: It was a hand-drawn tiered racing form with names and point values scribbled in each box. Shadow was looking at it upside down, not that it mattered, seeing as how he couldn't read.

"Look here." She pointed to the first box. "You won

four points for coming in second in yesterday's race. That's a good start—real good."

Shadow wondered how many more points he'd need.

"You need seventy to secure a spot in the Derby."

His heart sank. That was a lot of points.

"Don't worry. I've got a plan." Shadow leaned in close. "There's one more Prep race coming up on Sunday. That's scored the same as this last one: ten points to win, four to place, two to show. I don't want to put too much pressure on you, boy, but we'll have to squeak out a win on that one. We need the ten to carry forward. That'll qualify us for the Championship Series. You follow?"

Shadow just stared at her blankly and she carried on.

"The Championship Series are higher stakes. That means the points go way up: fifty to win, twenty to place, ten to show. All you gotta do here is get on the board. Finish fourth or better in a couple of these races and we advance into the second leg of the series."

Shadow was doing his best to follow along, but it was a lot to take in.

"Now, those next races are what're called the springboards. A win here will earn you a whopping one hundred points. Ring that bell, you go straight to the front of the line: automatic qualification for the Derby. Great if it happens, but not essential. Just getting on the boards twice should be enough to put you over the top."

Somehow, Fyfe had made getting to the Derby seem possible. She had laid it all out there on that scrap of paper: all of Shadow's dreams, just within reach.

"If all else fails, there's the Wild Card race just before the Derby, but don't worry about that. You don't tussle with the Wild Card unless you're in dire straits."

Shadow nuzzled Fyfe. He may not have had a clue what she was talking about, but one thing was crystal clear: She believed he could do it.

"Fyfe!" Roscoe called to her from way back at the barn. "Breakfast!"

Fyfe folded up the piece of paper and shoved it into her pocket. "Let's keep this between us, okay?" she said to Shadow. She knew Roscoe didn't have any expectations of Shadow coming anywhere close to the Derby. He was just hoping to win enough races to earn the money they owed the bank. But Fyfe shared Shadow's propensity for pipe dreams and she had set her sights on Churchill Downs.

Just because they'd done well in their first race, it didn't mean their training was done. Far from it, in fact. Roscoe knew there was still work to do in building up Shadow's stamina. It wasn't enough to have speed. And it wasn't enough to have endurance. He had to have them *both*. Shadow had finished strong, but Roscoe had seen how he'd burned out early on, and he worried that Shadow had relied more on his heart than his hooves to carry him through.

So, first thing Monday morning, Roscoe mounted the saddle and gave a quick tap of his heel, spurring Shadow into a gallop. Lap after lap, they went around the apple trees, through the thickets of briar bushes, and behind the woodshed. But on their fourth lap, as they were rounding the back bend at the far edge of the property, Shadow noticed that the loose fence slat with the teeth marks that he and Fyfe never did get around to fixing was pushed way out again.

He couldn't see much—the property jutted up against the woods back there and it was shaded and dark—but as he got closer, a glint of light flashed in the red, beady, bloodthirsty eyes of a wild coyote. Just then, a strong breeze blew, setting the leaves in the trees all aflutter, breaking up the shade and bringing the coyote into full view. He had a limp chicken clenched in his jaw and was yanking its lifeless body through the hole in the fence—one swift tug and she was gone.

Raelynn!

Shadow startled. He couldn't help it. He reared back on his hind legs then bucked forward mightily, throwing Roscoe off him. Roscoe hit the ground hard and came down on his bad knee. He cried out in pain. A sound that terrible hadn't been heard on Flynn Farm since the day of Shadow's birth when Esther Mae wailed in agony much the same way. Roscoe couldn't stand. He lay in the dirt clutching his knee, which, under the fabric of his pants, appeared to have dislocated itself entirely, bulging out from the side of his leg.

Shadow raced back to the house where Fyfe was sitting out on the front porch, waiting for them to circle round again. When she saw Roscoe wasn't with Shadow, she knew something was wrong. She hopped on Shadow's back and he took her to Roscoe. Roscoe couldn't be moved, not even by cart, so Fyfe rode back to the house with Shadow and sent for the doctor.

By the time the doctor arrived, Roscoe's leg had begun to turn purple due to lack of circulation; the injury was keeping blood from flowing past his knee. Roscoe was trying his best not to notice this, as the threat of losing his leg was more than he could bear. The doctor administered a powerful drug to kill the pain and it all but knocked Roscoe out. Then he hurried him away to the hospital.

Shadow was plagued with terrible guilt over Roscoe's injury. And to make matters worse, he was also mourning the loss of his friend Raelynn. He was the only one who saw what happened, so he knew he had to be the one to tell the other animals. He walked into the barn with his head hung low.

"Guys, I'm afraid I have some terrible news. It's about Raelynn."

"Uh-oh. Should I sit down for this?" asked Raelynn, as she plopped down in her nest.

"Raelynn!" Shadow couldn't believe his eyes! "You're alive!"

"Alive and clucking. Why shouldn't I be?"

"I saw a coyote dragging a chicken into the woods, and I thought—"

"Hush now," Gladys interrupted, trying to spare the other animals the details.

"Are you sure? Maybe it was a fluff of cotton or something?" asked Red.

"It had feet."

"It could have been one of the Hickses' hens," suggested Scout. "They lost a couple a while back. He could have snatched the poor bird there, then cut across our farm to the woods."

"Whoever it was," Oats said, "I believe they deserve a moment of silence." The animals bowed their heads.

The good doctors at Saint Joseph's performed a three-hour emergency surgery on Roscoe's knee. Fyfe waited nervously in the hospital's front room, cursing the fact that horses were not allowed inside because, at this moment, she was petrified for her pa and in dire need of her best friend.

When Roscoe woke after the procedure there was a brief moment of relief when he realized he still had his leg. However, that was the end of the good news. The bad news was his knee was shot. Whatever movement he had managed through sheer will and determination before was now non-negotiable: He couldn't force it. Not with pain or by might. Not at all or ever again. Roscoe would never ride again.

When he was discharged from the hospital they gave him a cane to help him put one foot in front of the other, but this amounted to something of a scarlet letter for an ex-jockey like him, so he refused it, hobbling on his own, with a distinct limp but his head held high.

22

Back home, Fyfe tended to her father dutifully, to the extent her old man's pride would allow. Each night, Fyfe rubbed Tiger Balm onto his knee and she would marvel at it, thick with scar tissue and held together with pins and stitches, like Frankenstein's monster. It was during this ritual that Fyfe chose to broach what she knew would be a sensitive subject, and to get down to the business of things.

"Who's going to ride Shadow now, Pa?"

"The next race is in three days' time, Fyfe," explained Roscoe. "Any jockey worth his salt already has a horse."

"Well what happens if we don't find somebody?"

"He'll be forced to withdraw."

"Then I guess we better find somebody," said Fyfe.

"And how do you suppose we do that? We can't very well sit a sack of potatoes on his back, can we?"

Scoot Zeigler was the next best thing to a sack of potatoes. Now, two sacks of potatoes? That would have been a fair fight. Scoot was a two-bit rent-a-jockey who liked to have a nip every now and again—and again, and again. He resembled nothing of an athlete in his inebriated stupor—Roscoe had found him in one of Jessamine County's most ill-reputed watering holes, fishing cigarette butts out of half-drunk glasses of cheap whisky—but they had no other options. He was pudgy and bloated, so when he put on Roscoe's racing silks, they gapped between the buttons and strained at the seams. But Scoot had won more races than he'd lost in his gin-soaked career, and that would have to be good enough for now.

Shadow was nervous to face off against Bred Winner again, especially without Roscoe on his back. Fyfe's words reverberated in his head: "We'll have to squeak out a win. . . ." Anything less than first place and he didn't move on.

But come race day, he knew he'd have to put his nerves aside because, despite everything, one thing hadn't changed: the stakes were high and the Flynns were counting on him. Win the race or lose the farm.

Before the start of a race, a few of the jockeys were in the habit of congregating out by the horse trailers in the parking lot. They had a fraternity all their own and Roscoe knew a lot of the guys on the bill for the day, so he took a stroll out back to say hello and get the news. Of course, when Roscoe was on the circuit he'd been somewhat of a stranger in these circles, tending to keep to himself and his horse instead, but he was always welcome nonetheless.

"Shouldn't you be in your silks?" called his good buddy Arnaz.

"Not today, old friend. Not anymore," Roscoe said. His limp was impossible to hide. His knee was still tender from surgery and he cringed with every step.

"What happened?" asked Arnaz.

"Took a spill." Roscoe didn't like talking about his injury. He tried changing the subject, "You here with Abracadabra?"

"Nah, the boss didn't like the way she was running so he retired her for the season. He's had me on Say It Ain't So for the last couple races and, I gotta admit, I think it was the right move. We just raced Delta

Downs out in Calcasieu Parish and broke the track record by point-eight."

Roscoe whistled, impressed.

"Hey Roscoe, if you're not racing, who's on Shadow?" one of the other jockeys asked.

"Scoot Ziegler."

The guys tried to stifle a snicker. Never a good sign.

"Believe me, I *wish* it was me," said Roscoe. "I'd love another crack at Bred Winner."

"Didn't you hear?" Arnaz looked surprised. "The Colonel pulled him."

"Good afternoon, race fans! It's a beautiful day for a race, and today's race is gonna be a beaut!" Skip the Quip welcomed fans to the track. "Now clean the cotton out of your ears and listen up, because your ol' pal Skip is about to take you where none of you bums have ever gone before. I'm giving you an exclusive look behind the caviar curtain. That's right, I'm here in the clubhouse with Colonel Ansel Epsom himself." He tilted the microphone toward the Colonel. "Hey, Joe, what do you know?"

"I'm just here as a spectator today. My boy Bred Winner is back at home, training for the big show," said the Colonel.

"That's right, Bred Winner qualified for the Derby very early on, still in the Prep Season. Don't tell me you're planning to mothball him all the way 'til May?"

"Too early to tell, Skip. We'll be watching closely and make those decisions as they come."

"I guess that means you're here scoping out the competition, huh? No doubt you'll be keeping an eye on Shadow of a Doubt, who almost snatched the win right out from under you last time."

The Colonel frowned. He'd hoped Shadow would have been forgotten by now. But Skip kept on poking the bear.

"Famed jockey Roscoe Flynn took a nasty spill and is out of the game. They got Scoot Zeigler to take his place today. Apparently they dragged him out of the gutter, wrung him out, and dusted him off just in the nick of time."

The Colonel dismissed Skip with a wave of his hand. "I don't care if it's Roscoe, Scoot, or the Lone Ranger riding him. Shadow's last run was beginner's luck. It won't happen again."

It was with great difficulty and little grace that Scoot Zeigler hoisted his corpulent buttocks into the air, and settled into his mount on Shadow's racing saddle.

Then they took their place in the number nine stall at the starting gate.

As they were calling for the start of the race on the loudspeaker, once again Roscoe was held up in line at the betting window. No sooner did he get to the front of the line than he heard Fyfe whistling to him from the edge of the stands. When she got his attention, she crossed her fingers on both hands for luck, then crossed her arms in an X for good measure. This made Roscoe smile. Fyfe waved him over and ran back to the stands.

Roscoe looked at the track and saw Shadow at the starting gate, a tiny David in a lineup of hulking Goliaths, and his smile faded into a nervous clenched-jaw grimace.

Roscoe placed his bet and pocketed his ticket, and found his way through the crowd to Fyfe who was pressed up against the rail, calling to Shadow, trying to get his attention. He told her to leave the horse alone and let him concentrate on the race, but Fyfe was over the moon when Shadow finally looked her way, and she gave him a great big wave. Shadow neighed warmly in return.

"I've got a good feeling about this one," Fyfe said, and Roscoe put his arm around the sweet, idealistic girl's shoulder.

The starting shot sounded. Out of the gate, it was Say It Ain't So, Passing Fancy, Shadow of a Doubt, and My Two Cents. Rounding the first bend, it was Say It Ain't So, Shadow of a Doubt, and Passing Fancy, with My Two Cents falling back in the pack. Shadow cut to the inside, settling into the sweet spot on the rail. Say It Ain't So was in the lead by just one length, but sticking close enough to the rail to keep Shadow behind.

Say It Ain't So was a big horse. All power. His stride was long and heavy and he charged ahead like a locomotive: noisy and strong. Shadow had none of that. His legs were short and it took him two strides to equal one of Say It Ain't So's.

Scoot tugged on Shadow's reins and guided him to the outside, which was sudden death for a short strider. Skip couldn't believe what he was seeing. "Shadow of a Doubt gives up the inside rail to pass on the outside!" he said. "A move like that so early in the race could spell disaster for this little guy!"

It was, indeed, a bad move. Say It Ain't So picked up another length and Passing Fancy took command of the number two spot.

At that moment, Shadow knew what he had to do. He stopped listening to the stranger on his back and started listening to his gut. He let his instincts take over. Scoot was working him over for speed, but that's not how Shadow had been trained. Roscoe had taught him to give it everything he had, mane to tail. He didn't just race with his legs; he raced with his heart and his head, too.

At the first bend, Passing Fancy planted wide, kicking up a cloud of dirt for Shadow to choke on. He didn't have the speed he needed to get around the frontrunners, but he figured maybe he could go *through* them. Shadow was small, and he knew he had to find a way to use that to his advantage. So he zigged to the inside, past Passing Fancy, then zagged to the outside, bringing him side-by-side with Say It Ain't So.

"Don't count out Shadow of a Doubt just yet! He is back in it!" shouted Skip.

Shadow and Say It Ain't So were out in front of the pack. Shadow lost half a length, but he remembered his training, how endurance made all the difference, how patience was a virtue, and he hunkered down. Say It Ain't So had a solid lead, but Shadow was still pacing himself. He had more to give.

Say It Ain't So barreled into the turn first, followed closely by Shadow. Then Shadow saw that white line ahead and he knew he could take it. Shadow broke away.

"Say It Ain't So goes in to the straightaway with a commanding lead, but Shadow of a Doubt is looking to overtake him!" Skip prattled into the microphone, perched on the edge of his seat. "Here he comes! It's a dead heat now. They're barreling down the chute neck-and-neck. Shadow surges ahead! I can't believe it! Say It Ain't So is nipped at the wire by the hard-closing Shadow of a Doubt! Shadow of a Doubt takes the win by half a length! Look for everybody's favorite under-dog to move on to the Championship Series!"

"Favorite" was an understatement. The crowd went wild as Shadow crossed the finish line. The cheers were so loud they could have heard them in the next county.

Race fans cheer for lots of different reasons, and there's a world of difference between the polite *huzzah*s of the boxed seats and the brouhaha rumble of those flush in the stands. But a real, honest-to-goodness cheer sounds like something else altogether. It's got nothing to do with the payout or the odds. It tran-scends the exacta, the trifecta, and the superfecta. It's the sound of having your socks blown off. The roar of raw excitement. It's appreciation in its purest form, and the battle cry of the true fan. *That* was the cheer they cheered for Shadow. And they dang near shattered the Richter scale.

"Holy smokes! Just when you think he's done for—bam, zip, whiz!—he slips right out in front!" exclaimed Fyfe, beaming with pride. "Let's go cash in that ticket!"

"We can't." Roscoe fingered the ticket in his pocket. His expression was decidedly more serious than Fyfe's, but she was too caught up in the moment to notice.

"I know, I know," Fyfe said. "We can get old man Peckinpaw to cash it for us, if we buy him a Coke."

"No, Fyfe—"

"Sure he will!" Fyfe interrupted. "He might try and gouge us for a pretzel, too, but I'll talk him down. Unless we made real good odds, then it's pretzels all around!"

"That's not it, Fyfe. We can't collect on the ticket . . . because we didn't win."

"Sure we did! You must be delirious. Didn't you see? Shadow smoked 'em!"

"Shadow won. *We* didn't."

"You mean . . . ?" Fyfe couldn't believe it. It couldn't be true.

"I put it all on Say It Ain't So. I—I bet against

Shadow." Roscoe couldn't look at his daughter when he said this.

Fyfe's eyes flooded with tears. She could hardly speak. "How could you?"

"I was going to bet on Shadow, but when I got up to the window, I got scared. That little bit of money was everything we had in this world. I couldn't risk it all on hopes and dreams. So I made the safe bet. The odds on Say It Ain't So were two to one—practically a sure thing! Nobody thought Shadow would pull out the win. Nobody."

Fyfe did.

"Is it all gone then?" she asked.

"Everything."

"The entry fee for the next race too?"

"I'm sorry." Roscoe's voice broke.

"So that's it. Shadow won't race again." Tears cascaded down Fyfe's cheeks. Roscoe kneeled down, face-to-face with his daughter, both of them crying now. He hugged her to his chest, hoping to make her listen, to make her understand.

"Desperation drives a man to do foolish things, Fyfe. Stupid, petty, thoughtless things! I'm so sorry. Can you forgive me?"

"It's not that you lost the money. It's that you bet

against Shadow. That's *our* horse, Pa! And you turned your back on him. That'll break his heart. I know it will, because it broke mine." There was no kindness in her eyes now, no warmth left in her sad, little face.

Both father and daughter lay awake in their beds that night, staring up at the roof over their heads—a roof they might not be under much longer if they didn't come up with a way to make good on their delinquent mortgage. They'd won a modest purse in the last race, but it was barely enough to hold the bank at bay for another few weeks. It wouldn't even last them to the next race—and that's *if* there was another one.

They tossed and they turned and neither one slept a wink, Roscoe trying to figure out how he was going to scrape together the money to enter the next race, and Fyfe trying to figure how she was going to break it to Shadow that there might not *be* a next race.

23

THE NEXT MORNING, Roscoe prepared a warm and hearty breakfast of grits and biscuits. Fyfe came down to eat and slinked into her chair without saying a word. Roscoe joined her at the table with a steaming cup of joe.

"How'd you sleep?" he asked.

No answer. Fyfe shoveled the grits into her mouth without looking up.

"I put an extra pat of butter in there, just the way you like it."

Fyfe swallowed a few gulps of water without stopping to put her spoon down, then went right back to it.

"Look," Roscoe tried to reason. "I won't ask you to forgive me. That's too tall an order, I know. Just try to understand—"

"I understand alright. I understand that, not so long ago, you saw things differently. But something changed the day you got hurt in that race. And all that pride, and strength, and decency inside of you, well, you let them take it from you. Now there's a blackness in your heart. And that blackness is spreading. It's festering, and it's eating all of us up, bite by bite."

Roscoe couldn't deny it.

"I pity you, Pa. I can see now that you're just an empty shell of the man you once were. If a strong wind blew through here I think it might sweep you clear away. And I think that might be exactly what you *want*. I feel sorry for you, because you can't see goodness anymore, even when it's right in front of you. And feeling sorry for you ain't easy. You feel so dang sorry for yourself all the time there's barely any sorry left for the rest of us."

A hard lump formed in Roscoe's throat so that he couldn't speak.

"May I be excused?" said Fyfe, coldly.

He nodded and Fyfe got up from the table and went out to the barn, letting the screen door bang shut behind her. Roscoe sat there undisturbed for the next twenty minutes, praying for that strong wind.

. . .

Roscoe knew that by betting against Shadow, not only had he lost the money for Shadow to continue racing, but he'd also lost Fyfe's trust. Money comes and goes; he'd learned that the hard way after many years of booms and busts. But the way a child looks at her father, with respect befitting kings and admiration worthy of heroes, well, that was the best feeling in the whole wide world. And knowing he might never see that look again was agony. Roscoe would do anything to earn it back.

There was only one thing left to do, and Roscoe did not take the task lightly. He had to go to his friends and neighbors to ask for the money. He had to beg. But most of them had nothing but lint in their pockets themselves.

The manager of the Jockey Club down at the track agreed to let Roscoe set up a tin can and a sign asking for donations, but that went mostly overlooked, and yielded only a pittance of pocket change, some stray buttons, and one Canadian coin.

Roscoe even asked his pastor for help, but the holy man's collar kept him from getting involved in such matters as horse racing, gambling, and the lot.

Roscoe had nowhere left to turn. So, with his dignity sacrificed at the altar of necessity, he limped across the way to the Epsom estate. He was made to wait a good, long while before he was ushered into the Colonel's office. The dark wood parlor held bad memories for Roscoe. He took a seat across the desk from the Colonel, who was attending to some paperwork.

"Yes?" the Colonel said without looking up.

"I came to see about borrowing some money, Colonel. Not much, of course. Not much at all." The sound of the Colonel's fountain pen scratching across the grain of the paper distracted Roscoe. "I've lost Shadow's entry fee for the next race—"

"Lost it?"

"On a bet."

"Nasty business, gambling."

"Well, yes. It certainly seems to have turned out that way. But winning races is the only shot we've got at keeping the farm. And getting that entry fee back is the only shot we've got at winning. So you see, if I don't have that entry fee, it's all over. So I was hoping you might see fit to lend me the fee."

The Colonel looked up from his papers for the first time. Then he laughed. He laughed like he'd just been told the funniest joke he'd ever heard. "You want *me* to lend *you* the entry fee? Shadow dropping out is the best thing that could ever happen to me! Your horse is a threat to my horse. Why on God's green Earth would I give you the money to try to beat me?"

"I thought you might want a fair fight."

The Colonel laughed so hard his belly ached. "What about our history together suggests I would be interested in a fair fight?" The Colonel laughed Roscoe right out of his office.

Roscoe was about to go to the bank to see about an extension on his mortgage when the bank came to see him first. They sent a man by the name of Busy Lee Piedmont. He was a small, delicate fellow, with wire rimmed glasses and exceptionally soft hands. Roscoe begrudgingly invited him in and offered him some coffee. Busy Lee accepted and the two sat at the table with a fire crackling in the fireplace behind them and Scout lying out on the floor between their feet, gnawing on an old chicken bone.

Busy Lee began by informing Roscoe that he was several weeks behind on his mortgage payments to the bank, and that he owed a very large sum of money and had very little time in which to pay it. Roscoe was, of course, aware of this, and told the banker that he had a plan.

"Oh yes," Busy Lee interrupted. "I heard about your horse, Shadow. Winning race purses to pay off your debts." Busy Lee cracked a sheepish little smile in spite of himself. "It's quite the human-interest piece, indeed. However, as quaint a notion as it is, it's a drop in the bucket and your bucket has a hole in it, Mr. Flynn. It's not enough for him to win just some of the races. He has to win them *all*."

Roscoe didn't understand, so Busy Lee took the liberty of doing some calculations, because that's what bankers do for amusement, and concluded it would take every last penny of the Kentucky Derby prize to keep the bank at bay. Anything short of the whole enchilada would be insufficient and entirely all for naught. Roscoe had overlooked the small matter of interest in his plan and, as a result, had never figured on having to actually win the *Derby*. It was too big a thing to hope for from such a small horse.

"Then it's a lost cause," sighed Roscoe.

"Yes, I agree it's unlikely—" replied Busy Lee.

"It's impossible."

"How so, Mr. Flynn?"

"Because I don't even have the money for the next entry fee. Barring some kind of miracle, Shadow's done with racing."

"I see . . . ." The banker tightened his lips into a sympathetic bow. "Well, that's a shame."

Roscoe pleaded for just a little more time. But Busy Lee could not be swayed. Every extension had already been exhausted, every line of credit called in. Roscoe had until the first of June to pay what was owed, or the bank would seize the property.

24

Scout had been listening carefully to every word the banker said. As their conversation came to an end, he dropped his chicken bone and quickly scurried out the back door. He ran as fast as his four legs would carry him, straight to the barn where he found the rest of the animals. "Guys, we're in trouble . . ." he said.

Scout carefully recounted what had transpired between Roscoe and Busy Lee, leaving nothing out. When the other animals heard the bad news, there was a chorus of exclamations and astonishments, and Raelynn nearly fainted. Red fanned her with his feathers to revive her.

But it was Shadow who took the news hardest of all. How was it he couldn't race again, even though he'd won his last race? He hoped Scout had misunderstood. But Scout was certain. He heard what he heard and facts were facts.

"What do we do now?" asked Red, his voice fraught with worry.

"What *can* we do? Our goose is cooked!" cried Rae-lynn.

"We're doomed! This is the end! Oh, sweet mercy!" wailed Gladys. The panic spread among the animals like wildfire. Only Oats watched quietly from the corner.

"So that's it, huh? You're just giving up?" His tone was gruff. Oats was disappointed in his friends and wasn't afraid to let them know it. "The Flynns have always been kind to us. Taken good care of us. Fed us and loved us. They're good humans. And they've tried hard. But they've done all they can do. It's up to us now."

"Us? But what can *we* do?" asked Gladys.

"We don't give up without a fight, for one. We have to have faith."

"In what?"

"In faith."

And so they did. Each of them took turns hatching one harebrained, ridiculous, far-fetched money-making scheme after another. Though, to be fair, farm animals' occupations usually tend more toward the producing-milk or pulling-plows variety, and they are quite rarely relied upon for fundraising, general planning, pulling through in the clutch, and other such complicated tasks usually reserved for humankind. So to say they were slightly out of their league would be putting it mildly.

Scout suggested digging in the sand for loose change; but there was no beach to dig up. Red suggested swiping pies cooling on windowsills, but pastries were not an acceptable currency for payment of the race entry fee. Gladys suggested selling her own milk at market, but the animal-human communication barrier would keep them from conducting any financial transactions. Try as they might, they were coming up dry. Then, suddenly, it hit them—literally.

Oats had gotten up the courage to go across the way to snoop around the far side of the Epsom estate. He'd once heard some humans discussing whether money did or did not grow on trees, and had gleaned from this conversation that there was at least a possibility that this elusive money tree really did exist. Oats figured that, if it did, it most certainly would be growing on the ritzy Epsom estate. And if he found it, perhaps he could prune a few low-hanging leaves.

But no sooner had he set out on this reconnaissance mission, stealthily making his way along the dusty dirt road that stretched from the Flynn Farm to the Epsom estate, than a rumbly old freight truck came speeding by. The truck hit a pothole, which shook it on its axle, and a gigantic brown box jostled free from its cargo hold and came tumbling off the back. It landed right on top of Oats! Not knowing what had hit him Oats fought that cardboard box like he was the heavyweight champion defending his title, swatting at it with his hooves, giving it a powerful kick with his hind legs, biting, swearing, spitting, and wrestling with it. But when the dust settled and the truck had driven off, the big brown box was left on the side of the road.

Oats circled it once around, then back around the other way, sizing it up and looking it over. He didn't know what to make of it, so he clenched a torn corner between his teeth and dragged it back to the barn to show the others.

By the time he got there, the box was a little worse for wear, beaten up and dirty. But just the same, the other animals regarded the mysterious object with great curiosity and awe. What was it? Each took a turn poking and prodding it until finally it busted open. They all crowded around and they carefully peered inside to behold its precious contents: bow ties. Hundreds of them. Red ones, blue ones, white ones, black ones. They were the ready-made kind that fastened in the back, with the bow all neat and pretty.

"What are they?" Gladys wondered.

Of course none of the farm animals had ever seen a bow tie before so they hadn't a clue what they were. Oats pulled one out of the box.

Scout sniffed at it. "Looks like some kind of animal collar."

"For very fancy animals," said Shadow.

"Domesticated animals, no doubt," added Red.

"Maybe these are the kinds of collars worn by city-dwelling cats and dogs and cows and the like?" Rae-lynn chimed in.

"There are no city-dwelling cows, dummy!" countered Oats.

"And that silk is far too fine for any animal," added Gladys. "I saw a picture in one of Mother Flynn's magazines a long time ago where a lady had a tie like that in her hair. She used it to hold her curls in place."

"Don't be ridiculous," Red crowed. "These things

are far too restricting for humans to put on themselves."

Things began to get heated in the fancy-animal-collar versus ladies-headwear argument, until Oats stepped in. "The important question is: What do we do with them? We had faith and it was rewarded with these . . . whatever-they-ares. These doohickeys are Shadow's ticket to racing, if we can just figure out how to use them. We need to hatch a plan."

The animals scooped the bow ties back into the broken box and then hid it under a pile of hay for safekeeping until they could think up a better course of action.

But days went by and they came no closer to formulating a plan. They racked their brains, they observed the humans carefully, searching for clues for what to do with the curious strips of silk, Scout even consulted animals on neighboring farms, but all to no avail. They couldn't even figure out what the ties were—let alone what to do with them!

Race day came and at sunup they were still short the entry fee. With just hours to go, Shadow's chances of running it were shot. Shadow was inconsolable.

"I know you're sad, child. But we tried our best," said Gladys.

"I just thought, when Oats found all those fancy collars, maybe things had turned around, you know? I was foolish to think it would make any difference. I wish this stupid box hadn't come and gotten our hopes up!" He lashed out and smashed the pile of hay where the box was hidden, knocking it over with a blow from his hoof.

Just then, the barn door opened and in walked a sullen Fyfe. She came to break the news to Shadow that there would be no race today. She was oblivious to Roscoe's conversation with the banker, and to Scout bearing witness to that conversation, so there was no way she could have known that Shadow and the rest of the animals were already painfully aware that this was the end of the proverbial road.

"Shadow, I've got bad news," she began. "I'm afraid you can't race today. I am so, so sorry we let you down." Fyfe went to put her arms around Shadow's neck when she felt something odd. A red bow tie was caught in his mane! It had gotten tangled there when Shadow knocked the box over.

"What have you got there, boy?" Fyfe untangled the bow tie and looked it over with a furrowed brow. "Where did this come from?" Then she spotted the box, tattered, mud-stained, and half-hidden under a pile of hay. She opened it and her face lit up. She called for her pa, and Roscoe came running from the house. Fyfe showed him the box.

"Bow ties?" Roscoe scratched his head. "Where'd they come from?"

"No way of knowing."

"Well, I suppose we ought to put a sign up or something. Return them to their rightful owner."

"It's an unmarked box we found in our very own barn. Heck, Shadow was wearing one! He's a literal gift-horse, Pa. Don't look him in the mouth."

"What do *we* want with a bunch of bow ties?"

"Come with me." There was a fire in her eyes that Roscoe hadn't seen in far too long. He would have followed her to the ends of the earth in that moment. "I've got an idea!

A HAND-PAINTED SIGN READ:

BUY A BOW TIE TO HELP OUT THE LITTLE GUY!

Fyfe, Roscoe, and even Shadow all wore bow ties as they stood outside the racetrack barking to the crowd, "Racing isn't just for the rich! Watch the race the way they watch it up in the boxes! Get your bow ties here! Every penny sold goes toward Shadow of a Doubt's entrance fee!"

The bow ties were selling like hotcakes. People got a kick out of them, and Shadow had won a loyal following in his first two races that was eager to help him out now.

It was mostly regular Joes and plain folks who were buying the bow ties. They wore them like badges of honor, taking a stand for a fair fight and a level playing field, and sticking up for the "little guy."

"How many have we sold so far?" Fyfe asked her pa, stuffing a fistful of cash in her pocket.

"A hundred, at least."

"How much time we got left?"

"Twenty minutes."

Fyfe let out an excited hoot. "We might just make it!"

A sea of bow ties soon filled the stands. It was a sight to behold. Bow ties hung around naked necks without collared shirts, bow ties on factory workers and farmhands, bow ties on women. There were bow ties as far as the eye could see. The cheap seats never looked so classy.

Skip the Quip watched it all from his announcer's booth above, and it became clear to him this wasn't just a race, it was a revolution.

The door to the booth flung open and a breathless young clerk shoved a piece of paper into Skip's hand. Skip thumped two fingers on his microphone, getting the attention of every last man, woman, and child out there. "Ladies and gents, it's your ol' pal Skip here. It gives me enormous pleasure to inform you there's been a last-minute entry in the race. Shadow of a Doubt joins the final heat."

. . .

Roscoe cut through the bustling crowd in the stables with Shadow and Fyfe in tow. They were late. The other horses had already warmed up. Shadow would have to ride cold. They'd have to hurry just to make the starting shot. The other jockeys were starting to take their mounts.

"We'll split up," instructed Roscoe. "You find Scoot and wring him out. I'll get Shadow tacked up."

Fyfe found Scoot Ziegler in the Jockey Club, passed out at a table in the corner. She gave a firm tug on his sleeve to wake him.

"I said, put it on my tab . . ." he murmured, half-asleep.

"Scoot, get up. You gotta race."

He squinted in the light and flopped a pudgy hand over his eyes.

"What's this about racing? I'm the best doggone racer this side of . . . wherever we are."

"Come on, Scoot," Fyfe urged. "We made it. Shadow's in the race. You gotta get up."

"Shadow? Well, I'll be. I didn't think you'd be able to scrape together the dough. Sorry, kid, but I'm in no shape to race. Find yourself another jockey."

"Another jockey? The race starts in eight minutes!

There is no other jockey." Scoot rested his head on the table with a thud. "All we need's a warm body. Just go out there and Shadow will do the rest. Please! Get up!"

Scoot snored loudly. He was passed out cold and there wasn't a single thing that could be done about it.

Fyfe knew they were in trouble. Her first thought was that Roscoe would have to ride instead, but she knew he couldn't. Not with his knee the way it was. And she knew he wouldn't be any more amenable to her second thought either. . . .

Fyfe kept a lookout for Roscoe as she snuck back into the stable, but there was no sign of him. He was off sorting out the payment for Shadow's last-minute entry. She changed into Roscoe's racing silks, which were too big on her, pooling around her wrists and ankles. Thinking fast, Fyfe stripped them off again and layered a spare pair of britches and an extra jockey's vest under the uniform to fill out her frame. Plus, she figured, the extra padding couldn't hurt. Then she stuffed a couple of horseshoes in her waistband to give her a little extra weight for the weigh in.

Female jockeys were few and far between and stuck out like a sore thumb, so Fyfe knew that if she had any chance of blending in she'd need to disguise herself as a boy. She tucked her hair up into her helmet, then

took a bit of dirt from the stable floor, rubbed it between her hands, and patted it onto her chin, creating a hint of a five o'clock shadow. She turned around to face Shadow, a brand-new man.

"Wish me luck," Fyfe grunted, her voice an octave lower than usual. Shadow blustered. "Wish me luck?" she tried again, this time in a slightly higher, more believable pitch, of which Shadow seemed to approve.

Fyfe was nervous as she walked toward the official's table. She kept her legs wide and slightly bent at the knees, walking like the cowboys she'd seen in those old westerns her pa liked to watch. She handed her entry card to the stern-faced man behind the desk and he eyed her up and down.

"How old are you, son?"

Whew! *Son.* She'd passed the first step.

"Fifteen," she answered, knowing that was the minimum age for jockeys, even though it was a few years more than she could properly lay claim to.

"Kind of small for fifteen, aren't ya?" the race official challenged her. But Fyfe was cool under pressure. She looked around at the room full of jockeys, grown men no more than five and a half feet tall.

"Ain't we all?"

This elicited a chuckle from the curmudgeon behind the desk. "All right, son. Step on the scale."

She tenuously stepped on and waited for it to register.

"One hundred and seven," he announced. And then he stamped her race card. "Good luck."

Boy, oh boy, did she need luck. Fyfe and Shadow both were a bundle of nerves as she led him to the starting gate, though Fyfe breathed a sigh of relief that they had managed to slip out of the stables before Roscoe returned.

Fyfe's hand shook ever so slightly as she gripped Shadow's reins. In an effort to comfort her, Shadow blustered softly in her right ear, but it didn't do any good, seeing as how she was all but deaf on that side ever since Mud River. The damage to her inner ear had left her with balance issues too, but Fyfe wasn't one to readily admit her shortcomings, and she went to extraordinary lengths to cover up her handicap. Even Roscoe never knew just how bad it was.

Seeing how she couldn't hear him made Shadow worry for his ol' pal Fyfe, and how they would fare out there on the track. But there was no turning back now. Shadow took his place at the starting gate.

"Ladies and gentlemen," Skip's voice came over the loudspeaker, "I have some updates for the final race. First, Bred Winner has been scratched from the race card—again. Second, there is a change of jockey on the number five horse, Shadow of a Doubt. Scoot Ziegler will be replaced by Bluegrass Gibson."

Bluegrass Gibson. Fyfe had thought the name up in a hurry, but she was quite pleased with it now that she heard it on the loudspeaker. She chose "Bluegrass" because she was brimming with Kentucky pride. And "Gibson" because it sounded sophisticated, like a fancy drink or a model in a classy magazine. Years of hanging around the track had taught her that a little razzle-dazzle never hurt when it came to racing.

But there was one person in the arena who was neither razzled nor dazzled by the name. The second Roscoe heard the announcement he raced out to the stands. He knew every jockey this side of the Mason-Dixon and he'd never heard of Bluegrass Gibson.

He pushed and shoved his way through the crowd, right up to the rail. And then he saw her, perched atop Shadow in the number five post.

Roscoe was struck with a peculiar mix of anger and pride. He thought about stopping the race, exposing Fyfe's secret in order to protect her. But he knew it would destroy her. He'd already lost her trust once, and he might not be able to get it back if he lost it again.

He had mere seconds to make the biggest decision of his life and his mind was split in two. So he took a page from Shadow's book and went with his gut: He trusted her. She believed she could do this. He had to let her try.

26

Fyfe shifted nervously in the saddle. She looked out at the stands and saw bow ties for miles. "Well, boy," she said to Shadow, "this is bigger than you or me now. It's bigger than the farm, too. There's a whole heap of people out there waiting to watch a horse do a magic trick. Let's give 'em what they came for."

Shadow's eyes narrowed as he set his sights on the finish line. He remembered that Fyfe had told him he'd only need to come in fourth in the Championship races, but now, with Fyfe on his back and all those people rooting for him in the stands, it seemed like nothing less than first would do. He had the weight of the world on his shoulders, high expectations and crummy odds. But rather than weigh him down, somehow it lifted him up. He had something to prove.

Bang! The starting pistol fired and the gate flung open. The horses erupted out onto the track all at once. Roscoe's old pal Arnaz took easy command of the lead from his inside post position, and his horse Say It Ain't So soared out in the clear, kicking up a cloud of dirt in his wake.

Shadow was running in the middle of the pack, neck-and-neck with Who's Your Daddy, Passing Fancy, and Sassafras Sister. But Shadow had more to give. He tried to break away, but something was holding him back.

Fyfe couldn't get her stance right on account of her balance issues. Every time she tried to post up she'd fall back. She was used to riding Shadow around the farm, and she was even used to riding him fast. But what Shadow and those other horses did out there on the track reinvented fast, and she couldn't get up and stay up with that much speed underneath her. Her bad ear wouldn't allow it.

"Get up!" She heard her pa's voice yelling out from the stands, the consummate trainer that he was. "Get up there!" he pleaded. Without posting up, her weight was distributed all wrong and she was slowing Shadow down.

But she couldn't do it. She tried again and again. She wouldn't stop trying. Yet she felt defeated as she bumped back down in the saddle time after time.

Shadow lost ground at the bend and Who's Your Daddy and Sassafras Sister pulled ahead. But, if he could just hold his position, he'd finish fourth and still pick up the points he needed to move on. Then Passing Fancy overtook him.

Skip's voice sounded grim over the track's speakers. "Folks, it looks like everyone's favorite underdog story might not have a happy ending after all."

Back at the farm, all the animals were huddled up against the fence listening to the tinny broadcast of the race on the farmhands' radio over in the Epsom's barn.

"It's Say It Ain't So out in front by a mile, followed by Who's Your Daddy, Passing Fancy, and Sassafras Sister, with Shadow of a Doubt now trailing the pack," rattled Skip.

"Oh, heavens!" cried Gladys. "What's gotten into Shadow?"

"He can't lose now!" Raelynn hid her head under her wing. "They worked so hard just to get him in the race. He can't lose!"

Just then, Oats felt it. A single raindrop. It landed right on the end of his snout. His lips curled into a grin. "It's not over yet."

A fat raindrop splashed down on Fyfe's helmet. Then another one. And another one. And she lit up with that same thousand-watt smile. "You feel that, boy? It's raining! Someone upstairs just decided to play your handicap."

Ever since that day on the farm when Shadow burned up the track in the rain, Roscoe and Fyfe had known he was sensational in the soup. The sky opened up and let loose a torrential sun shower that drenched the track. While the other horses lost speed as their hooves lost traction and their turns got sloppy, Shadow gained ground.

As soon as they got a little momentum going, Fyfe managed to find her balance and post up. Now they were unstoppable.

"Woo-hoooo!" Fyfe let out a rallying cry as they turned the bend on the homestretch and *woosh*ed past the fans.

"Come on, Shadow! Come on, boy!" Roscoe shouted. His cheers echoed as excitement rippled through the stands.

"Ladies and gentlemen, this could be a major upset!" Skip's voice boomed. "Just a second ago Shadow of a Doubt was bringing up the rear, and now he's passing 'em all!"

The rain was devastating the competition. Who's Your Daddy, Say It Ain't So, and Passing Fancy all fell back. And Shadow took full advantage. Despite the wet track, he spiked, pivoted, and snaked his way through the pack.

Shadow had the finish line in his sights. Sassafras Sister still had half a length on him, but her hooves were heavy in the mud. Trying to pick up speed, she pushed off against the track harder and harder, which only made her hooves sink deeper and deeper into the mud. Shadow, light as a feather, floated across the finish line first.

The cheap seats burst into cheers. Strangers hugged one another and grown men had tears in their eyes. All those race fans in their not-so-fancy bow ties cheered for their underdog champion as they kicked up puddles.

No bottles of champagne were uncorked in the clubhouse; there was no polite applause of fashionably gloved hands. This victory belonged to the little guy.

Fyfe and Shadow waltzed through the Winner's Circle, giving the reporters just enough time to pop off a single blurry shot of them, and leaving before they could ask any questions. Then they retreated to the privacy of the paddocks where Fyfe stripped off her silks and slipped out the back before the rest of the jockeys were done taking their bows.

Meanwhile, Skip the Quip cut through the boisterous crowd to where Roscoe stood, his arms hanging over the shoulders of a couple race fans, a rare smile on his face.

"Roscoe Flynn, what a spectacular race! Who's this scrappy dynamo of a jockey that came out of nowhere? Who is Bluegrass Gibson?"

Roscoe was always reluctant to indulge Skip, but he couldn't pass up the chance to brag to the world about Fyfe.

"He's a very close friend of mine. Bluegrass . . . well, Bluegrass is living the dream."

"Couldn't have said it better myself, old sport." *That* was something Skip had never said before. "You caught a break with that sun shower. Do you think Shadow's win was all luck?"

"When a guy crosses the finish line at a marathon they don't ask him which way the wind was blowing. A win's a win."

"Fair enough, friend," Skip agreed. "But some people had written Shadow off as a gimmick, a fluke. What do you have to say to the naysayers now?"

"Well, I don't know if your radio waves reach way up there to the rarified air of the box seats, but if they do, I'd like to tell those folks: We're comin' for you. Roses aren't only for the rich."

"Does that mean you think your little horse can take on the Colonel's in the Derby?"

"We're ready. But I'm starting to wonder if maybe he's hiding. . . ."

The Colonel clicked off the radio. He was simmering. Roscoe Flynn had called him out! Behind him, Bred Winner lapped the barn's half-mile training track in a blur. *Ba-duhm, ba-duhm, ba-duhm.* Bianchi shouted through his megaphone, a full-fledged auditory assault, commanding the jockey to use his whip to spur Bred Winner on.

As the Colonel looked on, he contemplated whether all of it—the high-tech machines, the black market medicine, the do-or-die attitude—whether it was enough.

Ba-duhm, ba-duhm, ba-duhm.

There was no denying it: Shadow had given Bred

Winner a run for his money at that photo finish. Maybe he *was* running scared. Maybe Bred Winner wasn't such a sure thing after all. Determined to do something about it, the Colonel turned to Bianchi.

"How fast?" he asked, eyeing the horse.

Bianchi consulted his stopwatch, "Fifty-one point three seconds."

"It's not good enough," barked the Colonel.

"We'll get there. There's still time."

"Shadow of a Doubt is getting better with every race. I tossed that runt out years ago. I won't have him coming back to haunt me."

"We beat that horse before. We can do it again," Bianchi assured him.

"*We beat that horse before?* As though that race could be considered a true victory? Bred Winner eked out that 'W' by a pathetic fingernail margin," the Colonel said, looming over Bianchi menacingly.

Ba-duhm, ba-duhm, ba-duhm. Bred Winner bounded around the track, faster and faster.

"Weakness is a disease," the Colonel hissed. "It festers and eats away at you from the inside out, until you're lousy with gut rot and people regard you with pity. I've seen it in lame, busted-up horses, and mangy feral dogs, and now . . . well, now I see it in you. I cannot abide you spreading your sickness to my horse. I will not let you lead my horse down the road to defeat."

Ba-duhm, ba-duhm, ba-duhm.

"Sometimes it is not for us to lead the horse. Sometimes, we must let the horse lead us," Bianchi said timidly.

"Let the horse lead *us?*" the Colonel repeated.

Then, in a fit of rage, he grabbed a riding crop from where it hung on the stable wall, hopped the fence of the training track, and, when Bred Winner came around, he swatted at him violently.

"I am in charge!" shouted the Colonel. "I'll show you who makes the rules around here!" The crop cracked against the horse's hide and he whinnied in pain. He reared back and stopped and started in fear and confusion as the Colonel chased him with the whip. *Thwap! Thwap! Thwap!* "You will not fail me! I will not be disgraced!"

"Please, Colonel Epsom . . ." Bianchi interrupted in a most timid voice. "He is a good horse."

The Colonel reeled around. He had worked himself into a frenzy. His clothes were disheveled and his hair was mussed.

"*He's a good horse?*" the Colonel mimicked, toying

with Bianchi like a cat with a mouse. "And tell me, Bianchi, are you a good man?"

Bianchi didn't answer. He kept his eyes fixed on the ground.

"Hmm?" the Colonel asked again, drawing out the word. He put the riding crop under Bianchi's chin and lifted his head up so that their eyes met.

"I—I try to be," Bianchi stammered back.

Thwap! The Colonel whipped the riding crop across his cheek. "That horse will do as I say. And so will you."

The Colonel threw the crop to the ground, exhausted. "Nothing less than total victory will be tolerated." He looked around at the large and well-appointed barn. "All this? The Epsom name?" His tone became despondent. "We're nothing if we don't win. It's all we have."

27

THE NEXT DAY was a good one back on Flynn Farm. Shadow had spent the better part of the morning retelling the tale of how he pulled out a win from nowhere in yesterday's race, and the other animals hung on his every word. (Although Shadow considered this something of a dress rehearsal, since he would tell the story all over again later that night when he could steal a precious moment or two at the fence with Gilda. As far as he was concerned, a win wasn't a win until he could share it with his mama.)

Shadow's voice cracked with excitement as he recounted every harrowing detail to the animals in the barn. It could be easy to confuse Shadow's storytelling with bragging, but not if you knew him. He just wanted to share his big moment with his friends. After all, the way he saw it, he would never have gotten there if it weren't for them, so that win belonged to each and every one of them.

Of course no one fooled themselves into thinking they were out of danger on the farm. They'd picked up a little scratch on the last race, but it wasn't enough to make a difference. Not a real one anyhow. But they were still in it. They'd live to see another day. The fifty points they'd earned brought their grand total to sixty-four, just six shy of the price of admission at the Derby. They'd race again in two Saturdays and that could very well clinch it for them. And that was reason enough to allow themselves a few hours to celebrate.

Meanwhile Fyfe and Roscoe were having a celebration of their own out on the front porch. It was after breakfast and they still hadn't begun the day's work. They sat side by side in two rockers, each with an ice-cold glass of milk, his with a touch of brandy in it, hers with a touch of chocolate. They clinked glasses.

"To Shadow!" Fyfe toasted.

"To *you*," Roscoe answered back. "You did a bang-up job out there, kiddo."

Fyfe took a hearty gulp of her milk then let out a mighty belch.

"You wanna talk about it?" Roscoe asked.

"Nope." She buried her face back in her glass.

"Well, I do. It was a dirty trick, you pullin' the ol' switcheroo up there. You had no business riding in that race, and you can't just go doin' whatever you please without regard to consequence. There are risks involved in racing—big risks, daunting to grown men who've been doing it their whole lives. Risks far too great for you to take on at your age."

"But it's in my blood, Pa. All I've ever known is horse racing. All I've ever wanted to be was you."

This tugged good and hard on Roscoe's heart-strings, but he knew he couldn't give up any ground. "I won't tell you twice. . . ."

He broke from her stare and let his gaze wander off toward the horizon. He took a sip of his drink to disperse the tension.

"I am proud of you, Fyfe." Roscoe took another sip. "But don't ever do it again."

She smiled a devilish little grin. Then, down at the end of the front walk, she spotted Colonel Epsom starting up the path.

"What's he doing here?"

"I sure don't know, kiddo. . . ."

The Colonel finally reached the front porch. He didn't bother to remove his hat.

"Hello, Roscoe," said the Colonel.

"Go inside," Roscoe said to Fyfe.

"But Pa!"

"Get."

Fyfe reluctantly slinked inside the house.

"Upstairs, Fyfe," he said. Roscoe knew she was hiding just off to the side of the screen door, hoping to eavesdrop. Fyfe sighed and stomped off, and Roscoe listened to her footsteps as she tromped up the stairs to be sure she was really gone. Then he turned his attention to the Colonel. He regarded him with an odd look in his eye, like he was gazing through a looking glass of hurt feelings and ugly truths.

"As long as we've known each other, you've never been on my farm before."

"I'm not here for the tour, Roscoe. I'm here for the horse."

Roscoe let out an indignant laugh. "How do you figure?"

"You gave him to me," the Colonel said. "Three years ago."

"And you gave him back."

"I *loaned* him back. You were short a workhorse. That doesn't change the fact that he was, and still is, my property."

"I'm poor, not stupid. You'd do well not to confuse the two, Colonel. If you intend to take him, then you best come back with a lawyer and y'all can not take the tour together."

The Colonel didn't say anything. But he didn't leave either.

Roscoe eyeballed him. "I didn't think so."

"I'll buy him off you."

"He's not for sale."

"I'll give you a price that's more than fair. I'll give you however much you need to get out of hock on this patch of dirt, plus enough to buy a new plow horse. How does that sound? Because I imagine it sounds something like music to your ears."

Roscoe was considering it. How could he not?

"Will you race him?" he asked the Colonel.

"No. I have no intention of racing him, riding him, petting him, or any other nonsense. Hell, I don't intend to keep him. He was born a workhorse, and he'll die a workhorse. Maybe I'll let one of the stable boys take him off my hands."

"He deserves to race."

"Now is not the time to take the moral high ground. Now is the time to look out for your family."

"That's what I am doing. Fyfe has seen me lie down

for far too long. It's about time I stood for something," said Roscoe.

"Well, I suppose I should have expected as much. You're flying high now."

The Colonel started back down the path, then turned back and warned, "Careful not to fly too high, 'less you end up like Icarus. Burnt to a *crisp*." And for the first time since he'd set foot on the property, he smiled.

28

THE WAITRESS SET down a frothy mug of root beer next to two empties in the corner booth. Bobcat Cooley had been here less than thirty minutes and was already on his third pop. He was slurping them down faster than a castaway in the Mojave.

"Put a scoop 'a vanilla in there, will ya, sweetheart?"

Bobcat hailed from the Windy City and was befittingly somewhat of a blustery character. The waitress sighed and took the root beer back to the kitchen where she turned it into a float.

"Thanks," he said when she brought it back out. She'd gotten off on the wrong foot with him when she'd accidentally offered him a children's menu as he first sat down, on account of his size. At four foot nine Bobcat was short even for a jockey. She gave him the kids' menu and a pack of crayons and he gave her what for. By way of an apology, she brought him a cup of split pea soup on the house, but that did little to curb what could only be described as his voracious appetite. He scarfed down the soup and devoured a plate of chicken wings, sucking the bones dry, before moving on to apple pie with a slice of cheddar cheese on top, and, of course, the root beer float. He ate like someone who knew someone else was picking up the bill. And that someone else was Roscoe Flynn.

"I want in," he said between bites.

"What do you mean, in?" answered Roscoe, sitting on the other side of the booth with Fyfe.

"*In*. I want a piece of the action, a slice of the pie."

Fyfe looked hungrily at *his* pie, all gooey and delicious. Bobcat was the only one eating. There wasn't money enough for them to order anything else besides two free glasses of water.

"I already said I'd give you ten percent of the purse."

"I want thirty."

"If I give up thirty, there's not enough left for the bank."

Bobcat set down his fork for a second. "Look, you guys stand to make a pretty penny if your Shadow wins. Now, as the jockey, I can't bet the race. And at ten percent, the way I see it, I'd make more sitting in the stands and betting the long shot."

"Thirty percent's not an option," Roscoe replied, holding strong. "Look, I've done the math every which way and ten percent is as high as I can go. A penny more and I lose the farm."

"I don't know what to tell you, Flynn. Sell your motion picture rights or somethin'. Make up the difference however you want, but I don't ride for less than thirty. Period, end of discussion."

Roscoe stared Bobcat down, but the truth was, Bobcat had him over a barrel—and he knew it.

"Look, Flynn, I know as well as you do that every other decent jokey is spoken for by now. You should thank your lucky stars that my horse fell out and I'm available. Shiver Me Timbers gettin' that staph infection was the best thing that could'a happened to you. Really, who else are you gonna get?"

Fyfe leaned into her pa and with her most measured demeanor said, "May I speak with you privately for a moment?"

The door to the diner swung shut with a bang behind her as Fyfe stormed out in a huff. Roscoe folded his arms across his chest. He knew he was in for a fight.

"He's not our guy," said Fyfe.

"Says who?" answered Roscoe.

"You and me both, if you're being honest with yourself. Now let's pack it in and be on our way before he eats us out of house and home."

"His record is rock solid. There's no arguing with the numbers. We've got Oaklawn Park coming up and that's no joke. We need a professional."

"Not this one."

"You don't have to like him."

"Well, I don't."

"Horse racing ain't about making friends, Fyfe."

"Yeah, but it dang sure oughta be about horses. And that blowhard does not love horses. Did you hear how he talked about his horse falling out? Without a shred of remorse?"

"Shadow doesn't need a best friend. He's already got you. He needs a jockey."

"No reason I can't be both," said Fyfe.

"I can think of two hundred and six. That's how many bones are in the human body. And if you broke a single one of 'em out there, I don't know what I'd do."

"I already did it once and I was just fine."

"And as I said, I was not happy about it. It was one

thing when you *had* to ride. That was an exception. But now we've got choices."

"Giving up thirty percent? That's not a choice!"

"We'll bargain with him," said Roscoe.

"He won't budge. You know that as well as I do."

"Then we'll find somebody else!" Roscoe was losing patience.

"Don't you get it, Pa? You can scour the circuit. Heck, you can search the far corners of the world. You can find the winningest jockey, but he'll never know Shadow like I do. I know how he moves, how he thinks. I'm the one that should be on his back." There was no denying it: Fyfe and Shadow had something special together.

"That doesn't change the fact that you're not a jockey. You spent half the race in the saddle."

"I've got time to train. And the best trainer to teach me." Fyfe could see Roscoe's expression softening. "Look, Pa, Shadow knows what to do. All we need is a warm body up there, and I'm positively toasty."

Roscoe looked at her, all willful and defiant, knowing she was right, but not knowing what to do about it exactly.

His voice got soft and sentimental. "I've been

banged up and knocked around in this life, but if anything ever happened to you, Fyfe, it would flatten me out."

"Please, Pa. I'll never ask you for another thing as long as I live, because nothing else will ever be this important. You gotta let me ride."

Roscoe turned it over in his mind. There was no amount of prize money worth the risk. He'd lose the farm before he lost her. But on the other hand, how could he put it all on the line to give the horse a chance to chase his dreams and then deny the same chance to his own child?

Roscoe knew what racing had meant to him, how it made him feel alive and important, and he wanted all that for her. He'd broken seventeen bones in his career. He'd had three concussions and more fractures, sprains, and tears than he could count. But he wouldn't trade a second of it. And he knew in his heart of hearts that, try as he might, he couldn't keep Fyfe from it.

He reached out and snapped his fingers by Fyfe's right ear. The sound was sharp and loud but she didn't flinch.

"What are you gonna do about that?" Roscoe asked.

He knew more than he'd let on. He'd noticed her

balance problems in the last race and figured the trouble must be her inner ear. If she'd lied to him, if she'd tried to cover it up or make an excuse, he would have known she wasn't ready. He wouldn't have let her race. But she didn't.

"Train," Fyfe said, willfully.

"I want one hundred practice hours under your belt before Oaklawn. And if I say you're not ready, that's the end of it."

"Yes, sir."

He held out his hand and they shook on it.

Fyfe trained morning, noon, and night in the days leading up to the race. There wasn't a moment's rest for her and Shadow. Fyfe struggled with her balance. And every time she slipped or fell, Roscoe doubted whether he was making the right decision letting her ride. But each time she fell she got right back up again, and she kept on getting up until she put his mind at ease. That girl was all go, and there was no holding her back.

When all was said and done, Fyfe and Shadow trained for exactly one hundred and eleven and one half hours. But she could have trained for a million hours and it still wouldn't have calmed her nerves. Oaklawn Park was no ordinary race. The outcome could determine eligibility for the Derby. Shadow would need to finish third or better to secure a place in the big show, and the competition was stiff. Fyfe was all at once terrified and more excited than she'd ever been.

THE MORNING OF the race, it was still dark outside as Fyfe stood in front of a full-length mirror in her bedroom with her thumbs hitched in her belt loops and her jaw pushed out to accentuate a more masculine angle.

"No comment," she said to her reflection in the deepest voice she could muster. And then she sniffed aggressively. "No comment," she tried it again, getting into character. Then she took a few steps back and practiced her walk, posing at the end in front of the mirror: "Name's Bluegrass, Bluegrass Gibson."

"Fyfe." She whipped around to see Roscoe standing in the doorway. She wondered how long he'd been standing there. "Time to go."

· · ·

Oaklawn Park Race Track was located in Hot Springs, Arkansas, which was about a ten-hour drive away, so it was still before sun-up when they got on the road. Fyfe sat in the passenger seat, clutching her knees to her chest. Both she and Roscoe were quiet, neither knowing the right words for such a big occasion.

"You lead with your hips when you walk," Roscoe said, one hand on the wheel, both eyes on the road. "Boys lead with their chest. Watch out for that."

"Okay." Fyfe took it under advisement. She was nervous about pulling off her alter ego again and was grateful for all the help she could get.

"People will be curious about you, seeing as how you came out of thin air. Especially the other jockeys. Don't try and fight it. Go with it. You're little, you're weird, and you like it that way. They're gonna come at you with a thousand questions. Say as little as possible and when all else fails, talk about your horse. At the end of the day, that's the only thing that matters."

This was great stuff. Fyfe was soaking it all in and she was starting to feel more confident. "I was thinking he might hum," she said.

"Hum?"

"Yeah, Bluegrass could hum. That could be his *thing*."

Roscoe supposed he didn't see the harm in it. "If Bluegrass likes to hum, then who am I to stop him?" And that was all they said about it.

Fyfe stared out the window the rest of the ride, except for the few times she spun around in her seat and climbed up on her knees to check on Shadow in the metal trailer they were towing. This was the farthest she had ever been outside the state of Kentucky. They went for long stretches without seeing another car and it helped to quiet Fyfe's nerves. The emptiness of the road somehow made her feel protected. It was like it was just the three of them, rattling around in this great big world.

It was two o'clock by the time they arrived at the track, with not much time to spare. Roscoe was worn out from the drive but Fyfe fared better since he insisted on her taking a nap somewhere around hour seven (though he did wake her up when they crossed the state line so she could mark the occasion). The magnitude of the race hit them on sight. There was a crush of fans making their way through the front gates, and there was electricity in the air.

"He, Pa! Look over there!" Fyfe pointed at a fan in a tattered tweed jacket wearing a red silk bow tie. Then they noticed another bow tie, and another, and another. There was a whole slew of them. Roscoe stopped a man wearing a loose-fitting black one.

"Excuse me, but did you come all the way from Kentucky?"

"Sure did, brother. That horse of yours is something special. I'll follow him all the way to the Derby."

It was all a bit overwhelming. And a bit wonderful.

It came as no surprise that the Colonel was sitting out Bred Winner once again. But while Shadow had been relieved not to have to face Bred Winner in the past two races, now he was disappointed. Bred Winner was the only horse that had beaten him so far. He wanted a re-match. And so did the fans. Murmurs about the inevitable battle royal that would ensue if Shadow were to actually make it to the Derby were reaching a fever pitch.

The Colonel had gotten wind of these murmurs and found them to be quite unsettling. So he turned up at the track that day even though he didn't have a horse in the race, in an effort to show how unaffected he was (which, of course, was all an act) and reassure the world at large that Bred Winner was indeed a lock. The Colonel strode in on his figurative high horse and spotted Roscoe and Fyfe leading their literal horse back to the stables.

"Flynn!" the Colonel bellowed.

Roscoe sent Fyfe on ahead with Shadow, knowing she needed to get him to his stall quickly so she had time to change into her Bluegrass getup before the weigh in.

"You're not coming?" she whispered. She had counted on her father being by her side the whole time and the idea of going it alone terrified her.

"None of the other jockeys need their hands held. You've got to do it on your own," he replied. And he was right. It would be too conspicuous for him to accompany his jockey to the weigh in. It simply wasn't done. "You'll be fine." Roscoe ushered Fyfe along with a reassuring hand at her back, then he turned to face the Colonel.

"You remember Bianchi, my trainer," the Colonel said, thrusting a thumb toward his number two. Roscoe shook Bianchi's hand. Then the Colonel quickly dismissed his trainer. "I'll meet you up in the box. I believe you have another matter to attend to?"

"Of course," Bianchi said and excused himself politely.

"What do you want, Colonel?" Roscoe had no patience for his games today.

"I just wanted to wish you luck."

. . .

Over at the stables Fyfe had transformed into Blue-grass Gibson and nervously joined the end of the line of jockeys waiting to be weighed in. She wiped her sweaty palms on her silks.

"It's Gibson, right?" the jockey behind her in line asked. She nodded without turning around. "Your horse had a heck of a run in that mud! You sure didn't waste any time in the winner's circle though. I don't think the papers got a single shot of you!"

"Not everyone's looking to get famous, Monroe," the jockey in front of her chimed in.

"Hey, can I help it if the camera loves me?" the jockey behind her snapped back.

They seemed content to carry on a conversation about her without her actual involvement, which suited Fyfe just fine. In fact, they didn't seem to notice Bluegrass at all. It wasn't that Fyfe passed for a boy flawlessly, but the profession was filled with so many unusual characters that being funny-looking, or speaking in a warbling basso profondo, wasn't so out of the ordinary.

"Set him straight, will you, Gibson?" The jockey Monroe focused his attention back on her. "What's the point of racing if it ain't about the glory?"

Fyfe panicked. She'd have to answer this time. Then she remembered Roscoe's advice: just talk about her horse.

"You know Shadow once ate twenty-seven carrots in a single sitting?" she said.

Crickets. No one said a word. She knew immediately that was the wrong thing to say. Then, to fill the awkward silence, Fyfe began to hum. She fumbled her way through the first few bars of "My Old Kentucky Home" until, lo and behold, the jockey in front of her joined in. Pretty soon every jockey on that line was humming right along with her to the very last note. Then, to answer Monroe's question, and to summarize what Bluegrass Gibson had so poignantly made clear, the jockey in front of her answered:

"*That's* the point."

Bianchi was wracked with guilt as he tiptoed into the stable and snuck into Shadow's stall. As soon as Shadow saw Bianchi he knew the trainer had no business being there and he let out a loud neigh, but with Fyfe at the weigh-in and Roscoe being kept busy by the Colonel, no one was around to hear it. Shadow had seen the transformation in Bred Winner since he began training with Bianchi, and he knew

Bianchi was capable of horrible things. *Dangerous* things.

Shadow backed away, trying to get away from Bianchi, but Bianchi kept creeping toward him. Soon Shadow had pressed himself up against the back wall of the tiny stall, and there was nowhere else to go. He was trapped. Shadow reared back on his hind legs and roared in fear, a desperate cry for help, but it was no use. He couldn't be heard over the hustle and bustle of the stable, and his friends were too far away.

Bianchi pulled out a pair of bolt cutters. He reached underneath Shadow's saddle for the leather girth that ran under his belly, keeping the saddle in place, and clipped it once on each side of its metal buckle. He was careful not to cut clean through, since that would be easily detected when Roscoe checked the tack before the start of the race, yet still deep enough so that it would give way under enough pressure. Bianchi heard footsteps coming and he scurried off like a coward, just in the nick of time.

"How'd it go?" Roscoe asked, seeing Fyfe coming down the way.

"That humming thing worked like a charm! I knew I was onto something," Fyfe said.

As Roscoe did a final saddle check, Shadow bucked and fussed. He didn't understand exactly what Bianchi had done but he knew something wasn't right, and he needed to warn them.

"Easy, boy," Roscoe urged.

Fyfe looked at Shadow quizzically. "What's gotten into you?"

"Probably just pre-race jitters."

Worried, Fyfe stroked Shadow's mane but it did little to calm him.

"Ready?" Roscoe asked. It was time.

Roscoe gave Fyfe a leg up. He watched as she hooked her feet into the stirrups and the corner of his mouth drew up a little, though he was too nervous to actually laugh or smile.

"What?" Fyfe asked. She wanted in on the joke.

"Nothing."

"*What?*"

"It's just . . . well . . . you kind of look like me."

Fyfe beamed with pride.

Up in the cushy box seats, the Colonel was fanning himself, pretending it was hot when really it was anxiety that was causing him to sweat. Bianchi entered the box, looking a little green, riddled with guilt. He whispered into the Colonel's ear, "It's done."

30

SHADOW WAS GIVING Fyfe an awful lot of trouble as they made their way to the starting gate. It wasn't like him to be squirming like this before a race, and Fyfe wondered if it wasn't more than just nerves. He tried to turn around and head back for the stables, but Fyfe tugged on his reins and kept him on course, leading him into the starting corral. Shadow was out of time. He could feel Fyfe's weight shift on top of him as she dug in her heels and crouched up into position, her rear hovering in the air in perfect posture. This was it. Ready or not.

The starting shot rang out and the gate whipped open. But Shadow didn't move. All the other horses flew out of there, but Shadow didn't budge. "Hyah!" Fyfe signaled. But Shadow just stood perfectly still.

She gave a short kick and finally he sprang to life. He hadn't planned on going, but they'd trained so hard and for so long, that he'd followed her command on instinct—and then there was no turning back. Just like that, they were off.

It was a disastrous start. Sassafras Sister was in the lead, followed by Who's Your Daddy and Time in a Bottle. Shadow trailed the pack by more than three furlongs. Skip the Quip couldn't remember if a horse had ever come from this far behind before.

Shadow began steadily gaining on the pack, and by the back straight he'd closed the gap by half. That put him only a few lengths behind the next horse. A couple horses fell back and he overtook them. By then he'd earned a place in the fray. Fyfe knew he had a strong late kick in him, which would come in handy at the top of the stretch. Coming up on the bend, the pack was thick. Shadow lithely weaved in and out, finding the empty space to slip past Time in a Bottle and Who's Your Daddy—then cutting inside and stealing the rail! Sneaking right past Sassafras Sister, miraculously, Shadow pulled out in front as he hugged the turn. The crowd roared as the underdog took the lead. As he rounded the corner, the stands were on Fyfe's right side and her deaf ear muffled the cheers. It was a bizarre sensation and it almost caused her to lose her balance. She tried to shake it off. Roscoe looked on nervously.

Fyfe and Shadow held the lead. Sassafras Sister was coming back on them, but Shadow crossed to the outside and boxed her out. As Shadow leaned into the cut, Fyfe rocked right in the saddle. The shift in Fyfe's weight caused the saddle to pull against the broken buckle and, unbeknownst to Fyfe, the strap came loose on one side.

"Hyah! Hyah!" Fyfe signaled Shadow to go faster. Sassafras Sister was right on their heels. She nosed right, left, right again. She was looking for an opening and Shadow wasn't going to give it to her. She made a play for the inside straight and Shadow broke left. As he did, Fyfe leaned into it hard and in that instant the saddle's strap gave way.

Fyfe was thrown from the horse, but her boot caught in the stirrup as she went down and she was dragged like a rag doll for more than fifty feet before the saddle finally came free completely and she was released, a motionless, huddled heap in the dirt.

Shadow felt the saddle go and he panicked. He knew Fyfe must have fallen. He tried to stop but he couldn't. The momentum of the pack charging from behind him carried him away.

In a flash, Roscoe vaulted the fence from the stands and ran to Fyfe.

A stunned silence fell over the track. You could have heard a pin drop. Sassafras Sister crossed the finish line first and the pop of a champagne cork echoed from the Colonel's box.

Roscoe dropped to his knees and cradled Fyfe's limp body in his arms. Slowly, she opened her eyes and looked up at him. He burst into tears and wept with happiness and sadness all at the same time. She wasn't gone, but she was in an awful bad way.

"I can't move my legs, Pa."

"It's gonna be okay, kiddo." He glanced over his shoulder and saw a team of medics rushing out onto the field with a stretcher. "We're gonna get you to the hospital."

"No!" There was fear in her eyes. "No hospital. If they examine me they'll know I'm not who I said I was. They'll see I'm a girl and our standing will be wiped out. Take me home. Call Doc Crump."

"But Fyfe, you need help."

"If they take me it's all over, forever. Don't let them take me." Her eyes welled with tears. "Please . . . don't let them take me."

The medics were there now. All business in their

crisp white coats, they laid down the stretcher next to Fyfe. They reached for her, but Roscoe hugged her into his chest.

"Get back!"

The medics were confused.

"Please, Pa," she muttered.

"Leave us be," he shouted to the two men in white jackets. He looked down at his baby girl, tears trickling down her freckled cheeks. "Try not to let them see you cry," he whispered to her.

He picked up Fyfe and laid her down on the stretcher himself as the men in white coats looked on. Then he took hold of the stretcher's handles and lifted the top end of it, the bottom end raking the dirt behind him as he dragged Fyfe off the track. The medics chased after him, but Roscoe yelled at them to get back.

Roscoe limped worse than ever under the weight of the stretcher, and his walk was slow and uneven, but full of pride. All eyes were on him as he persevered, one crooked step at a time.

A thin man in a threadbare sweater watching from the stands leapt the fence and came out onto the track. A guard yelled at him and told him to get back, but the thin man didn't listen. He pushed his way past the guard, walked right past Roscoe, and grabbed hold of the stretcher at its other end, lifting up Fyfe's feet and helping Roscoe carry her.

Another man jumped the fence, and another, and another, until there was a whole mob of them at least one hundred strong. They crowded around that stretcher and they hoisted Fyfe up onto their shoulders, and they marched behind Roscoe in solidarity.

Doc Crump was waiting on their front step when they arrived. His thin lips twitched nervously as he eyed his watch, anxious to have a look at the patient. They must have passed a handful of hospitals and clinics on the way home but Fyfe refused to stop. It had to be Crump, and only Crump. Of course Roscoe had misgivings about Fyfe's unwillingness to seek help sooner, but seeing as how she was of sound mind and stable condition, he obliged.

The doctor helped Roscoe carry Fyfe inside the house and lay her out flat on the kitchen table. Her pain had mostly subsided, but she was still in shock and didn't speak a word now. Roscoe clutched her hand in his, her precious, delicate little hand, and every once in a while he'd give it a squeeze just to make sure she squeezed back. Crump conducted a thorough examination, and when he finished he requested a word in private with

Roscoe. Judging by his expression, Roscoe knew whatever he had to say, it wasn't good.

"I'm afraid the cumulative effect of her injuries is quite significant." The doctor began in a soft voice. "She's suffered various bone swells and contusions."

Roscoe couldn't bring himself to look the doctor in the eye. Instead he stared at his hands, studying the callouses on his fingers.

"She also has a herniated disc that's pinched a nerve along her spine. That's what's causing the numbness in her legs. There's quite a bit of inflammation there, but as the swelling goes down she should regain feeling. God willing, she'll be back on her feet in a few days' time."

"It doesn't exactly feel like God's in our corner, Doc."

"I can't make any promises."

"Fyfe's a fighter. She'll pull through," Roscoe said, sounding as though he was trying to convince himself. He was clearly scared. The doctor put on his hat to go, but Roscoe grabbed his elbow and stopped him.

"You'll keep our secret, won't you? If anyone finds out that Fyfe is Bluegrass Gibson, everything she's worked for will be undone."

The doctor frowned. "Forgive me for saying so, Mr. Flynn, but that girl doesn't need another fan. She needs a father." Crump shook his elbow free. "I'll have the druggist send a boy around with some prescriptions."

Roscoe carried Fyfe up to her bed and kneeled down next to her, his bum leg sticking out to the side. He held her hand and watched her every breath. She finally woke after having slept a solid thirteen hours, and rubbed the sandman's crust out of her eyes.

"How long 'til I can ride?" Her voice cracked from weariness and want of use.

Roscoe knew that question was coming all along. He had been dreading it. He put a hand on her leg to console her then, realizing she couldn't feel his touch, withdrew it and folded his hands in front of him on the mattress.

"I'm so, so sorry, kiddo."

Fyfe whipped her head away from Roscoe, trying to hide the tears that had flooded her eyes. "What does Doc Crump know anyway? I'll show him," she sputtered angrily.

"Fyfe, you need to accept the fact that—"

"Leave me alone," she interrupted. It was more than she could bear.

"There's more to this life than horses," Roscoe finished.

"Is there?" She turned back to face him, her eyes red and swollen. "Because horses and heartbreak are all I've ever known." A tear rolled down the side of her face and disappeared into her pillow. Roscoe reached out to wipe it away, but she stopped him, "Just leave me alone."

Fyfe and Roscoe were inches from each other, but in that moment they were worlds apart. He felt she'd been spared, and she felt she'd been damned. He saw the glass as half full, and she—she was drowning in it.

"I'll get some fresh linens for your pillow," Roscoe said. It was just an excuse to get away. The stench of sadness hung too thick in the air and Roscoe was suffocating. He hurried for the door but just as he reached for the knob, Fyfe's raspy voice stopped him:

"Is Shadow okay?"

Shadow had wandered out onto the makeshift track and was grazing aimlessly around the very edge of the farm.

"It's not your fault." Shadow looked up, surprised to see Oats out of the barn.

Shadow went back to grazing. Moving kept him from thinking too much, and his thoughts were ripping him apart. The guilt, the sorrow, the fear: It was all too much. Oats followed a few steps behind him.

"Then why do I feel so bad?" Shadow asked Oats.

"You lost the race and you lost your best friend all at once. Of course you feel bad."

"Scout overheard the doc. Fyfe won't ever ride again. That means even when she gets better, things won't be like they were between us."

"She'll still love you."

"I let her down. I let everybody down—Mama, Roscoe, you. Everybody was counting on me to save the farm, and I couldn't do it."

"For what it's worth, we probably never really had a chance." Oats's words were cold comfort. "It was foolish to think we did. We shouldn't have asked you to race. It wasn't fair."

"I could have gone my whole life believing I could have been a racehorse, instead of *knowing* I couldn't. I cracked the dream wide open and there was nothing inside. It was because Fyfe believed in me that she got hurt." Shadow stopped grazing and turned to face his friend. "Don't you see, Oats? I've been nothing all along. And nothing's all I'll ever be."

31

ABOUT A WEEK went by without much change. The doctor had expected Fyfe up and about by now, but it seemed her mental state had gotten the better of her physical one. She had fallen into a deep depression and it kept her from healing.

Time itself inched along and a sort of sullen status quo sunk in. But just when the Flynns had grown accustomed to how bad things had gotten, things got even worse. It was a little before suppertime when there came a knock on the front door. The unexpected visitor took Roscoe away from his daughter's bedside and he hurried downstairs, hoping to make the interruption brief.

"Good evening. Are you Roscoe Flynn?" the stranger asked.

"Yes."

"I'm Ronald Streeter, from the Racing Board. I tried calling but it seems your phone's been disconnected. So I figured I'd just come by and tell you in person. All things considered, it seemed like the right thing to do."

"Tell me what?" asked Roscoe.

"I'm afraid I have some bad news. Of course I'm something of a fan myself, though I probably shouldn't say it, so it's very difficult for me to tell you this."

"You better just come out with it, Mr. Streeter."

"Shadow has been disqualified from the circuit."

"On what grounds?"

"Interference. He tripped up two of the other horses after your jockey took the fall. I'm afraid that means he's no longer eligible for Grade One Stakes races . . . including the Derby. I'm sorry."

Fyfe had been listening intently to the stranger downstairs, and at hearing the news her face went hot and burned angry. Her eyes flooded with tears and even though she tried to hold them in, she couldn't. They streamed down her face and pooled in her ears.

Roscoe took the stairs slow as he tried to figure how to break the news to Fyfe, but soon as he set foot in the doorway of her room he could see she'd already heard. He sat on her bed and scooped her up, hugging her to him tight. Her tiny body heaved in his arms as she sobbed.

"Can you ever forgive me, Pa?" she sputtered through the tears.

Roscoe held her out at arm's length and stared at her hard, confused. "Forgive you?"

"It's my fault. The accident. If I hadn't lost my balance. . . ." She still knew nothing about her saddle having been sabotaged. To her mind, the deafness in her ear had caused her to go off-balance, and the saddle had come off as a result of her fall, not the other way around. "It's over. We're not going to race the Derby. It's all over."

"Listen to me," Roscoe said. "You accomplished something bigger than the Derby. You showed me what it was to believe in something so much that it came true. All those people out in the stands, even Shadow himself—you showed us all. I'd lost hope. But you made a believer out of me."

"But there's nothing left to believe in. Not anymore."

Every day since the accident, Fyfe had asked Roscoe when she would be able to ride again. And every day, his answer was the same: Not ever. Day in and day out, it had been the same routine, with Fyfe asking over and over, hoping to chip away at his resolve. It hadn't bothered Roscoe, not one bit. But, the day she stopped asking? That's when he started to worry. She'd given up hope. Broken bones would mend, but a broken spirit? That had a way of bringing a person to her knees.

Roscoe was a dutiful caretaker. He administered pills for the pain and changed Fyfe's bedpan. Every morning, noon, and night, he exercised her legs on doctor's orders, to keep the muscles from atrophying. She should have been walking by now, but still she'd made no progress. In an effort to boost her morale, Roscoe even went down to the drugstore and bought more ice cream than he could fit in the icebox. Tutti frutti with the dried candies and nuts mixed in— Fyfe's favorite. She choked down a couple bites so as not to hurt his feelings, knowing the trouble he'd gone through and the expense it had cost him to get it. But she wasn't in an ice cream mood. She'd spend most of the day sleeping, and most of her waking hours just staring off into nowhere. She shut the world out. It had let her down one too many times, and it looked like this time it was going to keep her down for good.

. . .

Across the way at the Epsom Estate, the Colonel stood staring out the second story window of his library. His gaze was fixed on the upstairs window of the Flynn farmhouse, through which he could see just the foot of Fyfe's bed and her feet, which hadn't moved for days. It was not lost on him that Bluegrass Gibson had mysteriously disappeared after the accident, and that Fyfe Flynn had turned up injured the very same day with no explanation at all.

He tried telling himself that, if she was man enough to ride in the first place, she was man enough to take a fall. But knowing he was responsible for those still little feet corroded his conscience like acid, eating away at his soul bit by bit. He'd never meant to hurt a child.

Mrs. Epsom sat in an armchair by a crackling fire with a heavy book spread open on her lap. She observed her husband at his perch, which he had frequented often since Fyfe's fall.

"Ansel, is there something I don't know?"

"Hedy, what you don't know could fill this whole godforsaken house."

She closed her book and removed her reading glasses. "Why don't you enlighten me, then?"

"Because," the Colonel answered wearily, "I know how much you love lookin' in the mirror, and I know how bad it feels not to be able to stand the sight of yourself." He turned to her, his face looking hard and full of lines. "We go to the races and you sit up there in the box seats with your ridiculous, fancy hats and when we win, as we always do, you clap your little hands politely. But I can't clap. My hands are too dirty. All the grime and the filth and the smut would go flying and it'd get all over everything.

"A legacy rests on my shoulders, Hedy. The Epsom family has always bred champions. For generations, we've been bringing winners into this world. . . ." He couldn't help but look back at Fyfe's window, drawn to the horrible sight of her small, motionless feet. "And taking losers out of it."

Mrs. Epsom just stared at him, her expression blank and unaffected.

"The odds are back in our favor," the Colonel said. "That's all you need to know."

The next morning, Roscoe and Fyfe were awakened by the soft *tap-tap-tap* of a hammer on their front door as the banker Busy Lee Piedmont posted a formal notice of eviction. He'd come round at sunup hoping they'd still be asleep. He didn't want to deliver the news face-to-face.

The doctor had been by the day before to check in on Fyfe, and he'd discovered that the swelling in her spine had gone down almost completely, and that she should have regained full feeling in her lower body. Based on his physical examination, the doctor concluded that she was at this point fully capable of walking, but as far as Fyfe could tell, she was no better at all. As it turned out, her physical recovery was progressing normally, but she was suffering from a mental block that kept her from knowing it. The mind has a way of playing tricks on a person. You can be right as rain, but if you believe you're sick your mind can poison you like cyanide itself.

Unfortunately, disorders of this kind were outside the scope of Doc Crump's schooling, and as such he could do nothing for her. The most he could offer was a wheelchair to provide her means of getting around, though he quite emphatically noted it was not medically necessary.

So when the banker's *tap-tap-tap* roused them from their slumber, it was no small matter for Roscoe to scoop Fyfe out of bed, carry her downstairs, and situate her in the wheelchair to see what all the fuss was about.

When they finally got to the front door, Busy Lee Piedmont was already halfway down the walk, scurrying away quick as a field mouse. He made the mistake of looking back over his shoulder. He would never forget the look on Roscoe Flynn's face when he laid eyes on that eviction notice, not if he'd lived to be a hundred years old. It's a horrible thing to see a man break, and even worse to know you had any part in it.

Busy Lee didn't know what to say. He had no kind words for Roscoe. No way to inspire even a shred of hope. So he fell back on formality. "You've got forty-five days to vacate. Bank will be by with a bulldozer after that."

Roscoe said nothing. Fyfe reached over from her wheelchair and shut the door.

The Flynns were no strangers to hard luck. They'd had more than their fair share of bad breaks in this life. And every time they thought it couldn't get any worse, somehow it did. But this time they'd sunk as low as they could go. Any lower and they'd be six feet under. What they needed now was a miracle. Only they learned quick that miracles didn't favor bootstrap folks like them, at least not in their dusty little corner of the world.

That evening after dinner, Fyfe sat out on the front porch for a good, long while. Since the spill, she'd spent precious little time outdoors and she was going stir-crazy from the stale air of the farmhouse. The night air was cool and a light breeze blew through every now and again. She watched the lightning bugs spark, their bellies twinkling like Christmas lights. She was going to miss this place.

When it was time to turn in, she went to open the screen door and the handle came off in her hand. An old piece of junk. She used her fingernails to pry the door open then wheeled herself into the house. She found Roscoe standing in the doorway to the kitchen, staring at the childhood height marks that had been carved into the aging wood of the doorframe for generations, awash in nostalgia. She put the handle down on the table with a clunk and the sound snapped Roscoe out of his daze.

"A good gambler knows when to fold. Give up, Pa. Let the bank take it."

Roscoe traced his finger over the tallest notch on the door, with the initials "F.F." and the words "age 12" scratched next to it.

"This place is our home, Fyfe. And it has been for four generations. It's our history. And it's our only shot at any kind of a future. We're horse people. Horse people need land."

"It's occurred to me that we might not be the people we thought we were."

He shook his head no. "I know *exactly* who you are. You're Bluegrass Gibson. And if we've learned anything at all, it's that I'm not a good gambler." He shot Fyfe a weary half smile.

"I won't lie to you, Fyfe. The bank might take this place from us. But if they do, they'll have to pry it from my tired, broken, bloodied hands."

T HE FOLLOWING FRIDAY afternoon, Roscoe was
upstairs in his bedroom, emptying out his closet.
He kept one pair of long johns for when the weather
turned, a sturdy pair of boots, a good pair of work
gloves, and the clothes on his back. Everything else he
gathered into a burlap sack, intending to sell it for
whatever it would fetch. Of course, he was no fashion
fiend, so there wasn't much there to begin with, and
what was there was modest. But they needed every last
penny.

He'd already sold off the dishes, the pots and pans,
and the kettle, saving only a can opener and a few odd
utensils. As he tied a knot on the top of the sack, he
glanced across the room to where his racing ribbons

and trophies were displayed, all bright and shiny. They were the last symbols of pride in that dilapidated old house. Mementos of his glory days. He'd have to hock those next. That would be the hardest part, he thought.

Just as he hefted the sack of clothes onto his back, there came an awful racket outside his window. He looked out to see a pickup truck barreling toward the house, the driver leaning on his horn.

Roscoe bounded downstairs and as soon as he opened the front door, Ronald Streeter, the man from the Racing Board, barged right in. He pushed past Roscoe with a sack of his own flung over his shoulder and laid it down with a thud on the kitchen table.

"What's all this?" Roscoe was short on patience these days.

Mr. Streeter opened the bag and a mountain of envelopes spilled out.

"Letters! Thousands of them. And I've got ten more bags of 'em out in my truck. All for you."

"For *me*?"

"Well, technically for your horse."

Roscoe picked up one of the envelopes and examined it. "Mr. Streeter, these letters are addressed to the Racing Board."

"That's right. All from good people like you and

me, asking the board to reconsider its decision to disqualify Shadow. Everyone knows something wasn't right with that last race, Mr. Flynn. Whether it's hearsay or just a hunch. We all know it."

Fyfe wheeled herself into the room, right up to the table, and started rooting through the pile of envelopes. Then she began opening and reading the letters.

"That means a lot. Really, it does," said Roscoe. "But I'm afraid it won't *do* much. With all due respect Mr. Streeter, the board is stubborn, and rules are rules."

"Maybe, but they can't ignore a public outcry like this. Why, the whole state of Kentucky's up in arms over your colt! That's what I'm here to tell you: The board has opened an official investigation into your case."

"Our *case*?" said Roscoe.

"Sure! They're going to arrange for a veterinarian to come out and have a look at Shadow, and they'll send a specialist to inspect your saddle and the rest of the tack. Now, it could all be nothing. If they find the accident to be the result of jockey error, or some fault of the horse, then the ruling stands. But if the people are right, and you and Shadow didn't get a fair shake, he might just get his shot after all."

"You're saying there's a chance?" asked Roscoe.

"I'm saying there's a *chance* there's a chance. Like you said, the board is stubborn."

"Look at these letters, Pa," said Fyfe. "Some of them are made out to Shadow himself." She was absorbed in the flurry of creased white papers. She read aloud, one after the next, "*. . . we believe in you . . . we're praying for you . . . we love you, Shadow . . . you can do it.*" She looked up at her father quizzically. "But we lost."

"You don't have to win to be a hero," Roscoe replied. He picked up the letters by the fistful and held them out to her as proof. "Look at all these people! We gave them something to believe in."

Fyfe picked up another letter. This one caught her by surprise.

"*Dear Bluegrass . . . don't give up.*"

And she didn't. After that, Fyfe's disposition changed completely. She was like a compass where the needle had gotten stuck, but then one good whack set it straight again. It would be going too far to say her faith in humanity had been restored, but she was strongly considering it, pending the outcome of the investigation.

The very next morning after Mr. Streeter's visit, she

wheeled herself outside and onto Shadow's practice track. It was the first time she'd gone farther than the front porch in over two weeks. She wasn't used to getting around in the wheelchair out in the dirt, and she struggled through every bump and divot. The wheels felt heavy and moved slowly, but, one spin at a time, she inched around that track. Ultimately she'd need to get her legs working again, but first she needed to get strong. She had to walk before she could run, and she had to roll before she could walk. About three quarters of the way around the track she began to doubt whether she could do it, but then she heard the familiar click of hooves behind her. She'd missed that sound. She looked over her shoulder and there was Shadow, cheering her on, just as she always did for him. He walked a step behind her the whole rest of the way, slow as could be. They carried on like this each morning thereafter—her rolling where he used to run.

Monday morning marked the arrival of the inspector and the vet: two very serious men. They were there at the direction of the Racing Board, which would be taking their findings under careful advisement. The vet greeted Roscoe with a firm handshake. The inspector's handshake was less firm but equally aggressive, making up what it lacked in strength with rigor. Roscoe offered them each a glass of water, seeing as how they were conducting their business on rather a warm day, but they declined (in unison) and informed him they were not at liberty to accept any gifts or favors. Their code of conduct was unduly strict about fraternization with any subject of, or related to, an official investigation, and so they carried out their duties with few words and unblemished impartiality.

The vet wasted no time and went straight to work. As he poked and prodded Shadow, the peanut gallery peered through the barn window. Oats, Gladys, Red, and Raelynn were dumbfounded.

"What on Earth is that man doing to Shadow?" Gladys wondered.

The vet slipped the magnifying bifocals that had been resting on his forehead down over his eyes and squinted through their thick lenses to take a closer look at a brush burn around Shadow's middle. He measured its every dimension then scribbled some notes in a tiny, leather-bound journal.

"I bet he's here to buy him!" crowed Red.

"Holy smokes! You think so?" Raelynn fluttered. The thought alone was enough to ruffle her feathers.

"Scout said he saw them hang an eviction notice the

other day," said Red. "The bottom's dropped out once and for all and now they're forced to sell us off."

"Poor Shadow!" cried Raelynn. "Do you think they'll let us say goodbye?"

"Quit your cluckin', you two!" grumbled Oats. "There could be a million reasons why that fella is . . ."—the vet lifted Shadow's tail—". . . having a peek."

"Name one," Red challenged.

Oats was hard-pressed for an answer, but Scout darted into the barn just in the nick of time, panting in excitement. "Did you hear? The Racing Board is here to inspect Shadow. There's a chance he could get back in the race!"

"See? There's one," Oats glommed on.

The inspector was just as thorough and every bit as deliberate as the vet. He snapped on a pair of rubber gloves before meticulously poring over each piece of riding equipment used in the race. Then he plucked at Shadow's beaten-up, secondhand saddlecloth with a large pair of metal tweezers.

Roscoe eyed him from the corner of the room, studying his expression, looking for a tell as to whether this thing was going their way. But the inspector's unflinching face provided no clues.

Next, the inspector hoisted the saddle, untouched and still caked in dirt from the fall, onto the table. He took one look at it then turned to Roscoe.

"I'll need to take this with me."

It took exactly four weeks for the Racing Board to reach a decision. With the Derby now less than a month away, Ronald Streeter returned once again to deliver the news in person. He rapped "Shave and a Haircut" on the Flynns' front door, and when Roscoe answered it he found him shaking the rain off himself like a wet dog on the porch. Mr. Streeter stepped inside and took off his coat, and Roscoe spotted a red satin bow tie hanging loosely around his neck, half tucked inside his shirt collar.

"What have you got that thing on for?" Roscoe asked gruffly, afraid to get his hopes up.

Fyfe wheeled into the room behind Roscoe.

"The Racing Board's investigation found irrefutable evidence of foul play," said Mr. Streeter. "Someone snapped your saddle clean in half. They have no choice but to allow Shadow back in the circuit!"

Roscoe let out a loud whoop. "That means he can race the Derby!" He was practically giddy.

"Yes, but he'll still have to qualify. No points were

awarded in his last race, which means he's still at sixty-four. That's six shy of qualifying. The Championship Series is over, so that gives him just one shot to pick up the split."

"Keeneland." Roscoe was one step ahead of him.

"That's right. The Wild Card race. Win and you're in." Mr. Streeter grinned. "Think you can be in Lexington in eight days?"

Roscoe looked to Fyfe, "What do you think, kiddo?"

"It's too good to be true, isn't it, Pa?" She looked from Roscoe to Mr. Streeter, afraid to let herself believe it.

Mr. Streeter smiled and got down on bended knee to tell Fyfe face-to-face. "It's official. Heck, it's all over the news. Practically the whole town's got their bow ties on." He straightened the fancy red bow around his own neck with a wink.

Without another word Fyfe spun her wheelchair and burned rubber for the back door.

"Where are you going?" Roscoe called after her.

"To tell Shadow!"

Roscoe and Mr. Streeter hurried after her, but Fyfe didn't get too far. It had been raining all day and the ground was muddy so when the wheels of her chair rolled into the patch of dirt and grass that stretched from the house out to the barn, they began to sink. Try as she might to push her wheels forward, she only succeeded in digging them in deeper. There were no two ways about it: she was stuck.

"Carry me, Pa!"

"You've got to walk, Fyfe. Doc says you can if you really want to. Only thing stopping you is you."

It was true. Her injuries had all but mended. Only, she'd come to rely on the chair so much, and for so long, that her legs had gone weak.

"I can't." She was scared to try. Why couldn't this—just this one moment in her whole hardscrabble life—be easy?

Roscoe held out his hand. "I'll help you."

Fyfe grabbed his hand and Roscoe pulled her onto her feet. Her legs were wobbly and gave out under her. Mr. Streeter swooped in and grabbed a hold of her other side. Before she knew it, and between the three of them, she was standing. They stumbled forward together, one slow, clumsy step at a time. They were soon drenched to the bone, ankle-deep in mud, but undeterred. Fyfe would have walked to the ends of the earth to get to Shadow right then.

When they finally reached the barn door, they didn't have a free hand among them, so Roscoe kicked it open. The animals startled, all of them except for Shadow. He'd been staring at that door every minute of every day since he and Fyfe were ripped apart out on that track. And when it swung open and Fyfe was standing on the other side of it, all soggy and scrawny, and weak at the knees? Well, he just looked like he'd been expecting her all along.

33

BA-DUHM! SHADOW'S HOOVES pounded the dirt mercilessly as he galloped around the training pen at breakneck speed. Around and around and around, then—*wham!* Roscoe put his shoulder into a bale of hay and checked Shadow into the railing. Shadow recovered quickly, rebounding off the fence, losing a little speed but keeping his footing.

"Good!" called Fyfe who was watching from the other side of the fence, leaning on a set of rickety crutches—an undeniable upgrade from the wheels she'd been using the past few weeks. She was her old self again, and now that Shadow was back in training, she knew he was, too.

"Bred Winner will try to box us in and take the inside," she explained as though she expected

Shadow to understand her. "That's his signature move. We have to be ready for him this time. Try it again, and this time don't give up the rail. Get right back on it."

Roscoe smiled with pride. Fyfe was smart as a fox, stubborn as a mule, and still foolhardy enough to talk to a horse.

"This is ridiculous," she said to Roscoe this time. "He can't train without a jockey. Here, let me at him." She made her way through the open gate of the pen, her crutches squeaking with every step.

"Kiddo, I meant what I said before. Your riding days are behind you."

"Doc Crump is a capable physician, but he's vastly underestimated me." She reached for Shadow's reins but Roscoe got to them first.

"It's not just Crump," Roscoe said.

Fyfe screwed her mouth into a tight frown. She'd just assumed that, now that Shadow was back in this thing, Bluegrass was, too.

"What happened last time wasn't my fault," Fyfe insisted. "I didn't fall because I wasn't good enough. I got taken down. It could have happened to anybody, even *you*—and it did a year ago."

A tinge of pain coursed through his bad knee with

the memory. He looked down at the source of so much agony, his face full of regret.

Fyfe lowered her eyes to find his. "What happened to me wasn't right. I deserve a second chance. I *need* it. And deep down, you know that . . . because you need it too."

She was right, of course. But that didn't factor in to his decision. His needs were irrelevant—had been since the day she was born. But he looked into those big wide eyes of hers and it was like he could see the future. One path led to security, but it came with great sadness. Without the incentive to get back on the horse, she would never fully recuperate. Her ailments would go on to plague her for the rest of her days, and eventually her spirit would wither, too. The intelligent, resourceful, plucky girl she once was would disappear forever.

The other path was paved with risk, but at the end was great reward. Not *reward* in the traditional sense. There would be just as many losses as victories. But it was a life full of possibility, where she knew her old man was in her corner and that he believed she could do whatever she set her mind to. On this path, she was happy.

He handed Fyfe the reins. She let go of her crutches, letting them fall away, then hoisted herself up into the saddle. She looked strong up there. She was more confident in the saddle than she was on her feet. She couldn't walk, but she could ride. She wrapped the reins around her hand, let out a "hyah" and took off.

While it may have felt like the whole world was rooting for them, truth was the odds weren't in their favor. They'd have to come from behind and the bookmakers were taking sixteen-to-one action on Shadow. He was a bona fide long shot.

The Wild Card race was just around the corner and the Derby was just two weeks after that. Shadow had been collecting dust for two and a half months—no racing, no training—and now he was suddenly being catapulted into the big leagues. It was like skipping grade school and going straight to college. He had a lot of ground to cover—and fast.

Meanwhile Bred Winner hadn't missed a beat. He was training long hours, day in and day out. He was like a machine. He ate, slept, and breathed *"Win."* And it seemed the only one who wanted it more than him was the Colonel. He had racked up hundreds of victories in his career but this one was different. This one he had to work for.

While Fyfe climbed back on Shadow for the first

time in weeks, Bred Winner trotted along on one of Bianchi's cold, clinical machines: a stationary gate with a motorized belt that turned around under his hooves. The faster it spun, the faster Bred Winner had to run to keep up with it. Meanwhile, he was connected to a medical device by a dozen long wires that threaded over his back and under his legs. It was an electrocardiogram machine that measured his heart rate, and right now it was off the charts.

"What's your doohickey say?" the Colonel asked, eyeing the contraption.

"One hundred and eight beats per minute, and he's barely at a trot." Bianchi looked worried. "It's not good, Colonel."

"What do you think he'll top out at?"

"One-twelve. One-fifteen, *maybe*."

"And then what?"

"Then his heart will explode." He said it as though it was obvious, strange a concept as it was.

"Can't you give him something to slow the heart? An injection of some kind?"

"Yes, but—"

"Then do it."

"Colonel, it is very dangerous. Not just for the body, but also for the mind. All this pushing, pushing, pushing, and now pulling the other way? It creates a sickness in the head. You don't know what he could do."

"You're supposed to be the man with the magic potion. I brought you a very long way, and put an awful lot of trust in you. So make it happen. I need that horse on point for the Derby, with his ticker intact." He picked up a syringe from the table and tossed it at Bianchi. "Whatever it takes."

At the end of another punishing day of training, Bred Winner was led back to his stall by a stable boy where he was bathed, groomed, and hand-fed like a king. As severe as his training regimen was, his pampering regimen was equally extreme.

No doubt about it, the competition was heating up now that the potential for a big Derby showdown between Shadow and Bred Winner was back on track. They amped up their training on both sides of the fence, but their methods were as different as night and day.

Fyfe rode Shadow around the track, timing his laps by counting "One Mis-sis-sip-pi, two Mis-sis-sip-pi, three Mis-sis-sip-pi . . ." while Bianchi timed Bred Winner on the second hand of a Swiss-calibrated chrome chronograph.

Shadow pulled a cart loaded up with logs around the track. On his second go-around, Fyfe and Roscoe sat on top of the logs to add extra resistance. On his third, Fyfe and Roscoe—and Oats—were now all in the cart, cheering him on.

At the end of the day, Roscoe gently lifted Shadow's leg to ice down his tendon. Shadow glanced over at the Epsom estate. He couldn't help but wonder what Bred Winner was doing across the way.

Bred Winner's hooves dangled in the air as he was lifted by a harness and pulleys six feet straight up. He was positioned above an oversized metal tub filled with water and was slowly lowered into it. Then a stable boy turned on the jets and a powerful rush of bubbles pushed Bred Winner back. He struggled against the current, galloping in place. As soon as he lost an inch of ground against the jet streams, Bianchi stepped into a pair of hip waders and climbed into the tank with him to administer another shot of "medicine."

Next door, Shadow settled down for a good night's rest, and Red and Raelynn snuggled next to him in his stall. Lights out for Bred Winner, too. Only he didn't sleep. He stared off into the dark, the moonlight glinting in his steely deadened eyes.

34

EVEN THOUGH THEY resided not a hundred yards from each other, and even shared a property line right down the middle, the Epsoms and the Flynns had been working hard to avoid each other over the past several weeks. There were no accidental run-ins at the mailbox, no neighborly nods from across the fence. It took a racing event to eventually bring them together: the Wild Card race at Keeneland.

Keeneland was the Hail Mary for horses on the bubble: The last chance for anyone who still needed a point or two to squeak by. Points were awarded on a 10-4-2-1 scale so, depending on their standing going into the race, the top finishers could go on to contend for Derby fame. But for Shadow, still six points shy of a qualifying score, it was first place or bust.

Despite Fyfe's determination, eight days just wasn't enough time for her to get back in fighting shape. She protested vehemently when Roscoe announced he would not allow her to jockey the Wild Card, but the reality was she, too, knew she wasn't ready, so she gave up the fight without much of a squabble.

Of course this meant she couldn't attend the race either. Fyfe Flynn couldn't very well show up on crutches when it was Bluegrass Gibson who'd taken the fall. And showing up in character as Bluegrass was absolutely out of the question. Sitting in the stands or even milling about in the paddock presented a minefield of opportunities to blow her cover. So Fyfe had to sit this one out. But, fortunately, top-shelf jockeys were lining up from Jessamine to Lexington to take a crack at Shadow.

"Hello, old friend," came a voice as Roscoe led Shadow into the stables. It was Arnaz. He was suited up in his silks with Shadow's number on his arm.

"Will you look at that?" Roscoe greeted him with a burly hug and a clap on the back, "Ángel Arnaz, on time for once in his life!"

Arnaz chuckled. He put his hand on Shadow's muzzle, getting a feel for the horse. The stables were always filled with a mixture of nerves and adrenaline before the start of the race, but Keeneland was different. It was wall-to-wall last-ditch ponies here, so the desperation was ratcheted up a notch. Arnaz's way of blocking it out was to connect the horse's *yin* to his *yang* and focus in on his partner for the race. He circled Shadow, giving him the once-over, keeping a hand on him at all times to reinforce their vocational bond with a physical one.

"How's he looking?" Arnaz asked Roscoe.

"A little rusty maybe. He's been cold for nearly seven weeks."

"How's he for speed?"

"A couple seconds off his best. But his stamina hasn't waned."

"Got it."

"He's not like other horses, Arnaz. He's all elbow grease, this one. He'll work for it. And just when you think he's spent, he'll dig deeper. Don't ever count him out."

"Reminds me of someone else I know."

"Get him to the top of the stretch and he'll pull through."

Arnaz nodded. "How's your man Bluegrass? Will he pull through, too?"

"Hope so."

"And how's Fyfe?" Arnaz locked eyes with Roscoe. There was something about the directness of both his question and his stare that caught Roscoe off-guard.

"How do you mean?"

"Haven't seen her around in a while, that's all."

"She's been putting in extra hours on the farm. Trying to turn that patch of dirt around."

Arnaz nodded again and hoisted himself up into the saddle. It was impossible to know whether Arnaz suspected anything, but he was a friend and Roscoe knew he wouldn't talk.

"Thanks for coming, Arnaz."

"Ahh, come on. You don't turn down a chance to be part of history." He tugged his helmet on and fastened its strap under his chin. "I just hope we win."

Roscoe smiled a thin, nervous smile.

As he headed to his spot in the stands, Roscoe wasn't at all surprised to see the Colonel standing at the rail, his fancy, tall-heeled, horsehair boot hitched on the bottom rung. He had come to Lexington under the guise of good sportsmanship. After all, Bred Winner would be running the Derby, and he wanted to scout out the final round of competition. But the truth was, there was only one horse he had come to see, and that was Shadow of a Doubt. He hoped that Keeneland would put an end to the rivalry between Shadow and Bred Winner. He hoped Shadow would lose, that he would fail to secure a spot in the Derby, and the rematch the newspapers, the radio announcers, and the American public had all been clamoring for would never take place.

As the horses lined up at the starting gate, it was clear who the crowd favorite was. At first, one solitary voice rang out from the crowd: "Sha-dow! Sha-dow!" Then another voice joined in, and another, until every bow-tie-wearing superfan was chanting his name. "Sha-dow! Sha-dow!" It was the anthem of the underdog.

The starting shot rang out and it was a melee from the get-go. On the first stretch, there was a pile-up at the rail with just a few ponies falling back. The rest of the pack was neck-and-neck. Sassafras Sister had the lead by a nose, and Shadow of a Doubt was off by three lengths. He bobbed and weaved, looking for an opening, but there was none. Arnaz spurred him on and charged straight up the middle, but Shadow was too little and got bounced out in between Time in a Bottle and Bingo Was His Name-O.

Finally, at the first bend, Shadow found a hole and

put Time in a Bottle and My Two Cents behind him.

Sha-dow! Sha-dow!

Going in to the back straight, the pack started to thin out, which gave Shadow more room to move. Inside, outside, inside, outside—he maneuvered past the other horses just as if they were apples on the Famous Flynn Apple Slalom. Then Shadow cut behind Bingo Was His Name-O and slipped by him right on the rail going into the final turn.

The chanting grew louder: *Sha-dow! Sha-dow!*

It was the top of the chute now, and Shadow was off a length-and-a-half from Sassafras Sister, the only horse still ahead of him. But she was on the fence and clinging to it for dear life. He had to make a move. It was now or never. Shadow broke away! He crossed to the outside and, just like Roscoe said he would, he dug deeper. Shadow began to gain ground. One length! Two lengths! Three full lengths! Shadow crossed the wire first and clinched it.

The crowd went berserk. Roscoe pulled his hat down low to hide his eyes, embarrassed that he might not be able to fight back tears. He couldn't believe it.

"Hey, you're Roscoe Flynn!" said a fan in a white bow tie. Roscoe looked up and then the man said the best five words Roscoe had ever heard his whole life: "See you at the Derby."

The normally reserved jockey couldn't control himself any longer. His emotions got the better of him and he latched onto the stranger, giving him a big old bear hug. Shadow was going to the Derby, and there wasn't a darn thing the Colonel could do to stop him.

Or was there?

After the race, the paddocks cleared out pretty quickly and Roscoe and Shadow were the last ones left.

"You enjoying all this song and dance?"

Roscoe looked over his shoulder to find the Colonel lurking behind him. He paid him no mind and went about his business, rinsing down Shadow. But the Colonel needled him again.

"You won't win the Derby," said the Colonel.

"You got some kinda crystal ball up there in your big ol' mansion that lets you see the future?" replied Roscoe.

"I've got something better. Call it an 'insurance policy'."

"And what's that?"

"Gilda Cage." The Colonel sensed Roscoe tense up.

"You have a soft spot for that old horse, don't you?"

Shadow snorted and balked. That was his mama the Colonel was talking about.

"Shadow of a Doubt crosses that finish line first, and it's curtains for Gilda."

"You're bluffing. She's of use to you as a breeder."

"I don't bluff." The Colonel sucked his teeth. "I'd put Gilda down like a rabid dog, then I'd sit down to dinner like nothing even happened."

Shadow made up his mind right then and there that he wouldn't race in the Derby. He would protect Gilda at any cost. And Roscoe was of the same mind. "We'll withdraw from the race," he said.

"You will do no such thing. You will race. And you will lose. The legend of Shadow of a Doubt dies at the Derby." The Colonel scraped the dirt off his boots. "Make it a good show though, huh? Wait to take the dive until the quarter mile. Keep 'em in suspense."

A smarmy Cheshire-cat grin crept across the Colonel's face. He knew he had Roscoe over a barrel, and he relished every second of it.

35

Roscoe had the unpleasant job of breaking the news to Fyfe when he returned to the farm. He knew she would be upset, so he suggested they go get a couple of ice cream sodas to celebrate winning the Wild Card. He hoped they would be a sugary distraction for Fyfe, but she had a one-track mind, and as soon as she hopped in the truck, she bubbled over with excitement, chattering away about the Derby. Roscoe didn't have the heart to let her carry on like that, knowing the corner the Colonel had backed them into, and so he broke the news to her right there in the front seat. Precocious as she was, Fyfe found the Colonel's threat a difficult concept to understand.

"Why don't we just buy Gilda from him?" asked Fyfe.

"First of all, we don't have the money. Second of all, he'd never sell."

"Why not? We'd offer him a good deal. We'll pay a king's ransom if we have to."

"Don't matter the price, kiddo."

"But he's a business man, isn't he?"

"Yes, but in this case, he's got another motive besides money. You see, it's what they call 'leverage.' He needs Gilda so he has something to hold over us, so we'll do what he wants."

"And if we don't?"

"The Colonel is a bad man, Fyfe. He'd hurt her just to spite us."

"Well, can't we save her somehow? We could sneak over there in the middle of the night when no one's lookin'—"

"They've got a dozen farmhands and just as many stable boys. We wouldn't get ten feet before they chased us down."

"Well we could try!" Fyfe protested.

"Say we did sneak her out. What would we do with her? Hide her on the farm right under their noses? The Colonel would call the authorities and we wouldn't have a leg to stand on. We got no claim to her, Fyfe.

Gilda is the Colonel's horse, and he can do with her what he'd like."

"But it's cruelty! Surely no one would abide by him mistreating an animal like that."

"That's true. But he hasn't done anything yet and there's no way to prove he intends to."

Fyfe racked her brain. "There's got to be a way!"

"Look, Gilda and I got history. She's a good horse. I couldn't bear to see her go out like that. And I know Shadow couldn't either. Or you. At some point all the strategy, and the planning, and the training, and the fighting—it all falls away. When a life hangs in the balance, nothing else matters."

"No. Of course not, Pa." Fyfe slumped down in the worn seat of the truck. "If it's all the same to you, maybe we should just go home. I don't much feel like ice cream anymore." She rested her head against the window and watched as the trees zipped by. Everything was moving so fast.

"It's a strange feeling," she said. "I always just figured no matter how it ended, it'd end out there, on the track."

While Fyfe wrestled with the unscrupulousness of life, the farm animals were none the wiser about the

Colonel's threat. Shadow didn't let on what had happened. He couldn't risk the possibility that the other animals might try to convince him to go for the win after all. The truth remained that if he didn't win the purse then they'd surely lose the farm, and any one of them could end up on the butcher's block or put out to pasture. Shadow knew it was hard to think with a clear head when your own tail was on the line.

Late that night, Shadow was asleep in his stall when he heard the creak of the barn door. He opened his eyes just in time to see a shadowy figure dart inside.

"Who's there?" asked Shadow.

No answer. Shadow was frightened. None of the other animals had heard the noise or seen the dark figure. They were still sound asleep. Shadow's eyes darted around the room.

"Hello?"

Shadow peered into the darkness but he couldn't see anything. "Scout, is that you . . . ?"

Then Shadow felt hot breath on the back of his neck. He turned to see a coyote perched on the stack of hay bales in the corner of his stall. But the coyote looked right through Shadow. A hunter tracking his prey, his beady bloodshot eyes fixed on Raelynn, sound asleep on her roost. He growled, and the musty smell of death hung thick on his breath.

In an instant, the coyote leapt toward Raelynn! Shadow darted in front of her but just as he did, Oats pushed him out of the way, throwing himself in between Shadow and the coyote. The coyote's fangs sunk into Oats's back and his claws tore bloody streaks through his skin. Oats cried out in pain and fell to the ground just as the boom of a rifle blast rang out and Roscoe came charging out from the house. The gunshot scared the coyote off and he slinked out of the barn, leaving a trail of bloody paw prints behind.

When Roscoe saw how badly Oats was hurt he wasted no time in ringing up Doc Crump. The doc sped right over, still in his pajamas, and found Roscoe in the barn, red up to his elbows, trying to stop Oats from bleeding out. He went straight to it and made quick work of stitching up the wound.

"I know you're no animal doctor, but I didn't know who else to call," explained Roscoe. "I normally tend to the animals myself, but never nothing serious like this."

"That's fine, Mr. Flynn. I'm glad you called. He nicked an artery. It needed proper medical attention. But he's stable, for now." Doc Crump dressed the stitches tenderly. "He'll need lots of rest, plenty of fluids. And keep him warm. That's important." He stood. "Do you have a hose?"

Out back, Roscoe ran the hose while the doc scrubbed the blood off his hands.

"First Fyfe, now him—seems like I've been out to your property more times than I care to count lately. If things keep going like this I'm going to have to rent a room here."

"If things keep going like this, pretty soon you'll be able to buy the whole dang place."

Inside the barn, Oats lay still, resting wearily. His eyes were open but he stared out at nothing. It was effort just to breathe, his chest rising and falling slowly. His hair was stained red. The coyote was a natural predator and, tragic as it was, such was the way of the world.

Raelynn regarded Oats with great sorrow. "It seems silly to say thank you," she said softly. "It's not nearly enough. I owe you my life."

"Let him get some rest," said Red, and he guided Raelynn back to her perch.

But Shadow didn't budge. He stood over Oats, watching his wounded friend with guilt. It should have been him lying there all stitched up.

"Why'd you go and do that, Oats?"

"What, and let you get all the glory?" Oats managed a weak little smile. But the truth of the matter was, he couldn't let Shadow get hurt. "You're the champ, Shadow," Oats sputtered. "You're gonna win. You have to win."

Shadow didn't have the heart to tell him he had no intention of winning. Instead he kneeled down beside him. His body heat would keep him warm. That was important. That was all he could do.

36

THE NEXT DAY, Shadow and Fyfe continued their training, business as usual. Only it wasn't. They were chasing a dream that had already died. Just going through the motions. Shadow couldn't shake the thought of poor Oats lying weak and helpless on the barn floor, having risked his life for nothing at all. He'd wished the coyote had bitten him instead.

They called it quits right about sundown that day, not knowing for certain whether they'd pick up again tomorrow. They'd been in the habit of training long into the night, but now . . . well, they didn't much see the point.

But when tomorrow came, Fyfe and Shadow once again did the only thing they knew how to do. They rode. They were both frustrated and angry at the world, and they took it out on the track. Fyfe got on

Shadow's back and they ran lap after lap around that farm until it was too dark to see, and they had no choice but to surrender for the day.

Their training wasn't about the outcome anymore; it was about the process. It was an outlet for them, and the only way they could feel whole. After two weeks of this, both Shadow and Fyfe were stronger and better prepared than they ever had been before. It was a bitter irony.

At last it was the night before the Kentucky Derby, and while under normal circumstances the farm would have been fraught with nervous energy, there was now an eerie calm in its place. Things had been somber ever since Oats was attacked. Fyfe gave the animals their dinner round about eight o'clock. She brought a special treat for Shadow, and one for Oats, too, giving them each a sparkly sugar cube for dessert. Shadow offered his to Oats, but he still wasn't well enough to eat it. Seeing as sweets were hard to come by, Shadow saved them for him, squirreling them away under one of his thick blankets until Oats had regained enough strength to give them a gnaw.

They all turned in a few hours later and the barn went dark and quiet. Only Shadow couldn't sleep. A little after midnight, he wandered out into the field back behind the barn. He figured he'd have a good graze, just him and the crickets.

He heard the patter of hooves and looked up to see Gilda bounding over the fence from the Epsom estate. She cleared it in one graceful stride. Shadow had never seen Gilda run before. He'd never seen her any which way but behind a fence since he was just a few months old. He was in awe. Her form was flawless. Her power was immense. She was majestic.

Shadow was speechless for a moment, then he finally mustered the words to say, "All these years, and you could jump that fence this whole time?"

"There's a time for following rules and a time for breaking them, child. I've waited out by this fence every night for two weeks and you haven't come to see me once. Now, either you're so preoccupied with running that Derby tomorrow that you forgot about your mama, or something ain't right."

"I've been afraid to see you."

"Afraid? What on Earth for?"

"Because what I gotta do, you won't be proud of."

"Stable boys say you're fixin' to take a fall."

"So you know?"

"I know no such thing. I told myself those stable

boys were full of the same stuff they been shoveling. My Shadow wouldn't throw the race."

"I don't have a choice in the matter, Mama."

"You always have a choice."

"The Colonel says I take the dive, or else . . . or else he'll put you down."

This part was news to Gilda and it came as a shock. She tried to hide her emotions best she could.

"You're not going to let some silly threat stand in your way, are you?" Gilda said. She knew the Colonel long enough to know he always made good on his threats, but she tried not to let on for Shadow's sake. "There's folks depending on you."

"I don't care. I don't care if we lose the farm. None of it matters if anything happens to you."

"This thing's bigger than the farm now, child. There's a whole lotta people counting on you. And they've got their hopes and dreams wrapped up in yours. If you race tomorrow and you don't win? Well, that's okay. Then it wasn't meant to be. But if you race and you don't *try*? Then you lost a whole lot more than the Derby, Shadow. You lost your pride."

"I didn't ask for any of this."

"But you did, Shadow. All those years you spent pulling the cart, going to bed every night dreaming of racing, knowing you were destined for so much more. You asked for this. And you had every right to. So don't be afraid to take what's yours now."

"But you mean more to me than any of it."

"I know, sweet child." She nuzzled him. Then it hit her that this would be the last moment they spent together. "If you don't win tomorrow, you'll lose the farm and they're going to take you away. If you do, I might not be here when you get back. Either way, I think this is goodbye."

Shadow nickered and nuzzled against his mama, but Gilda had to be strong for her child.

"For what it's worth," she whispered, "I hope I'm watching you in the winner's circle from up above, rather than watching them drag you away from behind a fence. I *had* my moment in the sun. Now it's time you get yours."

"Tell me you love me more than fifty-four red roses, Mama."

"I love you more than all the roses in the world— pink, white, red, or otherwise. You remember that, Shadow. Come what may. Your mama loves you so very much."

Shadow pressed his face against hers. He wanted to feel her touch. He wanted to absorb it and remember it. He wanted to never let it go.

37

THE FIRST SLIVER of early morning sun peeked over the horizon. Red strutted out to his perch, cleared his throat, and let rip a long, loud cock-a-doodle-doo. Oats's eyes fluttered open and he looked around at the other animals quietly starting their day.

"Hey guys, I lost a lot of blood, so I could be confused," Oats said, his voice weak. "But last time I checked, today was still the doggone Kentucky Derby."

It seemed the rascally old son of a gun was feeling just a touch better, and Oats's quip gave the rest of the animals permission to celebrate. After that they let loose. They were giddy with excitement and practically bouncing off the walls.

Gladys paced back and forth, trying to burn off her nervous energy. But she accidentally stepped on Raelynn's foot, and the tiny delicate bird bones crunched under the weight of her hoof. This set Raelynn off like a bomb. She hopped around, flapping her wings. She collided with Red so hard it shook a feather loose. "Is this *my* feather?" he clucked. He picked it up and examined it nervously. "Is this mine or yours?"

Just then, Scout slipped through the barn door and warned, "Fyfe's coming! It's time!" The news only amplified the animals' giddiness and launched them into full-blown hysteria.

"Everybody relax!" Oats walked tenderly out of his stall. "Shadow needs to concentrate."

It was, without a doubt, the single most important day of their entire lives. But somehow Shadow wasn't caught up in the hysteria. He was calm as could be.

Fyfe was done up in her racing silks, her hair pinned under her helmet and just a hint of a faux five o'clock shadow on her jaw. It was the first time she'd been Bluegrass since she'd been using the crutches and she had to re-learn how to walk like a man with them. She made it to the barn door and, just as she was about to push it open, she bent over and hurled her guts out. Nerves.

The animals beamed with pride, full of hope, as they watched Fyfe load Shadow into the trailer. She slammed the door shut and Roscoe started the ignition.

"Ladies and gentlemen, this is the day you've been waiting for all year! Top off those juleps and brush off your chapeaus because The Kentucky Derby is about to get underway!"

Skip the Quip was in rare form today. He wore a plaid sport coat and a straw hat and he talked so fast the microphone nearly started to smoke.

"But it's not all opera glasses and caviar today. We've seen a resurgence of the cheap seats as everyman fans have come out in droves to cheer on the underdog, last-minute contender in this race. Yes sir, they're backing that diminutive little pony, Shadow of a Doubt, who's out to prove it's not the size of the dog in the fight, but the size of the fight in the dog. It oughta be a real nail-biter out there today, folks. It's been a tumultuous season, but it all boils down to this race right here. This one's for all the marbles."

Roscoe and Fyfe pulled up to Churchill Downs and

they stopped for a moment, just to drink it in. The majesty of the structure, the history of the tradition, the thousands of fans swarming the entrance: You couldn't have dreamed a grander scene.

Roscoe turned off the truck and surveyed the mob of race fans. Fyfe still wasn't sure-footed and he worried the crush of the crowd would be too much for her.

"Wait here," he instructed. "I'll bring Shadow around to the paddock, then I'll come back and take you in separate." She nodded.

Roscoe unloaded Shadow from the trailer and as they made their way back through the crowd the strangest, most unexpected thing happened. Complete strangers rushed up to Roscoe, wanting to shake his hand or touch Shadow's mane for good luck. Roscoe didn't know what to make of it. Then he got a glimpse of a folded-up newspaper tucked under a man's arm.

"Can I see that paper?" asked Roscoe.

"Hey, you're Roscoe Flynn! You can *have* it. Good luck out there today. We're all rooting for you."

"Thanks, friend. We appreciate it."

Roscoe unfolded the paper. Plastered across the front page was a shot of him and Shadow. The national press had got hold of the story and had made it out to be a tale of redemption for the retired jockey. It went on to say how Roscoe had worked for the Colonel before his injury, and how now he'd returned to the track to race Shadow against the Colonel's Bred Winner. It even alluded to the mysterious circumstances around Roscoe's "accident." They'd blown the whole thing up to astronomical proportions and it suddenly wasn't just Bred Winner versus Shadow, it was the Haves versus the Have-Nots the world over. And this was about to be the final showdown.

"I quit!" The indignant jockey unlatched the strap on his helmet and threw it on the ground by Bred Winner's hooves. He had been making such a ruckus getting Bred Winner ready for the race that one of the stable boys had gone and fetched the Colonel, who was now on the receiving end of this outburst. "He tried to bite me!"

"It's just nerves," dismissed the Colonel.

"Nerves? Are you crazy? That horse is out of control. I don't know what you're giving him, but—"

"I don't like what you're implying, son," the Colonel interrupted.

The jockey glanced sideways at Bianchi, who was

burdened by guilt but stone silent all the same. Clearly neither one was going to admit any wrongdoing. Doping was illegal and grounds for disqualification from the race.

"I'm not going to break my neck out there. Find yourself another patsy."

"Listen to me, you insignificant little hood ornament," the Colonel began. "If that horse wants to bite you, you let it. Now get out there and bring me back a win or I'll see to it personally you never race again."

The jockey looked at the fire and brimstone burning behind the Colonel's eyes.

"You want this too bad."

"As though there's such a thing."

At that, the jockey turned and hung up his crop.

"PEOPLE DON'T WALK AWAY FROM ME!" the Colonel screamed.

"That's right." The jockey snapped the newspaper with the picture of Roscoe on the front page, "I heard they limp."

He walked off, leaving the Colonel fuming in his wake. He barked to the stable boy. "Go to the clubhouse and get Sal. Tell him to suit up. It's his lucky day."

The Colonel always had a spare jockey or two on

hand. This wasn't the first time one had been driven away by the combustible combination of his ambition and temper. He took Bianchi firmly by the arm and led him aside, out of earshot.

"What's going on with Bred Winner?" demanded the Colonel.

"We're pushing him too far, too fast. This isn't how the regimen was supposed to be administered. It was supposed to build up in his system over time."

"Well we're *out* of time. This is the Kentucky Derby! It all comes down to right now. If he doesn't win this race, he's finished."

"That's what I'm afraid of." Bianchi looked at the poor horse, his muscles twitching. "He'll either win, or die trying."

The Colonel grinned and clapped Bianchi on the back. "Good, because I'm ready to celebrate." He tugged out his pocket square and wiped his palms, as though he were literally washing his hands of all this messy business.

Roscoe hurried back to the truck to get Fyfe. He knew this should have been one of the happiest occasions of her life, but in a perverse reversal of fortune it had instead become one of her darkest days. Fyfe was solemn and joyless, the Colonel's threat weighing heavy on her mind, and Roscoe didn't know what to say to make it any better. But they had to carry on. He opened the car door and held out his hand to Fyfe.

"Come on. I'll take you around back."

"No, Pa. This here's Churchill Downs. I'm walking through the front door."

She took his hand and climbed down from the truck. He reached in the back for her crutches but when he handed them to her she shook her head no. She didn't want them. So Roscoe took hold of her firmly under her arm and she leaned on him instead. They walked slowly, one foot in front of the other, with their heads held high.

As they approached the gate, the hordes thickened and Fyfe faltered, jostled by the crush of people. A teen-age boy bumped into her and when he turned to apologize he recognized her as Bluegrass Gibson. Could it really be Bluegrass, down here with the masses, a big deal jockey shoulder-to-shoulder with the regular folk? The kid stopped in his tracks, staring in stunned silence for a moment. And then he started to clap. More and more people took notice and they started clapping too, until everyone was swept up in it.

Suddenly the crowd parted like the Red Sea, letting

Fyfe and Roscoe pass. Fyfe marched forward slowly, the rhythm of the applause like a drumbeat spurring her on. She tried to remember every face. She wanted to absorb every sound, every smell of this moment. She wanted these memories to last forever.

38

As much as the fans' support meant to Fyfe and Roscoe, sentimentality had no place in the paddock. When they got behind those doors it was all business. They went straight to work, grooming and saddling Shadow. With just a few minutes left to spare before she had to mount up, Fyfe couldn't resist taking one last look at the crowd. She peered out from the stables and saw the stands were packed to the rafters. Funny hats and fancy outfits were up top, and worn-out shoes and bow ties were on the bottom. She swallowed hard and hurried back to Shadow's stall, fast as she could on her crutches. She looked around for her pa, but he was gone.

"Has anyone seen Roscoe Flynn?"

A few of the other jockeys shook their heads.

Roscoe wasn't at the stables. He was at the betting window, where he'd spotted an old friend in line. Willie P. Cobb had worked at Churchill Downs for over two decades, handing out the racing forms.

"Do me a favor, Willie," Roscoe said as he sidled up next to him in line and jammed a wad of cash in his hand. "Put a little money down for me, huh?"

"What, you couldn't cut right up at the window?" joked Willie.

"You know how they are here, stricter than a grammar school teacher."

"Okay, Roscoe. Who you want it on?"

"On *my* horse. Who do you think?"

"I dunno. Just seems like gilding the lily, I guess. If your horse comes in first, you'll win the purse. What good will a little extra do ya? But if Bred Winner comes in first . . . you'll leave empty-handed."

Roscoe couldn't deny that Willie made a good point.

"Hedge your bets," Willie went on. "That's all I'm saying. Then either way you walk away with something."

Fyfe hoisted the saddle onto Shadow's back. This time she checked the buckle twice for safety. "My Old Kentucky Home" wailed to life in the background, at the hands of the brass band. She hummed along, as Bluegrass would do, and it reminded Shadow of how she used to sing that song to him as he fell asleep.

For the first time, something about their plan didn't feel quite right. Shadow had been certain of what he was going to do this whole time. But now, suddenly, he wasn't so sure anymore. His mind ping-ponged between all the people he knew were counting on him—the fans out in the stands, Oats and all the other animals back on the farm, Roscoe, Fyfe, and his mama, whose very fate hung in the balance. He was being pulled in so many directions, it was tearing him apart. He was in pieces, a million of them, and each one felt right and wrong all at the same time.

"I know. I feel it too," Fyfe said, like she could read his mind. She stroked his muzzle, comforting him.

"So what are we gonna do, boy?"

Roscoe and his friend Willie stepped up to the betting window. Roscoe clenched his jaw so tight the veins in his neck throbbed. He already knew how this race was supposed to end. Putting the money on Shadow would be a sucker's bet. But he'd made a promise to Fyfe never to take odds against Shadow again. Willie slid the money across the counter then turned to Roscoe.

"Well? What's it gonna be?"

Fyfe looked deep into Shadow's eyes, straight through to his soul. "Okay," was all she said, and then she climbed up into the saddle. She pulled a crumpled, black bow tie from her front pocket, and fastened it around her neck. They were going to race.

Fyfe and Shadow fell in line with the other horses and prepared to head out onto the track for the ceremonial lap before the start of the race. One by one, the horses paraded out. Many of them were familiar faces that had paved their road to the Derby: My Two Cents, Butterscotch Betty, Passing Fancy, Time in a Bottle, Say It Ain't So, and Bred Winner. Shadow was the last to go. There was a wave of polite applause as each competitor joined the line. But as soon as Shadow turned the corner, the crowd erupted. The cheers roared from the stands and washed over them, and Fyfe couldn't help but smile. She'd been to the Derby every year since she could remember, but she'd never seen it like this. It was magical. She gave a wave and the crowd went wild.

Fyfe scanned the stands and saw Colonel Epsom and

his wife perched up in the highest box seats. Mrs. Epsom absentmindedly clapped along until the Colonel admonished her and she folded her hands in her lap.

Then she spotted Roscoe as he made his way to the front and pressed up against the rail. She gave him a hopeful smile. The betting ticket in his hand was damp with perspiration. He was every bit as nervous as she was.

The horses took their places at the starting gate and waited. Shadow saw Bred Winner a couple posts over and the two horses locked eyes. Bred Winner's were full of venom, his stare icy and cold. Shadow tried to shake it off. He looked dead-ahead.

Then, amid all the hustle and bustle, Fyfe reached down and stroked Shadow's mane, her small fingers raking through his hair. Her touch calmed him and all the nerves, the noise, the screaming fans—they all faded away. It was just him and his best friend on his back.

Fyfe took up the reins and posted up in the saddle. She peered through the slats of the starting gate at the pristine stretch of dirt in front of them. Just like in life, at the Derby you only go around once. They had to make it count. Two minutes to make history.

The starting horn sounded and the gate swung open. Shadow bolted out so fast he grazed the gate before it even had a chance to open all the way. He was the first one out, nineteen other horses hot on his heels.

"And they're off!" Skip came to life over the loud-speaker. "Shadow of a Doubt is first out of the gate and the fans are going nuts for him! But, uh-oh, here comes trouble."

Bred Winner was closing in on him fast and hard.

He was a sprinter and Shadow didn't have enough speed to hold his lead down the chute. Bred Winner overtook him in a matter of seconds and kept going, full steam ahead. As Bred Winner barreled on, putting more and more space between him and Shadow, it shook Shadow's confidence. He dug deep for more speed but he was burning out too fast.

Here came the rest of the pack. Sassafras Sister and Time in a Bottle whizzed by, leaving Shadow a distant fourth, with Butterscotch Betty and My Two Cents on his tale. He was blowing it.

"Ease off! Get your head right." Fyfe shouted into his ear. "This is your race, Shadow. Race it your way."

"Bluegrass Gibson is coming back from a horrific fall in what's being hailed as the 'Battle over the Saddle'," said Skip, "and it seems like Bluegrass and Shadow may not have had the time they needed to get back in their groove."

But Shadow took Fyfe's coaching to heart. He pulled back and found his rhythm. The first turn was coming up fast and Shadow tried to get over on the inside rail. No dice; Sassafras Sister boxed him out. Bred Winner was still out in front. Time in a Bottle was gaining on him as they went into the turn, but Bred Winner planted wide and bumped up against him, knocking Time in a Bottle off course. He careened out and lost precious seconds. Time in a Bottle was out of the race. Bred Winner gave up some ground, too, and his lead narrowed to less than a length. Rounding the corner it was Bred Winner, Sassafras Sister, then Shadow.

Bred Winner charged down the back straight with such force that his hooves spiked divots in the dirt every time they struck the ground. Shadow was the exact opposite, light as a feather, like he was floating on air.

The second turn was in their sights. The gaps were closing and Bred Winner, Sassafras Sister, and Shadow were right on top of one another. The pressure was on. Bred Winner went into the turn hot. He had too much speed on him and, try as he might to rein him in, his jockey couldn't control him. Bred Winner took the turn wide and Shadow seized the opportunity to get in the pocket. He cut to the inside and hugged the rail so tight Fyfe's boot skimmed it!

"I've never seen a horse show that kind of precision on this track. Jack be nimble, Jack be quick, this pony's got a bag of tricks!" shouted Skip.

Shadow was out in front going into the final straightaway. But Bred Winner picked up speed coming out of the turn and the two of them were now in a dead heat.

"*This* is the show the people came to see!" Skip's voice boomed. "The epic rivalry between Shadow of a Doubt and Bred Winner is coming to a head right here, folks. It's the heart of gold versus the hooves of steel! Anything could happen."

But the Colonel knew precisely what was going to happen and his lips curled into a smug grin as he leaned back in his seat, waiting for the future to unfold as he'd written it. Any minute now, Shadow would pull back and his horse would cross the finish line first.

Down below, Roscoe white-knuckled the fence right at the sideline. He'd forgotten himself at the last turn when Shadow cut out in front, and for a moment he believed they really had a shot at this thing. The ride was fantastic, every single second of it. But it was about to come to an end.

"This is it—the last quarter mile!" clamored Skip.

Shadow and Bred Winner were neck-and-neck, exactly like they had been in that very first race together. Bred Winner watched Shadow out of the corner of his eye. He was huffing and puffing, breathing heavy. But Shadow just looked straight ahead.

Bred Winner started to run out of steam, but not Shadow. He was still going strong. Suddenly, Bred Winner realized Shadow wasn't giving up! Bred Winner tried desperately to speed up. He panted hard. Losing was not an option, not with the Colonel waiting for him when it was all over.

Bred Winner put his head down and charged Shadow with his shoulder. The two horses collided, sending Shadow into the fence. But Fyfe and Roscoe had trained him well and Shadow didn't miss a step. At that moment, Shadow knew nothing could stop him.

Bred Winner was growing tired. As a matter of fact, the whole pack behind them was tiring as well and, one by one, they were starting to slip away and fall back. The funny thing about the Kentucky Derby is, it's only two minutes, but at one-and-a-quarter miles, the track is a full eighth-of-a-mile longer than any qualifying race in the season. And for most horses, including Bred Winner, that extra eighth of a mile may as well have been a million miles.

But not for Shadow. He'd spent months pulling a plow around a track three times this long. His stamina could not be matched. While everyone else was slowing down, he was speeding up.

Roscoe looked down and stared hard at the ground. He couldn't bear to watch. But, all of a sudden, the roar of the crowd swelled to an uncharted decibel. Roscoe looked up just in time to see Shadow and Fyfe soar into first place. He opened his mouth to cheer them on, but he was so overcome that no sound came out. His eyes just welled with tears.

This was it: the final stretch. It all came down to Shadow, Bred Winner, and the white chalk line a hundred yards away, just like before. Only this time . . . Shadow of a Doubt hit the wire first!

"Shadow wins! Shadow wins!" Skip shouted from the announcer's box. "Ladies and gentlemen, he's done it! Shadow of a Doubt has proven once and for all, makes no difference the hand you're dealt—it's not bluffing if you believe it!" And the crowd went wild.

Within seconds, the rest of the horses rumbled across the finish line, all slowing to a trot. But not Shadow. He didn't stop at the finish line. He didn't stop for the flurry of newspaper reporters and photographers. He didn't stop for the Winner's Circle and the giant check. He didn't even stop for the blanket of roses. He kept right on running, straight out of Churchill Downs and right out onto the street. He ran and he ran and he ran for miles.

And Fyfe knew in an instant exactly where he was going. Shadow was determined to save Gilda. He had no idea how, he just knew he had to get home.

He raced down the long dirt road, and made it just in time to see Gilda glide over that fence between the Epsom Estate and the Flynn Farm. She soared through the air with such grace and then she hit the ground running.

Fyfe and Shadow watched as she tore across the field and disappeared into the woods behind the farm. A huge weight was lifted off Shadow's heart. She was safe. A few of the Epsom stable boys mounted up and took after her but it was mostly just a gesture. They

could never have caught her. Gilda always was the fastest horse they had.

Turns out Gilda didn't need saving after all. Like she said, she could jump that fence this whole time . . . .

A few minutes later, some confused reporters and spectators showed up at the farm. They'd followed Shadow there from Churchill Downs. They took photographs and everyone wanted to know why Shadow and Bluegrass left the racetrack, but Fyfe didn't answer.

Some of the papers put a spin on it and claimed it was an anti-establishment stand, the Everyman shirking the upper-crust trappings of the Derby, symbolically casting off the blanket of roses. But that wasn't it at all. Truth was, it all came down to loving someone more than fifty-four red roses.

39

You won't find Shadow of a Doubt in any record books. He was stripped of his title in the end. The Colonel exposed Bluegrass Gibson's true identity to the Racing Board and had the victory overturned. Of course, in doing so, he made Fyfe Flynn into something of a celebrity. Before she knew it, practically every news outlet in the country was telling the tale of the twelve-year-old girl who overcame a physical disability and tremendous adversity to win the Kentucky Derby. The title may have defaulted to Bred Winner as a technicality, but Shadow's legend remained intact.

Unfortunately, the Flynns didn't get to keep the prize money either. They had to forfeit the purse from the Derby along with the title. But once they became an overnight sensation in the press, the bank granted them a thirty-day reprieve, which came just in the nick of time to stave off foreclosure. That gave them a few weeks to get their affairs in order and, as it turns out, where there once was no work to be had for the man Colonel Epsom put out on the street, there was plenty for the man who had defeated him. Suddenly, Roscoe was in high demand. Believe it or not, there was more work than he could handle, which is why Fyfe got into the horse training business with her pa, lickety-split. Whether he was willing to admit it or not, she'd insisted that he needed her help. She understood horses better than anybody, and that alone made for an ace trainer.

Now that business was booming, Roscoe didn't have to worry too much about money troubles. They had enough to save Flynn Farm, and even had a little left over for some much-needed repairs and to hire Pike back.

As for the wager he placed at the Derby, well, they won that too. But he never cashed the ticket. He framed it.

"Shadow of a Doubt to WIN."

After all, the lesson was worth more than the prize.

It was a blow to Shadow, Fyfe, and Roscoe when

they lost the title and the purse, but in the end it didn't much matter. You see, winning isn't only about a title or a whole heap of prize money. The day the Racing Board made their decision, hundreds of people showed up at Flynn Farm. Fyfe peeked out the window and saw that none of them were wearing the bow ties she was used to seeing on their fans. She thought maybe they'd stopped believing, or that they were mad that Fyfe had tricked them. But Roscoe opened the door and the man at the front of the crowd handed him a blanket stitched together with fifty-four red bow ties. Shadow never got his blanket of red roses, but now he had something even better.

"Win or lose, he's still our hero," said the man.

And that made it all worthwhile.

The Colonel went on to win many more titles, but he never got over losing that one. The Flynns and the Epsoms didn't see much of each other after the Derby. On the rare occasion when Fyfe did catch a glimpse of the Colonel across the fence, she would thrust her arm up in the air and give him a big ol' friendly wave. She intended to "kill him with kindness," but Roscoe reminded her that murder of any sort, even if perpetrated with pleasantries and warm gestures, was wrong, so she reluctantly put an end to it.

Despite how their lives changed in the months following the Derby, one thing stayed the same on Flynn Farm. Busy as she was in her new role as a professional horse trainer, Fyfe still made time to ride Shadow every single day. It's been said that some people have an angel on their shoulder, but Shadow had his on his back.

Of course the very best part about the Flynns being able to stay in their home was that it meant all their animals were safe. That's really all they ever wanted. Oats made a full recovery, though he claimed his emotional scars ran deeper than his physical ones, and milked his one spectacular moment of heroism for years to come. For a Shetland pony, he played the part of the sacrificial lamb to a T.

In the end, Oats finally got that big promotion he'd been angling for and took up the job of draft horse at Flynn Farm. Of course, he was a might bit small to pull the plow, and to move it even an inch required the help of Gladys and Scout, and though Red and Raelynn weren't much use they pitched in too. (Oats coached the others in what he coined "plow face," a variation of the "race face" he taught Shadow, which hinged on a gunslinger's squint and a never-say-die snarl.) The whole lot of them, growling, flapping, squawking, and mooing, they'd dig in, one step at a time, and got the job done. It was a sight to behold all right. They were the only farm animals ever known to pull the plow by teamwork, but it suited them just fine.

Bred Winner was sold off to some bigwig in Bullitt County over in the Knobs. He fetched a pretty penny but his new owner didn't see much return on his investment. Bred Winner soon flamed out. And, truth be told, his passion was gone. After such a hollow Derby victory, "first place" had lost all meaning, and without that notion to chase around the track, he was just running in circles. After a string of unremarkable runs, his career was cut short mid-season and it brought him an unexpected sense of relief. He was sold again, this time to a breeder with a tiny sliver of land shoehorned in between a sleepy chicken farm and a shady creek, and for the first time in his life he was at peace.

As for Gilda, the Flynns never saw her again. But sometimes Shadow would just up and leave, disappearing for days at a time, and they'd know he was out in the wild, running free with his mama.

Every year on the anniversary of Shadow's Derby win, which of course was the same anniversary as the day Gilda ran away, Fyfe laid fifty-four red roses out back by the woods. Shadow had his bow tie blanket and that was all he needed, so Fyfe figured he'd want his mama to have the roses.

A Note About the Kentucky Derby

THE KENTUCKY DERBY is the most important horse race in the world. It has been held each year since 1875 and remains the longest, continuously held sporting event in U.S. history. The Derby takes place on the first Saturday in May at Churchill Downs in Louisville, Kentucky, and is known the world over as "The Most Exciting Two Minutes in Sports." It is a mere one and a quarter miles long, and only three-year-old thoroughbreds may compete.

Few horses will qualify to run "The Race for the Roses." A series of thirty-five races across the country pave the "Road to the Kentucky Derby" in the weeks leading up to the big event. Points are awarded on a sliding scale to the Top 4 finishers in each race. Only the twenty horses awarded the most points over the course of the season earn a post at the Kentucky Derby starting gate.

SKYLAR JAMES was born and raised in New York City. She learned to ride horses at the age of six and although her riding career was short-lived, lasting just one year, she is exceedingly proud of the red ribbon she won "that one time." She spent many an afternoon pressed up against the rail at the Meadowlands Racetrack, long before she was big enough to see over it. Skylar worked in charity, and before that in film and television, until she decided to chase her dreams and become a writer.

Fodor's 07

AA 4277 Boarding 3:70 PM

S0-AZT-271

LONDON

Where to Stay and Eat
for All Budgets

Must-See Sights
and Local Secrets

Ratings You Can Trust

Fodor's Travel Publications   New York, Toronto, London, Sydney, Auckland
www.fodors.com

FODOR'S LONDON 2007
Editor: Amy B Wang, Amanda Theunissen

Editorial Production: Linda K. Schmidt
Editorial Contributors: Rob Andrews, Ferne Arfin, Linda Cabasin, Ruth Craig, Christi Daugherty, Jessica Eveleigh, Adam Gold, Julius Honnor, Christina Knight, James Knight, Katrina Manson, Kristan Schiller, Hilary Weston, Alex Wijeratna
Maps and Illustrations: David Lindroth, *cartographer;* William Wu; additional cartography provided by Henry Columb, Mark Stroud, and Ali Baird, Moon Street Cartography; Bob Blake and Rebecca Baer, *map editors*
Design: Fabrizio La Rocca, *creative director;* Guido Caroti, *art director;* Chie Ushio, *designer;* Moon Sun Kim, *cover designer;* Melanie Marin, *senior picture editor*
Production/Manufacturing: Colleen Ziemba
Cover Photo (Covent Garden): David Noton/Masterfile

ISBN-10: 1-4000-1677-0

ISBN-13: 978-1-4000-1677-8

ISSN: 0149-631X

SPECIAL SALES
This book is available for special discounts for bulk purchases for sales promotions or premiums. Special editions, including personalized covers, excerpts of existing books, and corporate imprints, can be created in large quantities for special needs. For more information, write to Special Markets/Premium Sales, 1745 Broadway, MD 6-2, New York, NY 10019, or e-mail specialmarkets@randomhouse.com.

AN IMPORTANT TIP & AN INVITATION
Although all prices, opening times, and other details in this book are based on information supplied to us at press time, changes occur all the time in the travel world, and Fodor's cannot accept responsibility for facts that become outdated or for inadvertent errors or omissions. So **always confirm information when it matters,** especially if you're making a detour to visit a specific place. Your experiences—positive and negative—matter to us. If we have missed or misstated something, **please write to us.** We follow up on all suggestions. Contact the London editor at editors@fodors.com or c/o Fodor's at 1745 Broadway, New York, New York 10019.

PRINTED IN THE UNITED STATES OF AMERICA

10 9 8 7 6 5 4 3 2 1

Be a Fodor's Correspondent

Your opinion matters. It matters to us. It matters to your fellow Fodor's travelers, too. And we'd like to hear it. In fact, we *need* to hear it.

When you share your experiences and opinions, you become an active member of the Fodor's community. That means we'll not only use your feedback to make our books better, but we'll publish your names and comments whenever possible.

Here's how you can help improve Fodor's for all of us.

Tell us when we're right. We rely on local writers to give you an insider's perspective. But our writers and staff editors—who are the best in the business—depend on you. Your positive feedback is a vote to renew our recommendations for the next edition.

Tell us when we're wrong. We're proud that we update most of our guides every year. But we're not perfect. Things change. Hotels cut services. Museums change hours. Charming cafés lose charm. If our writer didn't quite capture the essence of a place, tell us how you'd do it differently. If any of our descriptions are inaccurate or inadequate, we'll incorporate your changes in the next edition and will correct factual errors at fodors.com *immediately.*

Tell us what to include. You probably have had fantastic travel experiences that aren't yet in Fodor's. Why not share them with a community of like-minded travelers? Maybe you chanced upon a beach or bistro or B&B that you don't want to keep to yourself. Tell us why we should include it. And share your discoveries and experiences with everyone directly at fodors.com. Your input may lead us to add a new listing or highlight a place we cover with a "Highly Recommended" star or with our highest rating, "Fodor's Choice."

Give us your opinion instantly at our feedback center at www.fodors.com/feedback. You may also e-mail editors@fodors.com with the subject line "London Editor." Or send your nominations, comments, and complaints by mail to London Editor, Fodor's, 1745 Broadway, New York, NY 10019.

You and travelers like you are the heart of the Fodor's community. Make our community richer by sharing your experiences. Be a Fodor's correspondent.

Happy traveling!

Tim Jarrell, Publisher

CONTENTS

ABOUT THIS
BOOK

Our Ratings

Sometimes you find terrific travel experiences and sometimes they just find you. But usually the burden is on you to select the right combination of experiences. That's where our ratings come in.

As travelers we've all discovered a place so wonderful that its worthiness is obvious. And sometimes that place is so experiential that superlatives don't do it justice: you just have to be there to know. These sights, properties, and experiences get our highest rating, **Fodor's Choice,** indicated by orange stars throughout this book.

Black stars highlight sights and properties we deem **Highly Recommended,** places that our writers, editors, and readers praise again and again for consistency and excellence.

By default, there's another category: any place we include in this book is by definition worth your time, unless we say otherwise. And we will.

Disagree with any of our choices? Care to nominate a place or suggest that we rate one more highly? Visit our feedback center a fodors.com.

Budget Well

Hotel and restaurant price categories from ¢ to $$$$ are defined in the opening pages of Chapter 15 and 16. For attractions, we always give standard adult admission fees; reductions are usually available for children, students, and senior citizens. Want to pay with plastic? **AE, D, DC, MC, V** following restaurant and hotel listings indicate if American Express, Discover, Diner's Club, MasterCard, and Visa are accepted.

Restaurants

Unless we state otherwise, restaurants are open for lunch and dinner daily. We mention dress only when there's a specific requirement and reservations only when they're essential or not accepted—it's always best to book ahead.

Hotels

Hotels have private bath, phone, TV, and air-conditioning and operate on the European Plan (a.k.a. EP, meaning without meals), unless we specify that they use the Continental Plan (CP, with a Continental breakfast), Breakfast Plan (BP, with a full breakfast), or Modified American Plan (MAP, with breakfast and dinner) or are all-inclusive (AI, including all meals and most activities). We always

list facilities but not whether you'll be charged an extra fee to use them, so when pricing accommodations, find out what's included.

Many Listings
★ Fodor's Choice
★ Highly recommended
⊠ Physical address
✛ Directions
🕮 Mailing address
☎ Telephone
🖷 Fax
⊕ On the Web
🖂 E-mail
🖾 Admission fee
🕓 Open/closed times
▶ Start of walk/itinerary
Ⓜ Metro stations
▭ Credit cards

Hotels & Restaurants
🏨 Hotel
🛏 Number of rooms
♨ Facilities
🍴 Meal plans
✕ Restaurant
🖎 Reservations
🏛 Dress code
🚬 Smoking
💂 BYOB
✕🏨 Hotel with restaurant that warrants a visit

Outdoors
🏌 Golf
⛺ Camping

Other
🕐 Family-friendly
🗊 Contact information
⇨ See also
⊠ Branch address
☞ Take note

WHAT'S WHERE

If London contained only its landmarks, it would still rank as one of the world's top destinations. But England's capital is much more. It's a heady mix of old and new, reflecting fast-moving changes in fashion, lifestyle, and architecture, with an unconquered heritage of more than 2,000 years of history. A city that loves to be explored, London beckons with great museums and galleries, shops and restaurants, royal pageantry, gracious parks and wild open spaces, quirky historical hideaways, and wholly unique neighborhoods.

WESTMINSTER & ROYAL LONDON

All things start at Westminster, where there is as much history in a few acres as in many entire cities. Ancient Westminster Abbey, crammed with memorials and monuments to the great and the good, can blind you to the spectacular surrounding Gothic splendor. Whitehall is both an avenue and the heartbeat of the British government; here is the prime minister's official residence, No. 10 Downing Street, and the Horse Guards, where two mounted sentries of the Queen's guard provide a memorable image. Whitehall leads to Trafalgar Square and the incomparable National Gallery, with the National Portrait Gallery just next door. From the grand Admiralty Arch, the Mall runs alongside the elegant St. James's Park, leading straight to Buckingham Palace, as unprepossessing on the outside as it is sumptuous inside. The streets are wide and the vistas long—the perfect backdrop for the pomp and pageantry of royal occasions.

ST. JAMES'S & MAYFAIR

St. James's and Mayfair form the core of the West End, the city's smartest and most desirable central area, where there is no shortage of history and gorgeous architecture, custom-built for ogling the lifestyles of London's rich and famous. Although many will say Mayfair is only a state of mind, the heart of Mayfair has shifted from the 19th-century's Park Lane to Carlos Place and Mount Street. Of course, the shops of New and Old Bond streets lure the wealthy, but the window-shopping is free. Mayfair is primarily residential, with two public grand houses to see: Apsley House, the Duke of Wellington's home, and, on elegant Manchester Square, the Wallace Collection, situated in a palatial town house filled with Old Master paintings and fine French furniture. The district of St. James's—named after the centuries-old palace that lies at its center—remains the ultimate enclave of the old-fashioned gentleman's London. Here you'll find Pall Mall, with its many noted clubs, including the Reform Club, and Jermyn Street, where you can shop like the Duke of Windsor.

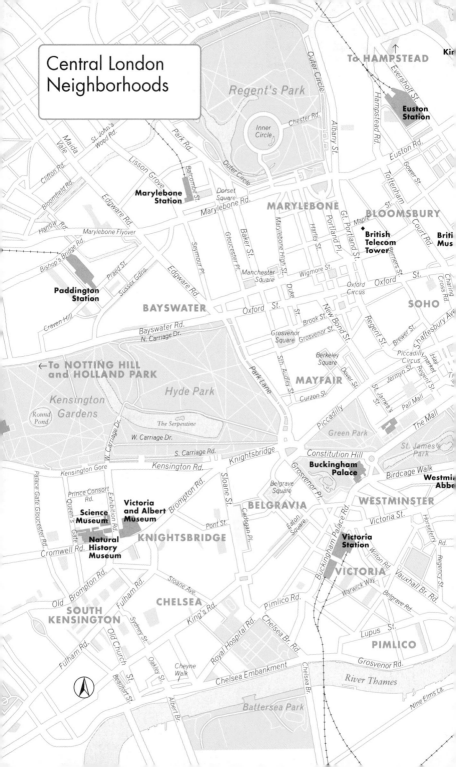

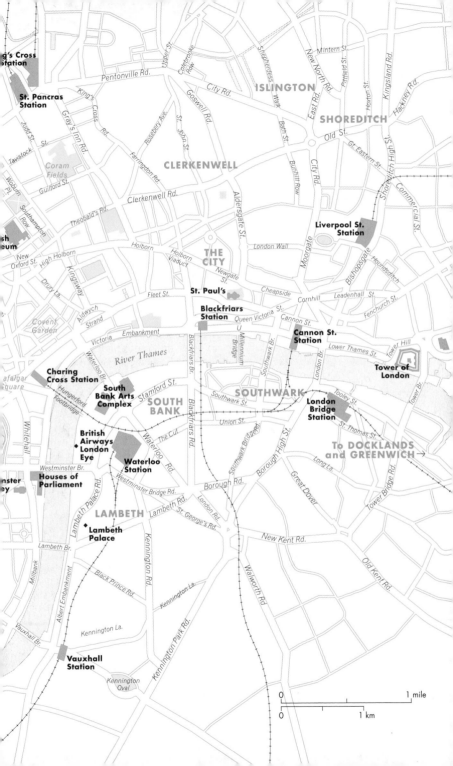

WHAT'S WHERE

SOHO & COVENT GARDEN	Once known infamously as London's red-light district, Soho these days is more stylish than seedy—now it's populated with film and record bigwigs (Sir Paul McCartney's offices are here). The area is not especially rich architecturally, but it is nonetheless intriguing. The density of Continental and Asian residents around quaint Soho Square means some of London's best restaurants—whether pricey Italian, budget Vietnamese, or the latest contemporary French opening—are in the vicinity. Shaftesbury Avenue cuts through the southern part of Soho; this is Theatreland, where you'll find almost 50 West End theaters. It's beloved by those who admire Shakespeare, Maggie Smith, and *Phantom*. To the south lie Leicester Square, London's answer to Times Square, and Charing Cross Road, the bibliophile's dream.
	Just east of Soho, Covent Garden is one of the busiest, most raffishly enjoyable parts of the city. Continental-style open-air cafés create a very un-English environment. Warehouses, once cavernous and grim, now accommodate fashion boutiques and a huge variety of shops favored by the trendy. A network of narrow streets, arcades, and pedestrian malls, the area is dominated by the Piazza, the scene of a food market in the 1830s and a flower market in the 1870s. Today the indoor-outdoor complex overflows with clothing shops, crafts stalls, and entertainers, and the modernized Royal Opera House opens onto the Piazza.
BLOOMSBURY & LEGAL LONDON	The literary set that made the name Bloomsbury world famous has left hardly a trace, but this remains the heart of learned London. The University of London is here; so are the Law Courts and the British Museum. With the British Library parked just north at St. Pancras, a greater number of books can probably be found in Bloomsbury than in all the rest of London. Virginia Woolf and T. S. Eliot would be pleased to note that some of London's most beautiful domestic architecture, elegant houses that would have been familiar to Dr. Johnson, still line the area's prim squares. At one, Charles Dickens worked on *Oliver Twist* at a tall upright clerk's desk.
THE CITY	Known as "the Square Mile," the City is to London what Wall Street is to Manhattan. As the site of the Celtic settlement the Romans called Londinium, this is the oldest part of London, yet thanks to blocks of high-rise apartments and steel skyscrapers, it looks like the newest. Within and around the capital-C

City are some of London's most memorable attractions, including St. Paul's Cathedral and storybook Tower Bridge. The sleekly modern Millennium Bridge links St. Paul's with the South Bank, while nearby, the glass-and-steel Swiss Re building (Sir Norman Foster's 30 St Mary Axe, known to all Londoners as "The Gherkin") is the most unusual addition to the City's 21st-century skyline. Charles and Diana tied the knot at St. Paul's, but they could have found other equally beautiful options here—St. Bride's (its distinctive multitiered spire gave rise to today's wedding cakes), St. Giles Without Cripplegate, and St. Mary-le-Bow. The infamous and wonderfully historic Tower of London is at the east border of the City.

THE EAST END

The 19th-century slums, immortalized by Charles Dickens and the evocative etchings of Gustave Doré, are a relic of the past. Today the area is a fascinating melting pot with a ramshackle beauty and a warm spirit of humor and friendliness. It has also become the fashionable epicenter of London's contemporary art scene, centering on the White Cube gallery in Hoxton and the Whitechapel Art Gallery. On Sunday you'll find 21st-century versions of the medieval fair: Spitalfields Market and Petticoat Lane. Brick Lane has another market straggling through old warehouses and side streets, as well as a profusion of some of the city's most popular curry houses and bagel bakeries. Nearby Columbia Road is a much-loved weekend flower market. Other engrossing sights include the Geffrye Museum and Design Centre, an overlooked cluster of wonderful historic interiors. Down by the river, sprawling eastward from Tower Bridge, the old docks have been regenerated into a modern landscape of glittering office developments.

THE SOUTH BANK

Totally rebuilt after the bombs of World War II flattened the remains of medieval Southwark (only a few stones of the Bishop of Winchester's Palace still stand), the South Bank has undergone a renaissance. If William Shakespeare returned today, however, he would be delighted to find a complete reconstruction of his Globe Theatre, not far from where the original closed in 1642. In fact, this side of the Thames—walk across the new Golden Jubilee Footbridges from Charing Cross and along the riverside embankment for great views of the city—has become a perch for diehard culture vultures: the Design Museum is here, as is the gigantic Tate Modern gallery, a new use for an old power station. The Millennium Bridge is a pic-

WHAT'S
WHERE

turesque pedestrian walkway to St. Paul's Cathedral. Nearby is the South Bank Arts Complex—with its Royal National Theatre and Royal Festival Hall. And who can resist the London Dungeon—a waxwork extravaganza featuring blood 'n' guts—where "a perfectly horrible experience" is guaranteed. Towering over all is the British Airways London Eye, the tallest observation wheel in Europe.

KENSINGTON & CHELSEA	Head first for the area's main attraction, the great museum complex of South Kensington. Raphael and Constable canvases, Ossie Clark couture, and William Morris chairs beckon at the Victoria & Albert Museum, a showcase for the decorative arts. Next to the V&A come the playful Science Museum and the gargantuan Natural History Museum. Most delightful are two historic homes: Leighton House, Lord Leighton's stunning Persian extravaganza, and the Linley Sambourne House, whose elegant Edwardian interiors were featured in *A Room with a View*. Regroup at Kensington Palace—its state rooms and royal dress collection are open for viewing—then repair to its elegant Orangery for a pot of Earl Grey.
	Chelsea has always beckoned to freethinkers and hipsters—from Sir Thomas More to Isadora Duncan (she couldn't find a place to stay her first night, so she decamped to the graveyard at Chelsea Old Church, which natives *still* insist is a lovely place to stay). Major sights include Christopher Wren's magisterial Royal Hospital, the site of the Chelsea Flower Show, Cheyne Walk, where Henry James and Dante Gabriel Rossetti once lived, and the King's Road, whose boutiques gave birth to the paisleyed '60s and the pink-haired punk '70s.
KNIGHTSBRIDGE & BELGRAVIA	Within Knightsbridge's cavalcade of streets lined with decorous houses are small, sleepy squares; delightful pubs nestled away in back lanes; and antiques shops, their windows aglow with the luminous colors of oil paintings. Not surprisingly, the capital's snazziest department stores, Harrods and Harvey Nichols, are also here.
	Just a short carriage ride from Buckingham Palace is Belgravia, London's most splendidly aristocratic enclave, with block after block of grand, porticoed mansions. Built in the mid-1800s, it is residential, untouched by neon, with an authentic vintage patina. Most of its streets are lined with terraced row houses, all painted Wedgwood-china white (to signify they remain the

	property of the Duke of Westminster). Pedigree-proud locations include Belgrave Square, Grosvenor Crescent, and Belgrave Place. Also check out the chic alleyways, called "mews."
NOTTING HILL & BAYSWATER	These are two of London's most fashionable and coveted residential areas. Notting Hill, around Portobello Road, is a trendsetting square mile of multiethnicity, galleries, small and exciting shops, and see-and-be-seen-in restaurants. The style-watching media dubbed the natives—musicians, novelists, and fashion plates—"Notting Hillbillies."
REGENT'S PARK & HAMPSTEAD	Helping to frame the northern border of the city, Regent's Park is home to the much-loved zoo and Regent's Park Open-Air Theatre. A walk around the perimeter of the park is a must for devotees of classical architecture; the payoff is a view of John Nash's Terraces, a grandiose series of white-stucco terraced houses, built around 1810 for the "People of Quality" who demanded London homes as nearly as possible resembling their grand country estates. In summer be sure to take in the rose-bedecked Queen Mary's Gardens. Next, head over to the open-air theater for, perhaps, a picture-perfect performance of *A Midsummer Night's Dream*.
	One of the great glories of Great Britain is the English village, and on the northern outskirts of London you'll find one of the most fetching: Hampstead. The classic Georgian houses, picturesque streets, cafés, and delis attract arts and media types and the plain wealthy. An amble along Church Row—possibly the finest terrace of 18th-century houses in London—will prove the pulling power of the area. London's most beautiful Vermeer painting is on view at Kenwood House (whose park hosts grand concerts and fireworks in summer). You can visit the Freud Museum and the Keats House, where the poet penned his immortal "Ode to a Nightingale." Or go bird-watching in the 800-plus emerald acres of Hampstead Heath.
DOCKLANDS	The epicenter of London's modern growth is the Isle of Dogs, once a neighborhood fit only for canines. Now you'll find the space-age architecture (Canary Wharf's No. 1 Canada Square being the most prominent, literally), waterways from the old docks, and the nifty overhead electric Docklands Light Railway linking buildings to wharves. The Museum in Docklands traces the history of this quarter. The Thames Barrier strides across the river, between the east end on the north bank and

WHAT'S
WHERE

	Greenwich on the south bank, and its visitor center and pedestrian walkway presents an exciting panorama.
GREENWICH	A quick 8-mi jaunt down the Thames will bring you past the National Maritime Museum and the *Cutty Sark* to Greenwich's Old Royal Observatory, where, if time stood still, all the world's timepieces would be off. When you tire of straddling the hemispheres at the Greenwich Meridian, take a stroll through the acres of parkland or, on weekends, the crafts and antiques markets. Sir Christopher Wren's Royal Naval College and Inigo Jones's Queen House both scale architectural heights, while Richard Rogers's defunct Millennium Dome encapsulates modern style, for better or worse. The pretty streets of Greenwich house numerous bookstores and antiques shops.
THE THAMES UPSTREAM	The most powerful palaces—Chiswick, Kew Palace and Gardens, Richmond, and Putney—were linked closely to London by the river. A river cruise along Old Father Thames to some of these famous places, enveloped with serenity and rolling greenery, makes an idyllic retreat from the city on a sweltering summer day. Stroll around and just enjoy the rural air or find your way out of the famous maze at Hampton Court Palace, England's version of Versailles.

LONDON
THEN & NOW

Roman & Saxon London

Since prehistoric times, scattered tribes lived off the wide stretch of tidal river and marshland that was to become London, and an Early Iron Age hamlet dating from 400 BC has been found at Heathrow. The full-scale Roman conquest of Britain by Claudius in AD 43 established the settlement of Londinium—which was promptly razed to the ground by the Celtic warrior queen Boudicca in her rebellion against foreign rule. Over the next four centuries, Londinium grew to be the largest city in Britannia, due to its advantageous position as a hub for trade with the rest of the colony, until the departing Roman eagle gave way to the Saxon wolf in AD 410. The influence of Augustine's Christian message on Saxon London sparked construction of its earliest churches, and the trading town of Ludenwic sprung up on the present site of Covent Garden and the Strand. After centuries of Viking raids, in 1042 the Saxon king Edward the Confessor moved his court out of the City to found a palace and abbey at Westminster.

Norman Conquest to the Great Fire

William the Conqueror's success at the Battle of Hastings in 1066 kicked off the Norman epoch. He cemented his authority over London with the construction of the White Tower, the four-turreted castle at the heart of the Tower of London, and granted a royal charter conferring certain rights and privileges on the city in 1067. Commerce flourished as the tradesmen (guilds) of the city received charters in the 14th century, but London's chronic industrial pollution and appalling sanitation resulted in a catastrophic brush with the Black Death 1348–58, which wiped out one third of the city's population. The Peasant's Revolt, which had gained momentum among the yeomen of Kent and Essex, and had destroyed part of the city, was put down at Smithfield in 1382.

Tudor London's arts scene flourished under Elizabeth I, as the playwrights Marlowe and Shakespeare delivered a string of hit plays to rapt London audiences at the Rose and Globe theaters, located on the south side of the river to ensure they escaped the censorship of the sober, hard-working City folk.

TIMELINE

ca. 400 BC	Early Iron Age hamlet built at Heathrow
AD 43	Romans conquer Britain, led by the emperor Claudius
60	Boudicca, queen of the Iceni, razes the first Roman Londinium
410	Roman rule of Britain ends
604	London's first bishop, Melitus, builds a cathedral in the name of St. Paul

886	Alfred the Great (871–899), king of the West Saxons, retakes the city; he is said to have "restored London and made it habitable"
1078	William the Conqueror (1066–87), Duke of Normandy, begins construction of the White Tower at the Tower of London
1191	First mayor of London elected
1265	First Parliament held in Westminster Abbey Chapter House

LONDON: THEN & NOW

Following the execution of Charles I at Banqueting House in 1649, after England's bitter civil war, London entered a morose period of Puritan privation under Oliver Cromwell, who shut the playhouses and cancelled Christmas. The Restoration of Charles II in 1660 brought an end to England's brief flirtation with republicanism.

Beset by the Great Plague, which had claimed 100,000 lives the previous year, London was teetering on the brink of collapse. The Great Fire of 1666, which started in the oven of the royal bakery on Pudding Lane, pushed the city over the edge. It burned for four days; London's medieval wooden buildings—including 87 churches and 13,000 houses—were destroyed, and 100,000 people were left homeless. However, this disaster gave the city a chance to start anew, and the king was determined to create a modern, well-built city that could rival other European capitals, with wide boulevards and grand piazzas.

Metropolitan Transformation

The rebuilding that took place in the wake of the Great Fire, led by the architect Sir Christopher Wren (whose churches, including St. Paul's Cathedral, still dominate London's skyline), revolutionized the city—but also polarized rich neighborhoods, predominantly to the west of the City, from poor ones, to the east. During the 18th century London grew enormously in power and wealth, and its streets and markets were enriched by immigrant communities arriving from all over the world. Institutions such as the Bank of England, the *Times* newspaper, and the ubiquitous coffeehouses reflected London's emergence as a financial center. In the meanwhile, the stomping grounds of the West End offered an alluring, dangerous cocktail of gambling and gin that ensnared citizens, rich and poor, and began to take its toll on the city.

Fueled by the Industrial Revolution and the British Empire, Victorian London continued to expand even farther, becoming the world's first megalopolis. The advent of the railways created suburbs that enabled the middle classes to escape the central slums, and London went on to score a world first with the opening of the underground railway in 1863, running between Farringdon and Paddington stations. The

city's Great Exhibition of 1851, the brainchild of Prince Albert, showcased Britain's industrial, military, and economic might.

Yet for all the brilliance on show within the glass walls of Crystal Palace, thousands of Londoners across the city remained in abject poverty. London's seedy underbelly was brutally exposed by the city's most famous serial killer, Jack the Ripper, who terrorized the sordid streets of the East End in 1888. Driven by a new sense of civic responsibility, lawmakers reformed child labor, education, and healthcare. Simultaneously, engineering advances enabled the construction of an adequate sewage system and much better city planning. By the time of Queen Victoria's death in 1901, the city's population had swelled to 4.5 million.

Modern Times

The first half of the 20th century brought the disasters of two world wars to the capital: the bombardment by German zeppelins in 1915 and the Blitz of World War II, in which 50,000 bombs were dropped on the city. London's postwar rehabilitation began with the coronation of a new monarch, Queen Elizabeth II, in 1952; the Clean Air Act of 1956 banished the "pea soup" smogs that had besmirched the city since the Industrial Revolution; and the 1960s gave birth to "swinging London," crowned by a soccer World Cup victory for England at Wembley stadium in 1966.

The 1980s saw the arrival of IRA terrorism on mainland Britain with Hyde and Regent's Park bombings, and the demise of the Greater London Council (GLC), led by Labour Party maverick Ken Livingstone, who was to return as the mayor of London in 2000. Poll tax riots in 1990 saw 200,000 protestors deluge Trafalgar Square, repeated in less violent form with the swathe of 2003 antiwar marches that saw a million people protest war in Iraq.

Inner London had swelled to more than 7 million people by the turn of the millennium, accounting for 15% of the country's population. In one traumatic week in July 2005, jubilation on the streets at news that the city was to host the 2012 Olympics turned to horror the following morning, as the city fell victim to multiple suicide-bomb attacks on rush-hour commuters, in which 56 people died.

1829–41	Trafalgar Square laid out
1834	Houses of Parliament gutted by fire
1849	Harrods opens as a small grocery store
1877	First Wimbledon tennis tournament
1946	Heathrow Airport opens
1976	Royal National Theatre opens
1981	Prince Charles marries Lady Diana Spencer in St. Paul's Cathedral
1984	The Thames Barrier, designed to prevent flooding in central London, is inaugurated
1991	The Channel Tunnel opens a direct rail link between Britain and Europe
2000	London welcomes the 21st century with the Millennium Dome, which closes the following year
2002	Princess Margaret, the queen's sister, dies at the age of 71; Queen Elizabeth the Queen Mother dies at 101; Queen Elizabeth II celebrates her Golden Jubilee
2005	Prince Charles marries Camilla Parker Bowles. 7/7 bomb blasts kill 56

ON THE
CALENDAR

Top seasonal events in and around London include the Chelsea Flower Show in May; Derby Day at Epsom Racecourse, Wimbledon Lawn Tennis Championships and Henley Regatta in June; and the London Arts Season from February through March, which combines many events in theater, art, and music with good deals on hotels and meals out.

There is a complete list of ticket agencies in *Britain Events,* available in person only from the Britain Visitor Centre. When in London, check the weekly magazine *Time Out,* available at newsstands, for an ongoing calendar of special events.

ONGOING Mar., Apr. & Sept.	The Chelsea Antiques Fair is a twice-yearly fair with a wide range of pre-1830 pieces for sale, attracting Sloane Rangers and serious collectors to the heart of London's antiques district in search of a bargain. ✉ *Old Town Hall, King's Rd., Chelsea SW3 5EE* ☎ *01444/482514* ⊕ *www.penman-fairs.co.uk.*
Mid-May–Late Aug.	Glyndebourne Festival Opera is a unique opportunity to see international stars in a bucolic setting, at a purpose-built opera house in the middle of the English countryside. Tickets go fast and early booking starts in early April. ✉ *Glyndebourne Festival Opera, Box 2624, Lewes, Sussex BN8 5UW* ☎ *01273/813813* ⊕ *www. glyndebourne.com.*
Late May–Late Aug.	Shakespeare Under the Stars gives you the chance to see the Bard's plays performed at Regent's Park Open-Air Theatre. There is nothing more magical than watching *A Midsummer Night's Eve* in the balmy summer air of a midsummer night's evening. Performances are usually Monday–Saturday at 8 PM, with matinees on Wednesday, Thursday, and Saturday. ✉ *Inner Circle, Regent's Park NW1 4NR* ☎ *020/7935–5756* ⊕ *www.openairtheatre.org.*
Mid-June–Early Sept.	Kenwood Lakeside Concerts offers fireworks and classical concerts in the park of London's regal stately house. Pack a picnic basket and a bottle of wine, arrive early for a lazy afternoon in Kenwood's luxurious grounds, listen to the orchestra start tuning up as the sun goes down, and then enjoy an evening of twinkling stars and bright strings. ✉ *Kenwood House, Hampstead La., Hampstead NW3* ☎ *020/8348–1286 information, 0870/333–6206 tickets.*
Mid-July–Mid-Sept.	Henry Wood Promenade Concerts (more commonly known as the "Proms") is a marvelous series of concerts at the Royal Albert Hall. While the infamous Last Night of the Proms is an opportunity for much patriotic flag-waving and singing along, other Proms show-

	case the hottest talents in classical music from around the world. Online booking opens late April, telephone booking mid-June. ✉ *Box Office, Royal Albert Hall, Kensington Gore, Kensington SW7 2AP* ☎ *020/7589–8212.*
WINTER Dec. 31	New Year's Eve at Trafalgar Square is a huge, freezing, sometimes drunken slosh through the fountains to celebrate the new year. Not organized by any official body, and only an event in the loosest sense, it's held in the ceremonial heart of London under an enormous Christmas tree, which is a gift from the people of Norway and set up from early December to early January. Unlike Americans, however, most Brits celebrate New Year's Eve at parties thrown at home.
Jan. 1	The London Parade is a U.S.-style extravaganza complete with 10,000 performers, including cheerleaders, floats, and marching bands, and is led by the Lord Mayor of London. It starts on the south side of Westminster Bridge at noon, passing Parliament Square, Whitehall, Trafalgar Square, Lower Regent Street, Piccadilly, and finishing in Berkeley Square around 3 PM. No tickets are required. ⊕ *www. londonparade.co.uk.*
Late Jan.	Charles I Commemoration is held on the last Sunday of the month, around the January 30 anniversary of the monarch's execution in 1649, and brings out Londoners dressed in 17th-century garb for a march tracing his last walk from St. James's Palace to the Banqueting House in Whitehall.
Late Jan./ early Feb.	Chinese New Year has its London heart in Soho. But the cries of "Kung Hei Fat Choi!" can be heard well beyond Chinatown: museums showcase Chinese treasures; Trafalgar Square and Leicester Square deck themselves up; the London Eye turns red; fireworks cascade over the city; and dragons dance through the narrow streets.
Mar. 31	The Head of the River Boat Race offers the spectacle of up to 420 eight-man crews dipping their 6,720 oars in the Thames as they race from Mortlake to Putney. The best view is from Surrey Bank above Chiswick Bridge (Tube to Chiswick); check *Time Out* for the starting time, which depends on the tide. The Oxford versus Cambridge University Boat Race takes place a week or two later, in the opposite direction but over the same 4½-mi course, carrying on a tradition going back to 1829. In 1912 both boats sank spectacularly. Around a quarter of a million people watch from the banks of the river.
SPRING Mid-Apr.	The Flora London Marathon is now the world's biggest, with a field in excess of 45,000. Race-day London takes on a festival atmosphere.

ON THE
CALENDAR

	Runners from all over the world start in Greenwich and Blackheath at 9–9:30 AM, then run via Docklands and Canary Wharf, the Tower of London, and Parliament Square to finish in the Mall. It's not so much the sporting prowess that attracts supporters all along the route, as the weird and wonderful outfits that runners wear. ⊕ *www.london-marathon.co.uk.*
Mid-May	The Punch and Judy Festival is held on the second Sunday in May and offers a May Fayre Procession in the morning, services at St. Paul's Church, then puppet shows and stalls until dusk. It's a lovely event for children of all ages. There is also a smaller event on the first Sunday in October. ⊠ *Covent Garden Piazza, London WC2* ☎ *020/7375–0441.*
Late May	The Chelsea Flower Show, Britain's most prestigious flower show, covers 22 acres for five days and is always graced by the Royals. It also a hosts a plethora of television gardening experts and horticulturists from across the country who have dedicated their lives to shrubs and plants. Book well ahead. ⊠ *Royal Hospital Rd., Chelsea SW3* ☎ *0870/906–3781* ⊕ *www.rhs.org.*
Early June	Derby Day is the best-known event on the horse-racing calendar, held at Epsom racecourse in Surrey, south of London. Like Royal Ascot (see below), it is an occasion for champagne, smart suits and ceremony. Oh, and of course a thrilling equine contest. *Information from United Racecourses Ltd.* ⊠ *Epsom Downs Racecourse, Epsom, Surrey KT18 5LQ* ☎ *013727/26311* ⊕ *www.epsomderby.co.uk.*
Mid-June	Royal Meeting at Ascot brings the horsey set and their enormous hats out in force the third week in June (Tuesday–Saturday; Thursday is the high-fashion Ladies Day). General admission is available but reserve months in advance; write for tickets to the Royal Enclosure (you must be sponsored). ⊡ *Protocol Office, American Embassy, 24 Grosvenor Sq., London W1A 1AE. General admission:* ⊠ *Ascot Racecourse, Ascot, Berkshire SL5 7JN* ☎ *01344/876876* ⊕ *www.royalascot.co.uk.*
Mid-June	Trooping the Colour, Queen Elizabeth's colorful official birthday parade, is held at Horse Guards, Whitehall, usually on the second or third Saturday of June. This ceremony has marked the sovereign's official birthday since 1748, and is arguably the proudest moment of the year for any guardsman from the elite regiments tasked with guarding the monarch. The drill, the tunics, and the boots on show will all have been polished to perfection. Write for tickets *only* between January 1 and February 28, enclosing a self-addressed stamped

	envelope. ⊠ *Ticket Office, Headquarters, Household Division, Horse Guards, Westminster SW1A 2AX* ☎ *020/7414–2479* ⊕ *www.royal.gov.uk.*
SUMMER Late June– Early July	Henley Royal Regatta, an international rowing event and top social occasion since 1839, takes place at Henley-upon-Thames, Oxfordshire. Even if you're not a rowing expert, it's worth it for the pomp and history. Most people hope for invites to the Steward's Enclosure (capped at 6,500 members, excluding guests), but the most important question of all: which hat to wear? ☎ *01491/572153* ⊕ *www.hrr.co.uk.*
Late June– Early July	The Wimbledon Lawn Tennis Championships are held at the All England Lawn Tennis and Croquet Club in Wimbledon. The only surviving grass court Grand Slam tournament produces, at its very best, thrilling games of serve and volley that are not seen anywhere else, and almost inevitable disppappointment for any British hopefuls taking part. Write early to enter the lottery for tickets for Centre and Number One courts; tickets for outside courts are available daily at the gate. ⊠ *All England Lawn Tennis Club Ticket Office, P.O. Box 98, Wimbledon SW19 5AE* ☎ *020/8971–2473* ⊕ *www.wimbledon.org.*
Late Aug.	Notting Hill Carnival is the biggest street party in Europe and one of its liveliest. For two days solid on the last Sunday and Monday in August, the streets of West London reverberate to the mesmerising tunes of steels bands and reggae sound systems set up at every street corner. The popular parade of floats takes place on the Sunday, with an array of incredible costumes, usually months in the making, while an inexhaustible supply of Caribbean joints provide soul food (jerk goat) for the weary, and the Red Stripe lager flows freely. ☎ *020/8964–0544.*
FALL Sept.	Open House is a rare one-day chance to view historic London interiors of buildings usually closed to the public. All manner of private residences, often belonging to the landed gentry, the newly famous, or simply scions of the art and design world, open up to a fascinated public. ☎ *020/7267–7644* ⊕ *www.londonopenhouse.org.*
Early Oct.	Pearly Harvest Festival Service draws a crowd of costermongers on the first Sunday in October to the Church of St. Martin-in-the-Fields, where the Pearly Kings and Queens strut their famous costumes. ⊠ *Trafalgar Sq., Covent Garden WC2* ☎ *020/7766–1100.*

ON THE CALENDAR

Early Nov.	**Lord Mayor's Procession and Show** is a procession for the lord mayor's inauguration that takes place from the Guildhall in the City to the Royal Courts of Justice. The long-running London tradition has happened ever since 1215. It is also a rare chance to see inside Mansion House, and brings a wonderful touch of color to London's commercial heart. ☎ *020/7332–1456* ⊕ *www.lordmayorsshow.org.*
Early Nov.	**Remembrance Sunday,** the Sunday closest to November 11, commemorates all those who have suffered and died in war. Much of the population wears poppies in the weeks leading up to the event and there's a ceremony at the Cenotaph in Whitehall, where the Queen and other dignitaries lay wreaths on the monument.
Nov. 5	**Guy Fawkes and Bonfire Night** celebrates a foiled 1605 attempt to blow up Parliament. Enormous amounts of fireworks are set off all over London, often at parks and open spaces in which attendance is free. One place to be is the bonfire festivity on Primrose Hill near Camden Town, another established event is at Alexandra Palace, near Muswell Hill, which looks out across the whole of the city. Southsiders should get down to Crystal Palace.

Experience London

WORD OF MOUTH

"The key to London's extraordinary museums and art galleries is that they're mostly free. So popping into several not only costs no money, but there are no ticket queues. And they'll still be there in a hundred years' time. Don't treat them like shrines: treat them like a city center park, that you just slip into for a couple of minutes. Above all, in London, be spontaneous."

—flanneruk

LONDON PLANNER

When to Go

The heaviest tourist season runs mid-April through mid-October, with another peak around Christmas—though the tide never really ebbs. Spring is the time to see the countryside and the royal London parks and gardens at their freshest; fall to enjoy near-ideal exploring conditions. In late summer, be warned: air-conditioning is rarely found in places other than department stores, modern restaurants, hotels, and cinemas in London, and in a hot summer you'll swelter. Winter can be rather dismal, but all the theaters, concerts, and exhibitions go full speed.

How's the Weather?

It's virtually impossible to forecast London weather, but you can be fairly certain that it will *not* be what you expect. It's generally mild—with some savage exceptions, especially in summer. In short, be prepared for anything: layers and an umbrella are your friends. The following are the average daily maximum and minimum temperatures for London.

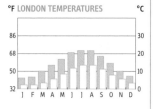

°F LONDON TEMPERATURES °C

Getting Around

London is, above all, a walker's city, and will repay every moment you spend exploring on foot. Of course, setting aside time for random wandering may be of dimished appeal when you're staring at a map with 30 minutes to scramble from one side of town to another. That said, here are your options for transportation within London:

■ By far the easiest and most practical way to get around is on the Underground, or "Tube." This, well, underground train system runs daily from early morning to night and provides a comprehensive service throughout the center with lines out to the suburbs. Tube fares can work out to be higher than bus fares, but if you're traveling a lot around town, you should buy a Travelcard pass (£4.50–£7 per day), which offers unlimited use of the Tube, buses, and the commuter rail.

■ The commuter rail system is an overground network that connects outlying districts and suburbs to the center. Prices are comparable to those of the Underground, and you can easily transfer between the Underground and other connecting rail lines at many Tube stations. Travelcards are also accepted on the overground commuter trains.

■ Buses crisscross all over town, and are a great way to see the city. Their routes are more complicated than the Tube, but by reading the route posted on the main bus stop and watching the route on the front of the bus, you won't go far wrong. Services are frequent.

■ Note: Transport for London, the Orwellian-named organization that runs the Tube and bus system in London, recently announced a major overhaul of the Tube that will cause considerable upheaval over the next decade. Lines are likely to be closed for long periods of time (particularly, in 2007, the Northern line) and there will be many disruptions to normal travel. Dates and plans are subject to change, so check the Transport for London Web site (⊕ www.tfl.gov.uk) for the most updated information before your trip.

London Hours

■ Most businesses are closed on Sunday and national (bank) holidays. Banks are open weekdays 9:30–4:30; offices are generally open 9:30–5:30.

■ The major national museums and galleries are open daily, with shorter hours on weekends than weekdays. Often there is one late-night opening a week.

■ The usual shop hours are Monday–Saturday 9–5:30. Around Oxford Street, Kensington High Street, and Knightsbridge, hours are 9:30–6, with late-night opening hours (until 7:30 or 8 PM) on Wednesdays or Thursdays.

Deal or No Deal?

	What it costs in London	What it costs in New York City
Movie ticket	£8–£12	$9–$13
Pair of theater tickets	£20–£70	$50–$200
Museum admission	Usually free; sometimes £5–£10	Usually $5–$10; sometimes free
Fast-food value meal	£4	$4
Tall latte	£2.15	$3.19
Pint of beer in a pub	£3 and up	$6 and up
1-mi taxi ride before tips	£5	$5
Subway ride within city center	£3	$2 city center
Bus ride within city center	£1.50	$2 city center

Addresses

Central London and its surrounding districts are divided into 32 boroughs—33, counting the City of London. More useful for finding your way around, however, are the subdivisions of London into postal districts. Throughout the guide we've given the full postal code for most listings. The first one or two letters give the location: N means north, NW means northwest, and so on. Don't expect the numbering to be logical, however. (You won't, for example, find W2 next to W3.) The general rule is that the lower numbers, such as W1 or SW1, are closest to the city center.

LONDON'S TOP ATTRACTIONS

Westminster Abbey

(A) The most exciting church in the land is the final resting place for the men and women who built Britain. Its great Gothic hall continues to play a part in the formation of the kingdom, having hosted nearly every coronation since 1308.

Buckingham Palace

(B) Not the prettiest royal palace, but a must-see for the glimpse it affords of modern royal life. The opulence of the state rooms open to the public provides plenty to gasp at, and don't forget the collection of china and carriages at the Queen's Gallery and Royal Mews next door.

St. Paul's Cathedral

(C) No matter how many times you have been before, the scale and elegance of Sir Christopher Wren's masterpiece never fail to take the breath away. Climb the enormous dome, third largest in the world, to experience the freaky acoustics of the Whispering Gallery, and higher still for fantastic views across London.

Tower of London

(D) The Tower is London at its majestic, idiosyncratic best. This is the heart of the kingdom—with foundations dating back nine centuries, every brick tells a story, and the axe-blows and fortunes that have risen and fallen within this turreted mini-city provide an inexhaustible supply of intrigue.

British Museum

(E) If you want to journey through time and space without leaving the confines of Bloomsbury, a visit to the British Museum has hours of eye-catching artifacts from the world's greatest civilizations, including the Elgin Marbles, the Rosetta Stone, and the Sutton Hoo treasure.

Shakespeare's Globe Theatre

(F) You can catch a Shakespeare play almost every night of the year in London. But standing on a floor of leaves and sawdust, and watching an offering from the Great Bard in a painstakingly re-created version of the galleried Tudor theater for which he wrote is a special thrill.

Greenwich Meridian Line

(G) Home of maritime London, Greenwich has a special charm. Most fun is climbing up to the Royal Observatory, surrounded by acres of green and magnificent river views, and straddling western and eastern hemispheres at 0° longitude.

Hampton Court Palace

(H) This collection of buildings and gardens won over Henry VIII to become his favorite royal residence. Its Tudor charm, augmented by touches from Wren, and a picturesque upstream Thames location make it a great day out—not even dour Oliver Cromwell, who moved here in 1653, could resist its charms.

Tate Modern

(I) More of an event than the average museum visit, Tate Modern, housed inside a striking 1930s power station, is a hip, immensely successful addition to the London gallery landscape. Passing judgment on the latest controversial temporary exhibit inside the giant turbine hall has become almost a civic pastime among art-loving Londoners.

National Gallery

(J) Whatever the collective noun is for a set of Old Masters—A palette? A canvas?—there are enough here to have the most casual art enthusiast purring with admiration. When you've finished, enjoy the newly pedestrian Trafalgar Square on the doorstep.

London's central parks

(K) With London's green spaces so broken up, it seems churlish to pick out only one. The four central parks are all within walking distance: pick St. James's Park for fairy-tale views; Green Park for hillocks and wide boulevards; Regent's Park for its open-air theater and the London Zoo; and Hyde Park for rowing on the Serpentine Lido.

FREE THINGS TO DO

The exchange rate may sting, but there's one conversion that'll never change: £0 = $0. Here are our picks for the top free things to do in London.

Free Art

Many of London's biggest and best cultural attractions are free to enter, and the number of museums offering free entry is staggering. (Donations are often more than welcome, and special exhibits usually cost extra.)

MAJOR MUSEUMS

British Museum
Burgh House and the Hampstead Museum
Clown's Gallery and Museum
Guildhall
Houses of Parliament
Imperial War Museum
Museum of Childhood
Museum of London
National Gallery
National Maritime Museum, Queen's House, and Royal Observatory
National Portrait Gallery
Natural History Museum
Royal Exchange
Science Museum
Sir John Soane's Museum
Tate Britain
Tate Modern
Theatre Museum
Victoria & Albert Museum
Wallace Collection

SMALLER GALLERIES

Hogarth House
ICA Gallery
Serpentine Gallery
Whitechapel Art Gallery
Courtauld Permanent Exhibition (Monday only)

Free Concerts

■ St. Paul's Cathedral, St. Martin's in the Fields, and St. James's Church, have regular lunchtime concerts, as does St. George Bloomsbury on Monday, Hyde Park Chapel on Thursday, and St. Giles in the Fields on Friday. There are regular organ recitals at Westminster Abbey.

■ Of the music colleges, the Royal Academy of Music, the Royal College of Music, the Guildhall, and the Royal Opera House have regular recitals, the Trinity College of Music holds recitals at lunchtime on Tuesday.

■ For contemporary ears, the area outside the National Theatre on the South Bank (known as the Djanogly Concert Pitch) reverberates to live world music weekdays at 6 PM, and on Saturday at 1 PM and 6 PM.

■ Another regularly excellent venue is the Spitz bistro and gallery, in Spitalfields market, which has free live jazz and classical gigs four times a week; get there early to bag a table.

■ You can catch decent open-mike nights for unsigned acts and singer songwriters at the River Bar (just south of Tower Bridge) every Wednesday, and Roadhouse (in Covent Garden) every Monday. Blues lovers should not miss the legendary Billy Chong Blues Revue band jam every Monday at the Globe pub in Hackney. The Palm Tree, in Mile End, is another great East End pub that has accomplished local jazz players on weekends.

(Almost) Free Theater & Opera

■ Sloane Square's Royal Court Theatre, one of the United Kingdom's best venues for new playwriting, has restricted-view, standing-room-only tickets at the downstairs Jerwood Theatre for 10 pence (yes, £0.10), available one hour before the performance.

- The Battersea Arts Club (BAC) has pay-what-you-can night on Tuesday for many of its shows.

- If all seats have been sold, the English National Opera sells standing tickets for the back of the Dress and Upper Circles at £5 each. Check at the box office.

- Standing tickets with obstructed views for the ballet or the opera at the Royal Opera House in Covent Garden start at £4.

Free (and Almost Free) Movies

- Free outdoor screenings of cult films (such as *Donnie Darko* and *Pulp Fiction*), sponsored by Stella Artois and held at different parks every year, have become a London summer institution: pack a picnic and stake out your spot early.

- The Prince Charles Cinema in the West End shows weekday matinees for £3.

Free Offbeat Experiences

- Go to the Public Record Office in Kew or Islington if you have a few hours to kill and want to track down some ancient branch of the family tree. Even if you don't have any leads, browsing through sheaves of ancient ledgers is great fun.

- If you came to London for spectacle, take a trip to a trial at the Old Bailey, the highest court in the land. Stories more twisted and compelling than anything on screen, strange costumes and wigs, command performances—it's true drama, without the West End ticket prices.

- London has some of the finest parks in the world, and enjoying them won't cost you a pretty pence. Keen ornithologists can join free bird-watching walks in Hyde Park, while dedicated strollers touched by royal nostalgia can take the 7-mi Diana, Princess of Wales Memorial Walk through Hyde, Green, and St. James's Parks.

- Although London's street markets are not in the habit of giving away merchandise for nothing, it's free to browse their stalls, taking in second-hand booksellers under Waterloo Bridge, fishmongers in Borough Market, and funky jewelry designers in Portobello.

- For human interest, you can't beat Covent Garden for its marvelous array of street performers and buskers, whose unlikely skills—imitating statues, balancing footballs on their noses, juggling fire, playing the banjo with their teeth—can hold any crowd's attention.

- There are free spectacles throughout the year, but one of the most warmly enjoyed is Guy Fawkes' Night (November 5), when parks throughout the country hold spectacular fireworks displays: Alexandra Palace and Ravenscourt Park are two of the best.

- On New Year's Eve thousands of revelers descend on Trafalgar Square and the South Bank to watch more free fireworks. The Underground usually runs all night, and is free into the new year.

- Finally, set aside time for random wandering. London is a great walking city because so many of its real treasures are untouted: tiny alleyways barely visible on the map, garden squares, churchyards, shop windows, sudden vistas of skyline or park. With comfortable, weatherproof shoes and an umbrella, walking might well become your favorite free activity here.

GREAT
ITINERARIES

No Time to Spare?

If you're caught on the hop, your best bet is to head for a bus that is heading over the river. You can't beat that combination of classic red, murky water, and the skyline.

Crowning Glories

This regal runaround packs more into a day than most cities can offer in a week. Hit Westminster Abbey early to avoid the crowds, then cut through St. James's Park to catch the Changing of the Guard at 11:20 AM at Buckingham Palace. (If the Palace doors are open, enjoy a peek at royal life.) Take a quick detour to the Tudor delights of St. James's Palace, old haunt of Charles I, before a promenade down the Mall past the Regency glory of Carlton House Terrace and through Admiralty Arch to Trafalgar Square.

■ TIP→ **Get an early start and a hearty breakfast, as this selection of treasures will likely keep you on your feet all day.**

Choose from the treasures of the National Gallery, the Who's Who of the National Portrait Gallery, or a brass rubbing in the crypt of St. Martin's-in-the-Fields if the children's interest is flagging. Suitably refreshed, this leaves a stately stroll down Whitehall—past Downing Street, Horse Guards Parade, and Banqueting House—to the Houses of Parliament, where you have the option of prebooking a tour, or trying to get in to see a debate.

■ TIP→ **Her Majesty's mounted guardsmen make a great photo op—you may even see Prince Harry, who joined the Regiment of the Blues and Royals, responsible for his grandmother's personal protection, after completing officer training at Sandhurst.**

If you have any time or energy left, stroll through Green and Hyde Parks to Kensington Palace, childhood home of Queen Victoria, and (for little aspiring princesses everywhere) the Royal Dress Collection.

Museum Magic

London has one of the finest collections of museums in the world, and certainly no other comparable city offers so much for free. Many resemble state-of-the-art, hands-on playgrounds; others take a more classical approach. One of the latter is the British Museum in Bloomsbury, an Aladdin's cave of artifacts from across the world. While in the area, pop into the nearby museum of architect Sir John Soane, the Theatre Museum, and, after spring 2007, the newly refurbished London Transport Museum.

■ TIP→ **The excellent restaurant in the British Museum's Great Court looks down on its library, where Karl Marx would shift uncomfortably, greatly afflicted by boils, as he researched** *Das Kapital.*

Alternatively, South Kensington's "Museum Mile" on Cromwell Road houses a triple-whammy that makes for a substantial day's-worth of diversion: the Victoria & Albert Museum, the Natural History Museum, and the Science Museum.

Retail Therapy

It's not hard to shop 'til you drop in London's West End. Start with the upscale on New Bond Street in order to save your afternoon frazzled look for nearby Oxford Street. Home to (take a deep breath here) Cerruti, Chanel, Cartier, De Beers, Dolce & Gabanna, Armani, Jimmy Choo, Versace, Swarovski, Bulgari, Tiffany, Prada, and Gucci, it's an awesome sweep of expense and elegance.

■ TIP→ **Men should not pass up a chance to browse the shirts on show at nearby Savile Row, famed for its high-quality tailoring.**

Oxford Street encompasses four Tube stations and is unbeatable for mass-market shopping. Run the gauntlet of high-street designers, cheap odds and ends, department stores, and ferocious pedestrians: it's seriously busy, but you're pretty much guaranteed a buy.

A more sedate but utterly fashionable experience can be found in Knightsbridge, wandering between Harvey Nichols and Harrods department stores. Take a south down Sloane Street to Sloane Square and head out along King's Road, home to boutiques galore and once capital of London's swinging sixties.

■ TIP→ To catch a glimpse of how to design your home to match your new couture clothes, visit the Conran Shop, at 81 Fulham Road, parallel to the Kings' Road.

To dip into the ever-expanding world of urban chic, try an afternoon in the Portobello street market in Notting Hill, where you can pick up remnants of various bygone ages: glassware, furniture, art and clothes, from boiler suits to Thai silk dresses. Portobello has wised up to tourist prices in recent years, so a trip out to Spitalfields (covered) market on a Sunday is worth considering, especially for a sample of the East End. Finally, for the younger crowd, Camden market has grunge and clubbing wear in spades.

Village People

Despite frequent traffic gridlock, London isn't designed on a grid. One of the benefits of this is a plethora of organic villages, each of which reveals a unique character. They are self-contained, boasting their own boutiques, theaters, local museums, parks, and prestigious residents. The easiest village to reach is Hampstead, 20 minutes from the city center by Tube, but a world away in character. It's home to a thriving arts scene, a history of left-wing poets and writers (including John Keats), some of the most gorgeous Georgian houses in London (hence the occasional jibe of "Champagne Socialism"), and a great range of smart shops, bistros, and French delicatessens.

■ TIP→ If you're in Hampstead, don't miss the chance to get out onto the Heath, moodier and wilder than many of London's other open spaces.

To the west, leave the slightly suburban center of Richmond behind to get down to the riverside, or head for the vast expanse of the park next door, which breaks all remaining links with city life.

The fantastic views bestowed on Greenwich, to the south of the Thames, ensure you never forget how close the city is—and yet this village's nautical past creates an almost seaside feel. The National Maritime Museum, the *Cutty Sark*, and its collection of fine buildings, as well as two very good markets, make it a worthwhile day trip.

To the east, Bethnal Green is a village in the midst of an urban renaissance. Visit the flower market of Columbia Road, the Children's Museum, and the paths along the canal.

■ TIP→ To appreciate fully how tribal London's villagers can be, try asking which part of the city they come from or live in. Some of the responses you'll get—"Haggerston," "Tufnell Park," "Turnham Green," "Camberwell," "Battersea"—indicate a dizzying array of identities, often consisting of a few neighboring streets.

(top) Big Ben and the Houses of Parliament at night. (bottom) The boys of Westminster Abbey Choir perform at Evensong.

(top) Horseback riding in Hyde Park. (bottom) Students study the Parthenon sculptures in the British Museum.

(top) Crossing the Millennium Bridge to St. Paul's Cathedral. (bottom) Raising a pint (or two) in a London pub.

(top) The ice-skating rink in the courtyard of Somerset House in winter. (bottom left) A compelling display of confectionery at Yauatcha in Soho. (bottom right) The Swiss Re Tower, one of the City's more recognizable buildings, at dusk.

(top) Design Museum, South Bank. (bottom) Museum-goers ponder an installation at the Tate Modern.

(top) The view mid-"flight" from a pod on the London Eye. (bottom) A cricket match in progress at Lord's.

(top) Changing of the Guard at Buckingham Palace. (bottom) The Great Court of the British Museum.

The London Eye and South Bank at night.

AUTHENTIC LONDON

It already feels like there's an impossible amount to do and see in London if you're a visitor, but imagine what it's like if you're a bona fide resident, with endless everyday choices and a check-list that never gets fully ticked off. Every weekend can take you somewhere new, catapulting you forward and backward in time, style, and experience. Here's a taster below.

Columbia Road Flower Market

Perfect for a Sunday morning potter, along with Londoners who are not quite sure what they're doing there either. The exotic selection of outsized and colorful plants dazzles, with cobbled alleys disappearing to hidden garden cafés.

A Football Match—Any Football Match

London doesn't get much more authentic than a 30,000-strong stadium on match day. In these emotional pressure-cookers, thousands of fans come to drink, swear, sing, and live every moment of their team's fortunes. Arsenal, Charlton Athletic, Chelsea, Fulham, Tottenham Hotspur, and West Ham United are the top-flight London clubs, although lower-division games (featuring Brentford, Crystal Palace, Millwall, Leyton Orient, or Queens Park Rangers) will be less heavily subscribed and cheaper to watch, with plenty of heart from the sidelines.

Bermondsey Antiques Market

If you want a brush with the cheeky types straight out of British gangster flicks, pop down to this former paradise for stolen goods. An old royal license (now canceled) ensured that stuff bought here did not have to be returned. Small stalls start setting up at 4 AM each Friday, so arrive early with a flashlight to scout for the best bargains. An ominous redevelopment of the market beckons, so enjoy its raffish charm while you can.

Smithfields Meat Market

If you're suffering from a little transatlantic jet lag, a visit to London's last remaining meat market, running until dawn on the edge of the City, provides a welcome late-night diversion. It's one of the few places you can see old-fashioned tradesmen at work. Nearby pubs have early-morning licenses and, naturally, serve some great cuts of meat.

Vauxhall City Farm

You have probably heard of London Zoo: this inner-city farm, just south of the river behind Britain's spy headquarters, is a much more hands-on day out for children, with donkey rides, lessons in pony grooming, and milking demonstrations all available.

Geffrye Museum

No visitor to a nation so obsessed with class should pass up the chance to peek into its drawing rooms. The Geffrye Museum does exactly this, with a selection of interiors from 1600 to the present day. Design tips abound for anyone looking to pick up on distinctive styles.

Go to a Greasy Spoon

The fatty delights of a classic London caff are best sampled after a night's excessive partying. A classic brunch will consist of fried bacon, sausage, egg, tomatoes, and mushrooms—and, for the adventurous, black pudding, washed down with a mug of strong tea. Take a selection of tabloid newspapers to peruse for the full effect.

Hoxton

The hip, urban cowboy in search of a culture fix can't get much trendier than London's brother-in-charms to Manhattan's Lower East Side, a district of mullet-headed

fashionistas, art school drop-outs, and angular City slickers. The White Cube gallery broke BritArt; a few drinks at Dragon Bar will break the ice with the locals.

Ronnie Scott's

Old Ronnie's tenor sax solos may no longer waft through the smoky haze of this infamous Soho jazz club, but his spirit lives on. The atmosphere is equally beguiling to aficionados and first-timers, and the acts, all top names from the world of jazz and blues, are brought alive by the intimate surroundings. The chips are good, too.

Visit an Ethnic Neighborhood

BRICK LANE

The home of London's sizable Bangladeshi community also borders the ubercool districts of Shoreditch and Hoxton. Packed out with zealous curry-house owners, it has many joints serving excellent chicken tikka masala, Britain's favorite curry dish.

BRIXTON

A focal point of London's African-Caribbean community, Brixton's Victorian streets offer nail and hair extension salons, jerk chicken joints, and market stalls selling yams and plantains. Ignore the sniffy remarks from types north of the river; Brixton's bars and clubs make it one of the best bets for a night out in London.

CHINATOWN

Soho's Gerrard Street, originally won by swordfight, became home to Hong Kong agricultural laborers following postwar immigration, and is a focal point of the city for annual celebrations of Chinese New Year. It's also a center for Cantonese and Szechuan cuisine: don't leave without trying crispy aromatic duck or dim sum dumplings.

EDGWARE ROAD

The modern tower blocks and offices of Edgware Road are unremarkable, but under this concrete burka, a host of souks stay open long into the night, serving superb *mezze* appetizers, sticky Arabian sweets, and strong coffee for an audience of hip, young Lebanese. For the full Middle East experience try the fragrant tobacco of a shisha pipe.

KILBURN

Driven to London by the potato famine of the 1840s, Kilburn's Irish community turn the streets green and gold on St. Patrick's Day (March 17). One of the best pints of Guinness east of the Irish sea is found at Biddy Mulligans pub, as well as some of the best live Gaelic music in town.

Highgate Cemetery

The timeless gaze of the stone angels that stand watch over this resting place of London souls is impossible to shrug off. Everlasting home to Communist theorist Karl Marx and novelist George Eliot, the 1839 Victorian cemetery of neo-Gothic statues and sarcophagi, fought over by the ivy, evokes a moving sadness and beauty.

"I have seen the Mississippi. That is muddy water. I have seen the St. Lawrence. That is crystal water. But the Thames is liquid history."
—John Burns

A TOUR OF THE THAMES

The twists and turns of the Thames River through the heart of the capital make it London's best thoroughfare and most compelling viewing point. Once famous for sludge, silt, and sewage, the Thames is now the cleanest city river in the world. Every palace, church, theater, wharf, museum, and pub along the bank has a tale to tell, and traveling on or alongside the river is one of the best ways to soak up views of the city.

A BRIEF HISTORY

The Thames has come a long way—and not just from its 344-km (214-mi) journey from a remote Gloucestershire meadow to the sea. In the mid-19th century, the river was dying, poisoned by sewers that flushed into the river. The "Big Stink" was so awful that cholera and typhoid killed more than 10,000 in 1853, and Parliament abandoned sitting in 1858. "The odour is hardly that of frankincense," said one contemporary of the 1884 drought that forced down water levels, leaving elegant Victorian nostrils exposed to slimy ooze on the banks.

Joseph Bazalgette, star civil engineer of his time, was commissioned to design a new sewage system, and by the 1900s nearly all was forgiven. (His efforts did not go unappreciated: Bazalgette was later knighted.) Today 7.2 million people get their drinking water from the Thames.

A marvelous array of boating options can put you port to starboard with ancient mariners, regatta rowers, houseboat gents, gin-palace queens, and even the odd naval officer. Lack sea legs? You can still enjoy the river: not much beats a wander beside London's waterway, strolling beneath strings of dangling lights at night, sipping the view from riverside cafés, or stepping out over splendid and inventive bridges to see skyline and water shimmer and sparkle.

ROWERS' ROW

Every spring Britain's oldest universities, Oxford and Cambridge, compete not with their brains but with their brawn, in the **Boat Race,** which began in 1829. The race is 4¼ miles upstream from Putney Bridge to Chiswick Bridge: expect clashing oars, clenched teeth, and the occasional sinking (there have been six). The best views are from Hammersmith at the Surrey bend, which is also where most of the pubs are clustered. ⊕ www.theboatrace.org

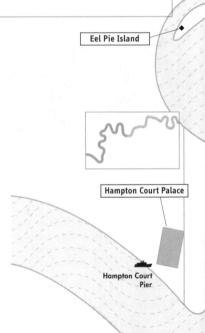

Eel Pie Island

Hampton Court Palace

Hampton Court Pier

1

A TOUR OF THE THAMES

HAMPTON COURT PALACE TO PUTNEY

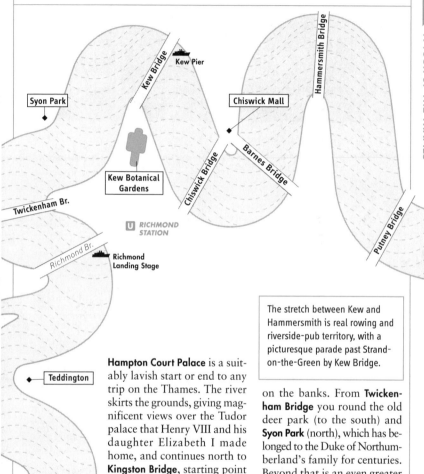

Kew Bridge

Kew Pier

Hammersmith Bridge

Syon Park

Chiswick Mall

Kew Botanical Gardens

Chiswick Bridge

Barnes Bridge

Twickenham Br.

Putney Bridge

U RICHMOND STATION

Richmond Br.

Richmond Landing Stage

The stretch between Kew and Hammersmith is real rowing and riverside-pub territory, with a picturesque parade past Strand-on-the-Green by Kew Bridge.

Teddington

Kingston Bridge

Hampton Court Palace is a suitably lavish start or end to any trip on the Thames. The river skirts the grounds, giving magnificent views over the Tudor palace that Henry VIII and his daughter Elizabeth I made home, and continues north to **Kingston Bridge**, starting point for the epic river voyage of Jerome K. Jerome's *Three Men in a Boat* and home to hectic summer regattas. At **Teddington**, where the poet Alexander Pope and writer Horace Walpole entertained their female admirers in the 18th century, the river turns tidal but remains quiet and unspoiled all the way to **Kew**, passing herons and fine stately homes standing proud

on the banks. From **Twickenham Bridge** you round the old deer park (to the south) and **Syon Park** (north), which has belonged to the Duke of Northumberland's family for centuries. Beyond that is an even greater treat—the UNESCO World Heritage Site of **Kew Botanical Gardens**. All manner of rowboats set up for one, two, four, or eight people pull hard under **Chiswick Bridge** and **Barnes (railway) Bridge,** past the expensive riverside frontage of **Chiswick Mall** and under **Hammersmith Bridge**, to **Putney** and **Fulham**— smart urban villages facing each other across the banks.

WANDSWORTH TO BLACKFRIARS

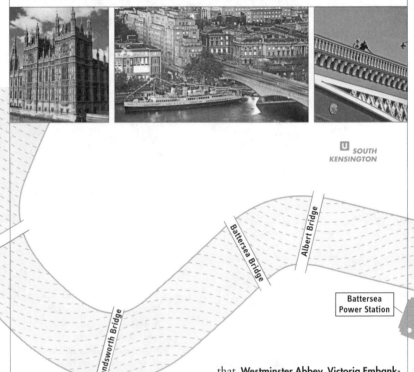

U *SOUTH KENSINGTON*

Battersea Bridge

Albert Bridge

Battersea Power Station

Wandsworth Bridge

Beyond **Wandsworth Bridge**, the early part of this stretch by **Battersea Bridge**, rebuilt in 1890, was London's real industrial heartland, the southern side chock full of cottage housing for laborers, artisans at work, and factories.

After **Albert Bridge**—glorious at night, with lights like luminescent pearls sweeping down on strings—the Thames is a metropolitan glory of a river, charging through fashionable **Chelsea** and past **Battersea Power Station**, under Chelsea, Vauxhall and Lambeth Bridges, with **Lambeth Palace** to the south.

The real treat of this stretch is the view of the **Houses of Parliament** and, beyond that, **Westminster Abbey. Victoria Embankment**, stretching all the way from Westminster to Blackfriars, was once all grim mudflats. In 1878 it became the country's first electrically illuminated street, and today it is all fine architecture, trees, and gardens—perfect strolling territory.

You can't miss the **British Airways London Eye**, whose parts were brought down the Thames one by one before being assembled on-location. Look out too for the London Aquarium and the Dalí show, housed in the baroque-style County Hall.

The **Golden Jubilee Bridges** by **Embankment**, two beautifully lit steel-cabled pedestrian walkways, are perfect for reaching the **South Bank**.

Look out for the golden eagle, a monument to World War I RAF fighters, and

Cleopatra's Needle, overlooking the Thames by Embankment, dates back to Heliopolis in 1450 BC. Look for World War II shrapnel gouges at the base.

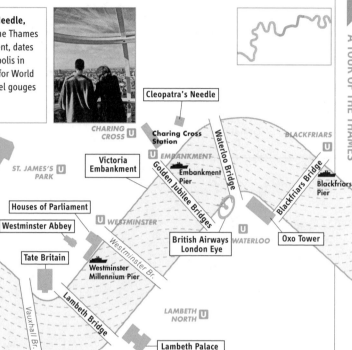

Cleopatra's Needle

CHARING CROSS U

Charing Cross Station

Waterloo Bridge

BLACKFRIARS U

U EMBANKMENT

Victoria Station

ST. JAMES'S U PARK

Victoria Embankment

Embankment Pier

Golden Jubilee Bridges

Blackfriars Bridge

Blackfriars Pier

U SLOANE SQUARE

Houses of Parliament

U WESTMINSTER

Chelsea Harbour Pier

Westminster Abbey

British Airways London Eye

U WATERLOO

Oxo Tower

Chelsea Br.

Tate Britain

Westminster Br.

Westminster Millennium Pier

Vauxhall Br.

Lambeth Bridge

LAMBETH NORTH U

Lambeth Palace

Cleopatra's Needle. For the ultimate double-decker bus-viewing moment, look at **Waterloo Bridge**, once known as Ladies Bridge because it was built by female labor during World War II. The bridge has great views of the South Bank.

Further on is the **Oxo Tower**, whose red-glass letters were designed in 1928 to spell out the brand name while circumventing tight laws on exterior advertising.

By **Blackfriars Bridge**, named after the monks who wore black robes and lived on the north bank during the Middle Ages, the river used to run red by the riverside tanneries and slaughterhouses.

A WHALE OF A TALE

In January 2006, newspapers across the country were full of photos of a northern bottlenose whale swimming past the House of Commons. The "little" lost mite (18 feet long and weighing 7 tons) had wandered up the estuary. Thousands came to watch the rescue mission, which failed when she died on a barge taking her to the open sea. But her memory will live on: her bones will be put on display in the Natural History Museum.

MILLENNIUM BRIDGE TO THAMES FLOOD BARRIER

Between Southwark and London bridges, look for the southside *Golden Hinde*, an exact scale reconstruction of Sir Francis Drake's galleon that sailed around the world.

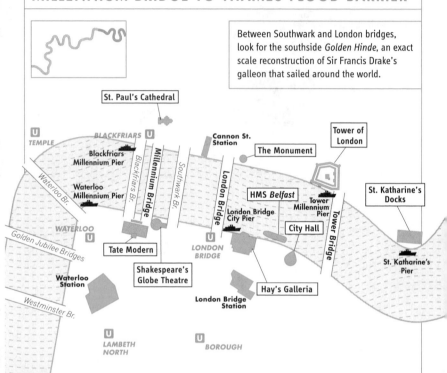

The **Millennium Bridge** is the newest span across the river: **St. Paul's Cathedral** and **Tate Modern** eye each other magnificently from either side of the once worryingly wobbly strip of a bridge. Farther on, the reconstructed **Shakespeare's Globe Theatre** is resplendent in whitewash and brown timber on the South Bank. **London Bridge** is admittedly not the river's finest, but it is the birthplace of the city. Some say the river ceases to be picturesque after St. Paul's, but we disagree: look for the flaming crown of the **Monument,** Sir Christopher Wren's tribute to those who died in the 1666 Great Fire of London.

Moored outside the Victorian shopping mall **Hay's Galleria** is **HMS** *Belfast,* Europe's last existing armored warship that saw action in World War II, now a floating naval museum on nine decks.

The splendid **Tower of London** sits proudly opposite the shining egg of **City Hall** (also

LONDON BRIDGE

Viking invaders destroyed London Bridge in 1014, hence the nursery rhyme "London Bridge is falling down." By 1962, London Bridge really *was* falling down again, its 1831 incarnation unable to take the strain of traffic. It was saved by American tycoon Robert McCulloch, who—possibly confusing the bridge with its much more splendid neighbor, Tower Bridge—bought it in 1968 for $2.46 million and had it shipped, stone by stone, to Lake Havasu in Arizona.

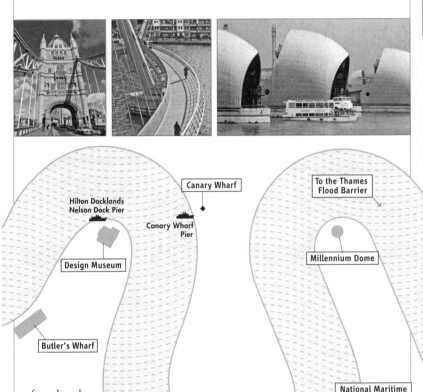

Canary Wharf

Hilton Docklands
Nelson Dock Pier

To the Thames
Flood Barrier

Canary Wharf
Pier

Design Museum

Millennium Dome

Butler's Wharf

National Maritime
Museum

Greenland
Pier

referred to by
the London
mayor Ken Liv-
ingstone as a
giant "glass testi-
cle"—a fine match
for its phallic friend
across the river, the **Swiss
Re Building,** aka the Gherkin,
both designed by a mischievous
Norman Foster). They frame the 1894
Tower Bridge, a magnificent feat of engineering and style, which leads past the
elegant confines of **St. Katharine's Docks,**
the trendy restaurants of **Butler's Wharf,**
and the **Design Museum.**

Masthouse
Terrace Pier

Greenwich
Pier

Cutty Sark

Royal Naval
College

sides of **Canary Wharf,** the city's new
business district, robotic in its modernity.

Step back in time at **Greenwich,** with the
Cutty Sark tea clipper, glorious **Royal
Naval College,** and the **National Maritime
Museum.** Round the bend and you're
back to the future, with the alien space-
ship **Millennium Dome** and the **Thames
Flood Barrier** looming.

For the pièce de résistance of London's
redevelopment, stay on the river until you
reach the bright lights and tall reflective

PLANNING

"On the smallest pretext of holiday or fine weather the mighty population takes to the boats," wrote Henry James in 1877. You can follow in the footsteps of James, who took a boat trip from Westminster to Greenwich, or make up your own itinerary.

■ Frequent daily tourist-boat services are at their height between April and October.

■ In most cases you can turn up at a pier, and the next departure won't be far away. However, it never hurts to book ahead if you can.

■ Westminster and Tower piers are the busiest starting points, usually with boats heading east.

■ TIP→ For a rundown of all the options, along with prices and timetables, contact **London River Services** (☎ 020/7222-1234 ⊕ www.tfl.gov.uk/river), which gives details of all the operators sailing various sections of the river.

■ The trip between Westminster Pier and the Tower of London takes about 30 minutes, as does the trip between the Tower and Greenwich.

■ A full round-trip can take several hours. Ask about flexible fares and hop on/off options at the various piers.

THE BEST WAYS TO EXPERIENCE THE THAMES FOR ...

Going off the beaten path (literally)	020/7928–3132 www.londonducktours.co.uk £17.50	
	London Ducktours offers sightseeing with a twist—amphibious patrol vehicles used in World War II have been painted like rubber duckies and traverse land and sea.	Departs from the London Eye (on land): Daily, according to demand, 10 AM–dusk. Approximately 1½ hours.
Saving time and money	020/7887–8888 www.tate.org.uk/tatetotate £4.30	
	The playfully polka-dotted **Tate Boat** ferries passengers across the river from the Tate Britain to the Tate Modern, with a stop at the London Eye in between.	Departs from the pier at either museum: Daily every 40 mins. Approximately 18 mins. one-way.
Impressing a date or client	0870/429–2451 www.bateauxlondon.com £19.50–£29.50 (lunch), £65–£99 (dinner)	
	For ultimate glamour (and expense), look into lunch and dinner cruises with **Bateaux London,** often formal affairs with surprisingly good two- to five-course meals. Variations include jazz brunch cruises on Sundays.	Departs from Embankment Pier: Daily 8 PM (boarding begins 45 mins. prior to departure). Approximately 3 hours.
Enjoying on-board entertainment	020/7740–0400 www.citycruises.com £62	
	The **London Showboat** lives up to its name, with four-course meals, snazzy cabaret acts from West End musicals, and after-dinner dancing.	Departs from Westminster Pier: Apr.–Oct., Wed.–Sun. 7 PM; Nov.–Mar., Thurs.–Sat. 7 PM (boarding begins 15 mins. prior to departure). Approximately 3½ hours.

Westminster & Royal London

2

WORD OF MOUTH

"One evening we attended Evensong at Westminster Abbey. It never ceases to amaze me how similar religious services are. Had I only been half awake, I might not have known I was in an Anglican church."

—geribrum

"The National Portrait Gallery is great because you feel immediately connected to the paintings as you recognize the subjects."

–sarahkay

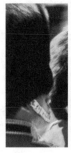

WESTMINSTER & ROYAL LONDON

Sightseeing
★ ★ ★ ★ ★

Nightlife
★ ★

Dining
★ ★ ★

Lodging
★

Shopping
★ ★

This is postcard London at its best. Crammed with red buses, dazzling sights, and ancient nooks and crannies, the area unites politics, high art, and religion. (Oh, and the Queen lives here, too.) Whether roaming above ground or deep beneath the surface, there are constant marvels. Such grand dames as Buckingham Palace, Big Ben, Westminster Abbey, and the National Gallery sit alongside lesser-known but nevertheless gallant knights of the realm: tiny, lovingly curated museums and buildings heavy with the lives and legacies of those who have shaped London's seat of power. If you have time to visit only one part of London, this is it.

What's Here

Royal London is so packed with sights it's difficult to know where to even *look* at times, let alone where to go, but the basic layout is simple if you think of three distinct areas—Buckingham Palace, Westminster and Whitehall, and Trafalgar Square—grouped at the corners of triangular St. James's Park.

Trafalgar Square is the official center of London, with **Nelson's Column** rising from the center. To its north, the **National Gallery** and **National Portrait Gallery** offer prime, mostly free, viewing of global art greats. Nearby **St. Martin-in-the-Fields** is one of London's best-loved churches, and has kept the homeless fed at lunchtime for decades.

From Trafalgar Square two roads lead to the homes of very different ideas of governance: **Whitehall** leads to the **Houses of Parliament,** while the **Mall,** a wide, pink boulevard beyond the stone curtain of **Admiralty Arch,** leads past **Carlton House Terrace** and the **Institute of Contemporary Arts** to the Queen's residence at **Buckingham Palace.** Heading down Whitehall, home to thousands of scurrying civil servants, the Queen's Lifeguards sit motionlessly on horses in front of Horse Guards Parade, while opposite is a historic warning to overweening royals, at the glorious Banqueting House. Its gorgeous painted ceiling, commemorating James I, would have been one of the final sights of his son, Charles I, who was executed here before a crowd of thousands in 1649.

Downing Street, diagonally opposite, is home to the prime minister, traditionally resident at the famed **No. 10,** along with his Chancellor and several other higher-ups. For an example of the famous British stiff upper lip in the face of adversity, the pristinely preserved **Cabinet War Rooms & Churchill Museum,** set underground near the Foreign Office, offer a rare insight into how military officials and civil servants went about their quest to win World War II. Whitehall also houses monuments to those lost in war, or to those who made the fight possible: look out for the **Cenotaph,** designed by Edwin Lutyens in 1920 in commemoration of the 1918 armistice. Parliament Square faces the neo-Gothic **Houses of Parliament,** set beside the Thames, where members of the Houses of Commons and Lords decide the laws of the day.

Westminster Abbey, a colossus of a parish church that once housed monks and even served as parliament for a few years, stands proudly opposite. It's also possibly the most celebrity-filled burial ground in the world—the final resting place of monarchs, poets, and politicians. In its shadow is the no less interesting **St. Margaret's Church,** home to intrigue throughout the ages and many a parliamentary wedding. For the headquarters of the Catholic church in the United Kingdom, visit the neo-Byzantine **Westminster Cathedral,** farther south alongside Victoria Street. A short trot along **Birdcage Walk,** on the south side of St. James's Park, takes you past **Wellington Barracks,** home to and museum of the Queen's Guard (visit the shop: a toy soldier lover's dream), until you reach the golden glint of the **Queen Victoria Memorial** in the middle of the roundabout facing Buckingham Palace. The building opens its doors to the public only in summer, but the next-door Queen's Gallery, open all year, is worth a visit for the impressive collection of paintings, furniture, and sparkling jewels acquired by successive royals, while **Royal Mews** houses the cars, carriages, and coaches fit for the Windsors. Finally, farther south toward Pimlico, **Tate Britain** is the focus of British artists of yesterday and today.

Places to Explore

Admiralty Arch. Gateway to the Mall—no, not an indoor shopping center but one of the very grand avenues of London—this is one of London's stateliest urban set pieces. On the southwest corner of Trafalgar Square, the arch, which was named after the adjacent Royal Navy headquarters, was designed in 1910 by Sir Aston Webb as part of a ceremonial route to Buckingham Palace. As you pass under the enormous triple archway—though not through the central arch, opened only for state occasions—the environment changes along with the color of the

GETTING ORIENTED

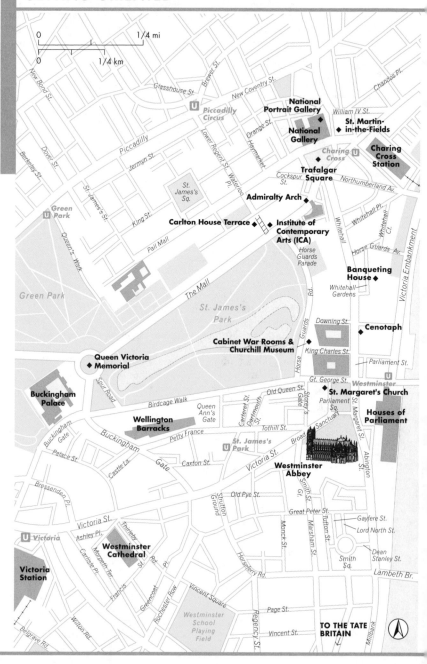

0   1/4 mi

0   1/4 km

New Bond St.

Glasshouse St.

Brewer St.

New Coventry St.

Chandos Pl.

Piccadilly Circus

National Portrait Gallery

William IV St.

St. Martin-in-the-Fields

Piccadilly

Orange St.

National Gallery

Charing Cross

Charing Cross Station

Dover St.

Jermyn St.

Lower Regent St.

Waterloo Pl.

Haymarket

Cockspur St.

Trafalgar Square

Northumberland Av.

Berkeley St.

St. James's St.

St. James's Sq.

King St.

Admiralty Arch

Green Park

Carlton House Terrace

Institute of Contemporary Arts (ICA)

Whitehall

Whitehall Pl.

Whitehall Ct.

Victoria Embankment

Queen's Walk

Pall Mall

Horse Guards Parade

Horse Guards Av.

The Mall

Banqueting House

Green Park

St. James's Park

Whitehall Gardens

Horse Guards Rd.

Downing St.

Cenotaph

Cabinet War Rooms & Churchill Museum

King Charles St.

Parliament St.

Queen Victoria Memorial

Spur Road

Gt. George St.

Westminster

Buckingham Palace

Birdcage Walk

Queen Ann's Gate

Carteret St.

Dartmouth St.

Old Queen St.

Storey's Gate

St. Margaret's Church

Parliament Sq.

St. Margaret St.

Houses of Parliament

Wellington Barracks

Petty France

Tothill St.

Broad Sanctuary

Buckingham Gate

Palace St.

Castle La.

Buckingham Gate

Caxton St.

Victoria St.

Westminster Abbey

Abingdon St.

Bressenden Pl.

Old Pye St.

Strutton Ground

Smith St. Gt.

Great Peter St.

Gayfere St.

Lord North St.

Victoria St.

Thirleby

Ashley Pl.

Victoria

Westminster Cathedral

Cartisle Pl.

Meredith Ter.

Monck St.

Marsham St.

Tufton St.

Dean Stanley St.

Smith Sq.

Lambeth Br.

Victoria Station

Francis

Greencoat Pl.

Rochester Row

Vincent Square

Horseferry Rd.

Page St.

Belgrave Rd.

Wilton Rd.

Westminster School Playing Field

Regency St.

Vincent St.

TO THE TATE BRITAIN

Millbank

TOP 5 REASONS TO GO

■ **Trafalgar Square:** Clamber onto one of the grand lions at the foot of Nelson's Column while waiting to meet someone.

■ **Cabinet War Rooms & Churchill Museum:** Listen to Churchill's wartime radio entreaties to the British people from this cavernous underground wartime hideout.

■ **Changing of the Guard:** Keep pace with the marching soldiers, resplendent in red and black, as they mark the daily routine.

■ **Tate Britain:** Stand in the Turner Room, face-to-face with the London scenes of Britain's greatest painter.

■ **Thames tours:** Ride a boat from Tate Britain to Tate Modern, and soak up the best views of Westminster and the London Eye en route.

FEELING PECKISH?

To the left of the visitor entrance to Westminster Abbey, you can get a coffee and a rich chocolate brownie (or three) from the vendor cart—nothing special, but cheap and useful on a chilly day.

Gordon's Wine Bar (⊠47 Villiers St. WC2N ☎020/7930-1408 ⊕ www.gordonswinebar.com), the oldest in London, is hidden below ground among vaulted brick arches and bathed in candlelight. A range of bottles will suit any budget, and buffet food includes excellent beef.

The good food and drink at **Inn the Park** (⊠ St. James's Park, SW1 ☎020/7451-9999 ⊕www.innthepark.com) is not always matched by great service, but the outdoor pinewood deck makes for fantastic people-watching in the early summer evenings.

GETTING THERE

Trafalgar Square—easy to access and smack dab in the center of the action—is a good place to start. Take the Tube to Embankment (District and Circle lines) and walk north until you cross the Strand, or alight at Charing Cross (Bakerloo, Jubilee, and Northern lines), where the Northumberland Avenue exit deposits you on the southeast corner of the Square.

MAKING THE MOST OF YOUR TIME

You could spend a lifetime absorbing the rich history of this part of London. More practically, try to leave at least two days if you want to dip into the full gamut of attractions without feeling horribly rushed.

If Royal London is what you want, make a day of Buckingham Palace, the Queen's Gallery, and the Guards Museum at Wellington Barracks. If you've a more constitutional bent, visit the Houses of Parliament and the Cabinet War Rooms.

NEAREST PUBLIC RESTROOMS

If you get caught short in Westminster Abbey, there are paid loos (50 p) across the street at the bottom of Victoria Street. Banqueting House and Queen's Gallery have some of the quietest, most dashing loos in London.

A BRIEF HISTORY

The Romans may have gunned for the City, but England's royals went for Westminster. London's home of democracy started out as Edward the Confessor's palace, when he moved his cramped court west in the 11th century. He founded Westminster Abbey in 1050, where every British monarch has been crowned since. Under the Normans, the palace of Westminster was an elaborate and French-speaking affair. The politicos finally got their hands on it in 1529 (when Henry VII and his court shifted up to the roomier Whitehall Palace), but nearly lost it forever with the Gunpowder Plot of 1605, when Catholic militants attempted to blow the prototypical Parliament to smithereens.

The magnificent Inigo Jones-designed Banqueting House is today's only surviving building of Whitehall Palace, and was the setting for the 1649 beheading of Charles I. Today's Westminster took shape during the Georgian and Victorian periods, as Britain reached the zenith of its imperial power. Grand architecture sprang up, and Buckingham Palace became the principal royal residence in 1837, when Victoria acceded to the throne. Trafalgar Square and Nelson's Column were built in 1843, to mark Britain's most famous naval victory, and the Houses of Parliament were rebuilt in 1858 in the trendy neo-Gothic style of the time.

road, for you're exiting frenetic Trafalgar Square and entering the Mall (rhymes with shall)—the elegant avenue that leads directly to the palace. ⊠ *The Mall, Cockspur St., Trafalgar Sq., Westminster, SW1* Ⓤ *Charing Cross.*

Banqueting House. This is all that remains today of the Tudor Palace of Whitehall, which was (according to one foreign visitor) "ill-built, and nothing but a heap of houses." James I commissioned Inigo Jones (1573–1652), one of England's great architects, to do a grand remodeling. Influenced during a sojourn in Italy by Andrea Palladio's work, Jones brought Palladian sophistication and purity back to London with him. The resulting graceful and disciplined classical style of Banqueting House must have stunned its early occupants. In the quiet vaults beneath, James would escape the stresses of being a sovereign with a glass or two. His son, Charles I, enhanced the interior by employing the Flemish painter Peter Paul Rubens to glorify his father all over the ceiling. As it turned out, these allegorical paintings, depicting a wise monarch being received into heaven, were the last thing Charles saw before he was beheaded by Cromwell's Parliamentarians in 1649. But his son, Charles II, was able to celebrate the restoration of the monarchy in this same place 20 years later. The old palace is also the setting for lunchtime concerts, held 1–2 PM. Call or check the Web site for details. ⊠ *Whitehall, Westminster, SW1A* ☎ *020/7930–4179, 0870/751–5178 recorded information, 0870/751–5187 concert tickets* ⊕ *www.hrp.org.uk* ✉ *£4.50,*

QUEEN VICTORIA MEMORIAL

You can't overlook this monument if you're near Buckingham Palace, which it faces from the traffic island at the west end of the Mall. The monument was conceived by Sir Aston Webb as the nucleus of his ceremonial route down the Mall to the Palace, and it was executed by the sculptor Thomas Brock, who was knighted on the spot when the memorial was revealed to the world in 1911. Many wonder why he was given that honor, since the thing is Victoriana incarnate: the frumpy queen glares down the Mall, with golden-winged Victory overhead and her siblings Truth, Justice, and Charity, plus Manufacture, Progress-and-Peace, War-and-Shipbuilding, and so on—in Osbert Sitwell's words, "tons of allegorical females . . . with whole litters of their cretinous children"—surrounding her. The Mall and Spur Rd., St. James's, SW1 Ⓤ Victoria, St. James's Park.

includes free audio guide ⊙ *Mon.–Sat. 10–5, last admission 4:30. Closed Christmas wk* Ⓤ *Charing Cross, Embankment, Westminster.*

FodorśChoice
★
Buckingham Palace. Buckingham Palace tops many a must-see list and has become perhaps *the* symbol of the royal family—although the building itself is no masterpiece and has housed the monarch only since Victoria (1819–1901) moved here from Kensington Palace on her accession in 1837. Compared to other great houses and palaces in London, it's a more modern affair. Originally Buckingham House and the home of George III, it was remodeled by John Nash on the accession of George IV in 1820. Nash overspent his budget by about half a million pounds and was dismissed by Parliament after George's death. Although Queen Victoria added the east front (by Edward Blore, facing the Mall) to accommodate her prodigious state entertaining, Nash's gorgeous designs can still be enjoyed at the core of the palace. The Portland stone facade dates only from 1913 (the same stone used for the Victoria Memorial outside the Palace and Admiralty Arch at the foot of the Mall), and the interior was renovated and redecorated only after it sustained World War II bomb damage.

The palace contains 19 state rooms, 52 royal and guest bedrooms, 188 staff bedrooms, 92 offices, and 78 bathrooms—a prerequisite for the 450 people who work there, and the mere 50,000 who are entertained during the year. The private royal apartments are in the north wing; when the Queen is in residence, the royal standard is raised. The state rooms are where much of the business of royalty is played out—investitures, state banquets, and receptions for the great and good—and these are open to the public while the royal family is away during the summer. A visit makes for a fascinating glimpse into another world: the fabulously gilt interiors are not merely museum pieces but pomp and pageantry at work. Highlights of the tour include the **Quadrangle,** bordered by the many offices and apartments for employees in this extraordinary miniature village. Beyond the gates you may see the changing of

Sightseeing on the Cheap

Join London's commuters on a double-decker bus. You can use your Zones 1 and 2 Travelcard on the following routes:

● **Bus 11:** King's Road, Sloane Square, Victoria Station, Westminster Abbey, Houses of Parliament and Big Ben, Whitehall, Trafalgar Square, the Strand, Fleet Street, and St. Paul's Cathedral.

● **Bus 12:** Bayswater, Marble Arch, Oxford Street, Piccadilly Circus, Trafalgar Square, Horse Guards, Whitehall, Houses of Parliament and Big Ben, Westminster Bridge.

● **Bus 19:** Sloane Square, Knightsbridge, Hyde Park Corner, Green Park, Piccadilly Circus, Shaftsbury Avenue, Oxford Street, Bloomsbury, Islington.

● **Bus 88:** Oxford Circus, Piccadilly Circus, Trafalgar Square, Whitehall, Houses of Parliament and Big Ben, Westminster Abbey, Tate Britain.

---

the guard, which adds to the experience. The **Grand Hall,** followed by the **Grand Staircase** and **Guard Room,** gives a taste of what's to follow: lines of cool marble pillars, gold leaf galore on ceilings and walls, and light, bright rooms with massive, twinkling chandeliers. Nash's ornate designs unfold through the numerous drawing rooms—beginning with the **Green Drawing Room**—each equally spectacular, filled with treasures brought from the Prince Regent's original palatial home, Carlton House. (Some of the most exquisite pieces in the world, such as the cabinet with gemstone-decorated panels and the precious Sèvres porcelain, found their way to the palace after the French Revolution.) The **Throne Room,** in opulent theatrical baroque style, has the original 1953 coronation throne, among others. The **Picture Gallery** is a feast of renowned art. The collection was begun by Charles I, and includes masterpieces by Rubens, Vermeer, Van Dyck, Cuyp, and Canaletto. (More from the Royal Collection can be seen in the **Queen's Gallery,** near the south side of the palace.) The **Ballroom** has videos of royal events, and you can also see the dubbing sword used in the investitures held here, where the Queen touches those to become "Sirs" and "Dames." The **State Dining Room,** with its elaborate ceiling and walls of kingly portraits, has views over the palace gardens. The **Blue Drawing Room** is splendor in overkill and the setting for prebanquet drinks. The bow-shape **Music Room** features lapiz lazuli columns between arched floor-to-ceiling windows, while the **White Drawing Room** is a sensation of white-and-gold plasterwork: a crescendo on which to end the tour.

Unless you have an invitation to one of the Queen's summer garden parties, the most you'll see of the 45-acre grounds is a walk along the south side. This addition to the tour gives views of the garden (west) front of the palace and the 19th-century lake. The walled oasis has plenty of wildlife—it contains more than 350 types of wildflowers.

Fodor's Choice ★ Behind the front palace gates, the **Changing of the Guard,** with all the ceremony monarchists and children adore, remains one of London's best free shows and culminates in front of the palace. Marching to live music, the guards proceed up the Mall from St. James's Palace to Buckingham Palace. Shortly afterward, the replacement guard approaches from Wellington Barracks via Birdcage Walk. Then within the forecourt, the old guard symbolically hands over the keys to the palace to the replacement guard. The ceremony, more properly known as **Guard Mounting,** lasts about 45 minutes and usually takes place on schedule, but the guards sometimes cancel because of bad weather; check the signs in the forecourt or phone. Get there by 10:30 AM to grab a spot in the best viewing section at the gate facing the palace, since most of the hoopla takes place behind the railings in the forecourt. Be sure to prebook tour reservations of the palace with a credit card by phone. ⊠ *Buckingham Palace Rd., St. James's, SW1* ☎ *020/7766–7300* ⊕ *www.royal.gov.uk* 🖼 *£14, includes audio tour, credit-card reservations subject to booking charge* ⊙ *Late July–late Sept., daily 9:45–6, last admission 3:45; confirm dates, which are subject to Queen's mandate. Changing of the Guard Apr.–July, daily 11:30 AM; Aug.–Mar., alternating days only 11:30 AM* 🚇 *AE, MC, V* Ⓤ *Victoria, St. James's Park.*

★ ♔ **Cabinet War Rooms & Churchill Museum.** It was from this small warren of underground rooms—beneath the vast government buildings of the Foreign Office—that Winston Churchill and his team directed Britain's troops in World War II. Designed to be bomb-proof, the complex is less museum, more fossilized time warp, as the whole has been preserved almost exactly as it was when the last light was turned off at the end of the war. Every clock shows almost 5 PM, and the furniture, fittings, and paraphernalia of a busy, round-the-clock war office are in situ, down to the colored map pins.

During air raids, the leading government ministers met here and the Cabinet Room is still arranged as if a meeting were about to convene. In the Map Room, the Allied campaign is charted on wall-to-wall maps with a rash of pin holes showing the movements of convoys. In the hub of the room, a bank of different-colored phones known as the "Beauty Chorus" linked the War Rooms to control rooms around the nation. The Prime Minister's Room holds the desk from which Churchill made his morale-boosting broadcasts; the Telephone Room (a converted broom cupboard) has his hotline to FDR. The PM's suite of rooms for dining, cooking, and sleeping are a recent restoration (2003). Telephonists and clerks who worked 16-hour shifts slept in lesser quarters in unenviable conditions; it would not have been unusual for a secretary in pajamas to scurry past a field marshal en route to a meeting.

By far the most exciting addition is the **Churchill Museum,** which opened in 2005 on the 40th anniversary of the great man's death. Different zones explore his life and achievements—and failures, too—through objects and documents, many of which, such as his personal papers, had not been revealed to the public. Central to the exhibition is an interactive timeline, with layers of facts, figures, and tales. If you visit in August, there are late-night openings and 1940s-style musical events; phone for details. ⊠ *Clive Steps, King Charles St., Westminster, SW1A* ☎ *020/7930–6961* ⊕ *www.iwm.org.uk* ⊡ *£11, includes audio tour* ⊙ *Daily 9:30–6; last admission 5* ⓤ *Westminster.*

Carlton House Terrace. This is a glorious example of Regency architect John Nash's genius. Between 1812 and 1830, under the patronage of George IV (Prince Regent until George III's death in 1820), Nash was the architect for the grand scheme of Regent Street and the sweep of neoclassical houses encircling Regent's Park. The Prince Regent, who lived at Carlton House, had plans to build a country villa at Primrose Hill (to the north of the park), connected by a grand road—hence Regent Street. Even though it was considered a most extravagant building for its time, Carlton House was demolished after the prince's accession to the throne. Nash's Carlton House Terrace, no less imposing, with white-stucco facades and massive Corinthian columns, was built in its place. It was a smart address and one that prime ministers Gladstone (1856) and Palmerston (1857–75) enjoyed. Today Carlton House Terrace houses the Royal College of Pathologists (No. 2), the Royal Society (No. 6, whose members included Isaac Newton and Charles Darwin), the Turf Club (No. 5), and, at No. 12, the **Institute of Contemporary Arts,** better known as the ICA. ⊠ *The Mall, St. James's, W1* ⓤ *Charing Cross.*

Downing Street. Looking like an unassuming alley but barred by iron gates at both its Whitehall and Horse Guards Road approaches, this is the location of the famous **No. 10,** London's modest version of the White House. Only three houses remain of the terrace built circa 1680 by Sir George Downing, who spent enough of his youth in America to graduate from Harvard—the second man ever to do so. **No. 11** is traditionally the residence of the chancellor of the exchequer (secretary of the treasury), and **No. 12** is the party whips' office. No. 10 has officially housed the prime minister since 1732. Just south of Downing Street, in the middle of Whitehall, you'll see the **Cenotaph,** a stark white monolith designed in 1920 by Edwin Lutyens to commemorate the 1918 armistice. On Remembrance Day (the Sunday nearest November 11, Armistice Day) it's strewn with red poppies to honor the dead of both world wars and all British and Commonwealth soldiers killed in action since; the first wreath is laid by the Queen and there's a march past by war veterans. ⊠ *Whitehall, Westminster, SW1* ⓤ *Westminster.*

🕙 **Horse Guards Parade.** Once the tiltyard of Whitehall Palace, where jousting tournaments were held, the Horse Guards Parade is now notable mainly for the annual Trooping the Colour ceremony, in which the Queen takes the Royal Salute, her official birthday gift, on the second Saturday in June. (Like Paddington

---

BEARSKIN, NOT BUSBY

While on duty, Guards soldiers are required to remain utterly aloof—they may not speak, may not swat errant flies from their noses, and in theory may not keel over under the weight of their enormous, saunalike hats. Called bearskins (not busbies, as is sometimes incorrectly assumed) after the material from which they are made, the headwear was taken as a trophy from the French after the victory of the Battle of Waterloo.

London's Great Architects

GREAT ARCHITECTURAL achievements in London have often been motivated by disasters and misfortunes. Like a phoenix, London rose from the ashes in a frenzy of rebuilding after the Great Fire of 1666 had destroyed four-fifths of the city. Three centuries later, more fire, caused by the German air raids in the Second World War, flattened huge chunks of London. Gray civic buildings and tower blocks rose from the rubble. As a result of these intense civic reconstructions, a few individuals had the opportunity to leave significant marks on the city.

Inigo Jones (1573–1652), one of England's first great architects, was almost single-handedly responsible for the resurgence of classical styles of architecture in the early 17th century. Often directly modeling his work after that of Italian architect Andrea Palladio, Jones was highly influential during his time, as the Palladian style quickly spread throughout England. His most famous works include St. Paul's Church at Covent Garden and the magnificent Banqueting House on Whitehall.

Sir Christopher Wren (1632–1723) was given the Herculean task of overseeing the rebuilding of London following the Great Fire. His ambitious plans for a complete redesign of the formerly medieval city, drawn up within a week after the fire, were shot down by landowners, businesspeople, and private citizens intent on a quicker reconstruction. It remains a mystery what effect Wren's membership in the secretive Masonic Lodge had on his efforts. Nevertheless, Wren was responsible for 51 new churches (all in the City) and the amazing St. Paul's Cathedral. Only 23 of the City churches still survive, the finest of which are St. Bride's (Fleet Street), St. Mary Abchurch (Abchurch Yard), and St. Stephen's Walbrook (Walbrook Street). A wander through the deserted streets of the City past the churches is a rewarding way to spend a weekend afternoon.

John Nash (1752–1835) completely re-designed a large section of the city stretching from the Mall northward to Regent's Park and also remodeled Buckingham Palace. He is largely responsible for the look of much of central London; it was his idea to clear Trafalgar Square of its royal stables to make room for the public space as it exists today. For an insight into Nash's vision for London, walk from Buckingham Palace along the Mall, past his white stucco Carlton House Terrace to your left. Walk across Trafalgar Square to Haymarket, where Nash built the Haymarket Theater. Then walk the length of Regent Street, passing on the way All Souls Church, Langham Place, and Park Crescent, which leads into Regent's Park from its southern end.

Bear, the Queen has two birthdays; her real one is on April 21.) There is pageantry galore, with marching bands—the occasional guardsman fainting clean away from the heat building up under his weighty bearskin—and throngs of onlookers. Covering the vast expanse of the square that faces Horse Guards Road, opposite St. James's Park at one end and Whitehall at the other, the ceremony is televised. At the Whitehall facade of

Horse Guards, the changing of two mounted sentries known as the **mounted guard** provides what may be London's most frequently exercised photo opportunity. ⊠ *Whitehall, Westminster, SW1* ☉ *Queen's mounted guard ceremony Mon.–Sat. 11 AM, Sun. 10 AM* Ⓤ *Westminster.*

NEED A BREAK?

The **Wesley Café** (⊠ Storey's Gate, Westminster, SW1 ☎ 020/7222-8010) is a popular budget haunt for office workers around Westminster. It's almost opposite Westminster Abbey, in the crypt of Central Hall, a former Methodist church. A meal costs around £5.

★ **Houses of Parliament.** Overlooking the Thames, the Houses of Parliament are, arguably, the city's most famous and photogenic sight, with the Clock Tower—which everyone calls Big Ben—keeping watch on the corner and Westminster Abbey ahead of you across Parliament Square.

> **TRIP TIP**
>
> The easiest time to get into the Commons is during an evening session—Parliament is still sitting if the top of the Clock Tower is illuminated.

The Palace of Westminster, as the complex is still properly called, was established by Edward the Confessor in the 11th century. It has served as the seat of English administrative power ever since. Henry VIII was the last king to hold court here, as after 1529 he moved a few steps away to the finer and more expansive Whitehall Palace. At the Reformation, the Royal Chapel was secularized and became the first meeting place of the Commons. The Lords settled in the White Chamber. These, along with everything but the **Jewel Tower** and **Westminster Hall,** were destroyed in 1834 when "the sticks"—the arcane elmwood "tally" sticks notched for loans paid out and paid back, kept beneath the Lords' Chamber, on which the court had kept its accounts until 1826—were incinerated, and the fire got out of hand. Westminster Hall, with its remarkable hammer-beam roof, was the work of William the Conqueror's son, William Rufus. It's one of the largest remaining Norman halls in Europe, and its dramatic interior was the scene of the trial of Charles I.

After the fire, Charles Barry and Augustus Pugin married their Renaissance and Gothic styles into the building you see today: Barry's classical proportions offset by Pugin's ornamental flourishes—although the latter were toned down by Gilbert Scott when he rebuilt the bomb-damaged House of Commons after World War II. The two towers were Pugin's work. The **Clock Tower** was completed in 1858 after long delays due to bickering over the clock's design. (Barry designed the faces in the end.) It contains the 13-ton bell

> **PHOTO OP**
>
> The best place for a photo opportunity alongside one of the guardsmen is at St. James's Palace, or try and keep up alongside them during the daily morning Changing the Guard. They leave St. James's at about 10:30 AM, for Buckingham Palace. Failing that, shuffle up to the mounted horse guards on the Whitehall side, there all day long.

known as Big Ben, which chimes the hour (and the quarters). At the southwest end of the main Parliament building is the 336-foot-high **Victoria Tower.**

The building itself, which covers 8 acres, is a series of chambers, lobbies, and offices joined by more than 2 mi of passages. There are two Houses, Lords and Commons. The former consists of hereditary peers— earls, lords, viscounts, and other aristocrats. The House of Commons is made up of 659 elected Members of Parliament (MPs). The political party with the most MPs forms the government, its leader becoming prime minister; other parties form the Opposition. Since 1642, when Charles I tried to have five MPs arrested, no monarch has been allowed into the House of Commons. The state opening of Parliament in November consequently takes place in the House of Lords. Visitors aren't allowed many places in the Houses of Parliament, though the Visitors' Galleries of the House of Commons do afford a view of democracy in process where the banks of green leather benches seat the opposing MPs. When they speak, it's not directly to each other but through the Speaker, who also decides who will get the floor each day. Elaborate procedures notwithstanding, debate is often drowned out by raucous jeers and insults. When MPs vote, they exit by the "Aye" or the "No" corridor, thus being counted by the party whips. In 2004 security in the chamber was spectacularly breached on two separate occasions, when fervent "father" protestors threw a purple flour–bomb from the Visitors' Gallery, after which a glass screen was installed. A later incident saw the traditionally dressed tail-coated security men wrestle "hunt" protestors to the floor of the chamber.

Other public areas of the 1,100-room labyrinth are punctuated with stirring frescoes commissioned by Prince Albert. You pass these on your way to the Visitors' Galleries—if, that is, you're patient enough to wait in line for hours (the Lords line is shorter) or have applied in advance for the special "line of route" tour for overseas visitors in summer opening (late July–August and mid-September–early October). Tickets can be prebooked by phone or on the Web site; alternatively, you can take a chance and buy same-day tickets from the ticket office opposite the Houses of Parliament. The tour takes you through the Queen's Robing Room, Royal Gallery, House of Lords, Central Hall (where MPs meet their constituents—the lucky ones get to accompany their MP to a prestigious tea on the terrace), House of Commons, and out into the spectacular Westminster Hall. Watch for the "VR" (Victoria Regina) monograms in the carpets and carving belying the "medieval" detailing as 19th-century work. The time to catch the action is Question Time— when the prime minister defends himself against the attacks of his "right honorable friends" on Wednesday between noon and 2:30 PM (it's also live on BBC2). Overseas visitors should check tour dates and details on

> ## A VIEW TO REMEMBER
>
> The most romantic view of the complex is from the opposite (south) side of the river, especially dramatic at night when the spires, pinnacles, and towers are floodlighted green and gold—a fairytale vision only missing the presence of Peter Pan and Wendy on their way to Never-Never Land.

the Parliament's Web site. The next best time to visit is either chamber's regular Question Time, held on Monday, Tuesday, and Thursday from noon to 2:30 PM.

For a special exhibition devoted to the "History of Parliament: Past and Present," head to the **Jewel Tower,** across the street from Victoria Tower,

> ### WHO WAS BIG BEN?
>
> Some say Ben was "Big Ben" Caunt, heavyweight boxing champ; others, Sir Benjamin Hall, the sizeable Westminster building works commissioner.

on Abingdon Street (also called Old Palace Yard), south of Parliament Square. Not to be confused with the other famed jewel tower at the Tower of London, this was the stronghold for Edward III's treasure in 1366. It's also one of the original parts of the old Palace of Westminster and still retains some original beams; part of the moat and medieval quay still remain. (The tower is run by English Heritage, with a small charge for entry.) Be sure to have your name placed in advance on the waiting list for the twice-weekly tours of the **Lord Chancellor's Residence,** a popular attraction since its spectacular renovation. ⊠ *St. Stephen's Entrance, St. Margaret St., Westminster, SW1* ☏ *020/7219–4272 Commons information, 020/7219–3107 Lords information, 020/7222–2219 Jewel Tower, 020/7219–2184 Lord Chancellor's Residence, 0870/906–3773 summer tours* ⊕ *www.parliament.uk* ✆ *Free, £7 summer tours* ☉ *Commons Mon. 2:30–10:30, Tues. and Wed. 11:30–7:30, Thurs. 11:30–6:30, Fri. 9:30–3 although not every Fri.; Lords Mon.–Thurs. 2:30–10; Lord Chancellor's Residence Tues. and Thurs. 10:30–12:30. Closed Easter wk, late July–early Sept., 3 wks for party conference recess mid-Sept.–early Oct., and 3 wks at Christmas* Ⓤ *Westminster.*

Institute of Contemporary Arts (ICA). Behind its incongruous white-stucco facade, at No. 12 Carlton House Terrace, the ICA has provided a stage for the avant-garde in performance, theater, dance, visual art, and music since it was established in 1947. There are two cinemas; a library of video artists' works; a bookshop; a café; a lively, hip bar; and a team of adventurous curators. ⊠ *The Mall, St. James's, SW1* ☏ *020/7930–3647* ⊕ *www.ica.org.uk* ✆ *1-day, weekday membership £1.50; weekends, £2.50; additional charge for cinema screenings* ☉ *Daily noon–9:30* Ⓤ *Charing Cross, Piccadilly Circus.*

▌ **NEED A BREAK?** The **ICAfé** is windowless but brightly lighted, with hot dishes, salads, quiches, and desserts. The upstairs bar has lighter food and windows overlooking the Mall. Both are open daily from noon and subject to the £1.50 one-day membership fee.

The Mall. This stately, 115-foot-wide processional route (pronounced like "shall") sweeping from Admiralty Arch to the Queen Victoria Memorial at Buckingham Palace is an updated 1904 version of the traditional rambling promenade that was used centuries before. The street was originally laid out around 1660 for the game of *paille-maille* (a type of croquet crossed with golf), which also gave the parallel road Pall Mall its

Modern Architecture

THE RENAISSANCE OF modern architecture in the capital has two major cues: the City boom and the brouhaha of the millennium. During the mid-'80s, the financial City deregulated and broke its boundaries socially, geographically—spreading east to Docklands—and architecturally, too. New buildings surged upward between the traditional classic pillars of Wren and Soane. Richard Rogers was responsible for the strident and beautiful Lloyds building in the City early on in 1986, although the sexiness stakes have been upped by Sir Norman Foster, whose recent portfolio includes the groundbreaking "Gherkin," the cucumber-shape tower for the Swiss Re headquarters (30 St. Mary Axe) in 2003, and, on the vegetable theme again, the mushroom-shape City Hall for the London Assembly headquarters by Tower Bridge in 2002. Other architects have complemented rather than outshone their neighbors, such as Stirling, who designed No. 1 Poultry to work with the surrounding Wren, Hawksmoor, and Lutyens designs.

The millennium celebrations also inspired many updates for old institutions, such as Norman Foster's awesome glass roofing and design of the Great Court at the British Museum. Glass is featured again in Rick Mather's revamp of the Maritime Museum and the Wallace Collection, and likewise in Dixon-Jones's internal facelift at the National Portrait Gallery and overhaul of the Royal Opera House. Richard Rogers broke the mold with the inspiring and controversial Millennium Dome, and not to be forgotten are other stars of the millennium: the bridges and the wheel. Foster's sculpted "blade of light" pedestrian footbridge had a wobbly beginning, but is now a firm attraction (at the doorstep of the tremendous Tate Modern powerstation makeover by Herzog & de Meuron). The Hungerford Bridge by Lifschutz Davidson from Charing Cross to the South Bank Arts Centre crept into the postmillennium, but is no less dazzling. The British Airways London Eye observation wheel by David Marks and Julia Barfield was almost eclipsed by the publicity surrounding the Dome downriver, yet it opened on time to spectacular success—and remains a tourist magnet and landmark on the constantly regenerating London horizon.

---

name, and it quickly became the place to be seen. Samuel Pepys, Jonathan Swift, and Alexander Pope all wrote about it, and it continued as the beau monde's social playground into the early 19th century, long after the game had gone out of vogue. ⊠ *The Mall, St. James's, SW1* Ⓤ *Charing Cross, Green Park.*

National Gallery. You could spend a day perusing one of the largest and best collections of western European paintings, and still not reach full immersion—all for free. Hard to believe that the nation's collection began with a nucleus of 38 paintings on show in a wealthy banker's house in Pall Mall (there's a painting of the paintings at the house of John Julius

Fodor'sChoice
★

Angerstein in the Victoria & Albert Museum). Even though the collection included works by Raphael, Rembrandt, Titian, and Rubens, it was hardly likely to rival the Louvre, so Parliament agreed in 1824 to a building in Trafalgar Square, the capital's central point. The gallery fills the north side of the square, with Nelson's column in the center, and after a welcome redesign, which stopped traffic roaring past the gallery door, pedestrians can now

> ## GOOD TO KNOW
>
> The question of what to see and where at the National Gallery has been solved with large plasma screen information systems, which highlight key paintings. Information boards with a color code for different eras of paintings—such as blue for 1250–1500—make orientation a breeze.

walk between the two and appreciate William Wilkins's impressive colonnaded neoclassic facade. By the end of the century, enthusiastic directors and generous patrons had turned the National Gallery into one of the world's foremost collections, with works from painters of the Italian Renaissance and earlier, from the Flemish and Dutch masters, the Spanish school, and of course the English tradition, including Hogarth, Gainsborough, Stubbs, and Constable.

The modern Sainsbury Wing, by American architect Robert Venturi, houses the Early Renaissance collection, and hosts excellent in-depth exhibitions, on themes or individual artists. The new Getty entrance at street level takes visitors into the updated east wing while the old stepped portico entrance on the first floor undergoes restoration. Gone is the previous dark, dingy Victorian atmosphere; now you progress into the gallery through a daylighted, bright stone staircase with sleek black marble into a modern double-level atrium. It makes a fabulous entrance to the revamped Central Hall and the marvelous Titian collection. Accompanying the redesign are superior visitor facilities, a better store for the must-have postcards and books, and a café. The completion of the building's overhaul entails renovating and updating the old portico entrance with its complicated and cramped stairways, while the basement floors will enjoy a renaissance with modern-day multimedia visitor facilities.

Worthy of a look are the exhibitions in the Sunley Room and Room 1, where works are organized along a theme, such as Bosch and Breugel, or focus on an artist, such as El Greco. Alternatively, begin at an "Art-Start" terminal in the Sainsbury Wing or East Wing Espresso Bar. The interactive screens give you access to information on all of the museum's holdings; you can choose your favorites, and print out a free personal tour map.

The following is a list of 10 of the most familiar works, to jog your memory, whet your appetite, and offer a starting point for your own exploration. The first five are in the Sainsbury Wing. In chronological order: (1) **Van Eyck** (circa 1395–1441), *The Arnolfini Portrait*. A solemn couple holds hands, the fish-eye mirror behind them mysteriously illuminating what can't be seen from the front view. (2) **Uccello** (1397–1475), *The Battle of San Romano*. In a work commissioned by the Medici family, the Florentine commander on a rearing white warhorse leads armored knights into battle against the Sienese. (3) **Bellini** (circa 1430–1516), *The Doge Leonardo Loredan.* The artist captured the Venetian doge's beatific expression (and snail-shell "buttons") at the beginning of his 20 years in office. (4) **Botticelli** (1445–1510), *Venus and Mars.* Mars sleeps, exhausted by the love goddess, oblivious to the lance wielded by mischievous putti and the buzzing of wasps. (5) **Leonardo da Vinci** (1452–1519), *The Virgin and Child.* This haunting black chalk cartoon is partly famous for having been attacked at gunpoint, and it now gets extra protection behind glass and screens. (6) **Caravaggio** (1573–1610), *The Supper at Emmaus.* A cinematically lighted, freshly resurrected Christ blesses bread in an astonishingly domestic vision from the master of chiaroscuro. (7) **Velázquez** (1599–1660), *The Toilet of Venus.* "The Rokeby Venus," named for its previous home in Yorkshire, has the most famously beautiful back in any gallery. She's the only surviving female nude by Velázquez. (8) **Constable** (1776–1837), *The Hay Wain.* Rendered overfamiliar by too many greeting cards, this is the definitive image of golden-age rural England. (9) **Turner** (1775–1851), *The Fighting Téméraire.* Most of the collection's other Turners were moved to the Tate Britain; the final voyage of the great French battleship into a livid, hazy sunset stayed here. (10) **Seurat** (1859–91), *Bathers at Asnières.* This static summer day's idyll is one of the pointillist extraordinaire's best-known works.

Glaring omissions from the above include some of the most popular pictures in the gallery, by Piero della Francesca, Titian, Holbein, Bosch, Bruegel, Rembrandt, Vermeer, Canaletto, Claude, Tiepolo, Gainsborough, Ingres, Monet, Renoir, and van Gogh. You can't miss the two most spectacular works on view—due to their mammoth size—Sebastiano del Piombo's *Sermon on the Mount* and Stubbs's stunning *Whistlejacket.* These great paintings aren't the only thing glowing in the rooms of the National Gallery—thanks to government patronage and lottery monies, salons here now gleam with stunning brocades and opulent silks. Rubens's *Samson and Delilah* has never looked better.

The collection of Dutch 17th-century paintings is one of the greatest in the world, and pieces by Hals, Hooch, Ruisdel, Hobbema, and Cuyp are shown in renewed natural light and gracious surroundings. ✉ *Trafalgar Sq., Westminster, WC2* ☎ *020/7747–2885* ⊕ *www. nationalgallery.org.uk* 🎟 *Free, charge for special exhibitions* ⊙ *Daily 10–6, Wed. until 9; 1-hr free guided tour starts at Sainsbury Wing daily at 11:30 and 2:30, and additionally 6 and 6:30 Wed, 12:30 and 3:30 Sat.* Ⓤ *Charing Cross, Leicester Sq.*

ART FOR KIDS

If you visit the National Gallery during the school vacations, there are special programs and trails for children that are not to be missed. Neither are the free weekday lunchtime lectures and Ten Minute Talks, which illuminate the story behind a key work of art. Check the information desk, or Web site, for details.

NEED A
BREAK?

The muraled **Crivelli's Garden Restaurant** (☎ 020/7747-2869) in the Sainsbury Wing of the National Gallery serves a fashionable lunch—mussels, gravlax, charcuterie, and salads, and has the added perk of a super view from huge windows overlooking Trafalgar Square. The ultracool **National Gallery Café** (☎ 020/7747-5945) in the east wing makes a fun stop, even if you're not visiting the gallery. Close to the Getty entrance, it offers a good range of snacks, lunches, and drinks, including traditional tea with scones. A children's menu is available, and it's open late (until 8:30 PM) on Wednesday.

★ ☼ **National Portrait Gallery.** An idiosyncratic collection that presents a potted history of Britain through its people, past and present, this museum is an essential stop for all history and literature buffs, where you can choose to take in a little, or a lot. The spacious, bright galleries are

> **DID YOU KNOW?**
>
> The miniature of Jane Austen by her sister Cassandra is the only likeness that exists of the great novelist.

accessible via a state-of-the-art escalator, which lets you view the paintings as you ascend to a skylighted space displaying the oldest works in the Tudor Gallery. At the summit, a sleek restaurant, open beyond gallery hours, will satiate skyline droolers. Here you'll see one of the best landscapes for real: a panoramic view of Nelson's Column and the backdrop along Whitehall to the Houses of Parliament. Back in the basement are a lecture theater, computer gallery, bookshop, and café.

Walking through the Photography Gallery is like looking at an upmarket celebrity or society magazine. In the Tudor Gallery—a modern update on a Tudor long hall—is a Holbein cartoon of Henry VIII; Stubbs's self-portrait hangs in the refurbished 17th-century rooms; and Hockney's appears in the modern Balcony Gallery, mixed up with photographs, busts, caricatures, and paintings. Many of the faces are obscure and will be just as unknown to you if you're English, because the portraits outlasted their sitters' fame—not so surprising when the portraitists are such greats as Reynolds, Gainsborough, Lawrence, and Romney. But the annotation is comprehensive, the layout is easy to negotiate—chronological, with the oldest at the top—and there's a separate research center for those who get hooked on particular personages. Don't miss the absorbing mini-exhibitions in the Studio and Balcony Galleries; and there are temporary exhibitions in the Wolfson Gallery, on subjects as diverse as "Below Stairs–400 Years of Servants' Portraits," to contemporary fashion photography from Terry O'Neill to Mario Testino. ⊠ *St. Martin's Pl., Covent Garden, WC2* ☎ *020/7312–2463 recorded information* ⊕ *www.npg.org.uk* ✉ *Free, charge for special exhibitions* ☉ *Mon.–Wed., weekends 10–6, Thurs. and Fri. 10–9* Ⓤ *Charing Cross, Leicester Sq.*

Fodor'sChoice
★ **The Queen's Gallery.** The former chapel at the south side of Buckingham Palace is now a temple of art and rare and exquisite objects, acquired by kings and queens over the centuries. Although Her Majesty

herself is not the personal owner, she has the privilege of holding these works for the nation. Step through the splendid portico (designed by John Simpson) into elegantly re-strained, spacious galleries whose walls are hung with some truly great works. An audio guide takes you through the treasures.

A rough timeline of the major monarch collectors starts principally with King Charles I. An avid appreciator of painters, Charles established the basis of the Royal Collection, purchasing works by Mantegna, Raphael, Titian, and Dürer (it was under royal patronage that Rubens painted the Banqueting House ceiling). During the Civil War many masterpieces were sold abroad and subsequently repatriated by Charles II. George III, who bought Buckingham House, scooped up a notable collection of Venetian (including Canaletto), Renaissance (Bellini and Raphael), and Dutch art (Vermeer), and patronized English contemporary artists such as Gainsborough, Hoppner, and Beechey. He also took a liking to American artist Benjamin West. The Prince Regent, George IV, transformed his father's house into a palace, filling it with fine art across the board from paintings to porcelain. In particular, he had a good eye for Rembrandt, contemporary equestrian works by Stubbs, and lavish portraits by Lawrence. Queen Victoria had a penchant for Landseer animals and landscapes, Frith's contemporary scenes, and portraits by Winterhalter. Finally, Edward VIII indulged Queen Alexandra's love of Fabergé, while many royal tours around the empire produced gifts of gorgeous caliber, such as the Cullinan diamond from southern Africa and the emerald-studded belt from India.

The Queen's Gallery displays merely a selection from the Royal Collection in themed exhibitions, while more than 3,000 objects reside in museums and galleries in the United Kingdom and abroad: check out the National Gallery, the Victoria & Albert Museum, the Museum of London, and the British Museum. ■ TIP➔ The E-gallery provides an interactive electronic version of the collection, allowing the user to open lockets, remove a sword from its scabbard, or take apart the tulip vases. It's probably the closest you could get to eyeing practically every diamond in the sovereign's glittering diadem. ⊠ *Buckingham Palace, Buckingham Palace Rd., St. James's, SW1* ☎ *020/7766–7301* ⊕ *www.royal.gov.uk* ✆ *£7.50, joint ticket with Royal Mews £11.50* ◷ *Daily 10–5:30; last admission 4:30* Ⓤ *Victoria, St. James's Park.*

Ⓒ **Royal Mews.** Fairy-tale gold-and-glass coaches and sleek Rolls-Royce state cars emanate from the Royal Mews, next door to the Queen's Gallery. The John Nash–designed Mews serves as the headquarters for Her Majesty's travel department (so beware of closures for state visits), complete with the Queen's own special breed of horses, ridden by wigged postilions decked in red-and-gold regalia. Between the stables and riding school arena are exhibits of polished saddlery and riding tack.

The highlight of the Mews is the splendid golden Coronation Coach, not unlike an art gallery on wheels, with its sculpted tritons and sea gods. Mews were originally falcons' quarters (the name comes from their "mewing," or feather shedding), but the horses gradually eclipsed the birds. Royal Household staff guide your tour. ⊠ *Buckingham Palace Rd., St. James's, SW1* ☎ *020/7766–7302* ⊕ *www.royal.gov.uk* ⌑ *£6, joint ticket with Queen's Gallery £11.50* ⊘ *Apr.–July and Oct., Sat.–Thurs. 11–4; Aug. and Sept., daily 10–5, no guided tours; last admission 45 min before closing* Ⓤ *Victoria, St. James's Park.*

↻ **St. James's Park.** With three palaces at its borders (the ancient Palace of Westminster, now the Houses of Parliament; the Tudor **St. James's Palace**; and Buckingham Palace), St. James's Park is acclaimed as the most royal of the royal parks. It's also London's smallest, most ornamental park, as well as the oldest; it was ac-

FodorsChoice ★

> **GREAT VIEWS**
>
> The bridge over the lake, universally referred to as the "duck pond," offers fantastic views of Buckingham Palace and the minarets of Whitehall.

quired by Henry VIII in 1532 for a deer park. The land was marshy and took its name from the lepers' hospital dedicated to St. James. Henry VIII built the palace next to the park, which was used for hunting only—dueling and sword fights were forbidden. James I improved the land and installed an aviary and zoo (complete with crocodiles). Charles II (after his exile in France and because of his admiration for Louis XIV's formal Versailles Palace landscapes) had formal gardens laid out, with avenues, fruit orchards, and a canal. Lawns were grazed by goats, sheep, and deer.

About 17 species of birds—including pelicans, geese, ducks, and swans (which belong to the Queen)—now breed on and around Duck Island at the east end of the lake, attracting ornithologists at dawn. Later on summer days the deck chairs (which you must pay to use) are crammed with office workers lunching while being serenaded by music from the bandstands. One of the best times to stroll the leafy walkways is after dark, with Westminster Abbey and

> **QUIRKY LONDON**
>
> Sir Walter Raleigh is among the notables buried at St. Margaret's, only without his head, which had been removed at Old Palace Yard, Westminster, and kept by his wife, who was said to be fond of asking visitors, "Have you met Sir Walter?" as she produced it from a velvet bag.

the Houses of Parliament rising above the floodlighted lake. ⊠ *The Mall or Horse Guards approach, or Birdcage Walk, St. James's, SW1* Ⓤ *St. James's Park, Westminster.*

St. Margaret's Church. Dwarfed by its neighbor, Westminster Abbey, St. Margaret's was founded in the 12th century and rebuilt between 1486 and 1523. As the parish church of the Houses of Parliament it's much sought after for weddings: Samuel Pepys married here in 1655, Winston Churchill in 1908. The east Crucifixion window celebrates another union, the marriage of Prince Arthur and Catherine of Aragon. Unfor-

Continued on page 68

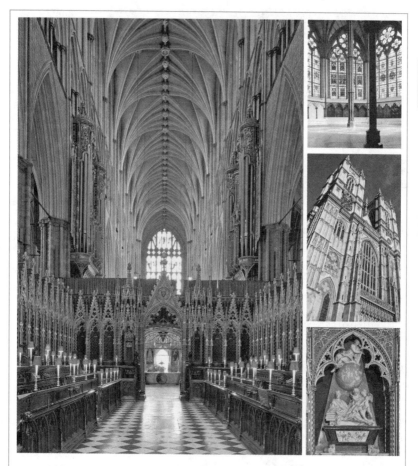

WESTMINSTER ABBEY

A monument to the rich—and often bloody and scandalous— history of Great Britain, Westminster Abbey rises on the Thames skyline as one of the most iconic sites in London.

The mysterious gloom of the lofty medieval interior is home to more than 600 statues, tombs, and commemorative tablets. About 3,300 people, from kings to composers to wordsmiths, are buried in the abbey. It has been the scene of 14 royal weddings and no less than 38 coronations—the first in 1066, when William the Conqueror was made king here.

TOURING THE ABBEY

There's only one way around the abbey, and as there will almost certainly be a long stream of shuffling tourists at your heels, you'll need to be alert to catch the highlights. Enter by the north door.

When you enter the church, look up to your right to see the **①painted-glass rose window,** the largest of its kind.

The **② Coronation Chair,** at the foot of the Henry VII Chapel, has been briefly graced by nearly every regal posterior since Edward I ordered it in 1301. Look for the graffiti on the back of the Coronation chair. It's the work of 18th- and 19th-century visitors and Westminster schoolboys who carved their names there.

In front of the **③ High Altar,** which was used for the funerals of Princess Diana and the Queen Mother, is a black-and-white marble pavement laid in 1268. The intricate Italian Cosmati work contains three Latin inscriptions, one of which states that the world will last for 19,683 years.

The **④ Chapel of Henry VII** contains the tombs of Henry VII and his queen, Elizabeth of York. Close by are monuments to the young daughters of James I, and an urn purported to hold the remains of the so-called Princes in the Tower—Edward V and Richard. Interestingly, arch enemies Elizabeth I and her half-sister Mary Tudor share a tomb here. An inscription reads: "Partners both in throne and grave, here rest two sisters, Elizabeth and Mary, in the hope of the Resurrection."

The **⑤ Chapel of St. Edward the Confessor** contains the shrine to the pre-Norman king. Because of its great age, it is closed off to the public; you must join a tour with the verger to be admitted to the chapel. (Details are available at the admission desk; there is a small extra charge.)

In the choir screen, north of the entrance to the choir, is a marble **⑥ monument to Sir Isaac Newton.**

A door from the south transept and south choir aisle leads to the calm of the **⑦ Great Cloisters.**

Geoffrey Chaucer was the first poet to be buried in **⑧ Poets' Corner** in 1400. Other memorials include: William Shakespeare, William Blake,

---

West Entrance

⑭

⑮

Nave

Choir

⑥

College Hall

Dean's Court

Deanery

⑬

⑦

Site of Refectory

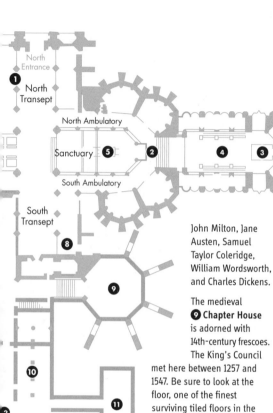

The **10 Abbey Museum** includes a collection of deliciously macabre effigies made from the death masks and actual clothing of Charles II and Admiral Lord Nelson (complete with eye patch).

The **11 Little Cloister** is a quiet haven, and just beyond, the **12 College Garden** is a delightful diversion. Filled with medicinal herbs, it has been tended by monks for more than 900 years.

John Milton, Jane Austen, Samuel Taylor Coleridge, William Wordsworth, and Charles Dickens.

The medieval **9 Chapter House** is adorned with 14th-century frescoes. The King's Council met here between 1257 and 1547. Be sure to look at the floor, one of the finest surviving tiled floors in the country.

The **13 Dean's Yard** is the best spot for a fine view of the massive flying buttresses above.

14 A plaque to Franklin D. Roosevelt is one of the Abbey's very few tributes to a foreigner.

The **15 Grave of the Unknown Warrior,** in memory of the soldiers who lost their lives in both world wars, is near the exit of the abbey.

QUIRKY LONDON

Near the Henry VII chapel, keep an eye open for St. Wilgefort, who was so concerned to protect her chastity that she prayed to God for help and woke up one morning with a full growth of beard.

A BRIEF HISTORY

960 AD Benedictine monastery founded on the site by King Edward and King Dunstan.

1045–65 King Edward the Confessor enlarges the original monastery, erecting a stone church in honor of St. Paul the Apostle. Named "west minster" to distinguish from "east minster" (St. Paul's Cathedral).

1065 The church is consecrated on December 28. Edward doesn't live to see the ceremony.

1161 Following Edward's canonization, his body is moved by Henry III to a more elaborate resting place behind the High Altar. Other medieval kings are later buried around his tomb.

1245–54 Henry III pulls down the abbey and starts again with a new Gothic style influenced by his travels in France. Master mason Henry de Reyns ("of Rheims") constructs the transepts, north front, and rose windows, as well as part of the cloisters and Chapter House.

1269 The new abbey is consecrated and the choir is completed.

1350s Richard II resumes Henry III's plan to rebuild the monastery. Henry V and Henry VII continue as benefactors.

1503 The Lady Chapel is demolished and the foundation stone of Henry VII's Chapel is laid on the site.

1540 The abbey ceases to be used as a monastery.

1560 Elizabeth I refounds the abbey as a Collegiate Church. From this point on it is a "Royal Peculiar," exempt from the jurisdiction of bishops.

1745 The western towers, left unfinished from medieval times, are finally completed, based on a design by Sir Christopher Wren.

1995 Following a 25-year restoration program, saints and allegorical figures are added to the niches on the western towers and around the Great West Door.

PLANNING YOUR DAY

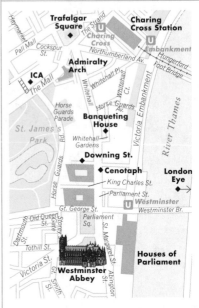

GETTING HERE: The closest Tube stop is Westminster. When you exit the station, walk west along Great George Street, away from the river. Turn left on St. Margaret Street.

CONTACT INFO: ✉ Broad Sanctuary, Westminster SW1 ☎ 020/7222-5152 ⊕ www. westminster-abbey.org.

ADMISSION: **Adults:** Abbey and museum £10. **Family ticket** (2 adults and 2 children): £22. **Children under 11:** free.

HOURS: The abbey is a house of worship. Services may cause changes to the visiting hours on any given day, so be sure to call ahead.
Abbey: Weekdays 9:30-3:45, Wed. until 6, Sat. 9:30-1:45; closes 1 hr after last admission.
Museum: Daily 10:30-4.
Cloisters: Daily 8-6.
College Garden: Apr.-Sept., Tues.-Thurs., 10-6; Oct.-Mar., Tues.-Thurs. 10-4.
Chapter House: Daily 10:30-4.

WHAT'S NEARBY: To make the most of your day, arrive at the abbey early (doors open at 9:30), then make an afternoon visit to the Parliament buildings and finish with a sunset ride on the **London Eye.** Post-flight, take a walk along the fairy-lit Embankment and have dinner (or a drink in the bar) with a view, at the OXO Tower Restaurant at **OXO Tower Wharf** (☎ 020/7803–3888). There's live jazz every evening starting at 7:30 PM.

Please note that overseas visitors can no longer visit **Parliament** during session. However, tours of the buildings are available in August and September. For more information and booking call ☎ 0870/90–3773. Also, it's advisable to prebook tickets for the London Eye. Do this online at www.londoneye.com, or call 0870/990–8883.

IN A HURRY?

If you're pressed for time, concentrate on the following four highlights: the Coronation Chair; Tombs of Queen Elizabeth I and Mary Queen of Scots in the Chapel of Henry VII; Poets' Corner; and Grave of the Unknown Warrior.

THINGS TO KNOW

■ Photography and filming are not permitted anywhere in the abbey.

■ In winter the interior of the abbey can get quite cold; dress accordingly.

■ For an animated history of the museum, join one of the tours that depart from the information desk at 10, 11, 2, and 2:30 daily.

■ Touring the abbey can take half a day, especially in summer, when lines are long.

■ To avoid the crowds, make sure you arrive early. If you're first in line you can enjoy parts of the abbey in relative calm before the mad rush descends.

■ If you want to study up before you go, visit www.westminster-abbey.org, which includes an in-depth history and self-guided tour of the abbey. Otherwise pick up a free leaflet from the information desk.

■ On Sundays the abbey is not open to visitors. Join a service instead. Check the Web site for service times, as well as details of concerts, organ recitals, and special events.

tunately, it arrived so late that Arthur was dead and Catherine had married his brother, Henry VIII. ⊠ *Parliament Sq., Westminster, SW1* Ⓤ *Westminster.*

🕒 **St. Martin-in-the-Fields.** The small medieval chapel that once stood here, probably used by the monks of

Westminster Abbey, was indeed surrounded by fields. These gave way to a grand rebuilding, completed in 1726, and St. Martin's grew to become one of Britain's best-loved churches. James Gibbs's classical temple-with-spire design became a familiar pattern for churches in early Colonial America. Though it seems dwarfed by the surrounding structures of Trafalgar Square, the spire is actually slightly taller than Nelson's Column, which it overlooks. It's a welcome sight for the homeless, who have sought soup and shelter here since 1914. The church is also a haven for music lovers; the internationally known Academy of St. Martin-in-the-Fields was founded here, and a popular program of concerts continues today. The church's musty interior is a wonderful place for music making—but the wooden benches can make it hard to give your undivided attention to the music. St. Martin's is often called the royal parish church, partly because Charles II was christened here. The crypt is a hive of lively activity, with a café and bookshop, plus the **London Brass-Rubbing Centre,** where you can make your own lifesize souvenir knight, lady, or monarch from replica tomb brasses, with metallic waxes, paper, and instructions provided from about £5; and the **Gallery in the Crypt,** showing contemporary work. ⊠ *Trafalgar Sq., Covent Garden, WC2* ☎ *020/7766–1100, 020/7839–8362 evening-concert credit-card bookings* ⊕ *www.stmartin-in-the-fields.org* ⊗ *Church daily 8–8; crypt Mon.–Sat. 10–8 (Brass-Rubbing Centre until 6), Sun. noon–6; box office Mon.–Sat. 10–5* Ⓤ *Charing Cross, Leicester Sq.*

NEED A BREAK? St. Martin's **Café in the Crypt,** with its high-arched brick vault, serves full meals, sandwiches, snacks, traditional tea, and wine. The choice here, which includes vegetarian dishes, is one of the best available for such a central location.

🕒 **Tate Britain.** The gallery, which first opened in 1897, funded by the sugar magnate Sir Henry Tate, is the older sister of Tate Modern, on the south bank of the Thames. Although the building is not quite as awe-inspiring as T.M., there have been updates to the interior, which make it a very user-friendly place to wander and explore great British art over 500 years from the 16th century to now and the latest wackiest Turner prize offerings. The Linbury Galleries on the lower floors stage temporary exhibitions, while the upper floors show the permanent collection. Each room has a theme and in-

FodorśChoice ★

cludes key works by major British artists: Van Dyck, Hogarth, and Reynolds rub shoulders with Rossetti, Sickert, Hockney, and Bacon, for example. Not to be missed is the generous selection of Constable landscapes.

The Turner Bequest consists of J. M. W. Turner's personal collection; he left it to the nation on condition that the works be displayed together. The James Stirling–designed Clore Gallery (to the right of the main gallery) opened in 1987 to fulfill his wish, and it should not be missed. The annual Turner Prize gets artists and nonartists into a frenzy about what art has come to—or where it's going.

You can rent an audio guide with commentaries by curators, experts, and some of the artists themselves. ⊠ *Millbank, Westminster, SW1* ☎ *020/7887–800, 020/7887–8008 recorded information* ⊕ *www.tate. org.uk* ☜ *Free, exhibitions £3–£10* ☉ *Daily 10–5:50* Ⓤ *Pimlico (signposted 5-min walk).*

NEED A BREAK?

Rather than walk back to Pimlico or Victoria, you may be tempted by two eateries right here. The **Café & Espresso Bar** has drinks, sandwiches, and cakes. The **Tate Restaurant** is almost a destination in itself, with its celebrated Rex Whistler murals and a daily fixed-price three-course lunch menu (around £15) and à la carte choices. Ingredients celebrate British produce, such as Cornish crab, Welsh lamb, organic smoked salmon, Stilton cheese, and seasonal vegetables. Vegetarian meals and children's-size portions are available. It's open Monday through Saturday noon to 3 and Sunday noon to 4.

Trafalgar Square. This is the center of London, by dint of a plaque on the corner of the Strand and Charing Cross Road from which distances on U.K. signposts are measured. It's the home of the **National Gallery** and the distinctive landmark, **Nelson's Column.** Great events, such as the Christmas Tree lighting ceremony, New Year's Eve, royal weddings, political protests, and sporting triumphs will always see the crowds gathering in the city's most famous square.

The commanding open space is built on the grand scale demanded by its central position in the capital of an empire that once reached to the farthest corners of the globe. From the 13th century it housed the Royal Mews for the royal hawks and falcons. As falconry became less popular, the space was used for horses stables and barracks until 1830, when John Nash had the buildings torn down as part of his Charing Cross Improvement Scheme. Nash exploited the square's natural incline—it slopes down from north to south—making it a succession of high points from which to look down the imposing carriageways that run dramatically away from it toward the Thames, the Houses of Parliament, and Buckingham Palace. Upon Nash's death, the design baton was passed to Sir Charles Barry and then to Sir Edwin Lutyens.

On the southern point of the square, en route to Whitehall, is the **equestrian statue of Charles I.** After the Civil War and the king's execution, Oliver Cromwell, then the leader of the "Commonwealth," commissioned a scrap dealer to melt the statue. The story goes that Rivett buried it in his garden and made a fortune peddling knickknacks wrought, he claimed, from its metal, only to produce the statue miraculously unscathed after the restoration of the monarchy—and to make more cash reselling it to the authorities. In 1767 Charles II had it placed where it stands today, near the spot where his father was executed in 1649. Each year, on January 30, the day of the king's death, the Royal Stuart Society lays a wreath at the foot of the statue. ⊠ *Trafalgar Sq., Westminster, SW1* Ⓤ *Charing Cross.*

Wellington Barracks. These are the headquarters of the Guards Division, the Queen's five regiments of elite foot guards (Grenadier, Coldstream, Scots, Irish, and Welsh) who protect the sovereign and patrol her palace dressed in tunics of gold-purled scarlet and tall fur "bearskin" helmets of Canadian brown bearskin. If you want to learn more about the guards, or view every kind of toy model soldier, visit the **Guards Museum**; the entrance is next to the Guards Chapel. ⊠ *Wellington Barracks, Birdcage Walk, Westminster, SW1* ☎ *020/7414–3428* 🎫 *£2* ☉ *Daily 10–4; last admission 3:30* Ⓤ *St. James's Park.*

Westminster Abbey See Page 63

Westminster Cathedral. Amid the concrete jungle of Victoria Street lies this remarkable neo-Byzantine find, seat of the Cardinal of Westminster, head of the Roman Catholic Church in Britain, and consequently London's principal Roman Catholic church. Faced with the daunting proximity of Westminster Abbey, the architect, John Francis Bentley, flew in the face of fashion by rejecting neo-Gothic in favor of the Byzantine idiom, which still provides maximum contrast today. The asymmetrical redbrick Byzantine hulk, dating only from 1903, is banded with stripes of Portland stone and abutted by a 273-foot-high campanile at the northwest corner, which you can scale by elevator. The interior is still incomplete, but worth seeing for its brooding mystery and its rich and colorful marble-work. Look out for the stations of the cross (stopping points for prayer or contemplation) by Eric Gill, the beautiful mosaic work on the roof of Holy Souls Chapel, and the striking baldachino—the enormous stone canopy standing over the altar and giant cross in front of it. The nave is the widest in the country and is constructed in green marble, which has a Byzantine connection—it was cut from the same place as the 6th-century St. Sophia's in Istanbul, and was almost confiscated by warring Turks as it traveled across the country. Just inside the main entrance is the tomb of Cardinal Basil Hume, who held the seat for more than 25 years. The Bell tower, containing Big Edward, can be climbed. There's a

FUN FACT

Queen Elizabeth II was the first reigning monarch since the Reformation ever to go inside Westminster Cathedral for a service.

café in the crypt. ⊠ *Ashley Pl., Westminster, SW1* ☏ *020/7798–9055* ⊕ *www.westminstercathedral.org.uk* ⊠ *Tower £2* ☉ *Cathedral daily 7–7. Tower Apr.–Sept., daily 9–5; Oct.–Mar., Thurs.–Sun. 9–5* Ⓤ *Victoria.*

Westminster & Royal London at a Glance

BF 10-5 W–Sun

SIGHTS
Admiralty Arch
Banqueting House
Buckingham Palace
Cabinet War Rooms
Carlton House Terrace
Cenotaph
Changing of the Guard
Houses of Parliament
London Brass-Rubbing
   Centre
Nelson's Column
No. 10 Downing Street
Queen Victoria Memorial
St. John's, Smith Square
St. Margaret's Church
St. Martin-in-the-Fields
Wellington Barracks
Westminster Abbey
Westminster Cathedral

MUSEUMS & GALLERIES
Churchill Museum
Gallery in the Crypt
Guards Museum
Institute of Contemporary
   Arts (ICA)
National Gallery
National Portrait Gallery
Royal Mews
The Queen's Gallery
Tate Britain

PARKS & GARDENS
Birdcage Walk
Horse Guards Parade
The Mall
St. James's Park
Trafalgar Square

WHERE TO STAY (⇨ Ch. 16)

BUDGET LODGING
James & Cartref House
New England Hotel

Vandon House Hotel
Windermere Hotel

MODERATE LODGING
Lime Tree Hotel

EXPENSIVE LODGING
City Inn Westminster
The Goring
Jolly Hotel St. Ermin's
No. 41
The Rubens at the Palace

ARTS & ENTERTAINMENT
   (⇨ Ch. 18)
St. John's, Smith Square,
   concert venue

SHOPPING (⇨ Ch. 19)

GIFTS
National Trust Gift Shop

St. James's & Mayfair

WORD OF MOUTH

"Even if it means a few steps out of your way, strolling through St. James's Park can be a way to get from A to B on some of your days."
—nessundorma

"The Sir John Soane museum is always good for an offbeat place to visit, and the Wallace Collection is also a fantastic place to spend a couple of hours—with lunch or tea and window shopping somewhere on Marylebone Street after."

—trvlgrl

www.fodors.com/forums

ST. JAMES'S & MAYFAIR

Sightseeing
★ ★ ★ ★

Nightlife
★ ★ ★

Dining
★ ★ ★ ★

Lodging
★ ★ ★ ★

Shopping
★ ★ ★ ★

Smart, stylish, and so British, St. James's and Mayfair comprise the heart and soul of London's West End. Walk along Oxford Street at a healthy clip and feel the history of old London and the chic tempo of new London keep step beside you. Along these streets you can also find the greatest concentration of fine hotels, posh department stores, opulent restaurants, swanky galleries, top auction houses, and international corporations—the sense of being somewhere important is all-encompassing in the sparkling streets of St. James's and Mayfair.

What's Here

Architecture buffs and fine-art connoisseurs will want to see the Christopher Wren–designed **St. James's Church** as well as **St. James's Square,** home of the London Library. The well-known quarters for gentlemen's clubs, **Pall Mall** is an excellent example of 18th- and 19th-century patrician architecture and home to **Waterloo Place,** where a number of famous statues have been erected, among them a stunning portrait of Florence Nightingale. An equally regal statue of Franklin D. Roosevelt, a British memorial to the 32nd U.S. President, rises to the occasion in the center of the distinguished **Grosvenor Square** across from the U.S. Embassy.

The **Royal Academy of Arts** is a cultured place to seek solace from swarming nearby Piccadilly Circus. At the opposite end of Piccadilly is another aesthete's lair, the grand home of the Duke of Wellington, **Apsley House** (or Wellington Museum); before it is **Wellington Arch.** Finally, fine-art enthusiasts should save an hour or two for **Hertford House** at **Manchester Square,** which contains the delightful (and not often crowded) **Wal-**

lace Collection, an exhibition of fine art and artifacts collected by four generations of Marquesses of Hertford.

Those for whom shopping is paramount will relish a mosey along **Old Bond Street, South Molton Street, Savile Row,** and **Jermyn Street,** where the most exclusive shops in London can be found. The somewhat overwhelmingly commercialized **Regent Street** is also fun for a few blocks if you fancy popping into the more modern department stores in town. Shoppers and historians alike will enjoy **Fortnum & Mason** at 181 Piccadilly. This old-fashioned fine-foods store feels lifted from another century with ornate murals decorating the walls, glass cabinets and brass fixtures casting a dazzling glow all around, and smiling salespeople tending to your every need (a rarity in London). Another historic shop (or group of shops) in this district is **Burlington Arcade.** Built in 1818 by the Earl of Burlington, this covered royal walkway is one of the most elegant places to purchase fine wares in London.

Finally, St. James's & Mayfair has a fascinating musical and oratorical heritage that spans several centuries. If you visit 25 Brook Street you'll be a guest in the former home of famed baroque composer Friedrich Handel. A painstakingly restored Georgian, the house is now a live-music venue with weekly recitals, as well as a museum of Handel's life, called **Handel House Museum.** At **Hanover Square** you'll come upon the splendid **St. George's Church,** where often during the holidays choral concerts are held. All Souls Church at **Portland Place** is home to innumerable classical concerts broadcast regularly by the BBC. Another notable musical site is No. 3 Savile Row, former headquarters of the Beatles' Apple Records label. If seeing this makes you want to "twist and shout," you might see fit to stop at **Speakers' Corner** in Hyde Park and join the ranks of figures such as Karl Marx, George Orwell, and Marcus Garvey, among others throughout history, who have exercised their right to let off steam in public.

Places to Explore

Apsley House (Wellington Museum). For Hyde Park Corner read "heroes corner"; even in the subway, beneath the turmoil of traffic, the Duke of Wellington's heroic exploits are retold in murals. The years of war against the French, and the subsequent final defeat of Napoléon at the Battle of Waterloo in 1815 made Wellington—Arthur Wellesley—the greatest soldier and statesman in the land. The house is flanked by imposing statues: opposite is the 1828 Decimus Burton **Wellington Arch** with the four-horse chariot of peace as its pinnacle (open to the public as an ex-

FodorsChoice ★

GETTING ORIENTED

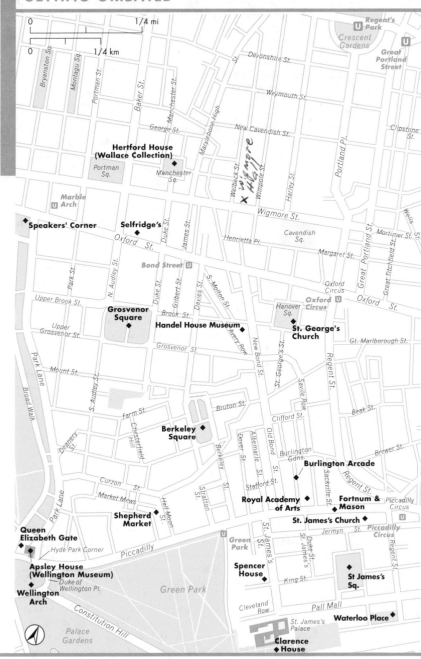

TOP 5 REASONS TO GO

■ **Claridge's Bar:** Unwind with afternoon tea at this art deco gem after a shopping spree in Mayfair.

■ **Fortnum & Mason:** Raid the chocolate counter—then raid the coffee counter across from it for a dose of exotic java to pair with your sweets.

■ **Oxford Street:** Wander up and down this always interesting street; in winter, bask in the brilliance of more than 250,000 light bulbs along 10 miles of cables used to decorate the street for the holidays.

■ **Royal Academy of Arts:** Visit the Summer Exhibition, a breathtaking affair showcasing some of the best sculpture and painting in the art world.

■ **Green Park:** Stroll along leafy paths through the undulating grass and trees, a lovely escape from the congestion of central London.

FEELING PECKISH?

Pret A Manger on busy Piccadilly, opposite the Royal Academy, has windows to watch the world go by. It's one of a high-standard chain of cafés that specializes in a small but gourmet selection of sandwiches and pastries for breakfast and lunch. Get there early if you want to beat the office crowd stampede. There's great coffee, too.

Yo! Sushi (⊠ Selfridges Food Hall, Oxford St.) is the healthiest (and perhaps least expensive) option for a quick bite in Mayfair. The place seats up to 45 people and serves fresh, reasonably priced sushi and—for those who aren't keen on raw fish—a substantial menu of hot foods as well. It's a fun stopover, too, inside one of the most glamorous shops in central London.

GETTING HERE

There are four Tube stops on the Central Line that will leave you smack in the center of these neighborhoods: Marble Arch, Bond Street (also Jubilee Line), Oxford Circus (also Victoria and Bakerloo lines), and Tottenham Court Road (also Northern Line). You can also take the Piccadilly or Bakerloo Line to the Piccadilly Circus Tube stop, the Piccadilly to the Hyde Park Corner stop, or the Piccadilly, Victoria, or Jubilee lines to the Green Park stop.

The best bus is the 8, which circles around via New Bond Street to Oxford Street, and skirts the eastern edge of Green Park to Grosvenor Place.

MAKING THE MOST OF YOUR TIME

Reserve at least a day to see the sites in St. James's and Mayfair, as this is one of London's most densely packed, dynamic districts. The only areas to avoid are the most popular commuter Tube stations at rush hour. At all costs, stay away from Oxford Circus around 5 PM, when rushing commuters can, at times, resemble an East African wildebeest migration. Other stations to avoid include Bond Street and Tottenham Court Road.

A BRIEF HISTORY

The name Mayfair derives from the 15-day May fair that was once held in the web of small streets known as Shepherd Market, but was brought to an end by the upper classes who lived there and felt it was drawing undesirables to their polished part of town. The beautiful St. James Park, meanwhile, stands as an idyllic emblem of this elite past: it's the oldest royal park in London and all that remains of the royal hunting grounds that once traversed the city to Islington, Marylebone, and Hampstead. Henry VIII acquired the park in 1532 for a deer park; he also built the neighboring, Tudor brick St. James Palace. Another historic site, Lancaster House, was built for the Duke of York in the 1820s, but is most famous as the locale of the 1978 conference that ended white rule in the African nation that is now Zimbabwe.

The equally illustrious Clarence House, built in 1825 for the Duke of Clarence (later William IV), is now the home of Prince Charles and Camilla Parker Bowles. And Spencer House, one of the most stunning 18th-century mansions in London, is home to the ancestors of the late Princess Diana of Wales. On a more somber note, if you follow the signs through Hyde Park you can find Marble Arch, once the city's gallows and now just a massive yet graceful arch that marks the merge of Bayswater Road and Oxford Street.

hibition area and viewing platform). Just behind Wellington Arch, and cast from captured French guns, the legendary **Achilles** statue points the way with thrusting shield to the ducal mansion from the tip of Hyde Park. Next to Apsley House is the elaborate gateway to the park, designed and built by Burton at the same time as the Wellington Arch.

Once known as No. 1, London, because it was the first and grandest house at the old toll gate from Knightsbridge village, this was long celebrated as the best address in town. Built by Robert Adam and later refaced and extended, this housed the Duke of Wellington from 1817 until his death in 1852. As the Wellington Museum, it has been faithfully restored, complete with Wellesley's uniforms, weapons, and his porcelain and plate collections (given by the grateful who were liberated by the Duke from the rule of the French). His extensive art collection includes Dutch Old Masters, Velázquez, Goya, and Rubens, as well as, ironically, portraits of his adversary Napoléon Bonaparte. The free audio guide highlights the most noted works and the superb decor. The most stunning is the Waterloo Gallery, where the annual banquet for officers who fought beside Wellington was held. With its heavily sculpted and gilded

A MUST-SEE AT THE WELLINGTON MUSEUM

Unmissable, in every sense (and considered rather too athletic for the time), is the gigantic Canova statue of a nude (but fig-leafed) Napoléon, which presides over the grand staircase that leads to the many elegant reception rooms.

ceiling, its feast of Old Master paintings on red damask walls, and commanding gray candelabra, it's a veritable orgy of opulence. There are commemorative weekends on either side of Waterloo Day, and the day itself when entry to the house is free, with special events and costumed guides. Telephone or check the Web site for details. ✉ *Hyde Park Corner* 🕾 *020/7499-5676* ⊕ *www.english-heritage.org.uk* ⊙ *Apr.–Nov., Tues.–Sun. 10–5; Dec.–Mar., Tues.–Sun. 10–4. Also open bank holiday Mon.* 🎟 *£4.95* Ⓤ *Hyde Park Corner.*

Bond Street. This world-class shopping haunt is divided into northern "New" (1710) and southern "Old" (1690) halves. On New Bond Street you'll find **Sotheby's,** the world-famous auction house, at No. 35. But there are other ways to flirt with financial ruin on Old Bond Street: the mirror-lined Chanel store, the vainglorious marble acres of Gianni Versace, and the boutique of the more sophisticated Gucci, plus Tiffany's British outpost and art dealers Colnaghi, Léger, Thos. Agnew, and Marlborough Fine Arts. **Cork Street,** which parallels the top half of Old Bond Street, is where London's top dealers in contemporary art have their galleries—where you're welcome to browse. Ⓤ *Bond St., Green Park.*

Burlington Arcade. Perhaps the finest of Mayfair's enchanting covered shopping alleys is the second oldest in London, built in 1819 for Lord Cavendish, to stop the hoi polloi from throwing rubbish into his garden at Burlington House, which is behind the arcade. It's still patrolled by top-hatted officials, who preserve decorum by preventing you from singing, running, or carrying open umbrellas. The arcade is also the main link between the Royal Academy of Arts and its extended galleries at 6 Burlington Gardens. ✉ *Piccadilly, Mayfair, W1* Ⓤ *Green Park, Piccadilly Circus.*

Clarence House. The London home of Queen Elizabeth the Queen Mother for nearly 50 years, Clarence House is now the Prince of Wales's residence. The Regency mansion was built by John Nash for the Duke of Clarence, who found living in St. James's Palace quite unsuitable. Since then it has remained a royal home for princesses, dukes, and duchesses, including the present monarch, Queen Elizabeth, after her marriage. The rooms have been sensitively preserved as the Queen Mother chose, with the addition of many works of art from the Royal Collection. You'll find it less palace, and more home (for the Prince and his sons William and Harry) with informal family pictures and comfortable sofas. The tour (by timed ticket entry only) is of the ground-floor rooms and includes the Lancaster Room, so called because of the marble chimneypiece presented by Lancaster county to the newly married Princess Elizabeth and

---

BERKELEY SQUARE

As anyone who's heard the old song knows, the name rhymes with "starkly." Not many of its original mid-18th-century houses are left, but look at Nos. 42–46 (especially No. 44, which the architectural historian Sir Nikolaus Pevsner thought London's finest terraced house) and Nos. 49–52 to get some idea of why it was once London's top address—not that it's in the least humble now. Snob nightclub Annabel's is one current resident. Berkeley Sq., Mayfair, W1 Ⓤ Green Park.

Royal Attractions

THE QUEEN AND THE ROYAL family attend approximately 400 functions a year, and if you want to know what they are doing on any given date, turn to the *Court Circular*, printed in the major London dailies, or check out the royal family Web site, ⊕ www.royal.gov.uk, for the latest pictures and events. Trooping the Colour is usually held on the second Saturday in June, to celebrate the Queen's official birthday. This spectacular parade begins when she leaves Buckingham Palace in her carriage and rides down the Mall to arrive at Horse Guards Parade at 11 exactly. To watch, just line up along the Mall with your binoculars!

Another time you can catch the Queen in all her regalia is when she and the Duke of Edinburgh ride in state to Westminster to open the Houses of Parliament. The famous gilded coach, such an icon of fairy-tale glamour, parades from Buckingham Palace,

escorted by the brilliantly uniformed Household Cavalry—on a clear day, it's to be hoped, for this ceremony takes place in late October or early November, depending on the exigencies of Parliament.

But perhaps the most relaxed, least formal time to see the Queen is during Royal Ascot, held at the racetrack near Windsor Castle—a short train ride out of London—usually during the third week of June (Tuesday–Friday). After several races, the Queen invariably walks down to the paddock on a special path, greeting race goers as she proceeds. Americans wishing to reserve a seat in the Royal Enclosure should apply to the **American Embassy** (✉ 24 Grosvenor Sq., Mayfair, London W1) before the end of March. But remember: you must be sponsored by two guests who have attended Ascot at least seven times before!

the Duke of Edinburgh. Like Buckingham Palace, Clarence House is open only in summer, and tickets must be booked in advance. ✉ *The Mall, St. James's, SW1* ☎ *020/7766–7303* ⊕ *www.royal.gov.uk* ✉ *£6* ☉ *Aug.–mid-Oct.* Ⓤ *Green Park.*

🕐 **Handel House Museum.** The former home of the composer, where he lived for more than 30 years until his death in 1759, is a celebration of his genius. It's the first museum in London solely dedicated to one composer, and that is made much of with room settings in the contemporary fine Georgian style. You can linger over original manuscripts (there are more to be seen in the British Library) and gaze at portraits, accompanied by live music—if the adjoining music rooms are being used by musicians in rehearsal. Some of the composer's most famous pieces were created here, including *Messiah* and *Music for the Royal Fireworks*. To hear a live concert here—there's a busy evening program of jazz and chamber music—is to imagine the atmosphere of rehearsals and "salon" music in its day. Handel House makes a perfect cultural pit-stop after shopping on nearby Bond and Oxford streets, and if you come on Saturday, there are free art and music activities for kids. The museum occupies both No. 25 and the adjoining house, where life in Georgian London is displayed in exhibit space (another musical star, Jimi Hendrix, lived here for a brief time in the 1960s, indicated by a blue plaque outside the house and a small exhibition of photos of the star). Occasional tours of the flat, currently administrative offices and not usually open to the public, can be arranged. Phone or check the Web site for details. ⊠ *25 Brook St., Mayfair, W1* ☎ *020/ 7495–1685* ⊕ *www.handelhouse.org* ✉ *£5* ✆ *Tues.–Sat. 10–6, Thurs. 10–8, Sun. noon–6* Ⓤ *Bond St.*

Grosvenor Square. This square (pronounced "*Grove*-na") was laid out in 1725–31 and is as desirable an address today as it was then. Americans certainly thought so—from John Adams, the second president, who as ambassador lived at No. 38, to Dwight D. Eisenhower, whose wartime headquarters was at No. 20. Now the ugly '50s block of the U.S. Embassy occupies the entire west side, and a British memorial to Franklin D. Roosevelt stands in the center. The little brick chapel used by Eisenhower's men during World War II, the 1730 Grosvenor Chapel, stands a couple of blocks south of the square on South Audley Street, with the entrance to pretty **St. George's Gardens** to its left. Across the gardens is the headquarters of the English Jesuits as well as the society-wedding favorite, the mid-19th-century Church of the Immaculate Conception, known as Farm Street because that's the name of the street on which it stands. ⊠ *Mayfair, W1* Ⓤ *Bond St.*

★ **Jermyn Street.** This is where the gentleman purchases his traditional fashion accessories. He buys his shaving sundries and hip flask from Geo. F. Trumper; briar pipe from Astley's; scent from Floris (for women, too—both the Prince of Wales and his mother are Floris customers), whose interiors are exceedingly historic and beautiful, or Czech & Speake; shirts from Turnbull & Asser; and deerstalkers and panamas from Bates the Hatter. Don't forget the regal cheeses from Paxton & Whitfield (founded in 1740 and a legend among dairies). Shop your way east along Jermyn Street, and you're practically in Piccadilly Circus. ⊠ *St. James's, SW1* Ⓤ *Piccadilly Circus.*

Marble Arch. John Nash's 1827 arch, moved to its present location in 1851, stands amid the traffic whirlpool where Bayswater Road segues into Oxford Street, and where Park Lane links up to the Wellington Arch at Hyde Park Corner. Search the sidewalk on the traffic island opposite the cinema to find the stone plaque that marks (roughly) the place where the Tyburn Tree stood for four centuries, until 1783. This was London's central gallows, a huge wooden structure with hanging accommodations for 21. Hanging days were holidays, the spectacle supposedly functioning as a crime deterrent. Oranges, gingerbread, and gin were sold, alongside "personal favors," to vast, rowdy crowds, and the condemned, dressed in finery for his special moment, was treated more as hero than as villain. Cross over (or under—there are signs to help in the labyrinth) to the northeastern corner of Hyde Park to Speakers' Corner. ⊠ *Park La., Mayfair, W1* Ⓤ *Marble Arch.*

NEED A
BREAK?

Sotheby's Café (✉ 34–35 New Bond St., Mayfair, W1) is a cut above the usual street café, as you would expect of this classy auction house on Bond Street. The lobster club sandwich is delicious, although not cheap.

Pall Mall. Like *the* Mall, Pall Mall rhymes with "shall" and derives its name from the old French mallet and ball game *paille-maille*. It was popular with English royals and aristocrats in the 17th and 18th centuries, particularly Charles II after his exile in France. To prevent disruption of the game by dust from the many passing carriages, the street was properly laid in 1660 and renamed Catherine Street (after Charles's queen, Catherine of Braganza), although it was always better known by the name of the game. Pall Mall was *very* fashionable, with No. 79 one of its livelier addresses, since Charles's gregarious mistress, Nell Gwyn, lived there.

The two best-known buildings, by James Barry, are the **Travellers' Club** and the **Reform Club,** both representatives of the upper-class gentleman's retreat that made St. James's the club land of London. The Reform is the most famous club of all, thanks partly to Jules Verne's Phileas Fogg, who accepted the around-the-world-in-80-days bet in its smoking room and was thus soon qualified to join the Travellers'. The RAC Club (for Royal Automobile Club, but it's never known as that), with its marble swimming pool, and the Oxford and Cambridge Club complete the Pall Mall quota; there are other, even older establishments—Brooks's, the Carlton, Boodles, and White's (founded in 1736, the oldest of all)—in St. James's Street around the corner, alongside *the* gentleman's bespoke shoemaker, Lobb's, and, at No. 6, *the* hatter, James Lock, which has one of the most historic store facades in the city—you half expect Lord Byron or Anthony Trollope to walk out the door. Waterloo Place, around the corner, is a continuation of this gentleman's quarter. ✉ *St. James's, SW1* Ⓤ *Piccadilly Circus.*

Piccadilly Circus. Although it may *seem* like a "circus" with its traffic and the camera-clickers clustered around the steps of **Eros,** the name refers to the five major roads that radiate from it. The origins of "Piccadilly" are from the humble tailor on the Strand named Robert Baker who sold picadils—a collar ruff all the rage in courtly circles—and built a house with the proceeds. Snobs dubbed his new-money mansion Piccadilly Hall, and the name stuck.

Eros, London's favorite statue and symbol of the *Evening Standard* newspaper, is not in fact the Greek god of erotic love at all, but the angel of Christian charity, commissioned in 1893 from the young sculptor Alfred Gilbert as a memorial to the philanthropic Earl of Shaftesbury (the angel's bow and arrow are a sweet allusion to the earl's name). It cost Gilbert £7,000 to cast the statue he called his "missile of kindness" in the novel medium of aluminum, and because he was paid only £3,000, he promptly went bankrupt and fled the country. (Not to worry—he was knighted in the end.) Beneath the modern bank of neon advertisements are some of the most elegant Edwardian-era buildings in town. ✉ *St. James's, W1* Ⓤ *Piccadilly Circus.*

Regent Street. This curvaceous thoroughfare was conceived by John Nash and his patron, the Prince Regent—the future George IV—as a kind of ultracatwalk from the Prince's palace, Carlton House, to Regent's Park (then called Marylebone Park). The section between Piccadilly and Oxford Street was to be called the Quadrant and lined with colonnaded shops purveying "articles of fashion and taste," in a big PR exercise to improve London's image as the provincial cousin of smarter European capitals. The scheme was never fully implemented, and what there was fell into such disrepair that, early this century, Aston Webb (of the Mall route) collaborated on the redesign you see today. It's still a major shopping street. Hamleys, the gigantic toy emporium, is fun; and since 1875 there has been Liberty, which originally imported silks from the East then diversified to other Asian goods, and is now best known for its "Liberty print" cottons, its jewelry department, and—still—its high-class Asian imports. The mock-Tudor interior, with stained glass and beams taken from battleships, is worth a look. ✉ *Mayfair, W1* Ⓤ *Piccadilly Circus, Oxford Circus.*

★ **Royal Academy of Arts.** Burlington House was built in the Palladian style for the Earl of Burlington around 1720, and it's one of the few surviving mansions from that period. The chief occupant today is the Royal Academy of Arts (RA), and a statue of one of its famed members, Sir Joshua Reynolds, with artist's palette in hand, is prominent in the piazza of light stone and fountains by Michael Hopkins. It's a tranquil, elegant space for sculpture exhibits, and has a café with outdoor tables in summer. Further exhibition space has been afforded with the opening of 6 Burlington Gardens, the old Museum of Mankind, reached through the elegant walkway of Burlington Arcade. An Armani retrospective proved an equally stylish choice for the opening exhibition in autumn 2003. The collection of works by Academicians past and present as well as its most prized piece, the *Taddeo Tondo* (a sculpted disk) by Michelangelo of the Madonna and Child, on display in the Sackler Wing. The RA has an active program of temporary exhibitions; hugely successful exhibitions here have included Sensation (1997), Monet in the 20th Century (1999), Van Dyck (1999), and the Genius of Rome (2001). Every June, the RA puts on the **Summer Exhibition,** a huge and always surprising collection of sculpture and painting by Royal Academicians and a plethora of other artists working today. ✉ *Burlington House, Piccadilly, Mayfair, W1* ☏ *020/7300–8000, 020/7300–5760 recorded information* ⊕ *www.royalacademy.org.uk* ✉ *Admission varies according to exhibition* ☉ *Sat.–Thurs. 10–6, Fri. 10–10* Ⓤ *Piccadilly Circus, Green Park.*

NEED A BREAK?

The Royal Academy Restaurant has hot dishes at lunchtime, very good vegetarian options, and an extensive salad selection that is inexpensive for such a posh location. It's open weekdays 10–5:30, with a dinner menu on Friday from 6:15 to 10:30.

St. James's Church. Set back from the street behind a courtyard, the church is filled most days with an antiques and crafts market. Completed in 1684, this was the last of Sir Christopher Wren's London churches and his own favorite. It contains one of Grinling Gibbons's finest works, an ornate limewood reredos (the screen behind the altar). The organ is a survivor of Whitehall Palace and was brought here in 1691. A 1940 bomb scored a direct hit here, but the church has been completely restored, albeit with a fiberglass spire. It's a lively place, offering all manner of lectures and concerts. The courtyard hosts different markets: on Tuesday antiques and small collectibles; Wednesday to Saturday arts and crafts. ✉ *Piccadilly, St. James's, W1* ☎ *020/7734–4511, 020/7381–0441 for concert program and tickets* ⊕ *www.st-james-piccadilly.org* Ⓤ *Piccadilly Circus, Green Park.*

St. James's Palace. With its solitary sentry posted at the gate, this surprisingly small palace of Tudor brick was once a home for many British sovereigns, including the first Elizabeth and Charles I, who spent his last night here before his execution. Today it's the working office of another Charles—the Prince of Wales. The front door actually debouches right onto the street, but he always uses a back entrance. Royals who live within the palace are Princess Alexandra and her husband, Sir Angus Ogilvy. Matters to ponder as you look (you can't go in): the palace was named after a hospital for women lepers, which stood here during the 11th century; Henry VIII had it built; foreign ambassadors to Britain are still accredited to the Court of St. James's even though it has rarely been a primary royal residence; and the present Queen made her first speech here. Friary Court out front is a splendid setting for Trooping the Colour, part of the Queen's official birthday celebrations. Everyone loves to take a snap of the scarlet-coated guardsman standing sentinel outside the imposing Tudor gateway. Note that the changing of the guard at St. James's Palace only occurs on days when the guard at Buckingham Palace is changed. See entry for Buckingham Palace for details. ✉ *Friary Court, St. James's, SW1* ⊕ *www.royal.gov.uk* Ⓤ *Green Park.*

St. James's Square. One of London's oldest and leafiest squares was also the most snobbish address of all when it was laid out around 1670, with 14 resident dukes and earls installed by 1720. Since 1841, No. 14—one of the several 18th-century residences spared by World War II bombs—has housed the **London Library,** founded by Thomas Carlyle, and which, with its million or so volumes, is considered the best private humanities library in the land. You can go in and read the famous authors' complaints in the comments book—but not the famous authors' books, unless you become a member. ✉ *St. James's, SW1* ⊕ *www.londonlibrary.co. uk* Ⓤ *Piccadilly Circus.*

★ **Selfridges.** With its row of massive Ionic columns, this huge store was opened three years after Harry Gordon Selfridge came to London from Chicago in 1906. Now British-run, Selfridges rivals Harrods in size and stock, and it's finally rivaling its glamour, too, since investing in major face-lift operations. (For more on Selfridges, see Chapter 19, Shopping.) ✉ *400 Oxford St., Mayfair, W1* ☎ *020/7629–1234* ⊕ *www. selfridges.co.uk* ⊘ *Weekdays 10–8, Sat. 9:30–8, Sun. 11:30–6* Ⓤ *Marble Arch, Bond St.*

★ **Spencer House.** Ancestral abode of the Spencers—Diana, Princess of Wales's family—this great mansion is perhaps the finest example of 18th-century elegance, on a domestic scale, extant in London. Superlatively restored by Lord Rothschild, the house was built in 1766 by Palladian architect John Vardy for the first Earl Spencer, heir to the first Duchess of Marlborough. Henry Holland, who was employed by the Prince Regent, added modifications. The gorgeous Doric facade, its pediment adorned with classical statues, makes immediately clear Earl Spencer's passion for the Grand Tour and the classical antiquities of the past. Inside, James "Athenian" Stuart decorated the gilded State Rooms, including the Painted Room, the first completely neoclassical room in Europe. The most ostentatious part of the house (and the Spencers did not shrink from ostentation—witness the £40,000 diamond shoe buckles the first countess proudly wore) is the florid bow window of the Palm Room: covered with stucco palm trees, it conjures up both ancient Palmyra and modern Miami Beach. The garden, of Henry Holland design, has been restored with planting of the time. Both the house and garden can be seen by guided tour only in limited numbers, so book in advance. ✉ *27 St. James's Pl., St. James's, SW1* ☏ *020/7499–8620* ⊕ *www.spencerhouse.co.uk* ☏ *£9* ⊙ *Sept.–Dec. and Feb.–July, Sun. 10:45–4:45; guided tour leaves approx. every 25 min; tickets on sale Sun. at 10:30. Garden: late May–July, separate charge and tour* Ⓤ *Green Park.*

★ ㉚ **Wallace Collection.** Assembled by four generations of Marquesses of Hertford and given to the nation by the widow of Sir Richard Wallace, illegitimate son of the fourth, this collection of art and artifacts is important, exciting, undervisited—and free. As at the Frick Collection in New York, Hertford House itself is part of the show: the fine late-18th-century mansion, built for the Duke of Manchester, contains a basement floor with educational activities, several galleries, and a courtyard, covered by a glass roof, with exhibit space and an upscale restaurant.

The first marquess was a patron of Sir Joshua Reynolds, the second bought Hertford House, the third—a flamboyant socialite—favored Sèvres porcelain and 17th-century Dutch painting; but it was the eccentric fourth marquess who, from his self-imposed exile in Paris, really built the collection, snapping up Bouchers, Fragonards, Watteaus, and Lancrets for a song (the French Revolution having rendered them dangerously unfashionable), augmenting these with furniture and sculpture and sending his son Richard out to do the deals. With 30 years of practice behind him, Richard Wallace continued acquiring treasures after his father's death, scouring Italy for majolica and Renaissance gold, then moving most of it to London. Look for Rembrandt's portrait of his son, the Rubens landscape, Gainsborough and Romney portraits, the Van Dycks and Canalettos, the French rooms, and of course the porcelain. The highlight is Fragonard's *The Swing,* which conjures up the 18th-century's let-them-eat-cake frivolity better than any other painting around. Don't forget to smile back at Frans Hals's *Laughing Cavalier* in the Big Gallery or pay your respects to Thomas Sully's enchanting *Queen Victoria,* which resides in a rouge-pink salon (just to the right of the main entrance). There is a fine collection of armor (which you can try on for size) and weaponry in the basement as a break from all the upstairs gentility. ⊠ *Hertford House, Manchester Sq., Mayfair, W1* ☏ *020/7563–9500* ⊕ *www.wallacecollection.org* ⊡ *Free, charge for special exhibitions* ⊘ *Daily 10–5* Ⓤ *Bond St.*

NEED A BREAK?

Café Bagatelle brings the outside in, in the elegant setting of the glass-roofed sculpture garden of the Wallace Collection. It's a little taste of France with a sophisticated lunch menu to match the ambience. If you don't want to indulge your budget too much you can just linger over coffee or afternoon tea, and drink in the surroundings. It's open daily 10–4:30.

Wellington Arch. Opposite the Duke of Wellington's mansion, Apsley House, this majestic stone arch surveys the busy traffic rushing around Hyde Park Corner. Designed by Decimus Burton and built in 1828, it was created as a grand entrance to the west side of London and echoes the design of that other landmark gate, Marble Arch. Both were triumphal arches commemorating Britain's victory against France in the Napoleonic Wars, and both were moved after their construction to ease the Victorian traffic situation. The Wellington Arch was constructed at the same time as the Apsley Gate (also Burton's design); you'll see the same highly ornamental green gates within the Wellington Arch. Atop the building, the Angel of Peace descends on the quadriga, or four-horse chariot of war. This replaced the Duke of Wellington on his horse, which was considered too large and hence moved to army barracks in Aldershot. A step inside the arch reveals the stories behind the building and statue, and explores other great arches across the world. Without doubt, the highlight is to walk around the top of the arch and enjoy the brilliant panoramas over the park, including glimpses into the private gardens of Buckingham Palace. In summer, Wellington Arch is the starting point for English Heritage themed walks. ⊠ *Hyde Park Corner, Mayfair, SW1* ☏ *020/7930–2726* ⊕ *www.english-heritage.org.uk* ⊡ *£3* ⊘ *Apr.–Oct., Wed.–Sun. 10–5; Nov.–Mar., Wed.–Sun. 10–4* Ⓤ *Hyde Park Corner.*

St. James's & Mayfair at a Glance

SIGHTS		WHERE TO EAT (⇨ Ch. 15)
All Souls Church	Royal Academy of Arts	MODERATE DINING
Clarence House	Wallace Collection	Bellamy's, *French*
London Library	PARKS & GARDENS	Cafe at Sotheby's,
Marble Arch	Green Park	*Afternoon Tea*
St. James's Church	Grosvenor Square	Momo, *North African*
St. James's Palace	Pall Mall	Patisserie Valerie at Sagne,
Spencer House	Piccadilly Circus	*Afternoon Tea*
Wellington Arch	Portland Place	Veeraswamy, *Anglo-Indian*
MUSEUMS & GALLERIES	St. George's Gardens	The Wolseley, *Austrian*
Apsley House (Wellington Museum)	St. James's Park	EXPENSIVE DINING
	St. James's Square	Angela Hartnett's Menu,
Handel House Museum	Speakers' Corner	*Contemporary*
	Waterloo Place	

Brown's, *Afternoon Tea*
Claridge's, *Afternoon Tea*
Fortnum & Mason,
    Afternoon Tea
Gordon Ramsay at
    Claridge's, *French*
Greenhouse, *Contemporary*
Le Caprice, *Contemporary*
Le Gavroche, *French*
Locanda Locatelli, *Italian*
L'Oranger, *French*
Mirabelle, *French*
Nobu, *Japanese*
The Ritz, *Afternoon Tea/*
    Continental
The Square, *French*
Sketch: Gallery,
    Contemporary

WHERE TO STAY (⇨ Ch. 16)

MODERATE LODGING
22 York Street
Best Western Shaftesbury
Bryanston
Durrants

EXPENSIVE LODGING
22 Jermyn Street
Brown's
Chesterfield Mayfair
Claridge's
The Connaught
The Dorchester
Dukes
Le Meridien Piccadilly
The Leonard
Marriott Park Lane
The Metropolitan
No. 5 Maddox Street
Park Lane Sheraton
The Ritz
The Stafford

PUBS & NIGHTLIFE
    (⇨ Ch. 17)
American Bar, *bar*
Claridge's Bar, *bar*
Dover Street Restaurant &
Jazz Bar, *jazz & blues*
Hush, *bar*
Late Lounge @ Cocoon,
    bar
The Running Horse, *pub*
Ye Grapes, *pub*

ARTS & ENTERTAINMENT
    (⇨ Ch. 18)
ICA Cinema, *film*
St. James's Church, *concert*
    venue

SHOPPING (⇨ Ch. 19)

DEPARTMENT STORES
Debenhams
Fenwick
John Lewis
Liberty
Marks & Spencer
Selfridges

MARKETS & MALLS
Bond Street
Burlington Arcade
Jermyn Street
Regent Street
Savile Row
Shepherd Market
South Molton Street

ACCESSORIES
Connolly
James Lock & Co. Ltd
Mulberry
Swaine, Adeney, Brigg

ANTIQUES
Grays Antique Market

ART GALLERIES & CRAFTS
Colefax & Fowler
Linley

AUCTIONS
Sotheby's

BOOKS
Bernard J. Shapero Rare
Books
Hatchards
Maggs Brothers Ltd
Simon Finch Rare
    Books Ltd
Waterstone's

CLOTHING
Browns
Dover Street Market
Favourbrook
Gieves and Hawkes
Jigsaw
Kilgour, French & Stanbury
Nicole Farhi
Ozwald Boateng

Please Mum
Rigby & Peller
Thomas Pink
Turnbull & Asser
Vivienne Westwood

FOOD
Berry Bros. & Rudd
Charbonnel et Walker
Fortnum & Mason
Paxton & Whitfield

GIFTS
Past Times

HOUSEHOLD ITEMS/
FURNITURE
Paul Smith

JEWELRY
Asprey
Garrard
Wright & Teague

MUSIC
HMV

PERFUME/COSMETICS
Floris

SHOES
John Lobb
Rupert Sanderson

STATIONERY & GRAPHIC
ARTS
Smythson of Bond Street

TOYS
Armoury of St. James's

3

Soho &
Covent Garden

WORD OF MOUTH

"The main business for buskers [in Covent Garden] is in the daytime, when the shops and stalls are open. The area is full of interesting-looking shops . . . . West from the piazza, King Street takes you towards Leicester Square via New Row to St. Martin's Lane, but before you cross over towards Charing Cross Road, turn left and look for Goodman's Court for echoes of Victorian back alleys."
—PatrickLondon

SOHO & COVENT GARDEN

Sightseeing
★ ★ ★

Nightlife
★ ★ ★ ★

Dining
★ ★ ★ ★

Lodging
★ ★

Shopping
★ ★ ★

Once a red-light district, the Soho of today delivers more "grown-up" than "adult" entertainment. Its theaters, restaurants, pubs, and clubs merge with the first-run cinemas of Leicester Square and the venerable venues (Royal and English National Operas) of Covent Garden to create the mega-entertainment district known as the West End. During the day, Covent Garden's historic piazza is packed with shoppers and sightseers, while Soho reverts to the business side of its lively, late-night scene—ad agencies, media, film distributors, actors, agents, and casting agents all looking for each other.

What's Here

This is one of London's oldest districts. The streets turn and wind, or end abruptly in blank walls, and it's easy to lose your sense of direction and get lost. Even Londoners carry local maps they consult now and then. But having what locals would call "a good mooch around," is half the fun.

Unless you're involved in the media and movie business or looking to buy some fruit and vegetables at the **Berwick Street Market** (Shopping, Chapter 19), Soho is more of a nighttime entertainment district than a place for strolling and sightseeing. If you like theater, head for the half-price ticket kiosk in **Leicester Square** early; browse a bit in the antiquarian booksellers along tiny **Cecil Court,** between Charing Cross Road and St. Martin's Lane; then aim for **Cleopatra's Needle** on Victoria Embankment near Embankment Station. From there you can ferret your way to the Strand through the small 18th- and early-19th-century lanes, passing the **Adam Houses** along the way.

The Savoy, just off the strand in its own little court is a good place to have a posh (and expensive) cream tea or a cocktail in the American Bar. **Somerset House** is just beyond, after the intersection with a half-circular road, the Aldwych. The **Courtauld Institute Gallery** and its shop are just under the Aldwych's archway. Once you've gone through the entry, a huge 18th-century piazza opens out. The former government buildings around it, built for George III, have only been opened to the public since the Millennium and now house several good museums. It's lovely to stop here for a snack or a tea in warm weather and watch London children playing in the new fountains. In winter an outdoor skating rink is set up.

Covent Garden starts north of the Strand. Drury Lane intersects the middle of Aldwych, passing one of London's oldest playhouses, **Theatre Royal, Drury Lane.** If you take a right onto Russell Street you come to the corner of Bow Street, one of the area's best intersections for things to do. Standing on the corner, you'll be within about 50 paces of **Bow Street Magistrates' Court,** the **Royal Opera House,** the **Theatre Museum,** and, when it reopens in late 2007, **London's Transport Museum.** You'll also be in sight of the Covent Garden Piazza, bustling with tourists and shoppers and loads of ways to spend your money.

It's likely that entertainers will be regaling the crowds in front of **St. Paul's Church,** known as the actor's church, on the west end of the market. They may look like ordinary buskers, but this is hallowed ground—the first Punch and Judy show was performed here—and they've had to pass strict auditions to be licensed. If they make you smile, don't forget to leave a coin.

North of Long Acre, catercorner to the Tube station, and closed to traffic halfway down, is **Neal Street,** one of Covent Garden's liveliest and most youthful pedestrian shopping areas. Here you can buy everything you never knew you needed—apricot tea, sitars, vintage aviators' jackets, silk kimonos, Alvar Aalto vases, halogen desk lamps, shoes with heels lower than toes, collapsible top hats, and all the clubbing gear a teenager could wish for.

Off Neal Street, on Earlham Street, is **Thomas Neal's**—a new, upscale, designer clothing and housewares mall named after the founder (in 1693) of the star-shape cobbled junction of tiny streets nearby, called **Seven Dials**—a surprisingly residential enclave, with lots going on behind the tenement-style warehouse facades.

On Shorts Gardens, off Neal Street, is **Neal's Yard** (note the comical, water-operated wooden clock), originally just a whole-foods wholesaler and now an entire holistic village, with therapy rooms, an organic bakery and dairy, a great vegetarian café, and a medical herbalist's shop reminiscent of a medieval apothecary.

Places to Explore

The Adam Houses. All that remains to hint at what was once a regal riverfront row of houses are a few of the surrounding buildings, but such is

GETTING ORIENTED

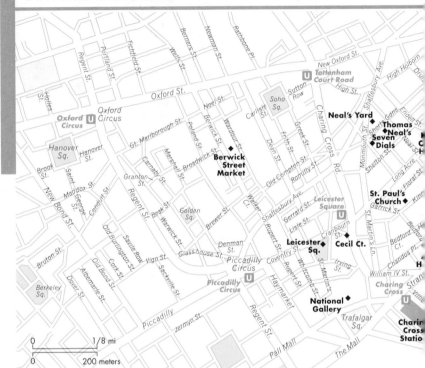

GETTING THERE	TOP 5 REASONS TO GO
Take any train to the Piccadilly Circus station (on the Piccadilly and Bakerloo lines or Leicester Square and Northern lines for Soho). Get off at Covent Garden on the Piccadilly Line for Covent Garden and Embankment (Bakerloo, Northern, District and Circle lines) or Charing Cross (Northern, Bakerloo and main railway lines) for the area south of the Strand.	■ **Hearing Big Ben:** Let its surprisingly familiar chimes waft down as you stroll down the Embankment.
	■ **Royal Opera House:** Applaud as a ballerina collects roses at the end of her performance.
	■ **Courtauld Gallery:** Admire your favorite impressionist painting up close in the Courtauld Gallery, then discover Cranach the Elder's mischievous *Adam and Eve*.
	■ **Somerset House:** Watch the skaters and ice-wall climbers on a December evening.
	■ **Soho's Chinatown:** Eat the best Singaporean, Thai, and Malaysian food outside of Asia.

MAKING THE MOST OF YOUR TIME

You can comfortably tour all the sights in Covent Garden in a day. Visit the small but perfect Courtauld Gallery on Monday before 2 PM when it's free. That leaves plenty of time to visit the marketplace, watch the street entertainment, and do a bit of shopping, with energy left over for a night on the town (or "on the tiles," as the British say) in Soho.

FEELING PECKISH?

The enormous **Chuen Cheng Ku** (⊠ 17 Wardour St., Soho, W1 ☎ 020/7437-1398) in Soho's Chinatown serves dim sim from steaming carts all day and through dinner, in an atmosphere like something out of an old movie.

Maison Bertaux (⊠ 28 Greek St., Soho, W1 ☎ 020/7437-6007) has been around since the end of the 19th century. Decor is spartan but fab French cakes, tarts, and savory quiches more than make up for that. Nobody's mother ever baked this well.

Neal's Yard Bakery & Tearoom (⊠ 6 Neals Yard, Covent Garden, WC2 ☎ 020/7836-5199) sells vegetarian food, delicious cakes, and salad-filled sandwiches in a relaxed, kid-friendly atmosphere.

GAY LONDON

The bars and clubs along Old Compton Street in Soho are popular with affluent, stylish gay men. There are some very smart nightclubs in the area. **Madame Jo Jo's** (⊠ 8-10 Brewer St. ⊕ www.madamejojos.com) has been around for nearly 50 years, with a range of different, popular club nights. The club's **Kitsch Cabaret,** which can be booked online, is so popular (with straights as well as gays) that it's booked up weeks in advance.

A BRIEF HISTORY

In the 18th century, Casanova lived and loved here before returning to Venice. Almost as soon as development covered what had been a royal park and hunting ground, Soho earned a reputation for entertainment, bohemianism, and cosmopolitan tolerance. When the minions of public decency decided to end Soho's sex trade in 1991, with tough licensing laws and zero-tolerance of soliciting, they cracked down on an old Soho tradition that still resurfaces from time to time.

For centuries Soho was also an immigrant slum. French Hugenots in the 1680s, followed by Germans, Russians, Poles, Greeks, Italians, and Chinese, settled and brought their ethnic cuisines with them. So when dining out became fashionable after World War I, Soho was the natural place for restaurants to flourish.

For 300 years, Covent Garden was a convent garden. In 1630, Inigo Jones turned it into Britain's first planned public square. But wealthy Londoners preferred their own gated gardens, and within 50 years the piazza became a fruit-and-vegetable market. Despite the development of the Royal Opera in the 19th century, the area became run-down and was scheduled to be demolished in the 1970s. A local campaign saved it and the restored market opened 1980.

their quality that they are worth a detour off the Strand to see. The work of 18th-century Scottish architects and interior designers, John, Robert, James, and William Adam, known collectively as the Adam brothers, the original development, called Adelphi Terrace (from the Greek *adelphoi* for brothers), was damaged in the 19th century, during the building of the Embankment and demolished in 1936 to be replaced by an art deco tower. What remains is now protected and gives a glimpse of former grandeur. Nos. 1–4 Robert Street and Nos. 7 and 10 Adam Street are the best. At the **Royal Society of Arts** (✉ 8 John Adam St. ☏ 020/7930–5115 ⊕ www.rsa.org.uk ✉ Free ☉ 1st Sun. of month, 10–1), you can see a suite of Adam rooms; no reservations are required. ✉ *The Strand, Covent Garden, WC2* Ⓤ *Charing Cross, Embankment.*

Bow Street Magistrates' Court. This was where the prototype of the modern police force first operated. Known as the Bow Street Runners (because they chased thieves on foot), the runners were the brainchild of the second Bow Street magistrate—none other than Henry Fielding, the author of *Tom Jones* and *Joseph Andrews*. The late-19th-century edifice on the site went up during one of the Covent Garden market improvement drives. ✉ *Bow St., Covent Garden, WC2* Ⓤ *Covent Garden.*

Cleopatra's Needle. Off the triangular-handkerchief Victoria Embankment Gardens is London's *very oldest thing*, predating its arbitrary namesake, and London itself, by centuries. The 60-foot red-granite obelisk was erected at Heliopolis, in lower Egypt, in about 1475 BC, then moved to

Alexandria, where in 1819 Mohammed Ali, the Albanian-born viceroy of Egypt, presented it to the British to commemorate Admiral Lord Nelson and the Battle of the Nile. The British, though grateful, had not the faintest idea how to get the 186-ton gift home, so they left it there for years until an expatriate English engineer contrived an iron pontoon to float it to London via Spain. The sphinxes are a later British addition, damaged in the Blitz. Future archaeologists will find an 1878 time capsule underneath, containing the morning papers, several Bibles, a railway timetable, some pins, a razor, and a dozen photos of Victorian pinup girls. ⊠ *Embankment, Covent Garden, WC2* Ⓤ *Charing Cross, Embankment.*

> ### FEELING PECKISH?
>
> Although they may set out a few tables, the coffee shops and snack bars along the Covent Garden market buildings are more geared to take-away than comfortable coffee breaks or lunches. They can be overpriced and of iffy quality. Head for Soho when the munchies strike.

Ⓒ **Courtauld Institute Gallery.** One of London's most beloved art collections, the Courtauld is in the grounds of the renovated, grand 18th-century classical **Somerset House.** Founded in 1931 by the textile magnate Samuel Courtauld to house his remarkable private collection, this is one of the world's finest impressionist and Postimpressionist galleries, ranging from Bonnard to van Gogh. A déja vu moment with Cézanne, Degas, Seurat, or Monet awaits on every wall (Manet's *Bar at the Folies-Bergère* is the star), with bonus post-Renaissance works thrown in. Botticelli, Brueghel, Tiepolo, and Rubens are also represented, thanks to the exquisite bequest of Count Antoine Seilern's Princes Gate collection. German Renaissance paintings, bequeathed in 1947 include the colorful and delightfully wicked *Adam and Eve* by Lucas Cranach the Elder. There are also some bold and bright Fauvist paintings. ⊠ *The Strand, Covent Garden, WC2* ☎ *020/7848–2526* ⊕ *www.courtauld.ac.uk* 🖃 *£5, free Mon. 10–2, except bank holidays* ☉ *Daily 10–6; last admission 5:15* Ⓤ *Covent Garden, Holborn, Temple.*

★ **Covent Garden Piazza.** The restored 1840 market building around which Covent Garden pivots is known as the Piazza. Inside, the shops are mostly higher-class clothing chains, plus a couple of cafés and some knickknack stores that are good for gifts. There's the superior **Apple Market** for crafts on most days, too. If you turn right, you'll reach the indoor **Jubilee Market,** which, with its stalls of clothing, army surplus gear, and more crafts and knickknacks, is disappointingly ordinary. In summer it may seem that everyone you see around the Piazza (and the crowds are legion) is a fellow tourist, but there's still plenty of office life in the area. Londoners who shop in the area tend to head for Neal Street

> ### HERE'S WHERE
>
> The small and intimate **Donmar Warehouse** theater is part of the Seven Dials complex. It's where film director Sam Mendes *(American Beauty, Road to Perdition, Jarhead)* made his name.

and the area to the left of the subway entrance rather than the touristy market itself. By the church in the square, street performers—from global musicians to jugglers and mimes—play to the crowds, as they have done since the first English Punch and Judy Show, staged here in the 17th century. ☒ *Covent Garden, WC2* Ⓤ *Covent Garden.*

Leicester Square. This square (pronounced "Lester") is showing no sign of its great age. Looking at the neon of the major movie houses, the fast-food outlets (plus a useful Häagen-Dazs café), and the disco entrances, you'd never guess it was laid out around 1630. By the 19th century it was already bustling and disreputable,

and now it's usually one of the few places crowded after midnight—with suburban teenagers, backpackers, and London's swelling ranks of the homeless. That said, it's not a threatening place, and the liveliness can be quite cheering. But be on your guard—any place so full of tourists and people a little the worse for wear is bound to attract pickpockets, and Leicester Square certainly does. In the middle is a statue of a sulking Shakespeare, clearly wishing he were somewhere else and perhaps remembering the days when the cinemas were live theaters—burlesque houses, but live all the same. Here, too, are figures of Hogarth, Reynolds, and Charlie Chaplin, and underneath, but not visible, is a £22 million electrical substation. On the northeast corner, in Leicester Place, stands the church of **Notre Dame de France,** with a wonderful mural by Jean Cocteau in one of its side chapels. ☒ *Covent Garden, WC2* Ⓤ *Leicester Sq.*

London's Transport Museum. Normally housed in the old Flower Market at the southeast corner of the Covent Garden Piazza, the museum is closed for redevelopment and not scheduled to reopen until late 2007. Most exhibits have been moved to a temporary location, the Museum Depot in the West London suburbs. The Depot is occasionally open for guided tours and open weekends. Visit the museum Web site for access information and to see if a public opening coincides with your London visit. ⊕ *www.ltmuseum.co.uk.*

Royal Opera House. In the past it was Joan Sutherland, Rudolf Nureyev, and Margot Fonteyn, and now Bryn Terfel, Placido Domingo, and Sylvie Guillem wow the audience. Tickets are top dollar (£50–£180), but worth it if you love the red-and-gold Victorian surroundings, which always give a very special feel to the performance. London's premier opera and ballet venue was designed in 1858 by E. M. Barry, son of Sir Charles, the House of Commons architect, and is the third theater on the site. The first theater opened in 1732 and burned down in 1808; the second opened a year later, only to succumb to fire in 1856.

The entire building has been overhauled spectacularly while keeping the magic of the grand Victorian theater. Without doubt, the glass-and-steel Floral Hall (so badly damaged by fire in the 1950s it was used only for storing scenery) is the most wonderful feature; you can wander around and drink in (literally, in the foyer café) the interior during the day. The same is true of the Amphitheatre Bar and Piazza concourse, which give a splendid panorama across the city. There are free lunchtime chamber concerts and lectures as part of the policy to dispel the Opera House's elitist tag. For more on the Royal Opera House, see Arts & Entertainment, Chapter 18. ⊠ *Bow St., Covent Garden* ☎ *020/7304–4000* ⊕ *www.royaloperahouse.org* Ⓤ *Covent Garden.*

St. Paul's Church. If you want to commune with the spirits of Vivien Leigh, Noël Coward, Edith Evans, and Charlie Chaplin, this might be just the place. Memorials to them and many other theater greats are found in this 1633 work of the renowned Inigo Jones, who, as the King's Surveyor of Works, designed the whole of Covent Garden Piazza. St. Paul's has been known as "the actors' church" since the Restoration, thanks to the neighboring theater district and St. Paul's prominent parishioners (well-known actors often read the lessons at services). Fittingly, its portico was where the opening scene for *Pygmalion* was staged. St. Paul's Church (Wren's St. Paul's cathedral is eastward in the City) is across the Covent Garden Piazza, often punctuated with street entertainers. They are continuing in a very old tradition. ■ TIP➔ London diarist Samuel Pepys, writing in the 17th century, reports watching the first Punch and Judy show in English on the Tuscan portico of this church. ⊠ *Bedford St., Covent Garden, WC2* Ⓤ *Covent Garden.*

FodorśChoice ★

Somerset House. An old royal palace once stood on the site, but the 18th-century building that finally replaced it was the work of Sir William Chambers (1726–96) during the reign of George III. It was built to house government offices, principally those of the Navy; for the first time in more than 100 years these gracious rooms are on view for free, including the Seamen's Waiting Hall and the Nelson Stair. In addition, the Navy Commissioners' Barge has returned to dry dock at the Water Gate. The rooms are on the south side of the building, by the river. The **Courtauld Institute Gallery** occupies most of the north building, facing the busy Strand. Between is the cobbled Italianate courtyard where Admiral Nelson used to walk, the scene of an ice rink in the winter holiday season as well as summer concerts and other cultural events. Cafés and a restored river terrace adjoin the property, and a stone-and-glass footbridge leads up to Waterloo Bridge, which you can walk across to get to the South Bank.

In the vaults of the house is **The Gilbert Collection,** a museum of intricate works of silver, gold snuff boxes, and Italian mosaics. The micromosaics on tables, portrait miniatures, and jewelry are made in such fine detail that you might think they're painted, so be glad if you're offered a magnifying glass—it's the best way to fully appreciate the fine detail. The **Hermitage Rooms** are the showcase for a selection of rotating exhibitions from the collections of the State Museum in St. Petersburg, and other Hermitage-related activities. The opening show consisted of a selection of jewels, antiquities, portraits, and miniatures amassed by Catherine the Great, one of the greatest collectors of all time. Subsequent exhibitions have included masterpieces of the Walpole Collection: Britain's first Prime Minister amassed works by such artists as Rembrandt, Rubens, Van Dyck, and Poussin, which were then sold to Catherine the Great. It's ironic that these pieces have returned to the country for the first time in more than 200 years. ✉ *The Strand, Covent Garden, WC2* ☎ *020/ 7845–4600 information, 020/ 7845–4630 Hermitage information* ⊕ *www.somerset-house.org.uk* 🎫 *Somerset House free, visit 1 collection £5, 2 collections £8, or get 3-day pass for unlimited visits over 3-day period to all collections £12* ⊙ *Daily 10–6; last admission 5:15* Ⓤ *Charing Cross.*

ICE-SKATING

It's hard to beat the skating experience at Somerset House, where during December and January a rink is set up in the spectacularly grand courtyard of this central London palace. Adults £9.50–£12, children £6. Popularity is enormous, and if you can't get a ticket, other venues such as Hampton Court and the Natural History Museum are following Somerset House's lead in having temporary winter rinks. ☎ 020/7845–4670 ⊕ www.somerset-house.org.uk/ icerink.

🎠 **Theatre Museum.** This mostly below-ground museum aims to re-create the excitement of theater itself. There are usually programs in progress allowing children to get in a mess with makeup or have a giant dressing-up session. Permanent exhibits paint a history of the English stage from the 16th century to Mick Jagger's jumpsuit, with tens of thousands of theater playbills and sections on such topics as Hamlet through the ages and pantomime—the peculiar British theatrical tradition when men dress as ugly women, known as Panto Dames, and girls wear tights and play princes. There's a little theater in the bowels of the museum and a ticket desk for "real" theaters around town, plus an archive holding video recordings and audiotapes of significant British theatrical productions. Like the London theater it represents, the museum is "dark" (closed) on Monday. ✉ *7 Russell St., Covent Garden, WC2* ☎ *020/7943–4700* ⊕ *www.theatremuseum.org* 🎫 *Free* ⊙ *Tues.–Sun. 10–6; last admission 5:30* Ⓤ *Covent Garden.*

Theatre Royal, Drury Lane. This is London's best-known auditorium and almost its largest. Since World War II, its forte has been musicals (past ones have included *The King and I, My Fair Lady, South Pacific, Hello, Dolly!,* and *A Chorus Line*)—though David Garrick, who managed it from 1747 to 1776, made its name by reviving the works of the by-then-obscure William Shakespeare. It enjoys all the romantic accessories of a London theater—a history of fires (it burned down three times, once in a Wren-built incarnation), riots (in 1737, when a posse of footmen demanded free admission), attempted regicides (George II in 1716 and his grandson George III in 1800), and even sightings of the most famous phantom of theaterland, the Man in Grey (in the Circle, matinees). The entrance is on Catherine Street. ✉ *Catherine St., Covent Garden, WC2* Ⓤ *Covent Garden.*

Soho & Covent Garden at a Glance

SIGHTS
The Adam Houses
Bow Street Magistrates'
  Court
Cleopatra's Needle
Leicester Square
Notre Dame de France
Royal Society of Arts
St. Paul's Church
Somerset House

MUSEUMS & GALLERIES
Courtauld Institute Gallery
The Gilbert Collection
Hermitage Rooms
Photographer's Gallery
Theatre Museum

WHERE TO EAT (⇨ Ch. 15)

BUDGET DINING
Bar Italia, *Café*
Food for Thought,
  Vegetarian
Maison Bertaux, *Café*
Market Place, *Latin*
Masala Zone, *Indian*
New Piccadilly, *Café*
Rock & Sole Plaice,
  Seafood

MODERATE DINING
Andrew Edmunds, *Eclectic*
Bertorelli's, *Italian*
Browns, *English*
Christopher's Grill,
  American
Joe Allen, *American*
L'Escargot, *Continental*
Orso, *Italian*
Randall & Aubin, *Seafood*
Rules, *English*
Smollensky's on the
  Strand, *American*

EXPENSIVE DINING
Asia de Cuba, *Pan-Asian*
Fung Shing, *Chinese*
The Ivy, *Contemporary*
J Sheekey, *Seafood*
Lindsay House, *Irish*
Savoy Grill, *Continental*
The Savoy, *Afternoon Tea*
Yauatcha, *Chinese*

WHERE TO STAY (⇨ Ch. 16)

EXPENSIVE LODGING
Covent Garden Hotel
Hazlitt's
The Howard Swissotel
One Aldwych
Radisson Edwardian
  Hampshire
Radisson Mountbatten
The Savoy
Soho Hotel
Trafalgar Hilton
Waldorf Hilton

PUBS & NIGHTLIFE
  (⇨ Ch. 17)
100 Club, *eclectic*
Ain't Nothin' but Blues
Amused Moose, *comedy*
Bar Rumba, *dance club*
The Borderline, *eclectic*
Box, *gay & lesbian*
Cafe des Amis, *bar*
Candy Bar, *gay & lesbian*
Comedy Store, *comedy*
De Hems, *pub*
The Edge, *gay & lesbian*
French House, *pub*
Friendly Society, *gay &*
  lesbian
G.A.Y, *gay & lesbian*
Heaven, *gay & lesbian*
Lamb & Flag, *pub*
The Living Room W1, *bar*
Milk & Honey, *bar*
Pizza Express, *jazz & blues*
Porterhouse, *pub*
Ronnie Scott's, *jazz*
Rupert Street, *gay &*
  lesbian
Sanctuary, *gay & lesbian*
The Shadow Lounge, *gay &*
  lesbian
Soho Theatre, *comedy*
St. James Tavern, *pub*
Tantra, *dance club*
Umbaba, *bar*
White Hart, *pub*

ARTS & ENTERTAINMENT
  (⇨ Ch. 18)
Curzon Soho, *film*
Donmar Warehouse

English National Opera
The London Coliseum
Royal Opera House
Soho Theatre
St. Martin-in-the-Fields
Theatre Royal, Drury Lane

SHOPPING (⇨ Ch. 19)

MARKETS & MALLS
Apple Market
Berwick Street Market
Jubilee Market
Seven Dials

ART GALLERIES & CRAFTS
Contemporary Ceramics
The Graphic Centre
Grosvenor Prints

BOOKS
Foyles
Stanfords Map & Travel
Tim Bryars Ltd

CLOTHING
Aquascutum
Koh Samui
Margaret Howell
Nicole Farhi
Paul Smith
River Island
Topshop

FOOD & GIFTS
Neal's Yard Dairy
Past Times
Soccerscene
The Tea House
The Vintage House

MUSIC
Blackmarket
MDC Opera Shop
Mr. CD
Virgin Megastore

PERFUME/COSMETICS
Lush
Penhaligon's
Pout
Space NK

SHOES
Shellys
Swear

TOYS
Benjamin Pollock's
Hamleys

4

Bloomsbury & Legal London

WORD OF MOUTH

"To me the British Museum is a destination that everyone should visit once in their life . . . . You could easily spend the entire day in the museum. So plan accordingly! The first time my wife and I visited we had a couple hours until closing and we thought 'eh, that's plenty of time.' We got the boot and we had barely left the first room. The next time we spent 4 hours in the Egyptian room. And this time we're taking another couple to share the experience."

–Kevin_C

BLOOMSBURY & LEGAL LONDON

Sightseeing
★ ★ ★

Nightlife
★ ★

Dining
★ ★

Lodging
★ ★ ★ ★

Shopping
★ ★

The hub of intellectual London, Bloomsbury is anchored by the British Museum and the University of London, which houses—among other institutions—the internationally ranked London School of Economics (LSE) and the School of Oriental and African Studies (SOAS). As a result, the streets and cafés around Bloomsbury's Russell Square are often crawling with students and professors engaged in heated conversation, while literary agents and academics surf the shelves of the antiquarian bookstores nearby.

What's Here

Perhaps the best-known square in Bloomsbury is the centrally located **Russell Square,** with gardens laid out by Humphry Repton, a prominent English landscape designer often considered the successor to Capability Brown. Then there's the charming **Bedford Square** and **Queen Square,** dominated by a handful of hospitals. Scattered about the **University College** campus are **Woburn Square, Torrington Square,** and **Gordon Square.** Gordon Square, at one point home to Virginia Woolf, the Bells, John Maynard Keynes (all at No. 46), and Lytton Strachey (at No. 51), is now the location of the **Percival David Foundation of Chinese Art.** The spectacular **British Library** is a few blocks north on Euston Road. The lovely **Tavistock Square** was, on a somber note, the site of one of the seven bombings that took place in London on July 7, 2005.

Though more often linked with its literary past—**Dickens House Museum,** where the author wrote *Oliver Twist,* is one of the most-visited sites in the area—Bloomsbury also happens to be where London's legal profession was born. In fact, the buildings associated with legal London were some of the only structures spared during the Great Fire of 1666, and so the serpentine alleys, cobbled courts, and historic halls frequented by the city's still-bewigged barristers ooze centuries of history. The massive, Gothic-style **Royal Courts of Justice** ramble for blocks all the way to the Strand, while the **Inns of Court—Gray's Inn, Lincoln's Inn, Middle Temple,** and **Inner Temple**—are where most British trial lawyers have offices even today. In the 14th century the inns were lodging houses where the barristers lived so that people would know how to easily find them (hence, the label "inn"). **Temple Church,** the 500-year old **Prince Henry's Room** and the **Staple Inn,** one of London's oldest surviving half-timber buildings, are also here.

Artists' studios and design shops share space with tenants near the **British Museum,** which offers up a dash of modernism with its sweeping glass-roof Great Court. Not far off on Little Russell Street, the **London Cartoon Museum** sells original published editorials and strip cartoons, while a bit farther north on Gordon Street the **Bloomsbury Theatre** presents foreign films, modern dance, and stand-up comedians. Guaranteed to raise a smile from the most blasé and footsore tourist is **Sir John Soane's Museum,** which hardly deserves the burden of its dry name.

Places to Explore

★ ☼ **British Library.** Since 1759, the British Library had been housed in the British Museum on Gordon Square. But space ran out long ago. The collection of around 18 million volumes now has a home in state-of-the-art surroundings, and if you're a researcher, it's a wonderful place to work (special passes are required). The library's treasures are on view to the general public: Magna Carta, a Gutenberg Bible, Jane Austen's writings, Shakespeare's First Folio, and musical manuscripts by Handel and Sir Paul McCartney are on show in the John Ritblat Gallery. Also in the gallery are headphones—you can listen to some of the most interesting snippets in a small showcase of the **National Sound Archive** stored here (it's the world's largest collection, but is not on view), such as the voice of Florence Nightingale, and an extract from the Beatles' last tour interview. The Workshop of Words, Sound & Images explores the vitality of the living word, and on weekends and during school vacations there are hands-on demonstrations of how a book comes together. Feast your eyes also on the six-story glass tower that holds the 65,000-volume collection of George III, plus a permanent exhibition of rare stamps. And if all that wordiness is just too much, you can relax in the library's piazza or restaurant, or take in one of the occasional free concerts in the amphitheater. ✉ *96 Euston Rd., Bloomsbury, NW1* ☎ *020/7412–7332* ⊕ *www.bl.uk* 🖃 *Free, charge for special exhibitions* ☼ *Mon. and Wed.–Fri. 9:30–6, Tues. 9:30–8, Sat. 9:30–5, Sun. 11–5 and bank holiday Mon.* Ⓤ *Euston, King's Cross.*

| British Museum | See Page 108 |

☼ **Dickens House Museum.** This is the only one of the many London houses Charles Dickens (1812–70) inhabited that's still standing, and it would

GETTING ORIENTED

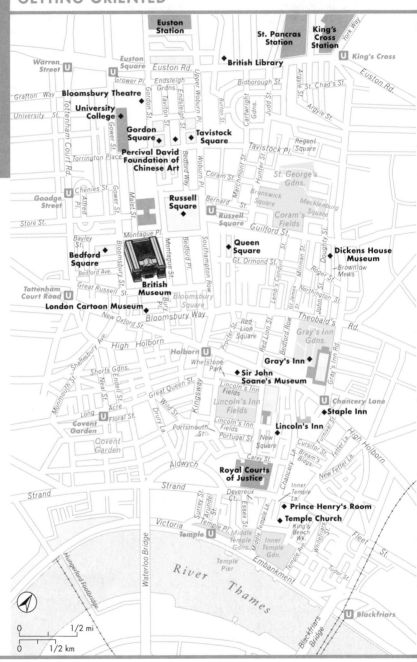

TOP 5 REASONS TO GO

- **British Museum:** It's never too late to start appreciating the treasures here that would take lifetimes to see.

- **British Library:** Lay eyes on the original Magna Carta, an actual Gutenberg Bible, copies of Jane Austen's writings, and Shakespeare's First Folio.

- **Museum Street:** Stroll along a street lined with independent galleries, antiquarian map shops, and delightful cafés.

- **Percival David Foundation:** Visit the most comprehensive collection of Chinese ceramics outside of China.

- **University of London:** Hang out at the Union with the day's paper while picking up the latest student fashion trends and eavesdropping on political discussions of the week's news.

FEELING PECKISH?

At **Alfred** (⊠ 245 Shaftesbury Ave.) sticky toffee pudding is the thing to order, and it should be slowly consumed.

The Hare and Tortoise Dumpling & Noodle Bar (opposite the Renoir Cinema on Brunswick Square) serves scrumptious Asian fast food until 10:30 PM, seven days a week. This bright café is a favorite with students and it's easy to see why: ingredients are all-natural, the portions huge, the service fast, and the bill always reasonable.

SAFETY

Come evening, avoid the region around King's Cross because it's known to be one of London's more unsavory neighborhoods, especially for nonnatives who don't know their way about town.

GETTING THERE

You can easily get to where you need to be on foot in Bloomsbury, and the Russell Square Tube stop on the Piccadilly Line leaves you right at the corner of Russell Square. The best Tube stops for the Inns of Court are Holborn on the Central and Piccadilly lines or Chancery Lane on the Central Line. Tottenham Court Road on the Northern and Central lines or Russell Square (Piccadilly Line) are best for the British Museum.

MAKING THE MOST OF YOUR TIME

Bloomsbury can be seen in a day, or in half a day, depending on your interests and your time constraints. If you plan to visit the Inns of Court as well as the British Museum, and you'd also like to get a feel for the neighborhood, then you may wish to devote an entire day to this literary and legal enclave. Unless you don't mind a lot of moving trucks, honking, and students carrying heavy loads through the streets, avoid Bloomsbury in mid-September, when the streets around Russell Square are filled with students moving into housing for the upcoming school session. (On the other hand, this air of activity does have its charms, too.)

5

A BRIEF HISTORY

Fundamental to the region's spirit of open expression and scholarly debate is the legacy of an elite corps of artists and writers who lived here during the first three decades of the 20th century. The "Bloomsbury Group" included the likes of Virginia Woolf, Lytton Strachey, and E. M. Forster, authors who—much like the Beat poets of San Francisco or the jazz artists of the Harlem Renaissance—defined their neighborhood as well as an entire era.

The neighborhood's very British-sounding name, however, stems from that of Norman landowner William de Blemund who, in 1201, acquired what was then just a rural patch of land. In the early 1660s the Earl of Southampton built what became Bloomsbury Square and later, in the 18th century, a cluster of wealthy landowners acquired additional land and developed the neighborhood's center. Bloomsbury Market opened in 1730, and today the district is home to some of London's most picturesque parks, squares, and buildings, as well as London's four Inns of Court.

have had a real claim to his fame in any case because he wrote *Oliver Twist* and *Nicholas Nickleby* and finished *Pickwick Papers* here between 1837 and 1839. The house looks exactly as it would have in Dickens's day, complete with first editions, letters, and a tall clerk's desk (where the master wrote standing up, often while chatting with visiting friends and relatives). "By Dickens!" (a previous generation's exclamation of surprise for "you don't say")—if it's "by him" or anything to do with him, then you can find it here, as this museum is a world authority on the great man. There's a treat for Lionel Bart fans—his score of *Oliver!* Down in the basement is a replica of the Dingley Dell kitchen from *Pickwick Papers*. A program of changing special exhibitions gives insight into the Dickens family and the author's works, with sessions where, for instance, you can try your own hand with a quill pen. Christmas is a memorable time to visit, as the rooms are decorated in traditional style: better than any televised costume drama, this is the real thing. ⊠ *48 Doughty St., Bloomsbury, WC1* ☎ *020/7405–2127* ⊕ *www.dickensmuseum.com* ⊠ *£5* ☉ *Mon.–Sat. 10–5, Sun. 11–5; last admission 4:30* Ⓤ *Chancery La., Russell Sq.*

Gray's Inn. Although the least architecturally interesting of the four Inns of Court and the one most damaged by German bombs in the 1940s, this still has its romantic associations. In 1594 Shakespeare's *Comedy of Errors* was performed for the first time in its hall—which was lovingly restored after World War II and has a fine Elizabethan screen of carved oak. You must make advance arrangements to view the Tudor-style Gray's Inn's Hall (apply in writing, in advance, to the administrator, the Under Treasurer), but you can stroll around the secluded and spacious gardens, first planted by Francis Bacon in 1606. ⊠ *Gray's Inn Rd., Holborn, Bloomsbury, WC1* ☎ *020/7458–7800* ☉ *Weekdays noon–2:30* Ⓤ *Holborn or Temple.*

★ **Lincoln's Inn.** There's plenty to see at one of the oldest, best-preserved, and most comely of the Inns of Court—from the Chancery Lane Tudor brick gatehouse to the wide-open, tree-lined, atmospheric Lincoln's Inn Fields and the 15th-century chapel remodeled by Inigo Jones in 1620. The wisteria-clad New Square, London's only complete 17th-century square, is not the newest part of the complex; in fact, the oldest-looking buildings are the 1845 Hall and Library, which you must obtain the porter's permission to enter. ⊠ *Chancery La., Bloomsbury, WC2* ☎ *020/7405–1393* ⊙ *Gardens weekdays 7–7, chapel weekdays noon–2:30; public may also attend Sun. service in chapel at 11:30 during legal terms* Ⓤ *Chancery La.*

Percival David Foundation of Chinese Art. This collection, belonging to the University of London, is dominated by ceramics from the Sung to Qing dynasties—from the 10th to the 19th century, in other words. It's on **Gordon Square,** which Virginia Woolf, the Bells, John Maynard Keynes (all at No. 46), and Lytton Strachey (at No. 51) called home for a while. ⊠ *53 Gordon Sq., Bloomsbury, WC1* ☎ *020/7387–3909* ⊕ *www. pdfmuseum.org.uk* 🖾 *Free* ⊙ *Weekdays 10:30–5* Ⓤ *Russell Sq.*

Prince Henry's Room. This is the Jacobean half-timber house built in 1610 to celebrate the investiture of Henry, James I's eldest son, as Prince of Wales; it's marked with his coat of arms and a PH on the ceiling. It's an entrance to the lawyers' sanctum, Temple, where the Strand becomes Fleet Street, and you can go in to visit the small Samuel Pepys exhibition. ⊠ *17 Fleet St., Bloomsbury, EC4* ☎ *020/7936–2710* ⊕ *www. cityoflondon.gov.uk* 🖾 *Free* ⊙ *Mon.–Sat. 11–2* Ⓤ *Temple.*

Royal Courts of Justice. Here is the vast Victorian Gothic pile containing the nation's principal law courts, with 1,000-odd rooms running off 3½ mi of corridor. And here are heard the most important civil law cases—that's everything from divorce to fraud, with libel in between—and you can sit in the viewing gallery to watch any trial you like, for a live version of *Court TV.* The more dramatic criminal cases are heard at the Old Bailey. Other sights are the 238-foot-long main hall and the compact exhibition of judges' robes. Check out the gift shop also, where useful items (such as umbrellas) are emblazoned with the royal courts' crest. ⊠ *The Strand, Bloomsbury, WC2* ☎ *020/7947–6000* ⊕ *www.open.gov. uk* 🖾 *Free* ⊙ *Weekdays 9:30–4:30; during Aug. there are no sittings and public areas close at 2:30* Ⓤ *Temple.*

★ **Sir John Soane's Museum.** Sir John (1753–1837), architect of the Bank of England, bequeathed his house to the nation on condition that nothing be changed. (Sir John owned Nos. 12, 13, and 14, Lincoln's Inn Fields, and recently No. 14 was added to the museum space.) He obviously had enormous fun with his home, having had the means to finance great experiments in perspective and scale and to fill the space with some wonderful pieces. There are also different exhibitions on subjects as broad and as varied as Sir John's interests: from early architecture to more modern art. In the Picture Room, for instance, two of Hogarth's *Rake's Progress* series are among the paintings on panels that swing away to reveal secret gallery pockets with more paintings. Everywhere mirrors and colors play tricks with light and space, and split-level floors worthy of a fairground fun house disorient you. In a basement chamber sits the vast 1300 BC sarcophagus

Continued on page 115

THE BRITISH MUSEUM

Anybody writing about the British Museum had better have a large stack of superlatives close at hand: most, biggest, earliest, finest. This is the golden hoard of nearly three centuries of the Empire, the booty brought from Britain's far-flung colonies.

The first major pieces, among them the Rosetta Stone and Elgin Marbles, were "acquired" from the French, who "found" them in Egypt and Greece. The museum has since collected countless goodies of worldwide historical significance: the Black Obelisk, some of the Dead Sea Scrolls, the Lindow Man. And that only begins the list.

The British Museum is a vast space split into 94 galleries, generally divided by continent or period of history, with some areas spanning more than one level. There are marvels wherever you go, and—while we don't like to be pessimistic—it is, yes, impossible to fully appreciate everything in a day. So make the most of the tours, activity trails, and visitors guides that are available (⇨ *Tours, page 114*).

The following is a highly edited overview of the museum's greatest hits, organized by area. Pick one or two that whet your appetite, then branch out from there, or spend two straight hours indulging in the company of a single favorite sculpture. There's no wrong way to experience the British Museum.

✉ Great Russell St., Bloomsbury WC1

☏ 020/7323–8920

⊕ www.thebritishmuseum.ac.uk

✉ Free; donations encouraged. Tickets for special exhibits vary in price.

☉ Galleries, including special exhibits, Sat.–Wed. 10–5:30, Thurs. and Fri. 10–8:30. Great Court Sun.–Wed. 9–6, Thurs.–Sat. 9 AM–11 PM. Reading Room library and information area daily 10–5:30, Reading Room viewing area Thurs. and Fri. 10–8:30.

Ⓤ Russell Square

(left) The Great Court
(top) *Cradle to Grave* by Pharmacopoeia

MUSEUM HIGHLIGHTS

Ancient Civilizations

The Rosetta Stone. Found in 1799 and carved in 196 BC by decree of Ptolemy V in Egyptian hieroglyphics, demotic, and Greek, it was this multilingual inscription that provided French Egyptologist Jean-François Champollion with the key to deciphering hieroglyphics. *Room 4.*

Colossal statue of Ramesses II. A member of the 19th dynasty (ca. 1270 BC), Ramesses II commissioned innumerable statues of himself—more than any other preceding or succeeding king. This one, a 7-ton likeness of his perfectly posed upper half, comes from his mortuary temple, the Ramesseum, in western Thebes. *Room 4.*

The Elgin Marbles. Perhaps these marvelous treasures of Greece shouldn't be here—but while the debate rages on, you can steal your own moment with them in the Parthenon Galleries. Carved in about 440 BC, these graceful decorations are displayed along with an in-depth, high-tech exhibit of the Acropolis; the **handless, footless Dionysus** who used to recline along its east pediment is especially well known. *Room 18.*

Mausoleum of Halikarnassos. All that remains of this, one of the Seven Wonders of the Ancient World, is a fragmented form of the original "mausoleum," the 4th-century tomb of Maussollos, King of Karia. The highlight of this gallery is the marble forepart of the **colossal chariot horse from the** *quadriga. Room 21.*

The Egyptian mummies. Another short flight of stairs takes you to the museum's most popular galleries, especially beloved by children: the Roxie Walker Galleries of Egyptian Funerary Archaeology have a fascinating collection of relics from the Egyptian realm of the dead. In addition to real corpses, wrapped mummies, and mummy cases, there's a menagerie of animal companions and curious items that were buried alongside them. *Rooms 62–63.*

Portland Vase. Made in Italy from cameo glass at the turn of the first century, it is named after the Dukes of Portland, who owned it from 1785 to 1945. It is considered a technical masterpiece—opaque white mythological figures cut by a gem-cutter are set on cobalt-blue background. *Room 70.*

(top) Portland vase
(bottom) Colossal statue of Ramesses II

The **Enlightenment Gallery** should be visited purely for the fact that its antiquarian cases hold the contents of the British Museum's first collections—Sir Hans Sloane's natural-history loot, as well as that of Sir Joseph Banks, who acquired specimens of everything from giant shells to fossils to rare plants to exotic beasts during his voyage to the Pacific aboard Captain Cook's *Endeavour. Room 1.*

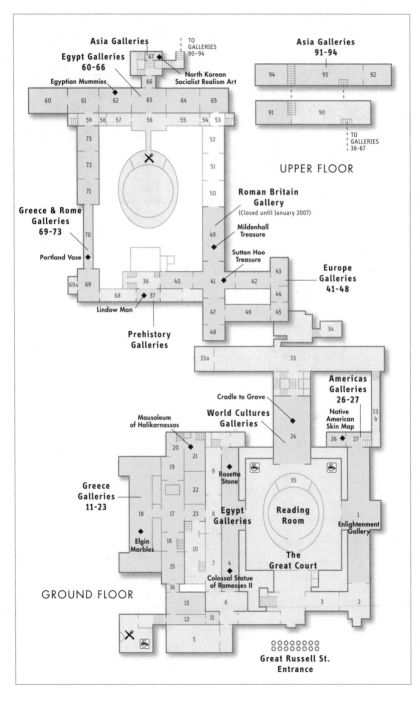

Asia Galleries

Egypt Galleries
60-66

Egyptian Mummies

TO
GALLERIES
90-94

67

66

North Korean
Socialist Realism Art

60 | 61 | 62 | 63 | 64 | 65

59 | 58 | 57 | 56 | 55 | 54 | 53

73

72

71

Greece & Rome
Galleries
69-73

70

Portland Vase

69a | 69

68 | 37

Lindow Man

Prehistory
Galleries

Asia Galleries
91-94

94 | 93 | 92

91 | 90

TO
GALLERIES
36-67

UPPER FLOOR

52

51

50

Roman Britain
Gallery
(Closed until January 2007)

49

Mildenhall
Treasure

Sutton Hoo
Treasure

36 | 40 | 41 | 42

43

44

Europe
Galleries
41-48

47 | 46 | 45

48

34

33a | 33

Americas
Galleries
26-27

Native
American
Skin Map

33
b

Cradle to Grave

World Cultures
Galleries

24

26 | 27

Mausoleum
of Halikarnassos

20

19

21

22

9 Rosetta
Stone

35

Greece
Galleries
11-23

18 | 17 | 23

8 Egypt
Galleries

Reading
Room

1
Enlightenment
Gallery

16

10

7 | 4

Colossal Statue
of Ramesses II

The
Great Court

Elgin
Marbles

15

14

GROUND FLOOR

13

12 | 11

5

3 | 2

00000000
00000000
Great Russell St.
Entrance

Asia

The Korea Foundation Gallery. Delve into striking examples of **North Korean Socialist Realism art** from the 1950s to the present and a reconstruction of a **sarangbang**, a traditional scholar's study, complete with hanji paper walls and tea-making equipment. *Room 67.*

World Cultures

Cradle to Grave. An installation by Pharmacopoeia, a collective of artists and a doctor, pays homage to the British nation's wellbeing—or ill-being, as it were. More than 14,000 drugs (the number estimated to be prescribed to every person in the U.K. in his lifetime) are encased in two lengths of nylon fabric resulting in a colorful tapestry of pills and tablets. *Room 24.*

The JP Morgan Chase North American Gallery. This is one of the largest collections of native culture outside of North America, going back to the earliest hunters 10,000 years ago. Here a 1775 **native American skin map** serves as an example of the importance of such documents in the exploration and cartography of North America. Look for the beautifully displayed **native American costumes.** *Room 26.*

The Mexican Gallery. The most alluring pieces sit in this collection side by side: a 15th-century **turquoise mask of Xiuhtecuhtli,** the Mexican Fire God and Turquoise Lord, and a **double-headed serpent** from the same period. *Room 27.*

Britain and Europe

The Mildenhall Treasure. This glittering haul of 4th-century Roman silver tableware was found beneath the sod of a Suffolk field in 1942. *Room 49.*

The Sutton Hoo Treasure. Next door to the loot from Mildenhall—and equally splendid, including brooches, swords, and jewel-encrusted helmets—the treasure was buried at sea with (it is thought) Redwald, one of the first English kings, in the 7th century, and excavated from a Suffolk field in 1938–39. *Room 41.*

Lindow Man. "Pete Marsh"—so named by the archaeologists who unearthed the body from a Cheshire peat marsh—was ritually slain, probably as a human sacrifice, in the 1st century and lay perfectly pickled in his bog until 1984. *Room 50.*

Colossal chariot horse from the *quadriga* of the Mausoleum at Halikarnassos

LOWER GALLERY

The three rooms that comprise the **Sainsbury African Galleries** are of the main interest here: together they present a staggering 200,000 objects, featuring intricate pieces of old ivory, gold, and wooden masks and carvings—highlighting such ancient kingdoms as the Benin and Asante. The displays include a collection of **55 throwing knives**; ceremonial garments including a dazzling pink and green **woman's coif** (*qufiya*) from Tunisia made of silk, metal, and cotton; and the *Oxford Man*, *a* 1992 woodcarving by Owen Ndou, depicting a man of ambiguous race clutching his Book of Knowledge.

THE NATION'S ATTIC: A HISTORY OF THE MUSEUM

The collection began when Sir Hans Sloane, physician to Queen Anne and George II, bequeathed his personal collection of curiosities and antiquities to the nation. The collection quickly grew, thanks to enthusiastic kleptomaniacs after the Napoleonic Wars—most notoriously the seventh Earl of Elgin, who obtained the marbles from the Parthenon and Erechtheion on the Acropolis in Athens during his term as British ambassador in Constantinople.

Soon thereafter, it seemed everyone had something to donate—George II gave the Royal Library, Sir William Hamilton gave antique vases, Charles Townley gave sculptures, the Bank of England gave coins. When the first exhibition galleries opened to visitors in 1759, the trustees agreed to admit only small groups guided by curators. The British Museum quickly became one of the most fashionable places to be seen in the capital, and tickets, which had to be booked in advance, were treated like gold dust.

The museum's holdings quickly outgrew their original space in Montague House. After the addition of such major pieces as the Rosetta Stone and other Egyptian antiquities (spoils of the Napoleonic War) and the Parthenon sculptures, Robert Smirke was commissioned to build an appropriately large and monumental building on the same site. It's still a hot ticket: the British Museum now receives more than 5 million visitors every year.

THE GREAT COURT & THE READING ROOM

The museum's classical Greek-style facade features figures representing the progress of civilization, and the focal point is the awesome Great Court, a massive glass-roofed space. Here is the museum's best-kept secret—an inner courtyard (now the largest covered square in Europe) that, for more than 150 years, had been used for storage.

The 19th-century Reading Room, an impressive 106-foot-high blue-and-gold-domed library, forms the centerpiece of the Great Court. The best way to marvel at it is to slip in, gaze at the 104,000 ancient tomes lining the shelves, and for a few moments join the weighty company of those who have used it as a literary and academic sanctuary over the past 150 years or so: H.G. Wells, Thomas Hardy, Lord Tennyson, Oscar Wilde, George Orwell, T.S. Eliot, and Beatrix Potter, to name a few.

(above) Reading Room

PLANNING YOUR VISIT

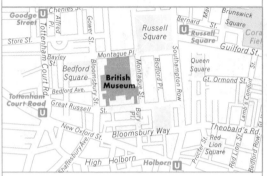

Tours

The **50-minute Eyeopener tour (free)** by museum guides does just what it says; ask for details at the information desk. The **90-minute Highlights tour (£8)** runs three times a day. After either of these tours, you can then dip back into the collections that most captured your imagination at your leisure.

An **audio version of the Highlights tour (£3.50)** is a less-animated but perhaps more relaxed way to navigate the galleries. Other audio tours focus on the Enlightenment and the Parthenon sculptures; another is designed for families.

Alternatively, the **Visitor's Guide (£5)** gives a brief but informative overview of the museum's history and is divided into self-guided themed tours.

Before you go, consider printing a **COMPASS tour (free)** from the museum's online navigation tool (www.thebritishmuseum.ac.uk/compass), which allows users to browse past and present exhibits as well as search for specific objects. A children's version can also be found here. Computer stations in the Reading Room offer onsite access to COMPASS.

■ TIP➔➔ The closest underground station to the British Museum is Russell Square on the Piccadilly line. However, since you will be entering via the back entrance on Montague Place, you will not experience the full impact of the museum's grand facade. To do so, alight at Holborn on the Central and Piccadilly lines or Tottenham Court Road on the Central and Northern lines. The walk from these stations is about 10 minutes.

WITH KIDS

■ Pick up the "Visiting with Children" leaflet, which has a guide to the top eight objects that attract the most attention from younger visitors.

■ The Reading Room has trails and activity backpacks for kids ages 2 to 6. There are also activity sheets for teens available.

■ Art materials are available for free from information points, where you can also find out about workshops, performances, storytelling sessions, and other free events.

■ Around the museum, there are Hands On desks open daily 11–4, which let visitors handle objects from the various collections.

WHERE TO REFUEL

The British Museum's self-service **Gallery Café** gets very crowded but serves a reasonably tasty menu beneath a plaster cast of a part of the Parthenon frieze that Lord Elgin didn't remove. It's open daily.

The **café in the Great Court** keeps longer hours and is a great place to people-watch and admire the spectacular glass roof while you eat your salad and sandwich.

If the weather is nice, exit the museum via the back entrance on Montague Place and amble over to **Russell Square,** which has grassy lawns, water fountains, and a glass-fronted café for post-sandwich coffee and ice cream.

of Seti I, lighted by a domed skylight two stories above. When Sir John acquired this priceless object for £2,000, he celebrated with a three-day party. The elegant, tranquil courtyard gardens with statuary and plants are now open to the public, and there's a below street-level passage, which joins two of the courtyards to the museum. ✉ *13 Lincoln's Inn Fields, Bloomsbury, WC2* ☎ *020/7405–2107* ⊕ *www.soane.org* ▣ *Free, Sat. tour £3* ☉ *Tues.–Sat. 10–5; also 6–9 on 1st Tues. every month; tours each Sat. at 2:30 PM* Ⓤ *Holborn.*

Temple. The entrance to Temple—the collective name for **Inner Temple** and **Middle Temple,** and the exact point of entry into the City—is marked by a young bronze griffin, the **Temple Bar Memorial** (1880), which makes a splendidly heraldic snapshot and marks the symbolic City border. (This replaced the Wren

---

KING'S CROSS STATION

Known for its 120-foot-tall clock tower, this yellow brick, Italianate building with large, arched windows was constructed in 1851–52 as the London terminus for the Great Northern Railway and routes to the Midlands, the north of England, and Scotland. Harry Potter and fellow aspiring wizards took the Hogwarts Express to school from the imaginary platform 9¾ (platforms 4 and 5 were the actual shooting site) in the movies based on J. K. Rowling's popular novels. The station has put up a sign for platform 9¾ if you want to take a picture there—but please don't try to run through the wall. Euston Rd. and York Way, Euston, NW1 ☎ 0845/748–4950 Ⓤ King's Cross

---

Temple Bar gateway dismantled in a Victorian road-widening scheme. The Temple Bar has now returned, opposite St. Paul's Cathedral.) In the buildings opposite is an elaborate stone arch through which you pass into Middle Temple Lane, past a row of 17th-century timber-frame houses, and on into Fountain Court. This lane runs all the way to the Thames, more or less separating the two Temples, past the sloping lawns of Middle Temple Gardens, on the east border of which is the Elizabethan **Middle Temple Hall.** If it's open, don't miss that hammer-beam roof, among the finest in the land. ✉ *Middle Temple La., Bloomsbury, EC4* ☎ *020/ 7427–4800* ☉ *Weekdays 10–11 and, when not in use, 2–4* Ⓤ *Temple.*

Temple Church. Featuring "the Round"—a rare circular nave—this church was built by the Knights Templar in the 12th century. The Red Knights (so called after the red crosses they wore—you can see them in effigy around the nave) held their secret initiation rites in the crypt here. Having started poor, holy, and dedicated to the protection of pilgrims, they grew rich from showers of royal gifts, until in the 14th century they were charged with heresy, blasphemy, and sodomy, thrown into the Tower, and stripped of their wealth. You might suppose the church to be thickly atmospheric, but Victorian and postwar restorers have tamed its air of antique mystery. Still, it's a very fine Gothic-Romanesque church, whose 1240 chancel ("the Oblong") has been accused of perfection. ✉ *The Temple, Bloomsbury, EC4* ☎ *020/7353–3470* ☉ *Wed.–Sat. 11–4, Sun. 1–4, and closures for special services* Ⓤ *Temple.*

University College. The college was founded in 1826 and set in a satisfyingly classical edifice designed by the architect of the National Gallery,

William Wilkins. In 1907 it became part of the University of London, providing higher education without religious exclusion. The college has within its portals the **Slade School of Fine Art,** which did for many of Britain's artists what the nearby Royal Academy of Dramatic Art (on Gower Street) did for its actors. On view inside is a fine collection of sculpture by an alumnus, John Flaxman. You can also see more Egyptian artifacts, if you didn't get enough at the neighboring British Museum, in the **Petrie Museum** (☎ 020/7679–2884 ⊕ www.petrie.ucl.ac.uk), accessed from Malet Place, on the first floor of the DMS Watson building. It houses an outstanding, huge collection of fascinating objects of Egyptian archaeology—jewelry, toys, papyri, and some of the world's oldest garments. It has proved so popular with schoolchildren that it's now open Saturday 10–1 in addition to Tuesday–Friday 1–5. The South Cloisters contain one of London's weirder treasures: the clothed skeleton of one of the university's founders, Jeremy Bentham, who bequeathed himself to the college. ⊠ *Gower St., Bloomsbury, WC1* Ⓤ *Euston Sq., Goodge St.*

Bloomsbury & Legal London at a Glance

SIGHTS
British Library
Gray's Inn
Inner Temple
Lincoln's Inn
Middle Temple
Royal Courts of Justice
Staple Inn
Temple
Temple Church
University College

MUSEUMS & GALLERIES
British Museum
Dickens House Museum
London Cartoon Museum
Percival David Foundation
  of Chinese Art
Petrie Museum
Prince Henry's Room
Sir John Soane's Museum

WHERE TO EAT (⇨ Ch. 15)

BUDGET DINING
Busabe Eathai, *Thai*
Lemonia, *Greek*
The Social, *English*
Yoisho, *Japanese*

MODERATE DINING
Crazy Bear, *Thai*
Fino, *Spanish*
North Sea Fish Restaurant,
  Seafood

EXPENSIVE DINING
Elena's L'Etoile, *French*
Galvin, *French*
The Providores & Tapa
  Room, *Eclectic*
Villandry, *French*
Hakkasan, *Chinese*

WHERE TO STAY (⇨ Ch. 16)

BUDGET LODGING
Alhambra Hotel
Arosfa Hotel
The Generator
Harlingford Hotel
Morgan Hotel
The Ridgemount
St. Margaret's
Tavistock Hotel

MODERATE LODGING
Blooms
The Buckingham
Novotel Euston

EXPENSIVE LODGING
Charlotte Street Hotel
Jurys Great Russell Street
Montague on the Gardens
myhotel bloomsbury
Sanderson

PUBS & NIGHTLIFE
(⇨ Ch. 17)
The Lamb, *pub*
Museum Tavern, *pub*

ARTS & ENTERTAINMENT
(⇨ Ch. 18)
Bloomsbury Theater
Peacock Theatre, *dance*
The Place, *dance*

SHOPPING (⇨ Ch. 19)

ACCESSORIES
James Smith & Sons Ltd

ART GALLERIES & CRAFTS
Contemporary Applied Arts

BOOKS/PRINTED MATTER
Gay's the Word
Gosh!
Waterstone's on Gower
  Street

HOUSEHOLD ITEMS
Heal's
Muji
Purves & Purves

The City

WORD OF MOUTH

"We arrived at the Tower of London just before 9:30 AM and went directly to the Crown Jewels, which were spectacular and completely uncrowded. I tried, unsuccessfully, to convince my dear husband that just ONE of those mere baubles would keep me happy forever . . . oh well, a girl can dream."

–fun4all4

THE CITY

The City, as opposed to the city, is the capital's fast-beating financial heart. Behind a host of imposing neoclassical facades lie the banks and exchanges whose frantic trade determines the fortunes that underpin London. But the "Square Mile" is much more than London's Wall Street—the capital's economic engine room also has currency as a religious and political center St. Paul's Cathedral has looked after Londoners' souls since the seventh century, and the Tower of London—that moat-surrounded royal fortress, prison, and jewel house—has taken care of beheading them. The City's maze of backstreets is also home to a host of old churches, marketplaces, and cozy pubs.

What's Here

There are many starting points to explore the City, but **Temple Bar Memorial,** at the top of the Strand, is the site of the only surviving entry point—the gate itself was removed in 1878 to widen the road. From here, **Fleet Street,** the site of England's first printing press, was the undisputed seat of British journalism until the 1980s. The church of **St. Bride's,** nearby, is another Wren minimasterpiece and still the church for journalists.

Nestled behind Fleet Street is **Dr. Johnson's House,** former home of the man who claimed that to be bored of London was to be bored of life. Eastward, **Ludgate Hill** provides the best approach to arguably London's most distinctive building, **St. Paul's Cathedral,** designed by Sir Christopher Wren and the fourth church to occupy the site. Opposite the Cathedral is **Temple Bar**, the original entrance to the City, painstakingly moved here brick-by-brick. To the south are clear views of the newly constructed **Millennium Bridge**, the pedestrian-only steel suspension bridge that links the City to the South Bank of the

HERE'S WHERE

The ancient church St. Bartholomew the Great makes a guest appearance in the film *Four Weddings and a Funeral*.

Thames. The **Central Criminal Court** (nicknamed **Old Bailey**), the highest court in the land, lies to the north, on the way to the famous 800-year-old **Smithfield Market**, whose Victorian halls are the site of a daily early-morning meat market.

Standing opposite is the ancient church of **St. Bartholomew the Great** and **St. Bartholomew Hospital**, both begun in 1123 by Henry I's favourite courtier Rahere, who caught malaria and, surviving, vowed to dedicate his life to serving the saint that had visited him in his fevered dreams.

The street named Little Britain leads to Aldersgate and the **Museum of London**, which also houses a portion of the original **Roman Wall** that ringed the City. This is a gateway to the modern **Barbican Centre**, a complex of arts venues and apartments that is all navigable above street level. To the southeast lies the **Guildhall**, headquarters of the Corporation of London that administers the City and the site of the only Roman amphitheater in London.

Nearby, the church of **St. Mary-le-Bow** and the narrow maze of streets just to its south, around **Bow Lane**, are great shopping haunts.

Cheapside leads to the epicenter of the City, the meeting point of a powerful architectural triumvirate: the **Bank of England**, the **Royal Exchange**, and **Mansion House**, where the Lord Mayor of the City of London (not to be confused with the Mayor of London, who works from City Hall on the South Bank) lives and entertains in traditionally lavish style. The Mansion House is next to another diverting and historic church, **St. Stephen Walbrook**, and the remains of the **Temple of Mithras**, at one time devoted to Bacchus, Roman god of wine and intoxication. Down King William Street lies **Monument**, built to commemorate the Great Fire of London of 1666. Northeast of its 202-foot-high tower are excellent views of two recent and unmissable additions to the City skyline: the **Lloyd's of London Building**, designed by Richard Rogers, and the **Swiss Re Tower**, designed by Norman Foster. From here, following the river east past Trinity Gardens, is one of London's most absorbing and bloody attractions, the **Tower of London. Tower Bridge** is a suitably giddying finale; wind down among the wharves of **St. Katherine's Dock**.

FLEET STREET

The newspapers have abandoned Fleet Street (also known as "The Street of Shame") for more modern offices on the fringes of the City, but for a taste of print pomp, savor the art deco chrome-and-black majesty of the old Daily Express building, home to the best selling British newspaper of all time in the postwar era, regularly shifting 4 million copies a day.

GETTING ORIENTED

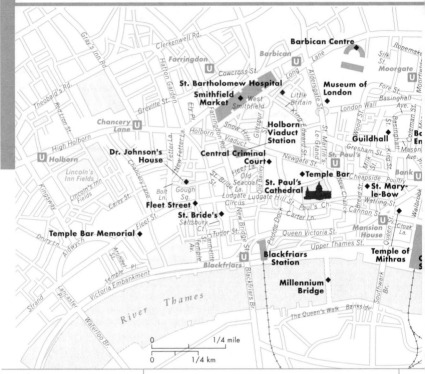

GETTING THERE	TOP 5 REASONS TO GO
The City is well served by the most concentrated selection of underground stops in London. St Paul's and Bank, on the Central Line, and Mansion House, Cannon Street, and Monument, on the District and Circle lines, deliver visitors to the heart of the City. Liverpool Street and Aldgate border the City's eastern edge, while Chancery Lane and Farringdon lie to the west. Barbican and Moorgate provide easy access to the theaters and galleries of the Barbican, while Blackfriars, to the south, leads to Ludgate Circus and Fleet Street.	■ **Monument:** Climb the 311 spiral steps to the top for dizzying views of the London skyline. ■ **St. Paul's Cathedral:** Talk into a wall of the Whispering Gallery and be heard on the opposite side. ■ **Tower of London:** Gaze in awe at the stunning Crown Jewels. ■ **Museum of London:** Relive the sights and sounds of Roman Londonium. ■ **Shops and the City:** Explore City outfitters and the upscale boutiques of Bow Lane and the Royal Exchange.

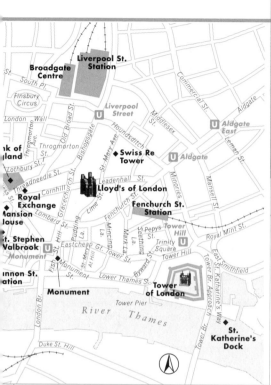

**MAKING THE MOST
OF YOUR TIME**

The "Square Mile" is as compact as the nickname suggests, with very little distance between points of interest, making it easy to dip into the City in short bursts. For full immersion in the Tower of London, set aside half a day, especially if seeing the Crown Jewels is a priority. Allow an hour minimum each for the Museum of London, St. Paul's Cathedral, and the Tower Bridge. On weekends, without the scurrying suits, the City is nearly deserted, making it hard to find lunch—and yet this is when the major attractions are at their busiest. So if you can manage to come on a weekday, do so.

A GOOD WALK

Crossing the Millennium Bridge from the Tate Modern to St. Paul's is one of the finest walks in London for views of the river and the cathedral that towers over it. Dubbed the "blaze of light," this shiny aluminum-and-steel construction is the first pedestrian-only bridge in central London in more than a century (the last being Tower Bridge in 1894).

FEELING PECKISH?

If you're in the City on a weekend, the friendly **Riverside Café Bar** (✉ St. Katherine's Way, E1 ☎ 020/7481-1464) is one of the few places you're sure to find a good cup of hot chocolate and hot and cold meals, with waterside views of the luxurious yachts and gin palaces moored at the docks.

Sweetings (✉ 39 Queen Victoria St., EC4 ☎ 020/7248-3062) is not cheap, and closed in the evenings, but it serves one of the best fish lunches in London. Not only can you refuel here on Dover sole and Black Velvet, the local brew, you can take time to observe the pinstripes at play in their natural habitat.

When you're done exploring Fleet Street, repair to the famed **Ye Olde Cheshire Cheese** (✉ 145 Fleet St., EC4 ☎ 020/7353-6170) for a pint of old-fashioned ale and a snack. It's one of London's best-loved pubs, rightly admired for its roaring log fires, and a dingy interior where you can imagine Johnson and Boswell getting together for a literary confab.

A BRIEF HISTORY

Rising from the mud of the Thames as the Roman settlement of Londinium, in AD 47, this is where the capital began. It gained immediate momentum as a trading center for materials and goods shipped in from all corners of the fledgling colony. Centuries later, William the Conqueror began building the palace that was to become the Tower of London. It went from being Henry III's defensive shelter in the 13th century to, by Tudor times, the world's most forbidding and grisly prison, where two of Henry VIII's six wives were executed. During the Middle Ages, powerful guilds that nurtured commerce took root, followed by the foundation of great trading companies, such as the Honourable East India Company, which started up in 1600.

The City's history has been punctuated by periods of chaos that have threatened to destroy it. The Great Fire of 1666 was the most serious, sparing but few of the cramped, labyrinthine streets, where the Great Plague of the previous year had already wiped out a huge portion of the population. Yet the gutted wastelands enabled a new start, driving out the plague-carrying rodents that had menaced London since the Middle Ages and forcing an architectural renaissance, led by Sir Christopher Wren. Further punishment came during the Blitz of World War II, when German bombers destroyed many buildings. Today's eclectic skyline reflects every period of its history, some sublime, some hideous.

Places to Explore

Bank of England. Known for the past couple of centuries as "the Old Lady of Threadneedle Street," after someone's parliamentary quip, the Bank of England, which has been central to the British economy since 1694, manages the national debt and the foreign exchange reserves, issues banknotes, sets interest rates, looks after England's gold, and regulates the country's banking system. Sir John Soane designed the neoclassic hulk in 1788, wrapping it in windowless walls, which are all that survives of his building. It's ironic that an executive of so sober an institution should have been Kenneth Grahame, author of *The Wind in the Willows*. This and other facets of the bank's history are traced in the Bank of England Museum (entrance is around the corner on Bartholomew Lane). The characterful furniture and paraphernalia in wood and brass contrast starkly with the interactive computer games where you can try your hand as a money-market dealer. There are gold bars on which to gaze, too, and fun facts on fraudsters of yesteryear. ⊠ *Threadneedle St., The City, EC4* ☎ *020/ 7601-5545* ⊕ *www.bankofengland.co.uk* ✉ *Free* ☉ *Weekdays and Lord Mayor's Show day, 2nd Sat. in Nov., 10–5* Ⓤ *Bank, Monument.*

Barbican Centre. With two theaters; the London Symphony Orchestra and its auditorium; the Guildhall School of Music and Drama; a major art gallery for touring and its own special exhibitions; two cinemas; a convention center; an upscale restaurant, cafés, and literary bookshops; and living space in some of the most desirable tower blocks in town, the Barbican is an enormous 1980s concrete maze that Londoners either love or hate. Navigation around the complex is via the yellow lines running, Oz-like, along the floors, with signs on the walls, although it's still easy to get lost. Actors rate the theater acoustics especially high, and the steep rake of the seating makes for a good stage view. The dance, music, and theater programs have been transformed into a yearlong fest named BITE, which stands for Barbican International Theatre Events, and encompasses dance, puppetry, and music. The emphasis is on presenting tomorrow's names today, although there are performances by established companies and artists, such as Merce Cunningham. ⊠ *Silk St., The City, EC2* ☎ *020/ 7638–8891 box office* ⊕ *www.barbican.org.uk* ✉ *Barbican Centre free, art gallery £6–£8, films £5–£7, concerts £5–£27, theater £3–£27* ☉ *Barbican Centre Mon.–Sat. 9 AM–11 PM, Sun. noon–11 PM; gallery Mon.–Sat. 10–7:30, Sun. noon–7:30; conservatory weekends noon–5:30 when not in use for private function; call first* Ⓤ *Moorgate, Barbican.*

Dr. Johnson's House. This is where Samuel Johnson lived between 1746 and 1759, compiling his famous dictionary in the attic as his health deteriorated. The only one of Johnson's residences remaining today, its elegant Georgian lines make it exactly the kind of place you would expect the Great Bear, as Johnson was nicknamed, to live. It's a shrine to a most literary man who was passionate about London, and it includes a first edition of his *Dictionary of the English Language* among the mementos of Johnson and his friend and diarist James Boswell. ⊠ *17 Gough Sq., The City, EC4* ☎ *020/7353–3745* ⊕ *www.drjh.dircon.co.uk* ✉ *£4.50* ☉ *May–Sept., Mon.–Sat. 11–5:30; Oct.–Apr., Mon.–Sat. 11–5; closed bank holidays* Ⓤ *Blackfriars, Chancery La.*

Guildhall. The Corporation of London, which oversees the City, has ceremonially elected and installed its Lord Mayor here for the last 800 years. The Guildhall was built in 1411, and though it failed to avoid either the 1666 or 1940 flames, its core survived. The Great Hall is a psychedelic patchwork of coats of arms and banners of the City Livery Companies, which inherited the mantle of the medieval trade guilds. Tradesmen couldn't even run a shop without kowtowing to these prototypical unions, and their grand banqueting halls, the plushest private dining venues in the City, are testimony to the wealth they amassed. Inside the hall, Gog and Magog, the pair of mythical giants who founded ancient Albion and the city of New Troy, upon which London was said to be built, glower down from their west-gallery grandstand in 9-foot-high painted lime-wood. The hall was also the site of famous trials, including that of Lady Jane Grey in 1553, before her execution at the Tower of London.

To the right of Guildhall Yard is the **Guildhall Art Gallery,** which includes portraits of the great and the good, cityscapes, famous battles, and a slightly cloying pre-Raphaelite section. The construction of the gallery led to the exciting discovery of London's only **Roman amphitheater,** which had lain underneath Guildhall Yard undisturbed for more than 1,800 years. It was excavated and now visitors can walk among

Continued on page 130

A *Da Vinci Code* Tour

CLOSE UP

ALTHOUGH THE REAL MEANING behind Leonardo Da Vinci's art is ultimately unknowable, the real-life places in which Dan Brown set his best-selling suspense novel, *The Da Vinci Code*, are known throughout the world, and the book has inspired travelers to visit them. All the London sights in the book are in a compact area east and south of Trafalgar Square and are accessible by bus or the Tube. In the order the sights appear in *The Da Vinci Code*—with one exception, King's College—you can easily walk this 2-mi route.

Langdon, Neveu, and Teabing's whirlwind of events begins in Paris, but midway through—realizing that the clue to the cryptex might not be in France but in England—the three board Teabing's private plane for London. Once on the ground, the threesome, hastily interpreting their latest cryptex clue, make a mad dash down Fleet Street to a Knights of the Templar fortress. To launch your own tour, take the Tube to St. Paul's station and head west on Ludgate Hill to **Fleet Street,** continuing until you get to Temple, where you'll see the Temple Bar Memorial, a young bronze griffin. Opposite the statue is an elaborate stone arch through which you pass into Middle Temple Lane, which runs south all the way to the Thames. **Temple Church** (⊠ Inner Temple La. off Fleet St., Bloomsbury Ⓤ Temple) will be on your left as you head toward the river. After you've explored the church, reverse course to the statue and continue west.

Along the Strand you'll pass by **King's College London** (⊠ The Strand, St. James's Ⓤ Temple) where, in the book, a portion of the second cryptex's message, "In London lies a knight a

Pope interred," finds new meaning for Langdon with the aid of a helpful King's College librarian's computer.

After exploring the campus, continue west on the Strand to Trafalgar Square. Just south of the square on Whitehall is the **Horse Guards Parade,** which edges **St. James's Park** (⊠ Middle Temple La., St. James's Ⓤ St. James's Park, Westminster). A character besotted with the Holy Grail has followed the trio to London, planning to usurp control of the secrets Langdon and Neveu continue to discover. Before he makes his move, though, he slips into St. James's Park to deal with an accomplice who has misbehaved.

Continue south to **Westminster Abbey** (⊠ South side of Parliament Sq., Westminster Ⓤ Westminster), the final scene of the trio's escapades in London. As Langdon and Neveu scour the **tomb of Sir Isaac Newton** for a final clue that will crack open the second cryptex, they receive a message from a rival character to meet in Westminster's **Chapter House.** In the ensuing struggle, they vanquish their nemesis. Sir Isaac Newton's grave and tomb are near the choir screen, at the north entrance to the choir.

An alternative to walking is to take Bus 11, which travels along Ludgate and Fleet Street to Trafalgar Square and Westminster. Note that Opus Dei's London office, which is mentioned in the book but is not open to the public, is more than 3 mi west of Westminster Abbey, just north (on Orme Court off Bayswater Road) of the northwest corner of Kensington Gardens. For full tours in the book's other key locales—Paris, Rome, and Scotland—pick up a copy of *Fodor's Guide to the Da Vinci Code.*

ST. PAUL'S CATHEDRAL

Sir Christopher Wren's maxim "I build for eternity" proves no empty boast.

Sublime, awesome, majestic, and inspirational are just some of the words to describe Wren's masterpiece, St. Paul's Cathedral—even more so now that it has been spruced up for its 300th anniversary in 2008.

This is the spiritual heart of the nation, where people and events are celebrated, mourned, and honoured. As you approach the cathedral your eyes are inevitably drawn skyward to the great dome, one of the largest in the world and an amazing piece of engineering. Visit in the late afternoon for evensong, and let the choir's voices transport you to a world of absolute peace in a place of perfect beauty, as pristine as the day it was completed.

TOURING ST. PAUL'S

Enter the cathedral via the main west entrance, and walk straight down the length of the nave to the central Dome Altar. Nobody can resist making a beeline for the dome, so start your tour beneath it, standing dead center on the beautiful sunburst floor, Wren's focal mirror of the magnificent design above. The dome crowns the center of the cathedral and rises to 364 feet. You will need to crick your neck upward for a remarkable spectacle—but save your strength for the "great climb" to get some fantastic views.

THE CATHEDRAL FLOOR

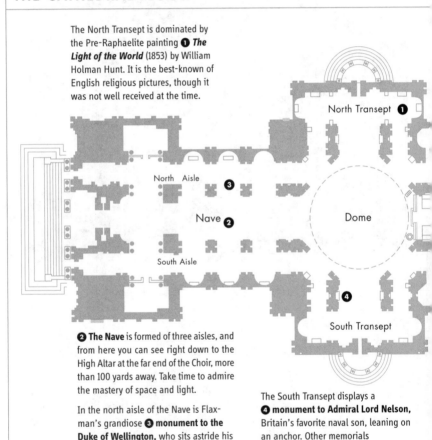

The North Transept is dominated by the Pre-Raphaelite painting ❶ *The Light of the World* (1853) by William Holman Hunt. It is the best-known of English religious pictures, though it was not well received at the time.

North Transept ❶

North Aisle ❸

Nave ❷

Dome

South Aisle

❹

South Transept

❷ **The Nave** is formed of three aisles, and from here you can see right down to the High Altar at the far end of the Choir, more than 100 yards away. Take time to admire the mastery of space and light.

In the north aisle of the Nave is Flaxman's grandiose ❸ **monument to the Duke of Wellington,** who sits astride his faithful charger, Copenhagen, the horse who carried him through the Battle of Waterloo.

The South Transept displays a ❹ **monument to Admiral Lord Nelson,** Britain's favorite naval son, leaning on an anchor. Other memorials commemorate the explorer Captain Robert Scott and the icon of British landscape painting, J.M.W. Turner.

6

CELEBRITY STATUS

St. Paul's has witnessed many momentous processions along its checkered nave. The somber state funerals of heroes Admiral Lord Nelson and the Duke of Wellington, and of Sir Winston Churchill, drew huge crowds. It was here, also, that the fairy-tale wedding of Prince Charles and Lady Diana Spencer took place, and the jubilees of Queen Victoria, George V, and the present Queen were celebrated.

The North Choir Aisle features the beautiful **❺ gilded gates** by Jean Tijou, perhaps the most accomplished artist in wrought iron of all time, as well as Henry Moore's sculpture **❻ *Mother and Child,*** its simple lines complementing the ornate surroundings.

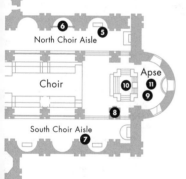

The South Choir Aisle contains a **❼ marble effigy of John Donne,** who was Dean of old St. Paul's for his final 10 years (he died in 1631). This is the only statue to have survived the Great Fire of London intact.

The Choir contains the **❽ Bishop's Throne** or cathedra, hence the name cathedral. Look aloft to the fabulous mosaics. Don't miss the exquisite, delicate carvings by Grinling Gibbons, in particular on the case of the **❾ great organ,** one of the Cathedral's greatest artifacts. It was designed by Wren and played by such illustrious figures as Handel and Mendelssohn.

❿ The High Altar, with its glorious canopy, is a profusion of marble and carved and gilded oak.

The Apse is home to the **⓫ American Memorial Chapel,** which honors the more than 28,000 U.S. soldiers who died while stationed in the U.K. during World War II. The lime-wood paneling incorporates a rocket as a tribute to the United States' achievements in space.

MUSICAL FRICTION

The organ, with its cherubs and angels, was not installed without controversy. The mighty instrument proved a tight fit, and the maker, known as Father Schmidt, and Wren nearly came to blows. Wren was reputed to have said he would not adapt his cathedral for a mere "box of whistles."

THE DOME

The dome is the crowning glory of the cathedral, a must for visitors.

At 99 feet, the ❶ **Whispering Gallery** is reached by 259 spiral steps. This is the part of the cathedral with which you bribe children—they will be fascinated by the acoustic phenomenon: whisper something to the wall on one side, and a second later it transmits clearly to the other side, 107 feet away. The only problem is identifying your whisper from the cacophony of everyone else's. Look down onto the nave from here and up to the monochrome frescoes of St. Paul by Sir James Thornhill.

More stamina is required to reach the ❷ **Stone Gallery,** at 175 feet and 378 steps from ground level. It is on the exterior of the cathedral and offers a vista of the city and the River Thames.

For the best views of all—at 280 feet and 530 steps from ground level—make the trek to the small ❸ **Golden Gallery,** the highest point of the outer dome. A hole in the floor gives a vertiginous view down. You can see the lantern above through a circular opening called the oculus. If you have a head for heights you can walk outside for a spectacular panorama of London.

The top of the dome is crowned with a ❹ **ball and cross.** At 23 feet high and weighing approximately 7 tons, it is the pinnacle of St. Paul's.

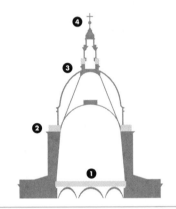

A BRIEF HISTORY

The cathedral is the masterpiece of Sir Christopher Wren (1632–1723), completed in 1710 after 35 years of building and much argument with the Royal Commission. Wren had originally been commissioned to restore Old St. Paul's, the Norman cathedral that had replaced, in its turn, three earlier versions, but the Great Fire left so little of it standing that a new cathedral was deemed necessary.

Wren's first plan, known as the New Model, did not make it past the drawing board; the second, known as the Great Model, got as far as the 20-foot oak rendering you can see here today before it, too, was rejected, whereupon Wren is said to have burst into tears. The third, however, known as the Warrant Design (because it received the royal warrant), was accepted, with the fortunate coda that the architect be allowed to make changes as he saw fit. Without that, there would be no dome, because the approved design had featured a steeple. Parliament felt that building was proceeding too slowly (in fact, 35 years is lightning speed, as cathedrals go) and withheld half of Wren's pay for the last 13 years of work. He was pushing 80 when Queen Anne finally coughed up the arrears.

■ TIP→ **To see Wren's Great Model, you must join a Triforium Tour (Mon. and Tues. at 11:30 and 2, Fri. at 2). These one-hour tours include a visit to the library and a glimpse of the famous geometrical staircase. The visit ends in the Trophy Room, where Wren's Great Model is on display. The tour costs £14 per person and includes entry to the cathedral and access to the crypt and galleries. It's best to book in advance by calling 020/7246-8357 or sending an e-mail to visits@stpaulscathedral.org.uk.**

THE CRYPT

A visit to the vast crypt is a time for reflection and contemplation, with some 200 memorials to see. If it all becomes too somber, take solace in the café or shop near the crypt entrance.

The ❶ **tomb of the Duke of Wellington** comprises a simple casket made from Cornish granite. He is remembered as a hero of battle, but his name lives on in the form of boots, cigars, beef Wellington, and the capital of New Zealand.

Here lies ❷ **Admiral Nelson,** killed at the Battle of Trafalgar in 1805. His body was preserved in alcohol for the journey home, and his pickled remains were buried here beneath Cardinal Wolsey's unused 16th-century sarcophagus.

Surrounded by his family and close to a plethora of iconic artists, musicians, and scientists, the ❸ **tomb of Sir Christopher Wren** is a modest affair. A simple slab marks the resting place with an inscription that concludes "Lector, si monumentum requiris, circumspice" (Reader, if you seek his monument, look around).

The beautiful ❹ **O.B.E. Chapel** (dedicated 1960) is a symbol of the Order of the British Empire, an order of chivalry established in 1917 by George V. The theme of sovereign and Commonwealth is represented in the glass panels.

The vast ❺ **treasury** houses the cathedral's plate, although a good deal has been lost or stolen over the centuries—in particular in a daring robbery of 1810—and much of the display comes from other London churches.

PLANNING YOUR DAY

WHAT'S NEARBY: After an early start and a morning spent at the cathedral, stroll over the Millennium Bridge (don't forget to look back for a great view of St. Paul's) and have lunch at Tate Modern. The restaurant at the top of the gallery has spectacular views of London.

CONTACT INFO: ✉ *St. Paul's Churchyard, Ludgate Hill EC4* Ⓜ *St. Paul's* ☎ *020/7236-4128* ⊕ *www.stpauls.co.uk*

ADMISSION: Adults: cathedral, crypt, ambulatory, and gallery £9. **Family ticket** (2 adults, 2 children): £21.50. **Children 7–16:** £3.50.

Tours: A guided tour of the cathedral and crypt lasts 1½–2 hours and costs £3. Tours start at 11, 11:30, 1:30, and 2. Rental audio tours cost £3.50 and last 45 min.

HOURS: The cathedral is a house of worship. Services may cause changes to the visiting hours on any given day, so be sure to call ahead.

Cathedral: Mon.–Sat. 8:30–4:30 (last admission at 4).
Shop: Mon.–Sat. 9–5, Sun. 10:30–5.
Crypt café: Mon.–Sat. 9–5, Sun. 10–5.

the remains, although most of the relics can be seen at the Museum of London, through which guided tours can be booked.

The 1970s west wing houses the **Guildhall Library**; it has mainly City-related books and documents, plus a collection belonging to one of the city livery companies, the Worshipful Company of Clockmakers, in the **Clockmakers' Company Museum,** with more than 600 timepieces on show, including a skull-faced watch that belonged to Mary, Queen of Scots. It's one of the most important horological collections in the country. ⊠ *Gresham St., The City, EC2* ☎ *020/7606–3030, 020/7332–3700 gallery* ⊕ *www.cityoflondon.gov.uk* 🎫 *Free; gallery and amphitheater £2.50* ⊙ *Mon.–Sat. 9:30–5; clockmaker museum weekdays 9:30–4:45; gallery Mon.–Sat. 10–5, Sun. noon–4, last admission 4:30 or 3:30* Ⓤ *St. Paul's, Moorgate, Bank, Mansion House.*

■ TIP➔ **Cheapside, running south of Guildhall, wasn't all that cheap actually. In 1500 one Italian visitor counted 52 goldsmiths shops and was blown away that London could boast more in the way of gold than Rome, Florence, or Milan.**

★ Ⓒ **Monument.** Commemorating the "dreadful visitation" of the Great Fire of 1666, this is the world's tallest isolated stone column. It is the work of Wren, who was asked to erect it "on or as neere unto the place where the said Fire soe unhappily began as conveniently may be." And so here it is—at 202 feet, exactly as tall as the distance it stands from Farriner's baking house in Pudding Lane, where the fire started. ⊠ *Monument St., The City, EC3* ☎ *020/7626–2717* ⊕ *www.towerbridge.org.uk* 🎫 *£2 combination ticket gives £1 discount off entry to Tower Bridge* ⊙ *Daily 10–5:40; hrs subject to change, call before visiting* Ⓤ *Monument.*

> **A VIEW TO REMEMBER**
>
> At the top of the Monument's 311-step spiral staircase (a better workout than any StairMaster) is a gallery providing fantastic views from the heart of the City and is helpfully caged to prevent suicidal jumps, which were a trend for a while in the 19th century.

★ Ⓒ **Museum of London.** If there's one place to get the history of London sorted out, right from 450,000 BC to the present day, it's here—although there's a great deal to sort out: Oliver Cromwell's death mask, Queen Victoria's crinolined gowns, Selfridges' art deco elevators, and the Lord Mayor's coach are just some of the goodies. The museum appropriately shelters a section of the 2nd- to 4th-century London wall, which you can view from a window inside. The displays—like one of the Great Fire, a 1940s air-raid shelter, a Georgian prison cell, a Roman living room, and a Victorian street complete with fully stocked shops—are complemented by rich soundscapes that atmospherically re-create London life through the ages. The archaeologists and curators at the museum regularly leap from AD to BC, as fresh building work in the city uncovers more treasures. None, though, have been as exciting as the ongoing project of preserving and displaying the Roman amphitheater at the Guildhall, and you can see the rewards of that excavation with the artifacts here. ⊠ *London Wall, The City, EC2* ☎ *020/7600–0807* ⊕ *www.museumoflondon.org.uk* 🎫 *Free* ⊙ *Mon.–Sat. 10–5:50, Sun.*

noon–5:50; last admission 5:30 Ⓤ *Barbican.*

Old Bailey. This, the present-day Central Criminal Court, is where Newgate Prison stood from the 12th century right until the beginning of the 20th century. Called by the novelist Henry Fielding the "prototype of hell," few survived for long in the version pulled down in 1770. Those who didn't starve were hanged, or pressed to death in the Press Yard, or they succumbed to the virulent gaol (the archaic British spelling of "jail") fever. The next model lasted only a couple of years before being torn down by raving mobs during the anti-Catholic Gordon Riots of 1780, to be replaced by the Newgate that Dickens described in several novels, including *Oliver Twist*. The Central Criminal Court replaced Newgate in 1907 and the most famous feature of the solid Edwardian building is the gilded statue of blind Justice perched on top; she was intended to mirror the dome of St. Paul's. More intriguing are the ghoulish proceedings that unfold inside, which are open to the public—Crippen and Christie, two of England's most notorious wife-murderers, were both tried here. The day's hearings are posted on the sign outside, but there are security restrictions, and children under 14 are not allowed in; call the information line first. ✉ *Newgate St., The City, EC4* ☎ *020/7248–3277 information* ⊕ *www.cityoflondon.gov.uk; proceedings available from www. hmcourts-service.gov.uk* ⊙ *Public Gallery weekdays 10:30–1 and 2–5 (approx); line forms at Newgate St. entrance; closed bank holidays and day after* Ⓤ *St. Paul's.*

St. Bartholomew the Great. Reached via a perfect half-timber gatehouse atop a 13th-century stone archway, this is one of London's oldest churches. With the Dissolution of the Monasteries, Henry VIII had most of it torn down; the Romanesque choir loft is all that survives from the 12th century. On the other side of the road, the church's namesake St. Bartholomew's Hospital is home to a small museum. Facing both is Smithfield's meat market. ✉ *Cloth Fair, West Smithfield, The City, EC1* ☎ *020/7606–5171* ⊕ *www.greatstbarts.com* 🎟 *Church free; museum £4* ⊙ *Church Tues.–Fri. 8:30–5 (Mar.–Oct. 8:30–4), Sat. 10–1:30, Sun. 8:30–1 and 2:30–8; museum Tues.–Fri. 10–4* Ⓤ *Barbican, Farringdon.*

St. Bride's. Appropriately named for anyone contemplating impending nuptials, the distinctively tiered steeple of this Christopher Wren–designed church gave rise to the shape of the traditional wedding cake. One early couple inspired to marry here

---

ICE-SKATING

Broadgate Ice is an outdoor rink for skaters of all abilities. It's open between November and April, and costs £8 a session, including skate rental, £5 for children. Call for opening times. Broadgate Arena, Eldon St., The City, EC2 ☎ 020/7505–4068 ⊕ www.broadgateice.co.uk Ⓤ Liverpool St.

TRIP TIP

If, for whatever reason, you're thirsting for a drink at 6 AM in the morning, head to the pubs around here, which are specially licensed to serve early-morning pints to market traders at the end of a hard day's night.

6

were the parents of Virginia Dare, the first European child born in colonial America in 1587. As St. Paul's (in Covent Garden) is the actors' church, so St. Bride's belongs to journalists, many of whom have been buried or memorialized here. The poet John Milton lived in the churchyard for a while, and by 1664 the crypts were so crowded that diarist Samuel Pepys, who was baptized here, had to bribe the grave digger to "justle together" some bodies to make room for his deceased brother. Now the crypts house a museum of the church's rich history, and a bit of Roman sidewalk. ✉ *Fleet St., The City, EC4* ☎ *020/7427–0133* ⊕ *www.stbrides.com* 🖅 *Free* ☽ *Weekdays 8–6, Sat. 11–3, Sun. for services only 10–1, 5–7:30; crypt closed Sun.* Ⓤ *Chancery La.*

St. Mary-le-Bow. This church is another classic City survivor; various versions have stood on the site since the 11th century. In 1284 a local goldsmith took refuge here after committing a murder, only to be killed inside the church by enraged relatives of his victim. The church was abandoned for a time afterward, but started up again, and was rebuilt in its current form after the Great Fire. Wren's 1673 incarnation has one of the most famous sets of bells around—a Londoner must be born within the sound of the "Bow Bells" to be a true cockney. The origin of that idea was probably the curfew rung on the bells during the 14th century, even though "cockney" only came to mean Londoner three centuries later, and then it was an insult. The Bow takes its name from the bow-shape arches in the Norman crypt. The garden contains a statue of local boy Captain John Smith, who founded Virginia in 1606 and was later captured by Native Americans. ✉ *Cheapside, The City, EC2* ☎ *020/7248–5139* ⊕ *www.stmarylebow.co.uk* ☽ *Mon.–Thurs. 6:30 AM–5:45 PM, Fri. 6:30 AM–4 PM* Ⓤ *Mansion House.*

> **DID YOU KNOW?**
>
> The traditional definition of "Cockneys"—East End London residents with their own accent and dialect—is that they were born within hearing distance of the bells of St Mary-le-Bow church. The Cockney dialect includes rhyming slang ("apples," as in "apples and pears," to mean "stairs") and adapting Yiddish words such as schtum and kosher. In recent years, the term "mockney" has become a light-hearted term of abuse for posh types who try to sound Cockney.

St. Paul's Cathedral   **See Page 125**

NEED A BREAK?

The **Place Below** (☎ 020/7329–0789), in St. Mary-le-Bow's crypt, is packed with City workers weekdays at lunchtime—the self-service vegetarian menu includes soup and quiche, which are particularly good. Lunches are served from 10:30 until 2:30, weekdays only. It's also open for breakfast.

St. Stephen Walbrook. This is the parish church many think is Wren's best, by virtue of its practice dome, which predates the one at St. Paul's by

Continued on page 140

THE TOWER OF LONDON

The Tower is a microcosm of the city itself—a sprawling, organic hodgepodge of buildings that inspires reverence and terror in equal measure. See the block on which Anne Boleyn was beheaded, gaze at the Crown Jewels, and pay homage to the ravens who keep the monarchy safe.

An architectural patchwork of time, the oldest building of the complex is the fairytale White Tower, conceived by William the Conqueror in 1078 as both a royal residence and a show of power to the troublesome Anglo-Saxons he had subdued at the Battle of Hastings. Today's Tower has seen everything, as a palace, barracks, a mint for producing coins, an archive, an armoury, and the Royal menagerie (home of the country's first elephant). Equally enticing is the stunning opulence of the Crown Jewels, kept on-site in the heavily fortified Jewel House. Most of all, though, the Tower is known for death: it's been a place of imprisonment, torture, and execution for the realm's most rabid traitors. These days, unless you count the killer admission fees, there are far less morbid activities taking place in the Tower, but it still breathes London's history and pageantry from its every brick and offers hours of exploration.

TOURING THE TOWER

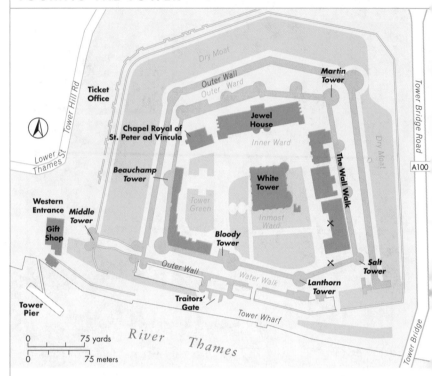

Entry to the Tower is via the **Western Entrance** and the **Middle Tower,** which feed into the outermost ring of the Tower's defenses.

Water Lane leads past the dread-inducing **Traitors' Gate,**

GOLD DIGGER?

Keep your eyes peeled as you tour the Tower: according to one story, Sir John Barkstead, goldsmith and Lieutenant of the Tower under Cromwell, hid £20,000 in gold coins here before his arrest and execution at the Restoration of Charles II.

the final point of entry for many Tower prisoners.

Toward the end of Water Lane, the **Lanthorn Tower** houses by night the ravens who keep the kingdom safe, and by day a timely high-tech reconstruction of the Catholic Guy Fawkes's plot to blow up the Houses of Parliament in 1605.

The **Bloody Tower** earned its name as the apocryphal site of the murder of two young princes, Edward and Richard, who disappeared from the Tower after being put there in 1483 by their uncle, Richard III. Two little skeletons (now in

Westminster Abbey) were found buried close to the White Tower in 1674 and are thought to be theirs.

The **Beauchamp Tower** housed upper-class miscreants: Latin graffiti about Lady Jane Grey can be glimpsed today on its walls.

Like a prize gem set at the head of a royal crown, the **White Tower** is the Tower's centerpiece. Its four towers dominate the Inner Ward, a fitting and forbidding reminder of Norman strength at the time of the conquest of England.

ROYAL BLING

The Crown of Queen Elizabeth, the Queen Mother, from 1937, contains the exotic 105-carat Koh-i-Noor (mountain of light) diamond.

Jewel House, Waterloo Barracks

Once inside the White Tower, head upstairs for the **Armouries,** where the biggest attraction, quite literally, is the well-endowed suit of armor worn by Henry VIII. There is a matching outfit for his horse.

Other fascinating exhibits include the set of Samurai armor presented to James I in 1613 by the emperor of Japan, and the tiny set of armor worn by Henry VIII's young son Edward.

The **Jewel House** in **Waterloo Barracks** is the Tower's biggest draw, perfect for playing pick-your-favorite-crown from the wrong side of bulletproof glass. Not only are these crowns, staffs, and orbs encrusted with heavy-duty gems, they are invested with the authority of centuries of monarchical power in England, since the 1300s.

Outside, pause at **Tower Green,** permanent departure point for the few prisoners whose executions were considered too sensitive for the vagaries of nearby Tower Hill. The Tower's most famous female victims—Anne Boleyn, Margaret Countess of Salisbury, Catherine Howard, and Lady Jane Grey—all went this decorous way.

Behind a well-kept square of grass stands the **Chapel Royal of St. Peter ad Vincula,** a delightful Tudor church and final resting place of six beheaded Tudor bodies. ▇ TIP → **Visitors are welcome for services and can also enter after 4:30 PM daily.**

The **Salt Tower,** reputedly the most haunted corner of the complex, marks the start of the **Wall Walk,** a bracing promenade along the stone spiral steps and battlements of the Tower that looks down on the trucks, taxis, and shimmering high-rises of modern London.

The Wall Walk ends at the **Martin Tower,** an old home of the Crown Jewels and now host to an exhibit that explains the art of fashioning royal headwear and includes 12,314 cut and uncut diamonds and the frames of five royal crowns.

On leaving the Tower, browse the **gift shop,** and wander the wharf that overlooks the Thames, leading to a picture-postcard view of Tower Bridge.

TIME KILLERS

Some prisoners managed to keep themselves plenty amused: Sir Walter Raleigh grew tobacco on Tower Green, and in 1561 suspected sorcerer Hugh Draper carved an intricate astronomical clock on the walls of his Salt Tower cell.

WHO ARE THE BEEFEATERS?

First of all, they're not technically known as Beefeaters, but as Yeoman Warders, first appointed as special bodyguards to King Henry VII following the Battle of Bosworth Field in 1485. No one quite knows where the term "Beefeater" originated: it may be from the French *buffetiers* (palace guards) or from "befeathered," in relation to their hats, although the most likely origin is that these guards could eat from the King's table.

Originally, the Yeoman Warders also served as jailers of the Tower, doubling as torturers when necessary. (So it would have been a Beefeater tightening the thumb screws, or ratchetting the rack another notch on some unfortunate prisoner. Smile nicely.) Today 36 Yeoman Warders, along with the Chief Yeoman Warder and the Yeoman Gaoler, live within the walls of the Tower with their families, in accommodations in the Outer Ward. They stand guard over the Tower, conduct tours, and lock up at 9:53 PM every night with the Ceremony of the Keys.

■ TIP→ Tickets to the Ceremony of the Keys are available by writing several months in advance; check the Tower Web site for details.

HARK THE RAVENS!

Legend has it that should the hulking black ravens ever leave, the White Tower will crumble and the kingdom fall. Charles II, no doubt jumpy after his father's execution and the monarchy's short-term fall from grace, made a royal decree in 1662 that there should be at least six of the carrion-eating nasties present at all times. There have been some close calls. During World War II, numbers dropped to one, echoing the precarious fate of the war-wracked country. In 2005, two (of eight) died over Christmas when Thor—the most intelligent but also the largest bully of the bunch—killed new recruit Gundolf, named after the Tower's 1070 designer. Pneumonia put an end to Bran, leaving lifelong partner Branwen without her mate.

■ DID YOU KNOW? In 1981 a raven named Grog, perhaps seduced by his alcoholic moniker, escaped to an East End pub after 21 years at the Tower. Others have been banished for "conduct unbecoming."

The six that remain, each one identified by a colored band around a claw, are much loved by the Yeoman Warder Raven Master for their fidelity (they mate for life) and their cheek (capable of 440 noises, they are witty and scolding mimics). It's not only the diet of blood-soaked biscuits, rabbit, and scraps from the mess kitchen that keeps them coming back. Their lifting feathers on one wing are trimmed, meaning they can manage

the equivalent of a lop-sided air-bound hobble but not much more. For the first half of 2006 the ravens were moved indoors full-time as a preventive measure against avian flu but have since been allowed out and about again. In situ they are a territorial lot, sticking to Tower Green and the White Tower, and lodging nightly by Wakefield Tower. They've had free front-row seats at all the most grisly moments in Tower history—Anne Boleyn's execution included.

■ TIP→ Don't get too close to the ravens: they are prone to pecking and not particularly fond of humans, unless you are the Tower's Raven Master.

And *WHAT* are they wearing?

A pike (or halberd), also known as a partisan, is the Yeoman Warder's weapon of choice. The Chief Warder carries a staff topped with a miniature silver model of the White Tower.

Anyone who refers to this as a costume will be lucky to leave the Tower with head still attached to body: this is the ceremonial uniform of the Yeoman Warders, and it comes at a cool £13,000 a throw.

The black Tudor bonnet is made of velvet; the blue undress consists of a felt top hat, with a single Tudor rose in the middle.

This Tudor-style ruff helps date the ceremonial uniform, which was first worn in 1552.

Insignia on a Yeoman Warder's upper right arm denote the rank he carried in the military.

The medals on a Yeoman Warder's chest are more than mere show: all of the men come from distinguished careers as senior non-commissioned officers (think screaming company sergeant major) in the army, navy, and air force.

This version of the royal livery bears the insignia of the current Queen ("E" for Elizabeth) but originally dates from Tudor times. The first letter changes according to the reigning monarch's Christian name; the second letter is always an "R" for *rex* (king) or *regina* (queen).

Slits in the tunic date from the times when Beefeaters were expected to ride a horse.

Red socks and black patent shoes are worn on special occasions. Visitors are more likely to see the regular blue undress, introduced in 1858 as the regular working dress of the Yeoman Warders.

The red lines down the trousers are a sign of the blood from the swords of the Yeoman Warders in their defense of the realm.

(IN)FAMOUS PRISONERS OF THE TOWER

Anne Boleyn   Lady Jane Grey   Sir Walter Raleigh

Sir Thomas More. A Catholic, Sir Thomas steadfastly refused to attend the coronation of Anne Boleyn (Henry VIII's second wife) or to recognize the multi-marrying king as head of the Church of England. Sent to the Tower for treason, in 1535 More lost his head.

Anne Boleyn. The first of Henry VIII's wives to be beheaded, Anne, who failed to provide the king with a son, was accused of sleeping with five men, including her own brother. All six got the chop in 1536. Her severed head was held up to the crowd, and her eyes were said to be moving and her lips mouthing prayer.

Margaret, Countess of Salisbury. Not the best-known prisoner in her lifetime, she has a reputation today for haunting the Tower. And no wonder: the elderly 70-year-old was condemned by Henry VIII in 1541 for a potentially treacherous bloodline (she was the last Plantagenet princess) and hacked to death by the executioner after she refused to put her head on the block like a common traitor and attempted to run away.

Queen Catherine Howard. Henry VIII's fifth wife was locked up for high treason and infidelity and beheaded in 1542 at age 20. Ever eager to please, she spent her final night practicing how to lay her head on the block.

Lady Jane Grey. The nine-days-queen lost her head in 1554 at age 16. Her death was the result of sibling rivalry gone seriously wrong, when Protestant Edward VI slighted his Catholic sister Mary in favor of Lady Jane as heir, and Mary decided to have none of it.

Guy Fawkes. The man who tried to bring down the Houses of Parliament and kill the king in the deadly Catholic Gunpowder Plot of 1605 was first incarcerated in the chambers of the Tower, where King James I requested he be tortured in ever-worsening ways. Perhaps unsurprisingly, he confessed. He met his seriously grisly end in the Old Palace Yard at Westminster, where he was hung, drawn, and quartered in 1607.

Sir Walter Raleigh. Once a favorite of Elizabeth I, he offended her by secretly marrying her Maid of Honor and was chucked in the Tower. As a conspirator against James I, he paid with his life. A frequent visitor to the Tower (he spent 13 years there in three stints), he managed to get the Bloody Tower enlarged on account of his wife and growing family. He was finally executed in 1618 in Old Palace Yard, Westminster.

Josef Jakobs. The last man to be executed in the Tower was caught as a spy when parachuting in from Germany and executed by firing squad in 1941. The chair he sat in when he was shot is preserved in the Royal Armouries' artifacts store.

FOR FURTHER EVIDENCE...

A trio of buildings in the Inner Ward, the **Bloody Tower, Beauchamp Tower,** and **Queen's House,** all with excellent views of the execution scaffold in Tower Green, are the heart of the Tower's prison accommodations and home to a permanent exhibition about notable inmates.

TACKLING THE TOWER (without losing your head)

☎ 0870/756-6060 ⊕ www.hrp.org.uk ⌑ £15, children 16 and under £9.50, children under 5 free. Family tickets (2 adults, 3 children) £43 ⊙ Mar.-Oct., Tues.-Sat. 9-6, Sun. and Mon. 10-6; last admission at 5. Nov.-Feb., Tues.-Sat. 9-5, Sun. and Mon. 10-5; last admission at 4 Ⓤ Tower Hill

■ TIP➜ You can buy tickets from automatic kiosks on arrival, or up to seven days in advance at any Tube station. Avoid lines completely by booking by telephone (☎ 0870/756-7070, weekdays 9–9, weekends 10–5) or online.

WITH KIDS: The Tower's centuries-old cobblestones are not exactly stroller-friendly, but strollers are permitted inside most of the buildings. If you do bring one, be prepared to leave it temporarily unsupervised (the stroller, that is—not your child) outside the White Tower, which has no access. There are baby-changing facilities in the Brick Tower restrooms behind the Jewel House.

■ TIP➜ Tell your child to find one of the Yeoman Warders if he or she should get lost; they will in turn lead him or her to the Byward Tower, which is where you should meet.

MAKING THE MOST OF YOUR TIME: Without doubt, the Tower is worth two to three hours. A full hour of that would be seriously well spent

by joining one of the Yeoman Warders' tours. It's hard to better their insight, vitality, and humor—they are knights of the realm living their very own fairytale castle existence.

The Crown Jewels are worth the wait, the White Tower is essential, and the Medieval Palace and Bloody Tower should at least be breezed through.

■ TIP➜ It's best to visit on weekdays, when the crowds are smaller.

IN A HURRY? If you have less than an hour, head down Wall Walk, through a succession of towers, which eventually spit you out at the Martin Tower. The view over modern London is quite a contrast.

TOURS: Tours given by a Yeoman Warder leave from the main entrance near Middle Tower every half-hour from 10 AM to 4 PM, and last about an hour. Beefeaters give occasional 30-minute talks in the Lanthorn Tower about their daily lives. Both tours are free.

GOOD SOUVENIRS: You can live like a king yourself with a few choice purchases in the Tower gift shop: an elegant bottle of walnut or bramble liqueur goes for £8.50, and sparkling tiaras start at £39.99. Regal on a budget? Pick up a Mario Testino postcard of Princess Diana for £0.75.

some 30 years. Yet there's far more to the history of the Church than as a dry run for its next-door big brother. There has been a church here since the 7th century, built on the site of an older Roman shrine. Inside the church, called "the most perfectly proportioned interior in the world" by one admirer, two sights warrant investigation: Henry Moore's 1987 central stone altar, which sits beneath the dome ("like a lump of Camembert," say critics), and, well, a telephone—an eloquent tribute to that savior of souls, Rector Chad Varah, who founded the Samaritans, givers of phone aid to the suicidal, here in 1953. ⊠ *Walbrook St., The City, EC4* ☎ *020/ 7626–8242* ☉ *Mon.–Thurs. 10–4, Fri. 10–3* Ⓤ *Bank, Cannon St.*

Ⓒ **Tower Bridge.** Despite its venerable,
Fodor'sChoice nay, medieval, appearance, this is a
★ Victorian youngster. Constructed of steel, then clothed in Portland stone, it was deliberately styled in the Gothic persuasion to complement the Tower next door, and it's famous for its enormous bascules—the "arms," which open to allow large ships through. Although this still happens occasionally, when river traffic was dense the bascules were raised about five times a day.

The exhibition **Tower Bridge Experience** is a fun tour inside the building to discover how one of the world's most famous bridges actually works, and to see the fantastic views on the outside. First, take in the romance of the panoramas from the east and west walkways between those grand turrets. On the east, the modern superstructures and ships of Docklands, and west, the best look at the steel and glass "futuristic mushroom" that is Greater London Assembly's City Hall, the Tower of London, St. Paul's, and the Monument. Then back down to the nitty gritty of the inner workings, which you learn about through hands-on displays and films. ☎ *020/7403–3761* ⊕ *www.towerbridge.org.uk* ☎ *£5.50; joint ticket available for Monument* ☉ *Daily 9:30–5:30; last entry at 5* Ⓤ *Tower Hill.*

> **QUIRKY LONDON**
>
> There's no missing the **Swiss Re Building,** also known as "The Gherkin," the Norman Foster masterpiece completed in 2003. It surges above Richard Rogers's mold-breaking Lloyd's of London, directly opposite, with its sculpted cucumberlike form. Spiraling light wells appear to wrap around the 40-story building, forming its distinctive shape; between are levels of office space, many of which are still unfilled. The two-tone diamond-pattern glazing—dark for the light wells and light for the office levels—gives the effect of a techno maypole, which can be appreciated for miles around. 30 St. Mary Axe, The City, EC3 Ⓤ Bank, Monument, Liverpool St., Aldgate

Tower of London   See Page 133

The City at a Glance

SIGHTS
Bank of England
Central Criminal Court
  (Old Bailey)
Dr. Johnson's House
Guildhall
London Bridge
Lloyds of London
Mansion House
Millennium Bridge
Monument
Roman Wall
Royal Exchange
St. Bartholomew the Great
St. Bartholomew Hospital
St. Bride's
St. Mary-le-Bow
St. Paul's Cathedral
St. Stephen Walbrook
Swiss Re Building
Temple Bar
Temple Bar Memorial
Temple of Mithras
Tower of London
Tower Bridge

MUSEUMS & GALLERIES
Barbican Gallery
The Curve
Museum of London

WHERE TO EAT (⇨ Ch. 15)

BUDGET DINING
E Pellicci, *English*
Simpson's Tavern, *English*
Sông Qué Café,
  Vietnamese

MODERATE DINING
Coach & Horses, *English*
The Eagle, *Mediterranean*
Moro, *Mediterranean*
The Real Greek, *Greek*
St. John Bread & Wine,
  Contemporary

EXPENSIVE DINING
Chez Bruce, *French*
Club Gascon, *French*
Gaucho Grill, *Latin*
Plateau, *French*
St. John, *Contemporary*
Sweetings, *Seafood*

WHERE TO STAY (⇨ Ch. 16)

BUDGET LODGING
City of London YHA

EXPENSIVE LODGING
Crowne Plaza London–
  The City
The Grange City
Great Eastern
Malmaison
The Rookery
Threadneedles

PUBS & NIGHTLIFE
  (⇨ Ch. 17)
Black Friar, *pub*
Ye Olde Cheshire Cheese,
  pub

ARTS & ENTERTAINMENT
  (⇨ Ch. 18)
Barbican Centre, *dance/
  film/theater*

SHOPPING (⇨ Ch. 19)

MARKETS & MALLS
St. Katherine's Dock
Smithfield Market

6

The East End

WORD OF MOUTH

"I've posted about Spitalfields before. I think it's a great way to spend a Sunday morning. Depending on your stamina there are four East End markets going on, in order from earliest to latest opening: Brick Lane, Columbia Road Flower Market, Petticoat Lane, and Spitalfields (my favorite of the four)."

—obxgirl

THE EAST END

Sightseeing
★ ★ ★

Nightlife
★ ★ ★ ★ ★

Dining
★ ★ ★

Lodging

Shopping
★ ★ ★ ★

Made famous by Dickens and infamous by Jack the Ripper, the East End is one of London's most hauntingly evocative neighborhoods. It may have fewer conventional tourist attractions but is rich in folk history, architectural gems, and feisty burgeoning culture. This is where you'll see trends being set by young, rakish hipsters dressed in vintage clothing mixed up with original pieces by young, local design talent. Once the focus of a large Jewish community, the area is now populated by students, creative types, and Bengali immigrants, whose influence is everywhere from innumerable curry houses to glittering sari shops to colorful street festivals. To experience the East End at its most lively, make sure you visit on the weekend—here it's possible to shop, eat, drink, and party your way through a whole 72 hours.

What's Here

Near the Aldgate East Tube stop, behind Houndsditch, is the **Bevis Marks Spanish and Portuguese Synagogue,** London's oldest synagogue, named after the street on which it stands.

The George Yard Buildings once stood behind No. 90 Whitechapel High Street; nowadays you'll come across the famous **Whitechapel Art Gallery** instead. A few steps east is the **Whitechapel Bell Foundry**; and, nearby, Osborn Street, which soon becomes **Brick Lane,** home to the **Old**

Truman Brewery. ■ TIP→ The Sunday morning junk market on Brick Lane adds further complements to the rewarding vintage-clothes shopping in this area.

On the west end of Fournier Street, sits Nicholas Hawksmoor's masterpiece, **Christ Church, Spitalfields,** along with some fine early Georgian houses. On Lamb Street are the two northern entrances to **Spitalfields Market.** ■ TIP→ Look out for work by young designers, whose one-off accessories make original gifts. If you have kids, they might have fun going to **Spitalfields City Farm,** a few blocks away on Weaver Street. On Folgate Street, just off Commercial Street, is **Dennis Severs's House.**

Arnold Circus is a perfect circle of Arts and Crafts–style houses around a central raised bandstand; this is the core of the Boundary Estate— "model" housing built by Victorian philanthropists for the slum-dwelling locals and completed as the 20th century began. Two streets north is **Columbia Road,** which on Sunday (8–2) gets buried under forests of shrubs and blooms of all shapes and sizes during London's main plant and **flower market.** Prices are ultralow, and lots of the Victorian shop windows around the stalls are filled with horticultural wares, accessories, and antiques. ■ TIP→ Arrive early to see the market in full sway and at its best. You can pick up coffee and a bagel for breakfast here from food stalls on the street.

On Kingsland Road, the **Geffrye Museum** occupies a row of early-18th-century almshouses. That bastion of contemporary art, the **White Cube** gallery, lies to the west in trendy Hoxton Square. To the east, meanwhile, is the quirky **Bethnal Green Museum of Childhood.**

Farther east still, toward Mile End, are the former **Trinity Almshouses,** with the statue of William Booth on the very spot where the first Salvation Army meetings were held. On the northwest corner of Cambridge Heath Road, is the **Blind Beggar** pub, with the **Royal London Hospital** a few yards to the left and its **Archives** behind.

In the outlying Docklands area, accessed using the Docklands Light Railway (DLR), the **Ragged School Museum** and the **Museum in Docklands** reveal even more about the East End's fascinating history.

Places to Explore

☺ **Bethnal Green Museum of Childhood.** This is the East End outpost of the Victoria & Albert Museum—in fact, this entire iron, glass, and brown-brick building was transported here from South Kensington in 1875. Since then, believe it or not, its contents have grown into the biggest toy collection in the world. The central hall is a bit like the Geffrye Museum zapped into miniature: here are dollhouses (some royal) of every period. Each genre of plaything has its own enclosure, so if teddy bears are your weakness, you need waste no time with the train sets. The museum's title is justified upstairs, in the fascinating—and possibly unique— galleries on the social history of childhood from baby dolls to Beanie Babies. Free art "carts" of goodies are available on weekends for children over age three with a ticket from the admission desk. There's also a soft-play area for little kids so the "big" ones can gaze longer at the museum's collection, a daily dressing-up area with old-fashioned clothes,

Continued on page 149

GETTING ORIENTED

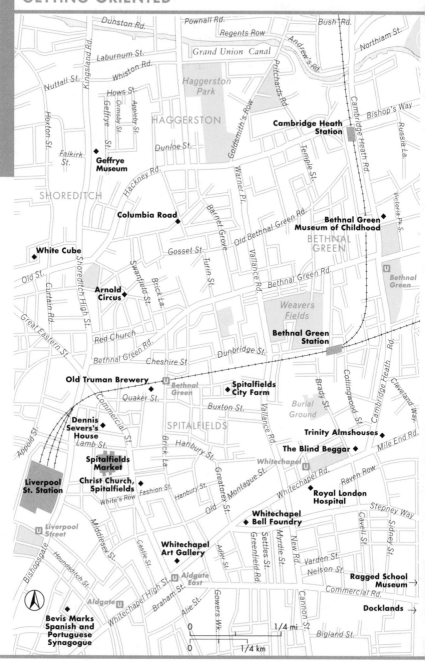

Dunston Rd.
Pownall Rd.
Regents Row
Bush Rd.
Northiam St.
Grand Union Canal
Andrew's Rd.
Laburnum St.
Whiston Rd.
Nuttall St.
Hows St.
Haggerston Park
Cambridge Heath Rd.
Bishop's Way
Russia La.
HAGGERSTON
Cambridge Heath Station
Geffrye St.
Ormsby St.
Appleby St.
Hoxton St.
Falkirk St.
Dunloe St.
Temple St.
Geffrye Museum
Hackney Rd.
Warner Pl.
Victoria Pk. S.
SHOREDITCH
Columbia Road
Barnet Grove
Old Bethnal Green Rd.
Bethnal Green Museum of Childhood
BETHNAL GREEN
White Cube
Gosset St.
Turin St.
Vallance Rd.
Bethnal Green
Old St.
Shoreditch High St.
Swanfield St.
Brick La.
Bethnal Green Rd.
Curtain Rd.
Arnold Circus
Weavers Fields
Great Eastern St.
Red Church
Bethnal Green Station
Bethnal Green Rd.
Cheshire St.
Dunbridge St.
Old Truman Brewery
Bethnal Green
Spitalfields City Farm
Brady St.
Collingwood St.
Cambridge Heath Rd.
Cleveland Way
Quaker St.
Buxton St.
Burial Ground
Commercial St.
SPITALFIELDS
Vallance Rd.
Trinity Almshouses
Mile End Rd.
Dennis Severs's House
Appold St.
Lamb St.
Brick La.
Hanbury St.
The Blind Beggar
Whitechapel
Spitalfields Market
Greatorex St.
Whitechapel Rd.
Raven Row
Liverpool St. Station
Christ Church, Spitalfields
Fashion St.
Hanbury St.
Old Montague St.
Royal London Hospital
Stepney Way
White's Row
Liverpool Street
Middlesex St.
Whitechapel Bell Foundry
New Rd.
Caveil St.
Sidney St.
Bishopsgate
Houndsditch St.
Castle St.
Whitechapel Art Gallery
Adler St.
Settles St.
Greenfield Rd.
Myrdle St.
Varden St.
Nelson St.
Ragged School Museum →
Aldgate East
Whitechapel High St.
Braham St.
Alie St.
Gowers Wk.
Cannon St.
Commercial Rd.
Docklands →
Aldgate
Bevis Marks Spanish and Portuguese Synagogue
Bigland St.

0 ——— 1/4 mi
0 ——— 1/4 km

TOP 5 REASONS TO GO

■ **Geffrye Museum:** Stroll around the walled herb garden, then have afternoon tea at the glass-fronted museum café.

■ **Columbia Road flower market:** Take advantage of jet lag and arrive early on a Sunday morning.

■ **Brick Lane shopping:** Poke about the thrift stores and vintage clothes shops on (and around) Brick Lane.

■ **Spitalfields Market:** Hunt for original accessories while eating organic chocolate cake on weekends.

■ **East End nightlife:** Have a hedonistic night out bar- and club-crawling in Hoxton and Shoreditch.

FEELING PECKISH?

At **Coffee@Brick Lane** (✉ 154 Brick La. ☎ 020/7247-6735), organic, shade-grown coffee in various guises is served in shabby-chic surroundings with worn Chesterfield sofas for lounging. Sandwiches and soups are basic but tasty.

The **Market Coffee House** (✉ 50-52 Brushfield St. ☎ 020/7247-4110) offers sandwiches such as Scotch beef with horseradish and watercress on a roll or bagel, along with fresh soup, ploughman's lunches, and English muffins.

SAFETY

Around the central hubs of Hoxton, Shoreditch, Spitalfields, and Brick Lane, you're unlikely to experience any trouble during daylight hours; even after dark it's relatively safe. However, if you're venturing into Whitechapel or out toward Bethnal Green and Mile End, be vigilant. Muggings are common and visitors should be on their guard at all times.

GETTING THERE

The best Tube stops to start from are Whitechapel or Aldgate East on the District-Hammersmith and City lines, or from Aldgate on the Metropolitan and Circle lines. For Ragged School and Docklands Museums, use the Docklands Light Rail (DLR) network.

MAKING THE MOST OF YOUR TIME

The East End isn't picturesque, but it's vibrant, colorful, and exciting. It offers adventure, and if you want to spend a lot of time here you'll enjoy exploring its hidden corners. Spitalfields Market bustles all weekend, while Brick Lane is at its best on a Sunday morning—which is, of course, also the time to visit Columbia Road for its glorious flower market. The White Cube and Whitechapel galleries are at the forefront of the contemporary art scene and, although both are small spaces, they certainly deserve an hour or two of your time.

As far as the nightlife goes, there's no time limit here. Start as soon as you like after your shopping—Hoxton's bars are your best bet—and finish as far into the following morning as your stamina will allow.

A GOOD WALK

There are some thrilling walks that illustrate the progress of Jack and other murderers around the East End: recommended is the **Blood and Tears Walk: London's Horrible Past** (☎ 020/7625-5155), which departs daily from Barbican Tube station.

A BRIEF HISTORY

The argument goes that the East End is the "real" London—since East Enders are born "within the sound of Bow Bells," they are deemed to be Cockney through and through. The district began as separate villages—Whitechapel and Spitalfields, Shoreditch, Mile End, and Bethnal Green—melding together during the 19th century. Nowadays it's home to Bengalis and more recent immigrants from other parts of the world, including China and Africa. Some of London's poorest communities live here, and the gang culture of such notorious East Enders as the Kray twins of the '60s is still a threatening force in this area—don't be alarmed, but do beware.

Two centuries earlier, neighboring Spitalfields provided sanctuary for the French Huguenots. They had fled here to escape persecution in Catholic France around 1685, and found work in the nascent silk industry, many of them becoming prosperous master weavers. Today Spitalfields and Shoreditch are London's most exciting bohemian neighborhoods, together with Hoxton, just north of here. There are stylish boutiques and cafés, artists' studios and galleries, thanks to the plentiful old, derelict, industrial spaces that were bought up cheaply and have been imaginatively remodeled.

Within the shadow of the City walls is London's oldest synagogue, the Bevis Marks, while Whitechapel is where the Salvation Army was founded and the original Liberty Bell was forged. However, what everyone remembers most about this area is the Victorian slum streets that were stalked by the most infamous serial killer of all, Jack the Ripper.

At No. 90 Whitechapel High Street once stood George Yard Buildings, where Jack the Ripper's first victim, Martha Turner, was discovered in August 1888. A second murder occurred some weeks later, and on Hanbury Street, behind a seedy lodging house at No. 29, is where Jack the Ripper left his third mutilated victim, "Dark" Annie Chapman. A double murder followed, and then, after a month's lull, came the death on this street of Marie Kelly, the Ripper's last victim and his most revolting murder of all. He had been able to work indoors this time, and Kelly, a young widow, was found strewn all over the room, charred remains of her clothing in the fire grate. Jack the Ripper's identity never has been discovered, although theories abound, which, among others, include a cover-up of a prominent member of the British aristocracy, the artist Walter Sickert, and Francis Twomblety, an American quack doctor.

and floor-size board games such as Snakes and Ladders—guaranteed to send parents into a world of nostalgia, and children to a tranquil land before techno took its hold. ⊠ *Cambridge Heath Rd., East End, E2* ☎ *020/8983–5200, 020/8980–2415 recorded information* ⊕ *www. museumofchildhood.org.uk* ⊠ *Free* ⊘ *Sat.–Thurs. 10–5:50; art workshop weekends 11, noon, 2, and 3* Ⓤ *Bethnal Green.*

Bevis Marks Spanish and Portuguese Synagogue. Named after the street on which it stands, this is London's oldest and most splendid synagogue. Embellished with rich woodwork for the benches and galleries, marble columns, and many plunging brass chandeliers, it's beautiful simplicity. The wooden ark resembles a Wren-style screen, and contains the sacred scrolls of the five books of Moses. When Cromwell allowed the Jews to return to England in 1655 (they had been expelled in 1290), there was no Jewish community, and certainly no place to worship openly. The site chosen to build a new synagogue in 1701 already had religious connections, as the house that stood here before, Burics Marks, was owned by the Abbot of Bury St. Edmunds; over the years the name reevolved. ⊠ *Bevis Marks, East End, EC1* ☎ *020/7626–1274* ⊘ *Mon.–Wed., Fri. and Sat. 11:30–1, Sun. 10:30–12:30* Ⓤ *Aldgate East, Liverpool St.*

The Blind Beggar. This is the Victorian den of iniquity where Salvation Army founder William Booth preached his first sermon. Also, on the south side of the street stands a stone inscribed HERE WILLIAM BOOTH COMMENCED THE WORK OF THE SALVATION ARMY, JULY 1865, marking the position of the first Sally Army platform; back by the pub a statue of William Booth stands where the first meetings were held. Booth didn't supply the pub's main claim to fame, though. The Blind Beggar's real notoriety dates only from March 1966, when Ronnie Kray—one of the Kray twins, the former gangster kings of London's East End underworld—shot dead rival "godfather" George Cornell in the saloon bar. The original Albion Brewery, celebrated home to the first bottled brown ale, was next door. ⊠ *337 Whitechapel Rd., East End, E1* Ⓤ *Whitechapel.*

Christ Church, Spitalfields. This is the 1729 masterpiece of Wren's associate, Nicholas Hawksmoor. Hawksmoor built only six London churches; this one was commissioned as part of Parliament's 1711 "Fifty New Churches Act." The idea was to score points for the Church of England against such nonconformists as the Protestant Huguenots. (It must have worked; in the churchyard, you can still see some of their gravestones, with epitaphs in French.) As the local silk industry declined, the church fell into disrepair, and by 1958 the structure was crumbling and had to be closed. After 25 years—longer than it took to build—the structure has now been completely restored, from the colonnaded portico and tall spire to its bold, strident baroque-style interior. As a concert venue, particularly during the annual Spitalfields Festival, it is truly beautiful. ■ TIP➔ **If you're lucky enough to be in town during the Spitalfields Festival held every summer and winter, then don't miss the chance to attend a classical concert in this atmospheric ecclesiastical venue.** ⊠ *Commercial St., East End, E1* ☎ *020/7247–7202* ⊘ *Tues. 11–4, Sun. 1–4* Ⓤ *Aldgate East.*

Street Stories

BRICK LANE AND THE NARROW streets running off it offer a paradigm of the East End's development. Its population has moved in waves: communities seeking refuge, others escaping its poverty.

Brick Lane has seen the manufacture of bricks (during the 16th century), beer, and bagels, but nowadays it's becoming the hub of artistic bohemia, especially at the Old Truman Brewery with its calendar of diverse cultural activities. It's also the heart of Banglatown—Bengalis make up one-third of the population in this London borough, and you'll see the surrounding streets have their names written in Bengali—and where you find some of the best Indian food in town, along with ethnic video shops, colorful saris, and stacks of sticky sweets. On Sunday morning the entire street is packed with stalls in a companion market to the nearby **Petticoat Lane.**

Flower and Dean streets, past the ugly 1970s housing project on **Thrawl Street** and once the most disreputable street in London, was where Abe Sapperstein, founder of the Harlem Globetrotters, was born in 1908.

Fournier Street contains fine examples of the neighborhood's characteristic Georgian terraced houses, many of them built by the richest of the early-18th-century Huguenot silk weavers (see the enlarged windows on the upper floors). Most of those along the north side of Fournier Street have now been restored by conservationists; others still contain textile sweatshops—only now the workers are Bengali.

North of the Christ Church, Spitalfields, is **Wilkes Street,** with more 1720s Huguenot houses, while neighboring **Princelet Street** was once important to the Jewish settlers. Where No. 6 stands now, the first of several thriving Yiddish theaters opened in 1886, playing to packed houses until the following year, when a false fire alarm, rung during a January performance, ended with 17 people being crushed to death and so demoralized the theater's actor-founder, Jacob Adler, that he moved his troupe to New York. Adler played a major role in founding that city's great Yiddish theater tradition—which, in turn, had a significant effect on Hollywood.

The Spitalfields Centre occupies and is raising funds to restore and open to the public the house at No. 19 Princelet Street, which harbored French Huguenots (the upper windows are wider than usual so the Huguenot silk weavers had light to work) and, later, Polish Jews (behind its elegant Georgian door, Jacob Davidson, a shoe warehouseman, formed the Loyal United Friendly Society and a tiny synagogue). Spitalfields's grand Georgian houses were crammed with lodgings and workshops for the poor and persecuted.

Elder Street, just off Folgate, is another gem of original 18th-century houses. On the south and east side of Spitalfields Market are yet more time-warp streets that are worth a wander, such as **Gun Street,** where artist Mark Gertler (1891–1939) lived at No. 32.

★ **Dennis Severs's House.** Enter this extraordinary time machine of a house with your imagination primed to take part in the plot. The Georgian terraced house belonged to the eponymous performer-designer-scholar from Escondido, California, who dedicated his life not only to restoring his house but also to raising the ghosts of a fictitious Jervis family that might have inhabited it over the course of two centuries. Dennis Severs created a replica of Georgian life, without electricity but with a butler in full 18th-century livery to light the candles and lay the fires—for the Jervises. The rooms are shadowy set pieces of rose-laden Victorian wallpapers, Jacobean paneling, Georgian wing chairs, baroque carved ornaments, "Protestant" colors (upstairs), and "Catholic" shades (downstairs). The "Silent Night" candlelight evenings, each Monday, are the most theatrical and memorable way to "feel" the house. Private visits by special arrangement are possible. ■ TIP→ A candlelight tour of Dennis Sever's House is a magical experience relished by both Londoners and out-of-towners. But make sure you plan your visit in advance, as competition to get on a tour can be tough. ✉ *18 Folgate St., East End, E1* ☎ *020/ 7247–4013* ⊕ *www.dennissevershouse.co.uk* ✆ *£8 for Sun., £5 for Mon. open house; £12 for candlelight Mon. evenings* ⊙ *1st and 3rd Sun. of month 2–5, 1st and 3rd Mon. noon–2. Call for hrs for "Silent Night" Mon., reservations essential* Ⓤ *Liverpool St.*

★ **Geffrye Museum.** An antidote to the grand, high-society town-house interiors of the rich royal boroughs in the center of town, here's where you can discover what life was like for the general masses. It's a small museum where you can walk through a series of room sets that re-create everyday domestic interiors from the Elizabethan period through postwar 1950s utility. Originally, the museum was a row of almshouses for the poor, built in 1716 by Sir Robert Geffrye, former Lord Mayor of London, which provided shelter for 50 pensioners over the course of 200 years. The houses were rescued from closure by keen petitioners (the inhabitants were relocated to a healthier part of town) and were transformed into the Geffrye Museum in 1914. The former almshouses were restored to their original condition, with most of the internal woodwork intact, including the staircase, upper floors, closets, and paneling. There are also displays on the almshouses' history and on the kinds of people who lived there. For the present, visits are restricted to prebooked tours on weekdays, and one Saturday a month without booking. Call ahead for details. To discover more, you can attend a regular "bring a room to life" talk. ✉ *Kingsland Rd., East End, E2* ☎ *020/7739–9893* ⊕ *www.geffrye-museum.org.uk* ✆ *Free* ⊙ *Tues.–Sat. 10–5, Sun. noon–5* Ⓤ *Old St., then Bus 243; Liverpool St., then Bus 149 or 242.*

★ ℭ **Museum in Docklands.** On a quaint cobbled quayside, beside the tower of Canary Wharf, this warehouse building alone is museum quality, quite apart from its interesting contents. With uneven wood floors, beams, and pillars, the museum used to be a storehouse for coffee, tea, sugar, or rum from the West Indies—hence the name West India Quay. The fascinating story of the old port and the river is told using films, together with interactive displays and reconstructions. Roaming visitor assistants are also on hand to help with further explanation and inter-

The East End Art Scene

IT WAS ONLY INEVITABLE that the once arty Islington area (the N1 postal district, which rubs streets with the less elegant end of the Regent's Canal toward the City, EC1) would become too expensive and gentrified for the artists themselves. Hoxton, on a corner of Islington just off the City Road, with its cheap industrial units and more artisan Georgian–Victorian terraced streets, was the logical next stop.

The seal of boho approval came when Damien Hirst's agent and the most important modern art dealer in town, Jay Jopling (married to artist-photographer Sam Taylor-Wood), set up the White Cube gallery at 48 Hoxton Square. Impoverished artists, however, are not newcomers to the area—in the 1960s, Bridget Riley set up an outfit here to find affordable studio space for British artists—but the latest wave this side of the millennium

has changed the face of this formerly down-at-the-heels neighborhood. It's now undeniably hip to be in Hoxton.

From the Barbican in the City to Whitechapel in the East End, as many as 30 art galleries have opened, showing the latest works of the YBAs (Young British Artists). A spread of trendy real estate has taken a firm grip across the City Road into E1, principally Shoreditch, Spitalfields, and "Banglatown"—the nickname for the neighborhood around Brick Lane where Bengali shops and homes have created a slice of South Asia. Where less-than-glam buildings for the poor (such as the Jewish Soup Kitchen off Commercial Street, Spitalfields) once stood are now loft-style luxury apartments. Boutiques, bars, clubs, and restaurants have followed in their wake, and the Eastside—as it has been coined—is unapologetically brimming with energy.

esting anecdotes. You can follow the Docklands story through the ages right up to the Docklands at War exhibition detailing the devastation of the Blitz, and the very latest developments with the arrival of newspaper headquarters (the *Times*) and financial institutions. To get a feel of how much the area is on the move—skyward as well as along the waterfront—journey here on the Docklands Light Railway (DLR) or by boat (pick up a leaflet of timetables and quays from Tube stations). ✉ *No. 1 Warehouse, West India Quay, Hertsmere Rd., East End, E14* ☎ *0870/444–3857* ⊕ *www.museumindocklands.org.uk* ✎ *£5; tickets valid for 1 yr* ⊗ *Daily 10–6; last admission 5:30* Ⓤ *Canary Wharf; DLR: West India Quay.*

Old Truman Brewery. This is the only one of the former East End breweries still standing. It's a handsome example of Georgian and 19th-century industrial architecture, and in 1873 was the largest brewery in the world. The buildings, which straddle Brick Lane, are a conglomeration of art, craft, and photo studios, and now established as capital cool. The Atlantis Gallery, host of the sell-out Body Worlds exhibition in 2002, is a major focus—visitors were crammed inside to watch a live autopsy as part of the exhibition. Less controversial events include fashion showcases for young, upcoming designers, and fringe events. The Vibe Bar is a hot spot to chill out behind a traditional Georgian facade. ⊠ *91 Brick La., East End, E1* ⊕ *www.trumanbrewery.com* Ⓤ *Aldgate East.*

☺ **Ragged School Museum.** In its time, this was the largest school in London and a place where impoverished children could escape their deprived homes to get free education and a good meal. The museum re-creates the children's experiences with a time-capsule classroom, dating from the 1880s. Even after their short school career, the students were helped to find their first jobs and a way out of their poverty. At home they were probably living in one room with the rest of their usually large family, eking out a sad life with little future prospect of improvement. The school was their passport to a better life.

It's an eye-opener for adults, and a fun time-travel experience for kids who get the chance to work with such materials as scratchy slates and chalks—just like Victorian kids did more than 100 years ago—in one of the many organized workshops. There are guided tours, an exhibit on the history of the area, a bookshop, and a café overlooking the Regent's Canal—which connects with Limehouse Basin by the river Thames—where you can take stock of the facilities young students have at their disposal today. ⊠ *46–50 Copperfield Rd., East End, EC3* ☎ *020/8980–6405* ⊕ *www.raggedschoolmuseum.org.uk* ⊠ *Free* ☉ *Wed. and Thurs. 10–5, 1st Sun. of month 2–5* Ⓤ *Mile End; DLR: Limehouse.*

Royal London Hospital. Founded in 1740, the Royal London was once as nasty as its then-neighborhood near the Tower of London. Waste was carried out in buckets and dumped in the street; bedbugs and alcoholic nurses were problems; but according to hospital records patients didn't die—they were "relieved." In 1757 the hospital moved to its present site, the building of which is the core of the one you see today. By then it had become one of the best hospitals in London, and it was enhanced further by the addition of a small medical school in 1785, and again, 70 years later, an entire state-of-the-art medical college. Thomas John Barnado, who went on to found the famous Dr. Barnado's Homes for Orphans, came to train here in 1866. Ten years later the hospital grew to become the largest in the United Kingdom, and now, though mostly rebuilt since World War II, it remains one of London's most capacious. To get an idea of the huge medical leaps forward, walk through the main entrance and garden to the crypt of St. Augustine with St. Philip's Church (alternatively, go direct two blocks south to the entrance on Newark Street), to the **Royal London Hospital Archives** (☉ Weekdays 10–4:30), where displays of medical paraphernalia, objects, and documentation illustrate the 250-year history of this East London institution. ⊠ *Whitechapel Rd., East End, E1* ☎ *020/7377–7608* ⊕ *www. rlhleagueofnurses.org.uk* ⊠ *Free* ☉ *Hospital and garden daily 9–6* Ⓤ *Whitechapel.*

☺ **Spitalfields City Farm.** This little farm, squashed into an urban landscape, raises a selection of farm animals, including some rare breeds, to help educate city kids in country matters. A tiny farm shop sells freshly laid eggs and organic seasonal produce. ⊠ *Weaver St., off Pedley St.,*

7

The Docklands Renaissance

BUT FOR THE RIVER, Roman Londinium, with its sea link to the rest of the world, would not have grown into a world power. Trade and people came and went on the water from the port, or Pool of London (some of the early American settlers to Virginia set sail from Blackwall, one of the numerous wharves and quaysides along the river). Life was played out by the riverside; palaces redolent of Venice—such as Lambeth, Greenwich, Somerset House, Westminster, and Whitehall—were built. Henry VIII erected dockyards at Woolwich and Deptford to relieve congestion at Billingsgate (fish market). Dock warehouses sprang up during the 18th century from the trade with the Indies for tea and coffee, spices, and silks (some now converted into museums and malls, such as Hay's and Butler's wharves). Along with others, West India and East India Docks were built in the 19th century, extending London's port some miles east, to Millwall and the Isle of Dogs.

Trade took a gradual downturn after World War II, leading to the docks' degeneration when larger vessels pushed trade farther downriver to Tilbury. It took a driverless railway and Britain's tallest building to start a renaissance. Now, what was once a desolate and dirty quarter of the East End is a modern piece of real estate, a peninsula of waterways with cutting-edge architecture, offices, water-based leisure and cultural activities, restaurants, and bars.

The best way to explore is on the Docklands Light Railway, whose elevated track appears to skim over the water past the swanky glass buildings where the railway is reflected in the windows. On foot, however, the Thames Path has helpful plaques along the way, with nuggets of historical information. Canary Wharf, 1 Canada Square (not open to the public), embodies the bold architecture of the Docklands, but a visit to one of the original dockside warehouses at West India Quay, to the Museum in Docklands (☎ 020/ 7001-9800), tells the story of days when boats and sailors, rather than blue-chip outfits, were all around here. Everything you could want to know about this fascinating place can be discovered in a series of displays and interactive zones: the water zone, dockwork, building, and early years. Some exhibits are scary—one, for example, reveals the grisly tortures meted out to pirates.

If you have time to travel farther downstream to the old Royal Dockyard at Woolwich, you'll find, adjacent to it, a brilliant exhibition of the Royal Artillery, *Firepower!* (☎ 020/ 8855-7755, www.firepower.org.uk, Woolwich Arsenal station). Complete with smoke and sound effects, it explores the role of the gunner in film, from the discovery of gunpowder to the Gulf War. Also on show are tanks and guns—some complete with battle scars, and most with individual investigative touch-screen storyboards. Housed in the old regal buildings of the Royal Arsenal leading down to the river shore, there's a powerful sense of the Thames and its lingering effect on the capital's history.

East End, E1 ☎ *020/7247–8762* ⊕ *www.spitalfieldscityfarm.org* 💷 *Free* ⊙ *Tues.–Sun. 10–4* Ⓤ *Aldgate East, Liverpool St.*

Spitalfields Market. There's been a market here since the mid-17th century, but the current version is overflowing with crafts and design shops and stalls, restaurants and bars (with a pan-world palette, from tapas to Thai), and different-purpose markets every day of the week. Part of the market is undergoing a redevel-

> **WHEN TO GO**
>
> The nearer the weekend, the busier it all gets, culminating in the arts-and-crafts and green market on Sunday—the best day to go.

opment program that retains the original "Horner Buildings" façade, while upgrading and expanding the market facilities within, with the arrival of both new shops and stalls on the Bishops Square side. For more on Spitalfields Market, see Shopping, Chapter 19. ✉ *65 Brushfield St., East End, E1* ☎ *020/7247–8556* ⊕ *www.spitalfields.co.uk* 💷 *Free* ⊙ *Daily 10–7; market stalls weekdays 10–3, Sun. 9:30–5* Ⓤ *Liverpool St.*

NEED A BREAK? In the new development at Spitalfields Market is **Canteen** (☎ 0845/656-1122), a large, open-plan eatery with long communal tables that serves predominantly British dishes made with additive-free ingredients. Hot chocolate with rum or freshly squeezed juices provide perfect liquid accompaniment.

White Cube. The original White Cube had cramped quarters in genteel St. James's—it was lured away by the massive open spaces of the East End's former industrial units. Damien Hirst, Tracey Emin, Gilbert and George, Sam Taylor-Wood, and other trailblazers have shown here, and gone on to become internationally renowned. The building looks, appropriately enough, like a white cube—it has a glassed-in upper level called "Inside the White Cube," where international guest curators are invited to show their projects. ✉ *48 Hoxton Sq., Hoxton, N1* ☎ *020/7930–5373* ⊕ *www.whitecube.com* 💷 *Free* ⊙ *Tues.–Sat. 10–6* Ⓤ *Old St.*

Whitechapel Art Gallery. Housed in a spacious 1901 art nouveau building, this has an international reputation for its shows, which are often on the cutting edge of contemporary art. The American painter Jackson Pollock exhibited here in the 1950s, as did pop artist Robert Rauschenberg in the '60s, and David Hockney had his first solo show here in the '70s. Other exhibitions highlight the local community and culture, and there are programs of lectures, too. The Whitechapel Café serves remarkably inexpensive, home-cooked, whole-food hot meals, soups, and cakes. ✉ *Whitechapel High St., East End, E1* ☎ *020/7522–7888* ⊕ *www.whitechapel.org.* 💷 *Free; charge for special exhibitions* ⊙ *Tues.–Fri. 11–5, Thurs. 11–9, weekends 11–6* Ⓤ *Aldgate East.*

Whitechapel Bell Foundry. This working foundry was responsible for some of the world's better-known chimes. Before moving to this site in 1738, the foundry cast Westminster Abbey's bells (in the 1580s), but its biggest work, in every sense, was the 13-ton Big Ben, cast in 1858 by George Mears and requiring 16 horses to transport it from here to

Westminster. The foundry's other important work was casting the original Liberty Bell (now in Philadelphia) in 1752, and both it and Big Ben can be seen in pictures, along with exhibits about bell making, in a little museum in the shop. Note: the actual foundry is off-limits, for health and safety reasons, but in the small front shop you can buy bell paraphernalia and browse through the historic photos. There are guided tours of the foundry on Saturday morning only, but bookings are usually made months in advance for larger groups. If you're going alone or with another person, you might be able to join a group (call for information and fees). ✉ *34 Whitechapel Rd., East End, E1* ☎ *020/7247–2599* ⊕ *www.whitechapelbellfoundry.co.uk* ✆ *Free* ☉ *Weekdays 9–5* Ⓤ *Aldgate East.*

The East End at a Glance

SIGHTS
Bevis Marks Spanish and
 Portuguese Synagogue
Christ Church, Spitalfields
Dennis Severs's House
Old Truman Brewery
Royal London Hospital
Trinity Almshouses
Whitechapel Bell Foundry

MUSEUMS & GALLERIES
Bethnal Green Museum
 of Childhood
Geffrye Museum
Museum in Docklands
Ragged School Museum
Royal London Hospital
 Archives
Vilma Gold
White Cube
Whitechapel Art Gallery

PARKS & GARDENS
Spitalfields City Farm

PUBS & NIGHTLIFE
 (⇨ Ch. 18)
333, *dance club*
93 Feet East, *eclectic music*
The Blind Beggar,
 historic pub
Cargo, *dance club*
Comedy Café, *comedy club*
Fabric, *dance club*
Hoxton Square Bar &
 Kitchen, *bar*
Ocean, *eclectic music*
Prospect of Whitby, *pub*
Smiths of Smithfield, *bar*
Spitz, *eclectic music*
Sunday Sunday,
 gay & lesbian
Trade, *gay & lesbian*

SHOPPING (⇨ Ch. 19)
MARKETS & MALLS
Brick Lane
Columbia Road Flower
 Market
Spitalfields Market

ACCESSORIES
Bernstock Speirs

ART GALLERIES & CRAFTS
Lesley Craze Gallery

CLOTHING
Frockbrokers
Junky Styling
The Laden Showroom
Son of a Stag

The South Bank

WORD OF MOUTH

"The view from the London Eye is fantastic—and worth every penny.
You can see for miles, and get good views of St. Paul's, Trafalgar
Square, Buckingham Palace, and of course Parliament and West-
minster Abbey."

—jules4je7

THE SOUTH BANK

Culture, history, sights: the South Bank has it all. Stretching from the Imperial War Museum in the southwest as far as the Design Museum in the east, high-caliber art, music, film, and theater venues concertina up alongside the likes of an aquarium, a wine museum, historic warships, and a foodie-favorite market. Three structures dominate the skyline: the looming stack of Tate Modern, housed in an old power station; the distinctive OXO Tower; and the one ring to rule them all, the British Airways London Eye. Meanwhile pedestrians cross between the north and south banks using the futuristic Hungerford Bridge and the curvaceous Millennium Bridge, purposely dragging their feet as they go to take in the compelling views of the Thames.

What's Here

Lambeth Palace stands by Lambeth Bridge, with the delightful **Museum of Garden History** in St. Mary's church next door. A little farther east along Lambeth Road is the impressive **Imperial War Museum;** the best view of the Houses of Parliament can be had on the embankment between Lambeth and Westminster bridges.

A few steps from Westminster Bridge sits the **Florence Nightingale Museum,** with its entrance on Lambeth Palace Road. Back on the embankment is the former County Hall, which houses the **London Aquarium** and the surrealist museum **Dalí Universe.** Until the end of 2005 this was also home to the much-talked-about Saatchi Gallery, now relocated to Chelsea.

Standing proud above this company of sights is the **British Airways London Eye.** Continuing along the curve of the river, you come to Hungerford Bridge running parallel to the Charing Cross rail line. It deposits pedestrians at the **South Bank Centre,** home to the **Royal Festival Hall** (undergo-

> **TRIP TIP**
>
> Make sure you're hungry when you arrive at Borough Market as there's plenty of opportunity to taste the traders' delicious produce.

ing renovations until summer of 2007), the **Hayward Gallery,** the **National Film Theatre,** and the **Royal National Theatre.** This area is alive with activity, especially in summer, with skateboarders, urban runners, secondhand-book stalls, street entertainers, and a series of plaques annotating the buildings opposite.

The famous **OXO Tower** sits on Upper Ground in the Coin Street Community neighborhood. Here also is **Gabriel's Wharf,** a small marketplace of shops and cafés. Past Blackfriars Bridge are the monolithic **Tate Modern** and the miniscule **Bankside Gallery.** Stretching from the Tate back across the river to the St. Paul's Cathedral steps in the City is the now-wobble-free sweep of the **Millennium Bridge.**

After the Tate, it's the reconstructed Jacobean **Shakespeare's Globe Theatre** that steals the show. On the right of the theater is the 17th-century **Cardinal's Wharf,** where Wren lived while St. Paul's Cathedral was being built.

The well-signposted Thames Path leads downriver to **Vinopolis,** the world's first museum, shop, and restaurant complex celebrating wine—now with tributes to whiskey and gin as well. This stands at the entrance to a dark, cobbled alley, an appropriate route to the dismal **Clink Prison.** On Clink Street you can discern the west wall, with a rose-window outline, of the ruins of Winchester House, which was the palace of the Bishops of Winchester until 1626.

The red, yellow, and black *Golden Hinde* nestles in the dry St. Mary Overie Dock, while the legendary **Borough Market,** held every Friday afternoon and Saturday, is the rowdier neighbor of **Southwark Cathedral.** (For more on Borough Market, see Chapter 19, Shopping.) Joiner Street runs beneath the arches of London's first (1836) railway. On St. Thomas Street, the **Old Operating Theatre Museum** is overshadowed by London Bridge station.

Halfway down Tooley Street is the grisly **London Dungeon;** a little farther toward the river is **Hay's Galleria.** At the bottom of Morgan's Lane is **HMS** *Belfast.* Just before Tower Bridge is the massive, glass, Darth Vader–helmet building of **City Hall,** designed by the ubiquitous Sir Norman Foster and home to the London Assembly.

Past the bridge a path leads between cliffs of the good-as-new warehouses, now **Butlers Wharf**—but once the dingy, dangerous shadowlands where Dickens killed off Bill Sikes in *Oliver Twist.* Here are munch-monster center, the Gastrodrome, and the **Design Museum,** where you can take another long-lasting view of the Thames and Tower Bridge.

GETTING ORIENTED

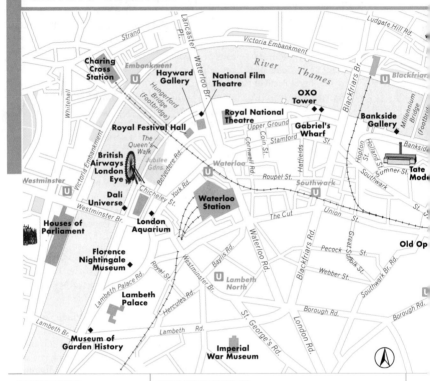

GETTING THERE	TOP 5 REASONS TO GO
For the South Bank use Westminster station on the Jubilee or Northern line, from where you can walk across Westminster Bridge; Embankment on District, Circle, Northern, and Bakerloo lines, where you can walk across Hungerford Bridge; or Waterloo on the Jubilee, Northern, and Bakerloo lines, where it's a five-minute walk to the Royal Festival Hall. In the east, alternatively, use Tower Gateway on the Docklands Light Railway (DLR). London Bridge on the Northern and Jubilee lines is a five-minute stroll from Borough Market and Southwark Cathedral.	■ **Hungerford Bridge:** Walk across the bridge at dusk, then east along a fairy-light embankment towards the OXO Tower. ■ **Shakespeare's Globe Theatre:** Catch a performance on a summer's eve. ■ **British Airways London Eye:** If you long to see London from a different perspective, look no farther. Take a flight on a clear day. ■ **Tate Modern:** Obsere one of the changing installations—always impressive and humbling—in the turbine hall. ■ **Borough Market:** Spend a Saturday morning gauging your way through stalls of organic produce.

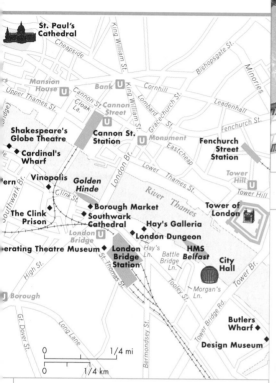

St. Paul's Cathedral

Cheapside

King William St.

Bishopsgate St.

Minories

Mansion House

Upper Thames St.

Bank

Cornhill

Leadenhall

Cannon St.

Cloak La.

Cannon Street

King William St.

Lombard St.

Gracechurch St.

Fenchurch St.

Shakespeare's Globe Theatre

Cannon St. Station

Monument

Eastcheap

Fenchurch Street Station

Cardinal's Wharf

London Br.

Lower Thames St.

Tower Hill

ern Br.

Vinopolis

Golden Hinde

River Thames

Tower Hill

Southwark Br.

Clink St.

Borough Market

Tower of London

The Clink Prison

Southwark Cathedral

Hay's Galleria

London Bridge

London Dungeon

erating Theatre Museum

London Bridge Station

Hay's Ln.

Battle Bridge Ln.

HMS Belfast

City Hall

High St.

St. Thomas St.

Tooley St.

Morgan's Ln.

Tower Br.

J Borough

Gt. Dover St.

Long Lane

Bermondsey St.

Tower Bridge Rd.

Butlers Wharf

Design Museum

0 ——— 1/4 mi

0 ——— 1/4 km

MAKING THE MOST OF YOUR TIME

Don't attempt the South Bank all in one go. Not only will you exhaust yourself, but you will miss out on the multifarious delights that it has to offer.

■ The Imperial War Museum demands a couple of hours, with the nearby Museum of Garden History providing an hour of further distraction.

8

■ To take in the South Bank galleries, such as Bankside and the Hayward, you'll need at least a day; the Tate Modern alone deserves a whole morning or afternoon, especially if you want to do justice to both the temporary exhibitions and the permanent collection.

■ The Globe Theatre requires about two hours for the exhibition theater tour and two to three hours for a performance. Finish with drinks or dinner at the OXO Tower or a stroll west along the riverbank and then across Hungerford Bridge.

FEELING PECKISH?

At Gabriel's Wharf have a sit-down meal at the **Gourmet Pizza Co.** (☎ 020/7928-3188) or grab a sandwich or coffee at one of the smaller establishments open during the day here.

For exquisite hand-made pastries, along with daily specials such as chicken paella or vegetarian moussaka, stop at the bijou premises of **Konditor & Cook** (✉ 10 Stoney St. ☎ 020/7407-5100), the star of the handful of eateries to be found at Borough Market.

SAFETY

At night, it's best to stick to where the action is, at the Butler's Wharf restaurants, the OXO Tower, the National Theatre, the National Film Theatre, and the Royal Festival Hall. Stray beyond these hubs and it begins to feel deserted.

A BRIEF HISTORY

Southwark, the oldest borough in England, was once infamous for being London's outlaw neighborhood. Although situated just across London Bridge, it was conveniently outside the city walls and laws and was therefore the ideal location for the theaters, taverns, and cock-fighting arenas—not to mention brothels—that served as after-hours entertainment in the Middle Ages. However, it was only the brave that chose to stay out once the sun had set on this side of the river. Following a matinee performance of *Henry V* or *Romeo and Juliet*, the hordes of plebeians that flocked to Shakespeare's popular Globe Theatre were more eager to scuttle back to the safety of their hearths than take their chances with whatever lurked in the shadows of a twilight South Bank.

For centuries the North London jibe about needing a passport to cross the mighty Thames may have held true. But, in the mid-20th century people began to hold their tongues as the South Bank emerged as one of the capital's most creative hubs. The development began in the 1950s with the construction of the Royal Festival Hall, part of the postwar, morale-boosting Festival of Britain in 1951, and was followed by the additions of the Hayward Gallery in the '60s and the Royal National Theatre in the '70s. In the '80s the Design Museum and wharfside developments at Gabriel's Wharf and Butlers Wharf attracted a fresh influx of residents and further development downriver; with the '90s came the refurbishment of the OXO Tower and the breathtaking reconstruction of Shakespeare's Globe Theatre. The architectural celebrations continued apace with showcase projects for the new millennium, such as Tate Modern and the British Airways London Eye—still a favorite with both Londoners and out-of-towners alike.

Even the previously lesser-frequented parts of the South Bank are now a magnet for visitors. The city's oldest market, Borough Market—or "London's Larder"—has become an essential foodie destination, where celebrity chefs go in search of farm-fresh produce. Just a short walk east, Bermondsey (or "Beormund's Eye" as it was known in Saxon times), with its artist studios and pretty streets, is being bought up by fashion-conscious homemakers in search of the new Hoxton.

Places to Explore

Bankside Gallery. Two artistic societies—the Royal Society of Painter-Printmakers and the Royal Watercolour Society—have their headquarters here. Together they mount exhibitions of current members' work, usually for sale, alongside artists' materials and books—a great place for finding that exclusive, not too expensive gift. There are also regular themed exhibitions. Note that the gallery usually closes for a few days between exhibitions, so check ahead for details before you go. ⊠ *48 Hopton St., South Bank, SE1* ☎ *020/7928–7521* ⊕ *www.banksidegallery. com* ⊠ *Free* ☉ *Daily 11–6* Ⓤ *Blackfriars, Southwark, St. Paul's.*

★ ☹ **British Airways London Eye.** To mark the start of the new millennium, architects David Marks and Julia Barfield conceived an entirely new vision: a beautiful and celebratory structure, which would allow people to see this great city from a completely new perspective—on a giant

> **DIMINISH YOUR EYE QUEUE**
>
> Buy your ticket online, over the phone, or at the ticket office in advance to avoid the long lines.

wheel. As well as representing the turning of the century, a wheel was seen as a symbol of regeneration and the passing of time. The London Eye is the largest observation wheel ever built, and in the top 10 tallest structures in London. From design to construction it took seven years to complete. The 25-minute slow-motion ride inside one of the enclosed passenger capsules is so smooth you'd hardly know you were suspended over the Thames, moving slowly round. On a clear day you can take in a range of up to 25 mi, viewing London's most famous landmarks from a fascinating angle. If you're looking for a special place to celebrate, champagne and canapés can be arranged ahead; check the Web site for details. ⊠ *Jubilee Gardens, South Bank, SE1* ☎ *0870/500–0600* ⊕ *www. ba-londoneye.com* ⊠ *£12.50* ☉ *June–Sept., daily 9:30 AM–10 PM; Oct.–May, daily 9:30–8* Ⓤ *Waterloo.*

Butlers Wharf. An '80s warehouse conversion of deluxe loft apartments, restaurants, and galleries, it is now mobbed thanks partly to London's saint of the stomach, Sir Terence Conran (also responsible for restaurants Bibendum, Mezzo, and Quaglino's). He has given it his "Gastrodrome" of four restaurants (including the fabulous Pont de la Tour), a vintner's, a deli, and a bakery. Try the Chop House bar for a great view of Tower Bridge. ⊠ *South Bank, SE1* Ⓤ *London Bridge or Tower Hill, then walk across river.*

☹ **The Clink Prison.** Giving rise to the term "clink," or jail, this institution was originally the prison attached to Winchester House, palace of the Bishops of Winchester until 1626. One of five Southwark establishments, it was the first to detain women, most of whom were called "Winchester geese"—a euphemism for prostitutes—which were endemic in Southwark, especially around the bishops' area of jurisdiction, which was known as "the Liberty of the Clink" so called because their graces' solution was to license prostitution rather than ban it. You'll discover, in graphic detail, how a grisly Tudor prison would operate on a code of cruelty, deprivation, and corruption. The museum is currently in the process of upgrading its displays and introducing new material to the exhibition, so expect to see some changes by the end of 2007. ⊠ *1 Clink St., South Bank, SE1* ☎ *020/7403–0900* ⊕ *www.clink.co.uk* ⊠ *£5* ☉ *Weekdays 10–6, weekends 10–9; last admission 1 hr before closing* Ⓤ *London Bridge.*

Dalí Universe. Here is Europe's most comprehensively arranged collection by master surrealist Salvador Dalí. The many exhibits—from art to sculpture, to furniture, to jewelry—are organized in themes (Sensuality and Femininity, Religion and Mythology, and Dreams and Fantasy), and thus the museum tries to give visitors a reflection of how Dalí thought out his work. There are more than 500 pieces on show, but highlights undoubtedly include the *Mae West Lips Sofa*, the *Lobster Telephone*, and *Spellbound* for the Hitchcock movie. Although there's much to take in, this museum has a much more commercial flavor and lacks the intimacy of other Dalí museums. ⊠ *County Hall, Riverside Bldg., Westminster Bridge Rd., South Bank, SE1* ☏ *0870/744–7485* ⊕ *www. daliuniverse.com* ✎ *£9.75* ⊙ *Daily 10–6:30; last entry at 5:30* Ⓤ *Waterloo, Westminster.*

☾ **Design Museum.** This was the first museum in the world to elevate everyday design and design classics to the status of art by placing them in their social and cultural context. Fashion, creative technology, and architecture are explored with thematic displays from the museum's permanent collection of design classics, and temporary exhibitions provide an in-depth focus on such subjects as the work of great designers such as Charles Eames and Isamu Noguchi, or thematic shows on the Bauhaus or erotic design. The museum looks forward, too, by showcasing innovative contemporary designs and technologies, an area that kids find absorbing (there are free activity packs to spark their interest further). All of this is supplemented by a busy program of lectures, events, and talks, including a workshop for kids. If you're in need of sustenance, there's the trendsetting Blueprint Café (designed by who else but Terence Conran), with its river terrace and superb views. For quicker snacks at a lower price, the museum's own café is on the ground floor beside the Thames footpath. The museum store sells good-quality, high-design products. Entry to both cafés and the store is free. ⊠ *28 Shad Thames, South Bank, SE1* ☏ *0870/833–9955* ⊕ *www.designmuseum.org* ✎ *£7* ⊙ *Mon.–Thurs. and weekends 10–5:45, last admission at 5:15; Fri. 10–10, last admission at 9:45* Ⓤ *London Bridge; DLR: Tower Gateway.*

Florence Nightingale Museum. Here you can learn all about the founder of the first school of nursing, that most famous of health-care reformers, "the Lady with the Lamp." See the reconstruction of the barracks ward at Scutari, Turkey, where she tended soldiers during the Crimean War (1854–56) and earned her nickname. Here you also find a Victorian East End slum cottage showing what she did to improve living conditions among the poor—and the famous lamp. The museum is in **St. Thomas's Hospital,** which was built in 1868 to the specifications of Florence Nightingale. Most of it was bombed to bits in the Blitz, then rebuilt to become one of London's teaching hospitals. ⊠ *2 Lambeth Palace Rd., South Bank, SE1* ☏ *020/7620–0374* ⊕ *www.florence-nightingale.co.uk* ✎ *£5.80* ⊙ *Weekdays 10–5, last admission 4, weekends 10–4:30, last admission 3:30* Ⓤ *Waterloo or Westminster, then walk over bridge.*

NEED A BREAK?

Gabriel's Wharf. This cluster of specialist shops, cafés, and restaurants is part of the Coin Street Community neighborhood and bustles with activity during the daytime. You can hire bicycles here from the London Bicycle Tour Company (☏ 020/7928–6838). ⊠ 52 Upper Ground, South Bank, SE1 ☏ 020/7401-2255 ⊕ www.gabrielswharf.co.uk ✎ Free ⊙ Shops and studios Tues.–Sun. 11-6 Ⓤ Blackfriars, Waterloo.

🕓 **Golden Hinde.** Sir Francis Drake circumnavigated the globe in this little galleon, or one just like it. This exact replica made a 23-year round-the-world voyage—much of it spent along U.S. coasts, both Pacific and Atlantic—and has settled here to continue its educational purpose. If you want information along with your visit, book a tour in advance. ⊠ *E St. Mary Overie Dock, Cathedral St., South Bank, SE1* ☎ *08700/11–8700* ⊕ *www.goldenhinde.co.uk* ⊟ *£3.50, £4.50 for prebooked guided tour* ⊗ *Times vary, call ahead* Ⓤ *London Bridge, Mansion House.*

Hay's Galleria. Hay's Wharf was built by Thomas Cubitt in 1857 on the spot where the port of London's oldest wharf had stood since 1651. It was once known as "London's larder" because of the quantity of edibles that landed here. It then wound down gradually and closed in 1970. In 1987 it was reborn as a small parade of bars and restaurants, offices, and shops, beneath an arched glass atrium roof supported by tall iron columns. The centerpiece is a fanciful kinetic sculpture by David Kemp, *The Navigators,* which looks like the skeleton of a pirate schooner crossed with a dragon and spouts water from various orifices. A handful of crafts stalls can be found here, along with the occasional string quartet. ⊠ *Battle Bridge La., South Bank, SE1* ☎ *020/7940–7770* ⊕ *www.haysgalleria.co.uk* Ⓤ *London Bridge.*

Hayward Gallery. The gray, windowless bunker tucked behind the South Bank Centre concert halls has had to bear the brunt of architectural criticism over the years, but that's changed with a foyer extension that gives more daylight, more space for exhibits, a café, and better access. The highlight of the project is an elliptical mirrored glass pavilion by New

> **MUST SEE**
>
> This is the one gallery you can't miss, literally, due to the multi-color neon tube sculpture atop the building, which blinks away through the night on the South Bank skyline.

York–based artist Dan Graham. The gallery encompasses a range of art media, crossing history and cultures, bridging the experimental and established. It's consistently on the cutting edge of new developments in art and critical theory, finding new ways to present the well known, from Picasso to Lichtenstein, and as a prominent platform for up-and-coming artists. ⊠ *South Bank Centre, South Bank, SE1* ☎ *020/7921–0813* ⊕ *www.hayward.org.uk* ⊟ *Mon. £4.50, Tues.–Sun. £9* ⊗ *Sat.–Mon., Thurs. 10–6, Tues. and Wed. 10–8, Fri. 10–9* Ⓤ *Waterloo.*

🕓 **HMS Belfast.** At 613 feet, this is one of the largest and most powerful cruisers the Royal Navy has ever had. It played an important role in the D-Day landings off Normandy, left for the Far East after the war, and has been becalmed here since 1971. On board there's a riveting outpost of the **Imperial War Museum,** which tells the Royal Navy's story from 1914 to the present and shows you about life on a World War II battleship (with interactive push button games and quizzes), from mess decks and bakery to punishment cells and from operations room to engine room and armaments. ⊠ *Morgan's La., Tooley St., South Bank, SE1* ☎ *020/7940–6300* ⊕ *www.iwm.org.uk* ⊟ *£8* ⊗ *Mar.–Oct., daily 10–6; Nov.–Feb., daily 10–5; last admission 45 min before closing* Ⓤ *London Bridge.*

★ ⟲ **Imperial War Museum.** Despite its title, this museum of 20th-century warfare does not glorify bloodshed but emphasizes understanding through evoking what life was like for citizens and soldiers alike through the two world wars. There's an impressive amount of hardware at the main entrance with accompanying interactive material, including a Battle of Britain Spitfire, a German V2 rocket, tanks, guns, and submarines—and from here you can peel off to the various sections of the museum. Sights, sounds, and smells are used to re-create the very uncomfortable Trench Experience in the World War I gallery, which is as equally effective as The Blitz Experience in the World War II gallery: a 10-minute taste of an air raid in a street of acrid smoke with sirens blaring and searchlights glaring. On the more pensive side, there's an equal amount of war art (by artists David Bomberg, Henry Moore, John Singer Sargent, and Graham Sutherland, to name a few), poetry, photography, and documentary film footage. There's also a permanent Holocaust exhibition, and a Crimes Against Humanity exhibition, which is not suitable for younger children. More recent wars attended by British forces are commemorated, too, and you can find out about those and the heroes who made the supreme sacrifice for them in the Victoria and George Cross Gallery. Don't miss the intriguing Secret War Gallery, which charts the history of agents' intrepid work in the wars and the inception of MI5 and MI6, the government's secret services.

The museum is housed in an elegant domed and colonnaded building, erected in the early 19th century to house the Bethlehem Hospital for the Insane, better known as the infamous Bedlam. By 1816, when the patients were moved here, they were no longer kept in cages to be taunted by tourists (see the final scene of Hogarth's *Rake's Progress* at Sir John Soane's Museum for some sense of how horrific it was), since reformers—and George III's madness—had effected more humane standards of confinement. Bedlam moved to Surrey in 1930. ⊠ *Lambeth Rd., South Bank, SE1* ☎ *020/7416–5320* ⊕ *www.iwm.org.uk* ▧ *Free* ⊙ *Daily 10–6* Ⓤ *Lambeth North.*

Lambeth Palace. For about 800 years this has been the London base of the Archbishop of Canterbury, head of the Church of England. Much of the palace is hidden behind great walls, and even the Tudor gatehouse, visible from the street, is closed to the public, but you can stand here and absorb the historical vibrations echoing from momentous events. These include the 1381 storming of the palace during the Peasants' Revolt against the poll tax and the 1534 clash of wills when Thomas More refused to sign the Oath of Supremacy claiming Henry VIII (and not the pope) as leader of the English Church, for which he was sent to the Tower and executed for treason the following year. ⊠ *Lambeth Palace Rd., South Bank, SE1* ⊕ *www.archbishopofcanterbury.org* Ⓤ *Waterloo.*

⟲ **London Aquarium.** This curved, colonnaded, neoclassic hulk once housed London's local government administration (now located at the Norman Foster–designed City Hall building farther downriver by Tower Bridge). Here's a dark and thrilling glimpse into the waters of the world, focused around a superb three-level aquarium full of sharks and stingrays, among other common and rarer breeds. There are also educational exhibits, hands-on displays, feeding displays, and piscine sights previously unseen on these shores. It's not the biggest aquarium you've ever seen—especially if you've been to SeaWorld—but the exhibit is well arranged on several subterranean levels, with areas for different oceans, water environments, and climate zones, including a stunning coral reef, and the highlight: the rain forest, which is almost like the real thing. There are regular feeding times and free talks throughout the day, while the aquarium also runs a conservation breeding scheme—so look out for new additions to the tanks. ⊠ *County Hall, Riverside Bldg., Westminster Bridge Rd., South Bank, SE1* ☎ *020/7967–8000* ⊕ *www.londonaquarium.co.uk* 🎫 *£9.75* ⊙ *Daily 10–6; last admission at 5* Ⓤ *Westminster, Waterloo.*

Ⓒ **London Dungeon.** Here's the goriest, grisliest, most gruesome attraction in town, where realistic waxwork people are subjected in graphic detail to all the historical horrors the Tower of London merely tells you about. Tableaux depict famous bloody moments—like Anne Boleyn's decapitation and the martyrdom of St. George—

> **CAUTION**
>
> Naturally, children absolutely adore this place, but be warned—nervous kiddies may find it too frightening. Expect long lines on weekends and during school holidays.

alongside the torture, murder, and ritual slaughter of lesser-known victims, all to a sound track of screaming, wailing, and agonized moaning. There are displays on the Great Fire of London and Jack the Ripper, and to add to the fear and fun, costumed characters leap out of the gloom to bring the exhibits to life. ⊠ *28–34 Tooley St., South Bank, SE1* ☎ *020/7403–7221* ⊕ *www.thedungeons.com* 🎫 *£14.50* ⊙ *Mid-Apr.–mid-July, daily 10–5:30; mid-July–mid-Sept., daily 10–7.30; mid-Sept.–mid-Nov., daily 10–5.30; mid-Nov.–mid-Apr. daily 10:30–5; phone to confirm dates* Ⓤ *London Bridge.*

Museum of Garden History. The first of its kind in the world, the museum is set in St. Mary's Church, next to Lambeth Palace. Founded in 1977, the museum has built up one of the largest collections of historic garden tools, artifacts, and curiosities, as well as an expanding library. Alongside the museum is a replica 17th-century knot garden, a peaceful haven of plants that can be traced back to that period. The garden also contains the tombs of the John Tradescants (the elder and younger), enthusiastic collectors of curiosities and adventurous plant hunters—who introduced many familiar blooms, such as lilac, to these shores—and memorials to William Bligh, captain of the *Bounty,* and the Sealy family of Coade stone fame. The shop has gifts in the plant vein, and a café. ⊠ *Lambeth Palace Rd., South Bank, SE1* ☎ *020/7401–8865* ⊕ *www.museumgardenhistory.org* 🎫 *Suggested donation £3* ⊙ *Daily 10:30–5* Ⓤ *Lambeth North.*

OXO Tower. Long a London landmark to the cognoscenti, the art deco–era OXO building has graduated from its former incarnations as a power-generating station and warehouse into a vibrant community of artists' and designers' workshops, a pair of restaurants, as well as five floors of community homes. There's an observation deck for a super river vista (St. Paul's to the east, and Somerset House to the west), and a performance area on the first floor, which comes alive all summer long—as does the entire surrounding neighborhood. All the designers and artisans rely on you to disturb them whenever they're open, whether buying, commissioning, or just browsing. The biggest draw remains the OXO Tower Restaurant extravaganza for a meal or a martini. ⊠ *Barge House St., South Bank, SE1* ☎ *020/7401–3610* ⊕ *www.oxotower.co.uk* ✍ *Free* ⊙ *Studios and shops Tues.–Sun. 11–6* Ⓤ *Blackfriars, Waterloo.*

Royal National Theatre. When this theater opened in 1976 Londoners generally felt the same way about this low-slung, multilayered "brutalist" block the color of heavy storm clouds and designed by Sir Denys Lasdun that they would feel a decade later about the Barbican Centre. But whatever its merits or demerits as a landscape feature, the Royal National Theatre has wonderful insides that are worth a tour.

SEEING STARS

The Royal National Theatre Company does not rest on its laurels: its productions list many of the nation's top actors (Sir Anthony Hopkins, Vanessa Redgrave, Sir Ian McKellen, Dame Judi Dench, and more) in addition to launching future stars.

Three auditoriums occupy the complex. The biggest one, the **Olivier,** is named after Sir Laurence, chairman of the first building commission and first artistic director of the National Theatre Company, formed in 1962. (In between the first proposal of a national theater for Britain and the 1949 formation of that building commission, an entire century had passed.) The **Lyttelton** theater has a traditional proscenium arch, and the little **Cottesloe** mounts studio productions and new work in the round. Interspersed with the theaters is a multilayered foyer with exhibitions, bars, and restaurants, and free entertainment. The whole place is lively six days a week. Because it's a repertory company, you'll have several plays from which to choose even if your London sojourn is short; but, tickets or not, wander around and catch the buzz. You may even bump into a star backstage. ⊠ *South Bank, SE1* ☎ *020/7452–3000 box office, 020/7452–3400 for tour* ✍ *Tour £5* ⊙ *Foyer Mon.–Sat. 10 AM–11 PM; 1-hr tour of theater backstage Mon.–Sat. 10:15, 12:30, and 5:30* ⊕ *www.nationaltheatre.org.uk* Ⓤ *Waterloo.*

Shakespeare & the Globe Theatre See Page 169

Southwark Cathedral. Pronounced "Suth-uck," this is the second-oldest Gothic church in London, after Westminster Abbey, with parts dating back to the 12th century. Although it houses some remarkable memorials, not to mention a program of lunchtime concerts, it's seldom visited. It was promoted to cathedral status only in 1905; before that it was the priory church of St. Mary Overie (as in "over the water"—on

Continued on page 174

"Within this wooden O..."

—William Shakespeare, Henry V

SHAKESPEARE &
THE GLOBE THEATRE

At Shakespeare's Globe Theatre, they say the Bard does not belong to the British; he belongs to the world. Not a day has gone by since the Restoration when one of his plays isn't being performed or reinterpreted somewhere. But here, at the site of the original Globe, in a painstaking reconstruction of Shakespeare's own open-air theater, is where seeing one of his plays can take on an ethereal quality.

If you are exceeding well read and a lover of the Bard, then chances are a pilgrimage to his Globe Theatre is already on your list. But if Shakespeare's works leave you wondering why exactly the play is the thing, then a trip to the Globe—to learn more about his life or to see his words come alive—is a must.

The Globe Theatre in Shakespeare's Day

In the 16th and 17th centuries, a handful of theaters—the Rose, the Swan, the Globe, and others whose names are lost—rose above the higgledy-piggledy jumble of rooftops in London's rowdy Southwark neighborhood. They were round or octagonal open-air playhouses, with galleries for the "quality" members of society, and large, open pits for the raucous mobs. People from all social classes, from royalty down to the hoi polloi, shared the communal experience of drama in these places. Shakespeare's Globe was one.

A fire in 1613 destroyed the first Globe, which was quickly rebuilt; however, Oliver Cromwell and waves of other reformers put an end to all the Southwark playhouses in the 1640s. By the time American actor and director Sam Wanamaker visited in 1949, the only indication that the world's greatest dramatist created popular entertainment here was a plaque on a brewery wall. Wanamaker was shocked to find that all evidence of the playwright's legendary playhouse had vanished into air.

And thereby hangs a tale.

Wanamaker's Dream

Over the next several decades, Wanamaker devoted himself to the Bard. He was director of the New Shakespeare Theatre in Liverpool and, in 1959, joined the Shakespeare Memorial Theatre Company (now the Royal Shakespeare Company) at Stratford-upon-Avon.

SHAKESPEARE'S ALL-TIME TOP 10

1. *Romeo and Juliet*. Young love, teenage rebellion, and tragedy are the ingredients of the greatest tearjerker of all time.

2. *Hamlet* (*right*). The very model of a modern antihero and origin of the most quoted line of any play: "To be or not to be..."

3. *A Midsummer Night's Dream*. Spells and potions abound as the gods use humans for playthings; lovers' tiffs are followed by happy endings for all.

4. *Othello*. Jealousy poisons love and destroys a proud man.

5. *The Taming of the Shrew*. The eternal battle of the sexes.

6. *Macbeth*. Ambition, murder, and revenge. Evil gets its just reward.

7. *The Merry Wives of Windsor*. A two-timing rascal gets his comeuppance from a pack of hysterically funny gossips.

8. *Richard III*. One of literature's juiciest villains. The whole audience wants to hiss.

9. *The Tempest*. On a desert island, the concerns of men amaze and amuse the innocent Miranda: "Oh brave new world, that has such people in't."

10. *King Lear*. A tragedy of old age, filial love, and grasping, ungrateful children.

SHAKESPEARE & THE GLOBE THEATRE

8

Finally, in the 1970s he began the project that would dominate the rest of his life: reconstructing Shakespeare's theater, as close to the original site as possible.

Today's Globe was re-created using authentic Elizabethan materials and craft techniques—green oak timbers joined only with wooden pegs and mortise-and-tenon joints; plaster made of lime, sand, and goat's hair; and the first thatched roof in London since the Great Fire. The complex,

200 yards from the site of the original Globe, includes an exhibition center, cafés, and restaurants. (The shell of a 17th-century-style theater, built adjacent to the Globe to a design by Inigo Jones, awaits further funds for completion.)

FUN FACT: Plays are presented in the open air (and sometimes the rain) to an audience of 1,000 on wooden benches in the bays, and 500 "groundlings," who stand on a carpet of filbert shells and clinker, just as they did nearly four centuries ago.

The eventual realization of Wanamaker's dream, a full-scale, accurate replica of the Globe, was the keystone that supported the revitalization of the entire district. The new Globe celebrates Shakespeare, his work, and his times, and as an educational trust it is dedicated to making the Bard continually fresh and accessible for new audiences. Sadly, Wanamaker died before construction was completed, in 1997. In Southwark Cathedral, a few hundred yards west of the Globe, a memorial to him stands beside the statue memorializing Shakespeare himself.

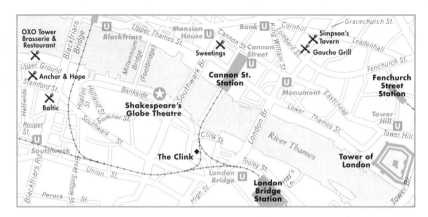

Seeing a Play at the Globe

✉ 21 New Globe Walk, Bankside, South Bank

☎ 020/7401-9919 box office, 020/7902-1400
New Shakespeare's Globe Exhibition

🌐 www.shakespeares-globe.org

🎫 Exhibition admission £9, family ticket
(2 adults, 3 children) £25; ticket prices for
plays vary (£5-£31).

🕐 Exhibition daily 10-5; plays May-early Oct.,
call for performance schedule.

Ⓤ Southwark, then walk to Blackfriars Bridge
and descend the steps; Mansion House,
then walk across Southwark Bridge;
Blackfriars, then walk across Blackfriars
Bridge; St. Paul's, then walk across
Millennium Bridge.

The season of plays is limited to the warmer
months, from May to the first week in October, with the schedule announced in late
January on the theater's Web site. Tickets
go on sale in mid-February. The box office
takes phone and mail orders as well as in-
person sales, but the most convenient way
to buy tickets is online. Book as early as
possible.

FUN FACT: "Groundlings"—those with £5
standing-only tickets—are not allowed to sit
during the performance. Reserve an actual seat,
though, on any one of the theater's three levels,
and you can join the "Elizabethan" crowd.

If you do have a seat, you can rent cushions for £1 (or bring your own) to soften
the backless wooden benches. A limited
number of backrests are also available for
rent for £3. The show must go on, rain or
shine, warm or chilly—so come prepared
for whatever the weather throws at you.
Umbrellas are banned, but you can bring
a raincoat or buy a cheap Globe rain pon-
cho, which doubles as a great souvenir.

MAKING THE MOST OF YOUR TIME
Give yourself plenty of time: there are several cafés and restaurants, as well as fascinating interactive exhibitions, and theater
tours with occasional live demonstrations.
Performances can last up to three hours.

WITH CHILDREN
Childsplay, a program for 8- to 11-year-
olds, is held once a month during
matinées. While Mom and Dad enjoy the
play, children—helped by actors, musi-
cans, and teachers—learn the background
and story and become accustomed to
Shakespearean language. By the time they
are admitted to the theater for the last 15
minutes of the play, the children have become Shakespeare enthusiasts for life.

A regular workshop for kids, run with the
Metropolitan Police, the National Archives,
and the National Forensic Service, uses
modern forensic techniques to solve real
Elizabethan crimes and mysteries.

Year-Round at Shakespeare's Globe

Shakespeare's Globe Exhibition is a comprehensive display built under the theater (the entry is adjacent) that provides background material about the Elizabethan theater and about the surrounding neighborhood, Southwark. The exhibition describes the process of building the modern Globe and the serious research that went into it.

FUN FACT: In Shakespeare's day, this was a rough part of town. The Bear Gardens, around the corner from the Globe, was where bear baiting, a cruel animal sport, took place. Farther along, the Clink (now a museum) was the local *gaol* (jail).

Daily live demonstrations include Elizabethan dressing, stage fighting, and swordplay, performed by drama students and stage-fighting instructors from the Royal Academy of Dramatic Art (RADA) and the London Academy of Music and Dramatic Art (LAMDA).

FUN FACT: Many performances are done in Elizabethan dress. Costumes are handmade from period materials—wool, silk, cotton, animal skins, and natural dyes.

Admission also includes a tour of the theater. On matinee days, the tour visits the archaeological site of the nearby (and older) Rose Theatre.

SPECIAL EVENTS

The Frost Fair, held annually the weekend before Christmas, commemorates several extraordinary winters in the 17th century when the Thames froze over and fairs took place on the ice. It includes street theater, Morris Dancing, sword fighting, and food and crafts stalls. Admission is £1, and there is special reduced admission to the Theatre and Exhibition during the fair.

Shakespeare's Birthday, April 23, is celebrated every year with free all-day admission to the theater and exhibitions, free performances, and public access to the Globe stage, giving all comers a chance to entertain the groundlings. The line of would-be thesps wraps around the block.

FUN FACT: Shakespeare's casts were all male, with young men and boys playing the female roles. A live demonstration in the costume exhibit shows how this was done—and how convincing it can be.

the South Bank). Look for the gaudily renovated 1408 tomb of the poet John Gower, friend of Chaucer, and for the Harvard Chapel. Another notable buried here is Edmund Shakespeare, brother of William. ⊠ *Montague Close, South Bank, SE1* ☎ *020/7367–6700* ⊕ *www.southwark.anglican.org* ✉ *Free, suggested donation £4* ⊙ *Daily 8–6* Ⓤ *London Bridge.*

Ⓒ
Fodor's Choice ★
Tate Modern. This ex-power station was built in the 1930s, and after a dazzling renovation by Herzog & de Meuron, provides a magnificent space for a massive collection of international modern art. The vast Turbine Hall is a dramatic entrance point to the museum. On permanent display in the galleries are classic works from 1900 to the present

> **WHEN TO GO**
>
> Avoid going to the Tate Modern on weekends, when visitor numbers are at their greatest. Visit during the week or join the cool crowd on Friday evenings when it's open until 10 PM.

day, by Matisse, Picasso, Dalí, Moore, Bacon, Warhol, and the most-talked-about British upstarts. The works are not grouped by artist but are arranged in themes that mix the historic with the contemporary—Landscape, Still Life, and the Nude—on different levels, reached by a moving staircase, which is a feature in itself. You could spend a visit merely exploring one floor, but that would be cowardly, as there's usually one major barnstorming exhibition to see (for which there is sometimes a charge), which is always the talking point of Londoners who have their fingers on the pulse. ⊠ *Bankside, South Bank, SE1* ☎ *020/7887–8888* ⊕ *www.tate.org.uk* ✉ *Free* ⊙ *Sun.–Thurs. 10–6, Fri. and Sat. 10–10* Ⓤ *Blackfriars, Southwark.*

Vinopolis. Spread over 2 acres between the Globe Theatre and London Bridge, you can take a virtual tour of the world's wine cultures, and have an opportunity to put your skills to the taste. The four restaurants claim to offer more wines by the glass than anywhere else in the city, and you can, of course, buy. Keep in mind that the last entry is two hours before the scheduled closing time, and you should allow at least two hours for a tour. ⊠ *1 Bank End St., South Bank, SE1* ☎ *0870/444–4777* ⊕ *www.vinopolis.co.uk* ✉ *Tues.–Thurs. £11.50, Fri.–Mon. £13.50* ⊙ *Mon., Fri., and Sat. noon–9, Tues.–Thurs. and Sun. noon–6* Ⓤ *London Bridge.*

The South Bank at a Glance

8

Kensington & Chelsea

WORD OF MOUTH

"I don't know how to properly describe the Chelsea Flower Show. For five days a year, it takes over the sizeable compound of the Royal Hospital Chelsea; enormous temporary buildings sprout from the parade grounds and entire landscapes are created that will endure just a week. The best thing I can say is this: if you are ever in London at the end of May, go. And don't settle, as we did, for a half-day ticket. Spring for the (gulp) full-day pass. You won't regret it."

–Neal_Sanders

KENSINGTON & CHELSEA

Sightseeing
★ ★ ★ ★

Nightlife
★

Dining
★ ★ ★ ★

Lodging
★ ★ ★

Shopping
★ ★ ★ ★

The Royal Borough of Kensington & Chelsea has always been home to world-famous movers and shakers. There are more blue plaques (historic markers) here than in any other part of London, three superb shopping districts, a royal palace, and one of the best concentrations of museums in the world. Kensington is the more established, conservative area, while Chelsea, equally well-heeled, basks in its literary and artistic connections: the youth culture of the '60s was virtually invented here. Today, though more comfortable than cutting-edge, it still attracts fascinating people to its villagelike neighborhoods.

What's Here

As you head north from the Thames, the Royal Borough changes, layer by layer. The lawns and parkland of Wren's impressive **Royal Hospital** stretch down to the river near Chelsea Bridge, in the southeast corner. It's about a mile west along the Embankment to **Cheyne Walk, Chelsea Physic Garden,** and **Carlyle's House,** with all their arty and historic associations. The blue plaques commemorating important residents along here are amazing. On the way, notice the **Albert Bridge,** a candy-color Victorian confection of a suspension bridge.

If you cut through the Royal Hospital grounds, which are open to the public, you'll emerge on Royal Hospital Road right next to the National Army Museum. If you're a shopaholic, zig-zag north, through pleasant residential streets to **King's Road** (Shopping, Chapter 19), for retail therapy and for a bit of culture at the newly relocated **Saatchi Gallery,** which is doing its best to restore the cutting edge to the neighborhood. Once you hit King's Road, ramble up and down the tiny Georgian lanes of pastel-color houses, especially **Jubilee Place** and **Burnsall Street,** that run off it to the north, leading to the hidden "village square" of **Chelsea Green.**

> ### LONDON AT NIGHT
>
> The Albert Bridge, alight with thousands of lights, its reflection sparkling on the river, is one of London's great romantic views.

Alternatively, if you'd rather just continue shopping, you can charge your way (literally) down King's Road, from Sloane Square to World's End. The shopping area recently christened as **Brompton Cross** doesn't appear on most maps, but if you aim west, as the crow flies, from Sloane Square to the intersection of the Fulham Road and Brompton Road, you'll find a small but choice collection of fashion and homeware shops (Shopping, Chapter 19).

Near South Kensington tube station is the heart of a small French community, centered around the French school, known as the **Lycée,** and a good place to look for a light snack or a coffee before attempting the South Kensington museums, the **Victoria & Albert Museum,** the **Science Museum**, and the **Natural History Museum,** around the corner.

The **Royal Albert Hall,** with its bas reliefs that make it look like a red-brick Wedgewood pot, is the next layer, about ¼ mi north, past the museums and Imperial College on Exhibition Road. Facing the Albert Hall, across Kensington Gore in Kensington Gardens, is the **Albert Memorial,** the recently regilded monument to Prince Albert, the British Empire, and all its interests. **Kensington Palace** and its **Orangery** is diagonally across the park, with the gated **Kensington Palace Gardens** running behind it.

Kensington High Street, together with **Kensington Church Street,** is yet another great shopping and snacking area. Turn into Derry Street or Young Street, on either side of Barkers Arcade, and enter **Kensington Square,** one of the most complete 17th-century residential squares in London. Holland Park is about ¾ mi farther west, with the entrance on Park Close, off Ilchester Road. Both **Leighton House** and the **Linley Sambourne House** are nearby as well.

Places to Explore

★ **Kensington Palace.** For more than 300 years, royals have lived here in grand style. The original building, Nottingham House, needed 12 years of renovation by Wren and Hawksmoor, who had been commissioned by King William III and Queen Mary to turn it into a proper palace. During the subsequent three reigns, it underwent much further refurbishment—accompanied by numerous royal deaths: William III died here in 1702, Queen Anne in 1714, George I in 1727, and George II in 1760, after which it ceased to be a royal residence. It was also here that the 18-year-old Princess Victoria was called from her bed in June 1837 by the Archbishop of Canterbury and the Lord Chamberlain, to be told of the death of her uncle, William IV, and her accession to the throne. The

GETTING ORIENTED

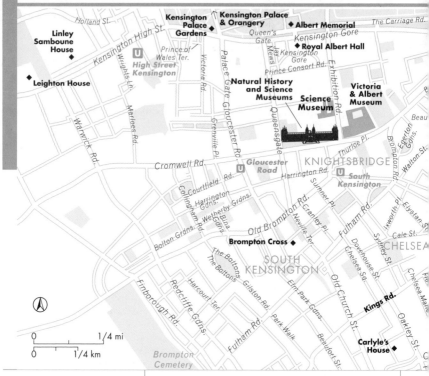

GETTING HERE

GETTING HERE

Depending on where you're headed, there are several useful Tube stations for Kensington & Chelsea: Sloane Square and High Street Kensington on the District and Circle lines; Earls Court on the Piccadilly Line; and South Kensington and Gloucester Road on the District, Circle, and Piccadilly lines.

TOP 5 REASONS TO GO

■ **The V&A Museum:** Sketch in the sculpture court, where even stools are provided—then have a glass of wine under the Chihuly chandelier.

■ **Natural History Museum:** Watch a child catch on that the museum's new animatronic T. rex has noticed *him*—and is licking its dinosaur chops.

■ **Science Museum:** Kids and you can enjoy this "painlessly educational" museum.

■ **The Proms:** Sing along at the end of a Proms concert in Royal Albert Hall. (Even better: watch the English concert-goers drop their inhibitions and join in, too

■ **King's Road pubs:** Chat with a Chelsea Pensioner, in full red-uniformed regalia, over a pint.

MAKING THE MOST OF YOUR TIME

You could fill three or four days in this borough: a shopping stroll along the length of King's Road is easily half a day. Add lunch and some time weaving back and forth between King's Road and the river and you can fill a day. Give yourself a half-day, at least, for the Victoria & Albert Museum and a half-day for either the Science or Natural History Museum.

A GOOD RUN

The short circuit around the Thames between Chelsea Bridge and Albert Bridge is a pleasant 1½-mi run. From Chelsea Bridge run west along Chelsea Embankment. The wooded park on the other side is Battersea Park with its Peace Pagoda in the middle. Turn left across the river on the Albert Bridge. Then turn left into Battersea park and run along the cinder path beside the river. Now the view is of Chelsea as well as the boats and barges on the river. There are good public bathrooms and drinking fountains in the park. Emerge from the park and turn left across Chelsea Bridge back to the starting point.

FEELING PECKISH?

The Café at the V&A (⊠ Victoria & Albert Museum, Cromwell Rd., SW7 ☎ 020/7581-2159) serves breakfast, light snacks, tea, and full meals throughout the day, all in a very grand room at modest prices. You can even have a buffet supper on late nights. Stop by just to see the authentic and original Arts & Crafts decor, one of William Morris' earliest commissions, with stained-glass panels by Edward Burne Jones.

NEAREST PUBLIC RESTROOMS

Peter Jones, the big department store in Sloane Square, has several large, clean restrooms that are free to use. Don't be shy about entering any pub and asking for the "loo." Even if you aren't a customer, nobody will mind. Usually, in this part of town, the restrooms are clean and well maintained.

State Apartments, including the late Princess Margaret's rooms are on show on the first floor. The Duke and Duchess of Gloucester and Prince and Princess Michael of Kent have apartments here, albeit very much private ones.

On the Garden Floor is the palace's visitor entrance, which takes you into the Red Saloon and Teck Saloon, where the **Royal Ceremonial Dress Collection** displays garments dating to the 18th century. State and occasional dresses, hats, shoes, and gloves from the present Queen's

PRINCESS DIANA
The late Diana, Princess of Wales lived here until her death in 1997 and is possibly most notable by the absence of references to her, save for the display of her dresses in the Royal Ceremonial Dress Collection. Her apartments were in the northwest wing of the palace. People still leave flowers at the palace gates for her, particularly on the anniversary of her death.

wardrobe are showcased, as are some incredible evening gowns worn by that most fashionable of royal icons, the late Princess Diana. Other displays interpret the symbolism of ceremonial court dress and also show the labor that went into producing this attire. Some dazzlers of note are the coronation robes of Queen Mary and George V and a regal mantua—a 6-foot-wide court dress that recalls the truth that part of the aristocratic game was to impress your fellow courtiers with your clothes.

Similarly, the State Apartments, especially the King's Apartments, reminded visitors none too subtly of regal power. The King's Grand Staircase is the impressive starting point of the tour, with superb trompe-l'oeil paintings by William Kent showing courtiers looking down. The Presence Chamber (used for formal receptions), painted with mythical gods in the Italian "grotesque" style, is a red-and-gold assault on the eyes, packed with paintings. Look out for the Grinling Gibbons cherubic overmantel carvings. Next follows the more intimate Privy Chamber, reflected by its comparatively tranquil decor. The Mortlake tapestries commissioned by Charles I represent the seasons, and the lavish painted ceiling alludes to the godlike status of monarchs. Roman columns and gilded decor in the Cupola Room, where Princess Victoria was christened, reminded the royal visitor that being admitted beyond the Presence Room was a mark of status (note that although the ceiling appears to be domed it's actually as flat as a pancake). These rooms lack chairs because only the monarch would have been seated.

Next come the rooms where Victoria had her ultrastrict upbringing, since restored with items that belonged to her and Prince Albert. Originally part of the King's Apartments, these bedrooms and dressing rooms seem pleasantly domestic compared with the grandeur of the state rooms. The King's Gallery, which precedes the private apartments of Queen Anne, and later of Queen Mary, returns to the gilded theme—by Thornhill (of St. Paul's Cathedral fame)—with rich red damask walls. The copies of Van Dyck's Charles I portraits (the originals are at the Queen's Gallery, Buckingham Palace) dominate the scene, along with two pieces by Tintoretto. The tour ends with the Queen's Staircase, which leads into the garden: undoubtedly the true natural gem of the palace,

A BRIEF HISTORY

Kensington and Chelsea were separate villages, each with royal connections, until united in 1965. Chelsea, south of King's Road (Charles II's private way from St. James to Fulham), was settled before the Domesday Book and already fashionable when two of Henry VIII wives lived there. Artists and writers flocked to the area in the 19th century, establishing a creative colony in Cheyne Walk; at one time Turner, Whistler, John Singer Sargent, Dante Gabriel Rossetti, and Oscar Wilde were residents. Creatives still come. In the '60s it was the turn of the Rolling Stones and the Beatles; in the '70s Bob Marley wrote "I Shot the Sheriff" in a flat off Cheyne Walk.

Kensington laid its first royal stake when King William III, fed up with the vapors of the Thames, bought a country place there in 1689 and converted it into Kensington Palace. Courtiers followed, but the village kept its rural quality well into the Victoria's reign when, in the building boom of the 1850s, large landowners developed their farms into vast tracts of smart town houses. Queen Victoria's consort, Prince Albert, added the jewel in the borough's crown when he turned the profits of the Great Exhibition of 1851 into South Kensington's metropolis of museums.

and which provided the original attraction for the green-thumbed William and Mary. If you visit in spring, the tulips, which were a favorite of Mary's, reign supreme in a riot of color. The Orangery, built for Queen Anne, was the scene of many a royal family party; you can take a cup of tea here, before admiring the Sunken Garden with its fountains and Tudor design which echoes Hampton Court.

The palace was also home to the late Princess Margaret, and a new photographic exhibition, "Number 1A Kensington Palace: from Courtiers' Lodgings to Royal Home," has opened in her former apartments. The Princess and Lord Snowdon transformed the place in the 1960s, mixing modern with 18th-century, a blend evidenced in the entrance hall, Snowdon's study, the guest bedroom, and garden room. ⊠ *The Broad Walk, Kensington Gardens, Kensington, W8* ☎ *0870/751–5180 advance booking and information* ⊕ *www.hrp.org.uk* ✉ *£11.50; discounted joint tickets for one other palace, specified at time of purchase, are available* ⊘ *Mar.–Oct., daily 10–6; Nov.–Feb., daily 10–5; last admission 1 hr before closing* Ⓤ *Queensway.*

Kensington Palace Gardens. Starting behind Kensington Palace, this is one of London's rare private roads, guarded and gated both here and at the Notting Hill Gate end. Part of the Crown Estate, a unique institution that holds private property for Britain through the Crown, it's open to pedestrian traffic. If you walk it, you can see why it earned the nickname "Millionaires' Row"—it's lined with palatial white-stucco houses designed by a selection of the best architects of the mid-19th century. ⊠ *Kensington, W8* Ⓤ *High St. Kensington.*

9

Linley Sambourne House. Filled with delightful Victorian and Edwardian antiques, fabrics, and paintings, the home of *Punch* cartoonist Edward Linley Sambourne in the 1870s is one of the most charming 19th-century London houses extant—small wonder that it was used in Merchant and Ivory's *A Room with a View*. An Italianate house, it was the scene for society parties when Anne Messel was in residence in the 1940s. Being Kensington, there's a royal connection, too: her son, Antony Armstrong-Jones, married the late Princess Margaret, and their son has preserved the connection by taking the name Viscount Linley. Admission is by guided tours, given by costumed actors. There are set tour times on weekends, and you can call in advance for a tour appointment on other days. ⊠ *18 Stafford Terr., Kensington, W8* ☎ *020/7602–3316* ⊕ *www.rbkc.gov.uk* 🖃 *£6* ☉ *Guided tours weekends 10, 11:15, 1, 2:15, 3:30* Ⓤ *High St. Kensington.*

Ⓒ **Natural History Museum.** Architect Alfred Waterhouse had relief panels
FodorśChoice scattered across the outrageously ornate French Romanesque–style
★ terra-cotta facade of this museum, depicting extant creatures to the left of the entrance, extinct ones to the right. Far from becoming crusty itself, the museum has invested millions in a superb modernization program, with more of the wow-power and interactives necessary to secure interest from younger visitors.

Upon entering the museum's central hall you'll come face-to-face with the most potent symbol of extinction—the dinosaurs—as a giant diplodocus skeleton dominates the many archways to the Life Galleries. From here you can follow the Waterhouse Way to further dinosaur exploration in Gallery 21, where velociraptors and oviraptors slug it out, *Jurassic Park*–style, in a vivid animatronic reconstruction. Don't be surprised when the dinos notice you—the fierce, animatronic Tyrannosaurus Rex senses when human prey is near and "responds" in character. Nearby, you can visit the first T. rex jaw ever discovered—its teeth are nearly 7-inches long. It's easy to spend all day here, but there are later developments of beastly evolution to discover: en route to the first of these, in the Human Biology Gallery (22), you pass through a birth-simulation chamber. In the Mammal Galleries (23 and 24), a massive 82-foot blue whale suspended on two levels is the centerpiece of the displays showing man's relationship with creatures large and small, from fossils to ferocious beasts. From here you can delve further into this field of biodiversity by continuing on to the new Darwin Centre, which showcases the museum's entire collection—all 22 million creatures—from a tiny Seychellian frog to the Komodo dragon lizard. In the Creepy Crawlies Gallery (33), there's a super-enlarged scorpion so nightmarish that it makes tarantulas seem cute. If this is your field of fun, then you might want to zip down to the basement for hands-on activities in the Investigate section, where you can handle actual objects, from old bones to bugs.

The Earth Galleries are also unmissable, if you have the time and stamina, and could make an alternative museum tour beginning, as there's a secondary museum entrance at the Exhibition Road end. No less stunning in effect, a giant escalator takes you into a globe, around which are representations of our solar system. There is a choice of lev-

Historic Plaque Hunt

AS YOU WANDER AROUND
London, you'll see lots of small, blue, circular plaques on the sides and facades of buildings, describing which famous, semifamous, or obscure but brilliant person once lived there. The first was placed outside Lord Byron's birthplace (now no more) by the Royal Society of Arts. There are around 700 blue plaques, erected by different bodies—you may even find some green ones which originated from Westminster City Council—but English Heritage now maintains the responsibility, and if you want to find out the latest, check the Web site www.english-heritage.org.uk. Below are some of the highlights:

James Barrie (100 Bayswater Rd., Hyde Park, W2); **Hector Berlioz** (58 Queen Anne St., Marylebone, W1); **Elizabeth Barrett Browning** (50 Wimpole St., Marylebone, W1); **Robert Browning** (17 Warwick Crescent, Hyde Park, W2); **Frederic Chopin** (4 St. James's Place, St. James's, W1); **Sir Winston Churchill** (28 Hyde Park Gate, Kensington, SW7); **Captain James Cook** (88 Mile End Rd., Mile End, E1); **T. S. Eliot** (3 Kensington Court Gardens, Kensington, W8); **Mahatma Gandhi** (20 Baron's Court Rd., West Kensington, W14); **George Frederic Handel** (25 Brook St., Mayfair, W1); **Karl Marx** (28 Dean St., Soho, W1); **Wolfgang Amadeus Mozart** (180 Ebury St., Belgravia, SW1); **Sir Isaac Newton** (87 Jermyn St., St. James's, SW1); **Florence Nightingale** (10 South St., Mayfair, W1); **George Bernard Shaw** (29 Fitzroy Sq., Bloomsbury, W1); **Percy Bysshe Shelley** (15 Poland St., Soho, W1); **Mark Twain** (23 Tedworth Sq., Chelsea, SW3); **Oscar Wilde** (34 Tite St., Chelsea, SW3); **William Butler Yeats** (23 Fitzroy Rd., Camden, NW1).

els—and Earth surfaces—to explore, such as "The Power Within" (Gallery 61), where you can feel an earthquake simulation and get the inside facts on volcanoes. ✉ *Cromwell Rd., South Kensington, SW7* ☎ *020/7942–5000* ⊕ *www.nhm.ac.uk* ✆ *Free* ☉ *Mon.–Sat. 10–5:50, Sun. 11–5:50, last admission 5:30, daily tours from main information desk* Ⓤ *South Kensington.*

Royal Albert Hall. This domed, circular 8,000-seat auditorium (as well as the Albert Memorial, opposite) was made possible by the Victorian public, who donated funds for it. More money was raised, however, by selling 1,300 future seats at £100 apiece—not for the first night but for every night for 999 years. (Some descendants of purchasers still use the seats.) The Albert Hall is best known for its annual July–September Henry Wood Promenade Concerts (the "Proms"), with bargain-price standing (or promenading, or sitting-on-the-floor) tickets sold on the night of concert. For more on Royal Albert Hall, see Arts & Entertainment, Chapter 18. ✉*Kensington Gore, Kensington, SW7* ☎*020/7589–8212* ⊕*www. royalalberthall.co.uk* ✆ *Prices vary with event* Ⓤ *South Kensington.*

Royal Hospital. The hospice for elderly and infirm soldiers was founded by Charles II in 1682 as his troops had hitherto enjoyed not so much as a meager pension and were growing restive after the civil wars of 1642–46 and 1648. Charles wisely appointed the great architect Sir Christopher Wren to design this small village of brick and Portland stone set in manicured gardens (which you can visit) surrounding the Figure Court—named after the 1692 bronze figure of Charles II dressed up as a Roman soldier—and the Great Hall (dining room) and chapel. The latter is enhanced by the choir stalls of Grinling Gibbons (who did the bronze of Charles, too), the former by a vast oil of Charles on horseback by Antonio Verrio, and both are open to the public.

The "Chelsea Pensioners" are recognizable by their traditional scarlet frock coats with gold buttons, medals, and tricorne hats. The pensioners celebrate Charles II's birthday—May 29, Oak Apple Day—by draping oak leaves on his statue and parading around it in memory of a hollow oak tree that expedited the king's miraculous escape from the 1651 Battle of Worcester. Also in May, and usually the third week, the Chelsea Flower Show, the year's highlight for thousands of garden-obsessed Brits, is held here. Run by the Royal Horticultural Society, the mammoth event takes up vast acreage here, and the surrounding streets throng with visitors. ⊠ *Royal Hospital Rd., Chelsea, SW3* ☎ *020/ 7730–0161* ⊕ *www.chelsea-pensioners.org.uk* 🎟 *Free* ☉ *Mon.–Sat. 10–noon and 2–4* Ⓤ *Sloane Sq.*

Saatchi Gallery. Charles Saatchi, who made his fortune building an advertising empire that successfully "rebranded" Margaret Thatcher's Conservative Party, is an astute art collector who has made acquisitions that regularly create headlines. Saatchi's personal collection, exhibited in his large private gallery, reflects the leading edge of the British avantgarde. Paula Rego, Damien Hirst, Rachel Whiteread, Janine Antoni, and Tracey Emin have all been shown. At this writing, the new Saatchi Gallery, relocated from the South Bank, was scheduled to reopen in early 2007; check the Web site for updated details. ⊠ *Duke of Yorks HQ Building, Kings Rd., Chelsea SW3* ☎ *020/7823–2363* ⊕ *www.saatchi-gallery. co.uk* Ⓜ *Sloane Sq.*

Ⓒ **Science Museum.** This, the third of the great South Kensington museums, stands behind the Natural History Museum in a far plainer building. It has loads of hands-on exhibits, with entire schools of children apparently decanted inside to interact with them; but it is, after all, painlessly educational. Highlights include the Launch Pad gallery, which demonstrates basic scientific principles (try the plasma ball, where your hands attract "lightning"—if you can get them on it); *Puffing Billy,* the oldest steam locomotive in the world; and the actual *Apollo 10* capsule. But don't be mistaken in thinking this is kids'-only territory—there's plenty here for all ages. The latest and best offering for that is the Wellcome Wing, a space-age addition devoted to contemporary science, medicine, and technology, which also includes a 450-seat IMAX cinema. Note that there's a special charge for the cinema shows, and for the special exhibitions. Science Night Sleepovers, held throughout the year, are kids' favorites. Groups of five to nine children, 8 to 11 years old, accompanied by an adult, get to play all night in this fabulous place. Check the Web site for the schedule. ⊠ *Exhibition Rd., South Kensington, SW7*

FodorsChoice ★

☎ 0/870–870–4868 ⊕ *www.sciencemuseum.org.uk* ✉ *Free* ☉ *Daily 10–6* Ⓤ *South Kensington.*

🐾 **Victoria & Albert Museum.** Recognizable by the copy of Victoria's impe-
Fodor'sChoice   rial crown on the lantern above the central cupola, this institution is al-
★   ways referred to as the V&A. It's a huge museum, showcasing the applied
arts of all disciplines, all periods, all nationalities, and all tastes, and it's
a wonderful, generous place to get lost in, full of innovation and completely devoid of pretension. Prince Albert, Victoria's adored consort, was
responsible for the genesis of this permanent version of the 1851 Great
Exhibition, and his queen laid its foundation stone in her final public London appearance, in 1899. From the start, the V&A had an important
role as a research institution, and that role continues today.

There are many beautiful diversions: one minute you're gazing on the
Jacobean oak four-poster Great Bed of Ware (one of the V&A's most
prized possessions, given that Shakespeare immortalized it in *Twelfth
Night*) and the next you're in the celebrated Dress Collection, coveting
a Jean Muir frock. ■ TIP→ **As a whirlwind introduction, you could take a
free, one-hour daily tour, or a 30-minute version on Wednesday evening. Otherwise, follow your own whims around the enormous space, but updated areas
of the museum are worthy destinations.**

The British Galleries are an ambitious addition that heralds British art
and design from 1500 to 1900. Here you'll see such major pieces as George
Gilbert Scott's model of the Albert Memorial, and the first-ever English fork made in 1632, but you'll also discover fascinating facts behind
the designs, such as the construction of a 16th-century bed and the best
way for women in cumbersome hooped skirts to negotiate getting in and
out of carriages. Throughout the galleries are interactive corners for all
ages, where you can discover, design, and build—from your own family emblem to period chairs. Free tours of the British Galleries depart
daily from the rear of the Cromwell Road entrance at 12:30 and 2:30
and last one hour.

The silver is amassed in the Whiteley Silver Galleries, opened in October 2002, which bring more than 500 shining examples together. From
ancient medieval reliquaries to the Napoleonic period, to contemporary
pieces, it's a stunning collection, and the largest in the United Kingdom.

Unchanged, but still spectacular, is the Glass Gallery, where a collection
spanning four millennia is reflected between room-size mirrors under
designer Danny Lane's breathtaking glass balustrade. ■ TIP→ **The V&A's
outstanding glass collection includes a massive Dale Chihuly chandelier in the
entrance dome—the only Chihuly piece on public display in the U.K.** Don't miss
the pure art, too: the Raphael Galleries house seven massive cartoons
the painter completed in 1516 for his Sistine Chapel tapestries (now in
the Pinoteca of the Vatican Museums in Rome). The shop is the museum in microcosm, and quite the best place to buy art nouveau or arts-
and-crafts gifts. ✉ *Cromwell Rd., South Kensington, SW7* ☎ *020/
7942–2000* ⊕ *www.vam.ac.uk* ✉ *Free* ☉ *Thurs.–Tues. 10–5:45, Wed.
and last Fri. of month 10–10; tours daily at 10:30, 11:30, 1:30, 3:30,
and Wed. at 7:30 PM* Ⓤ *South Kensington.*

9

Kensington & Chelsea at a Glance

SIGHTS
Albert Bridge
Albert Memorial
Kensington Palace
Leighton House
Linley Sambourne House
Royal Hospital
MUSEUMS & GALLERIES
Natural History Museum
Saatchi Gallery
Science Museum
Serpentine Gallery
Victoria & Albert Museum
PARKS & GARDENS
Chelsea Green
Chelsea Physic Garden
Holland Park
Kensington Square
WHERE TO EAT (⇨ Ch. 15)
BUDGET DINING
Chelsea Bun,
   American-Casual
Kandy Tea House,
   Afternoon Tea
MODERATE DINING
The Collection,
   Mediterranean
Lou Pescadou, *French*
The Pig's Ear,
   Contemporary
PJ's Bar & Grill,
   American-Casual
Wódka, *Polish*
EXPENSIVE DINING
Aubergine, *French*
Bibendum, *Contemporary*
Chutney Mary, *Anglo-
   Indian*
Gordon Ramsay at Royal
   Hospital Road, *French*
La Brasserie, *French*
The Orangery at Kensington
   Palace, *Afternoon Tea*
Racine, *French*
Tom Aikens, *French*
WHERE TO STAY (⇨ Ch. 16)
BUDGET LODGING
Abbey House
easyHotel
Holland House YHA

Hotel 167
Swiss House Hotel
The Vicarage
MODERATE LODGING
Aster House
Astons Budget Studios
Five Sumner Place
The Gallery
Kensington House Hotel
Number Sixteen
EXPENSIVE LODGING
Bentley Kempinski
Blakes
Cadogan
The Cranley
Eleven Cadogan Gardens
The Gore
Milestone Hotel &
   Apartments
myhotel chelsea
The Pelham
San Domenico House
PUBS & NIGHTLIFE
   (⇨ Ch. 17)
606 Club, *jazz & blues*
Admiral Codrington, *pub*
ARTS & ENTERTAINMENT
   (⇨ Ch. 18)
Holland Park Opera, *opera*
Royal Albert Hall,
   concert venue
Royal Court Theatre,
   theater
SHOPPING (⇨ Ch. 19)
DEPARTMENT STORES
John Lewis
ACCESSORIES
Accessorize
Lulu Guinness
ANTIQUES
Antiquarius
The Furniture Cave
Hope and Glory
ART GALLERIES & CRAFTS
Classic Prints
Designers Guild
Kelly Hoppen
AUCTIONS
Christie's
Lots Road Auctions

BOOKS/PRINTED MATTER
Children's Book Centre
John Sandoe Books, Ltd
Pan Bookshop
CLOTHING
Agnès B
Bamford & Sons
Betsey Johnson
Betty Jackson
Biondi
Brora
Collette Dinnigan
Daisy & Tom
Jaeger
Joseph
MiMi
Trotters
Vivienne Westwood
Zara
FLEA MARKETS
Orsini
VV Rouleau
FOOD
L'Artisan du Chocolat
Rococo
Whittard of Chelsea
GIFTS
General Trading Co
**HOUSEHOLD ITEMS/
FURNITURE**
Conran Shop
JEWELRY
Butler & Wilson
Les Néréides
Links of London
PERFUME/COSMETICS
Jo Malone
L'Artisan Parfumeur
SHOES
Franchetti Bond Ltd
Kate Kuba
Manolo Blahnik
Patrick Cox
**STATIONERY/GRAPHIC
ARTS**
Green & Stone
Ordning & Reda
TOYS
Early Learning Centre
Science Museum Gift Shop

Knightsbridge & Belgravia

WORD OF MOUTH

"We walked through small streets of Knightsbridge, just beautiful on a sunny crisp Sunday morning, and came along the side of the [Brompton] Oratory . . . . We had a few minutes to explore the Oratory (neo-renaissance style) before the 11:00 Mass, which was sung in Latin. It was quite the ethereal experience as we drifted into dozing with what sounded like the heavenly chorus for our lullabye. The homily was quite good (I was awake for that part), and the church was full."

—noe847

KNIGHTSBRIDGE & BELGRAVIA

Sightseeing
★

Nightlife
★

Dining
★★

Lodging
★★★

Shopping
★★★★

Britain's reputation as a nation of shopkeepers is well kept in Knightsbridge, home of Harrods, Harvey Nichols, and the latest international designers, as well as a clutch of jewelers where you can drop some serious cash on very serious baubles. In short: Knightsbridge is *must*-go territory for shopaholics. In Belgravia, to the east, the frenetic pace is replaced by all the peace and quiet money can buy. Grand, white terraces of aristocratic town houses, part of the Grosvenor estate, are owned by the Dukes of Westminster. Many are leased to embassies but a remarkable number remain homes of the discreet, private wealthy.

What's Here

There's no getting away from it. This is shop-til-you-drop territory of the highest order. With two world-famous department stores, **Harrods** and **Harvey Nichols,** a few hundred yards apart, and every bit of space between and around taken up with designer boutiques, chain stores, and jewelers, it's hard to imagine why anyone who doesn't like shopping would even think of coming here. This may be the day for Dad and the kids to visit the dinosaurs at the Natural History Museum in South Kensington (Chapter 9), so that Mom can spend money in peace.

If the department stores seem overwhelming, **Beauchamp Place** (pronounced "Beecham"), a left off Brompton Road and four streets west of Harrods, is a good tonic. It's lined with equally chic and expensive boutiques, but they tend to be smaller, more personal, and less hectic.

Another place to find peace and quiet (of a less expensive kind) is **Brompton Oratory,** the area's ornate and historic Catholic Church. If you're lucky, you may catch a rehearsal of the church's famous boys choir. Remember this is an active place of worship.

Once you've maxed out your credit cards, a peaceful stroll in Belgravia may be just the thing. Walk east along the Brompton Road until it ends at Knightsbridge (the name of a street as well as the district) across Sloane Street. Pass Harvey Nichols and turn right into **Lowndes Square.** At the bottom of the square, continue on Lowndes Street to **West Halkin Street,** which leads into **Belgrave Square.** These are some of the grandest houses in London and, although many of them are embassies, several are still private homes.

Leave the square along Belgrave Place, admiring the lovely, Westminster-white houses. **Eaton Square,** lined with substantial terraces, most divided into large flats or town houses, is the next major intersection. Often, the only people on the streets are professional dog walkers and chauffeurs. Turn right on Eaton Square, and right again after one block, onto **Elizabeth Street.** Some people call this area Belgravia, others Pimlico–Victoria. Either way, now that you've had a break, it's time to shop again, and this street is the place to be. ■ TIP→ **At the fabulous Chocolate Society you can drink and eat chocolate to die for, as well as buy some to take home.**

Places to Explore

Belgrave Square. The square, as well as the streets leading off it, are genuine elite territory and have been since they were built in the mid-1800s. The grand, porticoed mansions were created as town residences for courtiers, conveniently close to the monarch—-Buckingham Palace is

> **HERE'S WHERE**
>
> Fans of 1970s British television should note that Eaton Place was the home of the Bellamy's of *Upstairs, Downstairs* fame.

virtually around the corner. This district is wholly residential: other than the colorful flower seller who does business at the southwest corner of Belgrave Square, the area is untouched by neon or retail activity of any kind. The terraced row houses are almost all painted a pristine white to signify they're owned by Duke of Westminster, London's biggest landlord and one of Britain's richest men. Walk down Belgrave Place toward Eaton Place and you pass two of Belgravia's most beautiful mews: Eaton Mews North and Eccleston Mews, both fronted by grand Westminster-white rusticated entrances right out of a 19th-century engraving. ■ TIP→ **Traffic really whips around Belgrave Square so be careful.**

Brompton Oratory. This is a late product of the mid-19th-century English Roman Catholic revival led by John Henry Cardinal Newman (1801–90), who established the oratory in 1884 and whose statue you see outside. Architect Herbert Gribble, a previously unknown 29-year-old, won the competition to design the place, an honor that you may conclude went to his head when you see the vast, incredibly ornate interior. It's punctuated by treasures far older than the church itself, like

GETTING ORIENTED

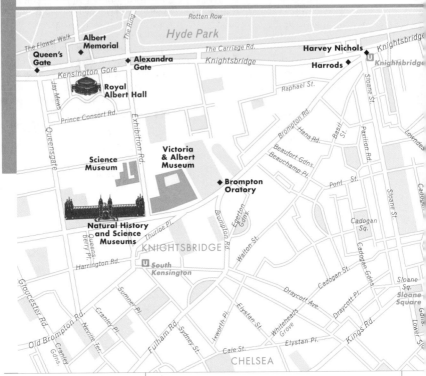

GETTING HERE

Knightsbridge is easy. Just take the Piccadilly Line to Knightsbridge Station. Hyde Park Corner on the Piccadilly Line is near the northeast corner of Belgrave Square while Victoria Station on the District, Circle, and Victoria lines or Sloane Square on the District and Circle lines are equidistant from the shops along Elizabeth Street.

NEAREST PUBLIC RESTROOMS

If you need a restroom, choose Harvey Nicks over Harrods. Harrods charges £1 to use its facilities.

TOP 5 REASONS TO GO

■ **Harrods food halls:** Notice the glistening mosaic of fresh fish under the actual mosaic ceilings of these esteemed underground culinary corridors.

■ **Harvey Nichols:** Find a designer dress in your size, for 80% off, in the Harvey Nicks January sales.

■ **Brompton Oratory:** Listen to the Schola Cantorum, with its brilliant boys choir, sing a Mozart Mass.

■ **Beauchamp Place:** Spot celebs at the latest hot restaurant while taking a break from your shopping marathon.

■ **Patisserie Valerie:** Sink your teeth into a Paris Brest pastry at the venerable, art nouveau patisserie on Brompton Road.

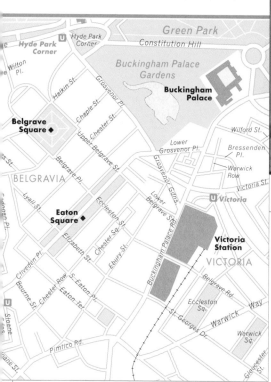

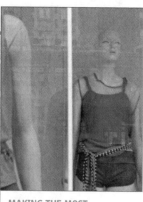

MAKING THE MOST OF YOUR TIME

Spending time here is mostly about stamina. If you're planning to seriously shop the big department stores, take a break between Harvey Nichols and Harrods to shop in smaller stores, stroll Beauchamp Place, or have a snack. To do justice to this area, don't plan on visiting far-away shopping neighborhoods on the same day. St. James's and Mayfair, including Fortum's and the Bond Street arcades, are close enough for determined shoppers.

There's not much to do in Belgravia besides soak up the atmosphere. It's nice for a leisurely stroll of an hour or less, but if you rush up and down its streets, you'll have missed the point.

SAFETY

Knightsbridge is a safe area, but beware of pickpockets in crowded Tube stations and department stores. Quiet Belgravia is so heavily watched by a mélange of doormen, chauffeurs, embassy security staff, and security cameras that it feels like the safest place on earth. Still, remain alert, and don't flash expensive watches and bling.

FEELING PECKISH?

With five branches, **Pâtisserie Valerie** (✉ 215 Brompton Rd., SW3 ☎ 020/7832-9971) is a London institution. The one down the road from Harrods, across from the Brompton Oratory, serves light meals and dazzling pastries in a bustling atmosphere.

Yo! Sushi is one of the quick, casual restaurants on Harvey Nichol's fifth floor. The **Café** on the fifth-floor is great for shopping breaks, light meals, and people watching as well.

A GOOD WALK

Just across Knightsbridge, at the end of Sloane Street, brave the complicated pedestrian crossing and go under the arch of the building that straddles the street. You'll be in Hyde Park, near the Hyde Park Barracks of one of the Queen's Household Regiments. If you're lucky, you may catch them exercising the horses on Rotten Row.

10

A BRIEF HISTORY

Like the Westbourne River, bridged in the ancient past to give this area its name, the history of Knightsbridge is buried under modern London. In the mid-16th century it was the site of a leper colony and considered a dangerous, malodorous place—a far cry from today, when the biggest dangers are to your bank balance. Belgravia is part of a nearly 300-acre central-London estate formed by a marriage of noble families in 1677. It was used as waste ground for grazing sheep until developed by Thomas Cubitt in the 19th century.

the giant *Twelve Apostles* in the nave, carved from Carrara marble by Giuseppe Mazzuoli in the 1680s and brought here from Siena's cathedral. The church conducts Sung Latin and Tridentine Masses. There are refreshments after the Sung Latin Mass on Sundays at 11. ☒ *Brompton Rd., Kensington, SW7* ☏ *020/7808–0900* ⊕ *www.bromptonoratory. com* ✉ *Free* ⊙ *6:30 AM–8 PM. Services weekdays 7 AM, 10, 12:30, and 6 PM; Sat. 7 AM, 8:30 Latin, 10, and 6 PM; Sun. 7 AM, 8, 9 Tridentine Latin, 10, 11 Sung Latin), 12:30, 4:30 PM, and 7* Ⓤ *South Kensington.*

Harrods. Just in case you don't notice it, this well-known shopping destination frames its domed terra-cotta Edwardian outline in thousands of white lights each night. The 15-acre Egyptian-owned store's sales weeks are world-class, and inside it's as frenetic as a stock-market floor. Its motto, *Omnia, omnibus, ubique* (Everything, for everyone, everywhere) is not too far from the truth. Don't miss the extravagant Food Hall, with its stunning art nouveau tiling in the neighborhood of meat and poultry and continuing on in the fishmongers' territory, where its glory is rivaled by displays of the sea produce itself. This is the place to acquire your green-and-gold souvenir Harrods bag, as food prices are surprisingly competitive. For more on Harrods, see Shopping, Chapter 19 ☒ *87–135 Brompton Rd., Knightsbridge, SW1* ☏ *020/7730–1234* ⊕ *www.harrods. com* ⊙ *Mon.–Sat. 10–7, Sun. noon–6* Ⓤ *Knightsbridge.*

Harvey Nichols. This is fashionista central and a must for anyone who has been watching *Absolutely Fabulous*, dahling—in which case you'll already know to call it Harvey Nicks. The housewares on the fourth floor are as deliciously of the moment as the clothing and accessories for men and women. For more on Harvey Nichols, see Shopping, Chapter 19 ☒ *109–125 Knightsbridge, Knightsbridge, SW1* ☏ *020/7235–5000* ⊕ *www. harveynichols.com* ⊙ *Mon.–Sat. 10–8, Sun. noon–6* Ⓤ *Knightsbridge.*

Knightsbridge & Belgravia at a Glance

SIGHTS
Brompton Oratory

PARKS & GARDENS
Beauchamp Place
Belgrave Square
Eaton Square
Lowndes Square

WHERE TO EAT (⇨ Ch. 15)

EXPENSIVE DINING
Amaya, *Indian*
Brasserie St. Quentin,
   French
The Capital, *French*
The Enterprise,
   Contemporary
Harrods, *Afternoon Tea*
La Poule au Pot, *French*
Le Cercle, *French*
Zafferano, *Italian*
Zuma, *Japanese*

WHERE TO STAY (⇨ Ch. 16)

MODERATE LODGING
Knightsbridge Green
Tophams Belgravia

EXPENSIVE LODGING
The Berkeley
The Beaufort
The Capital
Egerton House
The Franklin
The Halkin
Knightsbridge Hotel
The Lanesborough
L'Hotel
Mandarin Oriental
   Hyde Park

PUBS & NIGHTLIFE
   (⇨ Ch. 17)
Pizza Express, *jazz & blues*
Star Tavern, *pub*
The Blue Bar at the
   Berkeley Hotel, *bar*

SHOPPING (⇨ Ch. 19)

DEPARTMENT STORES
Harrods
Harvey Nichols

ACCESSORIES
Anya Hindmarch

Philip Treacy

ART GALLERIES & CRAFTS
Linley
Map House

AUCTIONS
Bonhams

CLOTHING
Agent Provocateur
Burberry
Egg
Hackett
Please Mum
Rigby & Peller

FOOD
The Chocolate Society

PERFUME/COSMETICS
Les Senteurs

SHOES
Jimmy Choo

10

Notting Hill & Bayswater

WORD OF MOUTH

"Half a mile east of Notting Hill is Bayswater, where the Tube station is surrounded by small cafés, restaurants, and shops, often with an Arabic flavor . . ."

—ben_haines_london

NOTTING HILL & BAYSWATER

Sightseeing
★ ★ ★

Nightlife
★ ★ ★

Dining
★ ★ ★

Lodging
★ ★ ★

Shopping
★ ★ ★ ★

North of the Royal Parks and once the estate of the Bishop of London's trustees, Bayswater is now a bustling hub of tourist restaurants, hotels, and high street shopping. To the west is the more enticing Notting Hill, a trendsetting square mile of ethnicity, music, and markets, with lots of restaurants to see and be seen in, as well as younger, more egalitarian modern-art galleries. The style-watching media have dubbed the local residents Notting Hillbillies. The whole area has mushroomed around one of the world's great antiques markets, Portobello Road. A Saturday morning spent here is almost obligatory, and people travel from all boroughs of the capital to soak up its chic, multicultural vibe, where the cool urban crowd meets and melds with the posh people of West London.

What's Here

In Bayswater, the main thoroughfare of **Queensway** is a rather peculiar, cosmopolitan street of ethnic confusion, late-night cafés and restaurants, a skating rink, and the **Whiteleys** shopping-and-movie mall. Turn left at the end into **Westbourne Grove,** however, and you've entered the Notting Hill of the film sets, replete with chic boutiques and charity shops laden with the cast-offs of the wealthy residents. You'll reach the famous **Portobello Road** after a few blocks, with the beautifully restored early-20th-century **Electric Cinema** at No. 191. Turn left for the Saturday antiques market and shops, right to reach the Westway overpass and the grocery and flea market. The stalls at **Westway Portobello Green Market** are occupied by junk, bric-a-brac, secondhand threads, and clothes and accessories by young, up-and-coming designers. Nearby on Acklam Road are the **Westbourne Studios,** an office complex with a gallery, restaurant, and bar open to the public, and the capital's best skateboarding park, **Bay Sixty6.**

QUEEN'S ICE BOWL

London's most central year-round ice-skating rink is the **Queens Ice Bowl,** where the per-session cost, including skate rental, is £6.50 for both adults and children. ✉ *17 Queensway, Bayswater, W2* ☎ *020/7229−0172* Ⓤ *Queensway.*

11

Places to Explore

Hyde Park & Kensington Gardens   See Page 203

★ **Portobello Road.** Tempted by tassels, looking for a 19th-century snuff spoon, an ancient print of North Africa, or a dashingly deco frock (just don't believe the dealer when he says the Vionnet label just fell off), or hunting for a gracefully Georgian silhouette of the Earl of Chesterfield? Head to Portobello Road, world famous for its Saturday antiques market (arrive before 9 AM to find the real treasures-in-the-trash; after 10, the crowds pack in wall to wall). Actually, the Portobello Market is three markets: antiques, "fruit and veg," and a flea market. The street begins at Notting Hill Gate, though the antiques stalls start a couple of blocks north, around Chepstow Villas. Lining the sloping street are also dozens of antiques shops and indoor markets, open most days—in fact, serious collectors will want to do Portobello on a weekday, when they can explore the 90-some antiques and art stores in relative peace. Where the road levels off, around Elgin Crescent, youth culture and a vibrant neighborhood life kick in, with all manner of interesting small stores and restaurants interspersed with the fruit and vegetable market. This continues to the Westway overpass ("flyover" in British), where London's best flea market (high-class, vintage, antique, and secondhand clothing; jewelry; and junk) happens Friday and Saturday, then on up to Golborne Road. There's a strong West Indian flavor to Notting Hill, with a Trinidad-style Carnival centered along Portobello Road on the August bank-holiday weekend. (For more on Portobello Road, see Shopping, Chapter 19.) Ⓤ *Notting Hill Gate, Ladbroke Grove.*

GETTING ORIENTED

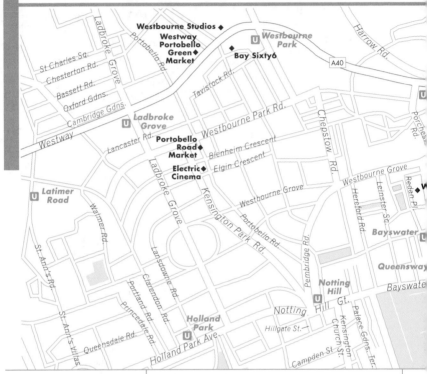

GETTING THERE

For Portobello Market and environs, the best Tube stops are Ladbroke Grove and Westbourne Park (Hammersmith and City lines); ask for directions when you emerge. The Notting Hill stop on the District, Circle, and Central lines enables you to walk the length of Portobello Road on a downhill gradient.

A GOOD WALK

To gape at Notting Hill's grandest houses, stroll over to Lansdowne Road, Lansdowne Crescent, and Lansdowne Square—two blocks west of Kensington Park Row.

TOP 5 REASONS TO GO

■ **Westbourne Grove:** People-watch at a sidewalk café in this swank section of the neighborhood.

■ **Portobello Road Market:** Seek and ye shall find; go early-morning antiques-hunting at London's most famous market.

■ **Notting Hill shopping:** Browse for vintage designer pieces at Notting Hill's numerous secondhand and retro clothing stores.

■ **Notting Hill Carnival:** Experience the explosion of color, culture, and music that is the Notting Hill Carnival, held over two days every August bank holiday.

■ **Electric Cinema:** Catch a movie reclined on a two-seater leather sofa, a beer and bar snacks at hand.

Westway

Royal
Oak

Bishop's Bridge Rd.

Eastbourne Ter.

Westbourne Ter.

Gloucester Ter.

**Paddington
Station**

Praed St.

Sussex Gardens

Sussex Place

Whiteleys

Leinster Gdns.

Queensway

Craven Hill

**Lancaster
Gate** U

Hyde Park Place

Rd.

*Kensington
Gardens*

E. Carriage Dr.

0 | 1/4 mi

0 | 1/4 km

Hyde Park

MAKING THE MOST OF YOUR TIME

Saturday is Notting Hill and Portobello Road's most fun and frenetic day. You could easily spend a whole day shopping, eating, and drinking here. You may prefer to start at the end of Portobello Road and work backward, using the parks for relaxation after your shopping exertions. Do the same on Friday if you're a flea-market fan. Sunday, the Hyde Park and Kensington Gardens railings all along Bayswater Road are hung with dubious art, which may slow your progress; this is also prime perambulation day for locals. The perimeter of the two parks alone covers a good 4 mi, and it's about half as far again around the remainder of the route. You could cut out a lot of park without missing out on essential sights and walk the whole thing in a brisk three hours.

SAFETY

At night, be wary of straying too far off the main streets as it gets "edgier" toward Ladbroke Grove's high-rise estates and the more deprived neighborhoods in the surrounding areas.

FEELING PECKISH?

For healthy fast food, it's hard to beat the canteen at **Fresh & Wild** (⌧ 208–212 Westbourne Grove ☎ 020/7229–1063). In addition to the stellar salad bar, there are daily hot specials. Once you've had your fill, stock up on tasty snacks from the store for later, too.

One price (£18), one meal, is the simple formula at the much-loved **Rodizio Rico** (⌧ 111 Westbourne Grove ☎ 020/7792–4035). The Brazilian fare consists of buffet salads, stews, and juicy steaks.

Tea houses are back in vogue in the capital, with celebrity clientele airing their graces at **Tea Palace** (⌧ 175 Westbourne Grove ☎ 020/7727–2600). Choose from 150 different infusions.

Notting Hill & Bayswater at a Glance

MUSEUMS
Jane Addams Hull-House
  Museum
Mexican Fine Arts Center
  Museum

WHERE TO EAT (⇨ Ch. 15)

BUDGET DINING
Alounak, *Middle Eastern*
Churchill Thai Kitchen, *Thai*
The Salusbury,
  Contemporary

MODERATE DINING
The Belvedere, *Continental*
Cow Dining Room,
  Contemporary
Electric Brasserie,
  Contemporary
Julie's, *English*
The Waterway,
  Contemporary

EXPENSIVE DINING
Clarke's, *Contemporary*
E&O, *Pan-Asian*
Harlem, *American–Casual*
Kensington Place,
  Contemporary
The Ledbury, *French*

WHERE TO STAY (⇨ Ch. 16)

BUDGET LODGING
Garden Court Hotel

MODERATE LODGING
Colonnade
The Columbia
Main House
The Pavilion
Portobello Gold
Vancouver Studios

EXPENSIVE LODGING
Abbey Court
Guesthouse West
The Hempel
K West
The Lennox
Miller's Residence
The Portobello

PUBS & NIGHTLIFE
(⇨ Ch. 17)
Beach Blanket Babylon,
  bar
Notting Hill Arts Club,
  dance club
Windsor Castle, *pub*

ARTS & ENTERTAINMENT
(⇨ Ch. 18)
The Electric Cinema, *film*

SHOPPING (⇨ Ch. 19)

MARKETS & MALLS
Portobello Road Market

ART GALLERIES & CRAFTS
Flower Space
Themes & Variations

BOOKS
Books for Cooks
Travel Bookshop

CLOTHING
Bamford & Sons

FOOD
The Spice Shop

GIFTS
The Cross

HOUSEHOLD ITEMS/
FURNITURE
Cath Kidston
Graham & Green

JEWELRY
Dinny Hall

MUSIC
Music & Video Exchange

PERFUME/COSMETICS
Diptyque

HYDE PARK & KENSINGTON GARDENS

Every year millions of visitors descend on the royal parks of Hyde Park and Kensington Gardens, which sit side by side and roll out over 625 acres of grassy expanses that provide much-craved-for respite from London's frenetic pace. The two parks incorporate formal gardens, fountains, sports fields, great picnic spots, shady clusters of ancient trees, and even an outdoor swimming pool.

Although it's probably been centuries since any major royal had a casual stroll here— you're more likely to bump into Madonna and Guy Ritchie than Her Royal Highness these days—the parks remain the property of the Crown, which saved them from being devoured by the city's late-18th-century growth spurt.

Today the luxury of such wide open spaces continues to be appreciated by the Londoners who steal into the parks before work for a session of tai chi, say, or on weekends when the sun is shining. Simply sitting back in a hired deck chair or strolling through the varied terrain is one of the most enjoyable ways to spend time here.

(counterclockwise from top right)
Morning fog on Rotten Row, Hyde Park

Albert Memorial

Diana Princess of Wales Memorial Playground

Inline-skating, Hyde Park

KENSINGTON GARDENS

Afternoon tea taken in the Orangery, a short walk from the Sunken Garden on the palace grounds, is a quintessentially English experience.

At the end of the 17th century, William III moved his court to the impeccably kept green space that is now **Kensington Gardens.** He was attracted to the location for its clean air and tranquillity and subsequently commissioned Sir Christopher Wren to overhaul the original redbrick building, resulting in the splendid **Kensington Palace.**

To the north of the palace complex is the early-19th-century **Sunken Gardens,** complete with a living tunnel of lime trees (i.e., linden trees) and golden laburnum.

On western side of the **Long Water** is George Frampton's 1912 *Peter Pan,* a bronze of the boy who lived on an island in the Serpentine and never grew up and whose creator, J.M. Barrie, lived at 100 Bayswater Road, not 500 yards from here.

Back toward Kensington Palace, at the intersection of several paths, is George Frederick Watts's 1904 bronze of a muscle-bound horse and rider, entitled **Physical Energy.** The **Round Pond** is a magnet for model-boat enthusiasts and duck feeders.

Near the Broad Walk, toward Black Lion Gate, is the **Diana Princess of Wales Memorial Playground,** an enclosed space with specially designed structures and areas on the theme of Barrie's Neverland. Hook's ship, crocodiles, "jungles" of foliage, and islands of sand provide a fantasy land for kids—more than 70,000 visit every year. Just outside its bounds is Ivor Innes's *Elfin*

When it first opened in 2003, the Diana Memorial Fountain averaged about 5,000 visitors per hour.

Oak, the remains of a tree carved with scores of tiny woodland creatures.

One of the park's most striking monuments is the **Albert Memorial.** This Victorian high-Gothic celebration of Prince Albert is adorned with marble statues representing his interests and amusements.

Diminutive as it may be, the **Serpentine Gallery** has not been afraid of courting controversy with its temporary exhibitions of challenging contemporary works.

HYDE PARK

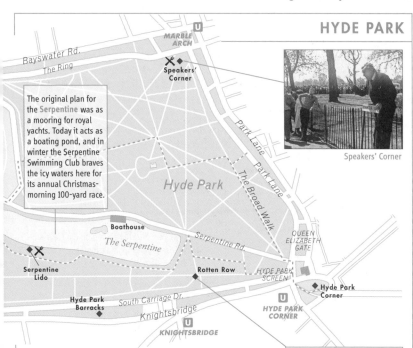

> The original plan for the Serpentine was as a mooring for royal yachts. Today it acts as a boating pond, and in winter the Serpentine Swimming Club braves the icy waters here for its annual Christmas-morning 100-yard race.

Speakers' Corner

Hyde Park was once the hunting ground of King Henry VIII. This stout, bawdy royal more or less stole Hyde Park, along with the smaller St. James's and Green parks, from the monks of Westminster in 1536. The public wasn't to be granted access to Hyde Park's delights until James I came to the throne and opened up limited parts to "respectably dressed" plebeians.

It was Charles I, in the 1700s, however, who was to shape the Hyde Park that visitors see today. Once he had created **the Ring** (North Carriage Drive), which forms a curve north of the **Serpentine** and boathouses, Charles allowed the general public to roam free. During the Great Plague of 1665, East Enders and City dwellers fled to the park, seeking refuge from the black bilious disease.

The stone **Serpentine Bridge**, built in 1826 by George Rennie, marks the boundary between Hyde Park and Kensington Gardens. **Rotten Row,** a corruption of the French *route de roi* (king's road), runs along the southeastern edge of Hyde Park and is still used by the Household Cavalry, who live at the **Hyde Park Barracks**—a high-rise and a long, low, ugly red block—to the left. This is where the brigade that mounts the guard at Buckingham Palace resides; you can see them at about 10:30 AM, as they leave to perform their duty in full regalia, plumed

> Rotten Row was the first artificially lit highway in Britain. In the late 17th century, William III was concerned that his walk to from Kensington Palace to St. James's Park was too dangerous, so he ordered 300 lamps to be placed along the route.

helmets and all, or await the return of the guard about noon.

On the south side of the 1930s **Serpentine Lido** (open to swimmers from June to September) is the £3.6 million oval **Diana Memorial Fountain.**

Ever since the 1827 legislation of public assembly, **Speakers' Corner** near Marble Arch has provided an outlet for political debate: on Sundays, it's an unmissable spectacle of vehement, sometimes comical, and always entertaining orators.

ENJOYING THE PARKS

Ride. **Hyde Park Riding Stables** keeps horses for hacking the sand tracks. Group lessons (usually just a few people) are £45 per person per hour. Private lessons are £50 Tuesday–Friday, £60 on weekends. ✉ 63 Bathurst Mews, Bayswater W2 ☎ 020/7723–2813 ⊕ www.hydeparkstables.com Ⓤ Lancaster Gate.

Row. **The Serpentine** has paddleboats and rowboats for £6 per person per hour, kids £2.50, March through October from 10 AM to 5 PM, later in good weather in summer. ☎ 020/7262–1330).

Run. You can run a **4-mi route** around the perimeter of Hyde Park and Kensington Gardens or a **2½-mi route** in Hyde Park alone if you start at Hyde Park Corner or Marble Arch and encircle the Serpentine.

Skate. On Friday, skaters of intermediate ability and upward meet at 8 PM at the Duke of Wellington Arch, Hyde Park Corner, for the **Friday Night Skate,** an enthusiastic two-hour mass skating session, complete with music and whistles. If you're a bit unsure on your wheels, arrive at 7:30 PM for the free lesson on how to stop. The **Sunday Rollerstroll,** a more laid-back version of the same thing, runs on Sunday afternoons; meet at 2 PM ⊕ www.thefns.com Ⓤ Hyde Park Corner.

Swim. **Serpentine Lido** is technically a beach on a lake, but a hot day in Hyde Park is surreally reminiscent of the seaside. There are changing facilities, and the swimming section is chlorinated. There is also a paddling pool, sandpit, and kids' entertainer in the afternoons. It's open daily from June through September, 10–5:30; admission £3.50, children £0.80 (£0.60 after 4 PM). ☎ 020/7706–3422 ⊕ www.serpentinelido.com Ⓤ Knightsbridge.

WHERE TO REFUEL

✗ The **Lido Café,** near the Diana Memorial Fountain, has plenty of seating with views across the Serpentine Lake.

✗ The **Honest Sausage** at Speakers' Corner is the place to grab a free-range sausage sandwich or organic bacon roll before enjoying the circus of debate.

✗ The **Broadwalk Café & Playcafe** next to the Diana Memorial Playground has a children's menu.

✗ The **Orangery** beside Kensington Palace is a distinctly more grown-up affair for tea and cakes.

SPEAKERS' CORNER

Once the site of public executions and the Tyburn hanging trees, the corner of Hyde Park at Cumberland Gate and Park Lane now harbors one of London's most public spectacles: Speakers' Corner. This has been a place of assembly and vitriolic outpourings and debates since the mid-19th century. The pageant of free speech takes place every Sunday afternoon.

Anyone is welcome to mount a soapbox and declaim upon any topic, which makes for an irresistible showcase of eccentricity—one such being the (now-deceased) Protein Man. Wearing his publicity board, the Protein Man proclaimed that the eating of meat, cheese, and peanuts led to uncontrollable acts of passion that would destroy Western civilization. The pamphlets he sold for four decades along the length and breadth of Oxford Street are now collector's items. Other more strait-laced campaigns have been launched here by the Chartists, the Reform League, the May Day demonstrators, and the Suffragettes.

PRACTICAL INFO

ADMISSION: Free for both parks

HOURS: Kensington Gardens 6 AM–dusk; Hyde Park 5 AM–midnight

CONTACT INFO: ☎ 020/7298–2100, ⊕ www.royalparks.gov.uk

GETTING HERE: Ⓤ **Kensington Gardens:** Kensington High Street, Queensway, Lancaster Gate, South Kensington. **Hyde Park:** Hyde Park Corner, Knightsbridge, Lancaster Gate, Marble Arch

EVENTS: Major events, such as rock concerts and festivals, road races, and talks, are regular features of the parks' calendar; check online for what's on during your visit.

Each summer, a different modern architect designs an outdoor pavilion for the Serpentine Gallery, the venue for outdoor film screenings, readings, and other such cultural soirees.

From June to August, Hyde Park hosts the Royal Parks Summer Festival, with live jazz evenings, opera, and plays all over the park grounds.

(left) Horseback riding, Hyde Park

(top) The Fountains, Kensington Gardens

(bottom) The Serpentine, Hyde Park

TOURS: There are **themed guided walks** about once a month, usually on Thursday or Friday afternoons. They are free but must be booked in advance. Check online or call the park offices for dates and details.

A 45-minute tour (£4.50) of the **Albert Memorial** is available. It's held at 2 and 3 PM on the first Sunday of the month. There's no need to book in advance unless you are part of a big group, in which case call 020/7495–0916.

Kensington Palace is open for tours daily 10–6 (last admission at 5). For tickets (£11.50) and information call 0870/751–5180 or visit www.historicroyalpalaces.org.

Regent's Park & Hampstead

WORD OF MOUTH

"Queen Mary's Rose Garden [in Regent's Park] was in the most magnificent bloom I have ever seen. There were so many roses they almost seemed artificial. And the aromas were intoxicating. Then I walked up north past the zoo and up Primrose Hill for the wonderful view over the whole city."

—janis

REGENT'S PARK & HAMPSTEAD

Sightseeing
★ ★ ★ ★

Nightlife
★ ★

Dining
★ ★

Lodging
★ ★

Shopping
★ ★ ★

If you feel the urge to escape the flurry of central London, hop the Tube north for an afternoon spent in the snug shelter of Regent's Park and Hampstead. A leisurely stroll along these peaceful streets, with gorgeous Georgian architecture and equally gorgeous inhabitants, will provide a taste of how laid-back (albeit moneyed) Londoners live. A longtime rendezvous of literati, these city districts contain two leafy parks, a handful of important historical sites, and some of the most stunning town-house architecture in the world (think any Merchant Ivory film). Excellent bookshops, contemporary boutiques, and cozy cafés line tree-shaded blocks abuzz with locals: you won't find souvenir stands here.

What's Here

Despite the proliferation of residential neighborhoods in Regent's Park, the region does include its share of tourist sites. The **Sherlock Holmes Museum** at the northern end of Baker Street is at the exact address of Holmes's fictional abode and contains wax figures in the exhibition area and an antiques shop on the ground floor. **Madame Tussaud's** is around the corner, and just inside the 112-acre **Regent's Park** along the Outer Circle is the **Regent's Park Open-Air Theatre** where, in summer, you can take in a Shakespeare play and a cocktail at the adjoining outdoor bar (that is, if you don't already have tickets for a match at the **Lord's Cricket Ground & Museum**). Design and art buffs will want to visit renowned 19th-century architect John Nash's **Cumberland Terrace** in the park. You may also wish to get a glimpse of **Kenwood House**, a 17th-century mansion containing a collection of priceless art, including Vermeer's *Guitar Player.*

If you're feeling energetic or if you have children to entertain, try wandering north within Regent's Park— past the daydreamers, dog-walkers, and soccer players—to the **London Zoo**, one of the oldest zoos in the world and still one of the best. Con-

> ## PRIMROSE HILL
>
> Primrose Hill offers some of the best views of the city and also happens to be the site of a series of well-known photographs of the Rolling Stones. Although the Stones also made music in this neighborhood, they did not use nearby Abbey Road studios where the Beatles famously recorded their entire output.

tinue your "urban safari" along **Regent's Canal** (the more common name for the Grand Union Canal) past bankside willows and the zoo animals to **Camden Lock**, where you'll come upon the stalls and merchants of colorful **Camden Market**. Or make the trek up **Primrose Hill**, both the name of the nearby neighborhood, and a 206-foot incline inside the park crisscrossed by walking paths every hundred yards or so.

A couple of noteworthy museums are also within walking distance from Regent's Park: the **Jewish Museum**, which traces the history of the Jewish community in Britain from the Norman Conquest to the present day, and the **London Canal Museum** where you can take a guided trip through London's slender waterways aboard a specially designed narrowboat. The **Freud Museum** is in the building where Sigmund Freud lived and worked just after he fled Austria following the German annexation of World War II, while Hampstead's oldest surviving house, **Fenton House,** is nearby on Hampstead Grove. George Eliot and Karl Marx are buried at **Highgate Cemetery**, adjacent to the immense **Hampstead Heath.** With its steep slopes toward Spaniard's Road, the heath offers views of the city comparable to those one would experience from the top of Primrose Hill.

Places to Explore

Camden Lock. What was once just a pair of locks on the Grand Union Canal has now developed into London's third-most-visited tourist attraction. It's a vast honeycomb of markets that sell just about everything, but mostly crafts, clothing (vintage, ethnic, and young designer), and antiques. Here, especially on a weekend, the crowds are dense, young, and relentless. You may tire of the identical T-shirts, pants, boots, vintage wear, and cheap leather on their backs and in the shops. Camden does have its charms, though. Gentrification has layered over a once overwhelmingly Irish neighborhood, vestiges of which coexist with the youth culture. Charm is evident in sections of the market itself as well as in other markets, including the bustling fruit-and-vegetable market on Inverness Street. Along the canal are some stylish examples of Nicholas Grimshaw architecture (architect of Waterloo Station), as well as the MTV offices. (For more on Camden Lock, see Shopping, Chapter 19.)

GETTING ORIENTED

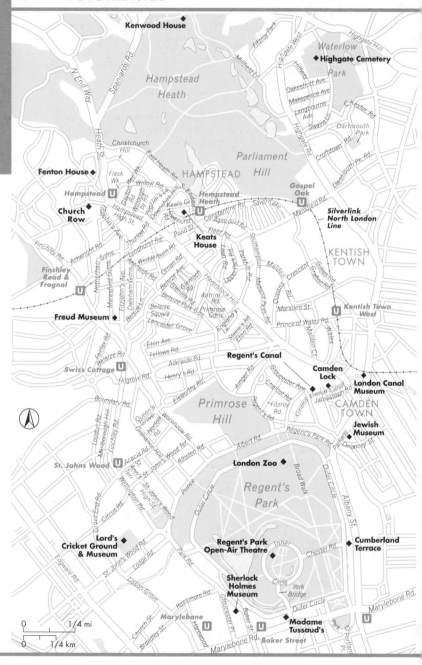

TOP 5 REASONS TO GO

■ **Primrose Hill:** Tackle the hill on a beautiful day with a friend, a stocked picnic basket, and a blanket, then enjoy the view from the top for a few long hours.

■ **Queen's Pub:** Nurse a pint at this Regent's Park Road pub where celebrities have been known to pop in.

■ **London Zoo:** Traipse through the walk-through forest and come face-to-face with a group of black-capped squirrel monkeys.

■ **Keats House:** Pick a plum from the tree planted outside on the original site that inspired "Ode to a Nightingale."

■ **Everyman Cinema:** Indulge in tapas and drinks at the cinema's sophisticated bar and lounge.

FEELING PECKISH?

For a substantial but still speedy meal on the hoof, stop at the **Hampstead Creperie** (✉ 77 Hampstead High St., Hampstead, NW3 ☎ 020/7372-0081), which serves authentic sweet and savory French crepes from a little cart on the street.

The excellent, thin-crust pizzas at **The Lansdowne** (✉ 90 Gloucester Ave., Primrose Hill, NW1 ☎ 020/7483-0409 Ⓜ Chalk Farm) are just as good as any Italian's. Atypical here are the pizza toppings: from fennel to chorizo to aubergine, they're anything but basic. The pub's low-key, family-friendly atmosphere makes the Lansdowne worth the walk to the topmost corner of Gloucester Avenue for a bite.

GETTING HERE

Reaching Hampstead by Tube is as easy as it looks: simply take the Edgewater branch of the Northern Line to the Hampstead stop. To get to Regent's Park, take the Bakerloo Line to Regent's Park Tube station or, for Primrose Hill, Swiss Cottage, St. John's Wood, and Belsize Park, the Swiss Cottage and St. John's Wood stops on the Jubilee Line or the Chalk Farm stop on the Northern Line.

MAKING THE MOST OF YOUR TIME

Depending on your pace, both Regent's Park and Hampstead can realistically be covered in a day. It might be best to spend the morning in Hampstead, then head south toward Regent's Park in the afternoon so that you're closer to central London come nightfall, if that is where your hotel is. It's advisable to stay out of Hampstead Heath and Regent's Park proper after nightfall unless there's an event (such as a play or concert) taking place on the greens.

A GOOD WALK

There really are no bad walks to be had in Hampstead. Once there, the village is best explored on foot, and Hampstead Heath will lead you by way of marked footpaths on a healthy jaunt through its sprawling green. The neighborhoods around Regent's Park—as well as the park itself—are also best explored on foot.

12

A BRIEF HISTORY

Much like New York City's Greenwich Village, the cliché about Regent's Park and its bordering enclaves (Primrose Hill, Swiss Cottage, and St. John's Wood) is that the majority of folks here claim to be artists—and yet the cost of a coffee at a café along Regent's Park Road will run you as much as, if not more than, one in Central London. In the last decade, real estate prices in these neighborhoods have skyrocketed and the elephants of the London Zoo now call some of the best-dressed folks in town neighbors.

In the early 18th century the commercial development of the mineral springs in Hampstead led to its success as a spa; people traveled from miles around to drink the pure waters from Hampstead Wells, and small cottages were hastily built to accommodate the influx. Though the spa phenomenon was short-lived, Hampstead remained a favorite place for many artistic figures whose legacies still permeate the landscape.

In December 2005 Hampstead was the site of the biggest fire in Europe since World War II. It erupted in one of its oil refineries: remarkably, no one was injured and the village suffered little damage.

✉ *Camden Lock, Camden High St., Camden Town, NW1* ⊕ *www.camdenlock.net* ⊙ *Daily 10–6* Ⓤ *Camden Town, Chalk Farm.*

NEED A BREAK? You will not go hungry in Camden Town. Among the countless cafés, bars, pubs, and restaurants, the following stand out for good value and good food. Within the market at Camden Lock there are various stalls selling the usual hot dogs, but you can also find good Chinese takeout, and other ethnic food if you don't mind standing as you eat outdoors, or finding a canalside bench. Alternatively, **Marine Ices** (✉ 8 Haverstock Hill, Camden Town, NW3 ☎ 020/7482–9003) has a window dispensing ice cream to strollers, and pasta, pizza, and sundaes inside. **Bar Gansa** (✉ 2 Inverness St., Camden Town, NW1 ☎ 020/7267–8909) offers tapas—small dishes for sharing—among other larger Spanish favorites, such as paella. **Wagamama** (✉ 3 Jamestown Rd., Camden Town, NW1 ☎ 020/7428–0751) has long bench tables with high stools, where you can eat utilitarian bowls of noodles of every description. It's great, filling food that pleases kids, too.

Fenton House. This is Hampstead's oldest surviving house. Now a National Trust property, it has an interesting collection of antiques and period interiors, along with some 17th-century-style gardens. Baroque enthusiasts can join a tour of the large collection of keyboard instruments, given by the curator, and there's a summer series of concerts on these very same instruments on Thursday evenings. Call ahead for details. ✉ *Hampstead Grove, Hampstead, NW3* ☎ 020/7435–3471 ⊕ *www.nationaltrust.org.uk* 🎫 *£4.90, joint ticket with 2 Willow Road*

£6.70 ✆ *Mar., weekends 2–5; Apr.–Oct., Wed.–Fri. 2–5, weekends 11–5* Ⓤ *Hampstead.*

Freud Museum. The father of psychoanalysis lived here for a year, between his escape from Nazi persecution in his native Vienna in 1938 and his death in 1939. Many of his possessions emigrated with him and were set up by his daughter, Anna (herself a pioneer of child psychoanalysis), as a shrine to her father's life and work. Four years after Anna's death in 1982 the house was opened as a museum. It replicates Freud's famous consulting rooms, particularly through the presence of *the couch.* You'll find Freud-related books, lectures, and study groups here, too. ✉ *20 Maresfield Gardens, Hampstead, NW3* ☎ *020/7435–2002* ⊕ *www.freud.org.uk* 🖃 *£5* ✆ *Wed.–Sun. noon–5* Ⓤ *Swiss Cottage, Finchley Rd.*

☾ **Hampstead Heath.** For an escape from the ordered prettiness of Hampstead, head to the heath—a wild park where wolves once roamed and washerwomen laundered clothes for aristocrats—which spreads for miles to the north. From its top, at Spaniards Road, there are stunning views for miles to the city. There are signposted paths, but these can be confusing. Maps are available from Hampstead newsagents and bookshops, or the information center at the Gospel Oak entrance, Gordon House Road, where you can also get details about the history of the Heath and the flora and fauna growing there. ✉ *Hampstead, NW3* ☎ *020/7482–7073 Heath Information Centre* ⊕ *www.cityoflondon.gov.uk* Ⓤ *Gospel Oak or Hampstead Heath Silverlink Line from Highbury & Islington underground for south of Heath; Hampstead underground, then walk through Flask Walk, Well Walk for east of Heath; Golders Green underground, then Bus 210, 268 to Whitestone Pond for north and west of Heath.*

Fodor'sChoice
★

NEED A BREAK?

Close by Hampstead Heath, walking east along Gordon House Road, a historic pub stands at the northwest edge, at the tollhouse between Spaniards Road and Hampstead Lane. The Spaniards Inn (✉ Spaniards Rd., Hampstead, NW3

HAMPSTEAD PONDS

Hampstead Ponds, three Elysian little lakes, are surrounded by grassy lounging areas. Originally the lakes were pits, where clay was dug out for making bricks up until the 19th century. The women's lake is particularly secluded (though crowded in summer) and is open all year, as is the men's. Opening times vary with sunrise and sunset. The Mixed Pond is open May through September, 7 AM to 7 PM. All have murky-looking but clean, fresh water, and all are free. Less murky is **Hampstead Lido,** open May through September. A swim here is £4 for the day (7 AM to 6:30 PM). In winter the pool is open mornings only (7 to 12:30, £2). The 1930s Grade II–listed swimming pool underwent a £2.9 million refurbishment in 2005. ✉ *E. Heath Rd., Hampstead, NW3* ☎ *020/7485–4491* Ⓤ *Tube or National Rail: Hampstead Heath.*

A Trip to Abbey Road

FOR COUNTLESS BEATLEMANIACS and baby boomers, No. 3 Abbey Road is one of the most beloved spots in London. Here, outside the legendary Abbey Road Studios, is the most famous zebra crossing in the world, immortalized on the Beatles' 1969 *Abbey Road* album. This footpath became a mod monument when, on August 8 of that year, John, Paul, George, and Ringo posed—walking symbolically *away* from the recording facility—for photographer Iain Macmillan for the famous cover shot. In fact, the recording facility's Studio 2 is where the Beatles recorded their entire output, from "Love Me Do" onward, including *Sgt. Pepper's Lonely Hearts Club Band* (early 1967).

The studios are closed to the public, but tourists like to Beatle-ize themselves by taking the same sort of photo. ⚠ **It's tempting to try and re-create *the* photo, but be careful: rushing cars make Abbey Road a** dangerous intersection. One of the best—and safer—ways Beatle-lovers can enjoy the history of the group is to take one of the smashing walking tours offered by the **Original London Walks** (☎ 020/7624-3978 ⊕ www. walks.com), including **"The Beatles In-My-Life Walk"** (11:20 AM at the Baker Street Underground on Saturday and Tuesday) and **"The Beatles Magical Mystery Tour"** (10:55 AM at Underground Exit 3, Tottenham Court Road, on Sunday and Thursday), which cover nostalgic landmark Beatles spots in the city.

Abbey Road is in the elegant neighborhood of St. John's Wood, a 10-minute ride on the Tube from central London. Take the Jubilee Line to the St. John's Wood Tube stop, head southwest three blocks down Grove End Road, and be prepared for a heart-stopping vista right out of Memory Lane.

☎ 020/8731-6571) is little changed since the early 18th century, when (they say) the notorious highwayman Dick Turpin hung out here. Keats also drank here, as did Shelley and Byron.

★ ☺ **Highgate Cemetery.** Highgate is not the oldest cemetery in London, but certainly it's the most celebrated. Such was its popularity that the acreage increased across the other side of the road, and this additional east side contains probably the most visited grave, of Karl Marx, where you also find George Eliot, among other famous names. The older west side was once part of a mansion owned by Sir William Ashurst, Lord Mayor of London in 1693. When the cemetery was consecrated in 1839, Victorians came from miles around to enjoy the architecture and the view. Both are impressive, from the moment you enter the grand wrought-iron gateway into a sweeping courtyard for horses and carriages. The highlight of the 20-acre site is the colonnaded Egyptian Avenue leading to the Circle of Lebanon, built around an ancient cypress tree—a legacy of Ashurst's garden—with catacombs skirting the edges. By the 1970s it was unkempt and neglected until a group of volunteers, the Friends of Highgate Cemetery, undertook the huge upkeep. Tours are arranged by the Friends, and among the numerous beautiful stone angels and beloved animals—memorials once hidden by wild brambles—they will show you the most notable graves, which include Michael Faraday and Christina Rossetti, each with their own, sometimes quirky, history. ■ TIP➔ Children under eight are not admitted; nor are dogs, cell phones, and video cameras. ⊠ *Swains La., Highgate, N6* ☎ *020/8340–1834* ⊕ *www.highgate-cemetery.org* ⊠ *£2, £3 for tours* ☉ *Call for opening times and visitor information; hrs vary according to whether a funeral service is scheduled* Ⓤ *Archway, then Bus 210 to Highgate Village.*

Jewish Museum. This museum tells a comprehensive history of the Jews in London from Norman times, though the bulk of the exhibits date from the end of the 17th century (when Cromwell repealed the laws against Jewish settlement) and later. The Ceremonial Art Gallery holds a collection of rare pieces, and the Audio Visual Gallery follows London Jewish life from cradle to grave. The museum's branch at the Sternberg Centre in Finchley covers social history, with changing exhibitions, and permanent exhibits and tape archives on the Holocaust, in the words of survivors. ⊠ *Raymond Burton House, 129 Albert St., Camden Town, NW1* ☎ *020/7284–1997* ⊕ *www.jewishmuseum.org.uk* ⊠ *£3.50* ☉ *Sun. 10–5, Mon.–Thurs. 10–4* Ⓤ *Camden Town* ⊠ *Sternberg Centre, 80 East End Rd., Finchley, N3* ☎ *020/8349–1143* ⊠ *£2* ☉ *Sun. 10:30–4:30, Mon.–Thurs. 10:30–5* Ⓤ *Finchley Central.*

Keats House. Here you can see the plum tree under which the young Romantic poet composed "Ode to a Nightingale," many of his original manuscripts, his library, and other possessions he managed to acquire in his short life. It was in February 1820 that Keats coughed blood up into his handkerchief and exclaimed, "I know the color of that blood; it is arterial blood. I cannot be deceived in that color. That drop of blood is my death warrant. I must die." He left this house in September, moved to Rome, and died of consumption there, in early 1821, at age 25. There are frequent guided tours and special events on Wednesday evenings (such as poetry readings); call or check the Web site for details. ⊠ *Keats House, Wentworth Pl., Keats Grove, Hampstead, NW3* ☎ *020/ 7435–2062* ⊕*www.keatshouse.org.uk* ⊠*£3, valid for 1 yr* ☉ *Apr.–Oct., Tues.–Sun. noon–5; Nov.–Mar., Tues.–Sun. 1–5* Ⓤ *Hampstead or overground Silverlink Hampstead Heath from Highbury & Islington.*

NEED A BREAK?

Hampstead is full of restaurants, including a few that have been here forever. Try the **Coffee Cup** (⊠ 74 Hampstead High St., Hampstead, NW3 ☎ 020/ 7435–7565), which has been serving English breakfasts all day to locals since the 1950s, from 8 until late (and you can get steak sandwiches and pasta, too). The **Hampstead Tea Rooms** (⊠ 9 South End Rd., Hampstead, NW3 ☎ 020/ 7435–9563) has been run by the same owners for more than 30 years, selling sandwiches, pies, pastries, and cream cakes, on drool view in the window. The quaintest pub in Hampstead, complete with fireplace and timber frame, is the **Hollybush** (⊠ 22 Holly Mount, Hampstead, NW3 ☎ 020/7435–2892), which dates back to 1807. Tucked away on a side street, it's open until 11 each night and serves traditional English lunches and dinners, often to the accompaniment of live Irish music.

★ ⓒ **Kenwood House.** Perfectly and properly Palladian, this mansion was first built in 1616 and remodeled by Robert Adam in 1764. Adam refaced most of the exterior and added the splendid library, which, with its curved painted ceiling, rather garish coloring, and gilded detailing, is the sole highlight of the house for decorative arts and interior buffs. What is unmissable here is the **Iveagh Bequest,** a collection of paintings that the Earl of Iveagh gave the nation in 1927, starring a wonderful Rembrandt self-portrait and works by Reynolds, Van Dyck, Hals, Gainsborough, and Turner. Top billing goes to Vermeer's *Guitar Player,* one of the most beautiful paintings in the world. In front of the house, a graceful lawn slopes down to a little lake crossed by a trompe-l'oeil bridge—all in perfect 18th-century upper-class taste. The rest of the grounds are skirted by Hampstead Heath. Nowadays the lake is dominated by its concert bowl, which stages a summer series of orchestral concerts, including an annual performance of Handel's *Music for the Royal Fireworks,* complete with fireworks. A popular café, the Brew House, is part of the old coach house, and has outdoor tables in the courtyard and terraced garden. ✉ *Hampstead La., Hampstead, NW3* ☎ *020/ 8348–1286* ⊕ *www.english-heritage.org.uk* ✉ *Free* ⊙ *House Apr.–Oct., daily 11–5; Nov.–Mar., daily 11–4. Gardens daily dawn–dusk* Ⓤ *Golders Green, then Bus 210.*

ⓒ **London Canal Museum.** Here, in a former ice-storage house, you can learn about the rise and fall of London's once extensive canal network. Outside, on the Battlebridge Basin, float the gaily painted narrow boats of modern canal dwellers—a few steps and a world away from King's Cross, which remains one of London's least salubrious neighborhoods. The quirky little museum is accessible from Camden Lock if you take the towpath. ✉ *12–13 New Wharf Rd., Camden Town, N1* ☎ *020/ 7713–0836* ⊕ *www.canalmuseum.org.uk* ✉ *£3* ⊙ *Tues.–Sun. 10–4:30; last admission 3:45* Ⓤ *King's Cross.*

★ ⓒ **London Zoo.** The zoo opened in 1828 and peaked in popularity during the 1950s, when more than 3 million people passed through its turnstiles every year. A modernization program focusing on conservation and education is underway. A great example of this is a huge glass pavilion—the Web of Life—which puts these aims into action. Other zoo highlights include the Casson Pavilion (which closely resembles the South Bank Arts Complex) and the graceful Snowdon Aviary, spacious enough to allow its tenants free flight. Recent additions include a desert swarming with locusts, meerkats perching on termite mounds, bats and hummingbirds, and an otter exhibit with underwater viewing. There's also a new walk-through forest where visitors can come face-to-face with a group of black-capped

HERE'S WHERE

The London Zoo's reptile house is a special draw for Harry Potter fans—it's where Harry first talks to snakes, to alarming effect on his horrible cousin.

squirrel monkeys. London zoo is owned by the Zoological Society of London (a charity), and much work is done here in wildlife conservation, education, and the breeding of endangered species. Male lion Lucifer was brought to the zoo in November 2004 in the hopes that he would breed with the young lioness Abi. For animal encounter sessions with keepers, and feeding times, check the information board at admission. ⊠ *Regent's Park, NW1* ☏ *020/7722–3333* ⊕ *www.londonzoo. co.uk* ⊠ *£13.50* ⊘ *Daily 10–4; last admission 1 hr before closing* Ⓤ *Camden Town, then Bus 274.*

Lord's Cricket Ground & Museum. If you can't manage to lay your hands on tickets for a cricket match, the next best thing is to take a tour of the spiritual home of this most British of games. Founded by Thomas Lord, the headquarters of the MCC (Marylebone Cricket Club) opens its "behind the scenes" areas to visitors. You can see the Long Room with cricketing art on display; the players' dressing rooms; and the world's oldest sporting museum, where the progress from gentlemanly village-green game to world-class sport over 400 years is charted. Don't miss the prize exhibit: the urn containing the Ashes (the remains of a cricket ball burned by Australia fans mourning their defeat at the hands of the MCC in 1883), and even smaller, the poor sparrow that met its death by a bowled ball. More up-to-date is the eye-catching Media Centre building, which achieved high scores in the architectural league. The tour is not available during matches, but the museum remains open. ⊠ *St. John's Wood Rd., St. John's Wood, NW8* ☏ *020/7616–8656* ⊕ *www.lords.org* ⊠ *£7, £2.50 museum only* ⊘ *Apr.–Sept., daily 10–2, not during major matches. Oct.–Mar., daily noon–2* Ⓤ *St. John's Wood.*

ⓒ **Madame Tussaud's.** One of London's busiest sights, this is nothing more and nothing less than the world's premier exhibition of lifelike waxwork models of celebrities. Madame T. learned her craft while making death masks of French Revolution victims, and in 1835 set up her first show of the famous ones near this spot. Nowadays, Superstars of Entertainment, in their own hall of the same name, outrank any aristocrat in popularity, along with a segment called the Spirit of London, and a Time Taxi Ride that visits notable Londoners from Shakespeare to Benny Hill. But top billing still goes to the murderers in the Chamber of Horrors, who stare glassy-eyed at visitors—one from an electric chair, one sitting next to the tin bath where he dissolved several wives in quicklime. What, aside from ghoulish prurience, makes people stand in line to invest in London's most expensive museum ticket? It's the thrill of rubbing shoulders with Shakespeare, Martin Luther King Jr., the Queen, and the Beatles—most of them dressed in their very own outfits—in a single day.

　■ TIP→ **Beat the crowds by calling in advance for timed entry tickets.** ⊠ *Marylebone Rd., Regent's Park, NW1* ☏ *0870/400–3000 for timed entry tickets* ⊕ *www.madame-tussauds.com* ⊠ *From £15; prices vary according to day and season, call for details, or check Web site* ⊘ *Weekdays 9:30–5:30, weekends 9:00–6:00* Ⓤ *Baker St.*

★ ⓒ **Regent's Park.** The youngest of London's great parks, Regent's Park was laid out in 1812 by John Nash, who worked for his patron, the Prince

Regent (hence the name), who was crowned George IV in 1820. The idea was to re-create the feel of a grand country residence close to the center of town, with all those magnificent white-stucco terraces facing in on the park. As you walk the Outer Circle, you'll see how successfully Nash's plans were carried out, although the focus of it all—a palace for the prince—was never actually built (George was too busy fiddling with the one he already had,

---

BOATING

You can spend a vigorous afternoon rowing about ✪ **Regent's Park Boating Lake** (☎ 020/7724–4069), where rowboats hold up to five adults and cost £6 per hour per person, £4.50 for kids, approximately March through October. Hours vary with daylight, weather, and park opening times.

Buckingham Palace). The most famous and impressive of Nash's terraces would have been in the prince's line of vision from the planned palace. **Cumberland Terrace** has a central block of Ionic columns surmounted by a triangular Wedgwood-blue pediment that's like a giant cameo. Snow-white statuary personifying Britannia and her empire (the work of the on-site architect, James Thomson) single it out from the pack. The noted architectural historian Sir John Summerson described it thus: "the backcloth as it were to Act III, and easily the most breathtaking architectural panorama in London."

As in all London parks, planting here is planned with the aim of having something in bloom in all seasons, but if you hit the park in May, June, or July, head first to the Inner Circle. Your nostrils should lead you to **Queen Mary's Gardens**, a fragrant 17-acre circle that riots with roses in summer and heather, azaleas, and evergreens in other seasons. The **Broad Walk** is a good vantage point from which to glimpse the minaret and golden dome of the **London Central Mosque** on the far west side of the park. If it's a summer evening or a Sunday afternoon, witness a remarkable phenomenon. Wherever you look, the sport being enthusiastically played is not cricket but softball, now Britain's fastest-growing participant sport (bring your mitt). You're likely to see cricket, too, plus a lot of dog walkers—not for nothing did Dodie Smith set her novel *A Hundred and One Dalmatians* in an Outer Circle house. ☎ 020/7486–7905 ⊕ *www.royalparks.gov.uk* ⊘ *5 AM–dusk* Ⓤ *Baker St., Regent's Park.*

Regent's Park Open-Air Theatre. The company has mounted Shakespeare productions here every summer since 1932; everyone from Vivien Leigh to Jeremy Irons has performed here. *A Midsummer Night's Dream* is the one to catch—never is that enchanted Greek wood more lifelike than it is here, augmented by genuine bird squawks and a rising moon. The park can get chilly, so bring a blanket; rain stops the play only when heavy. ✉ *Open-Air Theatre, Regent's Park, NW1* ☎ *0870/060–1811* ⊕ *www.openairtheatre.org* ⊘ *June–Aug., evening performances 7:30, matinees 2:30* Ⓤ *Baker St., Regent's Park.*

Sherlock Holmes Museum. Outside Baker Street station, by the Marylebone Road exit, is a 9-foot-high bronze statue of the celebrated detective. Keep your eyes peeled, for close by his image, "Holmes" himself, in his familiar deerstalker hat, will escort you to his abode at 221B Baker Street, the address of Arthur Conan Doyle's fictional detective. Inside, "Holmes's housekeeper" conducts you into a series of Victorian rooms full of Sherlock-abilia. It's all so realistic, you may actually begin to believe in Holmes's existence. ☒ *221B Baker St., Regent's Park, NW1* ☎ *020/7935–8866* ⊕ *www.sherlock-holmes.co.uk* ☒ *£6* ☉ *Daily 9:30–6* Ⓤ *Baker St.*

Regent's Park & Hampstead at a Glance

SIGHTS
Cumberland Terrace
Fenton House
Highgate Cemetery
Keats House

MUSEUMS & GALLERIES
Freud Museum
Jewish Museum
Kenwood House
London Canal Museum
Lord's Cricket Ground
    & Museum
Madame Tussaud's
Sherlock Holmes Museum

PARKS & GARDENS
Camden Lock
Hampstead Heath
Hampstead Ponds
London Zoo
Primrose Hill

Regent's Canal
Regent's Park

WHERE TO EAT (⇨ Ch. 15)

BUDGET DINING
Coffee Cup, *Café*
Mandalay, *Burmese*

MODERATE DINING
The Wells, *Contemporary*

WHERE TO STAY (⇨ Ch. 16)

BUDGET LODGING
La Gaffe
St. Christopher's Inn
    Camden

MODERATE LODGING
Four Seasons Hotel
Primrose Hill B&B

PUBS & NIGHTLIFE
(⇨ Ch. 17)
Lansdowne, *pub*
Spaniards Inn, *pub*

ARTS & ENTERTAINMENT
(⇨ Ch. 18)
Everyman Cinema Club,
    film
Kenwood House, *concert
    venue*
Open Air Theatre, *outdoor
    theater*

SHOPPING (⇨ Ch. 19)

MARKETS & MALLS
Camden Lock Market
Camden Market
Canal Market
Electric Market
Stables Market

ANTIQUES
Alfie's Antique Market

Greenwich

WORD OF MOUTH

"It was raining when I visited Greenwich, but armed with a sturdy brolly and an enthusiastic travel companion I still enjoyed my visit very much. The surrounding park area is also very beautiful and the town itself charming, even when the weather isn't perfect. . . .check what the Observatory's and Maritime Museum's winter hours are ahead of time, however. And I almost forgot about the *Cutty Sark*. Bundle up and enjoy!"

–Rebecka

GREENWICH

Sightseeing
★ ★ ★ ★

Nightlife
★

Dining
★ ★

Lodging
★

Shopping
★ ★ ★

Visit Greenwich and you'll discover what makes Londoners tick. Situated on the Greenwich Meridian Line at 0° longitude, this smart Thames-side town literally marks the beginning of time. For an island nation whose reputation was built on sea-faring adventure, Britain's centuries-old maritime tradition lays anchor here. Fans of elegant architecture will be in heaven-on-sea, while landlubbers can wander acres of rolling parkland and immaculately kept gardens. And while the world-famous *Cutty Sark* may have long since unloaded its last tea chest, trading traditions live on in Greenwich's maze of market stalls that sell a Davy Jones locker's worth of bric-a-brac, antiques, and retro gear.

What's Here

A visit to Greenwich feels like a trip to the country, but its key attractions are all fairly close to one another. The magnificent **Cutty Sark,** the world's last remaining tea clipper, with 11 mi of rigging overlooking the Thames, should be your first port-of-call in Greenwich. It's near the time machine–like entry point of the Greenwich Foot Tunnel that passes under the river.

The **Old Royal Naval College,** next door, is the village's most grandiose building, with an atmospheric history tour spanning the days when, as the Greenwich Hospital, wounded sea veterans were fed a daily diet of five pints of beer. Within the grounds are the immaculately preserved Chapel, designed by Sir Christopher Wren, and Painted Hall, with frescoes depicting scenes of naval grandeur (suitably pro-British for a dead Nelson to lay there in state in 1806).

Heading south, **Queen's House** (also known as the "House of Delight") has a good collection of oil paintings, including a wide-eyed seven-year-old Elizabeth I, scenes of Britain's seafaring ascent, and the occasional oceanic punch-up. An elegant colonnade connects to the **National Maritime Museum**, which has oodles of interactive exhibits that bring the seas to life: rigs creaking in the wind, sailors shouting, grainy footage of *The Titanic*, and the lucky toy pig that saved one little girl's life.

Behind the Maritime Museum, a path through **Greenwich Park**, into which Henry VIII introduced deer to give himself a good hunt, rises steeply to the **Royal Observatory**, where it's hard to resist the urge—no matter how old you are—to bestride two hemispheres by standing over the **Greenwich Meridian Line**.

Beyond the Wolfe Monument is **Ranger's House**, which houses the private art collection of 19th-century diamond millionaire Julius Wernher. Look out for a lovingly tended rose garden next to it, housing such eclectic species as Ice Cream, Tequila Sunrise, Remember Me, and Grandpa Dickson.

Down Croom's Hill, past rows of Georgian houses and the Roman Catholic Church is the **Fan Museum**, an idiosyncratic labor of love dedicated to treasured examples throughout the ages, from ivory, tortoiseshell, and mother-of-pearl exhibits right up to the modern extractor fan. **Greenwich Theatre**, opposite the Fan Museum, leads onto the main drag, Greenwich Church Street, with the bohemian **Village Market** on the corner and, a little farther on, the lively weekend **Greenwich Market**.

Heading east on the River Path takes in the delightful **Trafalgar Tavern**, with magnificent views over the Thames and gracious buildings on the right. Less than a mile farther on, toward north Greenwich, rises Richard Rogers's **Millennium Dome**. Farther downstream, in the next-door neighborhood of Woolwich, lies the **Thames Flood Barrier** and its adjacent visitor center.

Places to Explore

Cutty Sark. This sleek, romantic clipper was built in 1869, one of fleets and fleets of similar tall-masted wooden ships that plied oceanic highways of the 19th century, trading in exotic commodities—tea, in this case. The *Cutty Sark*, the only surviving clipper, was also the fastest, sailing the China–London route in

GETTING ORIENTED

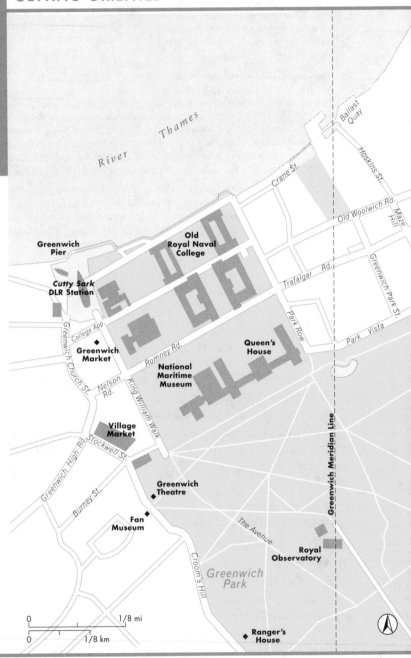

TOP 5 REASONS TO GO

- **Greenwich Meridian Line:** Stand astride time.

- **The *Cutty Sark*:** Sing sea-shanties on board the world's oldest tea clipper.

- **Trafalgar Tavern:** Take a pint and whitebait dinner over the night-lighted Thames on the tavern's terrace.

- **National Maritime Museum:** Relive the *Titanic's* last moments with rescued artifacts and underwater footage of the wreck.

- **Greenwich Market:** Rifle through retro lighting and clothing stalls.

FEELING PECKISH?

The **Gipsy Moth Pub** (✉ 60 Greenwich Church St., SE10 ☎ 020/8858-0786), behind the *Cutty Sark,* is the town's only memorial to another classic ship: the yacht that Sir Francis Chichester sailed single-handedly around the world in the 1960s. The galley here is expensive, but the beer garden makes up for it.

Goddard's Pie House (✉ 45 Greenwich Church St., SE10 ☎ 020/8293-9313 ⊕ www.pieshop.co.uk) is a classic pie-and-mash house established in 1890 and now in its fifth generation. Stop here for jellied eels, mash with the secret family "liquor," and rhubarb pie—it's hot, tasty, and excellent value.

Up by the Royal Observatory is **The Honest Sausage** (⊕ www. honestsausage.com) stall beside the Wolfe monument, serving delicious homemade organic sausages and huge jacket potatoes drenched in onion gravy. The views are great, too.

For the best pub in Greenwich, head for the **Trafalgar Tavern** (✉ Park Row, SE10 ☎ 020/8858-2909 ⊕ www. trafalgartavern.co.uk), with excellent views of the Thames. It's a grand place to have a pint and some upscale grub.

GETTING THERE

The Jubilee Line runs through Docklands from Canary Wharf to north Greenwich for the Millennium Dome. The zippy "driverless" Docklands Light Railway (DLR) runs to Cutty Sark station from Canary Wharf or Bank. Or take the DLR to Island Gardens and retrace the steps dockworkers used to take back and forth on the old Victorian Foot Tunnel under the river.

The best way to arrive, however—time and weather permitting—is like a sea admiral of old: by water. (For more on river ferries and cruising the Thames, *see* Chapter 1, Experience London.)

MAKING THE MOST OF YOUR TIME

Set apart from the rest of London, Greenwich is worth a day to itself, to make the most of walks in the rolling parklands and to immerse yourself in its richness of maritime art and entertainment. The boat trip takes about an hour from Westminster Pier (next to Big Ben), or 25 minutes from the Tower of London, so factor in enough time for the round-trip. For the craft markets, a weekend trip is best.

NEAREST PUBLIC RESTROOMS

There are paid toilets just beyond the nose of the *Cutty Sark* in front of the entrance to Greenwich Pier, but you're better off ducking into the tourist information center (at the nearby Old Royal Naval College), which is superb, unobtrusive, and helpful—and whose loos are free.

A BRIEF HISTORY

Although it's difficult to think of a more likeable neighborhood than Greenwich, this was not always the case. In the 17th century the diarist Samuel Pepys bemoaned the slew of invalids clogging up the streets. For almost 200 years, Greenwich Hospital was home to the war-wounded of the British Navy's numerous sea spats, who were housed at the Christopher Wren–designed building, one of the best-known in London. It closed in 1869, and was reincarnated as the Old Royal Naval College for training young officers and is the setting of many a blockbusting period film today.

Greenwich was originally home to one of England's finest Tudor palaces, and the birthplace of Henry VIII, Elizabeth I, and Mary I. Much of the palace fell into disrepair, but the site was reinvigorated with the construction of Queen's House—built by the masterful Inigo Jones in 1616 and considered the first "classical" building in England.

More recently, Greenwich became synonymous with the hopelessly ambitious Millennium Dome, which currently lies empty like an abandoned spaceship. However, there are plans to bring it to life again in 2007 as an entertainment and sports arena, and it's slated to host the gymnastics events of the 2012 Olympic Games in London.

1871 in only 107 days. Now the photogenic vessel lies in dry dock, a museum of one kind of seafaring life—and not a comfortable kind for the 28-strong crew, as you'll see. The collection of figureheads is amusing, too. ☒ *King William Walk, Greenwich, SE10* ☎ *020/8858–3445* ⊕ *www.cuttysark.org.uk* ☒ *£4.50* ☉ *Daily 10–5; last admission 4:30* Ⓤ *DLR: Cutty Sark.*

Fan Museum. In two newly restored houses dating from the 1820s, opposite the Greenwich Theatre, is this highly unusual museum. The 2,000 fans here, which date from the 17th century onward, compose the world's only such collection, and the history and purpose of these objects, often exquisitely crafted from ivory, mother-of-pearl, and tortoiseshell, are explained in satisfying detail. It was the personal vision—and fan collection—of Helene Alexander that brought it into being, and the workshop and conservation and study center that she has also set up ensure that this anachronistic art has a future. ■ **TIP→ If your interest is really piqued, you can attend fan-making workshops. Ask at the desk for details.** ☒ *12 Croom's Hill, Greenwich, SE10* ☎ *020/8305–1441* ⊕ *www. fan-museum.org* ☒ *£3.50* ☉ *Tues.–Sat. 11–5, Sun. noon–5* Ⓤ *DLR: Greenwich.*

Greenwich Market. You'll find this Victorian covered crafts market near the *Cutty Sark*, on College Approach. Established as a fruit-and-vegetable market in 1700, and granted a royal charter in 1849, the glass-roof market now offers arts and crafts Friday through Sunday, and antiques and collectibles on Thursday and Friday. Shopping for crafts is a pleasure, as in most cases you're buying directly from the artist. ✉ *College Approach, Greenwich, SE10* ☎ *020/7515–7153* ⊕ *www.greenwich-market. co.uk* ⊗ *Fri.–Sun. 9:30–5:30, Thurs. 7:30–5:30* Ⓤ *DLR: Cutty Sark.*

OFF THE BEATEN PATH

If you're around Greenwich Market during the weekend, the nearby **Village Market** on Stockwell Street has bric-a-brac and books, and it's well known among the cognoscenti as a good source for vintage clothing. On the opposite block to the Village Market, the weekend **Antiques Market** on Greenwich High Road has more vintage shopping, and browsing among the "small collectibles" makes for a good half-hour diversion.

★ ⊗ **National Maritime Museum.** Following a millennial facelift, one of Greenwich's star attractions has been completely updated to make it one of London's most fun museums. Its glass-covered courtyard of beautifully grand stone, dominated by a huge revolving propellor from a powerful frigate, is remniscent of the British Museum. The collection spans seascape paintings to scientific instruments, interspersed with the heroes of the waves. A new, permanent Nelson gallery was recently opened to celebrate the 250th anniversary of the Battle of Trafalgar, and contains the uniform he wore, complete with bloodstain, when he met his end there in 1805. Grapple hands-on with ropes, weights, rowing, and steering equipment, or catch a daily show at the planetarium (entry £3). Allow at least two hours in this absorbing, adventurous place; if you're in need of refreshment the museum has a good café with views over Greenwich Park. The **Queen's House** is home to the largest collection of maritime art in the world, including works by William Hogarth, Canaletto, and Joshua Reynolds. Inside, the Tulip Stair, named for the fleur-de-lis–style pattern on the balustrade, is especially fine, spiraling up without a central support to the Great Hall. The Great Hall itself is a perfect cube, exactly 40 feet in all three dimensions, decorated with paintings of the Muses, the Virtues, and the Liberal Arts. ✉ *Romney Rd., Greenwich, SE10* ☎ *020/ 8858–4422* ⊕ *www.nmm.ac.uk* ✉ *Free* ⊗ *Apr.–Sept., daily 10–6; Oct.–Mar., daily 10–5; last admission 4:30* Ⓤ *DLR: Greenwich.*

★ **Old Royal Naval College.** Begun by Christopher Wren in 1694 as a rest home, or hospital for ancient mariners, this became instead a school for young ones in 1873. Today the University of Greenwich and Trinity College of Music have classes here. You'll notice how the structures part to reveal the Queen's House across the central lawns. Behind the college are two buildings you can visit. The **Painted Hall,** the college's dining hall, derives its name from the baroque murals of William and Mary (reigned 1689–95; William alone 1695–1702) and assorted allegorical figures. James Thornhill's frescoes, depicting scenes of naval grandeur with a suitably pro-British note of propaganda, were painstakingly done over installments in 1708–12 and 1718–26, and good enough to earn him a knighthood. It's still used for dining, making

A VIEW TO REMEMBER

Construction on the Queen's House was only granted by Queen Anne on the condition that the river vista from the house was preserved, and there are few more majestic views in London than the awe-inspiring symmetry that Wren achieved.

merry, schools, and weddings today. In the opposite building stands the **College Chapel,** which was rebuilt after a fire in 1779 and is altogether lighter, in a more restrained, neo-Grecian style. ■ TIP→ **Trinity College of Music holds free classical music concerts in the chapel every Tuesday lunchtime.** ⊠ *Old Royal Naval College, King William Walk, Greenwich, SE10* ☎ *020/8269–4747* ⊕ *www.greenwichfoundation.org.uk* ⊠ *Free, guided tours £4* ⊙ *Painted Hall and Chapel Mon.–Sat. 10–5, Sun. 12:30–5, last admission 4:15; grounds 8–6* Ⓤ *DLR: Greenwich.*

Ranger's House. This handsome, early-18th-century villa, which was the Greenwich Park Ranger's official residence during the 19th century, is hung with Stuart and Jacobean portraits. But the most interesting diversion is the Wernher Collection, more than 650 works of art with a north European flavor, amassed by diamond millionaire

> **FUN FACT**
>
> Prance around the lightning-cracked Elizabeth Oak in Greenwich Park and you'll be in good historic company—it's so called after Elizabeth I's own flights of fancy in youth.

Julius Wernher at the turn of the 20th century. After making his money in diamond mining, he chose to buy eclectic objects, sometimes beautiful, often downright quirky, like the silver coconut cup. Sèvres porcelain and Limoges enamels, the largest jewelry collection in the country, and some particularly bizarre reliquaries form part of this fascinating collection. Wernher's American wife, Birdie, was a strong influence and personality during the belle epoque, which is easy to imagine from her striking portrait by Sargent. The house also makes a superb setting for concerts, which are regularly scheduled here. ⊠ *Chesterfield Walk, Blackheath, Greenwich, SE10* ☎ *020/8853–0035* ⊕ *www.english-heritage.org.uk* ⊠ *£5:30* ⊙ *Apr.–Sept., Wed.–Sun. 10–6; Oct.–Mar., by appointment only* ⊙ *Closed Jan. and Feb.* Ⓤ *DLR: Greenwich; no direct bus access, only to Vanbrugh Hill (from east) and Blackheath Hill (from west).*

★ ☺ **Royal Observatory.** Founded in 1675 by Charles II, this imposing institution was designed the same year by Christopher Wren for John Flamsteed, the first Royal Astronomer. The red ball you see on its roof has been there since 1833, and drops every day at 1 PM. This Greenwich Timeball and the Gate Clock inside the observatory are the most visible manifestations of Greenwich Mean Time—since 1884, the ultimate standard for time around the world. Greenwich is on the **prime meridian** at 0° longitude. A brass line laid among the cobblestones here marks the meridian, one side being the eastern, one the western hemisphere.

> **A GOOD WALK**
>
> Whether you go into the Royal Observatory or not, a walk up the steep path from the National Maritime Museum to the top of the hill gives you fantastic views across all of London, topped off with £1-a-slot telescopes to scour the skyline. Time it to catch the golden glow of late afternoon sun on Canary Wharf Tower and head back into town via the rose garden behind Ranger's House.

In 1948 the Old Royal Observatory lost its official status: London's glow had grown too intense, and the astronomers moved to Sussex, while the Astronomer Royal decamped to Cambridge, leaving various telescopes, chronometers, and clocks for you to view. An excellent exhibition on the solution to the problem of measuring longitude includes John Harrison's famous clocks, H1–H4, now in working order. There may be some closures to parts of the museum in preparation for the unveiling of Time and Space, a major development that adds a Planetarium and new galleries to the observatory. It's due to open in 2007. ⊠ *Greenwich Park, Greenwich, SE10* ☎ *020/8858–4422* ⊕ *www.rog. nmm.ac.uk* ⊠ *Free* ☉ *Apr.–Sept., daily 10–6; Oct.–Mar., daily 10–5; last admission 4:30* Ⓤ *DLR: Greenwich.*

> **DID YOU KNOW?**
>
> Right above the prime meridian line, a funky green laser shoots out across London, and at night it can be seen for several miles.

OFF THE BEATEN PATH

THAMES BARRIER VISITORS' CENTRE – Learn what comes between London and its famous river—a futuristic-looking metal barrier that has been described as the eighth wonder of the world. Multimedia presentations, a film on the Thames' history, working models, and views of the barrier itself put the importance of the relationship between London and its river in perspective. ⊠ *Unity Way, Eastmoor St., Woolwich, SE18* ☎ *020/8305–4188* ⊕ *www.thamesbarrierpark.org.uk* ⊠ *£1* ☉ *Apr.–Sept., daily 10:30–4:30; Oct.–Mar., daily 11–3:30* Ⓤ *National Rail: Charlton (from London Bridge), North Greenwich (Jubilee Line), then Bus 161 or 472.*

Greenwich at a Glance

SIGHTS	MUSEUMS & GALLERIES	PARKS & GARDENS
Cutty Sark	Fan Museum	Greenwich Park
Greenwich Meridian Line	National Maritime	SHOPPING (⇨ Ch. 19)
Millennium Dome	Museum	MARKETS & MALLS
Old Royal Naval College	Ranger's House	Antiques Market
Royal Observatory	Queen's House	Greenwich Market
Thames Flood Barrier	Thames Barrier Visitors'	Village Market
	Centre	

The Thames Upstream

WORD OF MOUTH

"[Hampton Court Palace is] a must-see part of your trip to London. You get to experience the feel of life in the castle more than in other royal palaces. You can take the tour at your own pace and there are all sorts of activities to keep you busy . . . . While we were there, there were games on the lawn in the courtyard for children. It's much more interactive and memorable overall than Windsor."

–Kim from Tennessee

THE THAMES UPSTREAM

Sightseeing
★ ★ ★ ★

Nightlife
★ ★

Dining
★ ★ ★

Lodging
★ ★

Shopping
★ ★

The upper stretch of the Thames unites a string of lustrous riverside pearls—Chiswick, Kew, Richmond, Putney—taking in friendly streets, horticultural delights, regal magnificence, and Henry VIII's fiendish outdoor labyrinth at Hampton Court Palace. Achieving a noble hat-trick of homes, gardens, and parks, the neighborhoods dotted along the way are as proud of their village-y feel as of their stately history, with many a pleasing pub nestled at the water's edge. After the bustle of the West End, here the pace slackens delightfully, and it becomes easy to forget you're in a capital city.

Chiswick & Kew

Chiswick is the nearest Thames-side destination to London, with Kew a mile or so beyond it. Much of Chiswick, developed at the beginning of the 20th century, is today a nondescript suburb. Incongruously stranded among the terraced houses, however, a number of fine 18th-century houses and a charming little village survive. The village atmosphere of Kew is still distinct, making this one of the most desirable areas of outer London. What makes Kew famous, though, are the Royal Botanic Gardens.

Places to Explore

▶ **Chiswick House.** Built circa 1725 by the Earl of Burlington (the Lord Burlington of Burlington House, Piccadilly, home of the Royal Academy, and, of course, the Burlington Arcade) as a country residence in which to entertain friends, and as a kind of temple to the arts, this is the very model of a Palladian villa, inspired by the Villa Capra near Vicenza in northeastern Italy. The house fans out from a central octagonal room in perfect symmetry, guarded by statues of Burlington's heroes, Palladio himself and his disciple Inigo Jones. Burlington's friends—Pope, Swift, Gay, and Handel among them—were well qualified to adorn a temple to the arts. Burlington was a great connoisseur and an important patron of the arts, but he was also an accomplished architect in his own right, fascinated by—obsessed with, even—the architecture and art of the Italian Renaissance and ancient Rome, with which he'd fallen in love during his Italian Grand Tour. Along with William Kent (1685–1748), who designed the interiors and the rambling gardens here, Burlington did a great deal toward the dissemination of Palladian ideals around Britain: Chiswick House sparked enormous interest, and you'll see these forms reflected in hundreds of later English stately homes both small and large. Sitting in acres of spectacular Italianate gardens filled with classical temples, statues, and obelisks, it's home to the sumptuous interiors of William Kent, including the Blue Velvet Room with its gilded decoration and intricate ceiling paintings. It also houses a fabulous collection of paintings and furniture. ⊠ *Burlington La., Chiswick, W4* ☎ *020/8995–0508* ⊕ *www.english-heritage.org.uk* ⊠ *£4* ☼ *Apr.–Oct., Sun., Wed.–Fri., and bank holidays 10–5, Sat. 10–2; closed some Sat. afternoons; Nov.–Mar., by appointment only* Ⓤ *Turnham Green, Chiswick.*

> ## BOAT RACES
>
> A great place to buy Hogarth prints is at **Fosters** (⊠ 183 Chiswick High Rd. W4 ☎ 020/8995-2768), the oldest shop in Chiswick. Run by a husband-and-wife team, the shop has its original Georgian frontage, creaking floorboards and a glorious number of original Victorian novels and essays. It also offers handwritten gift vouchers from £10 to £50,000.

14

Hogarth's House. Home to William Hogarth, the satirical painter and engraver, from 1749 until his death in 1764. Unprotected from the six-lane Great West Road, which remains a main route to the West Country, the poor house is besieged by surrounding traffic, but it's worth visiting for its little museum containing his amusing moralistic engravings, such as *Beer Street*, *Marriage a la Mode*, *The Harlot's Progress* and the most famous of all, the *Rake's Progress* series of 1735. ■ TIP➔ **Look out too for the 300-year old mulberry tree in the garden, a vain attempt to get silk worms to breed in England.** ⊠ *Hogarth La., Chiswick, W4* ☎ *020/8994-6757* ⊠ *Free* ☼ *Apr.–Sept., Tues.–Fri. 1–5, weekends 1–6; Oct.–Mar., Tues.–Fri. 1–4, weekends 1–5* Ⓤ *Turnham Green.*

NEED A BREAK? Pubs are the name of the game here at Chiswick's portion of the Thames. Many pubs sit on the bank of the river, offering watery vistas to accompany stout pints of brew. The **Bell & Crown** (⊠ 72 Strand-on-the-Green, Chiswick, W4 ☎ 020/8994-4164) is the first pub on the riverside path from Kew Bridge, with a riverside conservatory to check those breezes. The **Blue Anchor** (⊠ 13 Lower Mall, Hammersmith, W6 ☎ 020/8748-5774) is a cozy 18th-century watering hole, with rowing memorabilia lining the walls. The **Dove** (⊠ 19 Upper Mall, Hammer-

GETTING ORIENTED

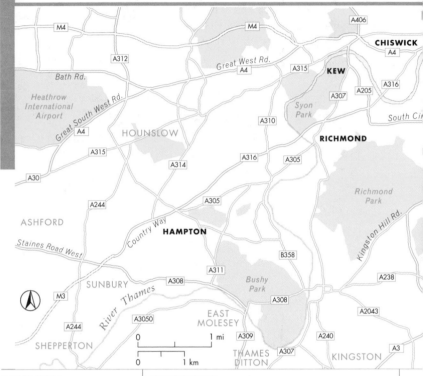

A GOOD WALK	GETTING THERE
From Chiswick House, follow Burlington Lane and take a left onto Hogarth Lane—anything but a lane—to reach Hogarth's House. Chiswick's Church Street (reached by an underpass from Hogarth's House) is the nearest thing to a sleepy country village street in all of London. Follow it down to the Thames and turn left at the bottom to reach the 18th-century riverfront houses of Chiswick Mall, referred to by locals as "Millionaire's Row." There are several pretty riverside pubs near Hammersmith Bridge.	The District Line is the best of the Tube options, stopping at Turnham Green (in the heart of Chiswick but a fair walk from the houses), Gunnersbury (for Syon Park), Kew Gardens, and Richmond. For Hampton Court, overland train is your only option: South West trains run from Waterloo, also stopping at Chiswick station (best for Chiswick House or Hogarth's House), Kew Bridge, Richmond (for Ham House), and St. Margaret's, best for Marble Hill House. Silverlink, another overland London service, also stops at Gunnersbury, Kew Gardens, and Richmond. A pleasant, if slow, way to go is by river. Boats depart upriver from Westminster Pier, by Big Ben, for Kew (1½ hours), Richmond (2–3 hours), and Hampton Court (3–4 hours depending on tides) several times a day in summer, less frequently from October through March. The boat trip is worth taking only if you make it an integral part of your day out, and be aware that it can get very breezy on the water.

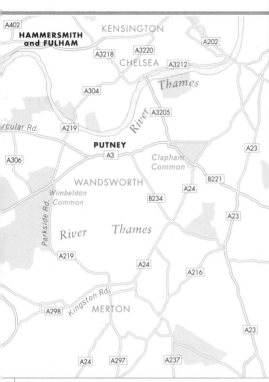

**MAKING THE MOST
OF YOUR TIME**

Hampton Court Palace requires at least half a day to experience the most of its magic, although you could make do with an afternoon at Richmond Park, or a couple of hours for any of the other attractions. Because of the distances involved between the sights, too much traveling eats into your day. The best option is to concentrate on one of the sights, adding in a brisk park visit, one stately home, and a riverside promenade, before rounding off with an evening pint.

NEAREST PUBLIC RESTROOMS

Richmond Park, Kew Gardens, and all the stately homes have public toilets available.

TOP 5 REASONS TO GO

■ **Hampton Court Palace:** Get lost in the leafy walls of the palace's maze as dusk falls.

■ **Richmond Park:** Take a misty early-morning stroll and catch sight of red deer.

■ **Richmond village:** Browse the antiques shops and go back in time.

■ **Kew Gardens:** Explore the giant stems of weird and wonderful plants at the Royal Botanic Gardens.

■ **Thames-side views:** Enjoy a pint from the creaking balcony of a centuries-old riverside pub as the boats row home.

smith, W6 ☏ 020/8748-5405) retains the charm of its 300-plus-year heritage. If you can find a spot on the tiny terrace it's a tranquil place to watch the energetic oarsmen.

★ ☺ **Kew Gardens.** The Royal Botanic Gardens at Kew are a spectacular 300 acres of public gardens, containing more than 30,000 species of plants. In addition, this is the country's leading botanical institute, and has been named a World Heritage Site by UNESCO. There are also strong royal associations. Until 1840, when Kew Gardens was handed over to the nation, it had been the grounds of two royal residences: the White House (formerly Kew House) and Richmond Lodge. George II and Queen Caroline lived at Richmond Lodge in the 1720s, while their eldest son, Frederick, Prince of Wales, and his wife, Princess Augusta, came to the White House during the 1730s. The royal wives were keen gardeners. Queen Caroline got to work on her grounds, while next door Frederick's pleasure garden was developed as a botanical garden by his widow after his death. She introduced all kinds of "exotics," foreign plants brought back to England by botanists. Caroline was aided by a skilled head gardener and by the architect Sir William Chambers, who built a series of temples and follies, of which the crazy 50-story **Pagoda** (1762), visible for miles around, is the star turn. The celebrated botanist Sir Joseph Banks (1743–1820) then took charge of Kew, which developed rapidly in both its roles—as a landscaped garden and as a center of study and research.

The highlights of a visit to Kew are the two great 19th-century greenhouses filled with tropical plants, many of which have been there as long as their housing. Both the **Palm House** and the **Temperate House** were designed by Sir Decimus Burton, the first opening in 1848, the second in 1899. The Temperate House was the biggest greenhouse in the world, and today contains the largest greenhouse plant in the world, a Chilean wine palm rooted in 1846. You can climb the spiral staircase almost to the roof and look down on this and the dense tropical profusion from the walkway. The **Princess of Wales Conservatory,** the latest and the largest plant house at Kew, was opened in 1987 by Princess Diana. Under its bold glass roofs, designed to maximize energy conservation, there are no fewer than 10 climatic zones.

Plants may be beautiful to look at, and they have many medicinal uses, but how many plants are used in making fabrics, paper, and many more items? In **Museum No. 1,** near the Palm House, an interesting exhibition of the economic botany collections shows which plants ". . . help the merchant, physician, chemist, dyer, carpenter and artisans to find raw materials of their profession correctly named." It's free, but opening hours are seasonal, so check beforehand. The plant houses make Kew worth visiting even in the depths of winter, but in spring and summer the gardens come into their own. In late spring the woodland nature reserve of Queen Charlotte's Cottage Gardens is carpeted in bluebells; a little later, the Rhododendron Dell and the Azalea Garden become swathed in brilliant color. High summer brings glorious displays of roses and water lilies, and fall is the time to see the heather garden, near the pagoda. Whatever time of year you visit, something is in bloom, and your journey is never wasted. The main entrance is between Richmond Circus and the traffic circle at Mortlake Road. ⊠ *Kew Rd., Kew* ☎ *020/8332–5655* ⊕ *www. kew.org* ⊠ *£11.75* ⊙ *Gardens Apr.–Oct., weekdays 9:30–6:30, weekends 9:30–7:30; Nov.–Mar., daily 9:30–4:30* Ⓤ *Kew Gardens.*

Kew Palace and Queen Charlotte's Cottage. To this day quietly domestic Kew Palace remains the smallest royal palace in the land. The house and gardens offer a glimpse into the 17th century. Originally known as the Dutch House, it was bought by King George II to provide more room in addition to the White House (another royal residence that used to exist on the grounds) for the extended royal family. In spring there's a romantic haze of bluebells. ⊠ *Kew Gardens, Kew* ⊕ *www.hrp.org.uk* ⊠ *£9.50.*

14

NEED A BREAK?

Maids of Honour (⊠ 288 Kew Rd., Kew ☎ 020/8940-2752), the most traditional of Old English tearooms, is named for the famous tarts invented here and still baked by hand on the premises. Tea is served in the afternoon, Tuesday–Saturday 2:30–5:30. If you can't wait for tea and want to take some of the lovely cakes and pastries to eat at Kew Gardens or on Kew Green, the shop is open Tuesday–Saturday 9:30–6 and on Monday until 1 PM.

Richmond

Named after the palace Henry VII built here in 1500, Richmond is still a welcoming and extremely pretty riverside "village," with many handsome (and expensive) houses, antiques shops, a Victorian theater, London's grandest stately home, and, best of all, the largest of London's royal parks.

Places to Explore

★ **Ham House.** To the west of Richmond Park, overlooking the Thames and nearly opposite the oddly named Eel Pie Island, the house was built in 1610 by Sir Thomas Vavasour, knight marshal to James I, then refurbished later the same century by the Duke and Duchess of Lauderdale, who, although not particularly nice (a contemporary called the duchess "the coldest friend and the most violent enemy that ever was known"), managed to produce one of the finest houses in Britain at the time. It's unique in Europe as the most complete example of a lavish Restoration period house, with a restored formal garden, which has become an influential source for other European palaces and grand villas. Produce from the garden can be enjoyed in the café in the Orangery. After considerable restoration, the library has been filled with 17th- and 18th-century volumes; the original decorations in the Great Hall, Round Gallery, and Great Staircase have been replicated; and all the furniture and fittings, on permanent loan from the V&A, have been cleaned and restored. The gardens and outhouses (Ice House and Still House) are worth a visit in their own right, and are more conveniently open year-round. A tranquil and scenic way to reach the house is on foot, which takes about 30 minutes, along the eastern riverbank south from Richmond Bridge. ⊠ *Ham St., Richmond* ☎ *020/8940-1950* ⊕ *www.nationaltrust.org.uk* ⊠ *House,* *gardens, and outhouses £8* ⊙ *House late Mar.–Oct., Sat.–Wed. 1–5; gardens all year, Sat.–Wed., 11–6* Ⓤ *Richmond, then Bus 65 or 371.*

Marble Hill House. On the northern bank of the Thames, almost opposite Ham House, stands another mansion, this one a near-perfect example of a Palladian villa. Set in 66 acres of parkland, Marble Hill House was built in the 1720s by George II for his mistress, the "exceedingly respectable and respected" Henrietta Howard. Later the house was occupied by Mrs. Fitzherbert, who was secretly married to the Prince Regent (later George IV) in 1785. Marble Hill House was restored in 1901 and opened to the public two years later, looking very much like it did in Georgian times, with extravagant gilded rooms in which Ms. Howard entertained famous poets and wits of the age, including Pope, Gay, and Swift. A ferry service operates during the summer from Ham House across the river; access on foot is a half-hour walk south along the west bank from Richmond Bridge. Group tours can be arranged. ✉ *Richmond Rd., Twickenham, Richmond* ☎ *020/8892–5115* ⊕ *www. english-heritage.org.uk* 🖃 *£4* ⊙ *Apr.–Oct., Sat. 10–2, Sun. and bank holidays 10–5; Nov.–Mar., prebooked tours only* Ⓤ *Richmond.*

⊙ **Richmond Park.** Charles I enclosed this one in 1637 for hunting purposes, like practically all the other parks. Unlike the others, however, Richmond Park still has wild red and fallow deer roaming its 2,470 acres of grassland and heath and the oldest oaks you're likely to see— vestiges of the forests that encroached on London from all sides in medieval times. White Lodge, inside the park, was built for George II in 1729. Edward VIII was born here; now it houses the Royal Ballet School. You can walk from the

> ## STAG LODGE STABLES
>
> Stag Lodge Stables has horses to ride in the big expanses of Richmond Park. Private lessons are £40 Tuesday to Friday, £50 on weekends. Riders with basic skills can rent a horse for a one-hour hack for £25, £35 on weekends. ✉ *Robin Hood Gate, Richmond Park, Richmond, TW10* ☎ *020/ 8974-6066* ⊕ *www.ridinginlondon. com* Ⓤ *Putney Bridge then Bus 85.*

park past the fine 18th-century houses in and around Richmond Hill to the river, admiring first the view from the top. ■ **TIP→ There's a splendid, protected view of St. Paul's Cathedral from King Henry VIII's Mound. Established in 1710, it measures 10 mi and is the bane of over-enthusiastic town planners. Find it and you have a piece of magic in your sights.** ☎ *020/ 8948–3209* ⊕ *www.royalparks.gov.uk* ⊙ *Mar.–Sept., daily 7 AM–dusk; Oct.–Feb., daily 7:30 AM–dusk* Ⓤ *Richmond.*

NEED A BREAK? The **Cricketers** (✉ Maids of Honour Row, Richmond Green, Richmond ☎ 020/ 8940-4372) serves a good pub lunch. The modern, partially glass-roof **Caffé Mamma** (✉ 24 Hill St., Richmond ☎ 020/8940-1625) is a good spot for inexpensive Italian food.

★ ⊙ **Syon House and Park.** The residence of Their Graces the Duke and Duchess of Northumberland, this is one of England's most sumptuous stately homes, and certainly the only one that's near a Tube station. Set in a 55-acre park landscaped by Capability Brown, the core of the house is Tudor—two of Henry VIII's queens, Catherine Howard and Lady Jane Grey, made pit stops here before they were sent to the Tower—but it was redone in the Georgian style in 1761 by famed decorator Robert Adam. He had just returned from studying the sites of classical antiquity in Italy and created two rooms here worthy of any Caesar: the entryway is an amazing study in black and white, pairing neoclassical marbles with antique bronzes, and the Ante-Room contains 12 enormous verdantique columns surmounted by statues of gold—this, no less, was meant to be a waiting room for the duke's servants and retainers. The Red Drawing Room is covered with crimson Spitalfields silk, and the Long Gallery is one of Adam's noblest creations (it was used by Cary Grant and Robert Mitchum for a duel in the 1958 film *The Grass Is Greener*). Elsewhere on the beautiful, rolling parkland is a Victorian glass conservatory that's famous among connoisseurs for its charm, not surprising as the designer, Fowler, was also responsible for the grand Covent Garden Flower Market. ■ TIP→ On certain bank holidays and Sundays you can take a miniature steam train ride in the grounds. Also within the grounds, but not part of the Syon enterprise, are a nature center and **The London Butterfly House** (☎ 020/8560–7272 ☉ Daily 10–3:30), with separate charges. ⊠ *Syon Park, Brentford* ☎ 020/8560–0882 ⊕ *www.syonpark.co.uk* 🖃 *£7.50 for house, gardens, conservatory, and rose garden; £3.75 gardens and conservatory* ☉ *House late Mar.–Oct., Wed., Thurs., Sun., and bank holidays 11–5; gardens daily 10:30–dusk* Ⓤ *Gunnersbury, then Bus 237 or 267 to Brentlea stop.*

Hampton Court Palace

Fodor'sChoice ★ Some 20 mi from central London, on a loop of the Thames upstream from Richmond, stands one of London's oldest royal palaces. It is actually two palaces in one: a magnificent Tudor redbrick mansion, begun in 1514 by Cardinal Wolsey, and a larger, late-17th-century baroque structure, where Christopher Wren designed the graceful south wing, one of the palace's many highlights.

From the information center in the main courtyard, you can choose which parts of the palace to explore—whether your taste is Tudor or baroque—based on a number of self-guided walking routes. Throughout the palace, costumed interpreters and special programs, such as cooking demonstrations in the cavernous Tudor kitchens, make history fun. As you progress into the State Apartments through halls hung with priceless paintings, you can easily imagine the ghost of Catherine Howard screaming her innocence of adultery to an unheeding Henry VIII. Other highlights in the Tudor portion include Henry's Great Hall and the Chapel Royal (with its fan vaulting and azure ceiling). The routes continue with the later King's (William's) Apartments, the Queen's Apartments, and the Georgian

GOOD TO KNOW

There's a map available to guide you around Hampton Court's notorious maze if you're pressed for time, but getting lost is much more fun.

Rooms. William and, especially, Mary loved Hampton Court and left their mark on the place—see their fine collections of Delftware and other porcelain. Be sure to look outside as you explore the baroque apartments. Famed throughout the world, the gardens were designed to please anyone gazing out the windows, as well as people strolling outside. ■ TIP➜ Come Christmas season, there's ice-skating on a rink before the West Front of the palace—an unmissable mixture of pageantry and pleasure.

The site beside the slow-moving Thames is idyllic, with 60 acres of fantastic ornamental gardens, lakes, and ponds, including William III's Privy Garden on the palace's south side. Its parterres, sculpted turf, and clipped yews and hollies—a hybrid of English and continental gardening styles—brilliantly set off Wren's addition. Other highlights are Henry VIII's Pond Garden, the enormous conical yews around the Fountain Garden, and the daffodil-lined paths of the Wilderness. On the east side of the house, 544 lime trees were replanted in 2004 along the Long Water, a canal built during the time of Charles II. The Great Vine, near the Banqueting House, was planted in 1768 and is still producing black Hamburg grapes. Perhaps best of all are the almost half mile of paths in the celebrated maze, which you enter to the north of the palace. It was planted in 1714 and is truly fiendish.

Royalty ceased living here with George III; poor George preferred the seclusion of Kew, where he was finally confined in his madness. The private apartments that range down one side of the palace are now occupied by pensioners of the Crown. Known as "grace and favor" apartments, they are among the most coveted homes in the country, with a surfeit of peace and history on their doorsteps. ⊠ *East Molesey on A308* ☎ *0870/752–7777* ⊕ *www.hrp.org.uk* ✉ *Palace, gardens, and maze £12.30, gardens only £4, maze only £3.50, park grounds free. Joint tickets available with Kensington Palace and Tower of London* ⊗ *State apartments Apr.–Oct., daily 10–6, last admission at 5; Nov.–Mar., daily 10–4:30; grounds daily 7–dusk* Ⓤ *Richmond, then Bus R68; National Rail, South West: Hampton Court Station, 35 min from Waterloo.*

The Thames Upstream at a Glance

SIGHTS
Chiswick House
Ham House
Hampton Court Palace
Hogarth's House
Kew Palace and Queen
  Charlotte's Cottage
Marble Hill House
Syon House

PARKS & GARDENS
Kew Gardens
The London Butterfly
  House

Richmond Park
Syon Park

WHERE TO EAT (⇨ Ch. 15)

MODERATE DINING
Chez Kristof, *French*
The Original Maids of
  Honour, *Afternoon Tea*

EXPENSIVE DINING
River Café, *Italian*

PUBS & NIGHTLIFE
  (⇨ Ch. 17)
Blue Anchor, *pub*
Bull's Head, *jazz & blues*
Cricketers, *pub*
Dove Inn, *pub*
Old Ship, *pub*

ARTS & ENTERTAINMENT
  (⇨ Ch. 18)
Riverside Studios, *dance/
  film*

14

Where to Eat

WORD OF MOUTH

"Brick Lane, in the East End, has become known for its many Indian eateries, shops, bakeries with windows stacked high with colorful sweets, etc. This street is so redolent of India and Pakistan you forget you're in London. Brick Lane is near the Petticoat Lane market."

–PalQ

Updated by
Alex Wijeratna

NO LONGER WOULD NOVELIST SOMERSET MAUGHAM be justified in warning, "To eat well in England, you should have breakfast three times a day." England is now one of the hottest places around for restaurants of every culinary flavor, with London at its epicenter. As anyone who reads the Sunday papers knows, London has enjoyed a huge boom in the restaurant sector. Among the city's 6,700 restaurants are "be-there" eateries, tiny neighborhood joints, gastro-pubs where young-gun foodniks find their feet, and swanky pacesetters where celebrity chefs launch their ego flights. Nearly everyone in town is passionate about food and will love telling you where they've eaten recently or where they'd like to go. You, too, will be smitten, since you will spend, on average, 25% of your travel budget on eating out. After feasting on modern British cuisine, visit one (or two) of London's fabulous pubs for a nightcap. Hit the right one on the right night and watch that legendary British reserve melt away. (⇨ For more on pubs, *see* Chapter 17, Pubs & Nightlife.)

To measure London's spectacular culinary rise, note that it was once a common dictum that the British ate to live while the French lived to eat. Change was slow in coming after the Second World War, when steamed pudding and boiled sprouts were still eaten daily by tweed-and-flannel–clothed Brits. When people thought of British cuisine, fish-and-chips came to mind, a dish that tasted best wrapped in newspaper. Then there was always shepherd's pie, ubiquitously available in pubs—though not made, according to the song from the musical *Sweeney Todd,* "with actual shepherd." Visitors used to arrive in London and joke that the reason Britain conquered half the world was that its residents probably wanted a decent meal. Didn't Britain invade India for a good curry?

Culinary London transformed as the capital built itself up as *the* key world finance center. New menus evolve constantly as chefs outdo each other, creating hot spots that are all about the buzz of being there. Master chefs from Europe such as Nico Ladenis and the Roux brothers showed the way, but it was a designer, Sir Terence Conran, who brought mega-restaurants to the middle classes. He started the revolution with Quaglino's, in 1993; his 480-seat Mezzo restaurant was the biggest in Europe when it opened, and he topped that with Bluebird in 1997, which came complete with grocery store, fishmonger, florist, and food market. Happily, though, the vogue has turned against mega-restaurants, and intimacy is returning.

DINING PLANNER

Top 5

■ **Anchor & Hope.** London's leading gastropub.

■ **Le Gavroche.** Clubby haute cuisine rated London's finest dining experience.

■ **St. John.** Adventurous eaters savor the challenge of Fergus Henderson's ultra-British cooking. Not for the faint-hearted.

■ **The Wolseley.** Viennese elegance for any budget at this grand, all-day café.

■ **Yauatcha.** Get your dim sum whenever you want it in this ultra *Sex in the City* setting.

Dining Hours, Reservations & Dress

In London you can find breakfast all day, but it's generally served between 7:30 and 10. Workmen's cafés and sandwich bars for office workers are sometimes open from 7:30, more upscale cafés from 9 to 10:30. Lunch is between noon and 2. Tea, often a meal in itself, is taken between 4 and 5:30; dinner or supper between 7:30 and 9:30, sometimes earlier. Many ethnic restaurants, especially Indian, serve food until midnight. Sunday is proper lunch day, and some restaurants will open for lunch only. Unless otherwise noted, the restaurants listed in this guide are open daily for lunch and dinner, but some restaurants do not open on Sunday (or Monday) at all. Reservations are always a good idea: we mention them only when they're essential or not accepted. Book as far ahead as you can, and reconfirm when you arrive. We mention dress only when men are required to wear a jacket or a jacket and tie.

WHAT IT COSTS In pounds

	££££££	££££	£££	££	£
AT DINNER	over £23	£20–£23	£14–£19	£10–£13	under £10

Prices are per person for a main course, excluding drinks, service, and V.A.T.

Paying & Tipping

American Express, Diners Club, MasterCard, and Visa are accepted almost everywhere, but a pub, small café, or ethnic restaurant might not take credit cards. Do not tip bar staff in pubs—although you can always offer to buy them a drink. In restaurants, tip 10%–15% of the check for full meals if service is not already included, a small token if you're just having coffee or tea. If paying by credit card, check that a tip has not already been included.

15

Prices

The democratization of restaurants in London has not translated into smaller checks, and London is not an inexpensive city. A modest meal for two can cost £35 (about $65) and the £100-a-head meal is not so taboo. Damage-control strategies include making lunch your main meal—the top places have bargain lunch menus, halving the price of evening à la carte—and ordering a second appetizer instead of an entrée, to which few places object. (Note that an appetizer, usually known as a "starter" or "first course," is sometimes called an "entrée," as it is in France, and an entrée in England is dubbed the "main course" or simply "mains.") Seek out fixed-price menus, and watch for hidden extras on the check: cover, bread, or vegetables charged separately, and service.

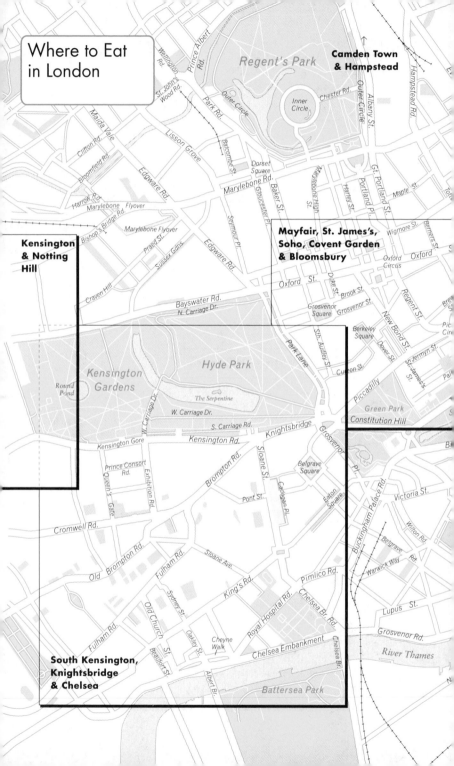

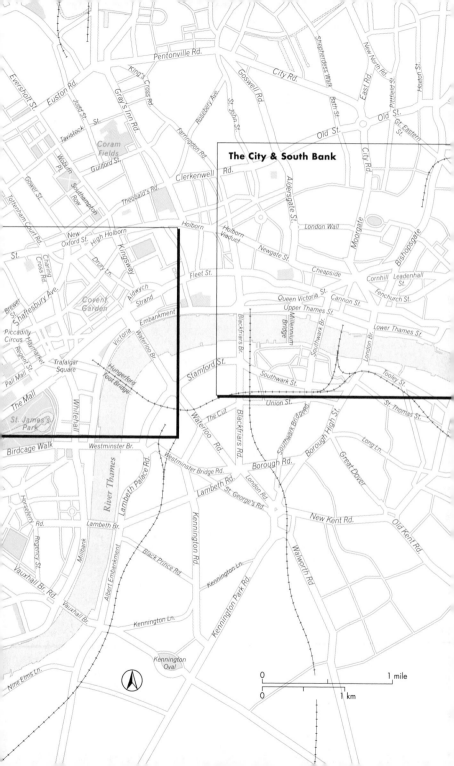

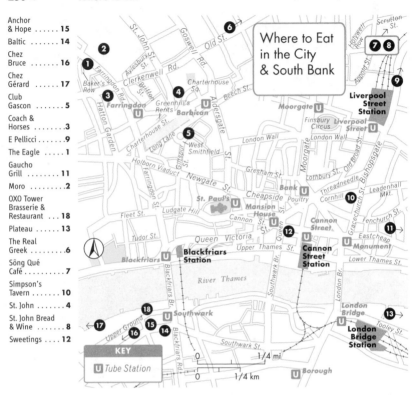

A major player at city tables is superchef-turned-mogul Marco Pierre White, whose restaurant empire includes Mirabelle, L'Escargot, and more. His onetime protégé, the gifted Gordon Ramsay, is picking up ground (and coverage in the press). Ramsay bestrides the London culinary scene like a colossus and has fingers in an assortment of merry pies. The rest of the much-lauded haute-cuisine scene is in world-class hands. Michel Roux Jr. commands at Le Gavroche, Eric Chavot sets a cracking pace at the Capital, and Tom Aikens has his eponymous place in Chelsea. There are, of course, many more stars of the celebrity variety (TV's "Naked Chef" Jamie Oliver is everywhere) and their latest activities, in the kitchen or otherwise, are tracked in any newspaper. To keep up with the whirl, each paper has reviewers aplenty. Read up on the top picks in the London *Evening Standard* (daily), *Time Out* magazine (weekly), or the food pages of the national newspapers, especially the weekend editions.

You can eat in London without breaking the bank. We've struck a balance in our listings and have included hip, scene restaurants, neighborhood spots, ethnic alternatives, gastro-pubs, quirky holdouts, and old favorites. There are upward of 80 cuisines offered in London, and ethnic restaurants have always been a good bet here, especially the thou-

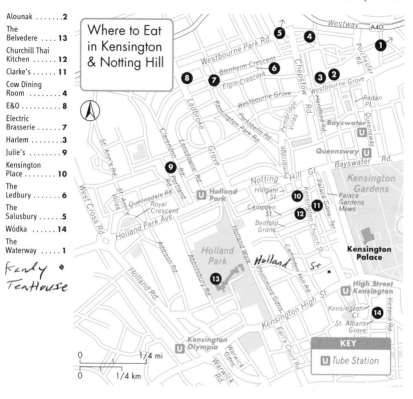

Kardy•
TeaHouse

sands of Indian restaurants, since Londoners now see a good curry as
their birthright. The assortment of foreign cuisines has broadened to include Malaysian, Japanese, Thai, Spanish, Turkish, Ethiopian, and
North African. With all this going on, traditional British food, when you
track it down, appears as just one more exotic cuisine in the pantheon.

**KEEP IN
MIND**

Two caveats: first, the "no smoking" trend is sweeping the London dining scene.
Tough legislation is going through Parliament on this, and an outright ban on smoking in public places—such as restaurants—is imminent at this writing. Second, beware of Sunday. Many restaurants are closed, especially in the evening; likewise
public holidays. Over the Christmas period, London virtually shuts down—it seems
only hotels are prepared to feed travelers. When in doubt, call ahead. It's a good
idea to book a table at all times.

Bloomsbury

There's a real contrast between Bloomsbury's two main dining districts, Marylebone and Fitzrovia. Marylebone is clean and village-y, with
a popular Sunday farmers' market and lots of local independent food
stores. Going hand-in-hand with the orderly vibe are precise, exemplary

Where to Eat in Mayfair, St. James's, Soho, Covent Garden & Bloomsbury

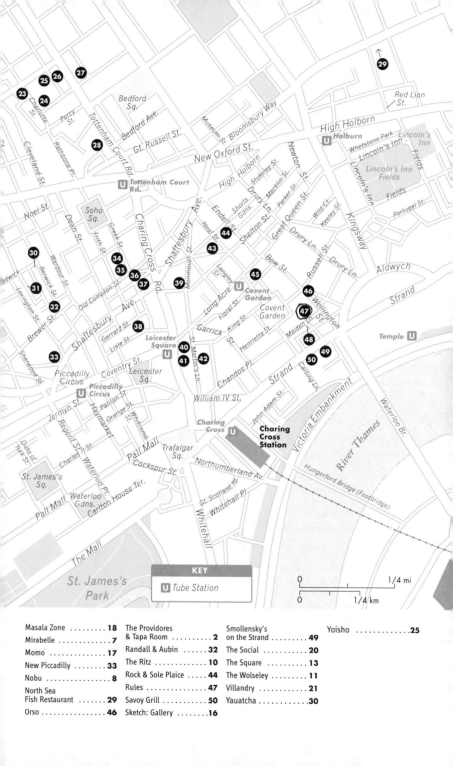

KEY

U *Tube Station*

restaurants. More central Fitzrovia, however, is media and advertising land, altogether more urban—and with a more decadent, expense account dining scene.

CHINESE
★ ££–£££££

✕ **Hakkasan.** It's *Crouching Tiger* territory at this lauded Cantonese basement restaurant off Tottenham Court Road. Ultra stylish and dimly lighted, Hakkasan is ideal for special occasions, with exquisite dim sum (lunch only), and a cracking cocktail scene. The à la carte menu is pricey. Its late-night days are Wednesday through Saturday (until 12:30 AM) and there's a two-hour time limit on tables. ✉ *8 Hanway Pl., Bloomsbury, W1* ☎ *020/7907–7000* ▭ *AE, MC, V* Ⓤ *Tottenham Court Rd.*

ECLECTIC
£££–££££

✕ **The Providores & Tapa Room.** Inventive Kiwi (New Zealand) chef Peter Gordon scores high with his Pacific Rim fusion cuisine in foodie-ville Marylebone. Have a sophisticated meal in the formal restaurant upstairs or try the more relaxed ground-floor Tapa Room. On the menu you'll find venison and coriander, kangaroo loin, guava sorbet, and roast *chioca* (a tuber similar to Jerusalem artichoke). ✉ *109 Marylebone High St., Bloomsbury, W1* ☎ *020/7935–6175* ▭ *AE, MC, V* Ⓤ *Baker St.*

ENGLISH
£

✕ **The Social.** Beautiful people colonize this friendly and hip DJ–bar, which offers great sounds and decent grub. The DJ sessions are eclectic (anything from electronica to salsa) and the food is English old-school comfort: bangers and mash, steak-and-Guinness pie, fish-finger sandwiches, and baked beans on toast. ✉ *5 Little Portland St., Bloomsbury, W1* ☎ *020/7636–4992* ▭ *AE, MC, V* Ⓤ *Oxford Circus.*

FRENCH
£££–££££

✕ **Elena's L'Etoile.** London's reigning monarch maitre d' Elena Salvoni MBE presided for years over L'Escargot in Soho, where she made so many friends that she opened her own place. This century-old 1950s-style Parisian hangout is one of London's few remaining unreconstructed French bistros. Traditional dishes of confit lamb, salmon cakes, crème brûlée, and apple tart are joined by newer treats, and most diners are guaranteed a smile from Elena even if they're not her politician-journalist-actor regulars. ✉ *30 Charlotte St., Bloomsbury, W1* ☎ *020/7636–7189* ▭ *AE, DC, MC, V* ☾ *Closed Sun. No lunch Sat.* Ⓤ *Goodge St.*

££–££££
Fodor'sChoice
★

✕ **Galvin.** London's lucky to have the Galvin brothers blazing a trail for the bistrot de luxe concept on Baker Street. The fêted chefs, Chris and Jeff, forsake Michelin stars and cut loose under the brasserie banner. An older crowd enjoys impeccable service in a handsome salon. There's no better crab lasagna in town, and the mains punch above their weight: daube of venison, pork with Agen prunes, halibut with brown shrimps. ✉ *66 Baker St., Bloomsbury, W1* ☎ *020/7935–4007* ▭ *AE, DC, MC, V* Ⓤ *Baker Street.*

££–££££

✕ **Villandry.** Heaven for food lovers, this posh gourmet deli is crammed with fancy French pâtés, continental cheeses, fruit tarts, biscuits, organic vegetables, and obscure breads galore. There's a bar, charcuterie, and fashionable dining room frequented by the extended New Labour gang. Breakfast is served from 8 AM. ✉ *170 Great Portland St., Bloomsbury W1* ☎ *020/7631–3131* ▭ *AE, MC, V* Ⓤ *Great Portland St.*

GREEK
£–££

✕ **Lemonia.** A superior version of London Greek near Regent's Park, Lemonia is large and light, and packed by night. Besides the usual *mezedes* (appetizers), *kleftiko* (baked lamb in lemon), and *stifado* (beef stewed in wine), there are interesting specials: quail, perhaps, or *gemista* (stuffed vegetables). ✉ *89 Regent's Park Rd., Bloomsbury, NW1* ☎ *020/7586–7454* ⌂ *Reservations essential* ☰ *MC, V* ☉ *No lunch Sat. No dinner Sun.* Ⓤ *Chalk Farm.*

JAPANESE
£–££
✕ **Yoisho.** The Japanese keep this undiscovered bistro-style restaurant mostly to themselves. It's tatty and poorly signed, but the food's famous, and a bargain for Fitzrovia. The grilled, skewered kushiyaki dishes—like pork belly or chicken heart—are delectable, and there are all sorts of dumplings, square omlets, rice balls, rice porridge, noodles, and raw fish. ✉ *33 Goodge St., Bloomsbury, W1* ☎ *020/7323–0477* ☰ *AE, MC, V* Ⓤ *Goodge St.*

SEAFOOD
£–£££
✕ **North Sea Fish Restaurant.** Come here and nowhere else for the national British dish of fish-and-chips—battered cod and thick fries with salt and vinegar. It's tricky to find: three blocks south of St. Pancras station, down Judd Street. They serve only freshly caught fish, which you can order grilled—though that would defeat the purpose. ✉ *7–8 Leigh St., Bloomsbury, WC1* ☎ *020/7387–5892* ☰ *AE, MC, V* ☉ *Closed Sun.* Ⓤ *Russell Sq.*

SPANISH
£–£££
✕ **Fino.** Pick away at a spread of fine modern Spanish tapas and enjoy a fashionable glass of sherry, too; but watch the bill—it all adds up in the end. Set in a plush basement, highlights include *pimentos de padron* (baby green peppers), stuffed courgette (zucchini) flowers, and fried squid. The meats are divine—Iberico ham, chorizo, and wind-dried beef. ▮ TIP➔ **The entrance is on Rathbone Street and set menus for £17.95 or £28 are the way to go.** ✉ *33 Charlotte St., Bloomsbury, W1* ☎ *020/7813–8010* ☰ *AE, MC, V* ☉ *Closed Sun.* Ⓤ *Goodge St.*

THAI
£–£££
✕ **Crazy Bear.** Lavish art deco styling is the draw at this glamour zone in Fitzrovia, ideal for cocktails in the basement lounge bar, and a cheeky Thai- and Asian-influenced meal upstairs. Head for the snapper with lemon zest, and end with cheesecake. ▮ TIP➔ **Admire the Murano chandelier, leather booths, ostrich-hide chairs, and the amazing mirrored loos.** ✉ *26–28 Whitfield St., Bloomsbury, W1* ☎ *020/7631–0088* ⌂ *Reservations essential* ☰ *AE, MC, V* ☉ *Closed Sun.* Ⓤ *Goodge St., Tottenham Court Rd.*

£
Fodor'sChoice
★
✕ **Busabe Eathai.** It's top value for money at this superior high–turnover Thai canteen. It's fitted with bench seats and hardwood tables but is no less seductive than the communal dining. The menu includes noodles, curries, and stir-fries; try chicken with butternut squash, cuttlefish curry, or seafood vermicelli (prawn, squid, and scallops). There are busier branches near Selfridges (8–13 Bird Street) and in Soho (106–110 Wardour Street). ✉ *22 Store St., Bloomsbury, WC1* ☎ *020/7299–7900* ⌂ *Reservations not accepted* ☰ *AE, MC, V* Ⓤ *Tottenham Court Rd.*

> **WORD OF MOUTH**
>
> "If you go [to Busabe Eathai] during regular lunch–dinner hours, be prepared to queue, cause they don't take reservations."
>
> –stadurst

Chelsea

Old money talks in this tony residential section, where some of London's finest establishments nestle in among the garden squares and stucco terraces. Gems like Tom Aikens and Racine may be peak performers, but they still fit snugly with the residential vibe.

AMERICAN-CASUAL
£££–££££

✕ **PJ's Bar & Grill.** Enter PJ's and adopt the Polo Joe lifestyle: wooden floors and stained glass, a slowly revolving propeller from a 1911 Vickers Vimy flying boat, and polo memorabilia. The place is relaxed and efficient, and the menu, which includes all-American staples like steaks, salads, and brownies, will please everyone except vegetarians. PJ's is open late and the bartenders can mix it all. Weekend brunch is popular with the beautiful Chelsea set. ⊠ *52 Fulham Rd., Chelsea, SW3* ☎ *020/7581–0025* ▭ *AE, DC, MC, V* Ⓤ *South Kensington.*

£

✕ **Chelsea Bun.** Get fed heaps for little moolah at this hybrid of an American diner and an English "greasy spoon" café. Expect a big menu with construction-buddy portions—burgers, salads, potato skins, all manner of breakfasts (including full English), pastas, and pies. ⊠ *9A Limerston St., Chelsea, SW10* ☎ *0870/780–3217* ▭ *MC, V* Ⓤ *Sloane Sq., then Bus 19 or 22.*

CONTEMPORARY
£–£££

✕ **The Pig's Ear.** Royal heir Prince William came with friends and split the bill in the first-floor dining room at this inventive gastro-pub, off the King's Road. Elbow in at the boisterous ground-floor pub area, or choose a restaurant vibe in the wood-panel salon upstairs. You'll find creative dishes on the short menu: shallot and cider soup, roast bone marrow, or skate wing and leaks are all typical, and executed . . . royally. ⊠ *35 Old Church St., Chelsea, SW3* ☎ *020/7352–2908* ⌲ *Reservations essential* ▭ *AE, DC, MC, V* Ⓤ *Sloane Sq.*

FRENCH
£££££

✕ **Aubergine.** Chef William Drabble's reputation soars at this refined haute cuisine restaurant off Fulham Road, which deals only in first-rate ingredients. Best-end lamb, braised pig's head, or monkfish carpaccio don't come much better, and service is gold standard. ◼ TIP→ **Enjoy a set lunch for £34.** ⊠ *11 Park Walk, Chelsea, SW10* ☎ *020/7352–3449* ⌲ *Reservations essential* ▭ *AE, DC, MC, V* ☉ *Closed Sun. No lunch Sat.* Ⓤ *South Kensington.*

£££££
Fodor'sChoice
★

✕ **Gordon Ramsay at Royal Hospital Road.** The famous Mr. Ramsay whips up a storm with white beans, lobster, foie gras, and shaved truffles. He's one of Britain's finest chefs, and wins the highest accolades here, where tables are booked months in advance. For £90, splurge on seven courses; for £70, dance through a three-course dinner; or try lunch (£40 for three courses) for a gentler check—but watch the wine and those extras. ⊠ *68–69 Royal Hospital Rd., Chelsea, SW3* ☎ *020/*

> **WORD OF MOUTH**
>
> "Gordon Ramsay at Royal Hospital Road: spectacular! My suggestion—go for lunch, late, and spend the afternoon. Still expensive, but worth it. You will have to make reservations exactly one month to the day at 9 AM—which means the middle of the night in the States."
>
> –JoeG

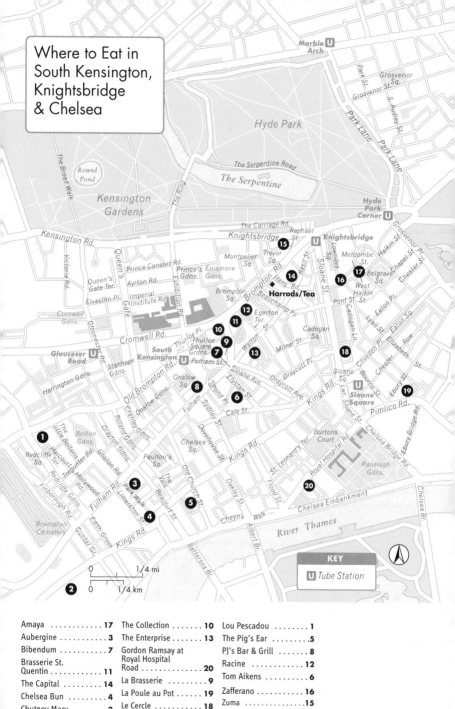

Where to Eat in South Kensington, Knightsbridge & Chelsea

7352–4441 or 020/7352–3334
🍴 *Reservations essential* 🍽 *AE,*
DC, MC, V 🕑 *Closed weekends*
Ⓤ *Sloane Sq.*

£££££ ✕ **Tom Aikens.** Wonder chef Tom
Fodor'sChoice Aikens trained under French legend
★ Joël Robuchon and excels at his slick modern eponymous restaurant. His constructions on the plate are intricate: many find delight with his pig's head with pork belly, poached oysters, and "piglet." There's a friendly sommelier to help navigate the hefty wine list. ✉ *43 Elystan St., Chelsea, SW3* ☎ *020/7584–2003* 🍴 *Reservations essential* 🍽 *AE, MC, V* Ⓤ *South Kensington.*

££–£££££ ✕ **Racine.** There's an upscale buzz at this star of the Brompton Road
Fodor'sChoice dining scene. Henry Harris's chic French brasserie excels because he does
★ the simple things well—and doesn't overcharge. Classics like calves' brain or smoked duck with French beans, or mussels with saffron mousse, hit the spot. Desserts and wines by the glass are fairly priced. ✉ *239 Brompton Rd., Chelsea, SW3* ☎ *020/7584–4477* 🍽 *AE, MC, V* Ⓤ *South Kensington.*

INDIAN ✕ **Chutney Mary.** London's stalwart romantic Indian holds its own as a
££–£££££ desired destination. Pan-continental dishes like Mangalore giant prawns and Goan chicken curry mingle with more familiar north Indian lamb or chicken tikka. Staff are gracious, lighting is muted, and desserts are worth a pop. ■ TIP→ **The three-course Sunday jazz brunch is good value at £16.50.** ✉ *535 King's Rd., Chelsea, SW10* ☎ *020/7351–3113* 🍴 *Reservations essential* 🍽 *AE, DC, MC, V* Ⓤ *Fulham Broadway.*

The City

The City district around Bank is a pinstripe central business district, which means it's relatively quiet on the streets after 9 PM.

CONTEMPORARY ✕ **St. John.** Most people love chef Fergus Henderson's ultra-British
££–££££ cooking at this converted smokehouse in Clerkenwell. His chutzpah is
Fodor'sChoice scary: one appetizer is pig skin, and others (calf brain or pig nose and
★ tail) are marginally less extreme. Entrées like bone marrow and parsley salad can appear stark on the plate but arrive with style. Expect an all-French wine list, plus malmseys and port. Try rice pudding with plums, or traditional English Eccles cakes. ✉ *26 St. John St., The City, EC1* ☎ *020/7251–0848 or 020/7251–4998* 🍴 *Reservations essential* 🍽 *AE, DC, MC, V* 🕑 *Closed Sun. No lunch Sat.* Ⓤ *Farringdon.*

★ **££–£££** ✕ **St. John Bread & Wine.** The canteen version of St. John in Clerkenwell is a winner no matter what meal of the day: have porridge and prunes for breakfast, seed cake and a glass of Madeira for "elevenses," oxtail and horseradish for lunch, and Gloucester Old Spot ham for dinner. The scrumptious bread is baked on-site, and the wine is mainly French. ■ TIP→ **It's good before or after a stroll around nearby Old Spitalfields or Brick Lane markets.** ✉ *94–96 Commercial St., The City, E1* ☎ *020/7247–8724* 🍽 *AE, MC, V* Ⓤ *Aldgate East, Liverpool St.*

Where to Refuel Around Town

WHEN YOU'RE ON THE GO or don't have time for a leisurely meal—and Starbucks simply won't cut it—you might want to try a local chain restaurant or sandwich bar where you can stop for a quick bite or get something to take out. Although many of London's chains serve relatively soulless fare, the ones listed below are fairly priced and committed to quality and using fresh ingredients.

Café Rouge: This classic 30-strong French bistro chain has been around for eons—it's so "uncool" that it's now almost fashionable. Nonetheless, it's still useful when out and about. ⊕ www.caferouge.co.uk

Carluccio's Caffé: Affable TV chef Antonio Carluccio's chain of 12 all-day traditional Italian café/bar/food shops are freshly sourced and make brilliant stops on a shopping spree. ⊕ www.carluccios.com

Ed's Easy Diner: Overdose on made-to-order hamburgers, onion rings, and thick milk shakes at this chain of shiny, retro '50s-theme American diners. ⊕ www.edseasydiner.co.uk

Giraffe: Kids and grown-ups enjoy burgers, salads, and smoothies at this 12-strong chain of animal-theme restaurants. Staff are all smiles, and the prices, cute. ⊕ www.giraffe.net

Gourmet Burger Kitchen (aka GBK): Kiwi Peter Gordon's line of six (and counting) burger joints is wholesome and handy, with Aberdeen Angus beef, lamb, or venison burgers. ⊕ www.gbkinfo.co.uk

Pizza Express: Serving tasty but utterly predictable pizzas, Pizza Express seems to be everywhere (there are 95 in London). Soho's branch has a cool live jazz program. ⊕ www.pizzaexpress.com

Pret a Manger: London's take-out supremo isn't just for sandwiches: there are wraps, noodles, sushi, salads, and tea cakes as well. ⊕ www.pretamanger.com

Ranoush Juice Bar: Chewy shwarmas proliferate at these late-night café and juice bars (open until 3 AM daily), which serve kebabs, falafal, and tabbouleh. There are three branches in Kensington and one on Edgeware Road. ⊕ www.maroush.com

Strada: Stop here for authentic pizzas baked over a wood fire, plus simple pastas and risottos. It's stylish, cheap, packed, and doesn't take reservations. ⊕ www.strada.co.uk

Tootsies Grill: This superior burger joint does yummy grilled burgers, fries, salads, steaks, BLTs, and chicken spreads. There's a children's meal for £4.95 and branches in Holland Park, Fulham, Chiswick, Ealing, Wimbledon, Kew, South Kensington, Parsons Green, Hampstead, and Oxford Circus. ⊕ www.tootsiesrestaurants.co.uk

Wagamama: Voted the capital's favorite restaurant, Londoners drain endless bowls of noodles at this chain of high-tech, high-turnover, high-volume Japanese canteens. ⊕ www.wagamama.com

15

ENGLISH
££–£££
Fodor'sChoice
★

✕ **Coach & Horses.** Farringdon's award-winning rare-breed gastro-pub gets it right on all levels. The inside feels like a proper English pub—retaining original wooden screens and etched glass—and there are quality ales and earnest service, and the kitchen excels through invention. You might find smoked mackerel, crispy pork belly, or Old Spot ham with fava beans and parsley sauce. ■ TIP→ Dine in the bar if you want that real English pub sensation. ✉ *26–28 Ray St., The City, EC1* ☎ *020/ 7278—8990* ☰ *AE, MC, V* Ⓤ *Farringdon.*

£–££

✕ **Simpson's Tavern.** A bastion of tradition, this back-alley chophouse was founded in 1757 and is as "rum and racuous" as ever. It's popular with ruddy–faced City folk, who come for old-school fare: steak-and-kidney pie, liver and bacon, chump chops, potted shrimps (served in small pots with butter), or the house specialty, "stewed cheese" (cheese on toast with béchamel and Worcestershire sauce). It's shared seating and service is "idosyncratic"—one of it's charms. ✉ *38½ Cornhill, at Ball Ct., The City, EC3* ☎ *020/7626–9985* ♨ *Reservations not accepted* ☰ *AE, DC, MC, V* ☺ *Closed weekends. No dinner* Ⓤ *Bank.*

£

✕ **E Pellicci.** Expect Cockney banter and all-day English breakfasts at this landmark café not far from Brick Lane. Absolutely tiny, with stained glass, deco marquetry, and pics autographed by *EastEnders* soap stars, it's the hole-in-the-wall for the breakfast Londoners adore: eggs, bacon, toast, baked beans, black pud, "bubble 'n' squeak" (cabbage and mashed potatoes), the works. Your arteries may clog up, but at least the wallet survives: almost everything's £4.60, including lasagna. ✉ *332 Bethnal Green Rd., The City, E2* ☎ *020/7739–4873* ☰ *No credit cards* ☺ *Closed Sun.* Ⓤ *Bethnal Green.*

FRENCH
£££££

✕ **Plateau.** Sir Terence Conran's Plateau is an excellent choice for a Canary Wharf business meal or for something more relaxed. In a slick all-white space, with tulip-shape chairs and floor-to-ceiling plate-glass windows overlooking Canada Square, Plateau has something for everyone; a bar, rotisserie, terrace, smoking room, and main restaurant. Mains like monkfish and leeks and sea bass and parsnip puree are mighty expensive, but this is Canary Wharf, where money, it seems, is no object. ✉ *Canada Place, Canary Wharf, The City, E14* ☎ *020/ 7715–7100* ♨ *Reservations essential* ☰ *AE, MC, V* Ⓤ *Canary Wharf.*

££££–£££££

✕ **Club Gascon.** It's hard to find a sexier place than this in London. Maybe it's the leather-wall interior, the cut flowers, cute service, or the way the tapas-style, modern, southwestern French cuisine is served (on a rock rather than on a plate). It must be the quality of the foie gras, which you could enjoy from start to finish: feast on duck foie gras "popcorn," and then have it for pudding with grapes and gingerbread. ✉ *57 W. Smithfield, The City, EC1* ☎ *020/7796–0600* ♨ *Reservations essential* ☰ *AE, MC, V* ☺ *Closed Sun. No lunch Sat.* Ⓤ *Barbican.*

GREEK
££–£££

✕ **The Real Greek.** Theodore Kyriakou lifts Greek cuisine up several notches at this Shoreditch favorite. Push costs down with a spread of *meze* (small appetizers) and *fagakia* (mid-size dishes). Lamb sweatbreads, grilled octopus, and Ismir squid with prunes recall a real taste of the mainland, and the all-Greek wine list is worth a sniff. ✉ *15 Hoxton Market, The City, N1* ☎ *020/7739–8212* ♨ *Reservations essential* ☰ *MC, V* ☺ *Closed Sun.* Ⓤ *Old St.*

LATIN
** £££–£££££**

✕ **Gaucho Grill.** Red in tooth and claw City finance traders can't get enough of the prime Argentine steaks served here—one of the capital's better steakhouse chains at Canary Wharf. Flown from Buenos Aires to outlets in St. James's, South Kensington, Hampstead, and the City, the steaks are cut to order. The grill's unreconstructed approach is great

WORD OF MOUTH

"As a kick start, I would suggest eating at least one good Indian meal (it's practically our national cuisine these days) and eating in at least one good gastro-pub."
–jenstu13

for a beef fix; leave the vegetarians at home. ✉ *29 Westferry Circus, Canary Riverside, The City, E14* ☎ *020/7987–9494* 🖃 *AE, DC, MC, V* Ⓤ *Canary Wharf.*

MEDITERRANEAN
★ **££–£££**

✕ **Moro.** Up the road from the City, near Clerkenwell and Sadler's Wells dance theater, is Exmouth Market, a cluster of cute shops, an Italian church, and more fine restaurants like Moro. The menu includes a mélange of Spanish and North African flavors. Spiced meats, Serrano hams, salt cod, and wood-fired and char-grilled offerings are the secret to Moro's success. There's a long zinc bar, the tables are small, and the only downside is the persistent noise. But then again, that's part of the buzz. ✉ *34–36 Exmouth Market, The City, EC1* ☎ *020/7833–8336* 🍴 *Reservations essential* 🖃 *AE, DC, MC, V* ☙ *Closed Sun.* Ⓤ *Farringdon.*

£–£££

✕ **The Eagle.** The Eagle spearheaded the welcome trend toward pubs serving good meals. As *the* original '90s gastro-pub, it belongs in the "Restaurants" section by virtue of its good-value Portuguese–Spanish food. You'll find about nine dishes on the blackboard menu daily—a pasta, three vegetarian choices, and a risotto usually among them. Many places in London charge twice the price for similar food. ✉ *159 Farringdon Rd., The City, EC1* ☎ *020/7837–1353* 🍴 *Reservations not accepted* 🖃 *MC, V* Ⓤ *Farringdon.*

SEAFOOD
££–£££££

✕ **Sweetings.** Uniquely English, Sweetings (est. 1889) is a time warp from the old imperial City of London days. There are certain things Sweetings *doesn't* do: reservations, dinner, coffee, and weekends. It does, however, do seafood. Not far from St. Paul's Cathedral, it's a "luncheon" choice for City gents. They drink tankards of black velvet (Guinness and champagne) and eat potted shrimp, Cornish brill, and roe on toast. The West Mersea oysters are fresh, and the desserts are public-school favorites like baked jam roll and "spotted dick" (suet pudding with currants). ✉ *39 Queen Victoria St., The City, EC4* ☎ *020/7248–3062* 🍴 *Reservations not accepted* 🖃 *AE, MC, V* ☙ *Closed weekends. No dinner* Ⓤ *Mansion House.*

VIETNAMESE
★ **£**

✕ **Sông Qué Café.** If you're in Hoxton and looking for an unpretentious place to eat, this Vietnamese canteen offers outstanding value for money. Block out the scruffy Kingsland Road location and tacky decor and instead dig into papaya salad, chili squid, Vietnamese pancakes, and *pho* (beef broth with rice noodles and rare steak). ✉ *134 Kingsland Rd., The City, E2* ☎ *020/7613–3222* 🖃 *AE, MC, V* Ⓤ *Old St.*

15

Covent Garden

Avoid tourist traps and fake razzmatazz in the heart of showbiz London. There are crowds until late in Theaterland, and you may see a star if you duck into the right venues. Look for thespians in London's former favorite, the Ivy, or J Sheekey and Orso. Covent Garden is always glamorous, and you might spot the A-list dining next to you at one of the hotel draws on St. Martin's Lane, like Asia de Cuba.

AMERICAN
★ £–£££

✕ **Joe Allen.** Thespians head here after curtain fall in Theaterland, but more for the basement Broadway buzz than the American comfort food. The menu is undemanding: pastrami and fig and black-bean soup are typical starters, and entrées include hamburgers, BBQ spare ribs and corn muffins, plus lamb and eggplant. There are Yankee desserts, such as grilled banana bread with ice cream and caramel sauce. Weekend brunch is enjoyable, too. ⊠ *13 Exeter St., Covent Garden, WC2* ☎ *020/7836–0651* ⌂ *Reservations essential* ⊟ *AE, MC, V* Ⓤ *Covent Garden.*

☾ £–£££

✕ **Smollensky's on the Strand.** This American-style bar-restaurant is useful if you have children in tow, especially at lunch on weekends, when the young are fed burgers and "kids' cocktails" and are taken off your hands by clowns and magicians. The grown-up menu favors red meat, with several cuts of steak, all served with fries and sauces. There are potato skins, salads, and other vegetarian choices, and sandwiches, inspired by American cuisines from New England to New Mexico. ⊠ *105 Strand, Covent Garden, WC2* ☎ *020/7497–2101* ⊟ *AE, DC, MC, V* Ⓤ *Charing Cross.*

CONTEMPORARY
£–£££££
Fodor'sChoice
★

✕ **The Ivy.** Though pushed from the highest reaches of London's restaurant heirarchy, Ivy is still hard to get into. In a wood-panel room with stained glass, a curious mix of celebs and out-of-towners dines on Caesar salad, salmon cakes, and English classics like shepherd's pie and rhubarb fool (stewed rhubarb and cream). For star-trekking ("Don't look now, dear, but there's Hugh Grant") this is the prime spot in London. The weekend set-price lunch is a bargain at £22.50. ■ TIP→ **Try walking in off the street for a table on short notice—it's known to work.** ⊠ *1 West St., Covent Garden, WC2* ☎ *020/7836–4751* ⌂ *Reservations essential* ⊟ *AE, DC, MC, V* Ⓤ *Covent Garden.*

CONTINENTAL
★ £££££

✕ **Savoy Grill.** Ambitious chef Marcus Wareing triumphs at this bastion of establishment power dining. Kind lighting, wood paneling, and silverplated pillars mark the classic art deco interior, and assembled CEOs, press barons, and politicians have warmed to Wareing's menu. On it are braised pork belly, calves' sweetbreads, an "Arnold Bennett" omelet (with smoked haddock and Gruyère béchamel sauce), and chateaubriand beef. ⊠ *The Savoy, Strand, Covent Garden, WC2* ☎ *020/7592–1600* ⌂ *Reservations essential* 𝚗 *Jacket required* ⊟ *AE, MC, V* Ⓤ *Covent Garden.*

ENGLISH
★ £££

✕ **Rules.** Come, escape from the 21st century. Opened in 1798, London's oldest restaurant—and gorgeous institution—has welcomed everyone from Charles Dickens to the current Prince of Wales. It's one of the single most beautiful dining salons in London: plush red banquettes and lacquered Regency yellow walls crammed with oil paintings, engravings, and Victorian cartoons. The menu includes fine historic dishes—try roast beef and Yorkshire pudding or the steak-and-kidney pudding for a taste of the 18th century. Daily specials will, in season, include game from Rules' Teesdale estate. ⊠ *35 Maiden La., Covent Garden, WC2* ☎ *020/ 7836–5314* ⊟ *AE, DC, MC, V* Ⓤ *Covent Garden.*

ITALIAN ✕ **Bertorelli's.** Across from the stage door of the Royal Opera House,
£–£££ Bertorelli's is reliable, chic, and convenient for pre- or post-performance meals. The food is tempting, and the menu is just innovative enough: typical dishes include asparagus ravioli, swordfish, and char-grilled beef with truffle oil. There's a café-bar below and a restaurant above, and branches at 19–23 Charlotte Street in Bloomsbury and 11–13 Frith Street in Soho. ⊠ *44A Floral St., Covent Garden, WC2* ☎ *020/7836–3969* ⊟ *AE, DC, MC, V* ⊘ *Closed Sun.* Ⓤ *Covent Garden.*

£–£££ ✕ **Orso.** Showbiz people gravitate to the mid-range Tuscan-inspired food here in Covent Garden. It's not surprising that Orso shares the same snappy attitude as its sister restaurant, Joe Allen. The menu changes daily but always includes excellent pizza and pasta dishes plus entrées based, perhaps, on zucchini and mascarpone or roast sea bass. ⊠ *27 Wellington St., Covent Garden, WC2* ☎ *020/7240–5269* ⚲ *Reservations essential* ⊟ *AE, MC, V* Ⓤ *Covent Garden.*

PAN-ASIAN ✕ **Asia de Cuba.** Like the trendy St. Martins Lane hotel it resides in, funky
£££–£££££ Asia de Cuba is designed by Philippe Starck. It's bold and loud—check out the dangly light bulbs, Latino music, library books, mini-TVs, and satin-clad pillars. The food is Pan-Asian fusion and you're encouraged to share the family portions. The miso black cod is delicious, as is the calamari salad. Cheap it ain't, but it's certainly disco. ⊠ *45 St. Martin's La., Covent Garden, WC2* ☎ *020/7300–5588* ⊟ *AE, DC, MC, V* Ⓤ *Leicester Sq.*

SEAFOOD ✕ **J Sheekey.** The A-list go here as an alternative to the Ivy. Sleek and
★ **££–£££££** discreet, and linked with Theaterland, J Sheekey is one of Londoners' favorite finds. It charms with wood paneling, alcove tables, cracked tiles, and lava-rock bar tops. Opt for jellied eel, Dover sole, fish stew, cod tongue, and famous Sheekey fish pie. ■ TIP→ **Save money with the weekend three-course lunch for £21.50.** ⊠ *28–32 St. Martin's Ct., Covent Garden, WC2* ☎ *020/7240–2565* ⊟ *AE, DC, MC, V* Ⓤ *Leicester Sq.*

£–££ ✕ **Rock & Sole Plaice.** The appalling pun announces London's oldest fish-and-chips joint, complete with inside seating. In addition to salmon, sole, and plaice, there's the usual cod and haddock—battered, deep-fried, and served with rough-cut french fries, ready for the salt and vinegar shakers. ⊠ *47 Endell St., Covent Garden, WC2* ☎ *020/7836–3785* ⊟ *MC, V* Ⓤ *Covent Garden.*

VEGETARIAN ✕ **Food for Thought.** Although this is an unfussy vegetarian restaurant
£ with no liquor license, you can often find a line of people down the stairs here. It has communal tables and the good-value menu of soups, stir-fries, casseroles, and the like changes daily. Wheat-free, GM (genetically modified) -free, and vegan options are available, too. Note that it closes at 8:30 PM. ⊠ *31 Neal St., Covent Garden, WC2* ☎ *020/7836–9072*

⊜ *Reservations not accepted* ▭ *No credit cards* ☉ *Closed Christmas wk* Ⓤ *Covent Garden.*

Hammersmith

The claim to fame of this Thames-side Georgian village outpost is that it's on the route of the annual Oxford and Cambridge University rowing river "boat race." It's home to a multitude of hearty neighborhood restaurants and a shining star, the River Café, that can still pull in foodies from the outer Hebrides.

FRENCH ✕ **Chez Kristof.** Chez Kristof cleans ups in Brackenbury village with this
£–££££ perfect neighborhood pitch on Hammersmith Grove. The corner site has a spare look—muted greys, whites, and browns—and attracts swarms of locals. The modern French brasserie food can be salty, but it's more hit than miss—razor clam stew, ox cheek, pig's head, or veal trotters all sing for their supper. Go for the buzz, the terrace tables in summer, or the relaxed but glamorous West End vibe. ⊠ *111 Hammersmith Grove, Hammersmith, W6* ☎ *020/741–1177* ⊜ *Reservations essential* ▭ *AE, DC, MC, V* Ⓤ *Hammersmith.*

ITALIAN ✕ **River Café.** This canteen-style destination Italian spot started a trend
£££££ with its single-estate olive oils, simple roasts, and impeccably sourced ingredients. Chefs Rose Gray and Ruth Rogers use ultrafresh, seasonal ingredients, so expect salmon with Sicilian lemons, calamari with red pepper salsa, and pork and pancetta—plus one of London's highest checks. But remember: if you snag an evening table, this is in distant Hammersmith, and you may be stranded if you haven't booked a cab. Note that tables must be cleared by 11 PM. ⊠ *Thames Wharf, Rainville Rd., Hammersmith, W6* ☎ *020/7386–4200* ⊜ *Reservations essential* ▭ *AE, DC, MC, V* Ⓤ *Hammersmith.*

Hampstead

This northern district has scores of chains, canteens, neighborhood joints, noodle bars, and gastro-pubs, but the trick is finding diamonds among the diamanté.

CAFÉS ✕ **Coffee Cup.** A Hampstead landmark, this smoky, dingy, uncomfort-
£ able café is cheap and lovable, and always packed. You can get grills, sandwiches, cakes, fry-ups, plus anything (beans, eggs, kippers, mushrooms) on toast—nothing whatsoever healthy or fashionable. The Coffee Cup has no liquor license, but does have outdoor seating in summer. ⊠ *74 Hampstead High St., Hampstead, NW3* ☎ *020/7435–7565* ⊜ *Reservations not accepted* ▭ *No credit cards* Ⓤ *Hampstead.*

CONTEMPORARY ✕ **The Wells.** This gastro-pub–restaurant hybrid rests in a sturdy 18th-
£–£££ century tavern at the foothills of Hampstead. It's not a bargain—this is Hampstead, after all—but the soups deliver (try Jerusalem artichoke with truffle). Upstairs is more expensive, but the real fun is at the ground floor bar, perfect for Sunday lunch after a romp on the Heath. ⊠ *30 Well Walk, Hampstead, NW3* ☎ *020/7794–3785* ▭ *MC, V* Ⓤ *Hampstead.*

Knightsbridge

Host to the food halls of Harrods and Harvey Nichols department stores—as well as to the stunning parade of fashion boutiques on Sloane Street—Knightsbridge, at last, has a deck of destination restaurants to complement its glitz. Zuma, Le Cercle, and the Capital are real leaders of the pack. Alas, it's oh-so expensive, but for nonhigh rollers there's always world-class window shopping to enjoy.

CONTEMPORARY
£–££££

✕ **The Enterprise.** A hot gastro-pub for upperclass "Sloanes" near Brompton Cross, the Enterprise is filled with decorative types who complement the striped wallpaper, Edwardian side tables covered with baskets, vintage books piled up in the windows, white linen, and fresh flowers. The heartiness of the room contributes to a fun experience. Like the decor, the menu is eclectic—venison and red wine or sea bass with roasted fennel. ✉ *35 Walton St., Knightsbridge, SW3* ☎ *020/7584–3148* ⊟ *AE, MC, V* Ⓤ *South Kensington.*

FRENCH
£££££

✕ **The Capital.** The haute cuisine is nearly peerless at this clublike dining room that retains a grown-up atmosphere and formal service. Chef Eric Chavot conjures up superb and classic French dishes. Try frogs' legs with veal sweetbreads, foie gras with pumpkin risotto, roast pigeon and bacon, or crab lasagna. Desserts follow the same exceptional route. ■ TIP➔ Bargain set-price lunch menus (£29.50) are more affordable than dinner (£48–£68). ✉ *22–24 Basil St., Knightsbridge, SW3* ☎ *020/7589–5171* ⚱ *Reservations essential* ⊟ *AE, DC, MC, V* Ⓤ *Knightsbridge.*

££££
Fodor'sChoice
★

✕ **Le Cercle.** Prepare to be wowed by knockout new French cuisine at this ground-breaking restaurant and bar set in a steep, slick basement off Sloane Square. The tapas-style portions of steak tartare, foie gras, pigs trotters, quails eggs, and wild mushrooms cry out to be shared. ■ TIP➔ Four to six dishes generally suffice; try wines by the glass for each round of surprises. ✉ *1 Wilbraham Pl., Knightsbridge, SW1* ☎ *020/7901–9999* ⚱ *Reservations essential* ⊟ *AE, MC, V* ✆ *Closed Sun. and Mon.* Ⓤ *Sloane Sq.*

££–££££

✕ **Brasserie St. Quentin.** French expats and locals frequent this popular slice of Paris in Knightsbridge. Every inch of France is explored—queen scallops, snails, pheasant, partridge, fillet of beef brioche, tarte tatin—in the bourgeois provincial comfort that so many London chains (Dômes) try for but fail to achieve. ✉ *243 Brompton Rd., Knightsbridge, SW3* ☎ *020/7589–8005* ⊟ *AE, DC, MC, V* Ⓤ *South Kensington.*

££–££££

✕ **La Poule au Pot.** Americans and the Chelsea set swoon over this candlelight corner of France in Belgravia, where exposed walls, rustic furniture, and potted roses on tables make for romantic meals. Though not spectacular, the country cooking is decent and rustic. The *poule au pot* (stewed chicken) and goose with butterbeans are strong and hearty, and there are fine classics, such as beef bourguignonne and French onion soup. ✉ *231 Ebury St., Knightsbridge, SW1* ☎ *020/7730–7763* ⚱ *Reservations essential* ⊟ *AE, DC, MC, V* Ⓤ *Sloane Sq.*

INDIAN
£–£££££

✕ **Amaya.** The demanding and hard-to-fool denizens of Knightsbridge (and beyond) have anointed Amaya the new posh Indian kid on the block. The dark-wood paneling, terra-cotta statues, rosewood candles, and

15

Afternoon Tea

THE ENGLISH AFTERNOON tea ritual has been quietly brewing among London polite society. Perhaps it's an anti-Starbucks thing, but nevertheless, it is now ever *so* fashionable to take afternoon tea.

So, what is afternoon tea, exactly? Well, it means real tea (English Breakfast, Ceylon, Indian, or Chinese—and preferably loose leaf) brewed in a china pot, and usually served with china cups and saucers and silver spoons any time between 3 and 5:30 PM daily. In particularly grand places—such as some bigger hotels—there should be elegant finger foods on a three-tiered silver tea stand: bread and butter, and crustless cucumber, watercress, and egg sandwiches on the bottom; scones with clotted cream and strawberry preserve in the middle; and rich fruitcake and fancies on top.

Dress is smart casual in posh hotels, and conversation should by tradition avoid politics and religion. Make reservations for all these below, unless otherwise noted.

✕ **Brown's.** This classic English town-house hotel gains handsomely from recent renovations and sets the standard at the Tea Room, where one of London's best-known afternoon teas is served. Brown's may rely on its reputation somewhat, but still, everyone swears by its divine armchairs. For £36.50, you get sandwiches, scones with cream and jam, tart, fruitcake, and shortbread. ⊠ *33 Albermarle St., Mayfair, W1* ☎ *020/7493-6020* ⊟ *AE, DC, MC, V* ⏱ *Tea daily 2-6* Ⓤ *Green Park.*

✕ **Cafe at Sotheby's.** What could be better than perusing the finest art, sculpture, and antiques at this famous

Mayfair auction house before afternoon tea? It's open from 9:30 AM and tends to book up days in advance. ⊠ *Sotheby's Auction House, 34 New Bond St., Mayfair, W1* ☎ *020/ 7293-5077* ⏱ *Reservations essential* ⊟ *AE, DC, MC, V* ⏱ *Tea weekdays 3-4:45* Ⓤ *Oxford Circus.*

✕ **Claridge's.** This is the real McCoy, with liveried footmen proffering sandwiches, scones, and superior patisseries (£31.50 for traditional tea, £40 for champagne tea) in the palatial yet genteel foyer, to the sound of the resident "Hungarian orchestra." ⊠ *Brook St., Mayfair, W1* ☎ *020/ 7629-8860* ⊟ *AE, DC, MC, V* ⏱ *Tea served daily at 3, 5, 5:30* Ⓤ *Bond St.*

✕ **Fortnum & Mason.** Upstairs at the Queen's grocers, three set teas are ceremoniously served: standard afternoon tea (sandwiches, scones, and cakes: £22.50), old-fashioned high tea (the traditional nursery meal, adding something more robust and savory: £24.50), and champagne tea (£27.50). ⊠ *St. James's Restaurant, 4th fl., 181 Piccadilly, St. James's, W1* ☎ *020/7734-8040 Ext. 2241* ⊟ *AE, DC, MC, V* ⏱ *Tea Mon.-Sat. 3-5:30* Ⓤ *Green Park.*

✕ **Harrods.** For sweet-tooths, the fourth-floor Georgian Restaurant at this well-known department store has a high tea that will give you a sugar rush for a week. ⊠ *87-135 Brompton Rd., Knightsbridge, SW3* ☎ *020/ 7730-1234* ⊟ *AE, DC, MC, V* ⏱ *Tea weekdays 3:30-5:30, Sat. 4-5:30* Ⓤ *Knightsbridge.*

✕ **Kandy Tea House.** This Sri Lankan-run tiny tearoom, off Kensington Church Street, specializes in Ceylon tea (including high grown from Nuwara Eliya). There's delightful cream tea (£8 per person) with homemade scones, clotted cream, and jam, or afternoon tea with cucumber sandwiches. ⊠ *4 Holland St., Kensington, W8* ☎ *020/7937-3001* ⊟ *MC, V* ⊙ *Wed.-Fri. noon-5 PM, weekends noon-6 PM* Ⓤ *High St. Kensington.*

✕ **The Orangery at Kensington Palace.** This Georgian, gorgeous, sunlight-flooded, yes, orangery is the perfect place for a light lunch or tea. You can get homemade soups and quiche, cakes, shortbread, pastries, and pots of Earl Grey. Go when it's balmy, or you'll freeze. ⊠ *Kensington Gardens, Holland Park, W8* ☎ *020/7376-0239* ⊟ *AE, MC, V* Ⓤ *High St. Kensington, Queensway.*

✕ **The Original Maids of Honour.** A trip to Kew Royal Botanical Gardens is topped off with tea at Maids of Honour. The family-run business is famous for its cakes—puff pastry with sweet curd—made from a secret recipe. Prices are low, there's outdoor seating, and it's near Kew's main Victoria Gate entrance. ⊠ *288 Kew Rd., Kew, TW9* ☎ *020/8940-2752* ⊟ *MC, V* ⊙ *Mon 9:30 AM-1 PM, Tues.-Sat. 9:30 AM-6 PM* Ⓤ *Kew Gardens.*

✕ **Patisserie Valerie at Sagne.** Scoff decadent patisseries with afternoon tea at this ever-reliable, reasonably priced, and stylish café. It's a perfect Marylebone High Street resting point, and you'll adore the towering cakes, chandelier, and murals on the walls. ⊠ *105 Marylebone High St., Marylebone, W1* ☎ *020/7935-6240* ⊟ *AE, MC, V* ⊙ *Weekdays 7:30 AM-7 PM, Sat. 8 AM-7 PM, Sun. 9 AM-6 PM* Ⓤ *Marylebone.*

✕ **The Ritz.** The Ritz's huge, stagy, sometimes cold and overly formal Palm Court orchestrates cake stands, silver pots, a harpist, and Louis XVI chaises, plus a great deal of rococo gilt and glitz, all for £34. Reserve four weeks ahead, more for weekends. ⊠ *150 Piccadilly, St. James's, W1* ☎ *020/7493-8181* ⊟ *AE, DC, MC, V* ⊙ *Tea daily 11:30, 1:30, 3:30, and 5:30* Ⓤ *Green Park.*

✕ **The Savoy.** The glamorous Thames-side hotel does one of the most pleasant teas (£28 or £35.50). Its triple-tier cake stands are packed with goodies, and its tailcoated waiters are wonderfully polite. ⊠ *Strand, Covent Garden, WC2* ☎ *020/7836-4343* ⊟ *AE, DC, MC, V* ⊙ *Tea daily 2-4, 4-6* Ⓤ *Charing Cross.*

15

sparkly chandelier set an upscale tone, but it's the spicy grilled fish and meats from the open show-kitchen that get the juices flowing. Watch the chefs produce goodies from the tandoor oven, *sigri* (a charcoal grill) and *tawa* iron skillet, but mind those prices—they're dangerously high. ⊠ *Halkin Arcade, 19 Motcomb St., Knightsbridge, SW1* ☎ *0870/780–8174* ⌖ *Reservations essential* ⊟ *AE, DC, MC, V* Ⓤ *Knightsbridge.*

ITALIAN
£££££
✕ **Zafferano.** Cartier-wearing Belgravians flock to Zafferano, one of London's best exponents of *cucina nuova*. The fireworks are in the kitchen, and *what* fireworks: venison and polenta, John Dory and green olives. The desserts are *delizioso*, especially the chocolate fondant tiramisu. ⊠ *15 Lowndes St., Knightsbridge, SW1* ☎ *020/7235–5800* ⌖ *Reservations essential* ⊟ *AE, DC, MC, V* Ⓤ *Knightsbridge.*

JAPANESE
£££££
✕ **Zuma.** Hats off to this fashionable, Tokyo-style Japanese restaurant. Superbly lighted and designed, with polished granite, blond wood, and exposed pipes, it includes a bar, robata grill, and sushi counter, which takes no reservations. Try the succulent soft-shell crab, black cod wrapped in papery hoba leaf, and *wagyuu* beef. A "sake sommelier" is on hand to help navigate their 30 varieties of rice wine. ⊠ *5 Raphael St., Knightsbridge, SW7* ☎ *020/7584–1010* ⌖ *Reservations essential* ⊟ *AE, DC, MC, V* Ⓤ *Knightsbridge.*

Mayfair

English Monopoly board's top site, Mayfair is central London's most aristocratic area, home to the crème de la crème. With an influx of hedge-fund and trading houses, there's no shortage of top-end talent to keep restaurants busy. From Le Gavroche to Nobu and the Greenhouse, it's quality all the way, with little for the budget-minded.

CONTEMPORARY
£££££
✕ **Angela Hartnett's Menu.** The old-world atmosphere at these mahogany-panel dining rooms in the quintessential English Connaught is refreshed, thanks to chef Hartnett's cuisine. The modern European menu (with homage to Italy, the Mediterranean, Pays Basque, and Spain) is a far cry from the steak-and-kidney pudding and carved beef-of-old-England days of yore—although some interpretations of die-hard Connaught classics remain. Enjoy tortelli with Swiss chard and sea bream and salsify. ⊠ *The Connaught, Carlos Pl., Mayfair, W1* ☎ *020/7592–1222* ⌖ *Reservations essential* ⊟ *AE, DC, MC, V* Ⓤ *Green Park.*

£££££
✕ **Greenhouse.** Hidden behind Mayfair mansions and approached via a spot-lighted garden, this elegant salon is for aficionados of top-class and inventive French cuisine at any price. Sit by the garden windows and feast on foie gras with espresso syrup and Amaretto foam, sea-urchin panna cotta, or Limousin veal sweetbreads. The epic 90-odd page wine

book spans 2,000 bins, including Château d'Yquem (1887–1990). ✉ *27A Hay's Mews, Mayfair, W1* ☎ *020/7499–3331* ⚲ *Reservations essential* ▭ *AE, DC, MC, V* ⊘ *Closed Sun. No lunch Sat.* Ⓤ *Green Park.*

FRENCH ✕ **Gordon Ramsay at Claridge's.** There's a grand and gracious atmosphere
★ **£££££** at one of London's favorite celebration restaurants (Prime Minister Tony Blair had his 50th here). Consider the three-course lunches (£30), or the opulent set dinners (£60 and £70). Try Gloucester Old Spot pork belly or foie gras and goose breast with Périgord truffle. Book months ahead—choosing a Sunday evening is more likely to yield success. Arrive early for drinks at Claridge's art deco cocktail bar, one of the sassiest in town. ✉ *Claridge's, Brook St., Mayfair, W1* ☎ *020/7499–0099* ⚲ *Reservations essential* 👔 *Jacket required* ▭ *AE, MC, V* Ⓤ *Bond St.*

£££££ ✕ **Le Gavroche.** Chef Michel Roux Jr. inherits the family culinary gene
Fodor's Choice and outperforms at this clubby haven, which some critics rate the best
★ dining in London. His mastery of classic French cuisine—formal, flowery, decorated—makes the fixed-price lunch seem relatively affordable at £44 (with a half bottle of wine, water, and coffee included). In fact, lunch may be the best way to eat here if you don't have an expense account, which most patrons clearly do. Book at least a week in advance. ✉ *43 Upper Brook St., Mayfair, W1* ☎ *020/7408–0881* ⚲ *Reservations essential* ▭ *AE, DC, MC, V* ⊘ *Closed 10 days at Christmas. No lunch weekends* Ⓤ *Marble Arch.*

£££££ ✕ **The Square.** Chef Philip Howard's sophisticated set menus, in the modern French haute tradition, include dishes such as foie gras with muscat grapes or Bresse pigeon with butternut squash, followed perhaps by bitter chocolate fondant. Some say the decor lacks in the character department, but everything else purrs along. The clientele is heavy on corporate executives who appreciate impeccable service. There's a long wine list and an expert sommelier. ✉ *6–10 Bruton St., Mayfair, W1* ☎ *020/ 7495–7100* ⚲ *Reservations essential* ▭ *AE, DC, MC, V* ⊘ *No lunch weekends* Ⓤ *Green Park.*

£££–£££££ ✕ **Mirabelle.** There's a foxy vibe at this established '50s Mayfair basement restaurant. The interior is lavish and sparkly, and the food is an excellent interpretation of French with a hint of Italian. Expect silky seafood (grilled skate wing and winkles) and some good meat creations—loin of lamb and daube of beef stand out. The chocolate fondant dessert is a clear knockout, as is the tarte tatin. ✉ *56 Curzon St., Mayfair, W1* ☎ *020/7499–4636* ⚲ *Reservations essential* ▭ *AE, MC, V* Ⓤ *Green Park.*

★ **££–££££** ✕ **Bellamy's.** The Mayfair society crowd loves this uppercrust French brasserie for simple reasons: the discreet front of house, reassuring menu, classy-but-restrained decor, and the fabulously priced all-French wine list. The carte weaves from scrambled eggs with Perigord truffles, through whitebait, coquilles St. Jacques, to entrecote of beef, rillettes of duck, and *iles flottantes* ("floating islands"—egg custard topped with egg whites). ■ TIP➔ **The entrance is through a posh delicatessen next to the restaurant.** ✉ *18–18A Bruton Pl., Mayfair, W1* ☎ *020/7491–2727* ▭ *AE, DC, MC, V* Ⓤ *Green Park.*

15

Dining with Children

UNLESS YOUR CHILDREN behave impeccably, the key is to avoid the high-class establishments; you won't find a children's menu there, anyway. London's many Italian restaurants and pizzerias are popular with kids. Or take the children to Chinatown: it's welcoming, and a colorful and interesting experience. China House serves kids' portions and Chinese arts-and-crafts activities from 1 PM to 4 PM every week. Activities vary but include magicians, caricaturists, and origami experts. Browns (the brasserie) and the ubiquitous Pizza Express chain are family-friendly. At Sweeney Todd's, clowns and magicians provide entertainment on weekends. Hard Rock Cafe and Capital Radio Café have lively, musical atmospheres. There's a colorful

interior, a children's menu, and a helpful staff at Giraffe. At the laid-back Carluccio's Caffé, there are half-portions for kids and scrumptious Italian food for parents.

Browns (⊠ 82–84 St. Martin's La., WC2 ☎ 020/7491–5050). **Capital Radio Café** (⊠ Leicester Sq., WC2 ☎ 020/7484–8888). **Carluccio's Caffé** (⊠ 236 Fulham Rd., SW10 ☎ 020/ 7376–5960). **China House** (⊠ 51 Marchmont St., WC1 ☎ 020/ 7836–1626). **Giraffe** (⊠ 7 Kensington High St., W8 ☎ 020/7938–1221). **Hard Rock Cafe** (⊠ 150 Old Park La., W1 ☎ 020/7629–0382). **Sweeney Todd's** (⊠ 3–5 Tooley St., SE1 ☎ 020/ 7407–5267). **Sticky Fingers** (⊠ 1A Phillimore Gardens, W8 ☎ 020/ 7938–5338).

ITALIAN
£££–£££££
Fodor'sChoice
★

✕ **Locanda Locatelli.** Chef Giorgio Locatelli has the golden touch—hence the mile-long waiting list at this sexy Italian restaurant, replete with convex mirrors, beige banquettes, and cherry-wood dividers. The food is accomplished—superb risottos, handmade pastas, gorgeous fish, beautiful desserts. Be bold and try the nettle risotto or calves' kidney, and lose yourself in the all-Italian wine list. ⊠ 8 Seymour St., Mayfair, W1 ☎ 020/ 7935–9088 ⌖ Reservations essential ▤ AE, MC, V Ⓤ Marble Arch.

JAPANESE
££££–£££££

✕ **Nobu.** Within the Metropolitan, a so-hip-it-hurts hotel, soccer (that's football to the English) stars—and occasionally their wives—haunt London's top celebrity hangout and pay silly money for new-style sashimi with a Peruvian touch. Nobu Berkeley, a spin-off, rocks nearby (no reservations for parties under six), and Ubon (that's "Nobu" backwards), a sister restaurant, thrives in the east-side Canary Wharf business section. ⊠ Metropolitan Hotel, 19 Old Park La., Mayfair, W1 ☎ 020/ 7447–4747 ⌖ Reservations essential ▤ AE, DC, MC, V Ⓤ Hyde Park.

Notting Hill & Bayswater

Notting Hill or Notting *Hell*? The invasion of bankers, brokers, yuppies, dinks (double income, no kids), Ruperts, and Camillas has skewed the mixed boho vibe of old. It doesn't seem right, but it's gentrify or die these days, so expect Bentleys and Rollers, and ridiculous prices. In summer, dining outdoors near Portobello Market is the thing to do.

AMERICAN-
CASUAL
£–££££

✗ **Harlem.** A hip, young party crowd heads to Harlem for the American soul food, DJ-bar, and late liquor license. There are gumbo, BBQ ribs, buttermilk chicken, blueberry cheesecake, and Brooklyn beers, but it's the pretty people and downstairs club (open until 2 AM Monday–Saturday) that really pull them in. ⊠ *78 Westbourne Grove, Notting Hill, W2* ☎ *020/7985–0900* ⌣ *Reservations essential* ▭ *AE, DC, MC, V* Ⓤ *Queensway.*

BURMESE
£

✗ **Mandalay.** Bargain hunters have caught on to the nifty value for money at this tiny, 20-seat stalwart canteen run by two smiling Burmese brothers. All dishes are less than £7; bookings are recommended. Don't go for romance, but instead tuck into Burmese tea-leaf or papaya and cucumber salad, any of the fritters, or chicken, shrimp, and lime soup—you'll leave with change from a £20 note. ⊠ *444 Edgware Rd., Notting Hill, W2* ☎ *020/7258–3696* ⌣ *Reservations essential* ▭ *AE, DC, MC, V* Ⓤ *Edgware Rd.*

CONTEMPORARY
£££££

✗ **Clarke's.** The great Sally Clarke's daily changing, no-choice set dinners (£36—£49.50) contain ultrafresh ingredients, plainly but perfectly cooked, accompanied by home-baked breads. ▧ TIP→ **Ask to sit in the more atmospheric basement with views of the open kitchen, perfect for a tête-à-tête.** ⊠ *124 Kensington Church St., Notting Hill, W8* ☎ *020/7221–9225* ⌣ *Reservations essential* ▭ *AE, DC, MC, V* ☉ *Closed Sun. No lunch Sat.* Ⓤ *Notting Hill Gate.*

£££–££££

✗ **Kensington Place.** A favorite among the local chatterati, KP is packed, informal, and noisy. A giant plate-glass window and mural are backdrops to fashionable food—seared scallops and pea puree and lemon tart are perennials—but it's the relaxed vibe that draws the faces. ⊠ *201 Kensington Church St., Notting Hill, W8* ☎ *020/7727–3184* ▭ *AE, DC, MC, V* Ⓤ *Notting Hill Gate.*

£££

✗ **Cow Dining Room.** A chic gastro-pub, the Cow comprises a faux-Dublin 1950s backroom bar that serves rock oysters, salmon cakes, baked brill, and Cornish crab. Upstairs the chef whips up Brit specialties—roast chicken, ox tongue, lambs' kidneys, and black pudding are typical temptations. Notting Hill locals love the house special in the bar area: draft Guinness with a pint of prawns. ⊠ *89 Westbourne Park Rd., Notting Hill, W2* ☎ *020/7221–0021* ⌣ *Reservations essential* ▭ *MC, V* Ⓤ *Westbourne Park.*

££–£££

✗ **The Waterway.** The Little Venice, canal-side aspect is the big appeal at this rated gastro-pub. In summertime the canal-facing outside terrace heaves with local glitterati, who enjoy Pimms, posing, and BBQ burgers. Inside is cosy like a chalet, with a friendly open bar—all browns and burgundy—and a dining area. Expect clean and serene cooking; roast cod and peas is typical, and recommended. ⊠ *54 Formosa St., Notting Hill, W9* ☎ *020/7266–3557* ▭ *AE, MC, V* Ⓤ *Warwick Ave. Gate.*

£–£££
Fodor$Choice
★

✗ **Electric Brasserie.** There's nowhere better for people-watching than the Electric on Portobello Road's market day. Go for the bustle of the interior, too—zinc fittings, mirrors, and flattering lighting—and expect oysters, steaks, chunky sandwiches, and seafood platters. Or just settle in at the bar with a long drink. ⊠ *191 Portobello Rd., Notting Hill, W11* ☎ *020/7908–9696* ▭ *AE, DC, MC, V* Ⓤ *Notting Hill.*

15

£–££ ✕ **The Salusbury.** Previously unknown, the Queen's Park section is dubbed "Notting Hill North" now thanks to winning venues like the Salusbury. Sitting at the heart of the neighborhood action, it's a noisy, fumy, residential boozer, with enough creative spunk in its two-star quality dining room to keep the trendy QP denizens coming back for more. The chops, braised meats, and slow roasts are mighty soothing during the cold winter months. ⊠ *50–52 Salusbury Rd., Notting Hill, NW6* 🕾 *020/7328–3286* ⊟ *MC, V* Ⓤ *Queen's Park.*

CONTINENTAL ✕ **The Belvedere.** There's no finer setting for a summer Sunday lunch
££–£££ than a table by the window—except, perhaps, one by the balcony if you're lucky—at this elegant restaurant in the middle of Holland Park. The menu sticks to brasserie favorites, ranging from filet of ling (cod) to partridge, and there are nice weekend three-course lunch deals for £22.50. ⊠ *Holland Park, off Abbotsbury Rd., Notting Hill, W8* 🕾 *020/7602–1238* ⌖ *Reservations essential* ⊟ *AE, MC, V* ☻ *No dinner Sun.* Ⓤ *Holland Park.*

ENGLISH ✕ **Julie's.** This cute '60s throwback with a pop-star past has two main
££–£££ parts: a stylish wine bar and a basement restaurant, both filled with Victoriana and ecclesiastical furniture. Bryan Ferry and Jerry Hall came in their heyday; now it's their kids who come for a nostalgia trip. The cooking is old-fashioned English (pheasant-and-hare terrine, guinea fowl, and figs) and Sunday lunches are popular. In summer there's a garden room for alfresco eating. ⊠ *135–137 Portland Rd., Notting Hill, W11* 🕾 *020/ 7229–8331* ⊟ *AE, MC, V* Ⓤ *Holland Park.*

FRENCH ✕ **The Ledbury.** Top-bracket fine dining has arrived at the doorstep of
££££–£££££ Notting Hill's ultra-high-net-worth citizens. Run by the team behind Chez Bruce in Wandsworth, Ledbury is where to go for highly refined cuisine. It's not cheap—£45 for a three-course dinner—but it's super smart and professional. Marvel at the loin of hare—and there's a short list of fine wines, including 20 half bottles, and seven sherries by the glass. ⊠ *127 Ledbury Rd., Notting Hill, W11* 🕾 *0207/7792–9090* ⊟ *AE, MC, V* Ⓤ *Westbourne Park.*

MIDDLE EASTERN ✕ **Alounak.** It may be raffish, but the Iranian food here is tried and true.
£–££ Locals come for the hot bread and kebabs that emerge from the clay oven by the door. Try the chicken kebab or the *zereshk polo* (chicken with Iranian berries). Take Iranian black tea and Persian sweets, but note the sour yogurt drinks are not to everyone's liking. ⊠ *44 Westbourne Grove, Bayswater, W2* 🕾 *020/7229–4158* ⊟ *DC, MC, V* Ⓤ *Queensway.*

PAN-ASIAN ✕ **E&O.** If you like star-spotting, you'll enjoy E&O, one of London's
★ £–££££ hippest scene bars and restaurants. E&O means Eastern and Oriental, and the intelligent mix of Chinese, Japanese, Vietnamese, and Thai cuisines includes *beaucoup* vegetarian options. Don't skip the dumplings, black cod, Thai rare-beef, or mango and papaya salads. ⊠ *14 Blenheim Crescent, Notting Hill, W11* 🕾 *020/7229–5454* ⌖ *Reservations essential* ⊟ *AE, DC, MC, V* Ⓤ *Ladbroke Grove.*

POLISH ✕ **Wódka.** This popular neighborhood restaurant is loaded with locals
££–£££ and often seems like it's hosting one big, modern Polish dinner party. Alongside the salmon, herring, caviar, and eggplant blinis, you might find partridge or roast duck. Order a carafe of the purest vodka in London; it's encased in ice and flavored (with cherries, bison grass, and black currant) by the owner, an erstwhile Polish prince. ⊠ *12 St. Alban's Grove, Kensington, W8* ☎ *020/7937–6513* ⌗ *Reservations essential* ⊟ *AE, MC, V* ☺ *No lunch weekends* Ⓤ *High St. Kensington.*

THAI ✕**Churchill Thai Kitchen.** There's a cult appeal to this super-value Thai kitchen
£ attached to a traditional English pub. With big portions of all dishes priced at £5.85, it's a bargain for this high-end postal district, and full most nights. The pad thai noodles are a good bet, as are the red-and-green curries. Mind the abundant foliage in the conservatory. ⊠ *Churchill Arms, 119 Kensington Church St., Notting Hill, W8* ☎ *020/7792–1246* ⊟ *MC, V* Ⓤ *Notting Hill Gate, High St. Kensington.*

15

St. James's

From swanky perennials (Le Caprice) to design-led emporiums (Sketch: Gallery) to grand cafés (the Wolseley) to classic institutions (the Ritz), it's hard not to find something that fits in St. James's, one of the smartest sections in London.

AUSTRIAN ✕ **The Wolseley.** Enjoy grand elegance at this classic run by Messrs.
£–££££ Corbin and King, London's top restaurateurs. Framed with black lac-
Fodor$Choice querware, the Viennese-style café begins its long, decadent days with
★ breakfast at 7 AM and is open until midnight. Linger morning, noon, and night for Nürnberger bratwurst, Wiener schnitzel, Hungarian goulash, and, for dessert, strudel and *kaiserschmarren* (pancake with stewed fruit). It's particularly ideal for sinful pastries and weekend afternoon tea. ⊠ *160 Piccadilly, St. James's, W1* ☎ *020/7499–6996* ⊟ *AE, DC, MC, V.*

CONTEMPORARY ✕ **Le Caprice.** The glossy '80s Eva Jiricna interior; the perfect service;
£££–£££££ the menu, halfway between Euro-peasant and fashion plate—Le Caprice commands the deepest loyalty of almost any restaurant in London because it gets everything right. From monkfish to forest berries and white chocolate sauce, the food has no business being so good. Frequented by the older variety of celebrity, Le Caprice has some of the best people-watching in town. ⊠ *Arlington House, Arlington St., St. James's, SW1* ☎ *020/7629–2239* ⌗ *Reservations essential* ⊟ *AE, DC, MC, V* Ⓤ *Green Park.*

£££–£££££ ✕ **Sketch: Gallery.** The global fashion crowd totally *gets* the unusual design aesthetic at Mourad Mazouz's gastro-emporium. "Momo's" madcap gamble is all about extremes. The lavish Gallery dining room (a true art gallery space by day) serves carbo-light contemporary cuisine to a funky beat and video projections, and turns into a club Friday and Saturday nights, as soon as staff clear the floor. There's also a bar, cakes in the Parlour Room, lunch in the Glade area, and a lauded "molecular gastronomy" (science-based cuisine) menu in the fine dining, first-

A Dish to Dye For

BEING A BRIT THESE DAYS does generally involve loving curry. Whether or not the British are proud of the exploits of the Empire, one happy consequence has been that tasty, spicy Indian cooking—in particular, chicken tikka masala—has overtaken fish-and-chips as the national dish. Going out for an Indian meal is practically a must when visiting London, and most locals can recommend a favorite restaurant. However, if your chicken tikka appears to glow back at you in a particularly alarming reddy-yellow way, you may have cause for concern.

It appears that Brits would judge the freshness of their chicken tikka not by its taste, but by the brightness of its dyed-orange color. Eager to oblige this expectation of an excitingly exotic hue, some restaurants overstepped the boundaries of the law until recently. In 2003 hungry members of the British Food Standards Agency (FSA) ordered chicken tikka masala from every Indian takeout in the county of Surrey, near London, and found that more than half

of them served up prohibited amounts of food dye.

And to really make you choke on your popadams, the FSA also discovered that same year that Indian spice manufacturers unwittingly had been using traces of the chemical Sudan-I, a carcinogen more commonly used to add a nice hue to your shoes when you give them a polish. This resulted in the mass removal of such products from shelves in many countries, including Britain.

So what are the chances that you'll now hold back from one of the greatest pleasures of modern-day British life? The answer is naan whatsoever. The Sudan-I scare was swiftly and efficiently dealt with as of July 2003, says the FSA. Meanwhile, even the levels of food dye in the Surrey curry scandal won't do you any harm—unless you wolf down a pound of chicken tikka masala a day for many years. Eat responsibly, folks.

–Adam Gold

---

floor Lecture Room, overseen by French legend Pierre Gagnaire. ⊠ 9 *Conduit St., St. James's, W1* ☎ *0870/777–4488* ⚷ *Reservations essential* 🖃 *AE, DC, MC, V* ☉ *Closed Sun.* Ⓤ *Oxford Circus.*

CONTINENTAL ✕ **The Ritz.** This palace of gilt, marble, mirror, and trompe l'oeil would
££££££ moisten Marie Antoinette's eye. Add the view over Green Park and the Ritz's sunken garden, and it seems beside the point to eat. But the cuisine stands up to the visuals, with super-rich morsels—foie gras, lobster, truffles, caviar—all served with a flourish. Englishness is wrested from Louis XVI by a daily roast from the trolley. A three-course lunch at £45 makes the check more bearable than the £75 you would pay for the Friday and Saturday cha-cha-cha dinner-dance (a dying tradition). ⊠ *150 Piccadilly, St. James's, W1* ☎ *020/7493–8181* ⚷ *Reservations essential* 🏛 *Jacket and tie* 🖃 *AE, DC, MC, V* Ⓤ *Green Park.*

FRENCH ✕ **L'Oranger.** The haute cuisine reaches great heights at this special es-
££££–££££££ tablishment in St. James's, whether leek-and-potato cappuccino, John

Dory with langoustine, or the orange soufflé. Service is formal, the conservatory is romantic, and there's a small courtyard where the last duel in London was fought. ⊠ *5 St. James's St., St. James's, SW1* ☎ *020/ 7839–3774* ⌕ *Reservations essential* ⊟ *AE, DC, MC, V* ⊘ *Closed Sun. No lunch Sat.* Ⓤ *Green Park.*

NORTH AFRICAN ✕ **Momo.** It's a fun ticket, so go if you can. Mourad Mazouz—"Momo"
★ **£££** to friends—rocks beau London with his Casbah-like restaurant off Regent Street. There are Moroccan rugs, fur-skin seats, plus a DJ and often live North African music. Downstairs is the members-only Kemia Bar, and next door is Mô—a cozy Moroccan tearoom, open to all. The cuisine, although good, doesn't *quite* live up to the electic atmosphere, but that doesn't stop everyone from having a good time. ⊠ *25 Heddon St., St. James's, W1* ☎ *020/7434–4040* ⌕ *Reservations essential* ⊟ *AE, DC, MC, V* Ⓤ *Piccadilly Circus.*

Soho

15

It's all food, food, and more food in Soho. Coffee shops, noodle stops, teahouses, pizza parlors, burger joints, sushi counters, juice stops, oyster bars, snack stands, cafés, bakeries, brasseries, and patisseries—to highlight but a few things going on in this crazy central London dining district.

CAFÉS ✕ **Bar Italia.** This well-established caffeine-and-stand-up-snack stop is
£ a 24-hour haven for Soho-ites, theatergoers, and late-night clubbers. Expect panettone and pizza, rich chocolate cake, and real cappuccino. The walls are full of nostalgic photos of Italian singers and sporting heroes, and it's the *primo* place in London to watch Italy play in soccer's World Cup. ⊠ *22 Frith St., Soho, W1* ☎ *020/7437–4520* ⊟ *AE, DC, MC, V* Ⓤ *Leicester Sq.*

£ ✕ **Maison Bertaux.** Romantics cherish this tiny, two-story '50s French patisserie because nothing's changed in decades. The pastries and gooey cakes are to die for and are baked on-site; the éclairs are stuffed with light cream, and the Black Forest gâteau is studded with Morello cherries. There are savories, and cute tea services; try not to drool on the window display on the way in or out. ⊠ *28 Greek St., Soho, W1* ☎ *020/7437–6007* ⊟ *No credit cards* Ⓤ *Leicester Sq.*

£ ✕ **New Piccadilly.** Nothing (not even the menu) has changed at this family-run diner since its opening in 1951. The upturned lampshades, Formica tables, and bench seats remain; tea is served in Pyrex, and the food's cheap and cheery. Steak, chips, and spaghetti are £6.50; a banana split, £1.75. Charm is its style. Note it closes at 8:30 PM. ⊠ *8 Denman St., Soho, W1* ☎ *020/7437–8530* ⊟ *No credit cards* Ⓤ *Piccadilly Circus.*

CHINESE ✕ **Fung Shing.** In terms of service and food, this cool-green restaurant
★ **£–£££££** is a cut above the other Lisle–Wardour Street Chinese restaurants. Especially fine and exciting dishes are the crispy baby squid, steamed scallops, and salt-baked chicken, served on or off the bone with a bowl of broth. Reserve a table in the airy backroom conservatory. ⊠ *15 Lisle St., Soho, WC2* ☎ *020/7437–1539* ⊟ *AE, DC, MC, V* Ⓤ *Leicester Sq.*

£–£££££
Fodor'sChoice
★

✕ **Yauatcha.** It's all-day dim sum at this superbly lighted slinky Soho classic. Expertly designed by Christian Liaigre—with a bar-length aquarium, candles, and starry ceiling—the food's a match for the *Sex in the City* setting. There are wicked dim sum (try prawn and scallops), dumplings, and cocktails, and upstairs is a modern pastry shop. ■ TIP→ Note the 90-minute turnaround on tables, and ask to dine in the more romantic basement at night. ✉ *15 Broadwick St., Soho, W1* 🕾 *020/7494–8888* 🖅 *Reservations essential* 🖃 *AE, MC, V* Ⓤ *Oxford Circus.*

CONTINENTAL
££–£££

✕ **L'Escargot.** Everyone feels classy at this old-time Soho haunt that serves French food in a sassy art deco ground-floor salon (there's also the Picasso Room, a first-floor formal dining area, replete with Picasso artwork). The fine wines go well with the wood-pigeon *pithiviers* (filled puff pastry), roast pheasant with juniper, or any of the grilled fish. Owned by restaurateur Marco Pierre White, L'Escargot is relaxed, reliable, grown-up, and glamorous. ✉ *48 Greek St., Soho, W1* 🕾 *020/ 7437–2679* 🖃 *AE, DC, MC, V* ☺ *Closed Sun.* Ⓤ *Leicester Sq.*

ECLECTIC
£–£££

✕ **Andrew Edmunds.** Rustic food at realistic prices defines this perpetually jammed, softly lighted restaurant—though you'll wish it were larger and the seats more forgiving. Tucked away behind Oxford and Carnaby streets, it's a favorite with the media crowd that comes for the daily-changing, fixed-price lunch menus. Starters and main courses draw on the taste of Ireland, the Mediterranen, and Middle East. ✉ *46 Lexington St., Soho, W1* 🕾 *020/7437–5708* 🖃 *MC, V* Ⓤ *Oxford Circus, Piccadilly Circus.*

ENGLISH
🐾 £–£££

✕ **Browns.** Crowd-pleasing, child-friendly English feeding is performed well at this comfortable colonial-style brasserie chain. Salads, burgers, and pastas dominate the menu, but don't overlook king prawns, lamb, roasted peppers, and especially the classic Browns steak-and-Guinness pie. The Browns chain is seven-strong—from Kew to the City. ✉ *82–84 St. Martin's La., Soho, WC2* 🕾 *020/7497–5050* 🖃 *AE, DC, MC, V* Ⓤ *Leicester Sq.*

INDIAN
£–££

✕ **Masala Zone.** The modern canteen approach—shared tables, slick service, and cheap eats—works well at Masala Zone, more a pit-stop than somewhere to linger. The thali option has lots of little portions with rice and *dahl* (lentils), and the samosas and *bhajis* are spicy and delicious. There are other branches at 80 Upper Street in Islington and 147 Earls Court Road in Kensington. ✉ *9 Marshall St., Soho, W1* 🕾 *020/ 7287–9966* 🖃 *MC, V.*

IRISH
★
£££–£££££

✕ **Lindsay House.** Irish chef Richard Corrigan fills up this creaky 1740s Georgian Soho town house with his personality and some of the finest food in town. He's known for his invention—combining scallops with pork belly and veal sweetbreads with cauliflower. He excels with Irish

CLOSE UP

Brunch in Britain?

BRUNCH, IN ALL HONESTY, *hasn't* taken root in Londoners' affections, although more establishments realize they need to keep their kitchens open longer to really turn a dime. Hence, a few decent brunch options are springing up—but mainly for the benefit of out-of-towners.

✕ **Butlers Wharf Chop House.** Brunch here, at £16.95 for three courses, is as British as it gets, with lobster mayonnaise, Stilton and celery soup, and a fabulous Thames-side setting. ✉ *36E Shad Thames, South Bank, SE1* ☎ *020/7403-3403* ▭ *AE, DC, MC, V* ✆ *Brunch served weekends noon–4* Ⓤ *Tower Hill.*

✕ **Christopher's Grill.** Imagine you're in Manhattan at this superior Covent Garden purveyor of American food. They serve everything from pancakes, steak, eggs, and fries to salmon cakes and Caesar salad. ✉ *18 Wellington St., Covent Garden, WC2* ☎ *020/7240-4222* ▭ *AE, DC, MC, V* ✆ *Brunch served weekends 11:30–3* Ⓤ *Covent Garden.*

✕ **Joe Allen.** A hangout famous among theater people, Joe Allen is a place to hide from the British weather and down Bloody Marys. Supplement that with a grilled-chicken sandwich or a salad of spicy sausage, shrimp, and new potatoes. ✉ *13 Exeter St., Covent Garden, WC2* ☎ *020/ 7836-0651* ▭ *AE, MC, V* ✆ *Brunch served weekends 11:30–4* Ⓤ *Covent Garden.*

✕ **The Ivy.** There's enough comfort food at the Ivy to banish the worst of hangovers. Eggs Benedict and kedgeree spring to mind as first choices. The tricky part is getting in. ✉ *1 West St., Covent Garden, WC2* ☎ *020/7836-4751* ✆ *Reservations essential* ▭ *AE, DC, MC, V* Ⓤ *Covent Garden.*

✕ **Veeraswamy.** It's been here since 1926, but the Chutney Mary group from Chelsea has taken it over and made the mezzanine-level space sleek, chic, and full of color. The brunch menu (£15.50 for two courses) is a great way to sample authentic regional Indian cuisines. You may be so taken with the aromatic fish and chicken dishes and mod-Euro-traditional Indian desserts that you'll want to come back for dinner. ✉ *Victory House, 99–101 Regent St., St. James's, W1* ☎ *020/7734-1401* ▭ *AE, DC, MC, V* ✆ *Brunch served Sun. 12:30–3* Ⓤ *Regent St.*

15

---

beef and mash, and his white asparagus and langoustine can't be bettered. Petits fours with coffee will send you home oh-so-happy. ✉ *21 Romilly St., Soho, W1* ☎ *020/7439–0450* ▭ *AE, DC, MC, V* ✆ *Closed Sun.* Ⓤ *Leicester Sq.*

LATIN
£–££ ✕ **Market Place.** It's blond wood all the way at this popular spot off Oxford Street, where a trendy new-media crowd, spread over two floors and a terrace, jams to the DJs every night. There's tasty Latin bar food (roast pumpkin empanadas are especially good), and the bar serves some exotic beers. ✉ *11 Market Pl., Soho W1* ☎ *020/7079–2020* ▭ *AE, MC, V* Ⓤ *Oxford Circus.*

£–£££ ✕ **Randall & Aubin.** Ed Baines's converted French butcher's shop is one of London's buzziest champagne-oyster bars. Go for Loch Fyne oysters, crab, or lobster and french fries. At peak times you'll spend a while at the bar waiting for a seat, but it's worth it. Another popular R&A operates at 329 Fulham Road in Chelsea. ⊠ *14–16 Brewer St., Soho, W1* ☎ *020/7287–4447* ⟨ *Reservations not accepted* ⊟ *AE, DC, MC, V* Ⓤ *Piccadilly Circus.*

The South Bank

From zero to hero in 10 years is a good description of the South Bank dining scene. Exciting things happen now at the formerly bleak south side of the Thames, with the more "push-it" venues—from Anchor & Hope to Baltic—given free reign to experiment.

CONTEMPORARY ✕ **OXO Tower Restaurant & Brasserie.** London has a room with a view—
£££–£££££ and what a view. On the eighth floor of the OXO Tower on the South Bank, this special-occasion restaurant serves Euro-Asian food with classy ingredients (lobster with dandelion salad). Ceiling slats turn from white to blue, but who notices, with St. Paul's Cathedral and the imperial London skyline across the water? ■ TIP→ **The brasserie is cheaper than the restaurant, but both have great river views, especially in summer, when there are tables on the terrace.** ⊠ *Barge House St., South Bank, SE1* ☎ *020/ 7803–3888* ⊟ *AE, DC, MC, V* Ⓤ *Waterloo.*

EASTERN ✕ **Baltic.** To dine well in South-
EUROPEAN wark—perhaps after an art trip to Tate Modern—come to this vodka-
£–£££ party playground. Slick white walls, wooden beams, exposed walls, and
★ an amber chandelier make this converted coach house a sexy spot for drinks or a decent East European meal. Under the same ownership as Chez Kristof in Hammersmith, Baltic serves fine blinis (with caviar or smoked salmon) and tasty gravlax. Siberian, rye, and rose petal are but a few of the killer vodkas on offer. ⊠ *74 Blackfriars Rd., South Bank, SE1* ☎ *020/7928–1111* ⊟ *AE, DC, MC, V* Ⓤ *Southwark.*

> **WORD OF MOUTH**
>
> "I can heartily recommend Baltic, a very cool Polish restaurant with great cocktails. It looks like it should be expensive but is actually quite reasonable." –Kate

ENGLISH ✕ **Anchor & Hope.** Great things at reasonable prices come from the open
££–£££ kitchen at this permanently packed, no-reservations gastro-pub on the
Fodor'sChoice Cut: smoked sprats, and crab on toast are two standouts. It's informal,
★ cramped, and highly original, and there are often dishes for groups (whole shoulder of lamb is a good'un.) Expect to share a table, too. ⊠ *36 The Cut, South Bank, SE1* ☎ *020/7928–9898* ⟨ *Reservations not accepted* ⊟ *MC, V* ⊙ *Closed Sun.* Ⓤ *Waterloo, Southwark.*

FRENCH ✕ **Chez Bruce.** It's a feat to wrest the title of London's favorite restau-
££££ rant from the Ivy, and even more so for a neighborhood joint south of the river on Wandsworth Common. Expect peerless yet relaxed service—and wonders from chef–proprietor Bruce Poole. Dive into the

On the Menu

IN LONDON, LOCAL COULD MEAN any global flavor, but for pure Britishness, roast beef probably tops the list. If you want the best-value traditional Sunday lunch, go to a pub. Gastro-pubs, where Sunday roasts are generally made with top-quality ingredients, are a good bet. The meat is usually served with crisp roast potatoes and carrots, and with the traditional Yorkshire pudding, a savory batter baked in the oven until crisp. A rich, dark gravy is poured on top.

Other tummy liners include shepherd's pie, made with stewed minced lamb and a mashed potato topping and baked until lightly browned on top; cottage pie is a similar dish, but made with minced beef instead of lamb. Steak-and-kidney pie is a delight when done properly: with chunks of lean beef and

ox kidneys, braised with onions and mushrooms in a thick gravy, and topped with a light puff-pastry crust.

Fish-and-chips, usually cod or haddock, comes with thick french fries. A ploughman's lunch in a pub is crusty bread, a strong flavored English cheese with bite (cheddar, blue Stilton, crumbly white Cheshire, or smooth red Leicester), and tangy pickles with a side salad garnish. As for puddings, seek out a sweet bread-and-butter pudding, served hot with layers of bread and dried fruit baked in a creamy custard until lightly crisp. And we musn't forget the English cream tea, which consists of scones served with strawberry jam and clotted cream, and sandwiches made with wafer-thin slices of cucumber—and, of course, plenty of tea.

15

lamb's tongue or calves' brains, or experiment with veal, liver, and kidney, and head out with rum baba. The wines are great, the sommelier's superb, and overall it's all rather lovely. ✉ *2 Bellevue Rd., South Bank, SW17* ☎ *020/8672–0114* ⌛ *Reservations essential* ▤ *AE, MC, V* Ⓤ *Wandsworth Common rail.*

££–£££ ✕ **Chez Gérard.** One of a first-rate chain of steak-*frites* (fries) restaurants—there are 11 across London—this one has widened the choice on the Gallic menu to include more for those who don't eat red meat: for example, cod with mussels and leeks. But for those who do, beef steak with shoestring fries and béarnaise sauce remains the reason to visit. ✉ *9 Belvedere Rd., South Bank, SE1* ☎ *020/7202–8470* ▤ *AE, DC, MC, V* Ⓤ *Waterloo.*

South Kensington

This wealthy residential zone has, in addition to its many white-stucco family houses, enough quality establishments to keep everyone on their toes. Centered around the fashion apex Brompton Cross, the typical dining clientele here is hot international money, *avec* perma-tan, Gucci threads, and Miu Miu sunglasses in the hair.

CONTEMPORARY

£££–£££££

✕ **Bibendum.** This converted 1911 Michelin tire showroom, adorned with awesome stained glass and art deco prints, remains a smooth-running, London showpiece. Chef Matthew Harris cooks with Euro-Brit flair. Try calves' brains, any risotto, Pyrenean lamb with garlic and gravy, or tripe (just as it ought to be cooked). The £28.50 fixed-price lunch menu is money well spent, especially on Sunday. ⊠ *Michelin House, 81 Fulham Rd., South Kensington, SW3* ☎ *020/7581–5817* ⌃ *Reservations essential* ⊟ *AE, DC, MC, V* Ⓤ *South Kensington.*

FRENCH

££–££££

✕ **La Brasserie.** This is a fine spot if you're on the South Kensington museum trail. Opening hours are long, and you can find everything from croque monsieur to tarte tatin. There's a cozy feeling on Sunday mornings, when the entire well-heeled neighborhood sits around reading the papers and sipping cappuccino. You can't hang out at peak dining hours, however. The food is reliable, if a little overpriced. ⊠ *272 Brompton Rd., South Kensington, SW3* ☎ *020/7584–1668* ⊟ *AE, DC, MC, V* Ⓤ *South Kensington.*

£–£££

✕ **Lou Pescadou.** Imagine a slice of the south of France, in sea-theme surroundings and with an emphatically French staff. Fish predominates here, and the menu changes often—don't miss the *soupe de poisson* (fish soup) with croutons and *rouille* (rose-color, garlicky mayonnaise). The mostly French wine list can be pricey. ⊠ *241 Old Brompton Rd., South Kensington, SW5* ☎ *020/7370–1057* ⌃ *Reservations essential* ⊟ *AE, DC, MC, V* Ⓤ *Earl's Court.*

MEDITERRANEAN

££–£££

✕ **The Collection.** Enter through a spotlighted tunnel over a glass drawbridge, make your way past the style police, and find yourself engulfed by a fashionable crowd. The huge warehouse setting, with industrial wood beams and steel cables, a vast bar, and a suspended gallery, makes a great theater for people-watching. Well-dressed wannabes peck at Mediterranean food with Japanese and Thai accents. ⊠ *264 Brompton Rd., South Kensington, SW3* ☎ *020/7225–1212* ⊟ *AE, MC, V* Ⓤ *South Kensington.*

Where to
Stay

WORD OF MOUTH

"There is not one neighborhood in London that is 'close to every-thing.' London is a very large city. What is most important in my opinion is to have easy (close) access to a Tube station, and, even better, if possible, to a station that serves more than one Tube line."

—elaine

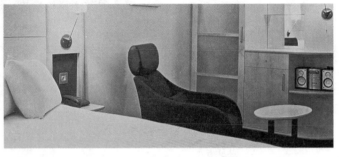

Updated by
Christi
Daugherty

YOU'LL FIND MANY THINGS IN LONDON HOTELS, including luxury, beauty, extraordinary service, and incredible views. One thing you'll look long and hard for, though, is a bargain. The market has always veered toward the expensive, and the dollars to pounds exchange rate hasn't been very helpful lately. If it's any consolation, though, you'll certainly get a lot for your money. You can relax in a brocade armchair while a butler serves you scones with Devonshire cream as thick as butter, or lounge on a handmade bed with strong coffee and fresh croissants as the Thames flows lazily outside. A modern convenience often absent even in the poshest of hotels is Wi-Fi service, and speedy broadband connections have only recently been introduced. However, barring connectivity, the sky's the limit in London hotels if your credit card extends that far.

The city's run-of-the-mill hotels are not so memorable. London is only just beginning to develop a base of moderately priced hotels that offer a high level of quality. Two new places that have opened in recent years—Zetter Rooms and Guesthouse West—represent moves in that direction, hopefully heralding a time when good, affordable London hotels will be the norm, rather than the rare exception.

At the budget level, B&Bs still dominate, and most are filled with as much chintz and as many antiques and resident pets as you might imagine. A fresh wind is the ultramodern, ultracheap "pod hotel"—loosely based on a concept popular in Tokyo. One, easyHotel, is a spinoff of the budget airline easyJet, and a similar version called "Yotel" is expected to open in early 2007. These are utterly floral-free establishments with tiny rooms holding just the basics—bed, shower, toilet—at very low prices. They are absolutely not for the claustrophobic, as the rooms, or pods as they're known, are tinier than a college dorm room. Slightly less drastic are the chain hotels with cookie-cutter furnishings and basic, modern conveniences that have opened in the center of town—the Best Western Shaftesbury and County Hall Travel Inn are both good examples. So, happily, your options will not be limited solely to cramped pods or flowery curtains. And even at the very bottom of the price scale, occasionally things can be trendy—just look at the slick simplicity of the Generator.

If you can spend a bit of money, London is the place to do it. Prices can soar into the empyrean, but many would argue that the best hotels are worth it. Take the Connaught, for example, a landmark hotel whose regulars (many of them quite famous) wouldn't consider staying any-place else. Its famous lobby is unadulterated by things modern; grandly faded, it's filled with oil paintings and antiques. One of the biggest hotel stories is the reopening of Brown's after renovations that lasted more than a year. The result is spectacular—cool neutral tones, chic furniture, and contemporary art have transformed the once traditional setting into a relaxing, modern oasis.

Notting Hill & Bayswater

Ah, trendy Notting Hill. Once an artsy, cheap, beautiful secret gem of a neighborhood, it has now been discovered—and it's still beautiful, but it's anything but cheap. A good portion of the city's most expensive real estate is here, and hotels are no exception. Bayswater, on the other hand, has long been where the city likes to keep its tourists, so there are plenty of hotels there, but not a whole lot else. Farther west, Shepherd's Bush is a bit grittier, but also has a funky, youthful spirit and many hotels and guesthouses, including plenty of budget options.

£££££ 🏨 **The Hempel.** Anouska Hempel first created the lush and lavish Blakes, then created virtually its opposite in the ultraminimalist Hempel, famed for its utter lack of any color except white—until recently, when splashes of color suddenly appeared here and there. But if you loved it in the days when it looked more like the inside of an empty refrigerator, never fear: there's still nothing jarring or extraneous here, and no visible means of support beneath the furniture. A word of warning: the Hempel appeals mainly to style hounds, and its stark, minimalist sensibility is not for everyone. ⊠ *31–35 Craven Hill Gardens, Bayswater, W2 3EA* ☎ *020/7298–9000* 🖶 *020/7470–4666* ⊕ *www.the-hempel.co.uk* ➲ *35 rooms, 12 suites* ♻ *Restaurant, room service, in-room fax, in-room safes, mini-bars, cable TV with movies, in-room VCRs, in-room data ports, 2 bars, lobby lounge, library, dry cleaning, laundry service, concierge, meeting rooms, parking (fee)* ➡ *AE, DC, MC, V* Ⓤ *Lancaster Gate.*

£££–£££££ 🏨 **The Portobello.** One of London's most famous hotels, the little Por-
Fodor'sChoice tobello (formed from two adjoining Victorian houses) is seriously hip,
★ attracting as many celebrities as ordinary folk, and garnering a stellar reputation in the process. It's certainly a quirky place, with each room individually decorated with random antiques, odd-but-luscious fabrics, statuary, and heaven-knows-what thrown in with a kind of designer abandon here and there. What you'll get for your money cannot be predicted—some rooms have balconies and claw-foot bathtubs; Room 16 has a round bed and an extraordinary Victorian "bathing machine" that actor Johnny Depp is said to have once filled with champagne for his then-girlfriend Kate Moss. ⊠ *22 Stanley Gardens, Notting Hill, W11 2NG* ☎ *020/7727–2777* 🖶 *020/7792–9641* ⊕ *www.portobello-hotel.co.uk* ➲ *24 rooms* ♻ *Restaurant, dining room, room service, fans, in-room safes, some in-room hot tubs, minibars, cable TV, in-room VCRs, in-room data ports, bar, lounge, babysitting, dry cleaning, laundry service, concierge, Internet, business services, car rental, no-smoking rooms; no a/c in some rooms* 🍽 *CP* ➡ *AE, MC, V* ⊘ *Closed 10 days at Christmas* Ⓤ *Notting Hill Gate.*

16

LODGING PLANNER

Top 5

■ **Cadogan.** Luxurious decor, at-your-fingertips service, and a bonus of colorful history—Lillie Langtry carried on an affair here with King Edward VII.

■ **Mandarin Oriental.** This exotic hotel never fails to amaze with its miles of marble, pleasant staff, gorgeous views of parks and city, and award-winning restaurants.

■ **Milestone.** Laid-back luxury: the fire-lighted lounge is open for drinks all night long, they'll pack a picnic for you to take to Kensington Park across the road, and the doorman is downright jolly.

■ **Number 16.** This beautiful hotel in South Kensington has spacious rooms with big, comfortable beds. The chic decor and friendly service make it a favorite.

■ **The Rookery.** A gem amid the brash, businesslike hotels of the financial district, the Rookery charms with imported antiques.

Which Neighborhood Is Right for Me?

The city's most famous expensive hotels are found in and around Piccadilly, but many lesser known yet equally luxurious options are in Knightsbridge, Kensington, and around Buckingham Palace. Aside from the excellent Generator hostel near Russell Square, quality budget options in such central locations are rare. Look for good deals around Russell Square in Bloomsbury, on the South Bank, in Bayswater, or farther out in Shepherd's Bush.

Facilities

The lodgings we list are the cream of the crop in each price category. We always list the facilities that are available, but we don't specify whether they cost extra. When pricing accommodations, always ask what's included and what costs extra. Modern hotels usually have air-conditioning. You should specify if you wish to have a double bed. All hotels listed have private baths unless otherwise noted. Whatever the price, *don't* expect a room that's large by American standards.

Prices

We've noted at the end of each review if breakfast is included in the rate (CP for continental breakfast daily and BP for full breakfast daily). Note: some establishments serve hearty breakfasts, others may have little more than coffee and rolls. There may be significant discounts on weekends and in the off-season. ■ TIP→ The **VisitLondon Accommodation Booking Service** (020/7932–2020, www.visitlondon.com) offers a best-price guarantee.

What It Costs In pounds

	£££££	££££	£££	££	£
HOTEL	over £250	£181–£250	£121–£180	£70–£120	under £70

Prices are for two people in a standard double room in high season, V.A.T. included.

££££   **K West.** Proud to be cooly modern, K West is hidden away inside an undistinguished glass-and-steel building in the bustling Shepherds Bush. The place can be a bit over-the-top and is probably unsuitable for children. The busy lobby houses the all-white K Lounge, and the minimalist approach continues in the bedrooms where dark wood, soft suede, and sleek beige walls and floors create a designer look; high-grade audio-visual equipment replaces the stimuli of the lounge. Suites have two-person baths and drawers labeled "smut," where you'll find "adult entertainment" supplies. ⊠ *Richmond Way, Shepherd's Bush, W14 OAX* ☎ *020/7674–1000* 🖷 *020/7674–1050* ⊕ *www.k-west.co.uk* ➥ *216 rooms, 6 suites* ♿ *Restaurant, room service, in-room safes, minibars, cable TV with video games, in-room DVDs, in-room data ports, gym, hot tub, massage, sauna, spa, steam room, bar, dry cleaning, laundry service, Internet, meeting rooms, parking (fee), no-smoking rooms* ☰ *AE, DC, MC, V* ⒪ *CP* Ⓤ *Shepherd's Bush (Central).*

£££–££££   **Abbey Court.** Sink deep into the Victorian era at this gracious white mansion on a quiet street off Notting Hill Gate. Dark-red wallpaper, gilt-frame mirrors, mahogany, and plenty of antiques decorate the little hotel. There are even more finds around the corner at the Saturday Portobello Road antiques market. Hardly all eye-candy, the hotel strives to meet the needs of business travelers with amenitites such as broadband Internet. A continental breakfast buffet is served in the conservatory. Bathrooms are tiny but modern: gray Italian marble, some with whirlpool baths. ⊠ *20 Pembridge Gardens, Notting Hill, W2 4DU* ☎ *020/7221–7518* 🖷 *020/7792–0858* ⊕ *www.abbeycourthotel.co.uk* ➥ *19 rooms, 3 suites* ♿ *Restaurant, room service, fans, in-room safes, in-room hot tubs, cable TV, in-room broadband, dry cleaning, laundry service, concierge, Internet, car rental, no-smoking rooms; no a/c* ☰ *AE, DC, MC, V* ⒪ *CP* Ⓤ *Notting Hill Gate.*

£££–££££   **The Lennox.** This sweet, white-stucco, Victorian row house changed its name and underwent a full renovation in 2006, which brought in tasteful new carpets, furniture, and curtains but did not dent the friendly, low-key personality. Bedrooms have a traditional feel, but much of the swagged floral drapery is gone, replaced by crisp, clean fabrics that lend some elegance. Bathrooms are small but modern. Staff are so friendly they verge on jolly, and the location in Notting Hill not far from the Portobello Road antiques market couldn't be leafier and lovelier. ⊠ *34 Pembridge Gardens, Notting Hill, W2 4DX* ☎ *0870/850–3317* 🖷 *020/ 7727–4982* ⊕ *www.thelennox.com* ➥ *20 rooms* ♿ *Dining room, room service, in-room safes, cable TV, in-room VCRs, in-room data ports, lobby lounge, dry cleaning, laundry service, Internet, business services, meeting rooms, parking (fee), some pets allowed; no a/c in some rooms* ☰ *AE, DC, MC, V* ⒪ *BP* Ⓤ *Notting Hill Gate.*

£££–££££   **Miller's Residence.** From the moment you ring the bell and are ushered up the winding staircase flanked by antiques and curios, you know you've entered another realm where history is paramount. The building is so packed with Jacobean, Victorian, Georgian, and Tudor antiques, that if it weren't so elegant it might remind you of your grandmother's attic. Run by Martin Miller of *Miller's Antique Price Guides* fame, this town house serves as his home, gallery, and B&B. Rooms are named

FodorśChoice ★

16

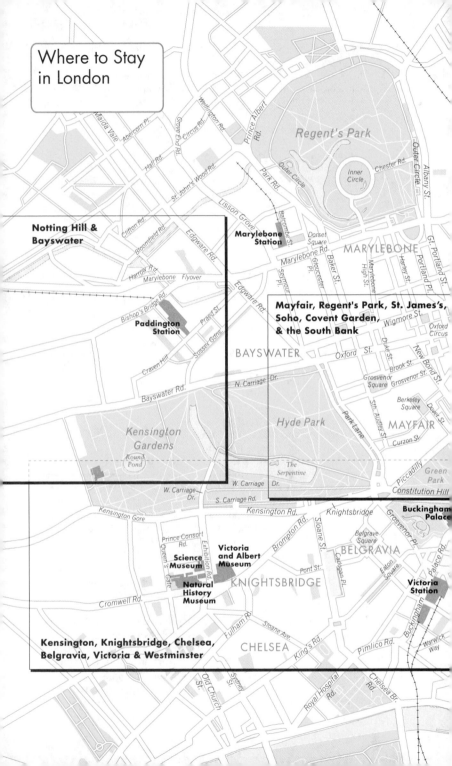

Where to Stay in London

Notting Hill & Bayswater

Marylebone Station

MARYLEBONE

Mayfair, Regent's Park, St. James's, Soho, Covent Garden, & the South Bank

Paddington Station

BAYSWATER

Regent's Park

Inner Circle

Buckingham Palace

Hyde Park

MAYFAIR

Kensington Gardens

Green Park

BELGRAVIA

Victoria Station

Science Museum

Victoria and Albert Museum

Natural History Museum

KNIGHTSBRIDGE

CHELSEA

Kensington, Knightsbridge, Chelsea, Belgravia, Victoria & Westminster

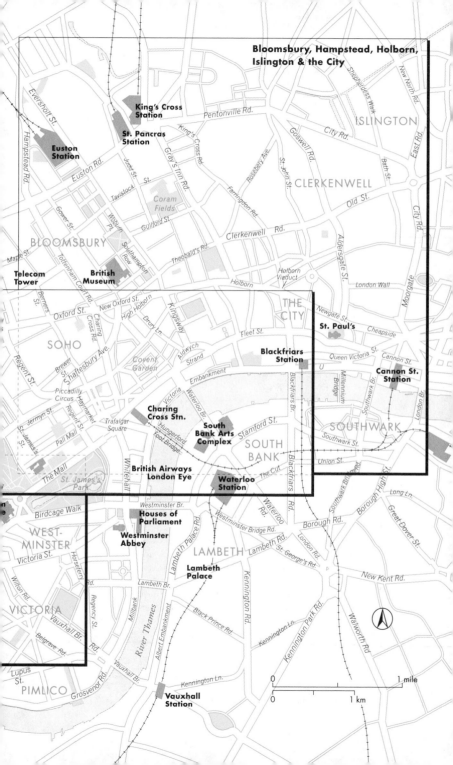

Bloomsbury, Hampstead, Holborn, Islington & the City

ISLINGTON

King's Cross Station

St. Pancras Station

Euston Station

CLERKENWELL

Coram Fields

BLOOMSBURY

Telecom Tower

British Museum

THE CITY

SOHO

St. Paul's

Blackfriars Station

Covent Garden

Cannon St. Station

Charing Cross Stn.

South Bank Arts Complex

SOUTHWARK

British Airways London Eye

SOUTH BANK

Waterloo Station

WEST-MINSTER

Houses of Parliament

Westminster Abbey

LAMBETH

Lambeth Palace

VICTORIA

River Thames

PIMLICO

Vauxhall Station

0   1 mile

0   1 km

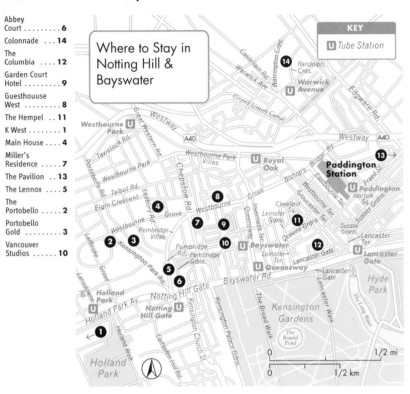

Where to Stay in Notting Hill & Bayswater

after Romantic poets. Sip a complimentary evening cocktail in the long, candlelight drawing room with fireplace, while mixing with other guests or the convivial staff. ✉ *111A Westbourne Grove, Notting Hill, W2 4UW* ☎ *020/7243–1024* 🖷 *020/7243–1064* ⊕ *www.millersuk.com* 🛏 *6 rooms, 2 suites* ⚬ *Dining room, fans, some in-room faxes, in-room data ports, lounge, dry cleaning, laundry service, concierge, Internet, meeting room; no a/c* ⊟ *AE, DC, MC, V* ⫻⦿⫻ *CP* Ⓤ *Notting Hill Gate.*

££–££££ ⊡ **Guesthouse West.** The idea behind this hip hotel is to offer high-class chic at moderate prices, and to a certain extent, it succeeds. The minimalist decor and technology—cool black-and-white photos and flat-screen TVs—are very stylish. Rooms, however, are truly tiny, and there's no room service offered. Nevermind, though, as the restaurant is handy and packed with locals, and the bar is a beautiful homage to the 1930s. ▣ TIP→ **The hotel's relationship with a local spa and restaurant provides guests with discounts, and there are guaranteed seats for shows at the small Gate Theatre.** If you fall deeply in love with the place you can "buy" a room for £235,000, which gives you "ownership" of it for 52 days of the year. ✉ *163–165 Westbourne Grove, Notting Hill, W11 2RS* ☎ *020/7792–9800* 🖷 *020/7792–9797* ⊕ *www.guesthousewest.com* 🛏 *20 rooms* ⚬ *Restaurant, cable TV, in-room DVDs, in-room data ports, Wi-Fi, bar, parking (fee), no-smoking rooms* ⊟ *AE, MC, V* Ⓤ *Notting Hill Gate.*

££–£££ 🏨 **Colonnade.** Near a canal filled with colorful narrow boats, this lovely town house rests beautifully in a quiet, residential area known as "Little Venice." From the Freud suite (Sigmund visited regularly in 1938) to the rooms with four-poster beds or balconies, you'll find rich brocades, velvets, and antiques. It's a former home, so each room is different; some are split-level. Extra touches in each are the bathrobe and slippers, bowl of apples, and CD player. The 1920s elevator and Wedgwood lobby fireplace add to the historic style of the place, but the new tapas bar is pleasantly modern. ✉ *2 Warrington Crescent, Bayswater, W9 1ER* ☎ *020/7286–1052* 🖷 *020/7286–1057* ⊕ *www. theetoncollection.com* 🛏 *15 rooms, 28 suites* 🍴 *Restaurant, dining room, room service, in-room safes, minibars, cable TV, in-room data ports, lobby lounge, wine bar, babysitting, dry cleaning, laundry service, business services, parking (fee), some pets allowed, no-smoking rooms* 🚭 *AE, DC, MC, V* Ⓤ *Warwick Ave.*

££–£££ 🏨 **Main House.** A brass lion door knocker marks the front door of the unassuming Main House. With just four rooms, it has a simple aim: to provide a good night's sleep in an interesting Victorian home. Furnished with clean white linens, chic modern furniture, and Asian art, the rooms are uncluttered and delightfully spacious. ■ TIP➔ **The tiny urban terrace is a great place for stargazing or reading the morning paper. A day rate at the local health club is available, too.** ✉ *6 Colville Rd., Notting Hill, W11 2BP* ☎ *020/7221–9691* ⊕ *www.themainhouse.com* 🛏 *4 rooms* 🍴 *Fans, in-room VCRs, in-room data ports, massage, bicycles, babysitting, dry cleaning, laundry service, Internet, meeting rooms, airport shuttle, parking (fee); no smoking* 🚭 *MC, V* ❚◯❚ *CP* Ⓤ *Notting Hill Gate.*

££–£££ 🏨 **Portobello Gold.** This no-frills B&B in the heart of the Portobello Road antiques area occupies the floor above the pub and restaurant of the same name. Flat-screen TVs are mounted on the wall, and the beds take up almost the entire room in the doubles. The best of the bunch is the split-level apartment (£££) with roof terrace, small kitchen, and soothing aquarium. The casual restaurant serves international food at reasonable prices, and there's an Internet café that charges £1 per half hour. ✉ *95–97 Portobello Rd., Notting Hill, W11 2QB* ☎ *020/7460–4910* ⊕ *www. portobellogold.com* 🛏 *6 rooms, 1 apartment* 🍴 *Restaurant, room service, cable TV, bar, laundry service, Internet* 🚭 *MC, V* ❚◯❚ *CP* Ⓤ *Notting Hill Gate.*

Fodor'sChoice ★

££ 🏨 **The Columbia.** The public rooms in these five adjoining Victorians are as big as museum halls. Some of the clean, high-ceiling bedrooms are very large (three to four beds) and have park views and balconies. Rooms are well decorated in creams and earth tones—they are not luxurious, but they're really a bargain in this price range. Given that, it's no surprise that the Columbia is popular with tour groups. ✉ *95–99 Lancaster Gate, Bayswater, W2 3NS* ☎ *020/7402–0021* 🖷 *020/ 7706–4691* ⊕ *www.columbiahotel.co.uk* 🛏 *103 rooms* 🍴 *Restaurant, in-room safes, bar, lobby lounge, dry cleaning, laundry service, concierge, meeting room; no a/c* 🚭 *AE, MC, V* ❚◯❚ *BP* Ⓤ *Lancaster Gate.*

££ 🏨 **The Pavilion.** This eccentric town house is another trendy address in London for fashionistas, actors, and musicians. Often used for fashion shoots, the kitsch bedrooms veer wildly from Moroccan fantasy (the

16

"Casablanca Nights" room) to acres of plaid ("Highland Fling") and satin ("Enter the Dragon"); you'll probably want to take some photos of your own here. ■ TIP→ **Triples and family rooms are ideal for groups looking for space *and* style.** ⊠ *34–36 Sussex Gardens, Bayswater, W2 1UL* ☎ *020/ 7262–0905* 🖷 *020/7262–1324* ⊕ *www.pavilionhoteluk.com* 🔄 *30 rooms* ⚭ *Room service, fans, cable TV, some in-room DVDs, in-room data ports, lounge, dry cleaning, laundry service, parking (fee), no-smoking rooms; no a/c* ▭ *AE, D, MC, V* ⟟⊙⟁ *CP* Ⓤ *Paddington, Edgware Rd.*

££ 🏨 **Vancouver Studios.** This little hotel in a Victorian town house is perfect for those wanting a home away from home. Rooms come with minikitchens, and you can even pre-order groceries to stock your minirefrigerator on arrival. Each studio has daily maid service as well as room service. Some rooms have working fireplaces, and one opens onto the leafy, paved garden. ⊠ *30 Prince's Sq., Bayswater, W2 4NJ* ☎ *020/ 7243–1270* 🖷 *020/7221–8678* ⊕ *www.vancouverstudios.co.uk* 🔄 *45 studios* ⚭ *Room service, kitchens, microwaves, refrigerators, in-room data ports, lounge, dry cleaning, laundry facilities, parking (fee); no a/c* ▭ *AE, DC, MC, V* Ⓤ *Bayswater, Queensway.*

£–££ 🏨 **Garden Court Hotel.** This attractive, small hotel is formed from two 19th-century town houses in a quiet garden square. Each room has a character of its own, some with original Victorian fittings. Note that some rooms are more recently refurbished than others. Rooms with toilet and shower cost an extra £30, and family-size rooms are in the ££ category. The paved garden is relaxing in good weather. ⊠ *30–31 Kensington Gardens Sq., Bayswater, W2 4BL* ☎ *020/7229–2553* 🖷 *020/7727–2749* ⊕ *www.gardencourthotel.co.uk* 🔄 *12 rooms, 10 with bath* ⚭ *Fans, cable TV, lounge, some pets allowed; no a/c, no smoking* ▭ *MC, V* ⟟⊙⟁ *BP* Ⓤ *Bayswater, Queensway.*

Bloomsbury & Holborn

These formerly parklike areas where Virginia Woolf and her literary circle once philosophized are now loud, bustling, businesslike neighborhoods to which much of London commutes wearily every day. It's also home to the British Museum, some wonderful restaurants, fabulous pubs, handy shopping, and excellent upscale hotels.

£££££ 🏨 **Sanderson.** This surreal urban spa sits in a converted textiles factory. From the moment you walk into the lobby, which is like a design museum for seating, and certainly once you get upstairs to see the billowy fabrics that serve as bathroom doors, you know that the Sanderson is walking to the beat of its own whimsical drum. The furniture is a mix of over-the-top Louis XV and postmodern pieces, and bedrooms have sleigh beds. Fitness addicts will find Agua (the "holistic bath house"), the in-room massage and spa serv-

> ### WORD OF MOUTH
>
> "I think Bloomsbury's the better location. You can hoof it to the theaters and not have to rely on the Tube, as you do from Kensington. We usually tried to fit in full days before the theater, and yet we liked to go back to the hotel to clean up and change before going out."   –Penny

ices, and the indoor-outdoor fitness classes just what the doctor ordered. Foodies should try the popular, sometimes controversial, Spoon restaurant. ⊠ *50 Berners St., Bloomsbury, W1T 3NG* ☎ *020/7300–1400* ⊞ *020/7300–1401* ⊕ *www.sandersonlondon.com* ⌁ *150 rooms* ⌂ *Restaurant, room service, some in-room faxes, in-room safes, mini-bars, cable TV, in-room VCRs, in-room data ports, gym, sauna, spa, billiards, 2 bars, lobby lounge, shop, babysitting, dry cleaning, laundry service, concierge, Internet, business services, meeting room, parking (fee), no-smoking rooms* ▭ *AE, DC, MC, V* Ⓤ *Oxford Circus, Tottenham Court Rd.*

££££–£££££ ▣ **Charlotte Street Hotel.** On a busy street in the media hub around Soho, this hotel fuses the modern and traditional. Bedrooms are beautifully decorated with unusual printed fabrics by designer and owner Kit Kemp, and bathrooms are lined with gleaming granite and oak, with walk-in showers and deep baths. Each bathroom has a flat-screen TV so you can catch up on the news while you soak with exclusive products by London perfumer Miller Harris. The restaurant, Oscar, is excellent. ■ **TIP→** There's a public screening room with Ferrari leather chairs for watching a movie at the Sunday-night dinner-and-film club. Or you might just want to read a paper by the fire in the drawing room. ⊠ *15 Charlotte St., Bloomsbury, W1P 1HB* ☎ *020/7806–2000, 800/553–6674 in U.S.* ⊞ *020/7806–2002* ⊕ *www.charlottestreethotel.com* ⌁ *44 rooms, 8 suites* ⌂ *Restaurant, room service, in-room safes, minibars, cable TV, in-room VCRs, in-room data ports, gym, bar, lobby lounge, cinema, library, dry cleaning, laundry service, concierge, Internet, business services, meeting rooms* ▭ *AE, DC, MC, V* Ⓤ *Goodge St.*

££££–£££££ ▣ **myhotel bloomsbury.** When myhotel opened in 1999 it was one of London's first minimalist boutique hotels. The town raved about its plain white walls, feng shui philosophy, and the flourish that consisted of a single perfect orchid in the foyer. But the London buzz has moved elsewhere, and myhotel is rushing to catch up. To that end, the cold white rooms are being repainted in bright colors, and all are being equipped with flat-screen TVs and Wi-Fi. The lobby, sushi restaurant, and trendy "mybar" still cling to their Spartan principles—for now. ⊠ *11–13 Bayley St., Bedford Sq., Bloomsbury, WC1B 3HD* ☎ *020/7667–6000* ⊞ *020/7667–6001* ⊕ *www.myhotels.com* ⌁ *76 rooms* ⌂ *Restaurant, room service, in-room safes, cable TV with movies, in-room DVDs, in-room broadband, gym, spa, bar, lounge, library, babysitting, concierge, Wi-Fi, business services, no-smoking floors* ▭ *AE, DC, MC, V* Ⓤ *Tottenham Court Rd.*

£££–£££££ ▣ **Montague on the Gardens.** What the hotel lacks in space it makes up for in charm with its yards of fabric covering the walls and ceilings. Converted from a row of 1830s Georgian town houses, the Montague keeps the antique look alive with its period furnishings and collection of objets d'art. Standard double rooms are small, but there are plenty of cozy public areas in which to unwind. The bar hosts jazz evenings, and the sitting room is filled with comfy, flowery furniture. The best views are from the small terrace and conservatories, where you can look out on a stretch of lawn running an entire city block. ⊠ *15 Montague St., Bloomsbury, WC1B 5BJ* ☎ *020/7637–1001*

16

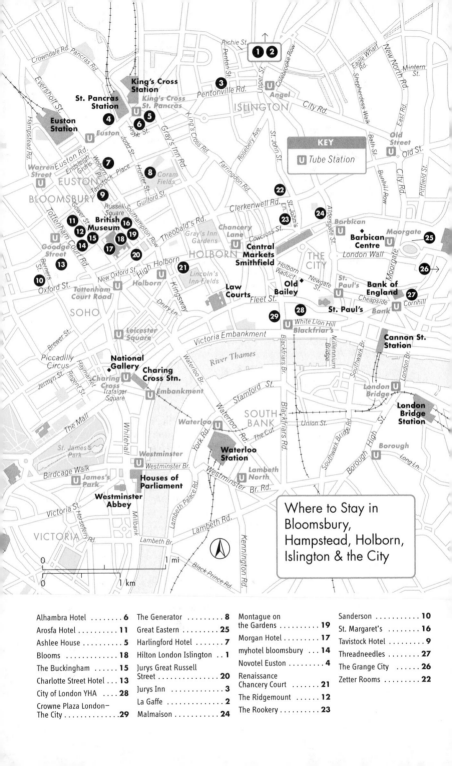

Where to Stay in Bloomsbury, Hampstead, Holborn, Islington & the City

0 ____ 1 mi
0 ____ 1 km

🖼 *020/7637–2516* ⊕ *www.redcarnationhotels.com* ⤢ *93 rooms, 11 suites* ⚭ *Restaurant, room service, some in-room faxes, some in-room safes, minibars, cable TV with movies, in-room data ports, gym, sauna, steam room, bar, lounge, dry cleaning, laundry service, concierge, Internet, business services, meeting rooms, no-smoking rooms* ▭ *AE, DC, MC, V* Ⓤ *Russell Sq.*

££££ 🖼 **Jurys Great Russell Street.** Originally designed by architect Sir Edwin Lutyens for the Young Women's Christian Association in the early 1930s, today this proud, neo-Georgian building is an upscale hotel aimed at corporate travelers during the week and leisure travelers on the weekend, when rates drop considerably. Throughout the reception area and lounge, much of the original design has been retained and the furniture is reproduction work. Rooms are fairly spacious and have a classic look to them, though they have all the perks of the 21st century. ⊠ *16–22 Great Russell St., Bloomsbury, WC1B 3NN* ☎ *020/7347–1000* 🖼 *020/7347–1001* ⊕ *www.jurysdoyle.com* ⤢ *124 rooms, 6 suites* ⚭ *Restaurant, room service, minibars, cable TV, in-room data ports, lounge, wine bar, library, dry cleaning, concierge, Internet, business services, meeting rooms, no-smoking rooms* ▭ *AE, DC, MC, V* Ⓤ *Tottenham Court Rd.*

£££–££££ 🖼 **Renaissance Chancery Court.** This landmark structure, built by the Pearl Assurance Company in 1914, has been transformed into a beautiful Marriott hotel. So striking is the architecture that the building was featured in the film *Howard's End.* The spacious bedrooms are popular with business travelers and the decor has a masculine edge—lots of leather and dark red fabrics. The day spa in the basement is a cocoon of peacefulness. There's marble everywhere, from the floors in public spaces and the massive staircase to the bathrooms. The restaurant, Pearl, is known for its modern European cuisine, and the bar, in an old banking hall, has elegant soaring ceilings. ⊠ *252 High Holborn, Holborn, WC1V 7EN* ☎ *020/7829–9888* 🖼 *0207/829–9889* ⊕ *www.renaissancehotels.com/loncc* ⤢ *343 rooms, 14 suites* ⚭ *Restaurant, room service, in-room safes, minibars, cable TV with video games, in-room data ports, gym, sauna, spa, steam room, bar, lobby lounge, shop, babysitting, laundry service, concierge, business services, meeting rooms, no-smoking rooms* ▭ *AE, MC, V* Ⓤ *Holborn.*

£££–££££ 🖼 **Zetter Rooms.** By day, the area between Holborn and Clerkenwell is
Fodor's Choice   all about business, and rare is the person not wrapped head-to-toe in
★   dark wool-blend, secured neatly with a silk tie. By night, though, those binds are loosened and it's all oh-so-trendy. London's latest "it" hotel reflects both personalities. The dizzying five-story atrium, art deco staircase, and slick restaurant are your first indications of what to expect at this converted warehouse: a breath of fresh air (and a little space) in London's mostly Victorian hotel scene. Rooms are smoothly done up in soft, dove-gray and vanilla fabrics, and the views from the higher floors are wonderful. It's all lovely to look at, and a bargain by London standards. ⊠ *86–88 Clerkenwell Rd., Holborn, EC1M 5RJ* ☎ *020/7324–4444* 🖼 *020/7324–4445* ⊕ *www.thezetter.com* ⤢ *59 rooms* ⚭ *Restaurant,*

16

room service, in-room safes, minibars, cable TV, in-room DVDs, in-room data ports, bar, lobby lounge, laundry service, concierge, Internet, business services, no-smoking floors ⊟ *AE, MC, V* Ⓤ *Farringdon.*

££–£££ ⬚ **Blooms.** This white Georgian town-house hotel is extremely handy for the British Museum (which is just around the corner), and offers a pleasant home away from home. Rooms are not too tiny by London standards, and are traditionally decorated with a light hand on the "floral" button. Those in the back of the hotel look out onto a leafy green garden. You can get good deals by booking in advance on the Internet, and on the whole, it's good value for the money. ⊠ *7 Montague St., Bloomsbury, WC1B 5BP* ☎ *020/7323–1717* 🖷 *020/7636–6498* ⊕ *www.bloomshotel.com* ⇥ *26 rooms, 1 suite* ♻ *Restaurant, room service, cable TV, bar, lounge, Internet, meeting rooms, some pets allowed; no a/c* ⊟ *AE, DC, MC, V* Ⓤ *Russell Sq.*

££–£££ **The Buckingham.** This Georgian town-house hotel near Russell Square is a great bargain for the money. Its spacious, attractively designed rooms are all studios and suites. Each has its own bijoux kitchenette, giving you an alternative to eating in restaurants every night. All have marble-and-granite bathrooms and plenty of amenities. Staff are friendly, and the location is an easy walk from the British Museum and Covent Garden. ⊠ *11–13 Bayley St., Bedford Sq., Bloomsbury, WC1B 3HD* ☎ *020/7636–2474* 🖷 *020/7580–4527* ⊕ *www.grangehotels.com* ⇥ *17 rooms* ♻ *Lounge, cable TV with movies, in-room broadband, no-smoking rooms* ⊟ *MC, V* Ⓤ *Tottenham Court Rd.*

£–£££ ⬚ **Novotel Euston.** Useful, but not all that stylish, this tower of a hotel is smack-dab in between King's Cross and Euston stations on busy Euston Road. It's popular with conference groups and business travelers, so all the guest rooms are generally pleasant, with good work spaces and comfortable beds. There's plenty of cappuccino on hand in the busy lobby, and the restaurant is handy, but not about to win culinary awards. One exception to the bland, businesslike atmosphere here is the spectacular view—from the upper floors you can see for miles. ⊠ *100–110 Euston Rd., Bloomsbury, NW1 2AJ* ☎ *020/7666–9000* 🖷 *020/7666–9100* ⊕ *www.novotel.com* ⇥ *309 rooms, 3 suites* ♻ *Restaurant, room service, in-room safes, minibars, cable TV with movies, in-room data ports, gym, massage, sauna, steam room, bar, lobby lounge, theater, dry cleaning, laundry service, concierge, Internet, business services, meeting rooms, no-smoking floors* ⊟ *AE, MC, V* Ⓤ *King's Cross, Euston.*

££ ⬚ **Harlingford Hotel.** The Harlingford is by far the sleekest and most contemporary of the Cartwright Gardens hotels. Bold color schemes and beautifully tiled bathrooms enliven the family-run place. ■ TIP➔ **The quad rooms are an excellent choice for traveling families.** ⊠ *61–63 Cartwright Gardens, Bloomsbury, WC1H 9EL* ☎ *020/7387–1551* 🖷 *020/7383–4616* ⊕ *www.harlingfordhotel.com* ⇥ *43 rooms* ♻ *In-room data ports, tennis court, lounge; no a/c* ⊟ *AE, DC, MC, V* ⦿ *BP* Ⓤ *Russell Sq.*

£–££ ⬚ **Arosfa Hotel.** The friendly owners, Mr. and Mrs. Dorta, set this B&B apart from the Gower Street hotel pack—that, and the fact that this was once the home of pre-Raphaelite painter Sir John Everett Millais. Rooms

FodorsChoice
★

are simple and comfortable. Those at the back are far quieter, though the double glazing somewhat tames the din of the students on their way to and from class at University College London. ⊠ *83 Gower St., Bloomsbury, WC1E 6HJ* ☎ *020/7636–2115* 🖷 *020/7636–2115* ⟿ *15 rooms* ⚖ *Dining room, fans, lounge; no a/c, no smoking* ═ *MC, V* ¶⊙| *BP* Ⓤ *Goodge St.*

£–££ 🏨 **Morgan Hotel.** This is a Georgian row-house hotel, family-run with charm and panache. The best rooms are the little apartments (£££), which give you a bit more space to move around in. The tiny, paneled breakfast room is straight out of an 18th-century dollhouse. Rooms have sunny decor; the ones in the back overlook the British Museum. ⊠ *24 Bloomsbury St., Bloomsbury, WC1B 3QJ* ☎ *020/7636–3735* 🖷 *020/7636–3045* ⊕ *www.morganhotel.co.uk* ⟿ *15 rooms, 5 apartments* ⚖ *In-room safes, some refrigerators, cable TV; no a/c* ═ *MC, V* ¶⊙| *BP* Ⓤ *Tottenham Court Rd. or Russell Sq.*

£–££ 🏨 **St. Margaret's.** A popular hotel near the British Museum and on a street Fodor'sChoice full of budget hotels, St. Margaret's has well-lighted rooms with high
★ ceilings in a Georgian-era building. The friendly family that runs the hotel is sure to welcome you by name if you stay long enough. Rooms are decorated with tasteful wallpaper and a light floral touch, as well as Georgian touches such as a fireplace and beautiful cornice moldings. All have huge windows and views of the leafy neighborhood. Internet access is free. ⊠ *26 Bedford Pl., Bloomsbury, WC1B 5JL* ☎ *020/7636–4277* 🖷 *020/7323–3066* ⊕ *www.stmargaretshotel.co.uk* ⟿ *64 rooms, 12 with bath* ⚖ *Dining room, fans, cable TV, lounge, Internet, no-smoking rooms; no a/c* ═ *MC, V* ¶⊙| *BP* Ⓤ *Russell Sq.*

£–££ 🏨 **Tavistock Hotel.** This big, sprawling hotel off Russell Square makes a handy, affordable base for exploring the British Museum and London's West End. The rooms are small and simply furnished, but clean and quiet with tea/coffemakers. The hotel itself has plenty of amenities, including a relaxed bar and restaurant. It won't win any design awards, but it's a solid option when money is an issue. ⊠ *Tavistock Sq., Bloomsbury, WC1H 9EU* ☎ *020/7278–7871 reservations, 020/7636–8383 hotel* 🖷 *020/7837–4653* ⊕ *www.imperialhotels.co.uk* ⟿ *343 rooms* ⚖ *Restaurant, lounge, cable TV, bar* ═ *MC, V* ¶⊙| *CP* Ⓤ *Russell Sq.*

£ 🏨 **Alhambra Hotel.** One of the best bargains in Bloomsbury, this family-run hotel has singles as low as £32 and doubles as low as £45. Rooms tend to be small and look dated, but they're definitely good value. Some rooms have a shower but no toilet; others have both. All rooms have a TV, all guests have access to free Wi-Fi, and tea/coffemakers are available on request. It's definitely not fancy, but it's certainly cheap. ⊠ *17–19 Argyle St., Bloomsbury, WC1H 8EJ* ☎ *020/7837–9575* 🖷 *020/7916–2476* ⊕ *www.alhambrahotel.com* ⟿ *52 rooms* ⚖ *Dining room, concierge, parking (fee), Wi-Fi, no-smoking rooms; no a/c, no room phones* ═ *AE, MC, V* ¶⊙| *BP* Ⓤ *King's Cross.*

£ 🏨 **Ashlee House.** This may be a hostel, but it attracts visitors of all ages, and is quite popular with older budget travelers, thanks to the lack of a curfew and a 24-hour reception desk. It has all the necessary hostel amenities including shared kitchen, free luggage storage, guided walking tours, and an Internet station. Staff are as cheerful as the decor, which

16

is all sunny yellows and vivid pinks. Prices range from £15 per person for a dorm room to £36 per person for a double. ⊠ *261 Gray's Inn Rd., Holborn, WC1X 8QT* ☎ *020/7833–9400* 🖷 *020/7833–9677* ⊕ *www.ashleehouse.co.uk* ⇗ *26 rooms, 175 beds* ⚭ *Dining room, lounge, laundry facilities, Internet, no-smoking rooms; no a/c, no room phones, no room TVs* ▭ *MC, V* ⊠ *CP* Ⓤ *King's Cross.*

£ 🔲 **The Generator.** This is where the young, enthusiastic traveler comes to find fellow partiers. It's also the cleverest youth hostel in town: set in a former police barracks, its rooms are designed like prison cells, making the most of the bunk beds and dim views. The Internet café provides handy maps and leaflets. The Generator Bar has cheap drinks and a rowdy crowd, and the Fuel Stop cafeteria provides inexpensive meals. There are singles, twins, and dormitory rooms, each with a washbasin, locker, and free bed linen. Prices run from £23 per person for a double room to £17 per person for a 14-bed dorm room. ⊠ *MacNaghten House, Compton Pl. off 37 Tavistock Pl., Bloomsbury, WC1H 9SE* ☎ *020/7388–7666* 🖷 *020/7388–7644* ⊕ *www.generatorhostels.com* ⇗ *215 beds* ⚭ *Restaurant, fans, lobby lounge, pub, sports bar, recreation room, shop, concierge, Internet, meeting rooms, airport shuttle, travel services, parking (fee), no-smoking floors; no a/c, no room phones, no room TVs* ▭ *MC, V* ⊠ *CP* Ⓤ *Russell Sq.*

£ 🔲 **The Ridgemount.** Rooms at this inexpensive guesthouse are clean and neat, and you cannot beat the location a few blocks away from the British Museum and London's West End theaters. The public areas, especially the family-style breakfast room, are rather sweetly cluttered Victorian-style parlors. Some rooms overlook a leafy garden and some have their own bathroom (for about £15 extra per night). ⊠ *65 Gower St., Bloomsbury, WC1E 6HJ* ☎ *020/7636–1141* 🖷 *020/7636–2558* ⊕ *www.ridgemounthotel.co.uk* ⇗ *32 rooms, 15 with bath* ⚭ *No-smoking rooms; no a/c, no room phones* ▭ *MC, V* ⊠ *BP* Ⓤ *Goodge St.*

The City

The City is also known as the Square Mile, because it is London's one-mile-square financial district, where most of the city's banks and financial corporations have their headquarters. The restaurants and upscale bars buzz during the week, but it can be quiet as a tomb here on weekends and after 8 PM.

£££££ 🔲 **Crowne Plaza London—The City.** The shell of an old stationery warehouse, on the former site of Henry VIII's Bridewell Palace, is now in its nth reincarnation as a polished hotel. Don't let its all-business appearance and financial-district location put you off: it's paces away from the Tube, and soundproof windows block out City noise (though some may find that an oxymoron come nightfall—if you're seeking a boisterous after-dark party scene, this is probably not the place for you). Minimalist rooms are smaller than typical Crowne Plaza but reasonable by London standards. Head down to the hotel's restaurant, Refettorio, for rustic Italian food (charcuterie, regional cheeses, homemade pastas) at its finest. ⊠ *19 New Bridge St., The City, EC4* ☎ *0870/400–9190* 🖷 *020/7438–8080* ⊕ *www.crowneplaza.com* ⇗ *203 rooms, 14 suites*

🍴 *Restaurant, café, room service, in-room safes, minibars, cable TV, some in-room DVDs, in-room broadband, gym, sauna, bar, dry cleaning, laundry service, concierge, Internet room, business services, meeting rooms, car rental, parking (fee), no-smoking rooms* Ⓤ *Blackfriars.*

£££££ 🏨 **Great Eastern.** This grand old Victorian railway hotel looks lavish and over-the-top on the outside, but inside it's all about modern, with polished wood, neutral colors, and contemporary art. You'll want for little here—there are five restaurants (serving sushi, seafood, brasserie fare, pub food, and haute cuisine, respectively), a popular bar, a gorgeous spa, and a boutique selling the covetable Ren bath products with which all the hotel's bathrooms are stocked. Rooms on the fifth and sixth floors are modern lofts, with lots of light. Note that with all the restaurants and bars, also used by locals, this is not a retreat from bustling London life. ✉ *Liverpool St. at Bishopsgate, The City, E2M 7QN* ☎ *020/7618–5010* 🖷 *020/7618–5011* ⊕ *www.great-eastern-hotel.co.uk* ⇄ *246 rooms, 21 suites* 🍴 *5 restaurants, 12 dining rooms, room service, some in-room faxes, in-room safes, minibars, cable TV with video games, in-room VCRs, in-room data ports, gym, spa, 2 bars, pub, library, shop, babysitting, dry cleaning, laundry service, concierge, Internet, business services, meeting rooms, car rental, no-smoking rooms* ▭ *AE, DC, MC, V* Ⓤ *Liverpool St.*

£££££ 🏨 **Threadneedles.** Owned by the people who run the Colonnade in Bayswater, Threadneedles is a first-rate boutique hotel. The building is a former bank, and the hotel has beautifully adopted the vast old banking hall, along with its luxurious marble and mahogany panels. Rooms are a good size for London, with big, comfortable beds and neutral coffee and cream colors, with dashes of deep burgundy. Bathrooms are modern and attractive, with plenty of marble. Given its location in the financial district, it's no surprise that this place looks as if it were custom-designed to please business travelers. ✉ *5 Threadneedle St., The City, EC2R 8AY* ☎ *020/7657–8080* 🖷 *020/7657–8100* ⊕ *www.theetoncollection.com* ⇄ *63 rooms, 6 suites* 🍴 *Restaurant, room service, in-room safes, in-room hot tubs, minibars, refrigerators, cable TV, in-room CDs, Wi-Fi, bar, lounge, dry cleaning, laundry service, concierge, meeting rooms, no-smoking floors* ▭ *AE, DC, MC, V* Ⓤ *Bank.*

★ 🏨 **The Rookery.** This is an extraordinary hotel, where each beautiful double room is decorated with a lavish, theatrical flair and an eye for history. Many have four-poster beds, each has a claw-foot bathtub, antique carved wooden headboard, and period furnishings, including exquisite salvaged pieces. In the Rook's Nest, the hotel's duplex suite, you can relax in an antique bath in the corner of the bedroom or enjoy a magnificent view of the City's historic buildings. The conservatory, with its small patio garden, is a relaxing place to unwind. ✉ *12 Peter's La., at Cowcross St., The City, EC1M 6DS* ☎ *020/7336–0931* 🖷 *020/7336–0932* ⊕ *www.rookeryhotel.com* ⇄ *30 rooms, 3 suites* 🍴 *Room service, fans, in-room safes, mini-*

££££–£££££

> **DID YOU KNOW?**
>
> An 18th-century hotel in the City, the Rookery is just steps away from the Jerusalem Tavern, from which it's said the Knights of St. John left to fight the Crusades.

16

bars, cable TV, in-room data ports, bar, lobby lounge, library, babysitting, dry cleaning, laundry service, concierge, meeting rooms, airport shuttle, car rental, parking (fee), no-smoking floors; no a/c ☰ *AE, DC, MC, V* Ⓤ *Farringdon.*

££££ 🏨 **The Grange City.** With an eye on business, this sleek hotel in London's City has everything the workaholic needs to feel right at home—chic bedrooms subtly decorated in creams and chocolates, modern furnishings, plenty of space (by London standards) in which to pace, broadband and direct-dial phones, and more. The women-only wing has extra amenities ranging from more powerful hair dryers to extra-secure doors with peep holes and chain-locks. Ladies (and gentlemen) can get some exercise in the hotel's magnificent columned swimming pool, and then linger over sushi at the Koto Japanese Restaurant or sip cocktails in the Isis Lounge. ⊠ *8–14 Cooper's Row, The City, EC3N 2BQ* ☎ *020/7863–3700* 🖷 *030/7863–3701* ⊕ *www.grangehotels.com* ↘ *307 rooms* ♤ *2 restaurants, room service, in-room safes, minibars, cable TV with video games, in-room broadband, gym, pool, sauna, spa, bar, lobby lounge, shop, in-room CDs, laundry service, concierge, business services, meeting rooms, no-smoking rooms* ☰ *AE, MC, V* Ⓜ *Tower Hill, Aldgate, Monument.*

££££ 🏨 **Malmaison.** Part of a small chain of well-regarded U.K. boutique hotels, this Clerkenwell address is very trendy, with contemporary furnishings, clean lines, and all the extras. Stylish rooms are well-decorated in neutral cream and beige, have huge beds and CD systems with a library of music on demand, as well as satellite TVs and free broadband. It prides itself on fast, quality room service, so breakfast in bed can be a pleasure. The whole package is a business traveler's dream. ⊠ *Charterhouse Sq., The City, EC1M 6AH* ☎ *020/7012–3700* 🖷 *020/7012–3702* ⊕ *www.malmaison.com* ↘ *95 rooms, 2 suites* ♤ *Restaurant, room service, in-room safes, minibars, cable TV, in-room broadband, gym, bar, babysitting, dry cleaning, laundry service, concierge, meeting room, no-smoking rooms* ☰ *AE, MC, V* ◉ *CP* Ⓤ *Barbican, Farringdon.*

£ 🏨 **City of London YHA.** The beautiful oak-panel chapel of this former choir school is now used as a meeting room, so, clearly, although concessions have been made at this hostel, there are still a few antique touches in the building. On your doorstep are St. Paul's Cathedral and the Millennium Bridge to the Tate Modern. Most of the rooms have four to eight beds, but there are a few singles, doubles, and triples. Cots can be provided for babies. ⊠ *36 Carter La., The City, EC4V 5AB* ☎ *0870/770–5764* 🖷 *020/7236–7681* ⊕ *www.yha.org.uk* ↘ *193 beds* ♤ *Restaurant, lounge, laundry facilities, Internet, meeting room; no a/c, no room phones, no room TVs, no smoking* ☰ *AE, MC, V* ◉ *BP* Ⓤ *St. Paul's.*

Hampstead & Islington

The leafy rolling hills of Hampstead and trendy shops and bars of Islington form some of the city's most sought after real estate—but still offer relatively good deals for visitors. Hampstead, with its vast green expanse of bucolic Hampstead Heath, is the more peaceful of the two, with steep streets lined with gorgeous Edwardian architecture. Islington lures with a buzzing nightlife and excellent restaurants. Both are about

15 minutes from the center by Tube. Best of all, because they're not in the city center, prices tend to be more moderate here.

ff–fff ☒ **Hilton London Islington.** Next door to the Islington Business Design Centre, this hotel is sleek and modern, standing out starkly in historic Islington. The hotel has standard, good-sized rooms with all the usual amenities meant to soothe the souls of the business travelers who make up most of its customers. For those with time for aesthetics, the rooms higher up have panoramic views. There's a relaxing spa for those worn down by jetlag. ✉ *53 Upper St., Islington, N1 0UY* ☎ *020/7354–7700* 🖷 *020/7354–7711* ⊕ *www.hilton.com* 🛏 *183 rooms, 6 suites* ⚅ *2 restaurants, coffee shop, room service, in-room safes, cable TV, in-room data ports, gym, hot tub, sauna, spa, steam room, bar, lobby lounge, babysitting, Internet, business services, meeting room, no-smoking rooms* ▭ *AE, DC, MC, V* ◯ *BP* Ⓤ *Angel.*

ff ☒ **Jurys Inn.** Just a 10-minute walk from King's Cross station, this non-descript, purpose-built, U.K. chain hotel provides low-price accommodations. The rooms are basic but spacious by London standards, and can accommodate up to three adults or a family of four. ■ TIP→ **Busy, trendy Upper Street, with its cafés, lively bars, and hip restaurants, is close by.** ✉ *60 Pentonville Rd., Islington, N1 9LA* ☎ *020/7282–5500* 🖷 *020/ 7282–5511* ⊕ *www.jurysinn.com* 🛏 *229 rooms* ⚅ *Restaurant, cable TV, in-room data ports, pub, babysitting, dry cleaning, laundry service, meeting rooms, parking (fee), no-smoking rooms* ▭ *AE, DC, MC, V* Ⓤ *Angel, King's Cross.*

ff ☒ **La Gaffe.** Italian Lorenzo Stella has welcomed people back to these early-18th-century shepherds' cottages, a short walk up one of Hampstead's magnificent hills, for more than 20 years. His restaurant has been going for nearly 40. Make no mistake: rooms are tiny, with showers only, but the popular wine bar and restaurant (which, naturally, serve Italian food) are yours to enjoy. Between the two wings of the hotel is a raised summer patio. ✉ *107–111 Heath St., Hampstead, NW3 6SS* ☎ *020/7435–8965* 🖷 *020/7794–7592* ⊕ *www.lagaffe.co.uk* 🛏 *18 rooms, 3 suites* ⚅ *Restaurant, café, fans, wine bar, laundry facilities, concierge, Internet, free parking; no a/c, no smoking* ▭ *AE, MC, V* ◯ *CP* Ⓤ *Hampstead.*

Kensington

One of London's most upscale neighborhoods, Kensington is a center of the tourist universe, and adjoining South Kensington blends right in. With lots of pricey boutiques, restaurants geared to expats and tourists, and plenty of popular bars and pubs, it has much to offer. Hotels in this area range from the very expensive to the affordable, and from the absurdly ornate to the resolutely basic.

fffff ☒ **Bentley Kempinski.** This opulent hotel is an elegant escape in Kensington. Housed in a creamy white Victorian building, its lobby is a gorgeous explosion of marble, with high ceilings, chandeliers and original architectural detail. The bedrooms are almost palatial by London standards, with silk wallpaper, golden furnishings, and fine marble bathrooms. The

16

two restaurants serve modern British cuisine with continental touches, while Malachite is a quiet bar for a brandy after dinner. Cigar lovers can drift to the Cigar Divan for Havana cigars and mature whiskies. The staff is obliging, and the marble Turkish steam room is a unique haven from the stresses of the day. ⊠ *27–33 Harrington Gardens, South Kensington, SW7 4JK* ☎ *020/7244–5555* 🖷 *020/7244–5566* ⊕ *www. thebentley-hotel.com* ⇄ *52 rooms, 12 suites* ♨ *2 restaurants, in-room fax, in-room safes, some in-room hot tubs, minibars, cable TV with movies and video games, in-room DVDs/VCRs, in-room data ports, gym, hair salon, spa, Turkish bath, bar, lounge, babysitting, dry cleaning, laundry service, concierge, Internet, business services, meeting rooms, airport shuttle, car rental, parking (fee), some pets allowed, no-smoking rooms* ▭ *AE, D, MC, V* Ⓤ *Gloucester Rd.*

£££££ ▦ **Blakes.** Designed by owner Anouska Hempel, Blakes is a fantasy packed with precious Biedermeier, Murano glass, and modern pieces collected from around the world. Rooms hark back to the days of the British empire, and include Chinese opium dens draped in lush red fabrics as well as bright spaces with classic colonial furnishings. The foyer sets the tone with piles of cushions, black walls, rattan, and bamboo. The exotic Thai restaurant is a trendy delight. ⊠ *33 Roland Gardens, South Kensington, SW7 3PF* ☎ *020/7370–6701* 🖷 *020/7373-0442* ⊕ *www.blakeshotels.com* ⇄ *38 rooms, 11 suites* ♨ *Restaurant, room service, some in-room faxes, in-room safes, minibars, cable TV, in-room VCRs, in-room data ports, Wi-Fi, gym, bar, babysitting, dry cleaning, laundry service, concierge, Internet, business services, meeting rooms, car rental, parking (fee); no a/c in some rooms* ▭ *AE, DC, MC, V* Ⓤ *S. Kensington.*

★ **£££££** ▦ **Milestone Hotel & Apartments.** This pair of intricately decorated Victorian town houses overlooking Kensington Palace and Gardens is an intimate, luxurious alternative to the city's more famous five-star hotels. Great thoughtfulness goes into the hospitality and everything is possible in this special place. You'll be offered a welcome drink upon arrival and, if you so desire, you can return to a post-theater midnight snack in your room or leave with a picnic for the park across the street. The staff is friendly and efficient, but never obsequious. Each sumptuous room is full of antiques; many have canopied beds. Our favorite is the Ascot Room, which is filled with elegant hats of the kind worn at the famous races. ⊠ *1 Kensington Ct., Kensington, W8 5DL* ☎ *020/7917–1000* 🖷 *020/7917–1010* ⊕ *www.milestonehotel.com* ⇄ *45 rooms, 12 suites, 6 apartments* ♨ *2 restaurants, room service, in-room fax, in-room safes, some kitchens, minibars, cable TV with movies, in-room VCRs, gym, hot tub, sauna, bar, lounge, babysitting, dry cleaning, laundry service, concierge, Internet, business services, meeting rooms, some pets allowed (fee); no smoking* ▭ *AE, DC, MC, V* Ⓤ *High St. Kensington.*

££££–£££££ 🏨 **Eleven Cadogan Gardens.** This aristocratic, late-Victorian, gabled town house has a clubby feel—there's no sign, just a simple 11 above the door. Antiques, landscape paintings and portraits, coupled with some of that solid, no-nonsense furniture that *real* English country houses have in abundance make it seem like you're staying in a family home. The best rooms are at the back, overlooking a private garden. If you want to spare no expense and hire a chauffeur-driven car, there's one standing by. The complimentary freshly baked cake for afternoon tea, and sherry and canapés in the evening are excellent. ✉ *11 Cadogan Gardens, Sloane Sq., South Kensington, SW3 2RJ* ☎ *020/7730–7000* 🖶 *020/7730–5217* ⊕ *www.number-eleven.co.uk* ⬠ *62 rooms* ⚐ *Dining room, room service, in-room safes, cable TV, in-room VCRs, in-room data ports, exercise equipment, massage, sauna, bar, dry cleaning, laundry service, concierge, Internet, business services, meeting rooms, airport shuttle, car rental; no a/c in some rooms, no kids* ▭ *AE, DC, MC, V* Ⓤ *Sloane Sq.*

££££–£££££ 🏨 **The Gore.** Just down the road from the Albert Hall, this friendly hotel is run by the same people who run Hazlitt's and the Rookery. The lobby looks like a set from a Luchino Visconti film, evoking centuries past. Upstairs are spectacular follylike rooms—Room 101 is a Tudor fantasy with minstrel gallery, stained glass, and four-poster bed, and Room 211, done in over-the-top Hollywood style, has a tile mural of Greek goddesses in its bathroom. As with anything eccentric, this place is not for everyone. ✉ *189 Queens Gate, Kensington, SW7 5EX* ☎ *020/7584–6601* 🖶 *020/7589–8127* ⊕ *www.gorehotel.com* ⬠ *54 rooms* ⚐ *Restaurant, room service, fans, in-room safes, minibars, cable TV, in-room VCRs, in-room data ports, bar, lounge, babysitting, dry cleaning, laundry service, concierge, meeting rooms, no-smoking floors; no a/c* ▭ *AE, DC, MC, V* Ⓤ *Gloucester Rd.*

££££–£££££ 🏨 **The Pelham.** Museum lovers flock to this sweet hotel across the street from the South Kensington tube station. The Natural History, Science, and Victoria & Albert museums are all a short stroll away, as is King's Road. At the end of a day's sightseeing, settle down in front of the fireplace in one of the two snug drawing rooms with their honor bars. The stylish, contemporary rooms by designer Kit Kemp have sash windows and marble bathrooms. Some top-floor rooms have sloping ceilings and casement windows. ✉ *15 Cromwell Pl., South Kensington, SW7 2LA* ☎ *020/7589–8288, 800/553–6674 in U.S.* 🖶 *020/7584–8444* ⊕ *www.firmdale.com* ⬠ *47 rooms, 4 suites* ⚐ *Restaurant, room service, some in-room safes, minibars, cable TV, in-room VCRs, in-room data ports, bar, concierge, business services, meeting rooms, parking (fee)* ▭ *AE, MC, V* Ⓤ *S. Kensington.*

££££ 🏨 **The Cranley.** Old-fashioned British propriety is the overall feeling here at this small, Victorian town-house hotel. High ceilings and huge windows make the bedrooms light and bright. The antique desks and four-poster or half-tester beds are in line with the period furnishings. Even

---

QUIRKY LONDON

The Gore has an eclectic selection of Victoriana, prints, etchings, antiques, and more than 4,000 original paintings.

16

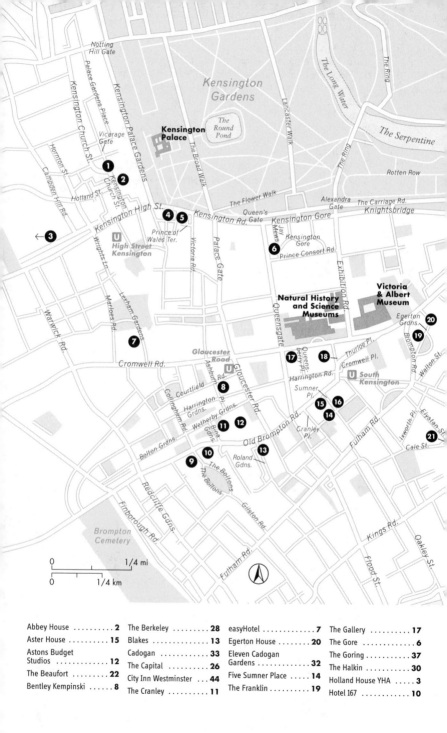

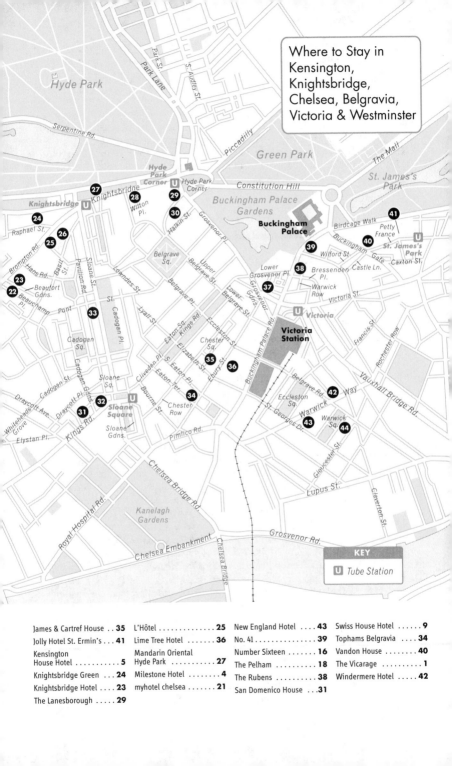

Where to Stay in Kensington, Knightsbridge, Chelsea, Belgravia, Victoria & Westminster

KEY

U *Tube Station*

the bathrooms have traditional Victorian fittings. Afternoon tea and evening canapés are complimentary. ■ TIP→ **Some rooms are big enough for families.** ⊠ *10–12 Bina Gardens, South Kensington, SW5 0LA* ☎ *020/7373–0123* 🖷 *020/7373–9497* ⊕ *www.thecranley.com* 🖎 *29 rooms, 5 suites, 4 apartments* ⚑ *Room service, in-room safes, some kitchens, cable TV, in-room VCRs, in-room data ports, babysitting, laundry service, concierge, Internet, business services, parking (fee), no-smoking rooms* ⊟ *AE, DC, MC, V* Ⓤ *Gloucester Rd.*

★ **£££–££££** 🖼 **Number Sixteen.** In a white-portico row of Victorian houses, close to the South Kensington Tube and a short walk from the Victoria & Albert Museum, Number Sixteen is a lovely, luxury B&B. Each room is different except for a uniform spaciousness (by London standards) and marble- and oak-clad bathrooms. The style is not so much interior-designed as understated—new furniture and modern prints are juxtaposed with yellowed oils and antiques. The staff is friendly, so lingering in the drawing rooms is a pleasure, and drinks are served in the charming garden in summer. ⊠ *16 Sumner Pl., South Kensington, SW7 3EG* ☎ *020/7589–5232, 800/553–6674 in U.S.* 🖷 *020/7584–8615* ⊕ *www.firmdale.com* 🖎 *42 rooms* ⚑ *Room service, in-room safes, minibars, cable TV, in-room VCRs, in-room data ports, bar, lounge, library, babysitting, dry cleaning, laundry service, concierge; no a/c in some rooms* ⊟ *AE, MC, V* ⎋ *CP* Ⓤ *S. Kensington.*

£££–££££ 🖼 **Kensington House Hotel.** This refurbished 19th-century town house off Kensington High Street has attractive, streamlined rooms with large windows and contemporary furnishings. Rear rooms have views of trees and mews houses, and all rooms have extras such as tea/coffeemakers and bathrobes. ⊠ *15–16 Prince of Wales Terr., Kensington, W8 5PQ* ☎ *020/7937–2345* 🖷 *020/7368–6700* ⊕ *www.kenhouse.com* 🖎 *41 rooms* ⚑ *Restaurant, room service, fans, in-room safes, cable TV, in-room data ports, bar, babysitting, dry cleaning, parking (fee), no-smoking rooms; no a/c* ⊟ *AE, DC, MC, V* ⎋ *CP* Ⓤ *High St. Kensington.*

£££ 🖼 **Five Sumner Place.** Once you've checked into this tall Victorian town house on a quiet residential street, you get your own key to the front door and make yourself at home. If the weather is pleasant, you can enjoy the small garden. In the morning, take breakfast in the conservatory. Guest rooms are simply decorated with pleasant Victorian detail and reproduction furniture. An elevator is available for those with mobility problems. ⊠ *5 Sumner Pl., South Kensington, SW7 3EE* ☎ *020/7584–7586* 🖷 *020/7823–9962* ⊕ *www.sumnerplace.com* 🖎 *17 rooms* ⚑ *Room service, minibars, in-room broadband, in-room data ports, parking (fee); no a/c, no smoking* ⊟ *AE, MC, V* ⎋ *BP* Ⓤ *S. Kensington.*

£££ 🖼 **The Gallery.** It's a small, Edwardian world apart from the bustling city, but it's a little pricey for what it has to offer. The Arts-and-Crafts–style living room has a piano, lush carpets, and cozy fires in the winter. Decor in the guest rooms is looking slightly dated, the floral fabric a bit old fashioned, but rooms are pleasant, with solid, comfortable beds, and the bathrooms have London's ubiquitous polished granite. ⊠ *10 Queensberry Pl., South Kensington, SW7 2E8* ☎ *020/7915–0000, 800/270–9206 in U.S.* 🖷 *020/7915–4400* ⊕ *www.eeh.co.uk* 🖎 *34 rooms, 2 suites* ⚑ *Room service, some in-room faxes, in-room safes, some in-room hot tubs, some* *minibars, cable TV, in-room data ports, bar, dry cleaning, laundry serv-ice, concierge, Internet, meeting rooms, airport shuttle; no a/c in some rooms* ⊟ *AE, DC, MC, V* ⦾ *BP* Ⓤ *S. Kensington.*

££–£££ ⬚ **Aster House.** Country-casual rooms fill this delightful guesthouse. ■ **TIP →** **The friendly owners go out of their way to make you feel at home and answer questions, even loaning guests a free cell phone to use while in town.** The conservatory where breakfast is served is an airy, light place, and the small garden at the back has a charming pond. Note that this is a five-story building with no elevator. ⊠ *3 Sumner Pl., South Kensing-ton, SW7 3EE* ☎ *020/7581–5888* 🖷 *020/7584–4925* ⊕ *www.welcome2london.com/asterhouse* ⬃ *14 rooms* ⌂ *Dining room, in-room safes, cable TV, lounge, Internet; no smoking* ⊟ *MC, V* ⦾ *BP* Ⓤ *S. Kensington.*

££–£££ ⬚ **Astons Budget Studios.** These three redbrick Victorian town houses on a residential street hold studios and apartments. All accommodations have concealed kitchenettes, and the apartments (£££) have marble bathrooms and trouser presses as well. The decor is a bit Scandinavian. ⊠ *31 Rosary Gardens, South Kensington, SW7 4NH* ☎ *020/7590–6000, 800/525–2810 in U.S.* 🖷 *020/7590–6060* ⊕ *www.astons-apartments.com* ⬃ *43 rooms, 12 suites* ⌂ *Dining room, fans, in-room safes, kitch-enettes, microwaves, refrigerators, cable TV, in-room data ports, concierge, Internet, business services, airport shuttle, car rental, park-ing (fee), some pets allowed, no-smoking floors; no a/c* ⊟ *AE, MC, V* Ⓤ *Gloucester Rd.*

££ ⬚ **Hotel 167.** This white-stucco, Victorian corner house just a two-minute walk from the V&A is no traditional old hostelry. With its strong abstract art pieces and black-and-white tiled floor, the lobby is unique, while the bedrooms are an unpredictable mélange of new and old furniture and colorful fabrics. The breakfast room–lounge is charm-ing, with wrought-iron furniture and sunny yellow walls. Its creative approach has been the subject of a novel ("Hotel 167" by Jane Solomon) and a song by the rock band Manic Street Preachers. ⊠ *167 Old Bromp-ton Rd., South Kensington, SW5 0AN* ☎ *020/7373–3221* 🖷 *020/7373–3360* ⊕ *www.hotel167.com* ⬃ *18 rooms* ⌂ *Dining room, mini-bars, cable TV; no a/c* ⊟ *AE, DC, MC, V* ⦾ *CP* Ⓤ *Gloucester Rd.*

££ ⬚ **Swiss House Hotel.** Those who come here expecting a mountainside chalet will surely be disappointed to see that it's yet another Victorian town house. Rooms can be quite small, but attractive, with polished wood floors, Scan-dinavian-style pine furniture, and simple dark-blue rugs. Back rooms have garden views and some single rooms are very tiny indeed. As for serv-ice, some aspects of the famous Swiss hospitality didn't make it across the border. ⊠ *171 Old Brompton Rd., South Kensington, SW5 0AN* ☎ *020/7373–2769* 🖷 *020/7373–4983* ⊕ *www.swiss-hh.demon.co.uk* ⬃ *15 rooms, 14 with bath* ⌂ *Dining room, fans, babysitting, parking (fee), no-smoking rooms; no a/c* ⊟ *AE, DC, MC, V* ⦾ *CP* Ⓤ *Gloucester Rd.*

££ ⬚ **The Vicarage.** The family-owned Vicarage sits on a leafy street off Kens-ington Church Street. The large Victorian house has an ornate lobby, with red wallpaper and rococo mirrors. Upstairs, the tiny rooms are painted in soft colors and filled with faux antiques—and perhaps are decked out in a bit too much floral fabric. The bright TV lounge seems

16

Where to Stay in Mayfair, Regent's Park, St. James's, Soho, Covent Garden, & the South Bank

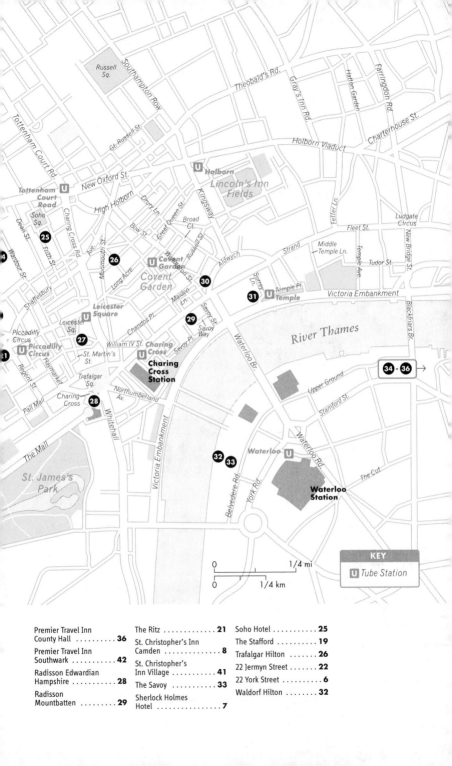

to urge you not to be such a separatist. A recent renovation means nine of the bedrooms now have bathrooms, while the rest share. ✉ *10 Vicarage Gate, Kensington, W8 4AG* ☎ *020/7229–4030* 🖷 *020/7792–5989* ⊕ *www.londonvicaragehotel.com* ⇌ *17 rooms, 9 with bath* ⚲ *Dining room, lounge; no a/c, no room TVs* ▭ *No credit cards* ⍟ *BP* Ⓤ *High St. Kensington.*

£–££ 🛏 **Abbey House.** The main attraction of this Victorian town house is its location near trendy Notting Hill and Kensington High Street's many shops. Inside, rooms look dated, and the decor is basic. Every room shares a bath with another. The slightly nicer, but still budget Vicarage is next door. There are stairs and no elevator here, so it can be a burden for those with mobility problems. ✉ *11 Vicarage Gate, Kensington, W8 4AG* ☎ *020/7727–2594* 🖷 *020/7727–1873* ⊕ *www.abbeyhousekensington.com* ⇌ *16 rooms without bath* ⚲ *Lounge, concierge; no a/c, no room phones* ▭ *No credit cards* ⍟ *BP* Ⓤ *High St. Kensington.*

£ 🛏 **easyHotel.** No London hotel received more attention in 2005 than budget easyHotel. Crammed into a big white town house are 34 tiny rooms, all with double bed and private bathroom, brightly decorated in the trademark orange-and-white of the Easy chain (which includes the Internet cafés "easyeverything" and the budget airline easyJet). The idea behind the hotel is to provide quality basics (bed, sink, shower, toilet) for little money. The tiny reception desk with one staff member can't offer much in terms of service, and if you want your room cleaned, it's an additional £10 a day. The concept is a huge hit—easyHotel is fully booked months in advance. ✉ *14 Lexham Gardens, Kensington, W8 5JE* ☎ *020/7216–1717* ⊕ *www.easyhotel.com* ⇌ *34 rooms* ⚲ *Cable TV; no a/c, no room phones, no smoking* ▭ *MC, V* Ⓜ *Gloucester Rd.*

£ 🛏 **Holland House YHA.** Part Jacobean mansion and part 1970s addition, this is certainly the most historic and pastoral of London's youth hostels. Dorm rooms overlook the wooded park, where black bunnies scamper and peacocks strut around the central Kyoto Gardens. Kensington High Street and civilization are just a few steps away. Inexpensive lunches and dinners are available. ✉ *Holland Walk, Kensington, W8 7QU* ☎ *0870/770–5866* 🖷 *020/7376–0667* ⊕ *www.hollhse.btinternet.co.uk* ⇌ *201 beds* ⚲ *Dining room, 4 tennis courts, lounge, recreation room, laundry facilities, Internet, meeting rooms; no a/c, no room phones, no room TVs, no smoking* ▭ *AE, MC, V* ⍟ *BP* Ⓤ *High St. Kensington.*

Knightsbridge, Chelsea & Belgravia

With Harrods, Harvey Nichols, and a glittering galaxy of posh department stores, exquisite clothing boutiques, and divine cafés, restaurants, and coffee shops, Knightsbridge and Chelsea are where the ladies who lunch live—and thus the hotels tend to be fabulous. There's plenty of space to park the Bentley, and the doormen here are terribly polite. By contrast, Belgravia is home to an assortment of budget hotels—perhaps nobody has told the Queen that they're in her neighborhood.

£££££ 🛏 **The Berkeley.** The elegant Berkeley successfully mixes the old and the new in a luxurious, modern building with a splendid penthouse swimming pool. The bedrooms either have swags of William Morris prints or are art deco. All have sitting areas, CD players, and big bathrooms with bidets. There are spectacular penthouse suites with their own conservatory terraces, and others with saunas or balconies. Dining venues include Marcus Wareing's high-class Pétrus restaurant, Gordon Ramsay's excellent and extremely popular Boxwood café, the eclectic and sumptuous Blue Bar, and the whimsical Caramel Room where morning coffee and decadent doughnuts are served. ⊠ *Wilton Pl., Belgravia, SW1X 7RL* ☎ *020/7235–6000, 800/637–2869 in U.S.* 🖷 *020/7235–4330* ⊕ *www.the-berkeley.com* 📑 *103 rooms, 55 suites* ⌕ *Restaurant, room service, in-room fax, in-room safes, some kitchens, minibars, cable TV, in-room VCRs, indoor-outdoor pool, gym, hair salon, sauna, spa, Turkish bath, bar, cinema, babysitting, dry cleaning, laundry service, concierge, Internet, business services, meeting rooms, airport shuttle, car rental, parking (fee), no-smoking floors* ⊟ *AE, DC, MC, V* Ⓤ *Knightsbridge.*

£££££ 🖭 **Cadogan.** This is both one of London's most beautiful hotels and one of its most historically naughty. A recent overhaul means much of its old stuffiness is gone—elegant golds and creams have replaced fussy florals. The drawing room has rich wood paneling and deep, comfortable armchairs, and is an excellent place for tea and people-watching. The sophisticated bar urges you to have a martini and a cigar. Breakfast offers healthy cereals and fruits alongside decadent pastries. ⊠ *75 Sloane St., Chelsea, SW1X 9SG* ☎ *020/7235–7141* 🖷 *020/7245–0994* ⊕ *www. cadogan.com* 📑 *65* ⌕ *Restaurant, room service, minibars, cable TV, in-room VCR, in-room data ports, Wi-Fi, tennis courts, bar, lounge, babysitting, dry cleaning, laundry facilities, concierge, no-smoking rooms* ⊟ *AE, MC, V.*

£££££ 🖭 **The Capital.** Reserve well ahead if you want a room here—as you must for a table in the hotel's popular, top-quality French restaurant. This grand hotel decanted into a private house is the work of the Levin family, who also own nearby L'Hotel, and it exudes their impeccable taste: fine-grain woods, original prints, and soothing, country-chic furnishings. ■ TIP→ **Ask for a front-facing room to get more space. If you're going for a deluxe double, ask for the L-shape rooms in the atmospheric Edwardian wing, where each room has a desk.** The staff is conscientious and friendly. ⊠ *22–24 Basil St., Knightsbridge, SW3 1AT* ☎ *020/759–1202, 800/ 926–3199 in U.S.* 🖷 *020/7225–0011* ⊕ *www.capitalhotel.co.uk* 📑 *40 rooms, 8 suites* ⌕ *Restaurant, dining room, room service, in-room safes, minibars, cable TV, in-room data ports, bar, lounge, babysitting, dry cleaning, laundry service, concierge, Internet, business services, meeting rooms, car rental, parking (fee), some pets allowed, no-smoking rooms* ⊟ *AE, DC, MC, V* Ⓤ *Knightsbridge.*

£££££ 🖭 **The Halkin.** Escape the clutter and flowery motifs of other hotels and chill-out in the understated design here: the clean-cut, white-marble, lobby bar has burgundy-leather bucket chairs; muted earth-tone bedrooms have bedside control panels for everything from lights to air-conditioning; in between are arresting, curved, charcoal-gray-and-chrome corridors. It's akin to staying in the Design Museum, except that you have Knightsbridge and Hyde Park practically on your doorstep, and the exceptional Nahm Thai restaurant in your lobby. The Shambhala Health Club at the nearby

Metropolitan Hotel is at your disposal as well. ⊠ *5 Halkin St., Belgravia, SW1X 7DJ* ☎ *020/7333–1000* 🖷 *020/7333–1100* ⊕ *www.halkin.co.uk* 🛏 *41 rooms* ♵ *Restaurant, some in-room faxes, in-room safes, cable TV with video games, in-room VCRs, in-room data ports, bar, babysitting, dry cleaning, laundry service, concierge, Internet, business services, parking (fee), no-smoking rooms* ▭ *AE, DC, MC, V* Ⓤ *Hyde Park Corner.*

£££££   🔲 **The Lanesborough.** Royally proportioned public rooms distinguish this
Fodor'sChoice   multimillion-pound, American-run conversion of St. George's Hospi-
★   tal. Everything undulates with richness—moiré silks and fleurs-de-lis in the colors of precious stones, magnificent antiques and oil paintings, hand-woven £250-per-square-yard carpet—as if Liberace and Laura Ashley had collaborated. To check in, sign the visitor's book, then retire to your room, where you are waited on by a personal butler. ■ TIP→ **Guests at the Lanesborough have their own private butlers.** Should you take the £5,000-per-night Royal Suite, the hotel will provide a chauffeur-driven Bentley and personal security guards. If you yearn for a bygone age and are very rich, this hotel is certainly for you. ⊠ *Hyde Park Corner, Belgravia, SW1X 7TA* ☎ *020/7259–5599, 800/999–1828 in U.S.* 🖷 *020/7259–5606, 800/937–8278 in U.S.* ⊕ *www.lanesborough.com* 🛏 *49 rooms, 46 suites* ♵ *2 restaurants, room service, in-room fax, in-room safes, some in-room hot tubs, some kitchens, minibars, cable TV with movies and video games, in-room broadband, exercise equipment, 2 bars, lobby lounge, library, babysitting, dry cleaning, laundry service, concierge, Internet, meeting rooms, car rental, parking (fee), no-smoking rooms* ▭ *AE, DC, MC, V* Ⓤ *Hyde Park Corner.*

Fodor'sChoice   🔲 **Mandarin Oriental Hyde Park.** Stay here, and the three greats of
★ £££££   Knightsbridge—Hyde Park, Harrods, and Harvey Nichols—are on your doorstep. Built in 1880, the Mandarin Oriental is one of London's most elegant hotels. Bedrooms are traditional Victorian with hidden high-tech gadgets (Wi-Fi is expected in late 2006) and luxurious touches—potted orchids, delicate chocolates, and fresh fruit. The service here is legendary and includes a butler on every floor. In 2005 Margaret Thatcher held her star-studded birthday party here. ⊠ *66 Knightsbridge, Knightsbridge, SW1X 7LA* ☎ *020/7235–2000* 🖷 *020/7235–2001* ⊕ *www.mandarinoriental.com* 🛏 *177 rooms, 23 suites* ♵ *2 restaurants, room service, some in-room faxes, in-room safes, minibars, cable TV, in-room VCRs, in-room data ports, gym, hot tub, sauna, spa, steam room, bar, babysitting, dry cleaning, laundry service, concierge, Internet, business services, meeting rooms, airport shuttle, car rental, parking (fee), no-smoking rooms* ▭ *AE, DC, MC, V* Ⓤ *Knightsbridge.*

£££££   🔲 **San Domenico House.** Until 2006 this place was known as the Sloane, and the new owners have kept things much as they were in that popular hotel. The decor is still lavish, with gorgeous antiques, luxurious curtains and bedding, and marble baths. But gone are the days when you could buy the furniture—it was too hard to find pieces to replace the beautiful antiques that the guests took home. The roof terrace, which has upholstered garden furniture and a panoramic view of Chelsea, is the best place to relax, and the staff are endlessly helpful. ⊠ *29 Draycott Pl., Chelsea, SW3 2SH* ☎ *020/7581–5757 or 800/324–9960 from the U.S.*

020/7584–1348 www.sandomenicohouse.com 14 rooms, 8 suites Dining room, in-room safes, cable TV, in-room VCRs, in-room data ports, lobby lounge, dry cleaning, laundry service, concierge, Internet, business services, parking (fee) AE, DC, MC, V Sloane Sq.

££££–£££££ **Knightsbridge Hotel.** Just off glamorous Knightsbridge near Harrods and Harvey Nichols in quiet Beaufort Gardens, this chic hotel is well placed for shoppers. The balconied suites and regular rooms are wrapped in bold fabrics, the beds piled high with warm duvets. All rooms have CD players, writing desks, and large granite-and-oak bathrooms. The fully loaded honor bar in the drawing room is an excellent place to unwind amid African sculptures and modern art. *10 Beaufort Gardens, Knightsbridge, SW3 1PT 020/7584–6300, 800/553–6674 in U.S. 020/7584–6355 www.knightsbridgehotel.co.uk 42 rooms, 2 suites Room service, in-room safes, minibars, cable TV, some in-room VCRs, in-room data ports, gym, bar, library, babysitting, dry cleaning, laundry service, concierge, Internet, meeting rooms, parking (fee) AE, MC, V Knightsbridge.*

£££–£££££ **myhotel chelsea.** This small, chic hotel tucked away down a Chelsea side street is a charmer. Rooms are bijoux small, but sophisticated, with mauve satin throws atop crisp white down comforters. Tiny bathrooms are made cheery with pale pink granite countertops. Flat-screen TVs, DVD players, and in-room Wi-Fi all set the place electronically ahead of many top-level London hotels. The beauty is in the details here—there's no restaurant, but the fire-warmed bar serves light meals and tea. There's no pool, but there's an excellent spa. The guest library has DVDs and books on loan, and offers a quiet place to relax. Best of all, you can get a good deal if you book in advance via the Web site. *35 Ixworth Pl., Chelsea, SW3 3QZ 020/7225–7500 020/7225–7555 www. myhotels.com 45 rooms, 9 suites Room service, fans, in-room safes, minibars, cable TV, in-room DVDs, Wi-Fi, gym, massage, spa, bar, library, lounge, babysitting, laundry service, some pets allowed, no-smoking floors AE, D, MC, V S. Kensington.*

££££ **The Beaufort.** This elegant pair of Victorian houses contains a guesthouse where you get a lot for your money. Guests get a front-door key, free run of the drinks cabinet in the drawing room, and an in-room CD player and radio. The high-ceiling, contemporary rooms have muted, sophisticated colors. Rates include flowers, fruit, chocolates, cookies, and water in your room; free e-mail and movies via the TV; cream tea in the drawing room; and membership at a local health club. Junior suites include a free one-way airport transfer. Four of the rooms have pretty wrought-iron balconies. *33 Beaufort Gardens, Knightsbridge, SW3 1PP 020/7584–5252 020/7589–2834, 800/584–7764 in U.S. www.thebeaufort.co.uk 20 rooms, 7 suites Room service, in-room safes, cable TV with movies and video games, in-room data ports, lobby lounge, babysitting, dry cleaning, laundry service, concierge, Internet, business services, meeting rooms, car rental, no-smoking rooms; no a/c in some rooms AE, DC, MC, V CP Knightsbridge.*

££££ **Egerton House.** This utterly peaceful, small hotel was the first in the group that includes the Franklin and Dukes hotels. Chintz, floral, or Regency-

16

stripe bedrooms overlook the gorgeous gardens in back or the redbrick facades of the buildings in the area; some have quirky shapes, one has a four-poster bed, and still others are bigger with closet space. The two drawing rooms, decorated in high-Victorian style, are good places to write letters or relax with a drink from the honor bar. ✉ *17–19 Egerton Terr., Knights-bridge, SW3 2BX* ☎ *020/7589–2412, 800/473–9492 in U.S.* 📠 *020/7584–6540* ⊕ *www.egertonhousehotel.co.uk* 🛏 *23 rooms, 6 suites* ⚭ *Dining room, room service, minibars, cable TV, some in-room VCRs, in-room data ports, bar, lounge, dry cleaning, laundry service, concierge, Internet, business services, meeting rooms, car rental, parking (fee), no-smoking rooms* ▭ *AE, DC, MC, V* Ⓤ *Knightsbridge, S. Kensington.*

££££ ▦ **The Franklin.** It's hard to imagine, while taking tea in this romantic hotel overlooking a quiet garden, that you're an amble away from busy Brompton and Cromwell roads and the splendors of the V&A Museum. A few of the rooms are small, but the marble bathrooms are not, and the large garden rooms and suites are romantic indeed. Some rooms have four-poster beds; all have antique furnishings. Tea is served daily in the lounge, and there's an honor bar. ✉ *28 Egerton Gardens, Knights-bridge, SW3 2DB* ☎ *020/7584–5533, 800/473–9487 in U.S.* 📠 *020/7584–5449, 800/473–9489 in U.S.* ⊕ *www.franklinhotel.co.uk* 🛏 *50 rooms* ⚭ *Dining room, room service, in-room safes, minibars, cable TV, some in-room VCRs, in-room data ports, bar, dry cleaning, laundry service, concierge, Internet, business services, meeting rooms, parking (fee), no-smoking rooms* ▭ *AE, DC, MC, V* Ⓤ *S. Kensington.*

£££–££££ ▦ **L'Hotel.** Rooms at this upscale B&B have an air of provincial France, with white bedcovers, pine furniture, and beige color schemes. It's like staying in a house—you're given your own front-door key, there's no elevator, and the staff leaves in the evening. Ask for a fireplace room: they're the biggest. Delicious breakfast croissants and baguettes are served in Le Metro cellar wine bar or brought to your room. You also have access to the restaurant and concierge services of the plush Capital Hotel, run by the same family, a few doors down the street. ✉ *28 Basil St., Knightsbridge, SW3 1AT* ☎ *020/7589–6286* 📠 *020/7823–7826* ⊕ *www.lhotel.co.uk* 🛏 *11 rooms, 1 suite* ⚭ *Restaurant, fans, minibars, cable TV, in-room VCRs, in-room data ports, bar, babysitting, dry cleaning, laundry service, concierge, Internet, parking (fee); no a/c* ▭ *AE, V* ⦿ *CP* Ⓤ *Knightsbridge.*

£££ ▦ **Knightsbridge Green.** Near Harrods and Hyde Park, this modern hotel has affordable triples and quads with sofa beds that are good for families. Rooms are rather plain and could use an update, but they have double-glaze windows that help muffle the sound of traffic on busy Knightsbridge. Breakfast can be delivered to your room, or you could linger in the lounge over complimentary tea and coffee. ✉ *159 Knights-bridge, Knightsbridge, SW1X 7PD* ☎ *020/7584–6274* 📠 *020/7225–1635* ⊕ *www.thekghotel.co.uk* 🛏 *28 rooms, 12 suites* ⚭ *In-room safes, cable TV, in-room data ports, babysitting, dry cleaning, concierge, Internet; no smoking* ▭ *AE, DC, MC, V* Ⓤ *Knightsbridge.*

£££ ▦ **Tophams Belgravia.** Family-owned since 1937, this place extends a warm welcome—and a good value. The hotel is in five linked Georgian houses. Bedrooms, which include family and four-poster rooms, are done in English country-house florals or deep greens and reds. ✉ *28 Ebury St., Belgravia, SW1W 0LU* ☎ *020/7730–8147* 🖷 *020/7823–5966* ⊕ *www.tophams.co.uk* ↰ *39 rooms* ⚐ *Restaurant, room service, cable TV, in-room data ports, bar, lobby lounge, babysitting, meeting room, parking (fee)* ⎮❍⎮ *BP* ▭ *AE, DC, MC, V* Ⓤ *Victoria.*

Mayfair to Regent's Park

Regal amid the noise of modern life, Mayfair is the kind of place where you inherit a home or you don't live there at all. Thus you almost have to be a tourist to get the chance to visit its leafy park-strewn streets. Regent's Park is almost exactly what you'd expect from the name: plenty of expensive hotels and exquisite service.

★ **£££££** 🖃 **Brown's.** Founded in 1837 by Lord Byron's "gentleman's gentleman," James Brown, this hotel consisting of 11 Georgian town houses holds a treasured place in London society. After being closed for more than a year, the venerable classic's reopening in late 2005 was hosted by former Prime Minister Margaret Thatcher. The transformation is extraordinary. Previously oak-panel, chintz-laden public spaces and thickly carpeted bedrooms with brocade wallpapers now speak with the accent of chic, contemporary style. Everything is done up in cool neutral tones of coffee and cream, beds are new and firm, bathrooms are filled with marble and high-end bath products. All rooms have broadband and office space. The staff are still exceedingly professional and helpful. It's still Brown's, only better. ✉ *34 Albemarle St., Mayfair, W1X 4BT* ☎ *020/7493–6020* 🖷 *020/7493–9381* ⊕ *www.brownshotel.com* ↰ *117 rooms, 12 suites* ⚐ *2 restaurants, room service, in-room broadband, in-room safes, minibars, cable TV, in-room data ports, gym, bar, lounge, meeting rooms* ▭ *AE, DC, MC, V* Ⓤ *Green Park.*

£££££ 🖃 **Chesterfield Mayfair.** Set deep in the heart of Mayfair, this hotel is the former town house of the Earl of Chesterfield. The welcoming wood-and-leather public rooms match the dark-wood furnishings in the snug bedrooms, which are done in burgundy, browns, and forest green. Double rooms may be on the small side, but they are elegant and the service is excellent. ✉ *35 Charles St., Mayfair, W12 SEB* ☎ *020/7491–2622* 🖷 *020/7491–4793* ⊕ *www.redcarnationhotels.com* ↰ *101 rooms, 9 suites* ⚐ *2 restaurants, room service, in-room fax, some in-room safes, some minibars, cable TV with movies, in-room data ports, exercise equipment, bar, library, dry cleaning, laundry service, concierge, Internet, business services, meeting rooms, no-smoking rooms* ▭ *AE, DC, MC, V* Ⓤ *Green Park.*

★ **£££££** 🖃 **The Connaught.** Make reservations well in advance for this very exclusive small hotel—it's the most understated of any of London's grand hostelries and is the London home-away-from-home for those who have inherited the habit of staying here from their great-grandfathers. The bar and lounges have the air of an ambassadorial residence, an impression re-inforced by the imposing oak staircase, butler on each floor, and dignified staff. Each bedroom has a foyer, antique furniture (if you don't like the desk, they'll change it), and fresh flowers. ■ TIP→ One of Britain's most famous chefs, Angela Hartnett, oversees the restaurants Menu and Grill, which share an exceptional approach to modern European cuisine. ⊠ *Carlos Pl., Mayfair, W1K 6AL* ☎ *020/7499–7070* 🖷 *020/7495–3262* ⊕ *www.savoy-group.co.uk* 🖙 *75 rooms, 27 suites* 🖒 *2 restaurants, room service, in-room fax, in-room safes, minibars, cable TV, in-room data ports, gym, massage, 2 bars, lobby lounge, babysitting, dry cleaning, laundry service, concierge, Internet, business services, meeting rooms, airport shuttle, car rental, travel services, parking (fee), no-smoking rooms* ▱ *AE, DC, MC, V* Ⓤ *Bond St.*

££££££
Fodor'sChoice
★

🛏 **The Dorchester.** Few hotels this opulent manage to be quite so charming. The glamour level is off the scale: 1,500 square yards of gold leaf and 1,100 square yards of marble. Bedrooms (some not as spacious as you might expect) have Irish-linen sheets on canopied beds, brocades and velvets, and Italian marble and etched-glass bathrooms with Floris toiletries. Furnishings throughout are opulent English country-house style, with more than a hint of art deco, in keeping with the original 1930s building. The hotel has embraced modern technology, though, and employs "e-butlers" to help guests figure out the advanced Web TVs in the rooms. ⊠ *Park La., Mayfair, W1A 2HJ* ☎ *020/7629–8888* 🖷 *020/ 7409–0114* ⊕ *www.dorchesterhotel.com* 🖙 *195 rooms, 55 suites* 🖒 *3 restaurants, in-room safes, minibars, cable TV with movies, in-room VCRs, in-room data ports, gym, health club, hair salon, spa, bar, lobby lounge, nightclub, shop, babysitting, dry cleaning, laundry service, concierge, Internet, business services, meeting rooms, car rental, parking (fee), no-smoking rooms* ▱ *AE, DC, MC, V* Ⓤ *Marble Arch, Hyde Park Corner.*

🐾 ££££££ 🛏 **The Landmark.** After a recent renovation, the Landmark is more luxurious than ever. Rich fabrics in neutral tones make the rooms soothing zones of relaxation, while high-speed Internet and doorbells that can be muted are welcome high-tech additions. The lovely, eight-story atrium Winter Garden is overlooked by odd-numbered rooms. Even standard rooms here are among the largest in London and have white marble bathrooms with plush robes. ■ TIP→ Despite all this luxury, it's worth mentioning that this is one of the few London grand hotels that doesn't force you to dress up. ⊠ *222 Marylebone Rd., Marylebone, NW1 6JQ* ☎ *020/ 7631–8000* 🖷 *020/7631–8080* ⊕ *www.landmarklondon.co.uk* 🖙 *299 rooms, 47 suites* 🖒 *2 restaurants, in-room fax, in-room safes, some kitchenettes, minibars, some microwaves, some refrigerators, cable TV with movies and video games, some in-room VCRs, in-room data ports, indoor pool, health club, spa, lobby lounge, piano bar, pub, shop, babysitting, dry cleaning, laundry service, concierge, Internet, business services, meeting rooms, no-smoking floors* ▱ *AE, DC, MC, V* Ⓤ *Marylebone.*

££££££ 🛏 **Le Meridien Piccadilly.** The massive 1908 building is fin-de-siècle elegant and carefully retains its exquisite architectural features. Guest rooms vary between "traditional" (read: outdated, standard decor) and "executive" (read: stylish, minimalist decor), as well as in size. A few on the seventh floor have balconies overlooking Piccadilly. ■ TIP→ **The hotel's Champneys, one of the most exclusive health clubs in London, is luxurious.** ✉ *21 Piccadilly, Mayfair, W1J 0BH* ☎ *020/7734–8000* 🖷 *020/7437–3574* ⊕ *www.lemeridien-piccadilly.com* ➮ *232 rooms, 35 suites* 🍽 *2 restaurants, room service, in-room fax, in-room safes, minibars, cable TV with movies and video games, in-room data ports, indoor pool, gym, health club, spa, billiards, squash, 4 bars, lobby lounge, library, babysitting, dry cleaning, laundry service, concierge, Internet, business services, meeting rooms, parking (fee), no-smoking rooms* ▭ *AE, DC, MC, V* Ⓤ *Piccadilly Circus.*

££££ 🖪 **Marriott Park Lane.** The ornate facade and beautiful interior of this swanky Marriott date to 1919, when the building was originally an apartment complex. Today its wonderful location at the Oxford Street end of Park Lane gives access to great shopping on Bond Street and lovely strolls through Hyde Park. The large hotel goes for a boutique feel. The sizeable bedrooms are standard Marriott fare. ■ TIP→ **The bar at the Marriott Park Lane has its own cocktail, the Crantini 140, a heady mix of white cranberries, vodka, and Cointreau.** ✉ *140 Park La., Mayfair, W1K 7AA* ☎ *020/7493–7000* 🖷 *020/7493–8333* ⊕ *www.marriott.com* ➮ *148 rooms, 9 suites* 🍽 *Restaurant, room service, in-room fax, in-room safes, minibars, cable TV with movies and video games, in-room data ports, indoor pool, gym, spa, babysitting, dry cleaning, laundry service, concierge, Internet, business services, meeting rooms, car rental, no-smoking rooms* ▭ *AE, DC, MC, V* Ⓤ *Marble Arch.*

££££ 🖪 **The Metropolitan.** This supertrendy hotel is one of the few addresses for visiting fashion, music, and media folk in London. Its Met bar has an exclusive guest list, and the restaurant is the famed Nobu, leased by Japanese wonder-chef Nobu Matsuhisa. The lobby is sleek and postmodern, as are the bedrooms, which have identical minimalist taupe-and-white furnishings. The best rooms overlook Hyde Park, but all have a groovy minibar hiding the latest alcoholic and health-boosting beverages. ✉ *Old Park La., Mayfair, W1K 1LB* ☎ *020/7447–1000, 800/337–4685 in U.S.* 🖷 *020/7447–1100* ⊕ *www.metropolitan.co.uk* ➮ *137 rooms, 18 suites* 🍽 *Restaurant, room service, in-room broadband, in-room fax, in-room safes, minibars, cable TV with movies and video games, some in-room VCRs, in-room data ports, gym, massage, bar, shop, babysitting, dry cleaning, laundry service, concierge, Internet, business services, meeting room, parking (fee), no-smoking floors* ▭ *AE, DC, MC, V* Ⓤ *Hyde Park Corner.*

££££ 🖪 **No. 5 Maddox Street.** At No. 5 Maddox, the apartmentlike rooms allow you to practically set up residence. Room service caters to your every whim, delivering groceries and lending out CDs, videos and DVDs, or even a bicycle. Deluxe suites have balconies and working fireplaces. Bedrooms have an understated Asian minimalist aesthetic with white-on-beige-on-brown color schemes and lots of bamboo. The minibars are stocked with everything from sweets to herbal tea, and you have access to a nearby health club. Note there's no elevator. ✉ *5 Maddox St., Mayfair, W1R 9LE* ☎ *020/7647–0200* 🖷 *020/7647–0300* ⊕ *www. no5maddoxst.com* ➮ *12 suites* 🍽 *Restaurant, room service, in-room* *fax, in-room safes, kitchens, minibars, microwaves, refrigerators, cable TV, in-room DVDs/VCRs, Wi-Fi, massage, babysitting, dry cleaning, laundry service, concierge, business services, parking (fee)* ▭ *AE, DC, MC, V* Ⓤ *Oxford Circus.*

£££££   🏨 **Park Lane Sheraton.** This is one of London's "old-school" classic hotels, with a long tradition of five-star style. While it's still a worthy option, it's looking a bit in need of a makeover these days, and is more than a little ragged around the edges. The choice of doubles ranges from regular ones with traditional-style furnishings to "smart" rooms, which include ergonomically designed chairs, extra outlets and lighting, and a combination printer/copier/fax machine. Many executive doubles have stunning views of Green Park, which is just across busy Piccadilly. The ballroom, of *Golden Eye* and *End of the Affair* fame, is exquisite. ⊠ *Piccadilly, Mayfair, W1J BX* ☎ *020/7499–6321* 🖷 *020/7499–1965* ⊕ *www.sheraton.com* 🛏 *268 rooms, 39 suites* ♨ *3 restaurants, room service, some in-room faxes, in-room safes, minibars, cable TV with movies, some in-room data ports, gym, hair salon, bar, lounge, babysitting, dry cleaning, laundry service, concierge, Internet, business services, meeting rooms, car rental, parking (fee), no-smoking rooms* ▭ *AE, DC, MC, V* Ⓤ *Hyde Park Corner.*

££££–£££££   🏨 **Dorset Square Hotel.** A fine pair of Regency town houses have the English country look with antiques, rich colors, and design ideas *House & Garden* subscribers would love. Rooms are quite small, but beautifully decorated and each has its unique style. ▪ TIP→ **The first-floor balconied Coronet rooms are the largest.** ⊠ *40 Dorset Sq., Marylebone, NW1 6QN* ☎ *020/7723–7874, 800/525–4800 in U.S.* 🖷 *020/7724–3328* ⊕ *www. dorsetsquare.co.uk* 🛏 *35 rooms, 3 suites* ♨ *Restaurant, room service, some in-room safes, minibars, cable TV, in-room VCRs, in-room data ports, lobby lounge, dry cleaning, laundry service, concierge, business services, parking (fee), some pets allowed, no-smoking rooms; no a/c in some rooms* ▭ *AE, MC, V* Ⓤ *Baker St.*

££££–£££££   🏨 **The Leonard.** Four 18th-century buildings make up a stunning, relaxed, and friendly boutique hotel. Shoppers will appreciate the location, just around the corner from Oxford Street. Rooms are decorated with a judicious mix of lived-in antiques and comfortable reproductions. For more elbow room, try one of the aptly named grand suites with palatial sitting rooms and tall windows. The roof garden is great for warm weather, and the welcoming lobby is stocked with complimentary newspapers to read by the fire. ⊠ *15 Seymour St., Mayfair, W1H 5AA* ☎ *020/ 7935–2010* 🖷 *020/7935–6700* ⊕ *www.theleonard.com* 🛏 *22 rooms, 21 suites* ♨ *Café, dining room, room service, in-room safes, some kitchens, minibars, cable TV, in-room VCRs, in-room data ports, gym, bar, lounge, babysitting, dry cleaning, laundry service, concierge, Internet, business services, meeting rooms, no-smoking rooms* ▭ *AE, DC, MC, V* Ⓤ *Marble Arch.*

£££–£££££   🏨 **Sherlock Holmes Hotel.** This was once a rather ordinary Hilton, until somebody noticed its location and had the arguably brilliant idea of making it a boutique hotel. Add a beautiful bar for a bit of local buzz, and—presto!—the place took off like a rocket. You might say it was elementary. With wood floors and leather furniture, said bar is marvelously relaxing; rooms have a masculine edge with lots of earth tones, pin-stripe sheets, and hyper-modern bathrooms. ■ TIP→ **Rooms are equipped with international electrical outlets, including those that work with American equipment.** ✉ *108 Baker St., Marylebone, W1U 6LJ* ☎ *020/7486–6161* 🖷 *020/7958–5211* ⊕ *www.sherlockholmeshotel.com* ⤵ *119* ♨ *Restaurant, room service, room TVs with movies, gym, spa, bar, concierge, no-smoking rooms* ▭ *AE, DC, MC, V* Ⓤ *Baker St.*

£££ **Best Western Shaftesbury.** When the Best Western chain set up house in the midst of historic London, it did an admirable job of fitting in, certainly using as much chrome and frosted glass as anybody could ask for. Complimentary newspapers are scattered about, and bedrooms are ultramodern, with neutral rugs, white walls, dark curtains, and sleek furniture. The price reflects all this effort, so it's not the typical Best Western bargain, but it's pleasant and ideally situated in the heart of Theaterland. ✉ *65–73 Shaftesbury Ave., Piccadilly, W1D 6EX* ☎ *020/7871–6000* 🖷 *020/7745–1207* ⊕ *www.bestwestern.com* ⤵ *69 rooms* ♨ *Cable TV, in-room DVDs, in-room broadband, business services, no-smoking rooms* ▭ *AE, MC, V* Ⓤ *Piccadilly Circus.*

£££ **Durrants.** A stone's throw from Oxford Street and the smaller, posher shops of Marylebone High Street, Durrants occupies a quiet corner almost next to the Wallace Collection. It's a good value for the area, especially if you like the old-English wood-paneling, leather armchairs, and dark-red patterned carpet. ■ TIP→ **Durrants has been a hotel since the late 18th century.** ✉ *26–32 George St., Mayfair, W1H 5BJ* ☎ *020/7935–8131* 🖷 *020/7487–3510* ⊕ *www.durrantshotel.co.uk* ⤵ *87 rooms, 5 suites* ♨ *Restaurant, dining room, room service, cable TV, in-room data ports, bar, babysitting, dry cleaning, laundry service, concierge, meeting rooms; no a/c in some rooms* ▭ *AE, MC, V* Ⓤ *Bond St.*

££ **Bryanston.** This family-run hotel, a few blocks north of Hyde Park and Park Lane, is an excellent value for the area. Three converted Georgian houses are decorated in traditional English style: open fireplaces, comfortable leather armchairs, oil portraits. The bedrooms are small and modernized, with a pink color scheme, creaky floors, and tiny bathrooms. ✉ *56–60 Great Cumberland Pl., Mayfair, W1H 8DD* ☎ *020/7262–3141* 🖷 *020/7262–7248* ⊕ *www.bryanstonhotel.com* ⤵ *81 rooms, 8 apartments* ♨ *Dining room, some kitchens, some microwaves, some refrigerators, cable TV, lobby lounge, lounge, pub, dry cleaning, laundry service, concierge, business services, meeting rooms, airport shuttle, parking (fee); no a/c* ▭ *MC, V* ⦿ *CP* Ⓤ *Marble Arch.*

££ **Four Seasons Hotel.** Alas, this has nothing to do with the Four Seasons opposite Hyde Park; there are no stunning views over the Thames, no soundless elevators. The hotel has, however, well-presented, Italianate bedrooms in soothing pastel colors, and is close to Regent's Park. The conservatory is a light, airy space for breakfast. ✉ *173 Gloucester Pl., Regent's Park, NW1 6DX* ☎ *020/7724–3461* 🖷 *020/7402–5594* ⊕ *www.4seasonshotel.co.uk* ⤵ *28 rooms* ♨ *Room service, fans, cable TV, in-room data ports, babysitting, dry cleaning, laundry service, Internet, business services, car rental, some pets allowed, no-smoking rooms; no a/c* ▭ *AE, DC, MC, V* ⦿ *CP* Ⓤ *Baker St.*

££ **22 York Street.** This Georgian town house has a cozy, family feel with

16

pine floors and plenty of antiques. Pride of place goes to the central, communal dining table where guests enjoy a rather varied continental breakfast of croissants, fruit, and cereal. A living room with tea/coffeemaker is at guests' disposal as well. The homey bedrooms are individually furnished with quilts and antiques. Triples and family rooms for four are available. ⊠ *22 York St., Mayfair, W1U 6PX* ☎ *020/7224–2990* 🖷 *020/ 7224–1990* ⊕ *www.22yorkstreet.co.uk* ⇨ *10 rooms* ⏦ *Cable TV, lounge; no a/c, no smoking* ☰ *AE, MC, V* ⏍ *CP* ⓤ *Baker St.*

£   ⌸ **St. Christopher's Inn Camden.** In bustling, hippie Camden Town just north of the center of London, this branch of a hostel and backpacker hotel chain is perfectly situated for wandering around Camden Lock and Camden Market. The decor is in the usual cheap and cheery hostel style, and is kept in good condition. There's no curfew, and you get key-card security and 10% off food and drink in the raucous Belushi's bar on the ground floor. Rooms range from doubles to 10-bed dorms; linens are free. The lounge has cable TV. ⊠ *48–50 Camden High St., Camden Town, NW1 0JH* ☎ *020/7407–1856* 🖷 *020/7403–7715* ⊕ *www. st-christophers.co.uk* ⇨ *52 beds, some without bath* ⏦ *Restaurant, bar, lounge, video game room, laundry facilities, Internet; no a/c, no room phones, no room TVs, no smoking* ☰ *MC, V* ⏍ *CP* ⓤ *Camden Town, Mornington Crescent.*

St. James's

Given its royal pedigree, it's no surprise that hotels in this tony area tend to be chic and accordingly expensive. For your money you get one of the city's best addresses, and a certain degree of classiness.

£££££   ⌸ **Dukes.** This small, exclusive, Edwardian-style hotel with a gas lantern–lighted courtyard entrance is in a discreet cul-de-sac. Overstuffed sofas, oil paintings of assorted dukes, and muted, rich colors create the perfect setting for sipping the finest dry martinis in town. ▮ TIP➡ **The hotel's trump card is that, for such a central location, it's peaceful and quiet.** The rooms are cozy, with floral prints and wood everywhere. ⊠ *35 St. James's Pl., St. James's, SW1A 1NY* ☎ *020/7491–4840, 800/ 381–4702 in U.S.* 🖷 *020/7493–1264* ⊕ *www.dukeshotel.co.uk* ⇨ *80 rooms, 9 suites* ⏦ *Restaurant, dining room, some in-room faxes, in-room safes, minibars, cable TV, some in-room VCRs, in-room data ports, gym, sauna, spa, steam room, bar, lobby lounge, dry cleaning, laundry service, concierge, business services, meeting rooms, parking (fee)* ☰ *AE, DC, MC, V* ⓤ *Green Park.*

£££££   ⌸ **The Ritz.** Uncapitalized, the word "ritz" has come to mean "posh" or "classy," and this is where the word originated. Memorialized in song by Irving Berlin, this hotel's very name conjures the kind of luxury associated with swagged curtains, handwoven carpets, and the smell of cigars, polish, and fresh lilies. The only thing that has been lost is a certain vein of moneyed naughtiness that someone like F. Scott Fitzgerald, at least, would have banked on. The bedrooms are bastions of pastel Louis XVI style, with gilded furniture and crystal chandeliers. With a ratio of two staff members to every bedroom, you're guaranteed personal service despite the hotel's massive size. ▮ TIP➡ **Formal dress is en-**

couraged, and jeans are not allowed in public areas. ⊠ *150 Piccadilly, St. James's, W1J 9BR* ☎ *020/7493–8181* 🖷 *020/7493–2687* ⊕ *www. theritzhotel.co.uk* 🛏 *133 rooms ⟡ 2 restaurants, room service, some in-room faxes, in-room safes, cable TV, some in-room VCRs, in-room data ports, gym, hair salon, bar, babysitting, dry cleaning, laundry service, concierge, Internet, business services, meeting rooms, car rental, parking (fee), no-smoking rooms* ▭ *AE, DC, MC, V* Ⓤ *Piccadilly Circus.*

★ **£££££** ▦ **The Stafford.** This is a rare find: a posh hotel that offers equal parts elegance and friendliness. It's hard to check in without meeting the gregarious manager, and his unshakable cheeriness must be infectious, for the staff are also upbeat and helpful. The location is one of the few peaceful spots in the area, down a small lane behind Piccadilly. Its 13 adorable carriage-house rooms, installed in the 18th-century stable block, are relative bargains; each individually decorated room has a cobbled mews entrance and gas-fueled fireplace, exposed beams, and CD player. The popular little American Bar has ties, baseball caps, and toy planes hanging from a ceiling modeled, presumably, on New York's 21 Club. A real find in the luxury category. ⊠ *St. James's Pl., St. James's, SW1A 1NJ* ☎ *020/7493–0111* 🖷 *020/7493–7121* ⊕ *www.thestaffordhotel.co.uk* 🛏 *81 rooms ⟡ Restaurant, dining room, cable TV, in-room data ports, bar* ▭ *AE, DC, MC, V* Ⓤ *Green Park.*

★ ▦ **Claridge's.** Stay here, and you're staying at a hotel legend (founded in **££££–£££££** 1812), with one of the world's classiest guest lists. The friendly, liveried staff is not in the least condescending, and the rooms are never less than luxurious. Enjoy a cup of tea in the lounge, or retreat to the stylish bar for cocktails—or, better, to Gordon Ramsay's inimitable restaurant. The bathrooms are spacious (with enormous showerheads), as are the bedrooms (Victorian or art deco). The grand staircase and magnificent elevator complete with sofa and driver are equally glamorous. Perhaps Spencer Tracy said it best when he remarked that, when he died, he wanted to go not to heaven, but to Claridge's. ⊠ *Brook St., St. James's, W1A 2JQ* ☎ *020/7629–8860, 800/637–2869 in U.S.* 🖷 *020/7499–2210* ⊕ *www.claridges.co.uk* 🛏 *203 rooms ⟡ Restaurant, in-room fax, in-room safes, some in-room hot tubs, minibars, cable TV with movies, in-room VCRs, in-room data ports, gym, hair salon, spa, bar, lobby lounge, shop, babysitting, dry cleaning, laundry service, concierge, Internet, business services, meeting rooms, airport shuttle, car rental, parking (fee), no-smoking rooms* ▭ *AE, DC, MC, V* Ⓤ *Bond St.*

🐧 **££££** ▦ **22 Jermyn Street.** This guesthouse is on a fashionable shopping street near Fortnum & Mason. Flexible room configurations, including sitting rooms that convert to bedrooms, mean families have plenty of space. In fact, the hotel rolls out the red carpet for children, providing anything from high chairs and coloring books to nannies and kids' bathrobes. For grown-ups, there is access to a nearby gym, complimentary newspapers, and a shoe shine. ⊠ *22 Jermyn St., St. James's, SW1Y 6HL* ☎ *020/7734–2353, 800/682–7808 in U.S.* 🖷 *020/7734–0750* ⊕ *www.22jermyn.com* 🛏 *5 rooms,*

16

ASK JEEVES
Bedrooms at Claridge's have bells to summon a maid, waiter, or valet.

13 suites & *Room service, in-room safes, minibars, cable TV with movies, in-room VCRs, in-room data ports, babysitting, dry cleaning, laundry service, concierge, Internet, business services, airport shuttle, car rental, parking (fee)* ⊟ *AE, DC, MC, V* Ⓤ *Piccadilly Circus.*

Soho & Covent Garden

These two areas may be close physical neighbors but they could hardly be more divergent in character. Funky Soho is busy, grimy, trendy, and happening—party central for London's young professionals, and home mostly to inexpensive hotels. Covent Garden is a tourist hub, with endless shopping and plenty of upscale hostelries.

£££££
Fodor's Choice
★

Covent Garden Hotel. In the midst of boisterous Covent Garden, this hotel is now the London home-away-from-home for a mélange of off-duty celebrities, actors, and style mavens. The public salons keep even the most picky happy: with painted silks, *style anglais* ottomans, and 19th-century Romantic oils, they're perfect places to decompress over a glass of sherry from the honor bar. Guest rooms are *World of Interiors* stylish, each showcasing matching-but-mixed couture fabrics to stunning effect. ■ TIP➜ **For £30 the popular Saturday-night film club includes dinner in the brasserie and a film in the deluxe in-house cinema.** ⊠ *10 Monmouth St., Covent Garden, WC2H 9HB* ☎ *020/7806–1000, 800/553–6674 in U.S.* 🖷 *020/7806–1100* ⊕ *www.firmdale.com* ↘ *55 rooms, 3 suites* & *Restaurant, room service, some in-room faxes, in-room safes, minibars, cable TV, in-room VCRs, in-room data ports, gym, spa, cinema, library, babysitting, dry cleaning, laundry service, concierge, Internet, business services, meeting rooms, car rental* ⊟ *AE, MC, V* Ⓤ *Covent Garden.*

£££££
Fodor's Choice
★

One Aldwych. An understated blend of contemporary and classic results in pure, modern luxury here. Flawlessly designed inside an Edwardian building, One Aldwych is coolly eclectic, with an artsy lobby, feather duvets, Italian linen sheets, and quirky touches (a TV in every bathroom, all-natural toiletries). It's the ultimate in 21st-century style, down to the awesome health club. Suites have amenities such as a private gym, a kitchen, and a terrace. Breakfast is made with organic ingredients. ■ TIP➜ **The pool at One Aldwych has speakers under water that play music you can hear when you dive in.** ⊠ *1 Aldwych, Covent Garden, WC2 4BZ* ☎ *020/7300–1000* 🖷 *020/7300–1001* ⊕ *www. onealdwych.co.uk* ↘ *93 rooms, 12 suites* & *2 restaurants, room service, in-room safes, some kitchens, minibars, cable TV with movies, in-room data ports, indoor pool, health club, spa, 3 bars, cinema, shop, dry cleaning, laundry service, concierge, business services, meeting rooms, parking (fee), no-smoking floors* ⊟ *AE, MC, V* Ⓤ *Charing Cross, Covent Garden.*

★ **£££££**

The Savoy. Does this grand hotel still measure up to its history? Absolutely. The art deco rooms are especially fabulous, but all rooms are impeccably maintained, spacious, elegant, and comfortable. A room facing the Thames costs a fortune and requires an early booking, but it's worth it. If in doubt, consider that Monet painted the view of the river from such a room. Bathrooms have original fittings, with sunflower-size showerheads. Top-floor rooms are newer and less charming. ⊠ *Strand, Covent Garden, WC2R 0EU* ☎ *020/7836–4343* 🖷 *020/ 7240–6040* ⊕ *www.savoy-group. com* 🛏 *263 rooms, 19 suites* 🛆 *3 restaurants, room service, in-room fax, in-room safes, minibars, cable TV with movies, in-room VCRs, in-room data ports, indoor pool, gym, hair salon, sauna, spa, steam room,*

HERE'S WHERE

The Savoy hosted Elizabeth Taylor's first honeymoon in one of its famous river-view rooms; and it poured one of Europe's first dry martinis in its equally famous American Bar, haunted by Hemingway, Fitzgerald, and Gershwin.

2 bars, lobby lounge, theater, shop, babysitting, dry cleaning, laundry service, concierge, Internet, business services, meeting rooms, parking (fee), no-smoking rooms ⊟ *AE, DC, MC, V* Ⓤ *Charing Cross.*

£££££   🖬 **Waldorf Hilton.** Following a massive overhaul, the Waldorf—once synonymous with luscious Edwardiana—now has frosted glass, white marble, and understated modern bedrooms. The "Art + Tech" rooms cater to modern travelers' demands with plasma-screen TVs, complimentary fruit, herbal teas, and soft drinks, as well as innovative safes with laptop chargers. The "contemporary" rooms have retained period features while incorporating all the new gadgets. The Palm Court was inspired by the ballroom on that famous luxury ship the *Titanic*—and even doubled for it in the eponymous Hollywood movie. After a century, the weekend tea dances with big-band music are still going strong. ⊠ *Aldwych, Covent Garden, WC2B 4DD* ☎ *020/7836–2400* 🖷 *020/7836–7244* ⊕ *www.hilton.com* 🛏 *303 rooms* 🛆 *Restaurant, room service, in-room safes, minibars, cable TV with movies and video games, in-room broadband, indoor pool, fitness classes, gym, hair salon, sauna, spa, steam room, bar, babysitting, dry cleaning, laundry service, concierge, Internet, business services, meeting rooms, parking (fee), no-smoking rooms* ⊟ *AE, DC, MC, V* Ⓤ *Charing Cross.*

££££–£££££   🖬 **The Howard Swissotel.** The rather spartan modern shell that encases the Howard Swissotel hides a contemporary, hip interior. It has a crisp brown color palette, with dark-wood furniture, light-wood floors, and lots of suede and leather, punctuated with bright white and red. Some rooms have spectacular river views, and all have Lavazza coffee machines. Suites have the option of a riverside balcony. There's alfresco dining in the Asian fusion restaurant in good weather. ⊠ *Temple Pl., Covent Garden, WC2R 2PR* ☎ *020/7836–3555* 🖷 *020/7379–4547* ⊕ *www.swissotel.com* 🛏 *189 rooms* 🛆 *Restaurant, room service, in-room safes, minibars, cable TV with movies, in-room data ports, bar, lobby lounge, dry cleaning, laundry service, concierge, Internet, business services, meeting rooms, parking (fee), no-smoking rooms* ⊟ *AE, D, MC, V* Ⓤ *Temple.*

££££–£££££   🖬 **Soho Hotel.** This redbrick, loftlike building opened its doors in 2004,
Fodor'sChoice   making it the first upscale hotel in gritty Soho. The sleek boutique
★   hotel's public rooms are boldly designed with bright fuschia and acid green, but the large bedrooms are much calmer, most with neutral, beige-and-cream tones, or subtle, sophisticated pinstripes, all offset by

16

modern furniture. The bar and restaurant, Refuel, is one of the city's hotspots, and there are movie-screening rooms downstairs, in case the wide-screen TVs in the rooms aren't big enough. ✉ *4 Richmond Mews, off Dean St., Soho, W1D 3DH* ☎ *020/7559–3000* 🖷 *020/7559–3003* ⊕ *www.sohohotel.com* ➴ *85 rooms, 6 apartments* ♧ *Room service, in-room DVDs, in-room broadband, gym, concierge, no-smoking rooms* ▤ *AE, MC, V* Ⓤ *Tottenham Court Rd.*

★ ££££ 🏨 **Hazlitt's.** Three connected, early-18th-century houses, one of which was the last home of essayist William Hazlitt (1778–1830), make up this charming Soho hotel. It's a disarmingly friendly place, full of personality but devoid of elevators. Robust antiques are everywhere, most beds are four-posters, and every room has a Victorian claw-foot tub in its bathroom. There are tiny sitting rooms, wooden staircases, and more restaurants within strolling distance than you could patronize in a year. ▌ TIP➜ This is *the* London address for visiting antiques dealers and theater and literary types. ✉ *6 Frith St., Soho, W1V 5TZ* ☎ *020/7434–1771* 🖷 *020/7439–1524* ⊕ *www.hazlittshotel.com* ➴ *20 rooms, 3 suites* ♧ *Room service, fans, minibars, cable TV, in-room VCRs, in-room data ports, dry cleaning, laundry service, concierge, Internet, meeting rooms, parking (fee), some pets allowed, no-smoking floors; no a/c in some rooms* ▤ *AE, DC, MC, V* Ⓤ *Tottenham Court Rd.*

££££ 🏨 **Radisson Edwardian Hampshire.** Right on Leicester Square and steps from the half-price ticket booth, this hotel is perfectly placed for theatergoers. Bedrooms are old-fashioned with plenty of rose prints, beige carpets, and flowery bedspreads, but bathrooms are modern. Public spaces exude plushness with thick carpets, gold chandeliers, and sparkling cut glass and mirrors. ▌ TIP➜ Rooms facing Leicester Square have lovely arched windows, but can be a bit noisier. ✉ *31–36 Leicester Sq., Covent Garden, WC2H 7LH* ☎ *020/7839–9399* 🖷 *020/7930–8122* ⊕ *www. radissonedwardian.com* ➴ *119 rooms, 5 suites* ♧ *Restaurant, room service, in-room safes, minibars, cable TV with movies, in-room data ports, gym, 2 bars, lobby lounge, babysitting, dry cleaning, laundry service, concierge, Wi-Fi, business services, meeting rooms, car rental, parking (fee), some pets allowed (fee), no-smoking floor* ▤ *AE, DC, MC, V* Ⓤ *Leicester Sq.*

££££ 🏨 **Radisson Mountbatten.** Named after the late Lord Mountbatten, last viceroy of India and favorite uncle of Prince Charles, the hotel reflects Mountbatten's life with photos of the estate where he lived, plus some Indian furnishings and animal prints and figurines. Service is excellent and rooms are quite small and understated, cooly decorated in neutral tones. Bathrooms have lashings of Italian marble. Corner suites have the best views of the city. ✉ *20 Monmouth St., Covent Garden, WC2H 9HD* ☎ *020/7836–4300* 🖷 *020/7240–3540* ⊕ *www.radissonedwardian. com* ➴ *143 rooms, 8 suites* ♧ *Restaurant, room service, some in-room faxes, in-room safes, minibars, cable TV with movies, in-room data ports, gym, bar, lobby lounge, babysitting, dry cleaning, laundry service, concierge, Internet, business services, meeting rooms, car rental, parking (fee), some pets allowed (fee), no-smoking floor* ▤ *AE, DC, MC, V* Ⓤ *Covent Garden.*

££££ 🖼 **Trafalgar Hilton.** This fresh, contemporary hotel defies the Hilton norm. The rooms here, in either sky-blue or beige color schemes, keep many of the 19th-century office building's original features, and some have floor-to-ceiling windows with expansive views of Trafalgar Square. Twenty-one rooms are split-level, with upstairs space for chilling out with a CD or DVD and sleeping space below. Bathrooms take the cake with deep baths, full-size toiletries, eye masks, and mini-TVs. ■ TIP→ **Go up to the roof garden for spectacular views of the Houses of Parliament, West-minster Abbey, and the British Airways London Eye, or ask for room 303 for ex-quisite views of your very own.** ⊠ *2 Spring Gardens, Covent Garden, SW1A 2TS* ☎ *020/7870–2900* 🖷 *020/7870–2911* ⊕ *www.hilton.com* ↳ *127 rooms, 2 suites* △ *Restaurant, room service, in-room safes, minibars, cable TV with movies and video games, in-room data ports, bar, dry cleaning, laundry service, concierge, Internet, business services, meeting rooms, parking (fee), no-smoking floors* ⊟ *AE, DC, MC, V* Ⓤ *Charing Cross.*

The South Bank

On the same side of the river as the cutting-edge Tate Modern, the artsy South Bank doesn't have many hotels, but those it does hold tend to be good deals; many people don't know how easy it is to cross the narrow Thames on one of the plentiful bridges, and how central you really are when you stay here.

£££££ 🖼 **London Marriott Hotel County Hall.** This exceptionally grand hotel has what many want—a view of the London Eye and the Houses of Parlia-ment across the Thames. The building is a mammoth, spectacular, ped-imented, and columned affair with bronze doors and marble lobby. Similarly, the decor in the guestrooms has a lot going on—floral bed-covers make strange bedfellows with chairs clad in pastel plaid, then there's bright sprigged carpet and wallpaper. Still, the views are lovely, and it's got all the businesslike bells and whistles you could ask for and a fantastic 24-hour health-and-fitness spa. ⊠ *County Hall, South Bank, SE1 7PB* ☎ *020/7928–5200* 🖷 *020/7928–5300* ⊕ *www.marriotthotels. com* ↳ *200 rooms* △ *2 restaurants, room service, in-room safes, mini-bars, cable TV with movies, in-room data ports, indoor pool, health club, hair salon, spa, 2 bars, babysitting, dry cleaning, laundry service, concierge, Internet, business services, meeting rooms, parking (fee)* ⊟ *AE, DC, MC, V* Ⓤ *Westminster.*

££££ 🖼 **London Bridge Hotel.** Just steps away from the London Bridge rail and Tube station, this thoroughly modern, stylish hotel is popular with busi-ness travelers. Most of the South Bank's attractions are within walking distance. Each sleek room is understated and contemporary. Three spa-cious two-bedroom apartments (£££££) come with kitchen, living room, and dining room. ⊠ *8–18 London Bridge St., South Bank, SE1 9SG* ☎ *020/7855–2200* 🖷 *020/7855–2233* ⊕ *www.london-bridge-hotel. co.uk* ↳ *138 rooms, 3 apartments* △ *Restaurant, room service, in-room safes, some kitchens, minibars, cable TV with movies, in-room broad-band, gym, sauna, bar, lobby lounge, dry cleaning, laundry service,*

16

concierge, meeting rooms, parking (fee), no-smoking floors ▤ *AE, DC, MC, V* Ⓤ *London Bridge.*

££ 🖼 **Premier Travel Inn County Hall.** Don't

Fodor'sChoice get too excited—this neighbor of the

★ riverfront Marriott is not next to it, but behind it, giving you a window onto the Marriott, not the Thames.

> **STAYING NEAR LONDON BRIDGE STATION?**
>
> Those staying at hotels near London Bridge Station can visit delightful Borough Market on Friday and Saturday for cheese, fresh falafel, and local London color.

Still, you get an incredible value, with the standard facilities of the cookie-cutter rooms of this chain. Best of all for families on a budget are the fold-out beds that let you accommodate two kids at no extra charge. *That's* a bargain. ⊠ *Belvedere Rd., South Bank, SE1 7PB* ☎ *0870/238–3300* 🖨 *020/7902–1619* ⊕ *www.premiertravelinn.com* ↪ *313 rooms* ⇗ *Restaurant, coffee shop, fans, in-room data ports, bar, business services, meeting rooms, parking (fee), no-smoking floors; no a/c* ▤ *AE, DC, MC, V* Ⓤ *Westminster.*

££ 🖼 **Premier Travel Inn Southwark.** Practically riverside, this branch of the Premier Travel Inn chain has an excellent location across the cobbled road from Vinopolis, where you can do extensive wine-tastings. Rooms have desks, tea/coffeemakers, and the chain's signature 6-foot-wide beds (really two zipped together). Family rooms can accommodate four people. The nautical Anchor restaurant and pub is adjacent to the hotel. ⊠ *34 Park St., South Bank, SE1 9EF* ☎ *020/7089–2580 or 0870/990–6402* 🖨 *0870/990–6403* ⊕ *www.premiertravelinn.com* ↪ *56 rooms* ⇗ *Cable TV, in-room data ports, parking (fee), no-smoking rooms* ▤ *AE, DC, MC, V* Ⓤ *London Bridge.*

£ 🖼 **St. Christopher's Inn Village.** Named for the patron saint of travelers, St. Christopher's Inn is the headquarters of this small hostel chain. Rooms are cheerful and have swipe-card access and shared bathrooms. The hostel's most endearing features are its rooftop sauna and open-air hot tub. For entertainment, try the sports bar downstairs. Other hostels in the chain are just down the street: Original at 121 Borough High Street, SE1 1NP, and Orient Espresso at 59 Borough High Street, SE1 1NE. These hostels are also booked through the Village. ⊠ *161–165 Borough High St., South Bank, SE1 1HR* ☎ *020/7407–1856* 🖨 *020/ 7403–7715* ⊕ *www.st-christophers.co.uk* ↪ *166 beds at Village, 50 beds at Original, 36 beds at Orient Espresso; all without bath* ⇗ *Restaurant, outdoor hot tub, sauna, pub, laundry facilities, Internet, no-smoking rooms; no a/c, no room phones, no room TVs* ▤ *MC, V* Ⓤ *London Bridge, Borough* ⑩ *CP.*

Westminster & Victoria

Westminster may be a bit stuffy and touristy, but it's home to Parliament, Westminster Abbey, and the Queen—things simply don't get handier for visitors. This is a busy, hectic, part of town, where historic monuments come at you fast and furious, but there are a few gorgeous parks to take the edge off.

£££££ 🖼 **No. 41.** This luxurious abode is not a formulaic, paint-by-numbers hotel. Its designer credentials are clear everywhere, from the unusual tiled floors to the extraordinary furnishings, which seem to have been drawn from every corner of the globe. The staff cocoons and pampers its guests—sit for a second and someone will offer you tea, cocktails, water—anything that crosses your mind can be yours in a second. Rooms, some of them split-level, are filled with high-tech gadgets to keep you in touch with the office back home. When you're not working, you can relax on the butter-soft leather sofa in front of the fireplace, recline on the exquisite bed linens and feather duvets, or luxuriate in the marble bath. A "whatever, whenever" button on the telephone connects you with the helpful, amiable staff. ⊠ *41 Buckingham Palace Rd., Victoria, SW1W 0PS* ☎ *020/7300–0041* 🖷 *020/7300–0141* ⊕ *www.41hotel. com* 🛏 *14 rooms, 4 suites* ◊ *Room service, in-room fax, in-room safes, some in-room hot tubs, minibars, cable TV with movies and video games, in-room broadband, in-room VCRs, in-room data ports, lounge, babysitting, dry cleaning, laundry service, concierge, Internet, business services, meeting rooms, car rental, parking (fee), no-smoking rooms* ▭ *AE, DC, MC, V* ⵙ *CP* Ⓤ *Victoria.*

£££££ 🖼 **The Rubens at the Palace.** This hotel, which looks out over the Royal Mews of Buckingham Palace, provides the sort of deep comfort needed to soothe away a hard day's sightseeing, with cushy armchairs crying out for you to sink into them with a cup of Earl Grey. With decent-sized rooms—not quite furnished like the ones at the palace, it must be said—and a location that couldn't be more central, this hotel is a favorite with tour groups. ⊠ *39 Buckingham Palace Rd., Westminster, SW1W 0PS* ☎ *020/7834–6600* 🖷 *020/7233–6037* ⊕ *www.rubenshotel.com* 🛏 *160 rooms, 13 suites* ◊ *2 restaurants, room service, some in-room faxes, in-room safes, some minibars, cable TV with movies, some in-room VCRs, in-room data ports, lobby lounge, piano bar, babysitting, dry cleaning, laundry service, concierge, Internet, business services, meeting rooms, parking (fee), no-smoking floors* ▭ *AE, DC, MC, V* Ⓤ *Victoria.*

££££–£££££ 🖼 **The Goring.** Buckingham Palace is just around the corner, and visiting VIPs use the Goring as a convenient, suitably dignified base for royal occasions. The hotel, built in 1910 and now run by third-generation Gorings, retains an Edwardian style. It's a bit fussy—striped wallpaper and floral curtains are combined with patterned carpets and brass fittings—and will never be described as "modern," but it has a classy, old-fashioned style. ⊠ *15 Beeston Pl., Grosvenor Gardens, Victoria, SW1W 0JW* ☎ *020/7396–9000* 🖷 *020/7834–4393* ⊕ *www.goringhotel.co.uk* 🛏 *68 rooms, 6 suites* ◊ *Restaurant, room service, in-room safes, in-room hot tubs, cable TV with movies, in-room data ports, gym, bar, babysitting, dry cleaning, laundry service, concierge, business services, meeting rooms, parking (fee), no-smoking rooms* ▭ *AE, DC, MC, V* Ⓤ *Victoria.*

££££–£££££ 🖼 **Jolly Hotel St. Ermin's.** The hotel is just a short stroll from Westminster Abbey, Buckingham Palace, and the Houses of Parliament. An Edwardian anomaly in the shadow of modern skyscrapers, the hotel is set on a tiny cul-de-sac courtyard. The lobby is an extravaganza of Victorian baroque—all cake-frosting stuccowork in shades of baby blue and creamy white. Guest rooms are tastefully decorated, but some are quite small. ■ TIP→ **The Cloisters restaurant at the Jolly Hotel St. Ermin's is an ornately carved 19th-century Jacobean-style salon, and one of the most magnificent rooms in which to dine in London.** ✉ *2 Caxton St., Westminster, SW1H 0QW* ☎ *020/7222–7888* 🖷 *020/7222–6914* ⊕ *www.jollyhotels.it* ⥃ *277 rooms, 8 suites* ♿ *Restaurant, room service, some in-room safes, minibars, cable TV with movies, in-room data ports, bar, lounge, babysitting, dry cleaning, laundry service, meeting rooms, parking (fee), no-smoking rooms* ▭ *AE, DC, MC, V* Ⓤ *St. James's Park.*

🐾 **££££** ▨ **City Inn Westminster.** In a rather stark steel-and-glass building steps from the Tate Britain, this member of a small U.K. chain has some rooms with spectacular views of Big Ben and the London Eye. Extras like floor-to-ceiling windows, CD players, and flat-screen TVs complement the contemporary, monochrome guest rooms. Cots, baby baths, Nickelodeon, special menus, and baby food are all on tap for kids. The restaurant and bar serve modern British cooking. ✉ *30 John Islip St., Westminster, SW1P 4DD* ☎ *020/7630–1000* 🖷 *020/7233–7575* ⊕ *www. cityinn.com* ⥃ *444 rooms, 16 suites* ♿ *Restaurant, room service, in-room safes, minibars, cable TV, in-room DVDs, in-room data ports, gym, bar, lobby lounge, babysitting, dry cleaning, laundry service, concierge, Internet, business services, meeting rooms, parking (fee), no-smoking rooms* ▭ *AE, MC, V* Ⓤ *Pimlico.*

££–£££ ▨ **Lime Tree Hotel.** On a street filled with budget hotels, the Lime Tree stands out for its gracious proprietors, the Davies family, who endeavor to provide a homey atmosphere as well as act as concierges. The flowery rooms include tea/coffeemakers. The triples and quads are suitable for families, but children under five are not allowed. The simple breakfast room covered with notes and gifts from former guests opens onto a garden. ✉ *135–137 Ebury St., Victoria, SW1W 9RA* ☎ *020/7730–8191* 🖷 *020/7730–7865* ⊕ *www.limetreehotel.co.uk* ⥃ *25 rooms* ♿ *Fans, in-room safes; no a/c, no kids under 5* ⦿ *BP* ▭ *MC, V* Ⓤ *Victoria.*

££ ▨ **James & Cartref House.** Husband-and-wife team Derek and Sharon James run these two town houses. All rooms are equipped with washbasins and tea/coffeemakers. Though the rooms are small and basic, they are well taken care of by the extremely pleasant proprietors. ✉ *108 and 129 Ebury St., Victoria, SW1W 9QD* ☎ *020/7730–6176* 🖷 *020/7730–7338* ⊕ *www. jamesandcartref.co.uk* ⥃ *19 rooms, 13 rooms with bath* ♿ *Fans; no a/c, no smoking* ⦿ *BP* ▭ *AE, MC, V* Ⓤ *Victoria.*

££ ▨ **New England Hotel.** This family-run B&B in a 19th-century town house is cheap(ish) and cheerful. The power showers, comfortable beds, and electronic key cards are pluses in this price category, but there's nothing fancy about the interior, and the bright color scheme is a bit startlingly cheerful. ✉ *20 Saint George's Dr., Victoria, SW1V 4BN* ☎ *020/ 7834–8351* 🖷 *020/7834–9000* ⊕ *www.newenglandhotel.com* ⥃ *25* *rooms ♿ Fans, cable TV, in-room data ports, meeting room, parking (fee), no-smoking floors; no a/c ⊟ AE, DC, MC, V ⦿ BP Ⓤ Victoria.*

£–££ ⌂ **Vandon House Hotel.** Popular with students, backpackers, and families on a budget, this simply decorated hotel is close to Westminster Abbey and Buckingham Palace. Singles and some twin rooms share bathrooms, but the rest are en suite with a shower only. The family rooms include a double bed and camp-style bunk bed, which could result in scuffles over who must sleep where. It's undeniably a friendly little place. ⊠ *1 Vandon St., Westminster, SW1H 0AH ☎ 020/7799–6780 🖷 020/ 7799–1464 ⊕ www.vandonhouse.com ⤵ 32 rooms ♿ Lounge, laundry service, Internet, meeting rooms, airport shuttle; no a/c, no smoking ⊟ MC, V ⦿ CP Ⓤ St. James's Park.*

£–££ ⌂ **Windermere Hotel.** This sweet, inexpensive hotel will not let you forget that it stands on the site of London's first B&B, which opened here in 1881. It's draped in charmingly sunny floral fabrics, kept in good taste by the antique beds and faux-antique fans in the rooms. Bathrooms are thoroughly modern, and the attached restaurant, small though it may be, is actually quite good. The Windermere is an excellent budget option. ⊠ *142–144 Warwick Way, Victoria, SW1V 4JE ☎ 020/7834–4163 🖷 020/7630–8831 ⤵ 22 rooms ⊕ www.windermere-hotel.co.uk ♿ Room service, cable TV, in-room data ports, bar, no-smoking floors ⊟ MC, V Ⓤ Victoria.*

16

Bed-and-Breakfasts & Apartment Agencies

If hotels are not your style, or if you're looking for something economical for a week's stay, there are endless options. You can stay with London families in small, homey B&Bs for an up-close-and-personal brush with city life, relax in a pied-à-terre, or rent an entire house—comfortable in the knowledge that you won't be startled awake by housekeeping the next morning. The benefits of using a B&B agency are substantial—the price is cheaper than a hotel room of comparable quality, you have access to the kitchen so you don't have to eat every meal in a restaurant, and yet you can usually arrange to have your breakfast prepared for you every day. The limitations are fairly minimal—although there is daily maid service, there is no staff at your beck and call should you want something at odd hours, and most are not located in the very center of the city (although many are in lovely and convenient neighborhoods like Notting Hill and Kensington). Prices for attractive rooms in privately owned homes start as low as £60 a night, and go up for more central neighborhoods and larger and more luxurious homes. It's an excellent option, both for seasoned travelers and for those trying to travel well without busting their budgets. Call around to find the place that's right for you.

CLOSE UP

Lodging Alternatives

APARTMENT RENTALS

For a home base that's roomy enough for a family and that comes with cooking facilities, consider renting furnished "flats" (what apartments are called in Britain). These can save you money, especially if you're traveling with a group. If you're interested in home-exchange, but don't feel like sharing, some home exchange directories list rentals as well. If you want to deal directly with local agents, get a personal recommendation from someone who has used the company; there's no accredited rating system for apartment rentals like the one for hotels. In addition to the options listed here, the London Tourist Board has accommodation lists; see also the "Bed-and-Breakfasts & Apartment Agencies" section above.

🔝 International Agents **At Home Abroad** ✉ 163 3rd Ave., No. 319, New York, NY 10003 ☎ 212/421-9165 🖨 212/533-0095 ⊕ www.athomeabroadinc.com. **Hideaways International** ✉ 767 Islington St., Portsmouth, NH 03801 ☎ 603/430-4433 or 800/843-4433 🖨 603/430-4444 ⊕ www.hideaways.com, annual membership $145. **Hometours International** ✉ 1108 Scottie La., Knoxville, TN 37919 ☎ 865/690-8484 or 866/367-4668 ⊕ thor.he.net/~hometour/. **Interhome** ✉ 1990 N.E. 163rd St., Suite 110, North Miami Beach, FL 33162 ☎ 305/940-2299 or 800/882-6864 🖨 305/940-2911 ⊕ www.interhome.us. **Vacation Home Rentals Worldwide** ✉ 235 Kensington Ave., Norwood, NJ 07648 ☎ 201/767-9393 or 800/633-3284 🖨 201/767-5510 ⊕ www.vhrww.com. **Villanet** ✉ 1251 N.W. 116th St., Seattle, WA 98177 ☎ 206/417-3444 or 800/964-1891 🖨 206/417-1832 ⊕ www.rentavilla.com. **Villas and Apartments Abroad** ✉ 183 Madison Ave., Suite 201, New York, NY 10016 ☎ 212/213-6435 or 800/433-3020 🖨 212/213-8252 ⊕ www.vaanyc.com. **Villas International** ✉ 4340 Redwood Hwy., Suite D309, San Rafael, CA 94903 ☎ 415/499-9490 or 800/221-2260 🖨 415/499-9491 ⊕ www.villasintl.com.

🔝 Local Agents **Acorn Apartments** ✉ 103 Great Russell St., WC1B 3LA ☎ 020/7813-3223 🖨 020/7813-3270 ⊕ www.acorn-apartments.co.uk, cost from £90. **The Apartment Service** ✉ 5 Francis Grove, Wimbledon SW19 4DT ☎ 020/8944-1444 🖨 020/8944-6744 ⊕ www.apartmentservice.com. **Landmark Trust** ☎ 01628/825925 ⊕ www.landmarktrust.org.uk, for London apartments in unusual and historic buildings.

UNIVERSITY HALLS OF RESIDENCE

University student dorms can be ideal for single travelers as well as those on a tight budget who want to come to London in summer when deals on other lodgings are scarce. Walter Sickert Hall has year-round lodging in its "executive rooms" (six single and three twin), and breakfast is even delivered to your room. Beds are usually available for a week around Easter, and from mid-June to mid-September in all the university accommodations around town. As you might expect, showers and toilets are shared, and there are no bellhops to carry your bags or concierges to answer your questions.

🔝 Universities **City University Hall of Residence: Walter Sickert Hall** ✉ Graham St., N1 8LA ☎ 020/7040-8822 🖨 020/7040-8825 ⊕ www.city.ac.uk/ems, costs £60 for a double year-round and includes continental breakfast. **London School of Economics Vacations** ☎020/7955-7575 🖷0207/955-7676 ⊕www.lsevacations.co.uk, costs £38 for a double without a toilet to £62 for a double with a toilet. You can choose from a variety of rooms in their five halls of residence around London. **University College London** ✉Residence Manager, Campbell House, 5-10 Taviton St., WC1H 0BX ☎020/7679-1479 🖷020/7388-0060, costs £35-£40 for a double and is open from mid-June to mid-September.

HOME EXCHANGES

If you would like to exchange your home for someone else's, join a home-exchange organization, which will send you its updated listings of available exchanges for a year and will include your own listing in at least one of them. It's up to you to make specific arrangements. 🇫 Exchange Clubs **HomeLink International** ⌖ Box 47747, Tampa, FL 33647 ☎813/975-9825 or 800/638-3841 🖷813/910-8144 ⊕www.homelink.org; $110 yearly for a listing, online access, and catalog; $70 without catalog. **Intervac U.S.** ✉30 Corte San Fernando, Tiburon, CA 94920 ☎800/756-4663 🖷415/435-7440 ⊕www.intervacus.com; $125 yearly for a listing, online access, and a catalog; $65 without catalog.

HOSTELS

No matter what your age, you can save on lodging costs by staying at hostels. In some 4,500 locations in more than 70 countries around the world, Hostelling International (HI), the umbrella group for a number of national youth-hostel associations, offers single-sex, dorm-style beds and, at many hostels, rooms for couples and family accommodations.

Membership in any HI national hostel association, open to travelers of all ages, allows you to stay in HI-affiliated hostels at member rates; one-year membership is about $28 for adults (C$35 for a two-year minimum membership in Canada, £14 in the United Kingdom, A$52 in Australia, and NZ$40 in New Zealand); hostels charge about $10-$30 per night. Members have priority if the hostel is full; they're also eligible for discounts around the world, even on rail and bus travel in some countries. Members of the Boy Scouts may want to consider London's useful Baden-Powell House, which offers rooms for as little as $25 a night for Scouts and their families, and to non-Scouts for slightly more. 🇫 Organizations **Baden-Powell House** ✉65-67 Queens Gate, London SW7 5JS ☎020/7584-7031 🖷020/7590-6902 ⊕www.scoutbase.org.uk/hq/bph/index.htm. **Hostelling International-USA** ✉8401 Colesville Rd., Suite 600, Silver Spring, MD 20910 ☎301/495-1240 🖷301/495-6697 ⊕www.hiusa.org. **Hostelling International-Canada** ✉205 Catherine St., Suite 400, Ottawa, Ontario K2P 1C3 ☎613/237-7884 or 800/663-5777 🖷613/237-7868 ⊕www.hihostels.ca. **YHA England and Wales** ✉Trevelyan House, Dimple Rd., Matlock, Derbyshire DE4 3YH, UK ☎0870/870-8808, 0870/770-8868, or 0162/959-2600 🖷0870/770-6127 ⊕www.yha.org.uk. **YHA Australia** ✉422 Kent St., Sydney, NSW 2001 ☎02/9261-1111 🖷02/9261-1969 ⊕www.yha.com.au. **YHA New Zealand** ✉Level 1, Moorhouse City, 166 Moorhouse Ave., Box 436, Christchurch ☎03/379-9970 or 0800/278-299 🖷03/365-4476 ⊕www.yha.org.nz.

16

££–££££ 🏠 **Coach House London Vacation Rentals.** Stay in the properties of Londoners who are temporarily away. Apartments and houses are primarily in Notting Hill, Kensington, and Chelsea. The extra touches—airport pickup, complimentary breakfast provisions, and a welcome drink with a representative—make this service personal. Homes also come with a phone number to call for help in planning your stay. ⊠ *2 Tunley Rd., Balham, SW17 7QJ* ☎ *020/8772–1939* 🖨 *0870/1334957* ⊕ *www. chslondon.com* ⊟ *AE, MC, V* ☞ *Payment by credit card only; 10% deposit required.*

££ 🏠 **Bulldog Club.** This reservation service offers delightful little London flats in sought-after neighborhoods. A three-year membership is about £25, with most properties available for about £105 per night. Full English breakfasts as well as other goodies are often provided. Most of the properties are in Knightsbridge, Kensington, and Chelsea. ⊠ *14 Dewhurst Rd., Kensington, W14 0ET* ☎ *020/7371–3202, 877/727–3004 in U.S.* 🖨 *020/7371–2015* ⊕ *www.bulldogclub.com* ⊟ *AE, MC, V.*

££ 🏠 **London B&B.** This long-established family-run agency has some truly spectacular—and some more modest—homes in central London. Check many of them out via its Web site before making a commitment. The staff here is most personable and helpful. ⊠ *437 J St., Suite 210, San Diego, CA 92101* ☎ *800/872–2632* 🖨 *619/531–1686* ⊕ *www. londonbandb.com* ☞ *30% deposit required.*

££ 🏠 **Primrose Hill B&B.** This is a small, friendly bed-and-breakfast agency genuinely "committed to the idea that traveling shouldn't be a rip-off." Expatriate American Gail O'Farrell has family homes (to which you get your own latchkey) in or near village-y Hampstead, all of which are comfortable. This used to be one of those word-of-mouth secrets, but now that everyone knows, book well ahead. ⊠ *14 Edis St., Regent's Park, NW1 8LG* ☎ *020/7722–6869* ⊟ *No credit cards.*

££ 🏠 **Uptown Reservations.** As the name implies, this B&B booking service accepts only the more upscale addresses and specializes in finding hosted homes or short-term apartments for Americans, often executives of small corporations. Nearly all the 85 homes on its register are in Knightsbridge, Belgravia, Kensington, and Chelsea. The private homes vary, of course, but all are good-looking. Self-catering rentals—ideal for families—start at £550 per week. ⊡ *Box 50407, Chelsea, W8 5XZ* ☎ *020/7937–2001* 🖨 *020/7937–6660* ⊕ *www.uptownres.co.uk* ⊟ *AE, MC, V* ☞ *Facilities vary. Payment by bank transfer, U.S. check, or credit card; 20% deposit required.*

£–££ 🏠 **At Home in London.** This service offers rooms in private homes in Knightsbridge, Kensington, Mayfair, Chelsea, and West London. Prices are very competitive and include breakfast, and rooms are all approved by the agency. Prices start at £28 a night per room, making this a great alternative to budget hotels. ⊠ *70 Black Lion La., Hammersmith, W6 9BE* ☎ *020/8748–1943* 🖨 *020/8748–2700* ⊕ *www.athomeinlondon. co.uk* ⊟ *MC, V* ☞ *£7.50 per person booking fee.*

£ 🖥 **Host & Guest Service.** In business for 40 years, this service can find you a room based on a huge selection of B&Bs in London as well as the rest of the United Kingdom, even in rural areas. It's a great way to find excellent bargains in small hotels and guesthouses, knowing that all have been vetted by the agency. ✉ *103 Dawes Rd., Fulham, SW6 7DU* ☎ *020/7385–9922* 🖨 *020/7386–7575* ⊕ *www.host-guest.co.uk* ▭ *MC, V* ☞ *Full payment in advance.*

16

Pubs & Nightlife

WORD OF MOUTH

"Many London pubs have a fascinating history and decor. Whether it is a beamed medieval, or has "snobscreens," or a display of antiques the choice is wide. The one often chosen is Ye olde Cheshire Cheese where I have had a meal. It was like going into a rabbits warren and we sat somewhere down in a basement. I found it slightly chlostrophobic but not enough to spoil my meal."

—tod

Updated by
Kristan Schiller

London is a veritable utopia for excitement junkies, culture fiends, and those who—simply put—like to party. Virginia Woolf once wrote of London, "I step out upon a tawny-colored magic carpet . . . and get carried into beauty without raising a finger. The nights are amazing, with all the white porticoes and broad silent avenues. And people pop in and out, lightly, divertingly, like rabbits . . . "

Most who visit London will, like Woolf, be mesmerized by the city's energy, which reveals itself in layers. Whether you prefer a romantic evening at the opera, rhythm and blues with fine French food, the gritty guitar riffs of East London, a pint and gourmet pizza at a local gastropub, or swanky cocktails and sushi at London's sexiest lair, the U.K. capital is sure to feed your fancy.

PUBS

Even today, when TV keeps so many glued to hearth and home, the pub, or public house, or "local," is still a vital part of British life. It also should be a part of the visitor's experience, as there are few better places to meet the natives in their local habitat. There are hundreds of pubs in London—ever fewer of which still have original Victorian etched glass, Edwardian panels, and art nouveau carvings. The list below offers a few pubs selected for central location, historical interest, a pleasant garden, music, or good food, but you might just as happily adopt your own temporary local.

Just as smoking in all pubs that serve food is being made illegal, gastro-pub fever is sweeping London. At many places, char-grills are installed in the kitchen out back and nouveau pub grub, such as Moroccan chicken, is on the menu. Regardless of what you eat, however, you'll definitely want to order a pint.

■ TIP→ Remember that what Americans call beer, the British call lager. However, the real pub drink is "bitter," usually served at room temperature. There's a movement to bring back the traditionally prepared ale that is much less gassy. There are also plenty of other potations: stouts like Guinness and Murphy's are thick, pitch-black brews you'll either love or hate; ciders, made from apples, are an alcoholic drink in Britain (Bulmer's and Strongbow are the names to remember); shandies are a mix of lager and lemon soda; and black-and-tans are a blend of lager and stout

PUBS & NIGHTLIFE PLANNER

What to Wear

As a general rule, you can dress as you would for an evening in, say, New York City; however, you will see far fewer people in the upscale London nightspots wearing jeans and tennis shoes. British women are also prone to bearing a bit more skin, so that sparkly, backless top you were saving for a Caribbean soirée might be just as suitable for a night out in London, weather permitting. Certain clubs will require that gentlemen wear a jacket—in general, it's a good idea to wear one if you're not headed to the pub or a rock show.

Top 5

■ **Claridge's Bar.** This grande dame of London hotels features an art deco bar frequented by media people, socialites, *and* regular folks.

■ **Nordic.** ABBA posters, a disco ball, friendly patrons, and a supermodel-like (yet friendly) staff. Try the Longberry, a powdered sugar-top fruity concoction and quite possibly the most delectable drink in London.

■ **Milk & Honey.** Like speakeasies in Prohibition-era America, this no-sign joint may be nondescript on the outside but inside it's a high-style wonderland with hand-rolled Havanas and an otherworldly wine list.

■ **Notting Hill Arts Club.** A groovy, international crowd keeps things stirring night after night. If you want fun, this is where to find it.

■ **Shepherd's Bush Empire.** It's now been more than a decade since this former BBC studio started providing incredible acoustics for some of the best live shows in the world.

What's Happening Now

There are several Web sites, in addition to the print publications *The Evening Standard, Time Out London, Where London,* and *In London,* which will tell you who's playing where and when. Check out www.Londontown.com, www.AllinLondon.co.uk, www.Viewlondon.co.uk, or www.london.net/nightlife.

Getting Around

If you're out past 12:30 AM, the best way to get home is by taxi (the Tube stops running at 12:30 AM Mon.–Sat. and 11:30 PM on Sun.). The best place to hail a taxi is at the front door of one of the major hotels; you can also have the staff at your last stop of the evening call one for you.

Liquor Laws

At the end of 2005, England and Wales relaxed their licensing laws and as many as 5,200 drinking establishments in London extended their opening hours. The new era marks the most notable change since 1915 of what many feel were draconian liquor laws that required most pubs to close at 11 PM. And although it's controversial, the new development only translates into a modest increase in overall licensing hours; only 14 bars and clubs are now open until dawn, while the rest shut at midnight or a few short hours later.

17

named for the distinctive uniforms worn by early-20th-century British troops. Discuss your choice of drink with the barman, turn to your neighbor, raise the glass, and utter that most pleasant of toasts, "Cheers."

✗ **Admiral Codrington.** Named after a hero of the Napoleonic Wars, this rustic bar in a former market district was once the most popular meeting place for the upwardly mobile of Sloane Square (Lady Diana Spencer is said to have been a regular in her teaching days). The "Admiral Cod" as it's known, has recently been refurbished and now houses a modern courtyard with a removable glass roof, where excellent English fare is served at lunch and dinnertime; the adjoining original pub with its bare floorboards remains a popular spot with "Sloane Rangers." ⊠ *17 Mossop St., Chelsea, SW3* ☎ *0871/332–4123* Ⓤ *South Kensington.*

✗ **Black Friar.** A step from Blackfriars Tube stop, this spectacular pub has an arts-and-crafts interior that is entertainingly, satirically ecclesiastical, with inlaid mother-of-pearl, wood carvings, stained glass, and marble pillars all over the place. In spite of the finely lettered temperance tracts on view just below the reliefs of monks, fairies, and friars, there is, needless to say, a nice group of beers on tap from independent brewers. ⊠ *174 Queen Victoria St., The City, EC4* ☎ *020/7236–5474* Ⓤ *Blackfriars.*

✗ **Blue Anchor.** This unaltered Georgian pub has been seen in the movie *Sliding Doors* and was the site where *The Planets* composer Gustav Holst wrote his *Hammersmith Suite.* Sit out by the river, or shelter inside with a good ale. ⊠ *13 Lower Mall, Hammersmith, W6* ☎ *020/8748–5774* Ⓤ *Hammersmith.*

✗ **Cricketers.** You'll find bowls of noodles and weekly quiz nights at this understated pub in one of London's wealthiest neighborhoods. It's also a fine place for a Pimm's (a British gin-based liquor). ■ TIP➔ On a summer's day, Cricketers makes a sublime vantage point for the cricket and the frolicking that take place on Richmond Green. ⊠ *Maids of Honour Row, the Green, Richmond, TW9* ☎ *020/8940–4372* Ⓤ *Richmond.*

✗ **De Hems.** London's only Dutch pub, straddling Chinatown and Shaftesbury Avenue, was founded in 1902. There's Oranjeboom on tap among numerous other tasty and strong Dutch and Belgian beverages. Interestingly named Netherlands dishes (*bitterballen* and *vlammetjes*) are on the menu, and the place is almost always lively—sometimes bustling—up to the midnight closing time. ⊠ *11 Macclesfield St., Chinatown, W1* ☎ *020/7437–2494* Ⓤ *Piccadilly Circus.*

✗ **Dove Inn.** Read the list of famous ex-regulars, from Charles II and Nell Gwyn to Ernest Hemingway, as you wait for a beer at this very popular, very comely 16th-century riverside pub by Hammersmith Bridge. If the Dove is too full, stroll upstream along the bank to the Old Ship or the Blue Anchor. ■ TIP➔ Please note, you must be 18 to be admitted to this pub. ⊠ *19 Upper Mall, Hammersmith, W6* ☎ *020/8748–9474* Ⓤ *Hammersmith.*

✗ **The Fire Station.** Located in a 1910 firehouse, this lively pub is known for its English menu and unique architecture, with old red metal fittings and white-washed brick walls still intact. Friendly service and a convenient location near the Waterloo Tube make this a solid choice if you don't mind the spirited after-work crowd that often packs the bar. ✉ *150 Waterloo Rd., Waterloo, SE1* ☎ *020/7620–2226* Ⓤ *Waterloo.*

✕ **French House.** In the pub where the French Resistance convened during World War II, Soho hipsters and eccentrics rub shoulders now with theater people and the literati—more than shoulders, actually, because this tiny, tricolor-waving, photograph-lined pub is almost always packed. ✉ *49 Dean St., Soho, W1* ☎ *020/7437–2799* Ⓤ *Tottenham Court Rd.*

✕ **George Inn.** The inn overlooks a courtyard where Shakespeare's plays were once staged. The present building dates from the late 17th century, and is central London's last remaining galleried inn. Dickens was a regular, and the George is featured in *Little Dorrit*. Entertainments include Shakespeare performances, medieval jousts, and morris dancing. ✉ *77 Borough High St., South Bank, SE1* ☎ *020/7407–2056* Ⓤ *London Bridge.*

✕ **Island Queen.** This sociable Islington pub with ornate windows and warm, red decor has home-cooked food and a cozy upstairs lounge. Relax on the soft sofas with a Belgian beer, or shoot a game of pool. Playwright Joe Orton frequented the place; he lived—and died, murdered by his lover—next door. ✉ *87 Noel Rd., Islington, N1* ☎ *020/7704–7631* Ⓤ *Angel.*

✕ **The Lamb.** Step back in time inside this intimate pub and feel the presence of Charles Dickens and his contemporaries who drank here. For private chats at the bar, you can close the delicate countertop window to the bar staff, only opening it when you fancy another pint. ✉ *94 Lamb's Conduit St., Bloomsbury, WC1* ☎ *020/7405–0713* Ⓤ *Russell Sq.*

★ ✕ **Lamb & Flag.** This 17th-century pub was once known as the Bucket of Blood because the upstairs room was used as a ring for bare-knuckle boxing. Now it's a trendy, friendly—and bloodless—pub, serving food (lunch only) and real ale. It's on the edge of Covent Garden, off Garrick Street. ✉ *33 Rose St., Covent Garden, WC2* ☎ *020/7497–9504* Ⓤ *Covent Garden.*

✕ **Lansdowne.** An outstanding new chef and friendly service are the main draws at this unassuming Primrose Hill pub. The menu ranges from steaks and fresh fish to thin-crust pizzas with toppings such as olives, fennel, and chorizo. Celebrities like it here for the laid-back, neighborhood atmosphere—and the fact that they aren't fussed over—so if you're looking to heckle movie stars, visit the West End instead. ✉ *90 Gloucester Ave., Primrose Hill, NW1* ☎ *020/7483–0409* Ⓤ *Chalk Farm.*

✕ **Le Beaujolais.** Around 60 lovingly selected French wines are available here, where you can snack on charcuterie and homemade pâté while snug and warm under the bottle-laden ceiling. It's a romantic spot and can get crowded just before theater performances, but has room again once the shows begin. ✉ *25 Litchfield St., Leicester Square, WC2* ☎ *020/7836–2955* Ⓤ *Leicester Square.*

✕ **Mayflower.** An atmospheric 17th-century riverside inn with exposed beams and a terrace, this is practically the very place from which the Pilgrims set sail for Plymouth Rock. The inn is licensed to sell American postage stamps. ✉ *117 Rotherhithe St., South Bank, SE16* ☎ *020/7237–4088* Ⓤ *Rotherhithe.*

17

✕ **Museum Tavern.** Across the street from the British Museum, this aptly named Victorian pub makes an ideal resting place after the rigors of the culture trail. This heavily restored hostelry once helped Karl Marx unwind after a hard day in the Library. He could have spent his *Kapital* on any of six beers available on tap. ⊠ *49 Great Russell St., Bloomsbury, WC1* ☎ *020/7242-8987* Ⓤ *Tottenham Court Rd.*

★ ✕ **Old Ship.** This early-opening (9 AM) riverside pub is great for a Full English breakfast or pancakes in the morning, or roasts and a good pint later in the day. Sit on the bright balcony or terrace and watch the rowers and boating folk messing around on the Thames in front of you. ⊠ *25 Upper Mall, Hammersmith, W6* ☎ *020/8748-2593* Ⓤ *Ravenscourt Park.*

★ ✕ **Porterhouse.** With arguably the capital's best selection of beers, this oft-crammed pub is a true institution. In the enormous, brewerylike space you can choose from the 172 international bottles (originating from Estonia to Ethiopia, Indonesia to Israel) or nine draft beers brewed by Porterhouse itself in Ireland. Irish dishes include Carlingford mussels and the "Great Craic" burger—made with Irish Angus beef, Irish cheddar, and a "special relish"—that soaks up the beer beautifully. International sports on TV and live music five nights a week provide entertainment. ⊠ *21–22 Maiden La., Covent Garden, WC2* ☎ *020/7379-7917* Ⓤ *Covent Garden.*

✕ **Princess Louise.** This fine, popular pub has an over-the-top Victorian interior—glazed terra-cotta, stained and frosted glass, and a glorious painted ceiling. It's not all show, either; the food is a cut above normal pub grub, and there's a good selection of real ales. ⊠ *208 High Holborn, Holborn, WC1* ☎ *020/7405-8816* Ⓤ *Holborn.*

✕ **Prospect of Whitby.** Named after a ship, this is London's oldest riverside pub, dating from 1520. Once upon a time it was called the Devil's Tavern because of the lowlife criminals—thieves and smugglers—who congregated here. Ornamented with pewter ware and nautical objects, this much-loved "boozer" is often pointed out from boat trips up the Thames. ⊠ *57 Wapping Wall, East End, E1* ☎ *020/7481-1095* Ⓤ *Wapping.*

✕ **The Running Horse.** This traditional English pub sits on the site of a building that dated back to 1720 and became a tavern in 1738. With excellent soups and salads, outdoor seating, a pool table, and a juke box (plus, it's only a five-minute walk to the Bond Street tube) the Running Horse is the perfect stopover for those needing a break from a jaunt through elegant Mayfair. ⊠ *50 Davies St., Mayfair, W1K* ☎ *020/7493-1275* Ⓤ *Bond St.*

✕ **St. James Tavern.** This pretty pub is steps from Piccadilly Circus and five major West End theaters; another plus is that it stays open until 1 AM Thursday through Saturday. The interior has lovely hand-painted Doulton tiles depicting Shakespearean scenes. The kitchen prides itself on its fish-and-chips—in general, the Tavern's meals, cocktails, and shooters are among the best value in central London. ⊠ *45 Great Windmill St., Soho, W1* ☎ *020/7437-5009* Ⓤ *Piccadilly Circus.*

✕ **Sherlock Holmes.** This pub used to be known as the Northumberland Arms, and Arthur Conan Doyle popped in regularly for a pint. It figures in *The Hound of the Baskervilles,* and you can see the hound's head and plaster casts of its huge paws among other Holmes memorabilia in the bar. ⊠ *10 Northumberland St., Trafalgar Square, WC2* ☎ *020/ 7930–2644* Ⓤ *Charing Cross.*

Fodor's Choice ✕ **Spaniards Inn.** Ideal as a refueling point when you're on a Hamp-
★ stead Heath hike, this historic, oak-beam pub has a gorgeous garden, scene of the tea party in Dickens's *Pickwick Papers.* Dick Turpin, the highwayman, frequented the inn; you can see his pistols on display. Before Dickens, Shelley, Keats, and Byron hung out here as well. It's extremely popular, especially on Sunday, when Londoners roll in for the tasty dishes, crackling fire, and amusing dog-washing machine in the parking lot. ⊠ *Spaniards Rd., Hampstead, NW3* ☎ *020/8731–6571* Ⓤ *Hampstead.*

✕ **Star Tavern.** In the heart of elegant Belgravia, this pub has a Georgian-era facade straight off a postcard. The inside is charming, too: Victorian furnishings and two roaring fireplaces make this a popular spot and a great place to flop down with your armload of Knightsbridge shopping bags. ⊠ *6 Belgrave Mews W, Belgravia, SW1* ☎ *020/7235–3019* Ⓤ *Knightsbridge.*

Fodor's Choice ✕ **White Hart.** The drinking destination of the theater community for some
★ time now, this elegant, family-owned pub on Drury Lane is one of the best places to mix with cast and crew of the stage. A female-friendly environment, a cheery skylight above the lounge area, and well-above-average pub fare make the White Hart one of the most sociable pubs in London. ⊠ *191 Drury La., Covent Garden, WC2* ☎ *020/7242–2317* Ⓤ *Holborn.*

Fodor's Choice ✕ **White Horse.** This pub in well-to-do Parson's Green has a superb menu
★ with a beer or wine chosen to match each dish. Open early for weekend brunch, the "Sloaney Pony" (named for its wealthy Sloane Square clientele) is enormously popular and a place to find many a Hugh Grant and Liz Hurley lookalike. The owner is an expert on cask-condition ale, and there are more than 100 wines to choose from. ⊠ *1–3 Parson's Green, Parson's Green, SW6* ☎ *020/7736–2115* Ⓤ *Parsons Green.*

✕ **Windsor Castle.** Rest here if you're on a Kensington jaunt, and save your appetite for the food, especially on Sunday, when they do a traditional roast. On other days you may find oysters, salads, fish cakes, and steak sandwiches. In winter a fire blazes; in summer an exquisite patio garden awaits. ⊠ *114 Campden Hill Rd., Notting Hill, W8* ☎ *020/ 7243–9551* Ⓤ *Notting Hill Gate.*

✕ **Ye Grapes.** This 1882 traditional (noisy, and anti-chic) pub has been popular since Victoria was on the throne. It's in the heart of Shepherd Market, the village-within-Mayfair, and is still home-away-from-home for a full deck of London characters. ⊠ *16 Shepherd Market, Mayfair, W1* ☎ *No phone* Ⓤ *Green Park.*

✕ **Ye Olde Cheshire Cheese.** Yes, it's a tourist trap, but it's also an extremely historic pub (it dates from 1667), and it deserves a visit for its sawdust-covered floors, low wood-beam ceilings, and the 14th-century crypt of Whitefriars' monastery under the cellar bar. But if you want to see the set of 17th-century pornographic tiles that once adorned the upstairs you'll have to go to Blacks Museum. This was the most regular of Dr. Johnson's and Dickens's *many* locals. ⊠ *145 Fleet St., The City, EC4* ☎ *020/7353–6170* Ⓤ *Blackfriars.*

17

NIGHTLIFE

As is true of nearly all cosmopolitan centers, the pace with which bars and clubs go in and out of fashion is mind-boggling. The phenomenon of absinthe has been replaced by bourbon's bite and the frenzy for the perfect cocktail recipe, while the dreaded velvet rope has been usurped by the doorbell-ringing mystique of members-only drinking clubs. The understated glamour of North London's Primrose Hill, which makes movie stars feel so at ease, might be considered dull by the über-trendy clubgoers of London's West End, while the price of a pint in Chelsea would be dubbed blasphemous by the musicians and poets of racially diverse Brixton. Meanwhile, some of the city's most talked-about nightlife spots are turning out to be those attached to some of its best restaurants and hotels—no wonder when you consider the increased popularity of London cuisine in international circles. Moreover, the gay scene in London continues to flourish.

Whatever your pleasure, however your whim turns come evening, chances are you'll find what you're looking for in London's ever-changing arena of activity and invention.

Bars

Today the London bar scene is known for its bizarre blends, its pioneering panache, and its highly stylish regulars. Time was, bars in London were just a stopover in an evening full of fun—perhaps the pub first, then a bar, and then it's off to boogie the night away at the nearest dance club. These days, however, bars have become less pit stops and more destinations in themselves. With the addition of dinner menus, DJs, dance floors, and the still-new later opening hours, people now stay into the wee small hours of the morning at many of London's most fashionable bars. From exotic spaces designed to look like African villages to classic art deco creations to cavernous structures housed in old railway stations, London's bar culture is as diverse as it is delicious.

★ **American Bar.** Festooned with a chin-dropping array of club ties, signed celebrity photographs, sporting mementos, and baseball caps, this sensational cocktail bar has superb martinis. ■ TIP→ **Jacket required after 5 PM.** ✉ *Stafford Hotel, 16–18 St. James's Pl., St. James's, SW1A* ☎ *020/ 7493–0111* ⊙ *Weekdays 11:30 AM–11 PM, Sat. noon–3 PM and 5:30–11 PM, Sun. noon–2:30 PM and 6:30–10:30* Ⓤ *Green Park.*

Fodor'sChoice **Annex 3.** The same set behind the London-based Les Trois Garçons
★ and Loungelover (three antique dealers) now have this richly decorated den of cocktail inventions to add to their roster. Infused with purple-and-red decor, dimly lighted crystal chandeliers, and walls that resemble the side of a giant Rubik's Cube, the très chic Annex 3 just off Regents Street serves a colorful mix of traditional and fruity drinks that will please most palates (as well as Japanese-influenced modern European fare for those who wish to nibble as they nurse). ✉ *6 Little Portland St., Fitzrovia, W1W* ☎ *020/7631–0700* ⊙ *Mon.–Sat. noon–11 PM* Ⓤ *Oxford Circus.*

The Blue Bar at the Berkeley Hotel. With Wedgwood-blue walls, Indian-style glass lanterns, and cozy seating arrangements in every corner, this baroque-style hotel bar is the ideal spot for a secretive tête-à-tête. Nurse a Blue Bar Martini (served dry with a blue cheese-stuffed olive) while snacking on honeyed nuts and taking in eclectic music ranging from Brazilian jazz to Tom Waits. ⊠ *Wilton Pl., Knightsbridge, SW1* ☎ *020/7235–6000* ⊗ *Mon.–Sat. 4 PM–1 AM* Ⓤ *Knightsbridge.*

Beach Blanket Babylon. In Notting Hill, close to Portobello Market, this always-packed bar is distinguishable by its eclectic interior of indoor–outdoor spaces filled with Gaudí-esque curves and snuggly corners—like a fairy-tale grotto or a medieval dungeon. ⊠ *45 Ledbury Rd., Notting Hill, W11* ☎ *020/7229–2907* ⊗ *Mon.–Thurs. noon–11 PM, Fri. and Sat. noon–midnight, Sun. noon–10:30 PM* Ⓤ *Notting Hill Gate.*

Bug Bar. Inside the crypt of a church, this intimate vaulted bar with Gothic overtones has restaurant and lounge areas, and is also attached to the trendy dance club Mass. Brixton hipsters shake it up to top DJs spinning the decks, and knock back "Bugtai" shooters at the bar. ⊠ *Brixton Hill, under St. Matthew's Church, Brixton, SW2* ☎ *020/7738–3366* ⊗ *Wed.–Fri. 8 PM–2 AM, Sat. 8 PM–4 AM, Sun. 7 PM–2 AM* Ⓤ *Brixton.*

Cafe des Amis. This relaxed brasserie–wine bar near the Royal Opera House is the perfect pre- or post-theater spot—and a friendly enough place to go to on your own. More than 30 wines are served by the glass along with a good selection of cheeses. Opera buffs will enjoy the performance and production prints on the walls. ⊠ *11–14 Hanover Pl., Covent Garden, WC2* ☎ *020/7379–3444* ⊗ *Mon.–Sat. 11:30 AM–11:30 PM* Ⓤ *Covent Garden.*

Fodor'sChoice ★ **Claridge's Bar.** This elegant Mayfair meeting place remains unpretentious even when it brims with beautiful people. The bar has an art deco heritage made hip by the sophisticated touch of designer David Collins. A library of rare champagnes and brandies as well as a delicious choice of traditional and exotic cocktails—try the Black Pearl—will occupy your taste buds. Request a glass of vintage Cristal (the only bar in London that serves it) or a smoke from the menu of fine cigars in the Macanudo Fumoir. ⊠ *55 Brook St., Mayfair, W1A* ☎ *020/7629–8860* ⊗ *Mon.–Sat. 11–11, Sun. 4–8:30* Ⓤ *Bond St.*

Fodor'sChoice ★ **Crazy Bear.** This sexy basement bar with cowhide stools and croc-skin tables feels like Casablanca in Fitzrovia. As you enter Crazy Bear, a spiral staircase leads to a mirrored parlor over which presides a 1947 Murano chandelier; indeed, a suitably smoky, dimly lighted backdrop for Bogey and Bergman. But don't let the opulence fool you: waitresses here are warm and welcoming to an all-ages international crowd abuzz with chatter. ⊠ *26–28 Whitfield St., Fitzrovia, W1T* ☎ *020/7631–0088* ⊗ *Mon.–Sat. noon–11* Ⓤ *Goode St.*

★ **Dogstar.** This popular South London hangout is frequented by local hipsters and counterculture types. The vibe is unpretentious and hip, and the modern Caribbean cuisine is a treat. Visual projections light up the interior and top-name DJs play cutting-edge sounds free on weekdays. Move on to the nearby dance club, Mass, and your sampling of local Brixton life will be complete. ⊠ *389 Coldharbour La., Brixton, SW9*

☎ 020/7733–7515 🖃 Free–£5 ⊙ Mon.–Thurs. and Sun. noon–2 AM, Fri. and Sat. noon–4 AM Ⓤ Brixton.

Hackney Central. A welcome addition to the East London nightlife scene, this bar and music club is the new incarnation of Hackney's old Victorian railway station. DJs and live bands perform in the bar upstairs, while food and drink flow in the restaurant and bar downstairs. ⊠ Amhurst Rd., Hackney, E8 ☎ 020/8986–5111 ⊕ www.hackneycentral.com 🖃 Free–£15 ⊙ Sun.–Thurs. 11 AM–midnight, Fri. and Sat. 11 AM–2 AM Ⓤ National Rail: Hackney Central.

Harlem. Backed by music producer Arthur Baker (the Elbow Room), Harlem re-creates New York in more ways than one, not the least of which is its size: the two rooms together equal the dimensions of an average Manhattan apartment. However, funky DJs, fresh tunes, and reasonably priced drinks—not to mention the excellent soul food served in the first floor restaurant—give Harlem a vibe all its own. ⊠ 78 Westbourne Grove, Westbourne Grove, W2 ☎ 020/7985–0900 ⊙ Weekdays 8 AM–2 AM, Sat. 10 AM–2 AM, Sun. 10 AM–2:30 AM Ⓤ Westbourne Park.

Hoxton Square Bar & Kitchen. The rectangular concrete bar, reminiscent of a Swedish airport hangar, has long, comfortable sofas, plate-glass windows at the front and back, and outdoor tables overlooking leafy Hoxton Square. Enlarged with the purchase of the Lux cinema next door, there's now a designated restaurant area serving venison and the like. The music policy here is anything but house, and creative types give the place good business. ⊠ 2–4 Hoxton Sq., Hoxton, E1 ☎ 020/7613–0709 ⊙ Mon.–Sat. 11 AM–midnight, Sun. 11 AM–11:30 PM Ⓤ Old St.

Hush. Once inside it's easy to envision 007 waltzing up to this 1970s-style bar and ordering a round of martinis for the supermodels sitting halfway across the room. This two-floor cocktail bar and restaurant, co-owned by Roger Moore's son Geoffrey, certainly draws its share of beautiful people. The entire bar is decked out in modish black-and-white photographs of celebrities ranging from Richard Attenborough to Posh Spice. But Hush is not without its simpler charms: the entranceway is located in a quiet court decorated with garlands and ribbons at holiday-time. ⊠ 8 Lancashire Ct., Brook St., Mayfair W1S ☎ 020/7659–1500 ⊙ Mon.–Sat. 11 AM–2 AM Ⓤ Bond St.

Fodor'sChoice ★ **Late Lounge & Cocoon.** The "it" place of the moment, the pan-Asian restaurant Cocoon transforms itself into a sophisticated lounge (with DJ) Thursday through Saturday until 3 AM. Smack in the center of the West End on a landmark site, the Late Lounge with its soft peach decor and sanctuarylike setting serves caviar, oysters, a selection of appetizers, and desserts as well as champagne, sake, and cocktails with an oriental twist. If you're looking to make an impression, this sparkling spot holds sway. ⊠ 65 Regent St., St. James, W1B ☎ 087/1332–6347 ⊙ Thurs.–Sat. 11 PM–3 AM Ⓤ Piccadilly.

Fodor'sChoice ★ **The Living Room W1.** In the former post office that appeared on the cover of David Bowie's *Ziggy Stardust* album, this stylish oasis just off bustling Regent Street is arguably one of the most spacious spots in London without a dance floor. The restaurant–bar is actually part of a chain but feels like a stand-alone with live piano music emanating softly from the first-floor bar and a scrumptious international menu upstairs. The staff here is friendly and the atmosphere playful yet urbane. ⊠ *3–9 Heddon St., Soho, W1B* ☎ *0870/1662–225* ⊙ *Mon.–Sat. 10 AM–1 AM, Sun. 11 AM–midnight* Ⓤ *Piccadilly.*

Long Bar at Sanderson Hotel. Dubbed by Vanity Fair as a "magical stage set for the world's high-profile travelers," the Philippe Starck–designed Sanderson Hotel envelops visitors in a fantasyland setting of billowy white decor and glass dividers. The dramatic, high-ceiling Long Bar just off the lobby serves sushi and tapas as well as cocktails, providing a chic shopping break as well as an excellent perch for people-watching. ⊠ *50 Berners St., Fitzrovia, W1T* ☎ *020/7300–1400* ⊙ *Mon.–Sat. 11 AM–1 AM, Sun. 11 AM–10:30 PM* Ⓤ *Oxford Circus.*

Milk & Honey. An offshoot of the New York members-only drinking club, this unmarked bar feels like a Prohibition-era speakeasy with its call-ahead policy and doorbell entrance. Here cocktail maestro Dale DeGroff serves up more potent potions than the name suggests until 11 PM during the early half of the week. However, if you're unacquainted with the bar's rules of conduct, consider yourself forewarned: "Gentlemen will not introduce themselves to ladies. Ladies . . . if a man you don't know speaks to you, please lift your chin slightly and ignore him." ⊠ *61 Poland St., Soho, W1F* ☎ *020/7000–655469* ⊕ *www.mlkhny.com* ⊙ *Open to non-members weekdays 6 PM–11 PM, Sat. 7 PM–11 PM* ⚎ *Reservations essential* Ⓤ *Oxford Circus.*

Nordic. With Red Erik and Faxe draft beers, shooters called "Husky Poo" and "Danish Bacon Surprise," and crayfish tails and meatballs on the smorgasbord menu, Nordic takes its Scandinavian feel the whole way. This secluded, shabby-chic bar serves many couples cozied up among travel brochures promoting the Viking lands. The sassy, sweet Longberry is quite possibly the most perfect cocktail ever made. ⊠ *25 Newman St., Noho, W1* ☎ *020/7631–3174* ⊕ *www.nordicbar.com* ⊙ *Weekdays noon–11 PM, Sat. 6 PM–11 PM* Ⓤ *Tottenham Court Rd.*

★ **Oxo Bar.** The views of London are inspiring from this eighth-floor bar near the Tate Modern on the south bank of the Thames. Most people come to eat at the excellent restaurant, one of London's best, but the bar is a wonderful place in its own right, perfect for a predinner drink or a vertiginous nightcap. ⊠ *Bargehouse St., South Bank, SE1* ☎ *020/7803–3888* ⊙ *Mon.–Sat. 11 AM–11 PM, Sun. noon–10:30 PM* Ⓤ *Waterloo.*

Smiths of Smithfield. This loft-style megabar with exposed wood beams, steel columns, and huge windows overlooks the Victorian Smithfield's market. Have a beer in the airy ground-floor pub, a cocktail in the intimate champagne-cocktail bar upstairs (open until 1 AM on weekends), or some fine British Modern cuisine in the restaurants. The 7 AM opening hour captures the fallout from nearby clubs. DJs spin records here in the evenings Wednesday through Saturday. ⊠ *67–77 Charterhouse St., East End, EC1N* ☎ *020/7251–7950* ⊙ *Mon.–Wed. 7 AM–11 PM, Thurs. and Fri. 7 AM–12:30 AM, Sat. 10 AM–12:30 AM, Sun. 9:30 AM–10:30 PM* Ⓤ *Farringdon.*

Ten West. At this sprawling South Beach–inspired bar under the Westway on Ladbroke Grove, retro-pattern wallpaper and cushy chairs are offset by lipstick-red latticework railings and chandeliers with marquee-like dividers throughout. Copper tables highlight the main event: simple

17

canapés and cocktails with names like Collins Avenue and the Delano. Although the Miami theme borders on excessive, the tasty food and drinks somehow alleviate the overkill. ✉ *161–165 Ladbroke Grove, Ladbroke Grove, W10* ☎ *020/8960–1702* ⊕ *www.vertigo42.co.uk* ⊗ *Weekdays 5 PM–midnight, weekends noon–midnight* Ⓤ *Ladbroke Grove.*

Umbaba. Prince Harry holds court with his pals at this über-trendy Soho spot styled after a West African village, while society girls teeter about sporting studded tiaras, short skirts, and kitten heels. Rustic dark-wood furniture offsets walls glazed with geometric designs. But although the decor is unique, the drinks tasty, and the patrons pretty, the Africa theme feels a bit gauche when you consider that the cost of booking a table here could feed an entire African village. ■ TIP→ **Members must purchase a passport for the Republic of Umbaba, for £500 annually, but civilians will be admitted for a fee of £15–£20 if they call ahead.** ✉ *15–21 Ganton St., Soho, W1F* ☎ *020/7734–6696* ⊗ *Wed.–Sat. 10 PM–3 AM* Ⓤ *Oxford Circus.*

Comedy & Cabaret

Amused Moose. This dark Soho basement is widely considered the best place to see breaking talent as well as household names doing "secret" shows. Ricky Gervais and Eddie Izzard are among those who have graced this stage and every summer a handful of the Edinburgh Fringe comedians preview here. The bar is open late and there's a DJ and dancing until 5 AM after the show. ✉ *Moonlighting, 17 Greek St., Soho, W1* ☎ *020/8341–1341* ✆ *£10.50* ⊗ *Showtimes vary, call for details.* Ⓤ *Tottenham Court Rd.*

Banana Cabaret. This pub is one of London's finest comedy venues. Well worth the trek, it's only 100 yards from Balham station, and there's a minicab office close by for those tempted to make a long night of it. ✉ *Bedford Pub, 77 Bedford Hill, Balham, SW12* ☎ *020/8673–8904* ✆ *£12–£15* ⊗ *Fri. 7:30 PM–2 AM, Sat. 6:30 PM–2 AM* Ⓤ *Balham.*

Canal Café Theatre. You'll find famous comics and cabaret performers every night of the week in this intimate, picturesque, canal-side venue. The long-running NewsRevue is a topical song and sketch show every night, Thursday–Sunday. ✉ *Bridge House, Delamere Terr., Little Venice, W2* ☎ *020/7289–6054* ✆ *£5–£9* ⊗ *Mon.–Sat. 7:30 PM–11 PM, Sun. 7 PM–10:30 PM* Ⓤ *Warwick Ave.*

Comedy Café. In addition to lots of stand-up comedy, this popular dive in trendy Hoxton has Tex-Mex cuisine, an open mike on Wednesday, and late-night disco on weekends. ✉ *66 Rivington St., East End, EC2* ☎ *020/7739–5706* ✆ *Free–£15* ⊗ *Wed. and Thurs. 7 PM–midnight, Fri. and Sat. 6 PM–1 AM* Ⓤ *Old St.*

★ **Comedy Store.** Known as the birthplace of alternative comedy, this is where the U.K.'s funniest stand-ups have cut their teeth before being launched onto prime-time TV. Comedy Store Players entertain audiences on Wednesday and Sunday; the Cutting Edge team steps in every Tuesday; and weekends have up-and-coming comedians performing on the same stage as established talent. There's a bar with food also available. ■ TIP→ **Tickets can be booked through Ticketmaster or over the phone.** Note that children under 18 are not admitted to this venue. ✉ *1A Oxendon*

St., Soho, SW1 ☎ *0870/060–2340* 🖃 *£13–£15* ◷ *Shows Tues.–Thurs. and Sun. 8 PM–10:15 PM, Fri. and Sat. 8 PM–10:15 PM and midnight– 2:30 AM* Ⓤ *Piccadilly Circus, Leicester Sq.*

FodorsChoice   **Soho Theatre.** This innovative theater programs excellent comedy shows
★   by established acts and award-winning new comedians. The bar downstairs stays open until 1 AM. Check local listings or the Web site for what's on and book tickets in advance. ✉ *21 Dean St., Soho, W1* ☎ *0870/ 429–6883* ⊕ *www.sohotheatre.com* 🖃 *£5–£15* Ⓤ *Tottenham Court Rd.*

Dance Clubs

The city that practically invented raves is always on the verge of creating something new, and on any given night there's a club playing the latest in dance music. Because London is so ethnically diverse, the tunes that emanate from the DJ box are equally varied; an amalgamation of sounds infusing drum 'n' bass, hip-hop, deep house, Latin house, breakbeat, indie, and R&B.

The club scene here ranges from mammoth-size playgrounds like Fabric and Cargo to more intimate venues where you can actually hear your friends talk. Check the daily listings in *Time Out* for "club nights," which are themed nights that take place the same night every week, sometimes at the same clubs but often shifting locations. Another good way to learn about club nights is by picking up fliers in your favorite bar.

Bar Rumba. Though nothing special to look at, this smallish West End venue has a reputation for good fun. The staff is friendly and the club is almost always heaving with serious clubbers grooving to different styles of music each night. Stop by weekdays for cheap cocktails during happy hour. ✉ *36 Shaftesbury Ave., Soho, W1* ☎ *020/7287–2715* 🖃 *£3–£11* ◷ *Mon. and Wed.–Fri. 6 PM–3:30 AM, Tues. 6 PM–3 AM, Sat. 9 PM–4 AM, Sun. 8 PM–1:30 AM* Ⓤ *Piccadilly Circus.*

★   **The Cross.** Stone-floored and rustic, this theme-night, 650-capacity venue manages to be cool and comfortable at the same time. With interesting architectural touches such as wrought-iron railings and a Greek-style outdoor garden, the Cross lends itself to a mixed crowd. Theme nights vary from "polysexual" to gay to charity affairs to musically themed events. ↻ *Check Web site for details on theme nights and opening hrs* ✉ *Kings Cross Goods Yard, Arches 27–31, York Way, N1* ☎ *020/ 7837–0828* ⊕ *www.the-cross.co.uk* Ⓤ *Kings Cross.*

FodorsChoice   **Cargo.** Housed under a series of old railway arches, this vast brick-wall
★   bar, restaurant, dance floor, and live-music venue pulls an international crowd with its hip vibe and diverse selection of music. Long tables bring people together, as does the food, which draws on global influences and is served tapas-style. ✉ *83 Rivington St., Shoreditch, EC2* ☎ *0871/ 075–1741* ◷ *Mon.–Thurs. noon–1 AM, Fri.–Sun. noon–3 AM* Ⓤ *Old St.*

Elbow Room. This innovative club designed in '60s pool-hall chic has 11 tables, leather-booth seating, and a neon-lighted bar. ■ TIP→ **One of the best deals is the occasional Sunday Marmalade night, when indie bands play for free from 7 PM.** There are also branches in Shoreditch and Westbourne Grove. ✉ *89–91 Chapel Market, Islington, N1* ☎ *020/7278–3244*

17

Free–£5 ⊙ *Mon. 5 PM–2 AM, Tues.–Thurs. noon–2 AM, Fri. and Sat. noon–3 AM, Sun. noon–midnight* Ⓤ *Angel.*

The End. Co-owned by Mr. C (ex-MC of cult band the Shamen) and tech-house producer Layo, this intimate club was designed by clubbers for clubbers. Top-name DJs, a state-of-the-art sound system, and minimalist steel-and-glass decor—clubbing doesn't get much better than this. Next door, the AKA Bar (owned by same) is a stylish split-level Manhattan-esque cocktail bar with excellent food. ⊠ *18 West Central St., Holborn, WC1* ☎ *020/7419–9199* ⊕ *www.endclub.com* 💷 *£6–£15* ⊙ *Mon. 10 PM–3 AM, Wed. 10:30 PM–3 AM, Thurs. 10 PM–4 AM, Fri. 10 PM–5 AM, and Sat. 10 PM–7 AM. Also some Sun.* Ⓤ *Tottenham Court Rd.*

Fabric. This sprawling subterranean club has been *the* place to be for the past few years. "Fabric Live" hosts drum 'n' bass and hip-hop crews and live acts on Friday; international big-name DJs play slow sexy bass lines and cutting-edge music on Saturday. Sunday is "Polysexual Night." The devastating sound system and bodysonic dance floor ensure that bass riffs vibrate through your entire body. ■ TIP→ **Get there early to avoid a lengthy queue, and don't wear a suit.** ⊠ *77A Charterhouse St., East End, EC1* ☎ *020/7336–8898* ⊕ *www.fabriclondon.com* 💷 *£12–£15* ⊙ *Fri. and Sun. 9:30 PM–5 AM, Sat. 10 PM–7 AM* Ⓤ *Farringdon.*

KOKO. KOKO is the latest name for this Victorian theater, formerly known as Camden Palace, that's seen acts from Charlie Chaplin to Madonna, and genres from punk to rave. Updated with lush reds not unlike a cockney Moulin Rouge, this is still one of London's most stunning venues. Sounds of live indie-rock, cabaret, funky house, and club classics keep the big dance floor moving, even when it's not heaving. ⊠ *1A Camden High St., Camden Town, NW1* ☎ *0870/432–5527* ⊕ *www.koko.uk. com* 💷 *£3–£20* ⊙ *Wed., Fri., and Sat. 10 PM–3 AM* Ⓤ *Mornington Crescent, Camden Town.*

Mass. In what was previously St. Matthew's Church, but is now an atmospheric club with Gothic overtones, winding stone steps lead to the main room where an extended balcony hangs over the dance floor. An unpretentious and friendly crowd dances, on rotating club nights, to reggae, drum 'n' bass, and R&B. On Saturday afternoons there's a house session. ⊠ *Brixton Hill, St. Matthew's Church, Brixton, SW2* ☎ *020/ 7738–7875* 💷 *£5–£15* ⊙ *Wed. and Thurs., 10 PM–2 AM, Fri. 10 PM–6 AM, Sat. noon–7 PM and 10 PM–6 AM* Ⓤ *Brixton.*

Ministry of Sound. It's more of an industry than a club, with its own record label, online radio station, and international DJs. The stripped down warehouse-style club has a super sound system and pulls in the world's most legendary names in dance. There are chill-out rooms, two bars, and three dance floors. ⊠ *103 Gaunt St., South Bank, SE1* ☎ *020/ 7378–6528* 💷 *£10–£35* ⊙ *Fri. 10:30 PM–5 AM, Sat. 11 PM–7 AM* Ⓤ *Elephant & Castle.*

Notting Hill Arts Club. Rock stars like Liam Gallagher and Courtney Love have been seen at this small basement club-bar. An alternative crowd swills beer to eclectic music that spans Asian underground, hip-hop, Latin-inspired funk, deep house, and jazzy grooves. What it lacks in looks it makes up for in mood. ⊠ *21 Notting Hill Gate, Notting Hill, W11* ☎ *020/ 7460–4459* ⊕ *www.nottinghillartsclub.com* 💷 *Free before 8 PM, be-*

fore 6 PM on Sun., then £5–£8 ⊘ Mon.–Wed. 6 PM–1 AM, Thurs. and Fri. 6 PM–2 AM, Sat. 4 PM–2 AM, Sun. 4 PM–1 AM Ⓤ Notting Hill Gate.

Pacha. London's version of the Ibizan superclub is in a restored 1920s dancehall next to Victoria Coach Station. The classic surroundings—all wood and chandeliers—don't stop the sounds from being eminently up-to-date. The crowd is slightly older than average and stylish, but not necessarily as monied as you might expect. ⊠ Terminus Pl., Victoria, SW1 ☎ 020/7833–3139 ⊠ £15–£20 ⊘ Fri. 10 PM–4 AM, Sat. 10 PM–6 AM Ⓤ Victoria.

Tantra. This sexy dance club is decidedly not for wallflowers. With its starry ceiling and leather furnishings, the sweeping space is chock-full of fashionistas boogying the night away to the latest beats. Count on expensive food and drinks, but if you're up for a night of celeb-spotting and stargazing amidst the London elite, Tantra crowns the list. ⊠ 62 Kingly St., Soho, W1R ☎ 0871/075–1754 ⊘ Mon.–Sat. 10:30 PM–3 AM Ⓤ Piccadilly Circus.

333. This is *the* last word in dance music for the trendy Shoreditch crowd. Fashionable bright young things dance to drum 'n' bass, twisted disco, and underground dance genres. ■ TIP➔ **Sunday is gay night.** There are three floors. You can chill on leather sofas at the relaxed Mother Bar upstairs, open from 8 PM daily, which always has DJs. ⊠ 333 Old St., East End, EC1 ☎ 020/7739–5949 ⊕ www.333mother.com ⊠ Free–£10 ⊘ Tues. hrs vary, Fri. and Sat. 10 PM–5 AM, Sun. 10:30 PM–4 AM Ⓤ Old St.

Eclectic Music

The Borderline. This important small venue has a solid reputation for booking everything from metal to country and beyond. Oasis, Pearl Jam, Blur, Sheryl Crow, PJ Harvey, Ben Harper, Jeff Buckley, and Counting Crows have all played live here. ⊠ Orange Yard off Manette St., Soho, W1 ☎ 020/7434–9592 ⊠ £6–£15 ⊘ Mon.–Sat. 7 PM–3 AM, Sun. 7 PM–11 PM Ⓤ Tottenham Court Rd.

FodorśChoice **Carling Academy Brixton.** This legendary Brixton venue has seen it all—
★ mods and rockers, hippies and punks. Despite a capacity of almost 5,000 people, this refurbished Victorian hall with original art deco fixtures retains a clublike charm; it has plenty of bars and upstairs seating. ⊠ 211 Stockwell Rd., Brixton, SW9 ☎ 0870/771–2000 ⊠ £10–£30 ⊘ Opening hrs vary Ⓤ Brixton.

Lock 17. This midsize venue in the Camden Lock warehouses caters to the full spectrum of musical tastes—country, jazz, blues, folk, indie, and world beat. (■ TIP➔ **Note that on Friday and Saturday it becomes a comedy club, Jongleurs.**) ⊠ Camden Lock off Camden High St., Camden Town, NW1 ☎ 020/7267–1577 ⊠ £5–£20 ⊘ Sun.–Thurs. 7:30 PM–midnight Ⓤ Camden Town.

93 Feet East. Knowing nods greet the bands in this cool but friendly independent venue, with a courtyard out back for taking a breather. Up-and-coming guitar groups and blues acts find their way here, while house DJs get you moving and live hip-hop crews shake you off your seat with hefty basslines. Short films are shown here on Sunday. ⊠ 150 Brick La., East End, E1 ☎ 020/7247–3293 ⊕ www.93feeteast.co.uk ⊠ Free–£10

17

⊘ *Mon.–Thurs. 5 PM–11 PM, Fri. 5 PM–1 AM, weekends noon–1 AM* Ⓤ *Aldgate East.*

Ocean. Bhangra to blues, classical to country, rock to reggae. This state-of-the-art building sports three venues and bars, an atrium, and a café-bar. There are three rooms of resident DJs on Decks Territory Saturday. ⊠ *270 Mare St., East End, E8* ☎ *020/8533–0111* 🖃 *£6–£25* ⊘ *Mon.–Thurs. 10 AM–11 PM, Fri. and Sat. 11 AM–2 AM, Sun. 6 PM–10 PM* Ⓤ *British Rail: Hackney Central.*

100 Club. Since it opened in 1942, all the greats have played here, from Glenn Miller and Louis Armstrong on down to the best traditional jazz artists, British and American blues, R&B, and punk. This cool, inexpensive club now reverberates to rock, indie, and R&B—as well as a little jazz, of course. You can still take jitterbug and jive lessons from the London Swing Dance Society. ⊠ *100 Oxford St., Soho, W1* ☎ *020/7636–0933* ⊕ *www.the100club.co.uk* 🖃 *£7–£15* ⊘ *Mon. 7:30 PM–midnight, Tues.–Thurs. 7:30 PM–11 PM, Fri. 7:30 PM–12:30 AM, Sat. 7:30 PM–2 AM, Sun. 7:30 PM–11 PM* Ⓤ *Oxford Circus, Tottenham Court Rd.*

Shepherd's Bush Empire. Once a grand old theater and former BBC TV studio, this intimate venue with fine balcony views now hosts a great cross section of mid-league U.K. and U.S. bands. ⊠ *Shepherd's Bush Green, Shepherd's Bush, W12* ☎ *0870/771–2000* 🖃 *£10–£30* ⊘ *Opening hrs vary* Ⓤ *Shepherd's Bush (H&C).*

Spitz. In charming Spitalfields Market, where the City interfaces with the East End, this two-level venue has eclectic music that includes world-beat, folk, jazz, Americana, and electronic sounds. The downstairs bar and bistro has DJs and live jazz free on Friday nights. ⊠ *109 Commercial St., East End, E1* ☎ *020/7392–9032* 🖃 *Free–£15* ⊘ *Mon.–Sat. 10 AM–midnight, Sun. 10 AM–10:30 PM* Ⓤ *Liverpool St.*

12 Bar Club. This rough-and-ready acoustic club hosts notable singer-songwriters. Four different acts of new folk and contemporary country perform each night in this intimate venue. There's a good selection of bottled beer and gastro-pub food here. ⊠ *22–23 Denmark Pl., West End, WC2* ☎ *020/7916–6989* 🖃 *£5–£10* ⊘ *Mon.–Thurs. 7:30 PM–1 AM, Fri. and Sat. 7:30 PM–3 AM, Sun. 7:30 PM–midnight. Café opens at 11 AM, Mon.–Sat.* Ⓤ *Tottenham Court Rd.*

★ **Union Chapel.** This beautiful old chapel has excellent acoustics and sublime architecture. The beauty of the space and its impressive multicultural programming have made it one of London's best musical venues, especially for acoustic shows. Performers have included Ravi Shankar, Björk, Beck, Beth Orton, and Bob Geldof, though nowadays you're more likely to hear lower-key alternative country, world music, and jazz. ⊠ *Compton Terr., Islington, N1* ☎ *020/7226–1686 or 0870/120–1349* ⊕ *www.unionchapel.org.uk* 🖃 *Free–£25* ⊘ *Opening hrs vary* Ⓤ *Highbury & Islington.*

Jazz & Blues

Jazz in London is highly eclectic. You can expect anything from danceable, smooth tunes played at a supper club to groovy New Orleans–style blues to exotic world-beat rhythms, which can be heard at some of the less central venues throughout the capital. Musicians are a combination of Brits and visiting artists from the United States and elsewhere. London hosts two major jazz festivals each year at venues throughout the city: the **Soho Jazz Festival** in October, encompassing a range of traditional jazz and Dixieland; and the **London Jazz Festival** in November, which showcases top and emerging artists in experimental jazz.

Ain't Nothin' but Blues. The name sums up this bar that whips up a sweaty and smoky environment. Local musicians, as well as some notable names, squeeze onto the tiny stage. There's good bar food of the chili-and-gumbo variety. Most weekday nights there's no cover. ✉ *20 Kingly St., Soho, W1* ☎ *020/7287–0514* 💳 *Free–£5* ◷ *Mon.–Wed. 6 PM–1 AM, Thurs. 6 PM–2 AM, Fri. 6 PM–2:30 AM, Sat. 1 PM–2:30 AM, Sun. 7:30 PM–midnight* Ⓤ *Oxford Circus.*

★ **Bull's Head.** Its pleasant location (right on the Thames) and the big-name musicians who jam here regularly make the excursion to Bull's Head worthwhile. Jazz-and-blues shows start nightly at 8:30 PM (2 PM and 8 PM on Sunday). ■TIP➔ **They also offer 250 wines.** ✉ *373 Lonsdale Rd., Barnes Bridge, Barnes, SW13* ☎ *020/8876–5241* 💳 *£3–£10* ◷ *Mon.–Sat. noon–11 PM, Sun. noon–10:30 PM* Ⓤ *Hammersmith, then Bus 209 to Barnes Bridge.*

Dover Street Restaurant & Jazz Bar. Put on your blue-suede shoes and prepare to dance the night away—that is, after you've feasted from an excellent French Mediterranean menu. Fun for dates as well as groups, Dover Street Restaurant offers three bars, a DJ, and a stage with the latest live bands performing everything from jazz to soul to R&B, all this encircling linen-covered tables with a friendly wait staff catering to your every whim. ✉ *8–10 Dover St., Mayfair, W1X* ☎ *0871/332–4946* 💳 *£45* ◷ *Weekdays noon–3:30 PM and 7 PM–3 AM, weekends 7 PM–3 AM* Ⓤ *Green Park.*

★ **Jazz Café.** A palace of high-tech cool in bohemian Camden—it remains an essential hangout for fans of both the mainstream end of the repertoire and hip-hop, funk, rap, and Latin fusion. Book ahead if you want a prime table overlooking the stage, in the balcony restaurant. ✉ *5 Pkwy., Camden Town, NW1* ☎ *020/7916–6060 restaurant reservations, 0870/150–0044 standing tickets* 💳 *£10–£25* ◷ *Mon.–Thurs. 7 PM–1 AM, Fri. and Sat. 7 PM–2 AM, Sun. 7 PM–midnight* Ⓤ *Camden Town.*

Pizza Express. One of the capital's most ubiquitous pizza chains also runs a great Soho jazz venue. The darkly lighted restaurant hosts top-quality international jazz acts every night. The Italian-style thin-crust pizzas are good, too, though on the small side. The Hyde Park branch has a spacious jazz club in the basement that hosts mainstream acts. ✉ *10 Dean St., Soho, W1* ☎ *020/7439–8722* Ⓤ *Tottenham Court Rd.* ✉ *11 Knightsbridge, Hyde Park Corner, Knightsbridge, W1* ☎ *020/7235–5273* Ⓤ *Hyde Park Corner* 💳 *£10–£25* ◷ *Daily from 11:30 AM for food; music Sun.–Thurs. 9 PM–midnight, Fri. and Sat. 7:30 PM–midnight.*

Fodor's Choice ★ **Ronnie Scott's.** Since the '60s, this legendary jazz club has attracted big names. It's usually crowded and hot, the food isn't great, and service is slow—but the mood can't be beat, even since the sad departure of its eponymous founder and saxophonist. Reservations are recommended. ✉ *47 Frith St., Soho, W1* ☎ *020/7439–0747* 💳 *£15–£25 nonmembers, £5–£15 members, annual membership £100* ◷ *Mon.–Sat. 8:30 PM–3 AM, Sun. 7:30 PM–11 PM* Ⓤ *Leicester Sq.*

17

606 Club. Expect a civilized Chelsea club that showcases mainstream and contemporary jazz by well-known British-based musicians. ■ TIP→ **You must eat a meal in order to consume alcohol, so allow for an extra £10–£20.** Reservations are advisable. ⊠ *90 Lots Rd., Chelsea, SW10* ☎ *020/ 7352–5953* ⊕ *www.606club.co.uk* ☜ *£7–£9 music charge added to bill* ☾ *Mon.–Wed. 7:30 PM–1:30 AM, Thurs.–Sat. 8 PM–2 AM, Sun. 8 PM–12:30 AM* Ⓤ *Earl's Court, Fulham Broadway.*

Rock

Ever since the Beatles hit the world stage in the early 1960s, London has been at the epicenter of rock and roll. The city is a given stop on any burgeoning or established band's international tour. These days, since rock clubs have been granted later licenses, many shows now go past 11 PM. Fans here are both loyal and enthusiastic. It is, therefore, a good idea to buy show tickets ahead of time. The "NME Live" page at ⊕ www.nme.com is a comprehensive search engine where you can easily book tickets online.

The Astoria. This balconied theater hosts cutting-edge alternative bands (punk, metal, indie guitar). Shows start early, at 7 PM most nights; the building is often cleared, following gigs, for club events. ■ TIP→ **Note that it's closed on some Tuesdays and Wednesdays.** ⊠ *157 Charing Cross Rd., West End, W1* ☎ *020/7434–9592* ☜ *£8–£25* ☾ *Mon., Thurs., and Fri. 7 PM–4 AM, Tues., Wed., and Sun. 7 PM–midnight, Sat. 6 PM–4:30 AM* Ⓤ *Tottenham Court Rd.*

★ **Barfly Club.** At one of the finest small clubs in the capital, punk, indie guitar bands, and new metal rock attract a nonmainstream crowd. Weekend club nights upstairs host DJs who rock the decks. ⊠ *49 Chalk Farm Rd., Camden Town, NW1* ☎ *020/7691–4244* ☜ *£5–£8* ☾ *Mon.–Thurs. 7:30 PM–midnight, Fri. and Sat. 8 PM–3 AM, Sun. 7:30 PM–11 PM* Ⓤ *Camden Town, Chalk Farm.*

Forum. The best medium-to-big-name rock performers consistently play at the 2,000-capacity club. It's a converted 1920 art deco cinema, with a balcony overlooking the dance floor. Consult the Web site for current listings. ⊠ *9–17 Highgate Rd., Kentish Town, NW5* ☎ *020/7284–1001* ⊕ *www.meanfiddler.com* ☜ *£12–£25* ☾ *Opening hrs vary depending on concert schedule* Ⓤ *Kentish Town.*

The Garage. Popular with the younger set, this intimate, two-stage club has a solid reputation for programming excellent indie and rock bands, including American bands. Club nights start after the gigs on weekends. ⊠ *20–22 Highbury Corner, Islington, N1* ☎ *020/7607–1818* ☜ *£5–£12* ☾ *Mon.–Wed. 8 PM–11:30 PM, Thurs. 8 PM–2 AM, Fri. and Sat. 8 PM–3 AM, Sun. 7 PM–midnight* Ⓤ *Highbury & Islington.*

Water Rats. This high-spirited pub hosted Bob Dylan on his 1963 tour, as well as the first Oasis gig. Anything from alt-country, hip-hop, to indie guitar bands thrashes it out most nights of the week. ⊠ *328 Gray's Inn Rd., Euston, WC1* ☎ *020/7336–7326* ☜ *£5* ☾ *Mon.–Sat. 7:30 PM–11:30 PM* Ⓤ *King's Cross.*

The Gay Scene

The U.K. capital's gay and lesbian culture is as thriving as it is in New York or Los Angeles, with Soho serving as the hub of gay London. Clubs in London cater to almost every desire, whether that be the suited up Tommy Hilfiger-look-alike scene, cruisers taking on smoky dives, flamboyant drag shows, lesbian tea dances, or themed fetish nights. There's also a cornucopia of queer theatre and performance art that runs throughout the year. Whatever your tastes, you'll be able to satisfy them with a night on the town in London.

Choices are admittedly much better for males than females here; while many of the gay clubs are female-friendly, those catering strictly to lesbians are the minority. The National Film Board puts on the Gay and Lesbian Film Festival in March. Pride London in July (an annual outdoor event similar to Stonewall in New York) welcomes anyone and everyone. This extravagant pageant spirals its way through London's streets, with major events taking place in Trafalgar Square and Leicester Square, then culminates in Victoria Embankment with ticketed parties continuing on afterwards. Visit ⊕ www.pridelondon.org for details.

For up-to-date listings, consult *Time Out, Boyz, Gay Times, Attitude,* or the lesbian monthly, *Diva.* Online directories include Gay to Z (⊕ www.gaytoz.com) and Rainbow Network (⊕ www.rainbownetwork.com).

Bars, Cafés & Pubs

Most bars in London are gay-friendly, though there are a number of cafés and pubs that are known as gay hangouts after-hours. Here's a listing of just a few, which serve drinks until 11 pm, (10:30 pm on Sunday).

Box. True to its name, this modern, industrial-chic bar is small and square. It's a staple on the preclub circuit and gets packed to the hilt with muscular boys. For peckish punters there's food before 5 PM daily. ⊠ *32–34 Monmouth St., Soho, WC2* ☎ *020/7240–5828* ⊙ *Mon.–Sat. 11 AM–11 PM, Sun. noon–10:30 PM* Ⓤ *Leicester Sq.*

Candy Bar. The United Kingdom's first girls' bar is intimate, chilled, and cruisey, with DJs mixing the latest sounds. Men are welcome as guests. ⊠ *4 Carlisle St., Soho, W1* ☎ *020/7494–4041* ⊡ *£5 after 9 PM, Fri. and Sat.* ⊙ *Mon.–Thurs. 5 PM–11:30 PM, Fri. and Sat. 5 PM–2 AM, Sun. 5 PM–10:30 PM* Ⓤ *Tottenham Court Rd.*

The Edge. *Poseurs* are welcome at this hip hangout. Straight groovers mingle with gay men over the four jam-packed floors. In summer, sidewalk tables provide an enviable view of Soho's daily street theater. ⊠ *11 Soho Sq., Soho, W1* ☎ *020/7439–1313* ⊙ *Mon.–Sat. noon–1 AM, Sun. noon–10:30 PM* Ⓤ *Oxford Circus.*

Fodor'sChoice ★ **Friendly Society.** This haute moderne hotspot hops with activity almost any night of the week; the basement feels a bit like something out of Star Trek with its white-leather pod seats. Rumor has it that Madonna pops in from time to time, which makes sense as the place is known for being gay yet female-friendly. ⊠ *79 Wardour St., Soho, W1D* ☎ *020/ 7434–3805* ⊙ *Weekdays 4–11, Sat. 2–11, Sun. 2–10:30* Ⓤ *Leicester Sq.*

CAN I TAKE MY KIDS TO THE PUB?

As pubs increasingly emphasize what's coming out of the kitchen rather than what's flowing from the tap, whether to bring the kids has become a frequent question. The law dictates that patrons must be 18 years of age or older to drink alcohol in a pub unless they're having a meal in an area designated for eating. In such cases, 16-year-olds accompanied by an adult may drink beer or cider. Children 14 to 17 may enter a pub but are not permitted to purchase or drink alcohol, while children under 14 are not permitted in the bar area of a pub unless the pub has a "Children's Certificate" and they are accompanied by an adult. In general, however, pubs have a section set aside for families and welcome well-behaved children. If possible, it's probably best to call ahead—the bar staff will fill you in on their children's policy.

Rupert Street. For smart boyz, this gay chic island among the sleaze has a new loungey feel with brown-leather sofas and floor-to-ceiling windows. It's crowded and cruisey at night with preclubbers, civilized and café-like by day, with traditional British food served until 5 PM. ⊠ *50 Rupert St., Soho, W1* ☎ *020/7292–7141* ⊗ *Mon.–Sat. noon–11 PM, Sun. noon–10:30 PM* Ⓤ *Leicester Sq., Piccadilly Circus.*

Clubs

Many of London's best gay dance clubs are in mixed clubs like Fabric on themed nights designated for gays. Almost all dance clubs in London are gay-friendly, but if you want to cruise or mingle only with other gays, it's best to call ahead or check Web-site listings.

G.A.Y. London's largest gay party is at the Astoria on Monday, Thursday, Friday, and Saturday. Saturday night hosts big-name talent; regular guests include Kylie Minogue, Geri Halliwell, and a whole host of B-list TV celebrities. ■ TIP→ Buy advance tickets to avoid the long Saturday-night queue. ⊠ *157 and 165 Charing Cross Rd., Soho, WC2* ☎ *020/7434–9592* ⊕ *www.g-a-y.co.uk* 🎫 *£1–£15* ⊗ *Mon. and Thurs. 10:30 PM–4 AM, Fri. 11 PM–5 AM, Sat. 10:30 PM–5:30 AM* Ⓤ *Tottenham Court Rd.*

Fodor'sChoice
★ **Heaven.** With by far the best light show on any London dance floor, Heaven is unpretentious, loud, and huge, with a labyrinth of rooms, bars, and live-music parlors. Friday is predominantly straight, while on Saturday there's also a gay comedy night (£10, 7 PM–11:30 PM). If you go to just one club, Heaven should be it. ⊠ *The Arches, Villiers St., Covent Garden, WC2* ☎ *020/7930–2020* ⊕ *www.heaven-london.com* 🎫 *£4–£12* ⊗ *Mon. 10:15 PM–5:15 AM, Wed. 10:30 PM–3 AM, Fri. and Sat. 10:30 PM–6 AM* Ⓤ *Charing Cross, Embankment.*

Fodor'sChoice
★ **Sanctuary.** There's something for everyone at this Soho hotspot. If you're not in the mood to let loose to pumping house music on the dance floor downstairs, you can ascend to the candlelit upstairs and sip your cocktail on a shapely sofa. The pianist who regularly plays on the top floor has a loyal fan base, and there's a singer belting out show tunes on Wednesday. ■ TIP→ Straight-friendly Sanctuary's happy hour (daily 5 PM–8 PM) is great

value. ⊠ *4–5 Greek St., Soho, W1* ☎ *020/7434-3323* ⊙ *Mon.–Sat. 5 PM–2 AM, Sun. 5 PM–12:30 AM* Ⓤ *Tottenham Court Rd.*

★ **The Shadow Lounge.** This fabulous little lounge and dance club glitters with faux jewels and twinkling fiber-optic lights over its sunken dance floor, which comes complete with pole for those inclined to do their thing around it. It has a serious A-list celebrity factor, with the glamorous London glitterati camping out in the VIP booth. Members are given entrance priority when the place gets full, especially on weekends, so show up early or prepare to queue. ⊠ *5 Brewer St., Soho, W1* ☎ *020/7287-7988* 🎫 *Free–£10* ⊙ *Mon.–Wed. 10 PM–3 AM, Thurs.–Sat. 9 PM–3 AM* Ⓤ *Leicester Sq.*

Sunday Sunday. A longtime fave with the girls, this is a very camp and fun Sunday ballroom, Latin, line-dance, time-warp disco. Tea and biscuits are served until 7 PM. ⊠ *BJ's White Swan, 556 Commercial Rd., East End, E14* ☎ *020/7780-9870* 🎫 *£2* ⊙ *Sun. 5:30 PM–midnight* Ⓤ *Aldgate East.*

Trade. This London institution among the hedonistic muscle boys is now more than a decade old, and begins when many clubs are closing. ■ TIP→ It's on only once a month, so check the Web site for dates. When advertised, the club even serves breakfast, which is not half bad. ⊠ *Turnmills, 63 Clerkenwell Rd., East End, EC1* ☎ *020/7250-3409* ⊕ *www.tradeuk.net* 🎫 *£15* ⊙ *Dates vary, 5:30 AM–1 PM* Ⓤ *Farringdon.*

17

Arts & Entertainment

WORD OF MOUTH

"The Tate Modern is well worth a trip. It is huge with many exhibits. I am a bit of a philistine when it comes to art, and have to admit that I 'popped in' while passing, just to see what it was like. I was surprised to find I really enjoyed it, and spent a few hours there. I seem to remember that it is free (except any 'special' exhibitions). There are certainly areas where you can sit, and get an excellent view of the Thames."

—willit

Updated by
Julius Honnor

SHAKESPEAREAN THEATER AND MUSICAL EXTRAVAGANZAS, the high passions of soccer and the genteel obscurities of cricket, enormous art installations and tiny Renaissance still lifes, magnificent operatics and cutting edge physical theater—if you're into going out, London will fill your fancy.

The arts in London have acquired some shiny new buildings and renovated homes, largely as a result of National Lottery money and the involvement on and off the city's stages by high-profile Hollywood figures, such as Kevin Spacey, who have given the theatrical scene extra pizzaz. The Donmar, Almeida, and Royal Court theaters have all been renovated to reveal their stripped-down, essential structures. Saved from Bingo-hall oblivion, the legendary Hackney Empire theater is thriving again after a £15 million refurbishment. And there are new studios and a renovated theater for contemporary dance at the Place. But the biggest story is south of the river. Herzog and de Meuron's magnificent Tate Modern, in what was once the Bankside Power Station, is now cemented as one of the city's big attractions. The Tate has enlivened London's contemporary art scene and provides the main focus for a rejuvenated South Bank. Some of the more tourist-oriented shows and musicals suffer from a lack of visitors, but in many cases this economic pressure has made London's theatre more innovative and more accessible, creating a vibrant cultural scene in a better position than ever to play on the world stage.

Sport is taken increasingly seriously in Britain, nowhere more so than in the capital. Londoners may not be the fittest bunch—participation falls far short of enthusiasm of the armchair variety—but they can get excited by just about anything sporting. Winning the Olympics, to be staged in the city in 2012, only sharpened an existing enthusiasm for balls, wheels, and sports gear of all shapes and sizes, and the Olympics are already starting to bring increased investment into London's sporting facilities. Wimbledon, the London Marathon, and international cricket are the big one-off events, though the weekly matches of Premiership football dominate for most of the year. Getting hold of a ticket for the most prominent occasions can be difficult, but at all other levels (from lower-division football to greyhound racing) there's always a great selection of sporting entertainment on offer.

THE ARTS

Whether you fancy your art classical or modern, or as a contemporary twist on a time-honored classic, you'll find that London's arts scene pushes the boundaries. Watch a Hollywood star in a West End theater, or a troupe of Latin American acrobats. See a blockbuster contemporary art show at the Tate Modern, or a Toulouse-Lautrec retrospective at the Tate Britain. There are international theater festivals, innovative music festivals, and obscure seasons of postmodern dance. Celebrity divas sing original-language librettos at the Royal Opera House; the Almeida Opera is more daring with its radical productions of new opera and music theater. Shakespeare's plays are brought to life at the reconstructed Globe Theatre, and challenging new writing is produced at the Royal Court. Whether you feel like the lighthearted extravagance of a West End musical or the next shark-in-formaldehyde sculpture at the White Cube, the choice is yours.

Dance

Dance fans in London can enjoy the classicism of the world-renowned Royal Ballet, as well as innovative contemporary dance from several companies—Ballet Rambert, Matthew Bourne's Adventures in Motion Pictures, Random Dance Company, Michael Clark Dance Company, Richard Alston Dance Company, Wade McGregor, Charles Lineham Company, DV8 Physical Theatre, and Akram Khan—and scores of independent choreographers. The English National Ballet and visiting international companies perform at the Coliseum and at Sadler's Wells, which also hosts various other ballet companies and dance troupes. Despite ongoing refurbishment, the South Bank Centre has a seriously good contemporary dance program that continues to host top international companies and important U.K. choreographers, as well as multicultural offerings from Japanese Butoh and Indian Kathak to hip-hop. The Place and the Lilian Bayliss Theatre at Sadler's Wells are where you'll find the most daring, cutting-edge performances.

The biggest annual event is **Dance Umbrella** (☎ 020/8741–5881 ⊕ www.danceumbrella.co.uk), a six-week season in October and November that hosts international and British-based artists at various venues across the city.

The following theaters are the key dance venues. Check weekly listings for current performances and fringe venues.

The London Coliseum. The English National Ballet (www.ballet.org.uk) and other dance companies often perform in this Edwardian baroque theater (1904) with a magnificent auditorium and an illuminated globe, restored and reopened in 2004. ✉ *St. Martin's La., Covent Garden, WC2N* ☎ *020/7632–8300* Ⓤ *Leicester Sq.*

Peacock Theatre. Sadler's Wells' West End annex, this modernist theater near the University of London offers commercial dance as well as ballet. ✉ *Portugal St., Holborn, WC2* ☎ *020/7863–8222* Ⓤ *Holborn.*

The Place. The Robin Howard Dance Theatre is London's only theater ded-

18

ARTS & ENTERTAINMENT PLANNER

What's on Now

To find out what's showing now, the weekly magazine *Time Out* (£2.50, issued every Tuesday) is invaluable. The *Evening Standard* also carries listings, especially in the supplement "Metro Life," which comes with the Thursday edition, as do many Sunday papers and the Saturday *Independent*, *Guardian*, and *Times*. You can pick up the free fortnightly *London Theatre Guide* from hotels and tourist-information centers.

There are hundreds of small private galleries all over London with interesting work by famous and not-yet-famous artists. The bi-monthly free pamphlet "new exhibitions of contemporary art" ⊕ www.newexhibitions.com, available at most galleries, lists and maps nearly 200 art spaces in London. Expect to pay around £10 for entry into touring exhibitions, but most permanent displays and commercial galleries are free.

Top 5 for the Arts

■ **Stand with the 'plebs' in Shakespeare's Globe Theatre.** There are seats, but to really experience theater Shakespearean style you should stand in the yard, with the stage at eye-level.

■ **Visit the latest grand art installation in the Turbine Hall at the Tate Modern.** The enormity of the Tate's central space either intimidates or inspires artists challenged to fill it.

■ **Catch a world-class performance at the Proms.** There's a surprisingly down-to-earth atmosphere among the elated company at these great concerts.

■ **Enjoy a night at the National Film Theatre.** Mingle with the real aficionados at a showing of a black-and-white, little-remembered Hungarian classic.

■ **Watch a Hollywood star in a West End production.** Film stars often come to London to boost their artistic credibility in small-scale theaters.

Top 5 for Entertainment

■ **Ice-skate at Somerset House.** The courtyard of a grand old pile is a spectacular setting for a winter skate.

■ **Get late summer-evening returns at Wimbledon.** Play often continues well into warm sunny evenings on Wimbledon's show courts. Line up to get bargain returns from those who go home early.

■ **Watch a one-day international at Lords.** Cricket can go on and on, but a one-day international is short enough to guarantee some excitement and long enough to get some idea of the rules.

■ **Dress up for Ascot.** However much you spruce yourself up, you may still feel underdressed among the over-the-top fashions of the English upper classes.

■ **Watch a Premiership football game.** If you can manage to see a London derby, this is probably your best chance to understand the passionately tribal nature of the national game.

icated to contemporary dance. Resolution! is the United Kingdom's biggest platform event for new choreographers. ✉ *17 Duke's Rd., Bloomsbury, WC1* ☏ *020/7121–1100* ⊕ *www.theplace.org.uk* Ⓤ *Euston.*

Riverside Studios. The two performance spaces are noted for postmodern movement styles and performance art. ✉ *Crisp Rd., Hammersmith, W6* ☏ *020/8237–1111* ⊕ *www.riversidestudios.co.uk* Ⓤ *Hammersmith.*

Fodor'sChoice
★
Royal Opera House. The renowned Royal Ballet performs classical and contemporary repertoire in this spectacular state-of-the-art Victorian theater. ✉ *Bow St., Covent Garden, WC2* ☏ *020/7304–4000* ⊕ *www. royaloperahouse.org* Ⓤ *Covent Garden.*

Fodor'sChoice
★
Sadler's Wells. Random Dance Company has its home in this lovely modern theater, which produces an excellent season of ballet and contemporary dance. The little Lilian Bayliss Theatre here has more left-field pieces. ✉ *Rosebery Ave., Islington, EC1* ☏ *020/7863–8000* ⊕ *www. sadlers-wells.com* Ⓤ *Angel.*

South Bank Centre. A diverse and exciting season of international and British-based contemporary dance companies is presented in the Queen Elizabeth Hall and Purcell Room. The Royal Festival Hall will reopen for performances in 2007, after extensive renovations. ✉ *Belvedere Rd., South Bank, SE1* ☏ *0870/380–0400* ⊕ *www.rfh.org.uk* Ⓤ *Waterloo, Embankment.*

Classical Music

Whether you want to go hear cellist Yo-Yo Ma at the Barbican or a Mozart requiem by candlelight, it's possible to hear first-rate musicians in world-class venues almost every day of the year. The London Symphony Orchestra is in residence at the Barbican Centre, although other top orchestras—including the Philharmonia and the Royal Philharmonic—also perform here. The Barbican also hosts chamber-music concerts with such celebrated orchestras as the City of London Sinfonia. Wigmore Hall, a lovely venue for chamber music, is renowned for its song recitals by up-and-coming young singers. The South Bank Centre has an impressive international music season, held in the Queen Elizabeth Hall and the small Purcell Room while refurbishments, due for completion in spring 2007, close the Royal Festival Hall. Full houses are rare, so even at the biggest concert halls you should be able to get a ticket for £12. If you can't book in advance, arrive at the hall an hour before the performance for a chance at returns.

■ TIP➔ **Lunchtime concerts take place all over the city in smaller concert halls, the big arts-center foyers, and churches; they usually cost less than £5 or are free, and will feature string quartets, singers, jazz ensembles, or gospel choirs.** St. John's, Smith Square, and St. Martin-in-the-Fields are popular locations. Performances usually begin about 1 PM and last one hour.

Classical-music festivals range from the stimulating avant-garde Meltdown (programmed in 2005 by Patti Smith, ⊕www.rfh.org.uk/meltdown) at the South Bank Centre in June to the more conservative Kenwood Lakeside Concerts (⊕ www.picnicconcerts.com) from July through August, at which you can listen to classical music outdoors. There are also church hall recitals during December's Spitalfields Festival (⊕ www.

18

spitalfieldsfestival.org.uk), and in livery stables and churches in and around the city during the monthlong City of London Festival (⊕ www. colf.org) in June and July.

A great British tradition since 1895, the Henry Wood Promenade Concerts (more commonly known as the "Proms"; ⊕ www.bbc.co.uk/ proms) run eight weeks, from July to September, at the Royal Albert Hall. Despite an extraordinary quantity of high-quality concerts, it's renowned for its (atypical) last night, a madly jingoistic display of singing "Land of Hope and Glory," Union Jack–waving, and general madness. Demand for tickets is so high you must enter a lottery. For regular Proms, tickets run £4–£80, with hundreds of standing tickets for £4 available at the hall on the night of the concert. ■ TIP➔ **The last night is broadcast in Hyde Park on a jumbo screen, but even here a seat on the grass requires a paid ticket that can set you back around £20.**

Barbican Centre. Home to the London Symphony Orchestra (www.lso. co.uk) and frequent host of the English Chamber Orchestra and the BBC Symphony Orchestra, the Barbican has an excellent season of big-name virtuosos. ⊠ *Silk St., East End, EC2* ☎ *0845/120–7518 box office, 020/ 7638–4141* ⊕ *www.barbican.org.uk* Ⓤ *Barbican.*

Kenwood House. Outdoor concerts are held in the grassy amphitheater in front of Kenwood House on Saturday evenings from July to late August. ⊠ *Hampstead Heath, Hampstead NW3 7JR* ☎ *0870/333–6206* ⊕ *www.picnicconcerts.com* Ⓤ *Hampstead.*

★ **Royal Albert Hall.** Built in 1871, this splendid iron-and-glass–dome auditorium hosts a varied music program, including Europe's most democratic music festival, the Henry Wood Promenade Concerts—the Proms. The Hall is also open daily for daytime guided tours (£6). ⊠ *Kensington Gore, Kensington, SW7* ☎ *020/7589–8212* ⊕ *www.royalalberthall. com* Ⓤ *South Kensington.*

St. James's Church. The organ was brought here in 1691 after fire destroyed its former home, the Palace of Whitehall. St. James's holds regular classical-music concerts, including free lunchtime recitals several times a week. ⊠ *197 Piccadilly, St. James's, W1* ☎ *020/7381–0441 concert program and tickets* Ⓤ *Piccadilly Circus, Green Park.*

St. John's, Smith Square. This baroque church behind Westminster Abbey offers chamber music and organ recitals as well as orchestral concerts September through July. There are occasional lunchtime recitals for £7. ⊠ *Smith Sq., Westminster, W1* ☎ *020/7222–1061* ⊕ *www.sjss.org.uk* Ⓤ *Westminster.*

★ **St. Martin-in-the-Fields.** Popular lunchtime concerts (free but £3.50 donation suggested) are held in this lovely 1726 church, as are regular evening concerts. ■ TIP➔ **Stop for a snack at the Café in the Crypt.** ⊠ *Trafalgar Sq., Covent Garden, WC2* ☎ *020/7839–8362* ⊕ *www.smitf.org* Ⓤ *Charing Cross.*

South Bank Centre. Due to two years' renovation work begun in 2005, the Royal Festival Hall's large-scale choral and orchestral works—including its housing of both the Philharmonia and the London Philharmonic orchestras—will be taken on by the other South Bank Centre venues such as the Queen Elizabeth Hall, which hosts chamber orchestras and

CLOSE UP

The Arts for Free

MUSEUMS & GALLERIES

Perhaps no other city in the world can match up to London's offerings of free art. Most of London's museums and galleries do not charge entrance fees.

The monthly *Galleries* magazine, available from galleries themselves or online at ⊕ www.artefact.co.uk, has listings for all private galleries in the capital.

CONTEMPORARY MUSIC

Brixton's Dogstar pub has an excellent selection of DJs playing for free on weekday evenings. Ain't Nothing But the Blues in Soho has live blues most nights, often without a cover charge. Spitz, in Spitalfields Market, frequently has live music for free. The largest of the music superstores, such as Virgin Piccadilly and HMV Oxford Street, have occasional live performances of pop and rock bands, often to accompany album or single launches.

CLASSICAL MUSIC & JAZZ

The Barbican, the Royal National Theatre, and the Royal Opera House often have free music in their foyers or in dedicated spaces, usually of high standard. On the South Bank, free festivals and special performances often take place alongside the river.

Many of London's world-class music colleges give free concerts several times a week. The Royal Academy of Music and the Royal College of Music often have free concerts. St. Martin-in-the-Fields has free lunchtime concerts. Other churches, including Westminster Abbey and Christchurch Spitalfields, also have frequent free music. For the Proms, which run from July to September at the Royal Albert Hall, good seats are expensive, but hundreds of standing tickets are available at £4: not quite free, but a good value.

DRAMA & PERFORMANCE ARTS

Look out for occasional festivals where innovative performances take place on the South Bank. Check the newspapers and *Time Out* for upcoming performances.

PARK LIFE

London's parks come to life in summer with a wide-ranging program of music, dance, and visual arts. See ⊕ www.royalparks.gov.uk for details or phone ☎ 020/7298-2000 for a free printed program. Radio stations also organize free summer music concerts (generally aimed at the teenybopper set) in London parks, with lots of big-name pop stars, but entry is usually by ticket only and events are often oversubscribed.

RADIO & TELEVISION

With so much broadcast material made in London, much of it recorded in front of live audiences, there are often opportunities to watch a free quiz show, current affairs debate, comedy, or even drama. Check the BBC Web site for forthcoming recordings or call **BBC Studio Audiences** (☎ 020/8576-1227 ⊕ www.bbc.co.uk/tickets). **Hat Trick Productions** (☎ 020/7434-2451 ⊕ www.hattrick.co.uk) makes a number of good comedy programs, including the excellent satirical current affairs program *Have I Got News for You.*

18

A-team soloists, and the intimate Purcell Room, where you can listen to chamber music and solo recitals. ⊠ *Belvedere Rd., South Bank, SE1* ☎ *020/7960–4242* ⊕ *www.sbc.org.uk* Ⓤ *Waterloo.*

Fodor's Choice ★ **Wigmore Hall.** Hear chamber music and song recitals in this charming hall with near-perfect acoustics. Don't miss the mid-morning Sunday concerts. ⊠ *36 Wigmore St., Marylebone, W1* ☎ *020/7935–2141* ⊕ *www. wigmore-hall.org.uk* Ⓤ *Bond St.*

Film

There are many wonderful movie theaters in London and several that are committed to nonmainstream and repertory cinema, in particular, the National Film Theatre. Now almost 50 years old, the London Film Festival (⊕ www.lff.org.uk) brings hundreds of films made by masters of world cinema to London for 16 days each October into November, accompanied by often-sold-out events. The smaller, avant-garde Raindance Film Festival (⊕ www.raindance.co.uk) highlights independent filmmaking, also in October.

West End movie theaters continue to do good business. Most of the major houses, such as the Odeon Leicester Square and the UCI Empire, are in the Leicester Square–Piccadilly Circus area, where tickets average £10. Monday and matinees are often cheaper, at around £5–£7, and there are also fewer crowds.

Check out *Time Out* or the *Guardian's* "Guide" section (free with the paper on Saturday) for listings.

Barbican. In addition to Hollywood films, obscure classics and occasional film festivals with Screen Talks are programmed in the three cinemas here. Saturday Family Film Club often has animation for the entire family. ⊠ *Silk St., East End, EC2* ☎ *020/7382–7000 information, 020/ 7638–8891 box office* Ⓤ *Barbican.*

BFI London IMAX Cinema. The British Film Institute's glazed drum-shape IMAX theater has the largest screen in the United Kingdom (approximately 75 feet wide and the height of five double-decker buses) playing state-of-the-art 2-D and 3-D films. ⊠ *1 Charlie Chaplin Walk, South Bank, SE1* ☎ *0870/787–2525* ⊕ *www.bfi.org.uk/imax* Ⓤ *Waterloo.*

★ **Curzon Soho.** This comfortable cinema runs an artsy program of mixed rep and mainstream films. There's also a Mayfair branch. ⊠ *99 Shaftesbury Ave., Soho, W1* ☎ *0871/871–0022* Ⓤ *Piccadilly Circus, Leicester Sq.* ⊠ *38 Curzon St., Mayfair, W1* ☎ *020/7495–0500* ⊕ *www. curzoncinemas.com* Ⓤ *Green Park.*

★ **The Electric Cinema.** This refurbished Portobello Road art house screens mainstream and international movies. The emphasis is on comfort, with leather sofas, armchairs,

> **WORD OF MOUTH**
>
> "My daughter and I went to a movie in the Mayfair section of London. Not only were the seats reserved, but they were wonderfully upholstered and rocked back and forth. It was a struggle to watch the movie (as good as it was) versus taking a well-needed nap."
>
> –bronxgirl

footstools, and mini coffee tables for your popcorn. ✉ *191 Portobello Rd., Notting Hill, W11* ☎ *020/7727–9958 information, 020/7908–9696 box office* ⊕ *www.electriccinema.co.uk* Ⓤ *Ladbroke Grove, Notting Hill Gate.*

★ ۞ **Everyman Cinema Club.** Kick off your shoes, curl up on the large comfy sofas, and have tapas and champagne brought to you in front of an excellent selection of classic, foreign, cutting-edge, and almost-new Hollywood titles. This venue also screens major sports games and TV events, and is a popular place for Hampstead denizens to bring their kids. ✉ *5 Hollybush Vale, Hampstead, NW3* ☎ *020/7431–1777* ⊕ *www.everymancinema.com* Ⓤ *Hampstead.*

ICA Cinema. Underground and vintage movies are shown in the avant-garde Institute of Contemporary Arts. ✉ *The Mall, St. James's, SW1* ☎ *020/7930–6393 information, 020/7930–3647 box office* ⊕ *www.ica. org.uk* Ⓤ *Piccadilly Circus, Charing Cross.*

۞ **National Film Theatre (NFT).** With easily the best repertory programming in London, the NFT's three cinemas show more than 1,000 titles each year, favoring obscure, foreign, silent, forgotten, classic, noir, and short films over Hollywood blockbusters. ■ TIP→ **The London Film Festival is based here at the NFT; throughout the year there are minifestivals, seminars, and guest speakers. Members (£29.95) get priority bookings (useful for special events) and get £1 off each screening.** ✉ *Belvedere Rd., South Bank, SE1* ☎ *020/7633–0274 information, 020/7928–3232 box office* ⊕ *www. bfi.org.uk/incinemas/nft/* Ⓤ *Waterloo.*

Riverside Studios Cinemas. The selection at this converted movie studio changes almost daily. Admission fees are reasonable; £5.50 gets you entrance to a double bill. ✉ *Crisp Rd., Hammersmith, W6* ☎ *020/ 8237–1111* ⊕ *www.riversidestudios.co.uk* Ⓤ *Hammersmith.*

۞ **Tricycle Theatre.** Expect the best of new British, European, and World Cinema, as well as films from the United States. There are occasional Irish, Black, and Asian Film Festivals. ✉ *269 Kilburn High Rd., Kilburn, NW6* ☎ *020/7328–1900 information, 020/7328–1000 box office* ⊕ *www.tricycle.co.uk* Ⓤ *Kilburn.*

Opera

The two key players in London's opera scene are the Royal Opera House (which ranks with the Metropolitan Opera House in New York), and the more innovative English National Opera (ENO), which presents English-language productions at the London Coliseum. Only the Theatre Royal, Drury Lane, has a longer theatrical history than the Royal Opera House, and the current theater—the third to be built on the site since 1858—completed a monumental 16-year renovation in 1999.

Despite occasional performances by the likes of Björk, the Royal Opera House struggles to shrug off its reputation for elitism. Ticket prices rise to £180. It is, however, more accessible than it used to be—the cheapest tickets are just £4. Conditions of purchase vary; call for information. Prices for the ENO are generally lower, ranging from £8 to £80. You can get same-day balcony seats for as little as £5.

18

Almeida Opera and BAC Opera produce opera festivals that showcase new opera and cutting-edge music theater. In summer, Holland Park Opera presents the usual chestnuts in the open-air theater of leafy Holland Park. Bring a picnic and an umbrella. Serious opera fans should not miss the Glyndebourne Festival, where Pavarotti made his British debut. It's the jewel in the crown of the country-house opera circuit, and the greatest opera festival in the United Kingdom.

International touring companies often perform at Sadler's Wells, Barbican, South Bank Centre, and Wigmore Hall, so check the weekly listings for details.

★ **Almeida Theatre.** The Almeida Opera Festival in July has an adventurous program of new opera and music theater. ⊠ *Almeida St., Islington, N1* ☎ *020/7359–4404* ⊕ *www.almeida.co.uk* Ⓤ *Angel.*

BAC Opera. New and often avant-garde opera is presented at the BAC Opera Festival. ⊠ *Lavender Hill, Battersea, SW11* ☎ *020/7223–2223* ⊕ *www.bac.org.uk* Ⓤ *Clapham Junction.*

English National Opera. ENO produces innovative opera for lower prices than the Royal Opera House. The company is based at the London Coliseum. ⊠ *St. Martin's La., Covent Garden, WC2* ☎ *0870/145–0200* ⊕ *www.eno.org* Ⓤ *Leicester Sq.*

★ **Glyndebourne.** Fifty-four miles south of London, Glyndebourne is one of the most famous opera houses in the world. Six operas are presented from mid-May to late-August. The best route by car is the M23 to Brighton, then the A27 toward Lewes. There are regular trains from London (Victoria) to Lewes with coach connections to and from Glyndebourne. Call the information office for information about recommended trains for each performance. ⊠ *Lewes, BN8 5UU* ☎ *01273/812321 information, 01273/813813 box office* ⊕ *www.glyndebourne.com.*

Holland Park Opera. In summer new productions and well-loved operas are presented against the remains of Holland House, one of the first great houses built in Kensington. Ticket prices range from £30 to £40. ⊠ *Holland Park, Kensington High St., Kensington, W8* ☎ *020/7602–7856* ⊕ *www.operahollandpark.com* Ⓤ *Kensington High St.*

FodorśChoice
★ **Royal Opera House.** Original-language productions are presented in this extravagant theater. ■ TIP➔ **If you can't afford £100 for a ticket, consider showing up in the morning (the box office opens at 10 AM, but queues for popular productions can start as early as 7 AM) to purchase a same-day seat, of which a small number are offered for £10 to £50.** There are free lunchtime recitals most Mondays in the Linbury Studio Theatre and occasional summer concerts broadcast live to a large screen in Covent Garden Piazza. ⊠ *Bow St., Covent Garden, WC2* ☎ *020/7304–4000* ⊕ *www.royalopera.org* Ⓤ *Covent Garden.*

Theater

In London the play really *is* the thing, and chances are good you can see a Sam Mendes Off-West End production, the umpteenth production of *Les Misérables,* a Peter Brook deconstruction of Shakespeare, innovative physical theater from *Le Théatre de Complicité,* the latest offering from *Cirque du Soleil* or Robert Lepage, or even a fringe production above a pub. West End glitz and glamour continue to pull in the audiences, and so do the more innovative players. Only in London will a Tuesday matinee of the Royal Shakespeare Company's *Henry IV* be sold out in a 1,200-seat theater.

In London the words "radical" and "quality," or "classical" and "experimental," are not mutually exclusive. The Royal Shakespeare Company (⊕ www.rsc.org.uk) and the Royal National Theatre Company often stage contemporary versions of the classics. The Almeida, Battersea Arts Centre (BAC), Donmar Warehouse, Royal Court Theatre, Soho Theatre, and the Old Vic attract famous actors and have excellent reputations for new writing and innovative theatrical languages. These are the places that shape the theater of the future, the venues where you'll see an original production before it becomes a hit in the West End. (And you'll see them at a fraction of the cost.)

Another great thing about the London theater scene is that it doesn't shut down in summer—it's business as usual for the Royal Shakespeare Company and Royal National Theatre. From mid-May through mid-September you can see the Bard served up in his most spectacular manifestation—at the open-air reconstruction of Shakespeare's Globe Theatre. In addition, the Open Air Theatre presents a season of Shakespeare-under-the-stars, from the last week in May to the third week in September, in lovely Regent's Park. **London Mime Festival** (⊕ www.mimefest.co.uk) happens in January. Some theater festivals take place throughout the year, so unlike other cities, there's always something good to see in London. **L.I.F.T.** (⊕ www.liftfest.org.uk), the London International Festival of Theatre, stages productions at venues throughout the city. **B.I.T.E.** (the Barbican International Theater Events) presents top-notch, cutting-edge performances. Check *Time Out* for details. The Web sites ⊕ www. whatsonstage.com and ⊕ www.officiallondontheatre.co.uk are both good sources of information about performances.

18

Theater-going isn't cheap. Tickets under £10 are a rarity; in the West End you should expect to pay from £15 for a seat in the upper balcony to at least £25 for a good one in the stalls (orchestra) or dress circle (mezzanine). However, as the vast majority of theaters have some tickets (returns and house seats) available on the night of performance, you may find some good deals. Tickets may be booked through ticket agents, at individual theater box offices, or over the phone by credit card; be sure to inquire about any extra fees. All the larger hotels offer theater bookings, but they tack on a hefty service charge.

Ticketmaster (☎ 0870/060–0800 ⊕ www.ticketmaster.co.uk) sells tickets to a number of different theaters, although they charge a booking fee. You can book tickets in the

CAUTION	

Be very wary of ticket touts (scalpers) and unscrupulous ticket agents outside theaters and working the line at TKTS (a half-price ticket booth)—they try to sell tickets at five times the price of the ticket at legitimate box offices. You might be charged £200 or more for a sought-after ticket (and you'll pay a stiff fine if caught buying a scalped ticket).

A BRIEF HISTORY

London's theatrical past goes back to the streets, marketplaces, and cathedrals that were once the backdrop for medieval mystery plays. Theaters here, which are some of the finest gems in the world, embody this history.

The first permanent theater, the Theatre, was built by Richard Burbage in Shoreditch in 1576, and was soon followed by Shakespeare's Globe Theatre on the South Bank—where the Bard's plays were staged alongside brothels, bearbaiting, and cock-fighting pits. The Puritans put an end to the fun, and the next dramatic boom didn't happen until after the Restoration of 1660, with the building of the Theatre Royal, Drury Lane (1662), and the Royal Opera House (1732).

Most of London's theaters were built toward the end of the Victorian era, when Shaftesbury Avenue cut through the Soho slums and theaters like the Shaftesbury (1886) and Aldwych (1905) became the center of London's theater scene. Covent Garden became host to frothy Edwardian theater facades along St. Martin's Lane and the Strand. The 1930s saw the emergence of jazzy art deco theaters until the outbreak of World War II, and the 1970s saw the first intervention of state funding and the concrete Brutalist-style architecture of the Barbican Centre and National Theatre.

In more recent years, lottery funds have subsidized renovations of existing spaces like the Royal Court, as well as new construction, most of which has resulted in unremarkable, modernist structures. Sitting in an exquisite Edwardian theater, soaking up the intricate plasterwork and plush boxes, even ordering a drink at the classy bar during intermission, are a big part of the theater-going experience.

United States through **Keith Prowse** (✉ 234 W. 44th St., Suite 1000, New York, NY 10036 ☎ 800/669–8687 ⊕ www.keithprowse.com). For discount tickets, **Society of London Theatre** (☎ 020/7557–6700) operates TKTS, a half-price ticket booth (no phone) on the southwest corner of Leicester Square, and sells the best available seats to performances at about 25 theaters. It's open Monday–Saturday 10 AM–7 PM, Sunday noon–2 PM; there's a £2 service charge. Major credit cards are accepted.

★ **Almeida Theatre.** This Off-West End venue premieres excellent new plays and exciting twists on the classics. Hollywood stars often perform here. ✉ *Almeida St., Islington, N1* ☎ *020/7359–4404* ⊕ *www.almeida.co. uk* Ⓤ *Angel, Highbury & Islington.*

★ **BAC.** Battersea Arts Centre has an excellent reputation for producing innovative new work. Check out Scratch, a monthly, pay-what-you-can night of low-tech cabaret theater by emerging artists, and the BAC Octoberfest of innovative performance. Tuesday shows also have pay-what-you-can entry. ✉ *176 Lavender Hill, Battersea, SW11* ☎ *020/ 7223–2223* ⊕ *www.bac.org.uk* Ⓤ *British Rail: Clapham Junction.*

Barbican Centre. Built in 1982, the Barbican Centre puts on a number of performances by British and international theater companies as part of its year-round **B.I.T.E.** (Barbican International Theatre Events), which also features ground-breaking performance, dance, drama, and music theater. ☒ *Silk St., East End, EC2* ☎ *020/7638–8891* ⊕ *www.barbican.org.uk* Ⓤ *Barbican.*

Fodor'sChoice
★
Donmar Warehouse. Hollywood stars often perform here in diverse and daring new works, bold interpretations of the classics, and small-scale musicals. It works both ways, too—former director Sam Mendes went straight from here to directing *American Beauty.* ☒ *41 Earlham St., Covent Garden, WC2* ☎ *0870/060–6624* ⊕ *www.donmar-warehouse.com* Ⓤ *Covent Garden.*

★ **Hackney Empire.** The history of this treasure of a theater is drama in its own right. Charlie Chaplin is said to have appeared here during its days as a thriving variety theater and music hall in the early 1900s. Sixty years later its glory had all but completely faded, and it was reduced to operating as a bingo hall. But in 1984 preservationists managed to get the building listed as a grade II historic site and, bingoers evicted, the Empire was resurrected. Badly in need of restoration, it closed in 2001 for a £15 million overhaul, and three years later, in January 2004, the curtain went up on the new-old Empire shining again. ☒ *291 Mare St., Hackney, E8* ☎ *020/8985–2424* ⊕ *www.hackneyempire.co.uk* Ⓤ *National Rail: Hackney Central.*

The Old Vic. American actor Kevin Spacey is the artistic director of this grand 1818 Victorian theater, one of London's oldest. Legends of the stage have performed here, including John Gielgud, Vivian Leigh, Peter O'Toole, Richard Burton, Judi Dench, and Laurence Olivier, who called it his favorite theater. After decades of financial duress threatening to shut it down, the Old Vic is now safely under the ownership of a dedicated trust and is thriving again. ☒ *The Cut, Southwark, SE1* ☎ *0870/060–6628* ⊕ *www.oldvictheatre.com* Ⓤ *Waterloo.*

Fodor'sChoice
★
Open Air Theatre. On a warm summer evening, classical theater in the pastoral, and royal Regent's Park is hard to beat for magical adventure. Enjoy a supper before the performance and during the intermission on the picnic lawn, and drinks in the spacious bar. ☒ *Inner Circle, Regent's Park, NW1* ☎ *0870/060–1811* ⊕ *www.openairtheatre.org* Ⓤ *Baker St., Regent's Park.*

★ **Royal Court Theatre.** Britain's undisputed epicenter of new writing, the RCT has produced gritty British and international drama since the middle of the 20th century, much of which gets produced in the West End. ■ TIP➜ **Don't miss the best deal in town—£7.50 tickets on Monday.** ☒ *Sloane Sq., Chelsea, SW1* ☎ *020/7565–5000* ⊕ *www.royalcourttheatre.com* Ⓤ *Sloane Sq.*

18

★ **Royal National Theatre.** Opened in 1976, the RNT has three theaters: the 1,120-seat Olivier, the 890-seat Lyttelton, and the 300-seat Cottesloe. Musicals, classics, and new plays are in repertoire. ■ TIP→ **An adventurous new ticketing scheme means some Royal National Theatre performances can be seen for as little as £10.** It's closed Sunday. ⊠ *South Bank Arts Centre, Belvedere Rd., South Bank, SE1* ☏ *020/7452–3000* ⊕ *www.nt-online. org* Ⓤ *Waterloo.*

Fodor'sChoice **Shakespeare's Globe Theatre.** This faithful reconstruction of the open-★ air playhouse where Shakespeare worked and wrote many of his greatest plays re-creates the 16th-century theater-going experience. Standing room costs £5. The season runs May through September. For more on Shakespeare's Globe Theatre, *see* Chapter 8. ⊠ *New Globe Walk, Bankside, South Bank, SE1* ☏ *020/7401–9919* ⊕ *www.shakespeares-globe.org* Ⓤ *Southwark, Mansion House, walk across Southwark Bridge; Blackfriars, walk across Blackfriars Bridge.*

Soho Theatre & Writers' Centre. This sleek theater in the heart of Soho is devoted to fostering new writing and is a prolific presenter of work by emerging writers. ⊠ *21 Dean St., Soho, W1* ☏ *020/7478–0100* ⊕ *www. sohotheatre.com* Ⓤ *Tottenham Court Rd.*

☾ **Tricycle Theatre.** The Tricycle is committed to the best in Irish, African-Caribbean, Asian, and political drama, and the promotion of new plays. ⊠ *269 Kilburn High Rd., Kilburn, NW6 7JR* ☏ *020/7328–1000* ⊕ *www.tricycle.co.uk* Ⓤ *Kilburn.*

Contemporary Art

In the 21st century, the focus of the city's art scene has shifted from west to east, and from the past to the future. Helped by the prominence of the Tate Modern, London's contemporary art scene has never been so high-profile. In public-funded exhibition spaces like the Barbican Gallery, Hayward Gallery, Institute of Contemporary Arts, Serpentine Gallery, and Whitechapel Art Gallery, London now has a modern art environment on a par with Bilbao and New York. Young British Artists (YBAs, though no longer as young as they once were)—Damien Hirst, Tracey Emin, Gary Hume, Rachel Whiteread, Jake and Dinos Chapman, Sarah Lucas, Gavin Turk, Steve McQueen, and others—are firmly planted in the public imagination. The celebrity status of British artists is in part thanks to the annual Turner Prize, which always stirs up controversy in the media during a monthlong display of the work at Tate Britain.

British artists may complain about how the visual arts here are severely underfunded, and about the rough ride they get in the media, but where else would Damien Hirst's 6-meter-high bronze version of an anatomy model fetch £1 million? Hirst and his Goldsmith's College contemporaries were catapulted to fame in the late 1980s, when they rented an unused Docklands warehouse to put on seminal shows like "Freeze." It coincided with a recession that saw West End galleries closing, and a property slump that enabled young artists to open trendy artist-run places in the East End.

West End dealers like Jay Jopling and, in particular, the enigmatic advertising tycoon and art collector Charles Saatchi, championed these Young British Artists. Depending on who you talk to, the Saatchi Gallery is considered to be either the savior of contemporary art or the wardrobe of the emperor's new clothes. Since 1992 Saatchi has shown several shows of YBA, including the period's most memorable sculptures—Damien Hirst's shark in formaldehyde, *The Impossibility of Death in the Mind of the Living,* and Rachel Whiteread's plaster cast of a room, *Ghost.* The Saatchi Gallery will reopen in the Duke of York's Building in Chelsea in 2007, after its short-lived tenancy on the South Bank ended acrimoniously in 2005.

The South Bank, with the Tate Modern and the Hayward Gallery, may house the giants of modern art, but the East End is where the innovative action is. There are dozens of galleries in the fashionable spaces around Old Street. The Whitechapel Art Gallery continues to flourish, exhibiting exciting new British artists and, together with Jay Jopling's influential White Cube in Hoxton Square, is the new East End art establishment.

The **Contemporary Art Society** (☎ 020/7612–0730 ⊕ www.contempart.org.uk) runs bus tours (£25 per person) for serious art enthusiasts the last Saturday of every month (except July, August, and December). ■ TIP→ This is a great opportunity to get the inside scoop on off-the-beaten-track spaces. Book well ahead, as spaces fill up quickly.

Barbican Centre. Innovative exhibitions of 20th-century and current art and design are shown in the Barbican Gallery and **The Curve** (▭ Free ☽ Mon.–Sat. 11–8). Recent highlights have included the world-renowned photographer David La Chapelle, Grayson Perry's classical yet provocative vases, and architectural designs by Daniel Libeskind, who built the Jewish Museum in Berlin. ✉ *Silk St., East End, EC2* ☎ *020/7638–8891* ⊕ *www.barbican.org.uk* ▭ *£6–£8, tickets cheaper if booked online in advance* ☽ *Mon., Wed., Fri., and Sat. 11–8, Tues. and Thurs. 11–6, Sun. noon–6* Ⓤ *Barbican.*

The Blue Gallery. A west-to-east emigree, the Clerkenwell Blue Gallery exhibits contemporary paintings and photographs, many by award-winning young artists. ✉ *15 Great Sutton St., Clerkenwell, EC1V* ☎ *020/7490–3833* ⊕ *www.thebluegallery.co.uk* ▭ *Free* ☽ *Weekdays 10–6, Sat. 11–3* Ⓤ *Farringdon.*

★ **Hayward Gallery.** This modern art gallery is a classic example of 1960s Brutalist architecture. It's part of the South Bank Centre and is one of London's major venues for important touring exhibitions. ✉ *Belvedere Rd., South Bank Centre, South Bank, SE1* ☎ *0870/165–6000* ⊕ *www.hayward.org.uk* ▭ *£7.50, Mon. half-price* ☽ *Thurs. and Sat.–Mon. 10–6, Tues. and Wed. 10–8, Fri. 10–9* Ⓤ *Waterloo.*

Institute of Contemporary Arts. Housed in an elegant John Nash–designed Regency terrace, the ICA's three galleries have changing exhibitions of contemporary visual art. The ICA also programs contemporary drama, film, new media, literature, and photography. There's an arts bookstore, cafeteria, and bar. To visit you must be a member of the ICA; a day membership costs £1.50. ✉ *Nash House, The Mall, St. James's, SW1* ☎ *020/*

18

7930–3647 or 020/7930–0493 ⊕ *www.ica.org.uk* ✉ *Weekdays £1.50, weekends £2.50* ⊗ *Daily noon–7:30* Ⓤ *Charing Cross.*

★ **Lisson.** Owner Nicholas Logsdail represents about 40 blue-chip artists, including minimalist Sol Lewitt and Dan Graham, at arguably the most respected gallery in London. The gallery is most associated with New Object sculptors like Anish Kapoor and Richard Deacon, many of whom have won the Turner Prize. A new branch, Lisson New Space, down the road at 29 Bell Street, features work by younger up-and-coming artists. ✉ *52–54 Bell St., Marylebone, NW1* ☎ *020/7724–2739* ⊕ *www.lissongallery.com* ✉ *Free* ⊗ *Weekdays 10–6, Sat. 11–5* Ⓤ *Edgware Rd. or Marylebone.*

Photographer's Gallery. Britain's first photography gallery brought world-famous photographers like André Kertesz, Jacques-Henri Lartigue, and Irving Penn to the United Kingdom, and continues to program cutting-edge and provocative photography. The prestigious annual Deutsche Börse Photography Prize is exhibited and awarded here annually. There's a print sales room (closed Sunday and Monday), bookstore, and a café. ✉ *5 and 8 Great Newport St., Covent Garden, WC2* ☎ *020/7831–1772* ⊕ *www.photonet.org.uk* ✉ *Free* ⊗ *Mon.–Wed., Fri., and Sat. 11–6, Thurs. 11–8, Sun. noon–6* Ⓤ *Leicester Sq.*

Royal Academy. Housed in an aristocratic mansion and home to Britain's first art school (founded in 1768), the Academy is best known for its blockbuster special exhibitions—like the record-breaking Monet, and the controversial "Sensation" drawn from the Saatchi collection of contemporary British art. The annual Summer Exhibition has been a popular London tradition since 1769. ✉ *Burlington House, Soho, W1* ☎ *020/7300–8000* ⊕ *www.royalacademy.org.uk* ✉ *From £9, prices vary with exhibition* ⊗ *Sun.–Thurs. 10–6, Fri. and Sat. 10 AM–10 PM* Ⓤ *Piccadilly Circus.*

Saatchi Gallery. At this writing, Charles Saatchi's ultramodern gallery was set to reopen in the Duke of York's HQ building in Chelsea in early 2007; its short-lived tenancy on the South Bank ended acrimoniously in 2005. For more information, visit the Web site. ✉ *Duke of York's HQ, Sloane Sq., Chelsea SW3 4RY* ☎ *020/7823–2332* ⊕ *www.saatchi-gallery.co.uk* Ⓤ *Sloane Sq.*

Serpentine Gallery. In a classical 1930 tea pavilion in Kensington Gardens, the Serpentine has an international reputation for exhibitions of modern and contemporary art. Man Ray, Henry Moore, Andy Warhol, Bridget Riley, Damien Hirst, and Rachel Whiteread are a few of the artists who have exhibited here. ✉ *Kensington Gardens, South Kensington, W2* ☎ *020/7402–6075* ⊕ *www.serpentinegallery.org* ✉ *Donation* ⊗ *Daily 10–6* Ⓤ *South Kensington.*

Fodor'sChoice **Tate Modern.** This converted power station is the largest modern-art gallery
★ in the world: give yourself ample time to take it all in! The permanent collection, which includes work by all the major 20th-century artists, is organized thematically rather than chronologically, and alongside blockbuster touring shows and solo exhibitions of international artists. ■ TIP➔ **The café on the top floor has gorgeous views overlooking the Thames and St. Paul's Cathedral.** ✉ *Bankside, South Bank, SE1* ☎ *020/7887–8008* ⊕ *www.tate.org.uk* ✉ *Free–£8.50* ⊗ *Daily 10–6, Fri. and Sat. until 10 PM* Ⓤ *Southwark.*

★ **Victoria Miro Gallery.** This important commercial gallery has exhibited some of the biggest names on the British contemporary art scene—Chris Ofili, the Chapman brothers, Peter Doig, to name a few. It also brings in exciting new talent from abroad. ⊠ *16 Wharf Rd., Islington, N1* ☎ *020/7336–8109* ⊕ *www.victoria-miro.com* ⊡ *Free* ☉ *Tues.–Sat. 10–6* Ⓤ *Old St., Angel.*

Vilma Gold. This serious commercial gallery in Bethnal Green shows outré work by international and British artists. ⊠ *25B Vyner St., East End, E2* ☎ *020/8981–3344* ⊕ *www.vilmagold.com* ⊡ *Free* ☉ *Thurs.–Sun. noon–6* Ⓤ *Bethnal Green.*

★ **Whitechapel Art Gallery.** Established in 1897, this independent East End gallery is one of London's most innovative. Jeff Wall, Bill Viola, Gary Hume, and Janet Cardiff have exhibited here. ⊠ *80–82 Whitechapel High St., East End, E1* ☎ *020/7522–7888* ⊕ *www.whitechapel.org* ⊡ *Free–£8* ☉ *Tues.–Sun. 11–6, Thurs. 11–9* Ⓤ *Aldgate East.*

★ **White Cube.** Jay Joplin's influential gallery is housed in a 1920s light-industrial building on Hoxton Square. Many of its artists are Turner Prize stars—Hirst, Emin, Hume, et al., and many live in the East End, which supposedly has the highest concentration of artists in Europe. ⊠ *48 Hoxton Sq., East End, N1* ☎ *020/7749–7450* ⊕ *www.whitecube.com* ⊡ *Free* ☉ *Tues.–Sat. 10–6* Ⓤ *Old St.*

SPORTS & THE OUTDOORS

In the wake of London's successful bid to host the Olympics in 2012, the city's sporting credentials and sporting facilities are receiving a massive boost. The salaries of professional athletes in the United Kingdom may not be quite as high as they are in the United States, but don't believe for one second that the British aren't dead serious about sports. When things are going well for an English national team, especially in football, there's a definite "feel-good" factor that envelops the capital. And for spectators there's plenty to get excited about. Alongside the traditions of the Wimbledon Tennis Championships and boating on the Thames there's the slow tension of cricket, the multimillion pound industry that is modern football (soccer), the festive atmosphere of the Flora London Marathon, and possibilities to watch just about anything else sporting.

For participants, London is a great city for the weekend player of almost anything. It comes into its own in summer, when the parks sprout nets and goals and painted white lines, outdoor swimming pools open, and a season of spectator events gets under way. For more on Hyde Park in particular, *see* Chapter 11. In winter there's the opportunity to ice-skate in some of Britain's most spectacular locations. If you feel like joining in, the London version of *Time Out* magazine, available in newsstands, is a great resource. On the Web, Sport England (⊕ www.sportengland.org) has a good database of information on local clubs, facilities, and organizations. Check ⊕ www.royalparks. gov.uk for details on all of London's royal parks. The listings below concentrate on facilities available for various sports, and on the more accessible or well-known spectator events. Bring your gear, and branch out from that hotel gym.

Bicycling

London is becoming more cycle-friendly, with special lanes marked for bicycles on some streets, especially in central London, and a network of cycle-only lanes, often along canal paths. ■ TIP➔ **If you plan to cycle much in the city, get the excellent London Cycling Campaign maps, with detailed cycling routes through the city.** They're available free from bike shops, Tube stations, or by post via the Web site of **London Cycling Campaign** (☎ 020/7928–7220 ⊕ www.lcc.org.uk).

★ **London Bicycle Tour Company,** right beside the OXO Tower on the South Bank, offers 3½-hour bike tours of the East End and West End, for £15. Reserve in advance by phone or on the Internet. You can also go it alone: bikes can be rented for £2.50 an hour or £14 for a day (£7 for each subsequent day). Or, if you prefer, there are in-line skates, tandems, and rickshaws for rent. ✉ *1A Gabriel's Wharf, South Bank, SE1* ☎ *020/7928–6838* ⊕ *www.londonbicycle.com* Ⓤ *Waterloo.*

Cricket

Since England beat Australia in 2005, the game of cricket has enjoyed a renaissance.

Fodor's Choice **Lord's** has been hallowed turf for worshipers of England's summer game
★ since 1811. Tickets can be hard to procure for the five-day Test Matches (full internationals) and one-day internationals played here: obtain an application form and enter the ballot (lottery) to purchase tickets. Forms are sent out from mid-November or you can sign up online. Standard Test Match tickets cost between £26 and £48. County matches (Middlesex plays here) can usually be seen by lining up on game day. ✉ *St. John's Wood Rd., St. John's Wood, NW8* ☎ *020/7432–1000* ⊕ *www. lords.org* Ⓤ *St. John's Wood.*

★ The **Oval,** home of Surrey County Cricket Club, is an easier place than Lord's to witness the *thwack* of leather on willow, with tickets for internationals sold on a first-come first-served basis from late October. Though slightly less venerated than its illustrious cousin, the standard of cricket here is certainly no lower. ✉ *Kennington Oval, Kennington, SE11* ☎ *020/7582–6660* ⊕ *www.surreycricket.com* Ⓤ *Oval.*

Equestrian Events

RACING The main events of "the Season," as much social as sporting, occur just
★ outside the city. Her Majesty attends **Royal Ascot** (✉ Grand Stand, Ascot, Berkshire ☎ 01344/622211 ⊕ www.ascot.co.uk) in mid-June, driving from Windsor in an open carriage for a procession before the plebes daily at 2. You'll need to book good seats far in advance for this event, although some tickets—far away from the Royal Enclosure and winning post—can usually be bought on the day of the race for £10–£15. Grandstand tickets, which go on sale on the first working day of the year, cost

£52. There are also Ascot Heath tickets available for a mere £3, but these only admit you to a picnic area in the middle of the race course. You'll be able to see the horses, of course, but that's not why people come to Ascot. The real spectacle is the crowd itself: enormous headgear is de rigueur on Ladies Day—the Thursday of the meet—and those who arrive dressed inappropriately (jeans, shorts, sneakers) will be turned away from their grandstand seats.

Fodor'sChoice ★ **Derby Day** (✉ The Grandstand, Epsom Downs, Surrey ☎ 01372/470047 ⊕ www.epsomderby.co.uk), usually held on the first Saturday in June, is, after Ascot, the second biggest social event of the racing calendar; it's also one of the world's greatest races for three-year-olds. Lord Derby and Sir Charles Bunbury, the founders of the mile-and-a-half race, tossed a coin to decide who the race would be named after. It was first run in 1780.

Football

To refer to the national sport as "soccer" is to blaspheme. It is football, and its importance to the people and the culture of the country seems to grow inexorably. Massive injections of money from television, sponsorship, and foreign investors often fail to filter down through the game, leaving some lower-division clubs in financial difficulty, but public interest in millionaire players and high-profile foreign stars in the domestic game is immense. The domestic season (August through May) culminates in the FA Cup Final, traditionally the biggest day in the sporting calendar, for which tickets are about as easy to get as they are for the Super Bowl. Increasingly important, the European Champions League, a club competition, brings together many of the world's best players in a quest for continental glory and riches. The three or four top English clubs are involved. International matches are once again being held at Wembley since the rebuilding of the National Stadium was completed in 2006.

For a real sample of this British obsession, nothing beats a match at the home ground of one of the London clubs competing in the Premier League, and a taste of the electric atmosphere only a vast football crowd can generate. Try to book tickets (from about £25 upward) in advance. You might also check out London's lower-division games: though the standard of football in League Two may not match that of the Premiership, tickets are much cheaper and easier to get hold of, and the environment can be just as fervent. For more information on teams, games, and prices, look in *Time Out* magazine.

PREMIER LEAGUE TEAMS **Arsenal** is historically London's most successful club, and after winning the Premiership without losing a single game in 2004, overtook northern giant Manchester United as the team to beat. Their reign, however, was ended by London rivals Chelsea, and in Europe they have often been less successful. ✉ *Highbury, Avenell Rd., Islington, N5* ☎ *020/7704-4040* ⊕ *www.arsenal.com* Ⓤ *Arsenal.*

Charlton Athletic has more passion than money, but has now prolonged its stay in the top division long enough to be taken seriously, and has a

Making a Bet

HORSES, GREYHOUNDS, football, and whether it will snow on the roof of the Meteorological Office on Christmas Day are all popular reasons for a "flutter" in all corners of the capital. Now that technology and the abolition of tax on betting have encouraged a massive surge in Internet wagers, you don't even need to leave home to put a pound on just about anything you want, or any combination of likely or unlikely events. If you do, however, you'll find London's ubiquitous bookmakers (Ladbroke and William Hill are the biggest) to be increasingly comfortable places with live satellite link-ups to sporting events around the world. At both equine and canine racecourses these chains are also represented, but here they struggle to compete for attention with the furious calling and signaling of the traditional bookies, whose tictac communications provide an alternative form of entertainment on the track.

habit of outperforming expectations. ⊠ *The Valley, Floyd Rd., Greenwich, SE7* ☎ *020/8333–4010* ⊕ *www.cafc.co.uk* Ⓤ *National Rail: Charlton.*

Chelsea, adored by a mix of thugs and genteel West Londoners, is owned by one of Russia's richest men, and the extra cash has pushed the team up to a new level. They won the Premiership in 2005 and are now one of the best in Europe. ⊠ *Stamford Bridge, Fulham Rd., Fulham, SW6* ☎ *0870/300–2322* ⊕ *www.chelseafc.co.uk* Ⓤ *Fulham Broadway.*

Fulham has relatively little recent experience in the top division, but, under the same owner as Harrods, they certainly possess the money and the self-confidence to stay with the big boys. ⊠ *Craven Cottage, Stevenage Rd., Fulham, SW6* ☎ *0870/442–1234* ⊕ *www.fulhamfc.co.uk* Ⓤ *Putney Bridge.*

Tottenham Hotspur, or "Spurs," traditionally an exponent of attractive, positive football, has underperformed for many years, but in the last two or three seasons there have been some signs of a revival for the North London side. ⊠ *White Hart La., 748 High Rd., Tottenham, N17* ☎ *0870/420–5000* ⊕ *www.spurs.co.uk* Ⓤ *National Rail: White Hart La.*

West Ham is the team of London's East End. After years of failing to match the successes of their past they returned to top- flight football in 2005, and will look to stay as long as possible. ⊠ *Boleyn Ground, Green St., Upton Park, E13* ☎ *020/8548–2748* ⊕ *www.whufc.com* Ⓤ *Upton Park.*

Rugby

An ancestor of American football that's played unpadded, Rugby Union raises the British blood pressure (especially on the Celtic fringes) enormously. The popularity of the game in the capital has been on the up since England won the Rugby World Cup in 2003. To find out about top clubs playing rugby in and around the capital during the September to May season, peruse *Time Out* magazine. Rugby League, a slightly different game, is played almost exclusively in the north of England, but you can catch the one southern Super League team, Harlequins Rugby League, at the Twickenham Stoop.

★ **Twickenham** hosts the Rugby Union Six-Nations tournament, where relative newcomer Italy joins old-timers England, France, Scotland, Wales, and Ireland. During this competition, held January through March, rugby can rival even football for the nation's sporting attentions, and tickets for these matches are more precious than gold. The domestic Powergen Cup Final is fought out at Twickenham in early May. Harlequins and London Scottish are club teams that both play their rugby here. Harlequins (www.quins.co.uk) have now taken over the London Broncos rugby league club, which will now play under the name Harlequins RL at Twickenham. To get there, take National Rail to Twickenham station; the stadium is a 10-minute walk away. You can also take the Tube to Richmond and take a bus or walk 15 minutes to the ground. ⊠ *Twickenham Rugby Football Ground, Whitton Rd., Twickenham, TW2* ☎ *0870/143–1111* ⊕ *www.twickenhamstadium.com.*

Running

London is a delight for joggers. If you don't mind a crowd, popular spots include Green Park, which gets a stream of runners armed with maps from Piccadilly hotels, and—to a lesser extent—adjacent St. James's Park. Both can get perilous with deck chairs on summer days. You can run a 4-mi perimeter route around Hyde Park and Kensington Gardens or a 2½-mi route in Hyde Park alone if you start at Hyde Park Corner or Marble Arch and encircle the Serpentine. Most Park Lane hotels offer jogging maps for this, their local green space. Regent's Park has the most populated track because it's a sporting kind of place; the Outer Circle loop measures about 2½ mi.

Away from the center, there are longer, scenic runs over more varied terrain at Hampstead Heath: highlights are Kenwood, and Parliament Hill, London's highest point, where you'll get a fabulous panoramic sweep over the entire city. Richmond Park is the biggest green space of all, but watch for deer during rutting season (October and November). Back in town, there's a rather traffic-heavy 1½-mi riverside run along Victoria Embankment from Westminster Bridge to Blackfriars Bridge, or a beautiful mile among the rowing clubs and ducks along the Malls—Upper, Lower, and Chiswick—from Hammersmith Bridge.

18

ON THE SIDELINES

The **Flora London Marathon,** starting at 9:30 AM on a Sunday in April, is a thrilling event to watch as well as participate in. Join the throngs who look on and cheer as over 40,000 internationally famous and local runners tackle the 26.2-mi challenge, from Greenwich to the Mall. Entrants include most of the world's best marathon runners, and the number of participants makes it the planet's biggest marathon. Entry forms for the following year are available between August and October. The Web site (www.london-marathon.co.uk) has details, including pubs and entertainment along the route.

CLOSE UP

Wimbledon

THE WIMBLEDON LAWN TENNIS Championships are famous among fans for the green, green grass of Centre Court; for strawberries and cream; and for rain, which always falls, despite the last-week-of-June–first-week-of-July high-summer timing. This event is the most prestigious of the four Grand Slam events of the tennis year. Whether you can get grandstand tickets is literally down to the luck of the draw, because there's a ballot system (lottery) for advance purchase. To apply, send a self-addressed stamped envelope (or an international reply coupon) with the completed application form between August 1 and December 31, and hope for the best.

There are other ways to see the tennis. About 500 Centre and Number 1 and 2 Court tickets are kept back to sell each day and fanatics line up all night for these, especially in the first week. Afternoon tickets collected from early-departing spectators are resold (profits go to charity). These can be excellent grandstand seats (with plenty to see—play continues until dusk). ■ TIP→ **You can also buy entry to the grounds to roam matches on the outside courts, where even the top-seeded players compete early in the two-week period.** Get to Southfields or Wimbledon Tube station as early as possible and start queuing to be sure of getting one of these. ⌂ Ticket Office, All England Lawn Tennis & Croquet Club, Box 98, Church Rd., Wimbledon, SW19 5AE ☎ 020/8946-2244 ⊕ www.wimbledon.org.

If you don't fancy the crowds and snaking queues of Wimbledon, you can watch many of the top names in men's tennis play in the pre-Wimbledon **Stella Artois Tournament.** This, too, is usually oversubscribed, but you can join a mailing list and then apply online from January for a priority booking. ⌂ Queen's Club, Palliser Rd., West Kensington, W14 ☎ 020/7385-3421 ⊕ www.stellaartoistennis.com Ⓤ Barons Court.

If you don't want to run alone, call the **London Hash House Harriers** (☎ 020/8567-5712 ⊕ www.londonhash.org). They organize noncompetitive hour-long hare-and-hound group runs around interesting bits of town, with loops, shortcuts, and pubs built in. Runs start at Tube stations, usually at noon on Saturday or Sunday in winter, and at 7 PM on Monday in summer. The cost is £1.

Squash

There are four squash courts at **Finsbury Leisure Centre,** a popular sports center in the City frequented by execs who work nearby. You can book by phone without a membership, and you're most likely to get a court if you show up to play during Londoners' regular office hours, or possibly on weekends, when courts are less busy. A court costs £7.80 per 40 minutes for nonmembers, £5.40 off-peak (before 4:30 PM). ⊠ Norman St., Finsbury, EC1 ☎ 020/7253-2346 Ⓤ Old St.

Swimming

☺ **Chelsea Sports Centre,** with a renovated, early-20th-century 32- by 12-meter indoor pool, is just off King's Road, so it's usually busy, especially on weekends when it's packed with kids. Each swim costs £3. ⊠ *Chelsea Manor St., Chelsea, SW3* ☎ *020/7352–6985* Ⓤ *South Kensington.*

Oasis has a heated outdoor pool (open year-round) and a 32- by 12-meter indoor pool. Needless to say, both are packed in summer. A swim costs £3.30. ⊠ *32 Endell St., Covent Garden, WC2* ☎ *020/7831–1804* Ⓤ *Covent Garden.*

Tennis

★ Many London parks have courts that are often cheap or even free: **Holland Park** is one of the prettiest places to play, with six hard courts available all year. The cost here is £5.50 per hour but only borough residents can book in advance. ⊠ *Holland Park, W8* ☎ *020/7602–2226* Ⓤ *Holland Park.*

Islington Tennis Centre is about the only place where you don't need a membership to play indoors year-round, but you do need to reserve by phone. There are two outdoor courts, too, and coaching is available, as are "Pay and Play" sessions where you can turn up and be matched with a player of similar ability. Prices are £17.50 for the indoor courts and £7.80 for outdoors. Nonmembers can book up to five days ahead. ⊠ *Market Rd., Islington, N7* ☎ *020/7700–1370* ⊕ *www.aquaterra.org* Ⓤ *Caledonian Rd.*

☺ **Regent's Park Tennis Centre** has courts available to nonmembers for £9 an hour peak (weekdays 4 PM–9 PM, weekends all day) and £7 off-peak. There are also social tennis sessions every Sunday 1–4 PM, where you can arrive without a partner and get in on a game. Four courts are floodlighted for use in winter. Two junior courts are the centerpieces of the "Tennis Kid Zone," and there's also a café. ⊠ *York Bridge Rd., Inner Circle, Regent's Park, Marylebone, NW1* ☎ *020/7486–4216* Ⓤ *Regent's Park.*

18

Shopping

WORD OF MOUTH

"Portobello Road is best seen very early Saturday morning—and really no other tourist attractions are open then. So go to the market around 8 AM (earlier if you can manage, but on your first full day in London that might be difficult). By 10–10:30 AM it gets very crowded, so it is best to be leaving around then. Most tourist attractions open around 10, so the timing is perfect."

—janisj

Updated by
Ferne Arfin

NAPOLÉON WAS BEING SCORNFUL when he called Britain a nation of shopkeepers, but with shopping one of today's most popular leisure activities, Londoners have had the last laugh. Not only does London have some of the finest stores in the world, it also has plenty of them—from grand department stores to exquisite specialty and designer shops. Like most other major cities, London has its share of national and global chain stores, but individuality still rules here and the real pleasure is in nosing out the unique.

You can shop like royalty and have your undies custom-made at Her Majesty's corsetière Rigby & Peller in Knightsbridge, run down a leather-bound copy of *Wuthering Heights* at a Charing Cross bookseller, find antique toby jugs on Portobello Road, or drop in at Vivienne Westwood's landmark shop on the King's Road—Gwen Stefani and Kelly Osborne are fans. Whether you're out for fun or for fashion, London can be the most rewarding of hunting grounds.

Apart from bankrupting yourself, the only problem you may encounter is exhaustion. London is a town of many far-flung shopping areas. Real shophounds plan their excursions with military precision, taking in only one or two shopping districts in a day, with fortifying stops for lunch, tea, and a pint or glass of wine in the pub.

Shopping Districts

Brompton Cross

Chelsea, South Kensington, and Knightsbridge come together in a high-fashion crossroads near the beginning of the Fulham Road. The area has only been called Brompton Cross since the millennium but in terms of fashion, only the name is new. Josephs, the Conran Shop, Chanel, Ralph Lauren, Betsey Johnson, Paul & Joe, Betty Jackson, and a scattering of posh eateries make this the place where London's "It" girls shop and show off. Discrete and exclusive clothing, modern jewelry, and home accessory shops are tucked away round the corner on Draycott Avenue and Walton Street.

Camden Town

A metropolis of crafts and vintage-clothing markets spreads from Camden Town Underground Station all the way to the Roundhouse, Chalk Farm. It began around the rough tumble of canal-side buildings known as Camden Locks—still the most hectic fun. Every kind of alternative style—retro, Goth, New Romantic, New Age, Punk, hippy, "Annie Hall"—is catered to. ■ TIP→ **This is the place to see London street fashion "on the hoof."** Art, home furnishings, antiques, and bric-a-brac are in abundance as well. It's less frenetic midweek.

Chelsea

The King's Road, from its beginning at Sloane Square west to Vivienne Westwood's World's End shop, is where Chelsea promenades—especially on bright weekend days. The new Duke of York's Square, opened near the eastern end in

> **NOT TO BE CONFUSED WITH . . .**
>
> Camden Passage Antiques Market and Pierrepont Arcade is miles away, in terms of both ethos and geography, from Camden Town. This bustling pedestrian village of high-quality antiques shops, crammed into tiny 18th-century lanes near Angel Tube Station in Islington, is for serious collectors and lovers of genuine treasures. Visit Wednesday and Saturday, from early morning, or Thursday for the weekly book market.

2004–2005, is an enclave of fashion, jewelry, home decor, and beauty boutiques with several good cafés. Among the many independent shops, some originals—like R. Soles for cowboy boots and Boy for glam rocker style, have been around for decades. And no other London street has such a concentration and variety of shoe stores—everything from popular British chains to Manolo Blahnik's original Chelsea shop.

Covent Garden

The restored 19th-century market building—in a something-for-everyone neighborhood named for the market itself—houses mainly high-class clothing chains and good-quality crafts stalls. Neal Street and the surrounding alleys have amazing gifts of every type—bikes, kites, tea, herbs, beads, hats . . . you name it. Floral Street and Long Acre have designer and chain-store fashion in equal measure, and Monmouth Street, Shorts Gardens, and the Thomas Neal's mall on Earlham Street have trendy clothes for the young street scene. The area is good for people-watching, too.

Kensington

Kensington Church Street has become makeup and beauty central, with Mac, Space NK, and several other cosmetic and fragrance shops clustered among the shoe and fashion shops near the southern end. Venture farther north for serious fine antiques and glamorous chandeliers. And don't be afraid to duck into the little side streets for a changing selection of boutiques. Kensington High Street is a smaller, less crowded, and classier version of Oxford Street, with a selection of clothing chains and larger stores at the eastern end.

Knightsbridge

Harrods dominates Brompton Road, but there's plenty more, especially for the well-heeled and fashion-conscious. Harvey Nichols is the top clothing spot, and there are many expensive designers' showcases along Upper Sloane Street. Narrow Beauchamp (pronounced "Beecham") Place has more of the same, plus home furnishings, knickknacks, and

19

SHOPPING PLANNER

Top 5

■ **Portobello Road Market.** This market is still the best for size, variety, and sheer street theater.

■ **Harrods Food Halls.** Noisy, colorful, and tempting, the food halls have long been a favorite. The mosaic of fresh fish assembled every day is a must-see.

■ **Liberty.** In a classic, half-timbered building, the store's historic connection with William Morris and the Arts and Crafts movement is maintained in a focus on design and truly beautiful things.

■ **Selfridges.** This is the best department store in London, with an astonishing selection of goods at prices that range from budget to astronomical.

■ **Hamleys.** With floor after floor of treasures for every child on your list, this is *the* London toyshop.

A Word About Service

Don't take it personally if salespeople seem abrupt—even rude. Service with a smile is a new concept here, and it hasn't caught on everywhere.

Opening Hours

Most shops are open from about 9:30 or 10 AM to 6 or 6:30 PM. Some may open at 11 and stay open until 7. Because shop hours, particularly for the smaller shops, are varied, it's a good idea to phone ahead. Stores that have late shopping—and not all do—are usually open until 7 or 8 PM, on Wednesday or Thursday only. On Sunday, many shops open between 11 AM and noon and close at 5 or 6 PM.

Watch Your Language

The English have their own version of our mutual language. Here are a few confusing terms to watch for when out and about in the shops:

Pants means underwear. Every other type of long-legged bottoms (except jeans) are called **trousers.** **Knickers** are ladies' undies. If you want pantyhose, ask for **tights. Jumper** means sweater—unless it's a cardigan, in which case it's called a **cardie.** If you ask for a **sweater,** you may be offered a sweat shirt. Men use **braces** to hold up their trousers; in England **suspenders** is another word for garters. If you want some Adidas or Nike-type athletic shoes, ask for **trainers**—never sneakers. Don't ask for a **pocketbook** or a **purse** if you mean a handbag—the former will be incomprehensible while the latter will produce a coin purse. In the nightwear department, nightgowns are always **nighties** and bathrobes are always **dressing gowns.**

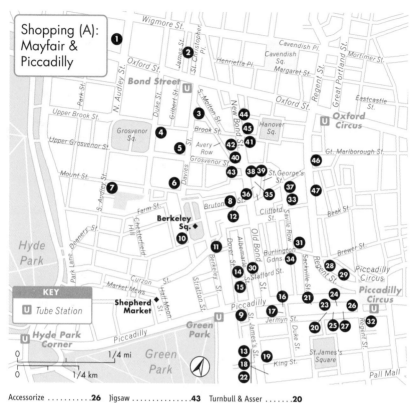

Shopping (A):
Mayfair &
Piccadilly

Know Your Shopping Personality

WHAT'S THE BEST PLACE to shop in London?" is an unanswerable question, akin to "How long is a piece of string?" There are thousands of shops in London and dozens of neighborhoods worth shopping in. Identify your shopping personality to narrow your choices for a successful day or half-day outing.

Department Store Aficionado. Do you like the buzz of a big store, want to look at many different kinds of merchandise in one place, finish your shopping list fast? Head for the department stores. Selfridges, Debenhams, John Lewis, and Liberty are all clustered in the area around Oxford Circus and Bond Street Tube stations. Harvey Nichols and Harrods share Knightsbridge Tube.

Fashionista. When only the best designers will do, start at Harvey Nichols, in Knightsbridge, then take in the designer boutiques along Sloane Street before boarding the Tube for Green Park. From there, head up New and Old Bond streets, finishing at Fenwick. If you still have time and energy, aim for St. Christopher Place W1 or South Molton Street W1 for more fashion boutiques.

Eclectic. If you don't like to be pinned down and like beautiful workmanship and originality, start at Liberty on Regent Street then head for either the Holland Park/Notting Hill or Marylebone neighborhoods. Both provide enough idiosyncratic lifestyle shops for hours of browsing.

Funky & Avant-Garde. Aim for the Spitalfields/Brick Lane area on a Sunday. Take the Tube to Liverpool Street or Aldgate East, then follow the crowds of trendies. Brick Lane runs parallel to Commercial Street (where Spitalfields Market is located). The ladder of small streets between them is good for surprises.

Easygoing. If you like popping in and out of different shops, a bit of people-watching, and a few good spots for coffee or lunch, the mile and a half of the Kings Road that starts in Sloane Square is ideal. You'll find small department stores like Peter Jones and Marks & Spencer, familiar chains, one-off boutiques, food and coffee shops, bookstores, electronics, music, children's goods, antiques, and high fashion all along the route.

such specialist collector's items as antique maps and globes. The kinds of restaurants favored by ladies who lunch—including the late Princess Diana's favorite, San Lorenzo—are tucked in between every few shops.

Marylebone

Between the Oxford Street of Selfridges and John Lewis and the main, east–west artery of the Marylebone Road, this quiet backwater is full of the kind of one-off shops that Londoners love. Marylebone High Street, once lined with local restaurants and practical shops, has kept a villagelike appeal while developing into a busy retail destination. Understated fashion shops for men and women, art galleries, sheet music and musical instrument shops, gourmet food emporiums, and patisseries jostle for space. Not far away, the jewel box–pretty shops on St. Christopher's Place and Gee's Court include the Queen's shoe-

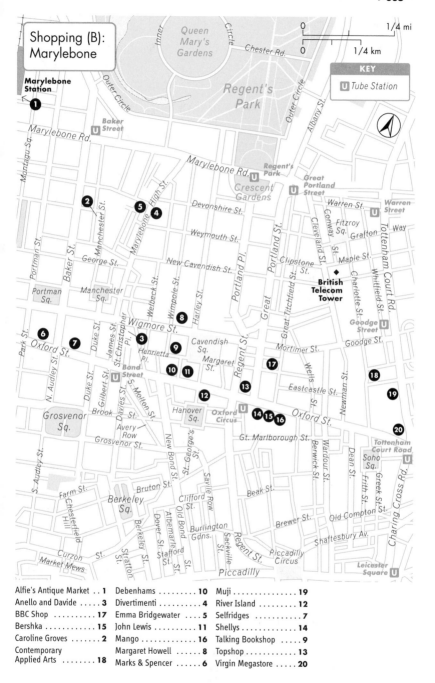

Shopping (B):
Marylebone

maker, Mulberry for leather goods, and Marimekko—still selling the Finnish fabrics that made it famous in the 1960s. Chiltern Street is also worth exploring for custom-made shoes, art galleries, and woodwind instruments.

Mayfair

Here you'll find Bond Street, Old and New, with desirable dress designers and jewelers, plus fine art on Old Bond Street and Cork Street. Old Masters, rare books, jewels worthy of a sheik's harem—this is the neighborhood to give your credit cards a real workout . . . or to people-watch the folks who do. South Molton Street used to be a fashion hotspot, but other than Browns—still a magnet for trendy label watchers—it has been taken over by coffee bars and cafés. The tailors of Savile Row are of worldwide renown, and you can order custom-monogrammed dinner plates at a 200-year-old shop on South Audley Street. When the astronomical prices leave you gasping, stop in at Fenwicks for some that are slightly less stratospheric.

Notting Hill

Branching off from the famous Portobello Road market, enclaves of boutiques sell young designers' wares, antiques, and things for the home—now favored stops for trendsetters. Go east to explore the Ledbury Road–Westbourne Grove axis. Kensington Park Road parallels the market, and farther west, Clarendon Cross has an eclectic mix of homewares, fine arts, and vintage clothes to die for. ■ TIP→ Whether you come on weekends when the Portobello Road market is in full swing, or on quieter weekdays, this is shopping for explorers who love pure, self-indulgent retail theater.

Oxford Street & Regent Street

A magnet for shoppers and tourists, overcrowded Oxford Street has some of London's great department stores in the run-up to Marble Arch—particularly Selfridges, John Lewis, and Marks & Spencer's flagship branch. Also here are interesting boutiques secreted in little St. Christopher's Place and Gees Court. East of a stretch of cheap and cheerful trendsetters around Oxford Circus, it all becomes pretty tacky. Give it a miss and hop on an eastbound bus toward Tottenham Court Road for Heal's, Habitat, Muji, and Purves & Purves for stylish gifts and homewares. Tottenham Court Road, around the corner from the British Museum, is also lined with shops selling computers, cameras, mobile phones, sound systems, and every kind of consumer electronics known to man.

Perpendicular to Oxford Street, the wider, curvier Regent Street has several department stores, including the legendary Liberty. Hamleys is the capital's toy center; other shops tend to be stylish men's chain stores or airline offices. There are also shops selling china and bolts of English tweed, but they tend to be aimed at the tourist market and charge tourist prices. "West Soho," around Carnaby Street went through a seedy period after the "Swinging Sixties," but is having a revival with loads of new shops selling trendy gear for young men.

Piccadilly & St. James's

The actual number of shops is small for a street of its length (Green Park takes up a lot of space), but Piccadilly fits in several quintessential

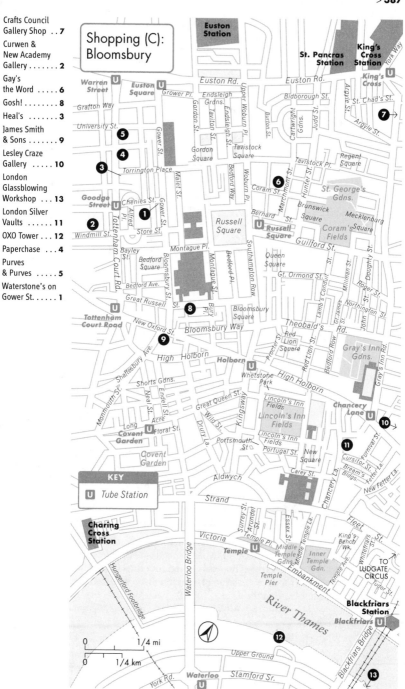

Shopping (C):
Bloomsbury

KEY

U Tube Station

0   1/4 mi

0   1/4 km

British emporiums. Fortnum & Mason is the star, and the historic Burlington Arcade is an elegant experience even for shop-phobics. ■ TIP➔ **If shopping on Piccadilly itself, keep in mind that the closer you get to Piccadilly Circus, the more the shops and goods reflect the more touristy nature of that end of the street.**

St. James's—where the English gentleman shops—has some of the most elegant emporiums for hats, handmade shirts, shoes, silver shaving kits, flasks, and traditional English hunting, fishing, and riding kits. Doorways often bear royal warrants, and shops along Jermyn Street, like Floris, have museum-quality interiors and facades. One traditional men's hatter, James Lock, has been in business since 1697.

Pimlico & Victoria

Not quite Belgravia, not quite anywhere really, this odd little corner of London, bounded by Lower Sloane Street, Pimlico Road, Ebury Street, and Elizabeth Street, is a center for very choice antiques, home decor, fashion, and food shops. This is where royals-who-retail ply their trade. Princess Margaret's son, David Linley, works in wood, and there's a farm shop owned by the Duchess of Devonshire. There are also hat makers, dress designers, artisan parfumeurs, and chocolatiers. If you're coming or going from Victoria Station or Victoria Coach Station, pass up the chain stores in the station mall and head here instead.

Spitalfields/East End/Hoxton

For the adventurous shopper who wants to sniff out the new and distinctive, the area around the freshened-up Spitalfields market is a fruitful hunting ground. The market operates daily and sells crafts and clothing with prices a little cheaper than those at Covent Garden. Lower rents mean more retail opportunities for young designers and purveyors of "cool" around Columbia Road (Open House), Cheshire Street (abé, Fred Bare, and MimiMika), and Brick Lane (Rokit), where there's fashion frocks, kits for men, jewelry and accessories, and the latest lifestyle must-haves for your home. The area around Brick Lane is especially good for lovers of vintage *clobber* (British slang for clothes). On Sunday, the Columbia Road flower market adds its own colorful excitement to the area. Keep in mind that many of the coolest shops and stalls are only open when the East End Markets (Columbia Road, Spitalfields, Brick Lane, Petticoat Lane, Whitechapel) are in full swing, so check the Market listings in this chapter to avoid disappointment.

A bit farther north in Shoreditch, near Old Street Tube station and Hoxton Square, followers of the Brit-Art gallery scene have begun to attract a new crop of fashion hopefuls. Check out the Hoxton Boutique, Wink, and Story for a combination of wearable fashion and wild, clubland looks that sail close to the edge.

Department Stores

London's department stores range from Harrods—practically a national monument on the tourist trail—to many mid-range stores that cater to Londoners' everyday needs. A few rise above the pack for their fashion (Harvey Nichols), originality (Liberty), or sheer excitement (the

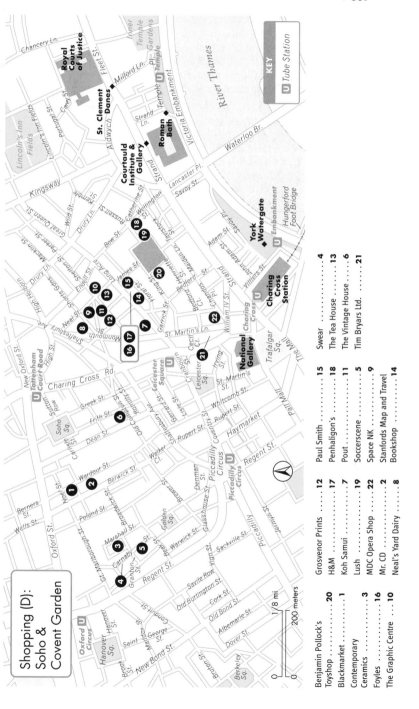

Shopping (D): Soho & Covent Garden

KEY
U Tube Station

Benjamin Pollock's Toyshop **20**
Blackmarket **1**
Contemporary Ceramics **3**
Foyles **16**
The Graphic Centre . . . **10**

Grosvenor Prints **12**
H&M **17**
Koh Samui **7**
Lush **19**
MDC Opera Shop **22**
Mr. CD **2**
Neal's Yard Dairy **8**

Paul Smith **15**
Penhaligon's **18**
Pout **11**
Soccerscene **5**
Space NK **9**
Stanfords Map and Travel Bookshop **14**

Swear **4**
The Tea House **13**
The Vintage House **6**
Tim Bryars Ltd. **21**

revamped Selfridges). The best are scattered about the West End on Oxford Street, Regent Street, and Knightsbridge. Some, like Marks & Spencer, another British institution now known mostly for clothing and food, have branches all over town. ■ TIP➜ Unless you have Olympic levels of stamina, aim to anchor a shopping day with only one or two department stores, dipping in and out of the nearby boutiques in between.

Debenhams. This large Oxford Street department store has moved up the fashion stakes. Years ago it wasn't on the hip shoppers' map, but with the arrival of the affordable Jasper Conran collection, wise-buying gals soon homed in. The "Designers at Debenhams" now features a changing list of fashionable names who design affordable clothes exclusively for this group of stores. In 2005–2006 the selection included Betty Jackson, Gharani Strok, Jasper Conran, Pearce Fionda, and John Rocha. Men's and children's wear as well as home accessories compete in the style stakes here, too. (⇨ Map B) ⊠ *334–348 Oxford St., Oxford Street, W1* ☎ *0844/561–6161* Ⓤ *Oxford Circus.*

Fenwick. Near the Oxford Street end of New Bond Street, Fenwick (pronounced *Fennick*) is a haven of realistically priced fashion in a shopping area where most things cost the earth. Five floors of chic clothes and accessories for men and women, lingerie, and home furnishings, highlight lesser known and emerging designers from all over Europe. Even the restaurants, Joe's on the second floor and Carluccio's in the basement, have style. Make sure to see the big selection of striking, semiprecious and costume jewelry on the ground floor. (⇨ Map A) ⊠ *63 New Bond St., Mayfair, W1* ☎ *020/7629–9161* Ⓤ *Bond St.*

Fodor'sChoice
★
Harrods. If you approach Harrods more as a tourist attraction than a fashion store you won't be disappointed. This Knightsbridge institution is an encyclopedia of luxury brands, with at least 500 departments and 20 restaurants packed onto seven floors across 4½ acres. In 2000, Harrods lost its Royal Warrants and some of its luster as a "top people's store." These days the fashion departments lean toward costly but safe. You'll be most impressed if you focus on the spectacular food halls, the huge ground-floor perfumerie, the marble clad accessory rooms, and the outrageous *Egyptian* escalator—at the bottom there's a tacky shrine to Diana and Dodi. ■ TIP➜ Be prepared to brave the crowds, and dress nicely, please—scruffy visitors are politely shown the door. (⇨ Map E) ⊠ *87 Brompton Rd., Knightsbridge, SW1* ☎ *020/7730–1234* Ⓤ *Knightsbridge.*

★ **Harvey Nichols.** It's a block away from Harrods, but Harvey Nicks is not competing on the same turf, because its passion is fashion, all the way. There are nearly six floors of it, including departments for dressing homes and men, but the woman who invests in her wardrobe is the main target. Accessories here are out of this world—you won't find a better hair-ornament selection in London. The fourth floor has a chic home-design department, stocking such names as Nina Campbell, Mulberry, Ralph Lauren, and Designers Guild. A reservation at the Fifth Floor restaurant is coveted, but you can drop in at the chic, if noisy, Café for panoramic views of Knightsbridge and its fashionistas. (⇨ Map E) ⊠ *109 Knightsbridge, Knightsbridge, SW1* ☎ *020/7235–5000* Ⓤ *Knightsbridge.*

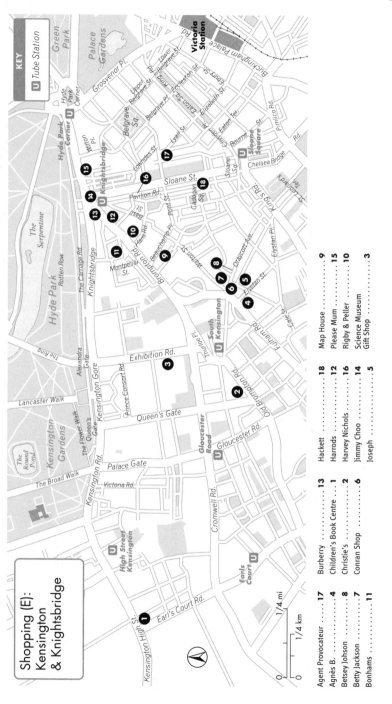

Shopping (E): Kensington & Knightsbridge

KEY
U Tube Station

Agent Provocateur **17**	Burberry **13**	Hackett **18**	Map House **9**
Agnès B. **4**	Children's Book Centre ... **1**	Harrods **12**	Please Mum **15**
Betsey Johson **8**	Christie's **2**	Harvey Nichols **16**	Rigby & Peller **10**
Betty Jackson **7**	Conran Shop **6**	Jimmy Choo **14**	Science Museum
Bonhams **11**		Joseph **5**	Gift Shop **3**

John Lewis. This store's motto is "Never knowingly undersold," and for all kinds of goods at sensible prices, John Lewis is hard to beat. Chelsea locals think of Peter Jones, its brother store in Sloane Square, Chelsea, for classic fashions and home accessories. In 2005 the Chelsea branch completed six years of modernization. Both stores have big dress and furnishing fabrics, needlework, and knitting departments. Their bespoke, lined draperies set the gold standard, not only in London but in smart, traditional homes all over Britain. (⇨ Map B) ⊠ *278 Oxford St., Mayfair, W1* ☎ *020/7629–7711* Ⓤ *Oxford Circus* ☞ *Peter Jones:* ⊠ *Sloane Sq., Chelsea, SW1* ☎ *020/7730–3434* Ⓜ *Sloane Sq.*

Fodor'sChoice
★
Liberty. With a wonderful black-and-white mock-Tudor facade, Liberty is a peacock among pigeons on humdrum Regent Street. In the 19th century, Liberty's designers, leaders in the art nouveau, Arts and Crafts, and aesthetic movements, created classic fabric and home-furnishing designs. Those Liberty prints are still world famous today. Inside, the store is a labyrinth of nooks and crannies stuffed with goodies, like a dream of an Eastern bazaar. The Asian department is rich with color; the jewelry department unusual and bohemian. Fashion, for men and women, focuses on quality and beautiful fabric. An altogether original store. (⇨ Map A) ⊠ *200 Regent St., Mayfair, W1* ☎ *020/7734–1234* Ⓤ *Oxford Circus.*

Marks & Spencer. A major chain of stores that's an integral part of the British way of life, Marks & Spencer was once known for its moderately priced practical clothes and knitwear. Since about 1998 the store has been struggling to find its place in the new retail environment, so what particular fashion incarnation is in-store when you arrive is anybody's guess. Some classics—like beautiful, moderately priced sweaters ("jumpers" in British parlance)—seem to be holding their own and the lingerie remains outstanding. Look for M&S Simply Food shops popping up all over the place and trading on the store's reputation for prepared dishes you can pass off as your own. They're a good source of shortbread, tins of British biscuits and sweets, and jars of condiments you can take home. The Marble Arch branch is the flagship, and its fast stock turnover ensures that it carries the latest from the M&S designers' stable. (⇨ Map B) ⊠ *458 Oxford St., Oxford Street, W1* ☎ *020/ 7935–7954* Ⓤ *Marble Arch.*

Fodor'sChoice
★
Selfridges. This giant, bustling store, now claiming to sell more than one million products, is giving Harvey Nicks a run for its money as London's leading fashion department store. It's packed to the rafters with high-profile, popular designer clothes for everyone in the family. Revamped for the millennium, the store launched itself into the 21st century by wrapping itself in the world's largest photographic artwork, by Sam Taylor Wood. The frenetic cosmetics department is one of the largest in Europe. There are so many zones with pulsating music that merge into one another—from fashion to sports gear to audio equipment—that you practically need a map. Don't miss the spectacular Food Hall. There's a theater-ticket counter and British Airways travel shop in the basement. The store is near the Marble Arch end of Oxford Street, which can be very crowded, especially in the holiday season. (⇨ Map B) ⊠ *400 Oxford St., Oxford Street, W1* ☎ *0870/837–7377* Ⓤ *Bond St.*

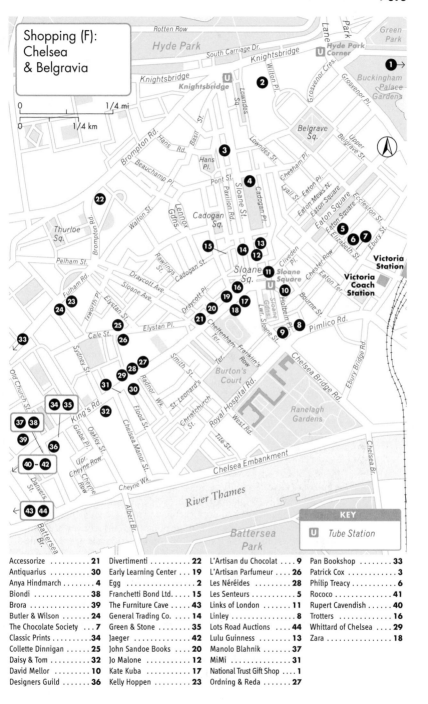

Shopping (F):
Chelsea
& Belgravia

KEY

🅄 Tube Station

Specialty Stores

Antiques

Investment-quality items or lovable junk, London has lots. Try markets first—even for pedigree silver, the dealers at these places often have the best wares and the knowledge to match. The Silver Vaults in Chancery Lane and Bermondsey are the best. Some say that Portobello Road has become a bit of a tourist trap, but if you acknowledge that it's a circus and get into the spirit, it's a lot of fun. Just don't expect many bargains. Kensington Church Street is *the* antiques-shopping street, with both prices and quality high. Early English and European pottery as well as Oriental art porcelains are a specialty. If you know your stuff (and your price limit), head out to Tower Bridge Road, south of the river, where there are mammoth antiques warehouses clustered around the Bermondsey market area. Some are open on Sunday. Farther west and north of the Thames, the Furniture Cave, at the corner of Lots Road, Chelsea, has one of the largest stocks around. Or you could try your luck at auction against the dealers. Summer is usually a quiet period, but at any other time there are plenty of bargains to be had.

Listed here is a selection of the hundreds of stores to whet your appetite.

■ TIP➡ Opening times vary: many places that are open on the weekend will close Monday or Tuesday.

★ **Alfie's Antique Market.** A huge and exciting labyrinth on several floors, it has dealers specializing in anything and everything, but particularly in textiles, furniture, and theater memorabilia. You won't be deliberately stiffed, but it's a caveat emptor kind of place, thanks to the amazing selection of merchandise. (⇨ Map B) ✉ *13–25 Church St., Regent's Park, NW8* ☎ *020/7723–6066* ⊗ *Closed Sun. and Mon.* Ⓤ *Edgware Rd.*

Antiquarius. At the Sloane Square end of King's Road is an indoor antiques market with more than 200 stalls selling collectibles, including items that won't bust your baggage allowance but may empty your bank account: art deco brooches, meerschaum pipes, silver salt cellars, and so on. (⇨ Map F) ✉ *131–145 King's Rd., Chelsea, SW3* ☎ *020/ 7351–5353* ⊗ *Closed Sun.* Ⓤ *Sloane Sq.*

The Furniture Cave. A vast warehouse of grand furniture, decorative salvage, and some high-quality reproductions, the Furniture Cave at the western edge of Chelsea is almost legendary. Here you might find a hardwood dining table capable of seating 30, chandeliers fit for a palace, stained-glass windows, and marble sculpture snatched from the destruction of an old church or a great country house. About 20 dealers spread out across acres of space over three floors. Much of the pine and reproduction furniture is quite affordable. (⇨ Map F) ✉ *533 King's Rd., Chelsea, SW10* ⊕ *www.furniturecave.co.uk* ☞ *Phone numbers and hrs vary with individual dealers* Ⓤ *Fulham Broadway or Earl's Court.*

Grays Antique Market. Dealers specializing in everything from Sheffield plate to Chippendale furniture assemble here under one roof. Bargains are not impossible, and proper pedigrees are guaranteed. Also try Grays in the Mews around the corner—it has more inexpensive, downscale merchandise. (⇨ Map A) ✉ *58 Davies St., Mayfair, W1* ☎ *020/*

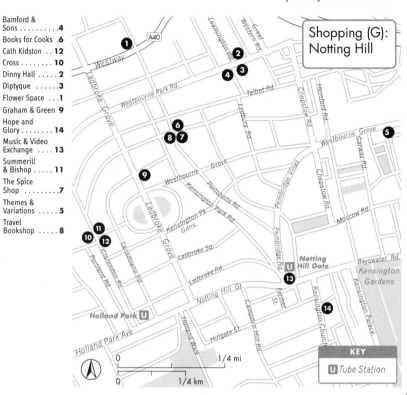

Shopping (G):
Notting Hill

KEY

Ⓤ *Tube Station*

19

7629–7034 ⊘ *Closed Sun.; open Sat. in Dec. only* Ⓤ *Bond St.* ✉ *1–7 Davies Mews, Mayfair, W1* ☎ *020/7629–7034* Ⓤ *Bond St.*

Hope and Glory. This is one of the many specialty stores in Kensington with commemorative china and glass from 1887 to the present; there are also affordable lesser pieces. The entrance is on Peel Street. (⇨ Map G) ✉ *131A Kensington Church St., Kensington, W8* ☎ *020/7727–8424* ⊘ *Closed Sun.* Ⓤ *Notting Hill Gate.*

★ **London Silver Vaults.** A basement conglomeration of around 40 dealers, it's a great place for the average Joe. Some pieces are spectacular, but you can also pick up a set of Victorian cake forks, jugs, cruet sets, candlesticks, and other smaller pieces for lower prices. ■ **TIP→ As an especially cool feature, most of the silver merchants actually trade out of room-size, underground vaults.** (⇨ Map C) ✉ *Chancery House, 53–64 Chancery La., Holborn, WC2* ☎ *020/7242–3844* ⊘ *Closed Sat. after 1, and Sun.* Ⓤ *Chancery La.*

Rupert Cavendish. This most elevated of dealers has the Biedermeier market cornered, with Empire and deco bringing up the rear. On a short stretch of the King's Road that's packed with high-quality antiques dealers, the shop is a museum experience. (⇨ Map F) ✉ *610 King's Rd., Fulham, SW6* ☎ *020/7731–7041* ⊘ *Closed Sun.* Ⓤ *Fulham Broadway.*

Auction Houses

A few pointers on going to auction: you don't need bags of money; the catalog prices aren't written in stone; and if you're sure of what you want when you view the presale, then bid with confidence. It's easy to get carried away in the excitement of the moment, so keep your limit in mind or take along a friend to remind you. Listed below are the main houses, which all deal in fine art and furniture. ■ TIP→ **If you find these are out of your budget, snoop around Lots Road in Chelsea, where you can find more budget-price contemporary furniture that compares favorably with the price of new.**

Bonhams. One of the more buyer-friendly places, this auction house has many interesting collections. Along with antiques, Bonhams specializes in 20th-century design. Its merger with the auction house Phillips, in 2002, increased the depth and scope of other specialty areas, such as Old Master paintings. Bonhams' Knightsbridge sales rooms are right across from Harrods. (⇨ Map E) ✉ *Montpelier St., Knightsbridge, SW7* ☎ *020/7393–3900* Ⓤ *Knightsbridge.*

★ **Christie's.** Look here for great English country-house furniture in varying states of repair, paintings, prints, carpets, lighting, plus all manner of bona fide treasures. It's amazing what can be classed as infinitely desirable with surprising price tags: the blue door from the film *Notting Hill* and the blue pinafore dress worn by Judy Garland in *The Wizard of Oz* went for a record £5,750 and £199,500, respectively. (⇨ Map E) ✉ *85 Old Brompton Rd., South Kensington, SW7* ☎ *020/7930–6074* Ⓤ *S. Kensington.*

★ **Lots Road Auctions.** Established in the 1970s by two former Christie's employees and one of the founders of the Furniture Cave, these weekly auctions, held at 1 PM and 4 PM every Sunday, offer a grab bag of fine antiques, good-quality used furniture, and out and out tat. Popular with decorators and locals on Sunday outings, these auction rooms, off the King's Road, are not in the least intimidating and a great place for beginners to get a taste for the sport. (⇨ Map F) ✉ *71–73 Lots Rd., Chelsea, SW10* ☎ *020/7376–6800* Ⓤ *Fulham Broadway or Earl's Court.*

Sotheby's. There's a well-publicized calendar of regular auctions for the well-heeled, but you can also just look, ponder possible purchases, or break for lunch in the superb café. (⇨ Map A) ✉ *34–35 New Bond St., Mayfair, W1* ☎ *020/7293–5000* Ⓤ *Bond St.*

Books

Charing Cross Road has long been a center of London bookselling. There's still quite a concentration of bookstores along its length, with specialist, antiquarian, and used bookstores tucked away in Cecil Court, a pedestrian alley linking it with St. Martin's Lane. But books are big business in London and the trade spreads into many corners of the city. Look, in particular, for the finest rare books around Mayfair. Bloomsbury, around London University and the British Museum, is good territory for used books and eccentric specialists. Every decent London High Street has its Waterstones, Ottakers, Borders, or local independent complete with coffee shops and, in some cases, even cocktail bars and jazz clubs.

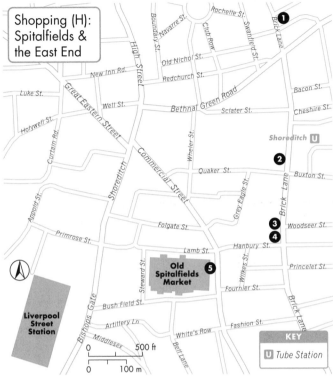

Shopping (H):
Spitalfields &
the East End

GENERAL **Foyles.** A quirky, labyrinthine, family-run business, this store was founded
Fodor'sChoice by the Foyle brothers, who sold their own secondhand textbooks from
★ the kitchen table after they failed the Civil Service exam. The Civil Service's loss was London book lovers' gain. Today Foyles' five floors
carry almost every title imaginable. One of London's best sources for
textbooks, the store stocks everything from popular fiction to military
history, sheet music, opera scores, and fine arts. Christina Foyle instituted a literary luncheon, which since 1930 has attracted more than 700
top authors to speak at the ballroom in Grosvenor House. In 1999, following Christina's death, the family undertook a massive modernization program—installing elevators and air-conditioning. The Silver
Moon for women, and Ray's Jazz, are stores within the store. There's
also a café. (⇨ Map D) ⊠ *113–119 Charing Cross Rd., Soho, WC2*
🕾 *020/7437–5660* Ⓤ *Tottenham Court Rd.*

Fodor'sChoice **Hatchards.** This is one of London's well-established bookshops, beloved
★ by writers themselves thanks to its cozy, independent character. Independence, however, is a matter of appearance only—Hatchards is owned
by the same corporate giant as the omnipresent Waterstones chain.
Nevertheless, you can revel in its old-fashioned charm while perusing
the well-stocked shelves lining the winding stairs. The staff has retained

19

old-fashioned helpfulness, too. (⇨ Map A) ✉ *187 Piccadilly, St. James's, W1* ☎ *020/7439–9921* Ⓤ *Piccadilly Circus.*

Pan Bookshop. This crowded, independent Chelsea bookshop is full of charm. The staff are dedicated booksellers who know about books, care about book lovers, and are known to take good care of local authors. Some sections, notably children's books, cookery books, philosophy, and travel, are among the best in London. (⇨ Map F) ✉ *158 Fulham Rd., Chelsea SW10* ☎ *020/7373–4997* Ⓤ *S. Kensington.*

John Sandoe Books, Ltd. Enter this tiny shop off the King's Road in Chelsea and you may feel as if you've stepped through a time portal to an earlier century. More than 25,000 books fill the three, dollhouse-size floors of an 18th-century house. Organization? Forget it! Only the staff, who share ownership of the shop, know where anything is. But they are knowledgeable, friendly, and full of great recommendations. You may be tempted to buy more than you can carry, but don't worry—they will pack and send your books anywhere in the world. Local writers, including William Boyd, Dame Muriel Spark, and Arabella Boxer, among others, are regulars and contribute to the shop's annual short publications. This is bookselling the way it used to be. (⇨ Map F) ✉ *10 Blacklands Terr., Chelsea, SW3* ☎ *020/7589–9473* Ⓤ *Sloane Sq.*

Waterstone's. For book buying as a hedonistic leisure activity, the monster-size store by Piccadilly Circus caters to all tastes. A sweeping staircase takes you up to the fifth-floor Studio Lounge, where until 10 PM you can sip a gin-and-tonic while browsing through a book and admiring the view. Waterstone's is the country's leading book chain, and they've pulled out all the stops to make this, their flagship, as comfortable and relaxed as a bookstore can be. (⇨ Map A) ✉ *203–206 Piccadilly, St. James's, W1* ☎ *020/7851–2400* Ⓤ *Piccadilly Circus.*

Waterstone's on Gower Street. Scholars prefer Waterstone's Gower Street branch (Bloomsbury, WC1), the chain's academic store and Europe's biggest academic book specialist. Located between London University and the Royal Academy of Dramatic Art, it was—under its old name, Dillons—the students' textbook source of choice. It still does a substantial business in second-hand textbooks and has a cozy coffee lounge as well as a comprehensive stock of highbrow books. (⇨ Map C) ✉ *82 Gower St., Bloomsbury, WC1* ☎ *020/7636–1577* Ⓤ *Euston Sq.*

SPECIALTY **Books for Cooks.** It may seem odd to describe a bookshop as delicious smelling, but between the products of its test kitchen and its regularly scheduled cookery demonstrations, Books for Cooks is hard to resist. Just about every world cuisine is represented on its shelves, along with the complete lineup of celebrity-chef editions. You can spend hours perusing the volumes over lunch or coffee and cakes in the shop's small restaurant. ■ TIP➔ **Before you come to London, visit the shop's Web site, www. booksforcooks.com, to sign up for a cookery class.** (⇨ Map G) ✉ *4 Blenheim Crescent, Notting Hill, W11* ☎ *020/7221–1992* Ⓤ *Notting Hill Gate.*

Children's Book Centre. Children are well-catered to in London bookshops generally. This one, in addition to the usual videos, CDs, DVDs, and other electronic paraphernalia kids demand, has the added treat of a basement full of toys. It's a very handy pacifier after you've done a bit of fashion shopping on Ken High Street. (⇨ Map

English Eccentrics

EVERY BIG CITY has the kind of specialist merchants that don't fit into any category but their own. London has more than its fair share of shops that cater to the individualist in all of us.

Anything Left-Handed. Lefties of the world unite: buy yourself all the elusive equipment you need for the kitchen (vegetable peelers, can openers), garden (pitchforks and pruners), and leisure. The helpful assistants give good advice— particularly for young kids. They'll try to source products not currently stocked. ✉ *57 Brewer St., Soho, W1* ☎ *020/7437-3910* Ⓤ *Piccadilly Circus.*

Farlows. When it comes to high-tone British-country pursuits, fishing (or angling as they call it here) is about as classy as it gets. Naturally, "one" must have the correct kit and the place to come for it is the flagship store of this most British of Britain's angling specialists. Incorporating House of Hardy rods and reels, the shop brings together the finest fishing equipment and clothing available anywhere. There are frequent fly-tying demonstrations and the assortment of about 3,000 feathery flies and lures is like a pick 'n mix of sweeties. ✉ *9 Pall Mall., St. James's, SW1* ☎ *020/7839-2423* Ⓤ *Piccadilly Circus.*

Holland & Holland. At this place for the hunting-and-shooting fraternity, bespoke is the byword. It has everything from guns (by appointment to the Duke of Edinburgh and the Prince of Wales) to complete hunting outfits, all with the Holland & Holland

brand label. Tailor-made travel wear (especially of the adventure variety) is also available. ✉ *31-33 Bruton St., Mayfair, W1* ☎ *020/7499-4411* Ⓤ *Bond St.*

The Kite Store. Purchase a whimsical kite here and spend a sunny day flying it on Primrose Hill (north of London Zoo), Parliament Hill, or, better still, Hampstead Heath's "kite hill." There are many different types here to suit different budgets and skill levels and most are pretty enough to grace the walls or ceiling of a lucky child's room. ✉ *48 Neal St., Covent Garden, WC2* ☎ *020/7836-1666* Ⓤ *Covent Garden.*

The Temple Gallery. Collectors will find the selection of early-Christian art and icons in this small gallery truly dazzling. Richard Temple has been honing his expertise in Byzantine iconography since the 1950s, scouring the world's auction markets for historically important works. Prices start at a few hundred pounds soaring to several thousands. ✉ *6 Clarendon Cross, Notting Hill, W11* ☎ *020/ 7727-3809* Ⓤ *Holland Park.*

VV Rouleau. This store stocks the most beautiful ribbons and trimmings for gifts, clothing, and home furnishings. The double-face satin ribbons, grosgrain, tartan, and velvet ribbons—in widths from 3mm to 100mm and in every possible color— are just what the well-dressed present is wearing. ✉ *54 Sloane Sq., Cliveden Pl., Chelsea, SW1* ☎ *020/7730-3125* Ⓤ *Sloane Sq.*

E) ✉ *237 High St. Kensington, Kensington,* W8 ☏ *020/7937–7497* Ⓤ *High St. Kensington.*

Gay's the Word. Bloomsbury is where academia, eccentricity, and independence of spirit come together. It's also where London's largest and oldest gay and lesbian bookshop is located. You'll find thousands of titles, from series literature and thoughtful nonfiction to erotica, multimedia, even comics. Opened in 1979, the shop has only recently had to compete with the Gay and Lesbian sections of some of London's mainstream bookstores—but it continues to lead the pack. (➪ Map C) ✉ *66 Marchmont St., Bloomsbury, WC1* ☏ *020/7278–7654* Ⓤ *Russell Sq.*

Gosh! "Holy inky fingers Batman! Is there a better comic book store in London?!" Probably not. Between the classic comics, graphic novels, manga, and independent minicomics this shop has got the genre covered. (➪ Map C) ✉ *39 Great Russell St., Bloomsbury, WC1* ☏ *020/ 7636–1011* Ⓤ *Tottenham Court Rd.*

Stanfords Map and Travel Bookshop. When it comes to encyclopedic coverage, there simply cannot be a better travel book and map shop on the planet. Stanfords is packed with a comprehensive selection of map and travel-book series. Their mail-order department is exemplary as well. Whether you're planning a junket to Surrey or a trip to the South Pole, this should be your first stop. (➪ Map D) ✉ *12 Long Acre, Covent Garden, WC2* ☏ *020/7836–1321* Ⓤ *Covent Garden.*

Talking Bookshop. An enormous selection of books for adults and children, on every form of recorded media is available here. MP3 downloads are scheduled to be added to the shop's selection in 2006. (➪ Map B) ✉ *11 Wigmore St., Marylebone, W1* ☏ *020/7491–4117* Ⓤ *Oxford Circus.*

Travel Bookshop. A short journey from the foodies' favorite (Books for Cooks), this store covers the world on its shelves. It's great for globetrotters and armchair travelers alike, and is the kind of crowded and dusty bookshop that makes a great movie backdrop. Which is probably why it was Hugh Grant's bookstore in the movie *Notting Hill.* (➪ Map G) ✉ *13 Blenheim Crescent, Notting Hill, W11* ☏ *020/ 7229–5260* Ⓤ *Notting Hill Gate.*

RARE & ANTIQUARIAN The English gentleman's library, with its glassed-fronted cabinets full of rare leather-bound books may be a film and literary cliché but there's no denying that London is one of the world's great centers for rare book collectors. Browsers will find several shops along Cecil Court, off Charing Cross Road. For the most exquisite books, especially travel and natural history volumes with beautiful color plates, visit Mayfair around Maddox and Conduit Streets.

Bernard J. Shapero Rare Books. Color plates are seen to best advantage in this bright, airy shop that vies with Maggs as one of the best antiquarian dealers in London. In addition to English and continental books that range from travel to medicine, there's also a gallery of maps and fine prints. (➪ Map A) ✉ *32 St. George St., Mayfair, W1* ☏ *020/ 7493–0876* Ⓤ *Oxford Circus.*

Maggs Brothers Ltd. How could any book lover resist a shop with such a deliciously Dickensian name? In a Georgian town house in one of Mayfair's elegant squares, Maggs was established in 1853, and is one of the world's oldest and largest rare-book dealers. Shop staff act as advisors to important collectors but they are, nonetheless, friendly and helpful to all interested visitors. (⇨ Map A) ⊠ *50 Berkeley Sq., Mayfair, W1* ☎ *020/7493–7160* Ⓤ *Green Park*.

Simon Finch Rare Books Ltd. Think Victoriana in all its glory. This shop specializes in fine English books from about 1800 to immediately before World War I. It's in the heart of Mayfair's rare-book territory, so convenient for a good afternoon's browse. (⇨ Map A) ⊠ *53 Maddox St., Mayfair, W1* ☎ *020/7499–0974* Ⓤ *Oxford Circus*.

Tim Bryars Ltd. Antiquarian books and maps, illustrated travel books, and natural-history texts are among the specialties here. If you love first-person accounts by intrepid travelers from the 18th and 19th centuries, this is the place to look. (⇨ Map D) ⊠ *8 Cecil Ct., Charing Cross Rd., Covent Garden, WC2* ☎ *020/7836–1901* Ⓤ *Leicester Sq*.

CDs & Records

The great megastores such as HMV and Virgin (which began as mail-order in the back pages of the music papers) that have taken over the globe started out in London. There are also specialty stores galore for cutting-edge music mixed by club DJs, and for stocking up your own collection of good old-fashioned vinyl. ■ TIP➔ **Before you get carried away, though, consider that CDs cost anywhere from 10% to as much as 50% more in the U.K. than they do in North America and continental Europe. So look for the kind of music you really can't find at home.**

Blackmarket. Indie, house, garage, world—this shop stocks the hottest club music around. They carry some CDs but this is really a shop for vinyl lovers. (⇨ Map D) ⊠ *25 D'Arblay St., Soho, W1* ☎ *020/7437–0478* Ⓤ *Oxford Circus*.

HMV. HMV Stores are all over London, with at least three branches on Oxford Street and a department in Selfridges. They tend to be crowded, and unless you know exactly what you want, the staff may seem too busy grooving to be of much help. (⇨ Map A) ⊠ *360 Oxford St., Mayfair, W1* ☎ *020/7514–3600* Ⓤ *Bond St*.

★ **MDC Opera Shop.** There's very little the helpful staff here doesn't know about opera and they'll guide you to the best performances of the best divas with the best conductors. The shop has also taken over some of the classical music stock of its late lamented sister operation MDC classical music that closed last year. (⇨ Map D) ⊠ *31 St. Martins La., Covent Garden, WC2* ☎ *020/7240–0270* Ⓤ *Covent Garden*.

Mr. CD. From jazz to heavy metal, with stops along the way for classical, techno and swing—this tiny shop packs it all in. Have a *mooch* around, as the British say, and you might be surprised at what you find. (⇨ Map D) ⊠ *80 Berwick St., Soho, W1* ☎ *020/7439–1097* Ⓤ *Oxford Circus*.

Music & Video Exchange. This store is fast becoming a destination for seekers of unusual and mainstream chart music as well as classical and pop. Young aspiring DJs can be seen rifling among the used discs and 12-inch records. (⇨ Map G) ⊠ *38 Notting Hill Gate, Notting Hill, W11* ☎ *020/7243–8573* Ⓤ *Notting Hill Gate*.

Virgin Megastore. This is Richard Branson's pride and joy (though his New York City store is even bigger). It's handy to have it all under one roof, but be prepared for an ear-blasting experience on the massive ground floor, which is stacked with current chart music. Other areas, with jazz and classics, are slightly more relaxed. Computer games are in vast supply. (⇨ Map B) ✉ *14–16 Oxford St., Soho, W1* ☏ *020/7631–1234* Ⓤ *Tottenham Court Rd.*

China & Glass

English bone china is legendary, and the famous brands—Royal Doulton, Spode, Wedgwood, Minton, and the like—are still made in England, most in the Derbyshire towns around Stoke-on-Trent known as "The Potteries." The top brands are all over London, with the best selections in Harrods, Selfridges, and John Lewis. Look for unusual or hard-to-find pieces, but don't expect many bargains, and remember that sale markdowns are likely to be seconds. Regent Street's china shops sell conventional tourist favorites at tourist prices. Look for smart modern designs and unusual European tableware in the shops listed below, as well as at some of the design and houseware shops listed later in this chapter.

Emma Bridgewater. Look here for fun and funky casual plates, mugs, jugs, and breakfast tableware designed with a sense of humor reflected in names like Hippy Hearts, Rise and Shine, and Black Toast. (⇨ Map B) ✉ *81A Marylebone High St., Marylebone, W1* ☏ *020/7486–6897* Ⓤ *Baker St. or Regents Park.*

★ **David Mellor.** Designer David Mellor has been creating modern cutlery in Sheffield stainless and silver plate since the 1950s. His cool and peaceful shop, tucked into a corner of Sloane Square, surrounds Mellor's own products with beautifully made, modern British tableware. (⇨ Map F) ✉ *4 Sloane Sq., Chelsea, SW1* ☏ *020/7730–4259* Ⓤ *Sloane Sq.*

★ **Divertimenti.** The store sells beautiful kitchenware, unusual culinary gifts—such as spoons made from polished horn—and lovely French pottery from Provence. If you've shopped the Chelsea store before, make a note that they've moved to Knightsbridge, closer to Harrods. (⇨ Maps B and F) ✉ *33–34 Marylebone High St., Marylebone, W1* ☏ *020/ 7935–0689* Ⓤ *Baker St. or Regents Park* ✉ *227–229 Brompton Rd., Knightsbridge, SW7* ☏ *020/7581–8065* Ⓤ *Knightsbridge.*

★ **Summerill & Bishop.** This little piece of Mediterranean country kitchen is in the middle of Notting Hill. Summerill & Bishop supplies French embroidered linen, Portuguese and Tuscan stoneware, natural candles and soaps, and all manner of authentic designer culinary ware for sleek city kitchens along with carefully chosen rustic antiques. (⇨ Map G) ✉ *100 Portland Rd., Notting Hill, W11* ☏ *020/7221–4566* Ⓤ *Holland Park.*

Thomas Goode. This gigantic luxury homeware shop in the middle of Mayfair has been in business at the same location since 1827. The china, silver, crystal, and linens are either of the store's own design and manufacture or are simply the best that money can buy. Originally, customers here were mainly international royals and heads of state. The store still holds three royal warrants, but today anyone who can afford it can have their own bespoke set of china. If such luxury is beyond you, visit anyway for the shop's museum. Displays include a 7-foot-tall china elephant, made for Goode by Minton and exhibited at the Paris exhibition of 1888. There's also a sample of the plates Prince Charles designed for his own household. (⇨ Map A) ⊠ *19 S. Audley St., Mayfair, W1* ☎ *020/7499–2823* Ⓤ *Green Park.*

Clothing

London is one of the world's fashion capitals, and every designer you've ever heard of is available. But it's London's eccentric street style that gives fashion here its edge. London women may not look as soignée as French or Italian women, but many are daring and colorful fashion risktakers. This is where the trends that show up on the European catwalks really begin.

What makes London clothes shopping so much fun—for both men and women—is that you can buy high-quality traditional British clothing, bespoke tailoring, today's best fashion labels, delicious vintage clothing, and outrageous directional street style without traveling farther than a couple of Tube stops.

ACCESSORIES **Accessorize.** Shrewd shoppers head here for the latest high-fashion items
★ at low prices. Beady bags, feathery jewels, devoré scarves—clever copies of each season's catwalk versions reach these stores fast. Part of the same group that owns Monsoon, they tend to promote the same color palettes. There are branches everywhere, but the shop across from Monsoon on the King's Road in Chelsea is particularly well stocked. (⇨ Maps A and F) ⊠ *102 King's Rd., Chelsea, SW3* ☎ *020/7591–0049* Ⓤ *Sloane Sq.*

★ **Anya Hindmarch.** Exquisite leather bags and witty, printed canvas totes are what made Hindmarch famous. Her designs are sold at Harrods and Harvey Nichols, but the real pleasure lies in her store, where you can see her complete collection of bags, shoes, and printed sweaters and tees. (⇨ Map F) ⊠ *15–17 Pont St., Belgravia, SW1* ☎ *020/7838–9177* Ⓤ *Sloane Sq., Knightsbridge.*

★ **Bernstock Speirs.** Makers of colorful modern, street-smart pull-on and trilby hats, Paul Bernstock and Thelma Speirs have collected Madonna, Alicia Keys, and James Brown into their cult following. (⇨ Map H) ⊠ *234 Brick La., Spitalfields/East End, E2* ☎ *020/7739–7385* Ⓤ *Old St., Bethnal Green.*

19

Connolly. The leather made by this elite company is the essence of Rolls-Royce elegance and Ferrari flash. Drivers leave their vehicles to be made over inside, but you can content yourself with the accessories: a pair of leather driving gloves or a leather driving helmet and goggles. Prices are on a prestige basis—high—although you could settle for a smaller-statement souvenir belt or cuff links. The term "speaking with a plum in one's mouth" was created for the Jeevesian staff here. (⇨ Map A) ⊠ *41 Conduit St., Mayfair, W1* ☎ *020/7439–2510* Ⓤ *Oxford Circus, Bond St.*

James Lock & Co. Ltd. Need a silk opera hat, with a fitted leather box to match? A custom-made trilby or a traditional tweed flat cap? James Lock of St. James's has been making men's (and lately women's) hats from its cozy little shop since 1676. Claiming to be one of the world's oldest family-run businesses, they have dressed the heads of Beau Brummel, Oscar Wilde, General de Gaulle, Jackie Onassis, Salvador Dali, and Frank Sinatra. Most notably, they made Admiral Lord Nelson's famous bicorn hat. Customers custom measurements are taken on a circa 1850's contraption called a *conformateur* and kept on file forever. A full selection of classic and traditional styles is available, or you can take home a souvenir miniature of Nelson's hat. (⇨ Map A) ⊠ *6 St. James's St., St. James, SW1* ☎ *020/7930–5849* Ⓤ *Green Park, Piccadilly Circus.*

James Smith & Sons Ltd. This has to be the world's ultimate umbrella shop, and a must for anyone interested in real Victorian London. Even if bespoke walking sticks and umbrellas are not on your shopping list, it's hard to resist a family-owned business that has traded since 1835 at the same New Oxford Street corner. Most of the shop fittings—made by a full-time shop fitter employed by Mr. Smith—have not changed in 140 years. This is a genuine landmark. (⇨ Map C) ⊠ *Hazelwood House, 53 New Oxford St., Bloomsbury, WC1* ☎ *020/7836–4731* Ⓤ *Tottenham Court Road, Holborn.*

★ **Lulu Guinness.** Bags and shoes made from beads, colored silks, and the loveliest designs are the trademark here, as are styles reflecting an off-beat sense of humor. Guinness's store is equally girlish and fun (*Vogue* covers adorn a see-through floor), with a downstairs salon where you can take tea. With boutiques in Hollywood and New York, Ms. Guinness plans to "bag" an increasingly starry clientele—just watch Oscar night. (⇨ Map F) ⊠ *3 Ellis St., Chelsea, SW1* ☎ *020/7823–4828* Ⓤ *Sloane Sq.*

Mulberry. This is Britain's entry in the luxury and fashion leathergoods market. Mulberry makes covetable, top-quality leather bags, belts, wallets, and cases for all sorts of things (even cell phone, computer organizer, and laptop cases). Separates in fine wools, fine cotton shirts, and silk scarves and ties have widened the collection. But the brand's standout feature is the ever-changing, fashion-savvy range of leather colors. The boutique-size store remains at St. Christopher's Place; the larger, main store is at New Bond Street. (⇨ Map A) ⊠ *11–12 Gees Ct., St. Christopher's Pl., Mayfair, W1* ☎ *020/7493–2546* Ⓤ *Bond St.* ⊠ *41–42 New Bond St., Mayfair, W1* ☎ *020/7491–3900* Ⓤ *Bond St.*

Philip Treacy. Treacy's magnificent hats are annual showstoppers on Ladies Day at the Royal Ascot races and regularly grace the pages of *Harper's Bazaar.* Part Mad Hatter, part Cecil Beaton, Treacy's creations always guarantee a grand entrance. Only the most serious fashion plates and exhibitionist hat wearers need apply, truly: the atelier is open by appointment only. Those on a budget can shoot along to Debenhams department store on Oxford Street, where Treacy has a diffusion line. (⇨ Map F) ⊠ *69 Elizabeth St., Pimlico & Victoria, SW1* ☎ *020/7730–3992* Ⓤ *Victoria.*

★ **Swaine, Adeney, Brigg.** This shop has been selling practical supplies for country pursuits since 1750. Not just for the horsey set, the store has golf umbrellas, walking sticks, and hip flasks—all beautifully crafted and ingenious. On a frosty morning, you shouldn't be without the umbrella with a slim tipple-holder flask secreted inside the stick. Herbert Johnson, hatter, is housed downstairs. (⇨ Map A) ⊠ *54 St. James's St., St. James's, SW1* ☎ *020/7409–7277* Ⓤ *Piccadilly Circus.*

CHILDREN'S   British children's wear has never been a bargain, and nothing is changed
WEAR   there. But since Britain has become more integrated with Europe, kids'

gear is more fashionable. Gone are the days when young London mums asked their friends to bring home French, Italian, or American kids clothes from their vacations abroad. Several of the lower-price adult chains, including H&M, Next, and Zara, have cheap and cheerful kids lines. There are several Gap Kids shops around town and even the supermarket chains Asda and Tesco are getting into the act with popular, bargain selections. In selected Jigsaw branches at Westbourne Grove and the Fulham Road, Jigsaw Juniors include classics with a twist for tweenies. But if you're looking for something more than run of the mill, expect to pay for it.

Daisy & Tom. Cool kids love this magical King's Road emporium. While they're riding the carousel, cuddling soft toys, or having a haircut, parents can be checking out high-fashion, top-label children's togs from Kenzo, IKKS, and Polo. Shoe shopping, for newborns to 10-year-olds, can actually be fun, and the colorful, packed bookshop has got to make a reader out of the most reluctant child. There's a soda fountain, too. (⇨ Map F) ⊠ *181–183 King's Rd., Chelsea, SW3* ☎ *020/7352–5000* Ⓤ *Sloane Sq.*

Please Mum. This Knightsbridge shop (between Harrods and Harvey Nicks) *is* the business and has been since 1971. It's where the celebrity sprogs of rock stars and cinema vedettes, along with international mini princesses and princelings, get their designer kit. The store caters to infants, toddlers, and tweens. If dressing your child in Armani, Versace, Moschino Bambino, Roberto Cavalli, Evisu, D&G, and a host of others sounds like fun, head for this fashion classic. A second shop, across from Selfridges, has similar goods. (⇨ Map A and E) ⊠ *85 Knightsbridge, Knightsbridge, SW1* ☎ *020/7486—1380* Ⓤ *Knightsbridge* ⊠ *24 Orchard St., Oxford Street, W1* ☎ *020/7486—3399* Ⓤ *Bond St.*

Trotters. Trotters has the latest lines for parents who want to dress their darlings in traditional styles. The shop stocks all the trendy kids' labels and caters from top to toe (there's a hairdressing service, plus shoes). There are also videos, toys, and books to keep tempers cool. It's at the Sloane Square end of the King's Road near the big Peter Jones branch of the John Lewis Department Store group. (⇨ Map F) ⊠ *34 King's Rd., Chelsea, SW3* ☎ *020/7259–9620* Ⓤ *Sloane Sq.*

GENERAL **Aquascutum.** Known for its trenchcoat classics, Aquascutum also stocks men's and women's clothing influenced by traditional British style. They keep up with the times, just about, but are firmly on the safe side. A new collection by their house designers, Michael Herz and Graeme Fidler, is an attempt to bring a youthful flair to the line. In addition to their new Regent Street Showroom, you can see most of their collection at Harrods, Selfridges, and other big department stores around town. (⇨ Map A) ⊠ *100 Regent St., Soho, W1* ☎ *020/7675–8200* Ⓤ *Piccadilly Circus.*

Burberry. The store tries to evoke an English heritage environment, with mahogany closets and stacks of neatly folded merchandise adorned with the trademark "Burberry Check" tartan. In addition to being seen on those famous raincoat linings, the tartan graces scarves, umbrellas, and even pots of passion-fruit curd and tins of shortbread. If you like showing off labels, what could be better? (⇨ Maps A and E) ⊠ 2

19

Brompton Rd., Knightsbridge, SW1 ☎ *020/7839–5222* Ⓤ *Knightsbridge* ⊠ *21–23 New Bond St., Mayfair, W1* ☎ *020/7839–5222* Ⓤ *Piccadilly Circus.*

Dover Street Market. Rei Kawakubo of Comme des Garçons has created this year's *must-visit* shop. On six floors of serendipity you might find clothing for men and women, objets d'arts, furniture, jewelry, whatever— all of it influenced by that design partnership's unique avant-garde perspective. Fancy a pair of Levi's or Keds customized by Junya Watanabe? How about customized Fred Perry polos or a limited-edition eau de cologne wrapped in its own handknit Fair Isle sweater. You never know what you will find, which is half the fun. (⇨ Map A) ⊠ *17–18 Dover St., Mayfair, W1* ☎ *020/7518–0680* Ⓤ *Green Park.*

Favourbrook. Actually three neighboring shops in St. James's, Favourbrook tailors formal-occasion wear for the chap who likes his morning suit or tux with a slightly boho twist. Handmade vests, jackets, and dresses are crafted from embroidered silks, brocades, velvets, and satins. The shops sell ready-to-wear as well as made-to-measure. Womenswear is at 18 Piccadilly Arcade, men's accessories at 19–21 Piccadilly Arcade, while the main shop is on Jermyn Street itself. (⇨ Map A) ⊠ *55 Jermyn St., St. James's, W1* ☎ *020/7491–2337* Ⓤ *Piccadilly Circus.*

H & M. The inexpensive clothing for men, women, and children here is virtually disposable casual wear. It's absolutely "in the moment" on first wearing—every season, top designers do a line (Stella McCartney, Karl Lagerfeld)—but one pass through the washing machine and the moment is over. There are branches all over, but the Covent Garden shop carries the best selection. (⇨ Map D) ⊠ *27–29 Long Acre, Covent Garden, WC2* ☎ *020/7395–1250* Ⓤ *Covent Garden.*

Jaeger. A real London classic, Jaeger has been making conservative but stylish clothing for men and women since the mid-19th century. It's particularly good for coats, suits, and separates. Founded around a Victorian "scientific" theory about the healthy properties of animal fibers (wool, camel's hair, silk, vicuña), the label has long since embraced a more modern approach. But its woolens and silks remain very collectible. There are several London branches. The King's Road store carries both the men's and women's lines. (⇨ Map F) ⊠ *145 King's Rd., Chelsea, SW3* ☎ *020/7352–1122* Ⓤ *Sloane Sq.*

★ **Jigsaw.** Popular with women in their twenties through forties, Jigsaw sells separates that don't sacrifice quality to fashion. There's a men's branch in Mayfair, and other branches around town. Kids get in on the act, too, with their own line, Jigsaw Junior. (⇨ Map A) ⊠ *126–127 New Bond St., Mayfair, W1* ☎ *020/7491–4484* Ⓤ *Bond St.*

★ **Junky Styling.** Gwen Stefani is a fan of outrageous designers Annika Sanders and Kerry Seager, who use their shop to create and showcase "deconstructed," limited-edition clothing. They started by recycling tailored clothes, for men and women, into wild clubbing outfits for themselves, and the business grew from there. New menswear, women's wear, and accessories blur the fine line between standing out in the crowd and sticking out like a sore thumb. Their one-off Wardrobe Surgery service will recycle your old threads into something wild and original. (⇨ Map H)

✉ *12 Dray Walk, Old Truman Brewery, 91–95 Brick La., Spitalfields/ East End, E1* ☎ *020/7247–1883* Ⓤ *Old St., Bethnal Green.*

★ **The Laden Showroom.** Victoria Beckham and Noel Gallagher are among the celebs who regularly check out new talent at this East End showroom for young designers. The store retails the work of 40 new designers, some selling no more than 12 items—so the look you find is likely to be exclusive. (⇨ Map H) ✉ *103 Brick La., Spitalfields/East Eng, E1* ☎ *020/7247–2431* Ⓤ *Aldgate East.*

Margaret Howell. British tailoring and traditional clothing styles combine with new fabrics and contemporary colors. Howell does floral prints and ruffles for women and uses soft, crumpled luxury fabrics for men. Recent ventures with Anglepoise, Erco, and several other manufacturers have brought the Margaret Howell look to contemporary housewares as well. (⇨ Map B) ✉ *34 Wigmore St., Soho, W1* ☎ *020/7009–9009* Ⓤ *Oxford Circus.*

★ **Paul Smith.** British classics with colorful and irreverent twists define Paul Smith's collections for both women and men. Beautifully tailored men's suits in exceptional fabrics might sport flamboyant linings or unusual detailing. Women's lines tend to take familiar and traditional British ideas and turn them on their heads with humor and color. In 2005 Smith added to his London presence with a home-furnishings shop in Mayfair. (⇨ Map D) ✉ *40–44 Floral St., Covent Garden, WC2* ☎ *020/ 7379–7133* Ⓤ *Covent Garden.*

★ **River Island.** With branches throughout the country, this chain targets young and dedicated fashion followers. Despite it's tweedy-sounding name, the look here is rock chick/clubland diva. Men's fashions are a bit more casual but equally trendsetting. There are 14 London shops, including one at Marble Arch, but the Oxford Circus superstore carries the entire line. (⇨ Map B) ✉ *301–306 Oxford St., Soho, W1* ☎ *020/ 7799–4018* Ⓤ *Oxford Circus.*

★ **Topshop.** This London standby has successfully made the transition from what the British call "cheap and cheerful" to a genuine fashion hotspot at affordable prices. Clothing is geared to the younger end of the market (although women who are young at heart will find plenty of wearable clothing here) and the aim is to copy catwalk trends as fast as possible. Every season, a changing selection of front-of-the-pack young designers do small collections, and buyers cruise the end-of-term design shows at St. Martin's School of Design for the next big thing. Topman brings the same fashion approach to clothing for younger men. (⇨ Map B) ✉ *214 Oxford St., Soho, W1* ☎ *020/7636–7700* Ⓤ *Oxford Circus.*

Zara. Zara has swept across the world (the price tags carry 25 flags and related prices) and has won a firm position in London. It's not hard to see why. The style is young and snappy, with clothes sorted into color groupings for work and play. Prices are unbelievably low, but this is disposable style. The new store at Duke of York's Square in Chelsea covers the company's entire range with a men's shop and a huge lower floor devoted to teens and snazzy kids' clothes. Accessories, shoes, bags, and outerwear are all coordinated so that every season's look turns the whole store into one, huge design statement. (⇨ Map F) ✉ *65 Duke of York's Sq., King's Rd., Chelsea, SW3* ☎ *020/7901–8700* Ⓤ *Sloane Sq.*

19

MENSWEAR Except for Jigsaw, all the stores listed in General Clothing have good selections of menswear, especially the sublime Paul Smith. The huge men's department in Harrods is one of the store's best, and Selfridges is another good choice with a big selection of designer men's suits. London's Savile Row tailors are still the spot where a man orders a bespoke suit once he has really "arrived." But with European designers like Armani and the moderately priced Emporio Armani making inroads, styles, even on this bastion of British traditionalism, are noticeably loosening up. Ozwald Boateng, with his sharp designs, colorful suitings and linings, is typical of the new wave of bespoke tailors. Those with more flash than cash should hotfoot to the trendsetting fashion chains: Topman, River Island, and Zara.

Bamford & Sons. The men's and boys' wear at Bamford & Sons combines the British heritage of tailoring and fabrics with a suave modernity. Dashing city wear, romantically nonchalant country clothes, plus fine leather and cashmere accessories are all available. (⇨ Map G) ⊠ *The Old Workshop, 79–81 Ledbury Rd., Notting Hill, W11* ☎ *020/ 7792–9350* Ⓤ *Notting Hill Gate* ⊠ *31 Sloane Sq. Chelsea, SW1* ☎ *020/ 7881–8010* Ⓤ *Sloane Sq.*

Gieves and Hawkes. One of the grandest of grand old names for London bespoke tailoring, this company made its name outfitting Britain's Royal Military officers and still supplies bespoke military uniforms. An alternative that costs about a quarter of the price, personal tailoring is a new four-week, made-to-measure service for men and women. Before you rush out for a bargain, consider that prices for a two-piece suit range from £695 to £1,600. (⇨ Map A) ⊠ *1 Savile Row, Mayfair, W1* ☎ *020/ 7434–2001* Ⓤ *Piccadilly Circus.*

Hackett. Started as a posh thrift shop, Hackett once recycled cricket flannels, hunting pinks, Oxford brogues, and similar British wear. Now it makes its own attire, and it has become a genuine—and very good—gentlemen's outfitter. (⇨ Map E) ⊠ *Main store: 137–138 Sloane St., Knightsbridge, SW1* ☎ *020/7730–3331* Ⓤ *Sloane Sq.*

Kilgour, French & Stanbury. Classic Savile Row tailoring has been updated with a luxury, ready-to-wear brand launched in 1998. The shop defines the essence of "Savile Row chic" as "lean shoulders, clean chest definition, and waisted silhouette" and does its best to provide it. Bespoke services include equestrian clothes and shirts as well as suits, and an "entry level bespoke" to ease customers into the concept. (⇨ Map A) ⊠ *8 Savile Row, Mayfair, W1* ☎ *020/7734–6905* Ⓤ *Piccadilly Circus.*

★ **Ozwald Boateng.** Ozwald Boateng's made-to-measure suits with their bright colors (even the more conservative suits sport bright silk linings), luxurious fabrics, and leading-edge styling used to be worn by rock and

---

PINKU WAISHATSU

The story goes that when Japanese businessmen first adopted Western-style white shirts they called them *waishatsu*, a name that eventually covered business shirts of any color. The British firm, Thomas Pink of Jermyn Street, quickly dominated the Japanese market. So, for a long time, a really fine business shirt in Japan was called a *pinku waishatsu*.

Bespoke London

HAVING ANYTHING made to order used to be an upper-class distinction in London. One had one's tailor, one's milliner, one's dressmaker, and so forth. Things are more democratic these days, but you can still have a remarkable number of things, besides Savile Row suits and shirts, custom-made.

Dress bespoke top to toe and inside out with undies from the Queen's corsetier, **Rigby & Peller**; hats from **Philip Treacy** and **James Lock**; suits and shirts—for both men and women—from **Gieves and Hawkes; Ozwald Boateng; Kilgour, French & Stanbury;** or **Turnbull & Asser.** Finish the look with bespoke or handmade shoes from **Caroline Groves, John Lobb,** or **Rupert Sanderson;** an umbrella or walking stick from **James**

Smith & Sons; and a bespoke briefcase from **Swaine, Adeney, Brigg.** Country leisure pursuits are looked after at **Farlows,** for bespoke fishing flies and lures; **Holland & Holland** for handmade English sporting guns, or **Biondi** for that important sunbathing necessity—a made-to-measure bikini. The ultimate bespoke service may be the one at **Thomas Goode,** where they'll help you design your own china pattern and produce a fine bone china service to your specifications.

If all this seems a bit astronomical for your purse, you can always pop into a branch of **Whittard of Chelsea.** They'll help you create your own blend of coffee or tea and pack it nicely for the trip home.

---

clubland luminaries. But the London scene has loosened up considerably since he opened his Savile Row atelier, and now any chap with enough alpha male confidence to cut a dash covets a Boateng (pronounced Bwateng) suit. If your wallet doesn't reach as far as bespoke, check out the ready-to-wear collection, along with accessories and scent, on Vigo Street. (⇨ Map A) ✉ *12A Savile Row, Mayfair, W1* ☎ *0870-/777–1377* Ⓤ *Piccadilly Circus.* (⇨ Map A) ✉ *9 Vigo St., Mayfair, W1* ☎ *020/ 7437–0620* Ⓤ *Piccadilly Circus.*

★ **Son of a Stag.** This line of outrageous clubland gear is available only here and in Milan. The style is aimed at young men with a sense of adventure who like to show up wearing something completely unexpected. (⇨ Map H) ✉ *The Old Truman Brewery, 9 Dray Walk, Brick La., Spitalfields, East End, E1* ☎ *0789/994–4444* Ⓤ *Liverpool St., Aldgate East.*

★ **Thomas Pink.** The firm still makes some of the best dress shirts—for men and women, around. Bespoke shirts for men are available at the Jermyn Street branch. (⇨ Map A) ✉ *85 Jermyn St., St. James's, SW1* ☎ *020/ 7930–6364* Ⓤ *Green Park, Piccadilly Circus.*

★ **Turnbull & Asser.** This is *the* custom shirtmaker, dripping exclusivity from every fiber. Twenty-eight separate measurements are taken and the cloth, woven to their specifications, comes in 1,000 different patterns— the cottons feel as good as silk. The first order must be for a minimum of six shirts, for around £140 each. There are less expensive, though still exquisite, ready-to-wear shirts available as well as jackets, cashmeres, suits, ties, and accessories. (⇨ Map A) ✉ *71–72 Jermyn St., St. James's, W1* ☎ *020/7808–3000* Ⓤ *Piccadilly Circus.*

19

WOMEN'S WEAR   As one of the world's great fashion capitals, London has shops to dress you in style—whether your style is rummage or royal, trendy or traditional. High-street chains like H&M, Top Shop, Next, and River Island take aim at the young, wild, and slim; John Lewis and Jaeger provide classics for the more sophisticated; and fashion-oriented department stores—Debenham, Harvey Nichols, Harrods, Selfridges, Liberty, Fenwick—cater for women of all ages and tastes.

★ **Agent Provocateur.** Created by Vivienne Westwood's son, these shops purvey sexy, naughty-but-nice lingerie in gorgeous fabrics and lace. Locations say a lot, and this retailer has branches in the almost-red-light area of Soho, around the corner from the Bank of England, and in stylish familyland Notting Hill. Selections are available in Selfridges and at Heathrow's Terminal 4 as well. (⇨ Map E) ✉ *16 Pont St., Knightsbridge, SW1* ☎ *020/7235–0229* Ⓤ *Knightsbridge, Sloane Sq.*

★ **Agnès B.** The chic and gamine, understated French clothing emphasizes simple, timeless pieces. Prices are mid-range, and given the level of quality, good value for the money. Sizing tends to the flatter, slimmer-hipped French ideal. There are various branches around London.(⇨ Map E) ✉ *111 Fulham Rd., Brompton Cross, SW3* ☎ *020/7225–3477* Ⓤ *S. Kensington.*

★ **Bershka.** The same Spanish company that has opened Zara shops all over the world is aiming for a younger, more street-savvy girl with Bershka. Think Bjork crossed with gypsies and you might be close—lots of bright colors and embroideries in unlikely places, light-hearted and full of surprises. (⇨ Map B) ✉ *221–223 Oxford St., Marylebone, W1* ☎ *020/7025–6160* Ⓤ *Oxford Circus.*

★ **Betsey Johnson.** She may have seen the back of 60, but designer Betsey Johnson has never outgrown her girly style. Youthful sportswear, dresses, clubbing gear, and party clothes look like they've been pulled together out of scraps of lace and tulle from Mommy's sewing box—lots of fun for the young at heart. (⇨ Map E) ✉ *106 Draycott Ave., ground fl., Brompton Cross, SW3* ☎ *020/7591–0005* Ⓤ *S. Kensington.*

★ **Betty Jackson.** A low-key fixture on the London fashion scene since the early 1980s, Betty Jackson uses beautiful fabrics and judicious layering and shaping to create modern yet timeless clothes that manage to look wonderful on women of any age. Her knitwear and jackets have a subtle Britishness. Look for her designs in Debenhams and in the Autograph collection at some branches of Marks & Spencer. (⇨ Map E) ✉ *311 Brompton Rd., Brompton Cross, SW3* ☎ *020/7589–7884* Ⓤ *S. Kensington.*

★ **Biondi.** London's only made-to-measure bikini service is available at this colorful resort-wear shop. Biondi staff will develop a bikini with a cut, fit, and design that's perfect for you—prices start at £150. The ready-to-wear swimwear and resort collection is inspired by South American, African, and Eastern motifs. The shop is a few doors away from the legendary Manolo Blahnik shop in Chelsea. (⇨ Map F) ✉ *55B Old Church St., Chelsea, SW3* ☎ *020/7349–1111* Ⓤ *Sloane Sq.*

Brora. The taste temperature is cool and conservative in this cashmere emporium for women and kids. There are dressed-up camisoles, sweaters, and cardigans; practical trousers; and noncashmere items such as picnic blankets and wash bags. Prices are surprisingly reasonable for such high-fashion products. There are branches in Notting Hill and Marylebone. (⇨ Map F) ⊠ *344 King's Rd., Chelsea, SW3* ☎ *020/7352–3697* Ⓤ *Sloane Sq.*

★ **Browns.** This shop—actually a series of small shops on South Molton Street—was a pioneer designer boutique in the 1980s and continues to talent spot the newest and best around. You may find the windows showcasing the work of top graduates from this year's student shows or displaying well-established designers such as Donna Karan, Yohji Yamamoto, Dries Van Noten, Clements Ribeiro, Anne Demeulemeester, or Hussein Chalayan. Browns has its own label as well as a bargain outlet at No. 50. (⇨ Map A) ⊠ *23–27 S. Molton St., Mayfair, W1* ☎ *020/7491–7833* Ⓤ *Bond St.*

Collette Dinnigan. One look at Dinnigan's highly ornamented, ultrafeminine signature logo and you should have a good idea of the kind of clothes she designs. The Australian designer's Chelsea Green shop looks a bit like a boudoir, complete with French chandelier. Inside, you'll find special-occasion dresses that tend toward the short and filmy, with hand embroidery and hand-applied beads. Think very delicate, very sexy, and very expensive. Halle Berry and Elle McPherson are among her fans. (⇨ Map F) ⊠ *26 Cale St., Chelsea, SW3* ☎ *020/7589–9686* Ⓤ *Sloane Sq.*

Egg. Almost hidden in the mews behind Harvey Nichols, this shop is the brainchild of Maureen Doherty, once Issey Miyake's right-hand person. She has described her customer as someone who likes clothes but is bored with fashion. Breezy, soft styles in silks and Indian cottons appeal equally to classy twentysomethings and women 50-plus. The shop is a former Victorian dairy. (⇨ Map F) ⊠ *36 Kinnerton St., Knightsbridge, SW1* ☎ *020/7235–9315* Ⓤ *Knightsbridge.*

Frockbrokers. A cross between a discount outlet and what Europeans call a "dress agency," this shop deals in designer clothing, jewelry, and accessories, and maternity and babywear that is usually new but occasionally "pre-owned." Unwanted designer presents, samples, press, and film pieces mingle with current and end-of-season bargains from the designers of the moment—or even the minute. If you love to browse for bargains and surprises, you'll have fun at Frockbrokers. (⇨ Map H) ⊠ *115 Commercial St., Spitalfields/East End, E1* ☎ *020/7247–4222* Ⓤ *Liverpool St.*

Joseph. Movie stars, models, and well-heeled women have frequented Joseph's many Knightsbridge and Chelsea shops for years. Known for a kind of luxe minimalism, Joseph Ettedgui's designs are simple, chic, and executed in beautiful fabrics. In particular, there are stylish women who swear by Joseph's bottom-flattering trousers. There's a menswear shop across the road at 74 Fulham Road and a great sale shop at 53 Kings Road. (⇨ Map E) ⊠ *77 Fulham Rd., Brompton Cross, SW3* ☎ *020/ 7823–9500* Ⓤ *S. Kensington.*

★ **Koh Samui.** Named for an exclusive Thai resort, this shop stocks designer clothes for the kind of young, elegant woman that thinks nothing of flying there for a week's detox at the drop of a hat. Designers of the mo-

19

ment are Tracey Feith, Christa David, Dries Van Noten, and the reborn Balenciaga label. Watch the pages of *Vogue* to see what's in stock tomorrow. (⇨ Map D) ⊠ *65 Monmouth St., Covent Garden, WC2* ☎ *020/7240–4280* Ⓤ *Covent Garden.*

★ **Mango.** Mango promises to dress and style the young, urban woman, from top to toe (including dresses, separates, accessories, and fragrance) in a global look. Of the three London stores, Oxford Street probably has the biggest selection. Look for Mango on Neal Street near Covent Garden and on Regent Street as well. (⇨ Map B) ⊠ *233 Oxford St., Marylebone, W1* ☎ *020/7534–3505* Ⓤ *Oxford Circus.*

★ **MiMi.** This tiny shop in the developing fashion enclave at the far end of the King's Road packs in more designers per square meter than you can shake your Christian Laboutin–shod foot at. Mimi Cherry picks the collections of the best established and newest designers to fill the two floors of her jewelbox of a shop. She's usually on hand to offer personal guidance about what will suit you. This is a relaxed, friendly place to shop for ready-to-wear designer gear. (⇨ Map F) ⊠ *250 Kings Rd., Chelsea, SW3* ☎ *020/7351–7192* Ⓤ *Sloane Sq.*

Nicole Farhi. Busy women willing to invest in quality value Nicole Farhi's softly tailored, functional dresses and separates. The style manages to be contemporary yet timeless, making these standbys in many a working-woman's wardrobe. The store has numerous locations around the city; the men's collection is available at a branch in Covent Garden. At the New Bond Street location, the downstairs in-store restaurant, **Nicole's** (☎ 020/7499–8408), is not just somewhere to resuscitate between purchases: Ms. Farhi designed the space and the menu to her own taste, and it's an extension of the fashion statement, a hot spot for lunching fashionistas who like to be seen. It's wise to reserve ahead. (⇨ Map A) ⊠ *158 New Bond St., Mayfair, W1* ☎ *020/7499–8368* Ⓤ *Bond St.* ☞ *Men's Collection:* ⊠ *11 Floral St., Covent Garden, WC2* ☎ *020/ 7497–8713* Ⓤ *Covent Garden.*

Rigby & Peller. Those who love luxury lingerie shop here for brands like La Perla and Gottex, as well as the corsetiere's own line. If the right fit eludes you, and you fancy being fitted by the Queen's corsetiere, have one made-to-measure. Most of the young royal and aristo women buy here, not just because the store holds the royal appointment, but because the quality and service are excellent and much friendlier than you might expect. (⇨ Map E) ⊠ *2 Hans Rd., Knightsbridge, SW3* ☎ *020/ 7589–9293* Ⓤ *Knightsbridge* ⊠ *22A Conduit St., Mayfair, W1* ☎ *020/ 7491–2200* Ⓤ *Oxford St.*

Vivienne Westwood. This is where it all started: the Pompadour-punk ball gowns, Lady Hamilton vest coats, and foppish landmark getups are the core of Westwood's first boutique in Chelsea, where you can still buy ready-to-wear under the sign of the spinning clock. The designer still represents the apex of high-style British couture, and the Davies Street boutique sells the Gold Label line of intoxicatingly glamorous creations: ready-to-wear or made-to-measure. At the Conduit Street branch in Mayfair, the story is the sharper Red Line: hot, pared-down catwalk versions. Menswear is also sold here. (⇨ Map A) ⊠ *6 Davies St., Mayfair, W1*

☎ *020/7629–3757* Ⓤ *Bond St.* ☞ *Original boutique:* ✉ *430 King's Rd., Chelsea, SW3* ☎ *020/7352–6551* Ⓤ *Sloane Sq. or Earl's Court* ✉ *44 Conduit St., Mayfair, W1* ☎ *020/7439–1109* Ⓤ *Bond St.*

Design

Britain has always encouraged design and applied arts. London, with its many design colleges, is a magnet for artisans and craftspeople in glass, textiles, jewelry making, ceramics, metal, leather, and woodwork. The Crafts Council Gallery Shop on Pentonville Road in Islington is a great place for an overview of modern, extremely imaginative, and often challenging handmade housewares, objets d'art, jewelry, and other design items.

★ **Colefax & Fowler.** The virtual birthplace of the English-country-house look, this is one of the most beautiful interior decorating shops in London. John Fowler, Lady Colefax, and Virginia-born Nancy Lancaster created the cozy yet grand style. Their legacy is preserved here in wallpapers and assorted antique accents. This shop is really more geared to interior design projects, but if you want to make your apartment back home into a mini-Chatsworth, be sure to stop here, if only to soak up the style. (⇨ Map A) ✉ *39 Brook St., Mayfair, W1* ☎ *020/7493–2231* ⊘ *Closed weekends* Ⓤ *Bond St.*

Contemporary Applied Arts. Expect to see quite a range of work by designers and craftspeople. Regular shows and exhibitions display everything from glassware and jewelry to furniture and lighting. (⇨ Map B) ✉ *2 Percy St., Bloomsbury, W1* ☎ *020/7436–2344* Ⓤ *Tottenham Court Rd.*

★ **Contemporary Ceramics.** A co-op of some of Britain's best ceramic artists, this modern store carries a wide spectrum of pottery, from beautifully tactile and practical housewares to avant-garde sculpture. A good selection of books on the subject is also available. (⇨ Map D) ✉ *7 Marshall St., Soho, W1* ☎ *020/7437–7605* Ⓤ *Oxford Circus.*

Crafts Council Gallery Shop. Within this shop lies a microcosmic selection of British craftspeople's work: jewelry, glass, ceramics, textiles, wood, and toys. The Crafts Council will also help you source individual craftspeople and artisans to arrange commissions. A gallery at the V&A Museum, long popular, closed in 2005, but is scheduled to reopen as a newly designed gallery in the spring 2006.(⇨ Map C) ✉ *44A Pentonville Rd., Islington, N1* ☎ *020/7806–2559* Ⓤ *Angel.*

Designers Guild. Though it sounds like a gallery for multiple designers, Designers Guild is actually the cheeky name of Tricia Guild's interior-design showcase, which occupies a corner in the fashionable enclave at the far end of the King's Road. Her fabrics, wallpapers, paints, furniture, and bed linens have inspired several decades worth of home owners and apartment dwellers, and her soft-furnishings book has taught many a budget-conscious do-it-yourselfer how to reupholster a sofa or make lined draperies. (⇨ Map F) ✉ *267–271 and 275–277 King's Rd., Chelsea, SW3* ☎ *020/7351–5775* Ⓤ *Sloane Sq.*

Flower Space. Step back in time when you enter this Portobello Road gallery and shop. The place is jam-packed with original 1960s and '70s

19

furniture, lighting fixtures, film posters, and objects for the home. Witty, colorful kitsch objects sit side by side with cool modernist furniture. Classic glassware, vintage collectibles, and objects from the decades that taste forgot—the 1960s Grundig speakers, a pair of cubes on sticks—have to be seen to be believed. (⇨ Map G) ✉ *301 Portobello Rd., Notting Hill, W11* ☎ *020/8968–9966* Ⓤ *Ladbroke Grove.*

Kelly Hoppen. Internationally regarded interior designer Kelly Hoppen's work has graced British Airways first class lounges, the Cartier Polo Marquee at Windsor, hotels, yachts, and private homes. In 2002, after 20 years as a top people's designer, she opened her flagship store on the Fulham Road, offering a combination of individually sourced items—antiques, art objects—as well as her own lines of bedlinens, furniture, fabrics, carpets, and paints. (⇨ Map F) ✉ *175–177 Fulham Rd., Brompton Cross, SW3* ☎ *020/7351–1910* Ⓤ *S. Kensington.*

★ **Lesley Craze Gallery.** Craze has cornered a design market in a fashionable spot on the edge of the city and filled it with jewelry by some 100 young British designers (fashion editors source upcoming talent here for their glossy spreads). In 2004 the separate textiles gallery was added to create a unified experience. With 40 textile artists represented, this is London's only gallery specializing in contemporary textiles. Prices are remarkably reasonable. (⇨ Map C) ✉ *33–35a Clerkenwell Green, East End, EC1* ☎ *020/7251–9200* Ⓤ *Farringdon.*

Linley. Is Viscount David Linley really, as some say, one of today's finest furniture designers? Or is it simply that he's the Queen's only nephew? It doesn't really matter. What does is that his work in wood is beautiful, covetable, and definitely the heirlooms of the future. His desks, chairs, and chests of drawers have one foot in the 18th century, another in the 21st. His sculptural furniture is often decorated with marquetry or parquetry—patterns or pictures worked in fine veneers. The large pieces are suitably expensive, but small desk accessories and objets d'art are also available. In 2005 Linley opened a new shop in Mayfair. (⇨ Map F) ✉ *60 Pimlico Rd., Pimlico and Victoria, SW1* ☎ *020/7730–7300* Ⓤ *Sloane Sq.* ✉ *46 Albemarle St., Mayfair, W1* ☎ *020/7290–1410* Ⓤ *Green Park.*

London Glassblowing Workshop. Visitors to Peter Layton's workshop can feel the heat of molten glass as they watch creative glassblowers and designers at work. In addition to Layton, a team of glassblowers produce their own work for sale or commission at the studio. For £250 you can sign up for a full-day lesson in glass-blowing. In addition to domestic pieces, Layton's glass work includes monumental sculpture and architechtural commissions. ■ TIP➔ Other craftspeople, printmakers, and artists work in the industrial area known as Leathermarket, south of London Bridge, so it's worth having a nose around to see what you can find. (⇨ Map C) ✉ *7 The Leathermarket, Weston St., South Bank, SE1* ☎ *020/ 7403–2800* Ⓤ *London Bridge.*

OXO Tower. Many varied artisans have to pass rigorous selection procedures to set up in the prime riverside workshops where they make, display, and sell their work. The workshops are glass-walled, and you're welcome to explore, even if you're just browsing. You can commission pieces, too—anything from a cushion cover to custom-made jewelry, furniture, and sculpture. There are 23 studios in all, spread over two floors, as well as exhibitions at Bargehouse and at *the.gallery@oxo*. The OXO Tower Brasserie & Restaurant on the top floor is noisy and overpriced, but with its fantastic view across the river, it's worth popping up for a drink. There's also a public terrace where you can take in the view. (⇨ Map C) ✉ *Bargehouse St., South Bank, SE1* ☎ *020/7401–2255* Ⓤ *Southwark.*

Themes & Variations. The name encapsulates the selection of styles and items found here, ranging from postwar to new-wave furniture, lighting, and decorative arts. Operated as a gallery, with changing exhibitions, you may find Master Glassworks by Yoichi Ohira, a collection of modernist furniture classics by the Italian MIM group or American Paul Evans, a selection of Georg Jensen silver jewelry, or a ceramic sculpture by 1950s Italian artist Professor Patterino. If you have a modernist space to fill, visit this gallery to wallow in the genre. (⇨ Map G) ✉ *231 Westbourne Grove, Notting Hill, W11* ☎ *020/7727–5531* Ⓤ *Notting Hill Gate.*

Food Halls & Stores

London excels at posh nosh. The selection has gotten even bigger with European integration. Ordinary Brits travel regularly to Europe now and expect their local supermarket to carry the foods they've tasted abroad. Many of London's finest food stores have been around for generations though. The Food Halls at Harrods are internationally famous, almost as much for the beautiful displays and ceramic-tile ceilings as for the packaged teas, chocolates, biscuits, fresh foods, and game. Don't miss the legendary fish displays. Selfridges is less daunting but more international in its selection. There are ingredients from around the world and a good kosher department—their man-size salt-beef sandwiches are a must. Marks & Spencer has made such a name for its food in recent years that it has opened a chain of M&S Simply Food stores. Look for them everywhere. Their packaged shortbreads, chocolates, and bottled sauces are great take-home gifts.

L'Artisan du Chocolat. *The Guardian* has called this the best chocolate shop in the United Kingdom. High praise when there are so many vying for the title. Imagine truffles that look like a box of South Sea pearls, the chocolate subtly scented with red fruits and jasmine. There are artful new creations every season. Leave the kiddies at home; this shop is total wish fulfillment for grown-up chocolate lovers. (⇨ Map F) ✉ *89 Lower Sloane St., Chelsea, SW1* ☎ *020/7824–8365* Ⓤ *Sloane Sq.*

Berry Bros. & Rudd. Londoners are relatively well-informed about wine. There are wine shops in every shopping district, and all the supermarkets sell high-quality selections. So a wine shop has to be really special to rise above the rest. This one is and it does. A family-run wine business since 1698, "BBR" stores its vintage bottles and casks in vaulted cellars that are more than 300 years old. The staff is extremely knowledgeable and the level of service simply unsurpassed. This is the kind of wine merchant that a lord of the realm might have turned to, in the past, to ensure a quality stock at home. Most of them still do. If you're in London when BBR holds a wine-tasting—or a dinner with a wine producer—try to attend. Dates are published on the company's Web site. (⇨ Map A) ✉ *3 St. James's St., St. James's, SW1* ☎ *020/7396–9600* ⊕ *www.bbr.com* Ⓤ *Green Park.*

Charbonnel et Walker. Britain's master chocolatier since 1875, this Mayfair shop was serving up beautifully packaged, high-quality chocolates long before most of the fashionable new brands appeared. Specializing in traditional sweets (violet and rose petal creams, for example), they will spell out a loved one's name, or any other message, in foil-wrapped chocolates around the edge of a huge, circular box; or fill up a flowered hatbox of chocs for the theater. ■ TIP➡ Some of their "drawing room" boxes are real works of art, and their drinking chocolate–coarsely grated fine chocolate in a tin–is worth carrying home in a suitcase. (⇨ Map A) ✉ *1 the Royal Arcade, 28 Old Bond St., Mayfair, W1* ☎ *020/7491–0939* Ⓤ *Green Park.*

The Chocolate Society. You can taste as well as buy at the Chocolate Society's shop—and you don't even have to be a member. Hot chocolate served in their small café contains 40 grams of pure chocolate. In addition to a wide choice of bonbons, truffles, and bars, the shop sells the Society's brownies, ice cream, and milk shakes. Yum. (⇨ Map F) ✉ *36 Elizabeth St., Pimlico and Victoria, SW1* ☎ *020/7259–9222* Ⓤ *Victoria, Sloane Sq.*

FodorsChoice   **Fortnum & Mason.** Although it's the Queen's grocer, this store is, para-
★   doxically, the most egalitarian of gift shops; it has plenty of irresistibly packaged luxury foods, stamped with the gold BY APPOINTMENT crest, for less than £5. Try the teas, preserves, blocks of chocolate, tins of pâté, or a box of Duchy Originals oatcakes—like Paul Newman, the Prince of Wales has gone into the retail food business. Stop for tea in the Patio Restaurant, overlooking the Food Hall. It's reasonably priced and a favorite with celebrity gents. (⇨ Map A) ✉ *181 Piccadilly, St. James's, W1* ☎ *020/7734–8040* Ⓤ *Piccadilly Circus.*

Neal's Yard Dairy. NYD favors a traditional approach to small independent British cheese makers. In a cobbled "yard" with neighboring natural and organic shops, you can try cheeses with names that evoke the countryside, such as Cornish Yarg and Sussex Golden Cross. Good baked breads are also sold in the Neal's Yard Bakery here. (⇨ Map D) ✉ *17 Shorts Gardens, Covent Garden, WC2* ☎ *020/7240–5700* Ⓤ *Covent Garden.*

★ **Paxton & Whitfield.** This is the most venerable of London's cheese shops, in business for more than 200 years. The fabulous aromas come from some of the world's greatest cheeses stacked on the shelves—in rounds, in boxes, and on straw, but always ready to be tasted. Whichever cheese is in season and ripe for eating is on display for sampling, and the staff is ready to help you pick the best wine to serve with it. (⇨ Map A) ✉ *93 Jermyn St., St. James's, SW1* ☎ *020/7930–0259* Ⓤ *Piccadilly Circus.*

★ **Rococo.** Chantal Coady writes, eats, and lives for chocolate. Vegetable fats are forbidden words in this cocoa fantasyland, and there are interesting and offbeat additions to the main chocolate recipe, such as essence of Earl Grey, thyme, pepper, and chili (remarkably tasty). There's also a branch in Marylebone. (⇨ Map F) ✉ *321 King's Rd., Chelsea, SW3*

☎ 020/7352–5857 Ⓤ *Sloane Sq.* ✉ *45 Marylebone High St., Marylebone, W1* ☎ 020/7935–7780 Ⓤ *Baker St.*

★ **The Spice Shop.** Birgit Erath set up a spice stall on Portobello Road as a weekend sideline while studying for a business degree in London. By the time she graduated, she had such a good business she opened her shop nearby. That was in the 1990s, and she hasn't looked back. Sourcing spices from all over the world, Birgit also creates her own blends and spice mixes. You can find any spice you can name among her usual stock of 2,500 products. (⇨ Map G) ✉ *1 Blenheim Crescent, Notting Hill, W11* ☎ 020/7221–4448 Ⓤ *Notting Hill Gate.*

The Vintage House. If whiskey is more to your taste than wine, you may want to visit the Vintage House, which has the country's largest selection of single malts, many notable for their age. In all, the shop carries 1,300 lines and is open late—to 11 PM most nights. (⇨ Map D) ✉ *42 Old Compton St., Soho, WC2* ☎ 020/7437–2592 Ⓤ *Piccadilly Circus, Leicester Sq.*

★ **Whittard of Chelsea.** If you're fussy about your coffee or tea, you need to visit Whittards, where they'll blend something for you if none of the on-hand blends hits the spot. Besides coffee and tea, you can buy chocolate (to eat or drink) along with high-quality coffee- and tea-making equipment, and trendy crockery. There are 120 stores in Britain, including 25 in London, so you're never far from a coffee fix. T-Zone shops on Carnaby Street and in Covent Garden sell only tea. (⇨ Map F) ✉ *184 King's Rd., Chelsea, SW3* ☎ 020/7376–4986 Ⓤ *Sloane Sq.*

Gifts

These selections are ideal for browsing and inspired gift-giving. They offer plenty of choice, a good range of prices, and the opportunity to find something different and special.

If you're hoping to find something particularly British, don't overlook London's museum shops. At the British Museum you might find reproductions of ancient Egyptian jewelry, or a dishcloth printed with the Rosetta Stone; at the Victoria & Albert look for Charles Rennie Mackintosh reproductions. The London Transport Museum sells transport models; the Natural History Museum has the largest selection of toy dinosaurs and real gemstones; the Science Museum carries models and items for would-be inventors, and the huge gift shop at the new Tate Modern on the South Bank is chock-a-block with books, posters, novelties, and art materials for BritArt lovers.

GENERAL **BBC Shop.** Whatever your favorite TV or radio show from the British Broadcasting Corporation, it's probably here in some form, from DVDs and computer games to books and toys. If you have a *Dr. Who* fan at home, this is the place to pick up a Tardis or an evil Dalek. Classic comedy by the Monty Python team shares shelf space with the latest giggles from *Little Britain.* (⇨ Map B) ✉ *50 Margaret St., Marylebone, W1* ☎ 020/7631–4523 Ⓤ *Oxford Circus.*

The Cross. This ultrachic Notting Hill/Holland Park cornucopia has something for everyone—even your pet pooch. Look for hedonistic, beautiful things: silk scarves, brocade bags, embroidered chinoiserie, fragrant candles, butterflies by Jade Jagger, and the kinds of toys and kiddie clothes that Gwyneth's little Apple might be wearing. (⇨ Map G) ⊠ *141 Portland Rd., Notting Hill, W11* ☎ *020/7727–6760* Ⓤ *Notting Hill Gate.*

General Trading Co. Known by its fans as the GTC, this eccentric shop is where aristocrats and royals place their wedding lists—not because the goods are expensive (though sometimes they can be) but because the gifts, furniture, and homewares are interesting, tempting, and usually one or two of a kind. The British Empire lives on here in goods that are sourced from the farthest corners of the world. ■ **TIP→ With quite a good selection of reasonably priced merchandise (alongside the astronomical), this shop is an amazing gallery of desirable things you don't need and never knew you wanted—but now can't live without.** (⇨ Map F) ⊠ *2 Symons St., Sloane Sq., Chelsea, SW3* ☎ *020/7730–0411* Ⓤ *Sloane Sq.*

★ **National Trust Gift Shop.** If you can't make it out to one of the country houses owned by the Trust, then this shop–information center in the old Blewcoats School is the next best thing. This "poor" school was built in the Georgian period for children by a local brewer. The infinitely original and covetable gifts include neat pots of conserves, chocolate, china, books, body-care products, and more, whose origins and design are based upon the Trust houses and estates around the nation. (⇨ Map F) ⊠ *23 Caxton St., Westminster, SW1* ☎ *020/7222–2877* Ⓤ *St. James's Park.*

Past Times. An enormous chain in Britain, this purveyor of all things nostalgic hasn't spread beyond France. Organized in period themes—Medieval, Celtic, Victoriana, Mackintosh and more—the shops sell a combination of reproductions (Celtic thistle pins for kilts) and *inspired-by* goods (jigsaw puzzles, calendars, and diaries). There's also a branch in the Covent Garden Market. (⇨ Map A) ⊠ *155 Regent St., Mayfair, W1* ☎ *08450/707–425* Ⓤ *Piccadilly Circus* ⊠ *19 Central Arcade, Covent Garden Market, Covent Garden, WC2* ☎ *08450/707–450* Ⓤ *Covent Garden.*

Soccerscene. At this mammoth temple to the world's most popular sport, you can grab any replica kit you care to mention (in Britain ask for your favorite team's "strip"). Beware of high prices. (⇨ Map D) ⊠ *56–57 Carnaby St., Soho, W1* ☎ *020/7439–0778* Ⓤ *Oxford Circus.*

The Tea House. Alongside the varieties of tea (including strange or rare brews like orchid, banana, Japanese Rice, and Russian Caravan) and a small selection of London cliché pots and caddies (London Bobby, taxi, bus, phone booth), there are beautiful, handcrafted or hand-painted teapots, Japanese ceramic tea sets, and sweet, "tea-for-one" pots that nest inside generous matching cups. All the teapots, accessories, and gadgets are sourced from the countries where tea is grown. (⇨ Map D) ⊠ *15A Neal St., Covent Garden, WC2* ☎ *020/7240–7539* Ⓤ *Covent Garden.*

PERFUMES &
COSMETICS
Both of London's most venerable perfumeries began life as barber shops. Mr. Floris brought his Mediterranean nose and perfumer's skill to London from Menorca, via Montpelier, 275 years ago. Mr. Penhaligon opened his shop about 135 years ago. Despite the advent of stylish new perfume and cosmetics shops, these grand old shops hold their own, and at least one, if not both, should be on the first time visitor's *must see* list.

Diptyque. Homes fragranced with candles and "burning essence" from this French luxury purveyor don't just smell lovely—they smell rich. Candles (available in 53 scents) in simple but elegant glass holders, spread subtle perfumes like Moss or Garden Mint. If you're fashion shopping in Notting Hill, be sure to drop in to this heady little shop. (⇨ Map G) ⊠ *195 Westbourne Grove, Notting Hill, W11* ☎ *020/7727–8673* Ⓤ *Notting Hill Gate.*

Fodor'sChoice
★
Floris. One of the most beautiful shops in London, Floris boasts gleaming glass and Spanish mahogany showcases (acquired from the Great Exhibition of 1851). Gift possibilities include swan's-down powder puffs, cut-glass bottles, and faux-tortoise shell combs that the shop has sold since the place opened in 1730. Queen Victoria used to dab her favorite Floris fragrance on her lace handkerchief. True to its origins as a barbershop, Floris makes scent for both men and women as well as shaving products. Look for beautifully packaged, intense bath essences and rose-scented mouthwash. (⇨ Map A) ⊠ *89 Jermyn St., St. James's, W1* ☎ *020/7930–2885* Ⓤ *Piccadilly Circus.*

Jo Malone. London's own passionate perfumer and cosmetician began blending scents and creams in the 1990s, and now has shops around the world. In addition to selling gorgeous products in discreet, modern packaging, the shops offer facials, treatments, and Fragrance Combining consultations. There are similar services at the 23 Brook Street Shop in Mayfair W1. (⇨ Map F) ⊠ *150 Sloane St., Chelsea, SW1* ☎ *020/ 7730–2100* Ⓤ *Sloane Sq.*

L'Artisan Parfumeur. Cognoscenti follow their noses to Chelsea Green, a tiny, hidden patch of grass north of the King's Road, for this tiny but very refined shop. A selection of highly original perfumes, candles, creams, and unusual scented trinkets (key chains with perfumed sachets, scented address books) might come in Wild Blackberry or Pineapple Creme, as well as floral, spicy, musk-based eau de parfums. (⇨ Map F) ⊠ *17 Cale St., Chelsea, SW3* ☎ *020/7352–4196* Ⓤ *Sloane Sq.*

Les Senteurs. An intimate, unglossy perfumery run by a French family, Les Senteurs sells some of the lesser-known, yet wonderfully timeless fragrances in town. Sample Creed, worn by Eugénie, wife of Emperor Napoléon III. (⇨ Map F) ⊠ *71 Elizabeth St., Pimlico and Victoria, SW1* ☎ *020/7730–2322* Ⓤ *Sloane Sq.*

Lush. This global favorite is crammed with fresh, pure, and wacky handmade cosmetics and bath products. Angels on Bare Skin is divine lavender cleansing mush. Banana Moon, Dirty Boy, and Pineapple Grunt are soaps sliced off huge slabs like cheese and paper-wrapped like sliced deli meat. Bath Bombs fizz furiously, then leave the water scattered with rosebuds or scented with honey and vanilla. (⇨ Map D) ⊠ *Unit 11, the Piazza, Covent Garden, WC2* ☎ *020/7240–4570* Ⓤ *Covent Garden.*

★ **Penhaligon's.** William Penhaligon, court barber at the end of Queen Victoria's lengthy reign, established this shop. He blended perfumes and toilet waters and often created private concoctions for such customers as Lord Rothschild and Winston Churchill, using essential oils and natural, sometimes exotic ingredients. You can buy the very same formulations today, along with soaps, talcs, bath oils, and accessories. You'll

19

find the strong whiff of Victoriana both inside and outside the flower-bedecked bottles and boxes. The shop is sumptuously outfitted with 19th-century perfumer furnishings. Modern times have had their influence with the introduction of pet products and a collection of leather accessories styled by designer-of-the-moment, Alice Temperly. (⇨ Maps A and D) ✉ *41 Wellington St., Covent Garden, WC2* ☎ *020/7836–2150* Ⓤ *Covent Garden* ✉ *16 Burlington Arcade, Mayfair, W1* ☎ *020/ 7629–1416* Ⓤ *Piccadilly Circus.*

Pout. The creators of Pout know that makeup is really all about fun and this is lippy (lipstick, Brit style) with a cheeky sense of humor. Product names include "Saucy Sadie," "Bite My Cherry," and "Tickle My Fancy." You can try before you buy, in a fun, girlie boudoir setup, complete with pink walls and love-heart seating. It's irresistible. (⇨ Map D) ✉ *32 Shelton St., Covent Garden, WC2* ☎ *020/7379–0379* Ⓤ *Covent Garden.*

Space NK. The brainchild of Nicky Kinnaird (NK), this shop specializes in discovering avant-garde makeup and cutting-edge, high-performance treatments. Lines change regularly because if you've heard of the brand, or it's being stocked in the department stores, Space NK has probably moved on. Regulars include Nars, Stila, and Laura Mercier; recent introductions (at this writing) included Yu-Be, Dr. Sebagh, Dr. Brandt, Dr. Lipp, and DuWop. Who knows what will be in this year. Bath and aromatherapy products usually include essential oils for moms and babies. There are branches across town, but the original is in Covent Garden. (⇨ Map D) ✉ *4 Thomas Neals, 37 Earlham St., Covent Garden, WC2* ☎ *020/7379–7030* Ⓤ *Covent Garden.*

STATIONERY & GRAPHIC ARTS **The Graphic Centre.** In the heart of London's advertising, design, and media communities, this huge store is packed to the rafters with papers, fine arts materials, office supplies, computer graphic supplies, and everything the budding anime or manga artist could wish for in the form of markers, Letraset, and other materials. (⇨ Map D) ✉ *16–18 Shelton St., Covent Garden, WC2* ☎ *020/7759–4500* Ⓤ *Covent Garden.*

Green & Stone. This fabulous cave of artist materials, papers, art books, antique frames, and mannequins is one of the longest-running shops on the Kings Road, with a distinguised arts pedigree. It began life in 1927 as part of the Chenil Gallery, under the directorship of Augustus John and George Bernard Shaw. At the current location since 1934, it's always crowded and popular. (⇨ Map F) ✉ *259 Kings Rd., Chelsea, SW3* ☎ *020/7352–0837* Ⓤ *Sloane Sq.*

Ordning & Reda. Cool, sleek Swedish stationery and useful pieces to dress up the drabbest of desks are sold in the hottest colors here. There are high-style knapsacks, too. (⇨ Map F) ✉ *186A King's Rd., Chelsea, SW3* ☎ *020/7351–1003* Ⓤ *Sloane Sq.*

Paperchase. The stationery superstore of London, it sells writing paper in every conceivable shade and in a dozen mediums. There are lovely cards, artists' materials, notebooks, and paperware. The three-floor store has a bookstore and café. There are new branches at 289 Kings Road SW3; the Piazza, Covent Garden WC2; and Euston Station NW1. (⇨ Map C) ✉ *213 Tottenham Court Rd., Bloomsbury, W1* ☎ *020/ 7467–6200* Ⓤ *Goodge St.*

Smythson of Bond Street. This is, hands down, the classiest stationer in Britain. No hostess of any standing would consider having a leather-bound guest book made by anyone else, and the shop's distinctive pale blue–page diaries and social stationery are British through and through. Bespoke stationery sets come with a form and a sample so that recipients can personalize their gift. There are branches on Sloane Street, in Harvey Nicks, and at Selfridges. (⇨ Map A) ✉ *40 New Bond St., Mayfair, W1* ☎ *020/7629–8558* Ⓤ *Bond St.*

TOYS & MODELS **Armoury of St. James's.** The fine toy soldiers and military models in stock here are collectors' items. Painted and mounted knights only 6 inches high can cost more than £1,000. Besides lead and tin soldiers, the shop has a full selection of regimental brooches, porcelain figures, military memorabilia, and antiques. (⇨ Map A) ✉ *17 Piccadilly Arcade, St. James's, SW1* ☎ *020/7493–5082* Ⓤ *Piccadilly Circus.*

Benjamin Pollock's Toyshop. This Covent Garden shop carries on in the tradition of its founder and namesake who sold "theatrical sheets" for toy theaters from the mid-19th century to his death in 1937. Robert Louis Stevenson was a fan who wrote, "'If you love art, folly, or the bright eyes of children, speed to Pollock's." Old-fashioned and magical toy theaters are the main stock in trade, but a selection of nostalgic puppets, mechanical toys, and zoetropes are also available. (⇨ Map D) ✉ *44 The Market, Covent Garden Piazza, WC2* ☎ *020/7379–7866* Ⓤ *Covent Garden.*

Early Learning Centre. This is the ultimate stop for toys and educational games for babies and preschool children. The products are all clearly marked to explain what is appropriate for different age groups, and the staff is patient and helpful. If you bring your kids, you can still shop in relative peace while your youngsters play on some of the equipment. There are organized play sessions every Tuesday from 9:30 to 11:30 AM (except in the Christmas shopping season) for parent and child. (⇨ Map F) ✉ *36 King's Rd., Chelsea, SW3* ☎ *020/7581–5764* Ⓤ *Sloane Sq.*

Fodor's Choice ★ **Hamleys.** Every London child puts a trip to Hamleys at the top of his or her wish list. A Regent Street institution, the shop has demonstrations, a play area, a café, and every cool toy on the planet—as soon as it's launched. The huge stock, including six floors of toys and games for children and adults, ranges from traditional teddy bears to computer games and all the latest technological gimmickry. It's a mad rush at Christmastime, but Santa's grotto is one of the best in town. And you can book Sunday-morning children's parties that include two hours of private access to the store. (⇨ Map A) ✉ *188–196 Regent St., Soho, W1* ☎ *0870/333–2455* Ⓤ *Oxford Circus.*

Science Museum Gift Shop. This store is best for imaginative toys and models, such as balsa-wood planes and "put-me-together" human skeletons. The books and puzzles are extensive and will satisfy the most inquiring minds. (⇨ Map E) ✉ *Exhibition Rd., South Kensington, SW7* ☎ *020/7942–4499* Ⓤ *S. Kensington.*

Housewares

London's main department stores, such as John Lewis, Harrods, and Selfridges, have just about everything you might need, but for something a little more cutting-edge, stroll along Tottenham Court Road to Heal's,

19

the ultimate designer furniture store. Terence Conran no longer owns Habitat, but his good design on a budget philosophy is still apparent. Muji takes home style a step farther by embracing clothes to match the furnishings. For handmade, eclectic designer pieces, you should head farther afield to David Mellor (covered in the China & Glass section) and Linley (covered in the Design section) in Chelsea.

Cath Kidston. The stock in trade here is a collection of bright, girly prints—ginghams, polka dots, and miles and miles of roses—pasted over everything in sight, from ceramics and bedlinens to fine china, stationery, and dog beds. There are a few clothing and nightwear lines for women and children, along with handbags, beach bags, and diaper bags of different sizes, but everything in this shop is basically a canvas for Kidston's sugary prints. You'll either love them or loathe them. (⇨ Map G) ⊠ *8 Clarendon Cross, Notting Hill, W11* ☎ *020/7221–4000* Ⓤ *Notting Hill Gate.*

★ **Conran Shop.** This is the domain of Sir Terence Conran, who has been informing British taste since he opened Habitat in the '60s. Home enhancers from furniture to stemware—both handmade and mass-produced, by famous names and young designers—are displayed in a suitably gorgeous building that is a modernist design landmark in its own right. The household articles are almost objets d'art. The Conran Shop on Marylebone High Street, Marylebone W1, has similarly beautiful wares. (⇨ Map E) ⊠ *Michelin House, 81 Fulham Rd., South Kensington, SW3* ☎ *020/7589–7401* Ⓤ *S. Kensington.*

Graham & Green. A Notting Hill stalwart before the area reached cult status, this lifestyle shop has something for everyone's home. Whether you prefer folksy, ethnic, European, or colonial, you can likely find cushions, throws, lanterns, mirrors, and more mundane housewares. Lately the store's sense of fun has extended to kids' stuff (like handmade fish kites), nightware, and unclassifiable must-haves like tidy little silk sleeping bags you can pop into your luggage if strange beds bring out the Howard Hughs in you. (⇨ Map G) ⊠ *4 and 10 Elgin Crescent, Notting Hill, W11* ☎ *0870/7727–4594* Ⓤ *Ladbroke Grove.*

Heal's. The king of the furniture shops lining Tottenham Court Road, Heal's has designs that combine modern style with classicism, particularly beds and seating. The prices are high, but the store makes for delightful browsing, and the kitchenware and decorative pieces are more affordable. At Christmastime, Heal's decorative baubles are gorgeous. There's another store at 234 King's Road, Chelsea SW3, that focuses more on accessories and lighting. (⇨ Map C) ⊠ *196 Tottenham Court Rd., Bloomsbury, W1* ☎ *020/7636–1666* Ⓤ *Goodge St.*

Muji. If you're into minimalism and you can see a pencil case as a style statement, you'll love this difficult to classify, Japanese-based chain. The merchandise is in complete harmony: white earthenware tableware on steel shelving, cream duvets on understated maple beds, gray towels, and skin-care products in white recyclable containers. Clothes—perfect white T-shirts, pants, and knits in linens and cottons—and stationery items round out the selection. A great store for browsers, there are branches everywhere: 187 Oxford Street, Soho W1; 135 Long Acre, Covent Garden WC2; 157 High Street Kensington, Kensington W8; 77 King's Road, Chelsea SW3. (⇨ Map B) ✉ *Unit 5, 6–17 Tottenham Court Rd., Bloomsbury, W1* ☎ *020/7436–1779* Ⓤ *Tottenham Court Rd.*

Paul Smith. The highly regarded British fashion designer, with successful, international collections for both men and women, opened his first exclusively home furnishings shop in Mayfair in 2005. Original, one-of-a-kind furniture pieces share space with what Smith terms "curiosities" in an ever changing selection, sourced from all over the world. (⇨ Map A) ✉ *9 Albemarle St., Mayfair, W1* ☎ *020/7493–4565* Ⓤ *Bond St.*

Purves & Purves. This is a great place, whether you want to spend £500 or £5. Modern furniture and kitchenware designs by Philippe Starck and cool Italian trendsetters are definitely upscale, almost investment pieces. Inexpensive, colorful, and witty gift items, such as bubbly plastic napkin rings, toothbrushes, or silly soap dishes, abound. The store also showcases many British designs. (⇨ Map C) ✉ *220–222 Tottenham Court Rd., Bloomsbury, W1* ☎ *020/ 7580–8223* Ⓤ *Goodge St.*

> **COME AGAIN?**
>
> Make sure you pronounce it "Purviss and Purviss" when asking for directions or you could get some funny looks.

Jewelry

If you are suddenly overcome with the need to invest in serious rocks, London won't let you down. All the major international players are here: Cartier, Tiffany, Bulgari, Fred, Boucheron, De Beers, Van Cleef and Arpels, Graff, Kutchinsky, David Morris, and Britain's own Mappin & Webb among them. Bond Street, in particular, is good hunting grounds for megawatt stocking fillers. ■ TIP➔ **Bargain hunters who know their gems head for Hatton Garden, London's traditional diamond center. It's lined with small, independent dealers in fine gemstones (set and loose), gold jewelry and bullion, pawnbrokers, safe deposits, and gemstone auction houses.** For creative, chic costume jewelry try Liberty or Harvey Nicks, and try Fenwicks on Bond Street for designer baubles in semi-precious stones and natural materials.

★ **Asprey.** Exquisite jewelry and gifts are displayed in a discreet and very British environment at the "global flagship" store—opened in 2004, designed by Lord Foster and British interior designer David Mlinaric. The setting reeks money, good taste, and comfort. If you're in the market for a six-branch Georgian candelabrum or a six-carat emerald-and-diamond brooch, you won't be disappointed. Bespoke jewelry is available as well. (⇨ Map A) ✉ *167 New Bond St., Mayfair, W1* ☎ *020/ 7493–6767* Ⓤ *Bond St.*

Fodor'sChoice
★ **Butler & Wilson.** Long before anybody ever heard the word "bling," this shop was marketing the look—in diamanté, colored rhinestones, and crystal—to movie stars and secretaries alike. Specialists in handmade, designer jewelry, they've added semi-precious stones and amber to the collections. The vintage-style clothes, once used only to display the jewelry, produced so many requests that they now sell filmy beaded dresses, handbags, and smashing capes as well. The crowded Chelsea Shop is

19

like being inside a giant's jewel box. There's also a smaller shop at 20 South Molton Street. (⇨ Map F) ⊠ *189 Fulham Rd., Chelsea, SW3* ☎ *020/7352–3045* Ⓤ *S. Kensington.*

Dinny Hall. Here you'll find a very simple collection of designs in mainly gold and silver. Pared-down necklaces with a single drop, delicate gold spot-diamond earrings, and chokers with delicate curls are indicative of the styles sold here. There's another branch at 54 Fulham Road, South Kensington SW3. (⇨ Map G) ⊠ *200 Westbourne Grove, Notting Hill, W11* ☎ *020/7792–3913* Ⓤ *Notting Hill Gate.*

Garrard. Formally known as "Garrard, the Crown Jeweler," this is the company that, since Queen Victoria's day, has set the Kohinoor diamond into more than one royal crown. Responsible for the upkeep of the crown jewels, this 270-year-old jeweler also created the Americas Cup in 1848. The focus is diamonds and precious gems in simple, classic settings. While the new Wings collection of pavé designs is definitely bling, tradition rules and you can still drop in to pick up a tiara of diamonds and rubies. (⇨ Map A) ⊠ *24 Albemarle St., Mayfair, W1* ☎ *020/7758–8520* Ⓤ *Bond St.*

Links of London. This company specializes in simple but weighty pieces in silver and 18 carat gold. Diamonds, pearls, and semi-precious stones are used sparingly. They are particularly good for charm bracelets and charms, with a changing selection every season. Besides the Sloane Square flagship, there are branches all over London and in most of the major department stores. (⇨ Map F) ⊠ *16 Sloane Sq., Chelsea, SW1* ☎ *020/7730–3133* Ⓤ *Sloane Sq.*

Les Néréides. This French costume jeweler handmakes deliciously frivolous concoctions built out of tiny beads, crystals, glass, pearls, embroidery, enameled flowers, and birds. The overall effect is fantasy vintage crossed with little girls' dreams. It's wearable for youthful, feminine women of any age. The shop is always packed. (⇨ Map F) ⊠ *166 Kings Rd., Chelsea, SW3* ☎ *020/7376–6270* Ⓤ *Sloane Sq.*

Wright & Teague. Designers of superb pared-down jewelry made of gold, silver, and understated gems, this husband-and-wife team has crafted an exquisite collection that is more affordable than the upscale international jewelers on the adjacent Bond Street block. They describe their design philosophy as "glamour with gravitas." (⇨ Map A) ⊠ *1A Grafton St., Mayfair, W1* ☎ *020/7629–2777* Ⓤ *Green Park.*

Prints

London prints, old and new, make great gifts. Below are some West End stores, but also try London's markets—in particular Camden Passage in Islington for fine antique prints, Antiquarius on the King's Road, and the shops lining Portobello Road. The antiquarian book sellers of Cecil Court, off Charing Cross Road, are sources of old prints, maps, and theater ephemera. Most of London's major galleries and museums have excellent art posters in their shops; check out the Tate Modern and Bankside Gallery (on the South Bank), Tate Britain, the National Gallery, and the Courtauld Institute—an often overlooked gem. In the bargain range, it's well worth making a date for one of the many art fairs dur-

Vintage London

THE BRITISH LOVE fancy-dress parties, year-round. A family "dressing-up box," where beautiful old favorites are saved for children's games, is common. Maybe that's why there's so much excellent vintage apparel around. Find throwaway retro from the recent past at Camden Market or on the fringes of Portobello Road and Brick Lane/Spitalfields. Here are some of the best:

Absolute Vintage is a warehouse of handpicked items from the 1930s through the 1980s, including more than 1,000 pairs of shoes, arranged on a rainbow wall of color. R&B star Kelis is reportedly a fan. ⊠ *15 Hanbury St., Spitalfields/East End, E1* ☎ *020/ 7247-3883* Ⓤ *Whitechapel, Liverpool St.*

Bertie Golightly has been wedged in between designer shops on one of London's most expensive shopping streets since 1980. "Lightly owned" is the word here for samples and previously owned designer clothes and accessories. ⊠ *48 Beauchamp Pl., Knightsbridge, SW3* ☎ *020/ 7584-7270* Ⓤ *Knightsbridge.*

Beyond Retro stocks 10,000 vintage and retro items for men and women. From cowboy boots to bowling shirts to prom dresses, they've got the largest collection of American Retro in the United Kingdom. Kiera Knightley and Kylie Minogue have been spotted here. ⊠ *110-112 Cheshire St., Spitalfields/East End, E2* ☎ *020/ 7613-3636* Ⓤ *Old St., Bethnal Green.*

Mary Moore Vintage is owned by sculptor Henry Moore's daughter, who turned a lifetime's passion for collecting into this little shop full of,

basically, her own wardrobe. Items from £90 to £1,000. ⊠ *5 Clarendon Cross, Holland Park/Notting Hill, W11* ☎ *020/7229-5678* Ⓤ *Holland Park.*

Orsini is a tiny but choice Kensington boutique. Eveningwear with Hollywood-style glamour is the trademark here, with clothes from the 1920s to the 1960s. ⊠ *76 Earls Court Rd., Kensington, W8* ☎ *020/ 7937-2903* Ⓤ *Earls Court or Kensington High St.*

Rokit consists of two shops along Brick Lane that stock everything from handbags and homewares to ball gowns, jeans, military, and Western wear. Magazine and rock stylists love it. ⊠ *101-107 Brick La., Spitalfields/ East End, E1* ☎ *020/7375-3864* Ⓤ *Aldgate E.*

Steinberg & Tolkien is a Kings Road institution with two packed floors of genuine vintage haut couture. There's very good—and pricey—designer costume jewelry and the boxy plastic handbags that were ultrachic in the 1950s. ⊠ *193 King's Rd., Chelsea, SW3* ☎ *020/7376-3660* Ⓤ *Sloane Sq.*

Virginia, Virginia Baker's collection of antique and vintage clothing, may be the best in London. Dresses, hats, and accessories from early Victorian (circa 1850) to the early 1930s are available. These are wearable collectors' items and priced accordingly. The shop is kept dark to protect the fabrics—ring the bell to enter. ⊠ *98 Portland Rd., Clarendon Cross, Holland Park/ Notting Hill, W11* ☎ *020/ 7727-9908* Ⓤ *Holland Park.*

19

ing the year, such as the **Affordable Art Fair** (☎ 020/7371–8787 ⊕ www. affordableartfair.co.uk) around March and October at Battersea Park, where you can bag original work for under £3,000.

Classic Prints. The dusty windows of this little shop always have something worth looking at. A few doors away from Green & Stone (see Stationery and Graphic Arts, above), it's worth browsing here if you're already on this choice stretch of the Kings Road. (⇨ Map F) ✉ *265 Kings Rd., Chelsea, SW3* ☎ *020/7376–5056* Ⓤ *Sloane Sq.*

Curwen & New Academy Gallery & Business Art Galleries. Formerly just the Curwen, this triumverate has regularly changing exhibitions of modern fine-art prints. (⇨ Map C) ✉ *34 Windmill St., Bloomsbury, W1* ☎ *020/7323–4700* Ⓤ *Tottenham Court Rd.*

★ **Grosvenor Prints.** London's largest collection of 17th- to early-20th-century prints includes a good selection of rare, early Americana. The main emphasis is London views and architecture as well as dogs and horses. It's an eccentric collection, with prices ranging from £70 into the thousands. (⇨ Map D) ✉ *19 Shelton St., Covent Garden, WC2* ☎ *020/ 7836–1979* Ⓤ *Covent Garden.*

Map House. Though a few items here are relatively inexpensive, this is mainly a shop for serious collectors of antique maps and globes—the sort of place that supplies prices on request. Much of its stock dates from the 16th century, and it's possible to buy a very rare, Ptolemaic worldview that dates from 1493. A gallery of fine botanical, animal, and cityscape prints are also antique collectibles. (⇨ Map E) ✉ *54 Beauchamp Pl., Knightsbridge, SW3* ☎ *020/7589–4325* Ⓤ *Knightsbridge.*

Shoes

It's no accident that Manolo Blahnik, the star footwear designer, made his name in London and still chooses to live here. The man who has shod fashionable women from Audrey Hepburn to Kate Moss and the "Sex and the City" girls, still trades from his original shop in Chelsea, off the King's Road. Jimmy Choo is another "native son" who began his career quietly in London's East End. Canadian-born Patrick Cox burst on the London scene in the 1990s, and has, as the British say, gone from strength to strength. Besides some very good British leather and shoe merchants, London is a magnet for the best in Italian, Spanish, Swiss, and French "pedi-couture." Stop in at one of the King's Road branches of Hobbs, Pied-A-Terre, or L. K. Bennett for British-designed, Italian-made shoes at more affordable prices.

★ **Anello and Davide.** Creators of the Beatles' famous Chelsea Boots, Anello and Davide have long been London's leading makers of bespoke theatrical and dancing shoes. Their new handmade, ready-to-wear line A&D, sold at their St. Christopher's Place shop, echoes many of its most famous, classic styles. Bespoke shoes are still available and, once they have taken your measurements, you can get them through mail order or online. (⇨ Map B) ✉ *20–21 St. Christopher's Pl., Marylebone, W1* ☎ *020/7935–7959* Ⓤ *Bond St.*

★ **Caroline Groves.** Made to measure, stunning women's shoes echo classics of the 1920s, '30s, '40s, and '50s. Caroline Groves considers herself more of a craftsperson than a designer. If you loved raiding your grandmother's attic for her favorite footwear, this is the place to visit. (⇨ Map B) ✉ *37 Chiltern St., Marylebone, W1* ☎ *020/7935–2329* Ⓤ *Baker St.*

★ **Franchetti Bond Ltd.** A combination of classic English styling and beautiful Florentine leathers, at (for London) moderate prices, makes this little shop behind Peter Jones a real find. The company specializes in tailored, ladylike footwear, and scrumptious handbags. If you visit in spring, stop here for the almost edible pastel loafers. There's a second branch in Burlington Arcade, Mayfair. (⇨ Map F) ✉ *12 Symons St., Chelsea, SW3* ☎ *020/7823–5550* Ⓤ *Sloane Sq.*

Jimmy Choo. It's the name on every supermodel's and fashion editor's feet. Choo's exquisite, elegant designs are fantasy itself, and he's become a contender for Manolo Blahnik's crown. These designs aren't cheap, but fans who would kill for these shoes probably could with their sharp, pointed toes and teetering stillettos. (⇨ Map E) ✉ *32 Sloane St., Knightsbridge, SW1* ☎ *020/7823–1051* Ⓤ *Knightsbridge.*

John Lobb. If you're planning to visit for your first pair of handmade shoes (after which your wooden "last," or foot mold, is kept), take note: this shop has a waiting list of six months plus, and only makes shoes for men. As well as plenty of time, you'll need plenty of money: around £1,500. But this buys a world of choice—from finest calf to exotic elk—and it will be your finest pair of shoes ever. (⇨ Map A) ✉ *9 St. James's St., St. James's, SW1* ☎ *020/7930–3664* Ⓤ *Piccadilly Circus.*

★ **Manolo Blahnik.** Blink and you'll miss the discreet sign of this little shoe shop. Here, in the heart of Chelsea, the man who single-handedly managed to revive the sexy stilletto and make it girly at the same time, has been trading since 1973. It's a must for shoe lovers with a healthy credit balance. If you're wearing your Manolos, hop on a bus or in a cab—the nearest Tube is about a mile and a half away. (⇨ Map F) ✉ *49–51 Old Church St., Chelsea, SW3* ☎ *020/7352–3863* Ⓤ *Sloane Sq.*

★ **Kate Kuba.** From comfy, practical Camper shoes made in Majorca to sexy spiked heels and boots, this shop always has an interesting selection of women's shoes—and a small selection for men, too. Prices, from moderate to expensive, are slashed during sales. It's tucked among several other good shoe stores in Chelsea's newest shopping area, Duke of York's Square. (⇨ Map F) ✉ *22 Duke of York Sq., Sloane Sq., Chelsea, SW3* ☎ *020/7259–0011* Ⓤ *Sloane Sq.*

Patrick Cox. The "Wannabe" shoe collection is affordable and irreverent, with retro designs and quirky materials and colors. His sophisticated signature collection is popular among trendsetters, while his famous and outrageous "Light Boot," for disco divas, uses fiber optics to set fire to the dance floor (only available at his main, Sloane Street store). (⇨ Map F) ✉ *129 Sloane St., Chelsea, SW3* ☎ *020/7730–8886* Ⓤ *Knightsbridge, Sloane Sq.*

★ **Rupert Sanderson.** Handmade designer shoes from a relative newcomer (he opened his Mayfair shop in 2004) combine bright colors, intricate effects, and a penchant for peep toes in very feminine shoes. Look for his sales, when prices can drop by half. (⇨ Map A) ✉ *33 Bruton Pl., Mayfair, W1* ☎ *0870/750–9181* Ⓤ *Bond St.*

19

Shellys. These are the kind of shoes drag queens wish they had small enough feet for. Around on the King's Road forever, with loads of London branches, these are outrageous, ultrafeminine, multicolor shoes, many on teetering heels and lofty platforms. Head here if you like to turn heads—and keep them turning. (⇨ Map B) ⊠ *266–270 Regent St., Soho, W1* ☎ *020/7287–0939* Ⓤ *Oxford Circus.*

Swear. The shoemaker for the movie *Star Wars* makes wild and funky shoes popular with iconoclasts, rubber fetishists, and anyone who can brave a platform two or three times bigger than the entire shoe itself. Styles tend to resemble trainers, sneakers, and workmen's boots on acid. (⇨ Map D) ⊠ *22 Carnaby St., Soho, W1* ☎ *020/77341–1690* Ⓤ *Oxford Circus.*

Street Markets

For London's most famous markets, and the one's worth making a special trip to visit, see page 429. The markets listed below are also worth visiting if you happen to be nearby or, in the case of Camden Passage, if you're a serious and knowledgeable antiques buyer.

Berwick Street. Soho's fruit, vegetable, and dairy market is not very different from many small neighborhood markets—except that the neighborhood is Soho. Shops lining the edges include some good Italian grocers, butchers, and fishmongers alongside shops selling theatrical fabrics and trimmings as well as those specializing in maribou-trimmed ladies undies and leather and rubber bondage gear! ⊠ *Soho, W1* ⊘ *Mon.–Sat. 9–5* Ⓤ *Oxford Circus, Piccadilly Circus.*

To Market, to Market   See Page 429

Camden Passage. Relatively new, as London markets go, this one set up in its 18th-century lanes in the early 1960s. Today around 350 antiques shops, and a small number of stalls open for business on Saturday and Wednesday. A few of the shops will open midweek by appointment. In its historic setting, this is an expensive hunting ground with most of the shops run by specialist dealers who will only haggle with specialist buyers and those in the trade. Despite the name, it's not in Camden but a couple of miles away in Islington. ⊠ *Islington, N1* ⊘ *Wed. 10 AM–2 PM, Sat. 10 AM–5 PM* Ⓤ *Angel.*

Covent Garden. Crafts stalls, jewelry designers, clothes makers—particularly of knitwear—potters, and many more artisans congregate in the undercover central area known as the Apple Market. Stall holders change depending on the day of the week, so if you see something you

Continued on page 435

TO MARKET, TO MARKET

Londoners love a good market. With their cluttered stalls and crowds of people, they are a visible reminder that, in this world of global chain stores and supermarkets, London is still, in many respects, an Old World European city.

Every neighborhood has its cluster of fruit, vegetable, and flower stalls, or its weekend car-boot sales—gigantic garage sales where ordinary people pay a fiver for the privilege of selling their castoffs. Some, like the North End Road Market in Fulham, run for miles. Others, like Brixton Market, Europe's biggest Caribbean-food market, specialize in ethnic ingredients and products. Still others crop up in the most unexpected places: on Berwick Street in the heart of Soho, for example, media moguls, designers, ad execs, actors, dancers, and ladies of the night mingle over the punnets of strawberries, wedges of cheddar, and slabs of wet fish.

The big specialty markets, open on weekends, are not only great for the occasional bargain but also for people-watching, photo ops, and all around great days out. And though the markets are popular with visitors, they aren't tourist traps. In fact, browsing the London markets is one of the few activities in London where natives and tourists mix and enjoy themselves as equals.

PORTOBELLO ROAD MARKET

🕐 Sat. 6–4:30

✉ Portobello Rd., Notting Hill

Ⓤ Ladbroke Grove (Hammersmith & City Line), Notting Hill (District, Circle, or Central Line), or Bus 52

☞ Antiques, fruits and vegetables, vintage clothing, household goods

London's most famous market still wins the prize for the all-around best. It sits in a lively multicultural part of town; the 1,500-odd antiques dealers don't rip you off (although you should haggle where you can); and it stretches over a mile, changing character completely as it goes.

The southern end is lined with antiques shops and arcades; the middle, above Elgin Crescent, is where locals buy fruits and vegetables. This middle area was the setting for the lovely sequence in the movie *Notting Hill* where Hugh Grant walks along the market and through the changing seasons. The section near the elevated highway (called the Westway) has the best flea market in town, with vintage-clothing stores along the edges. After that, the market trails off into a giant rummage sale of the kinds of cheap household goods the British call tat.

Some say Portobello Road has become a bit of a tourist trap, but if you acknowledge that it's a circus and get into the spirit, it's a lot of fun. Perhaps you won't find many bargains, but this is such a cool part of town that just hanging out is a good enough excuse to come. There are some food and flower stalls throughout the week, but to see the market in full swing, Saturday is the only day to come.

A PORTOBELLO DAY

In good weather the market gets very crowded by midday. For a Londoner's day at Portobello, come as early as you can (7 AM) and enjoy the market when the market traders have time for a chat and you can actually get near the stalls. By 10:30 you'll have seen plenty of the market and can stop for a late breakfast or brunch at the **Electric Brasserie** (✉ 191 Portobello Rd. ☎ 020/7908–9696), next to the area's famous Electric Cinema. If you still have the will to shop, move on to the less crowded boutiques along Westbourne Grove, Blenheim Crescent, or Ledbury Road.

BOROUGH MARKET

There's been a market in Borough since Roman times. This one, spread under the arches and railway tracks leading to London Bridge Station, is the successor to a medieval market once held on London Bridge. Post-millennium, it has been transformed from a noisy collection of local stalls to a trendy foodie center. Named the best market in London by a local magazine and the best market in Britain by a national newspaper, the Farmers Market held on Fridays and Saturdays has attracted some of London's best merchants of comestibles. Fresh coffees, gorgeous cheeses, olives, and baked goods complement the organically farmed meats, fresh fish, fruit, and veggies.

Don't make any other lunch plans for the day; celebrity chef Jamie Oliver's scallop man cooks them up fresh; wild boar sausages sizzle on a grill, and there is much more that's tempting to gobble on the spot. There are chocolates, preserves, and Mrs. Bassa's handmade Indian condiments to take home, but the best souvenirs are the memories.

⊙ **Fri. noon–4:30, Sat. 9–4**

⊠ Borough High St., South Bank

Ⓤ London Bridge (Jubilee or Northern Line), Borough (Nothern Line)

☞ Cheese, olives, coffee, baked goods, meats, fish, fruits, vegetables

---

A BARGAIN DAY ON THE SOUTH BANK
Combine a visit to the Tate Modern (free) and a walk across the Millennium Bridge from the Tate to St. Paul's with a Thames-side picnic of goodies foraged at Borough Market. The Italian cheese man brings a great selection direct from the Piedmont.

Or how about a wedge of Stinking Bishop cheese (Wallace and Gromit's favorite) from Neal's Yard Dairy? For about £3.50 you can buy a prawn wrap with crème fraîche, garlic, and chili from fishmonger Mr. Applebee.

A PUB RIGHT OUT OF DICKENS
On the way back to Borough Tube station, stop for a pint at the **George Inn** (⊠ 77 Borough High St., Southwark SE1 ☎ 020/7407–2056 Ⓤ London Bridge, Borough), mentioned by Dickens in *Little Dorrit*. This 17th-century coaching inn was a famous terminus in its day, and is the last galleried inn in London. Now owned by the National Trust, it is leased to a private company and still operates as a pub.

TO MARKET, TO MARKET

19

THE EAST END MARKETS

Brick Lane. The noisy center of the Bengali community is a hubbub of buying and selling. Sunday stalls have food, hardware, household goods, electrical goods, books, bikes, shoes, clothes, spices, and saris. The CDs and DVDs are as likely as not to be counterfeit, and the bargain iron may not have a plug—so be careful. But people come more to enjoy the ethnic buzz, eat curries and Bengali sweets, or indulge in salt beef on a bagel at Beigel Bake, London's 24-hour bagel bakery, a survivor of the neighborhood's Jewish past. Brick Lane's activity spills over into nearby Petticoat Lane Market with similar goods but less style.

From Brick Lane it's a stone's throw to the **Columbia Road Flower Market**. Only 52 stalls, but markets don't get much prettier or photogenic than this. Flowers, shrubs, bulbs, trees, garden tools, and accessories are sold wholesale. The local cafés are superb.

Stop to smell the roses and have Sunday brunch on Columbia Road before plunging into **Spitalfields**. Developers are in the process of changing the character of the covered market (once London's wholesale meat market) at the center of this area's boho revival. Plans under discussion include almost halving the space for stallholders but adding an extra market day. Currently, the Sunday market sells crafts, foods, antique and retro clothing, handmade rugs, soap filled with flowers and fruits, homemade cakes, and cookware. And, from Spanish tapas to Thai satays, it's possible to eat your way around the world.

BRICK LANE

🕐 **Sun. daybreak–noon**

✉ Brick La., East End

Ⓤ Aldgate East (Hammersmith & City or District Line), Shoreditch (East London Line)

☞ Food, hardware, household goods, electric goods, books, bikes, shoes, clothes, spices, saris

COLUMBIA ROAD FLOWER MARKET

🕐 **Sun. 8–2**

✉ Columbia Rd., East End

Ⓤ Old Street (Northern Line)

☞ Flowers, shrubs, bulbs, trees, garden tools, accessories

SPITALFIELDS

🕐 **Sun. 10–5**

✉ Brushfield St., East End

Ⓤ Liverpool St. or Aldgate (Hammersmith & City, Circle, or Bakerloo Line), Aldgate East (Hammersmith & City or District Line)

☞ Crafts, foods, antique clothing, rugs, soap, cakes, cookware

---

ONLY ON A SUNDAY
Sunday-only opening is the rule not only for the markets in the East End but also for most of the fashionable shops (elsewhere in this chapter) crammed into the lanes between these markets. It's the nursery for the designer names of the future, who come here to create their first and wildest collections.

BERMONDSEY

🕑 Fri. 4 AM–about noon

✉ Long La. and Bermondsey Sq., South Bank

Ⓤ London Bridge (Jubilee or Northern Line), Borough (Nothern Line)

☞ Antiques (silverware, paintings, furniture)

Come before dawn and bring a flashlight to bag a bargain antique at this famous market. Dealers arrive as early as 4 AM to snap up the best bric-a-brac and silverware, paintings, objets d'art, fine arts, and furniture. The early start grew out of a wrinkle in the law under which thieves could sell stolen goods with impunity in the hours of darkness when provenance could not be ascertained. That law was changed, and the market has been shrinking ever since.

Developers are sizing up the nearby outlets and warehouses that house the market spillover, so see this unique market while you still can. You can get here by walking from the London Bridge Tube station, or you can take a bus up Tower Bridge Road to Bermondsey Square. Better yet, have your hotel line up a car or minicab so you can arrive before public transit starts running.

THE CAMDEN MARKETS

CAMDEN MARKET
🕑 **Thurs.–Sun. 9–5:30**

CAMDEN LOCK MARKET, STABLES MARKET, AND CANAL MARKET
🕑 **Weekends 10–6**

ELECTRIC MARKET
🕑 **Sun. 9–5:30**

✉ Camden Town

Ⓤ Camden Town (Northern Line)

☞ Vintage clothing, antiques, jewelry, candlesticks, ceramics, mirrors, toys

Now that more stalls and a faux warehouse have been inserted into the surrounding brick railway buildings, some of the haphazard charm of this area—actually several markets gathered around a pair of locks in the Regent's Canal—is lost. Still, the variety of merchandise is mind-blowing: vintage and new clothes, antiques and junk, jewelry and scarves, candlesticks, ceramics, mirrors, and toys.

This is the closest thing London has to Les Puces, the Paris flea market, and though much of the merchandise is youth oriented, the markets have a lively appeal to aging hippies, fashion designers, and anyone with a taste for the bohemian who doesn't mind crowds and a bit of a madhouse scene. Camden is actually a collection of markets, cheek by jowl, each with slightly different, weekend opening hours.

THE GREENWICH MARKET

On Saturdays and Sundays the center of Greenwich becomes an enormous series of markets—antiques, arts and crafts, clothes, books, toys, marine paraphernalia, and flea-market miscellany. Less crowded than Camden, less touristy than Covent Garden, this part-indoor, part-outdoor market is surrounded by interesting shops and close to historic sites. If you make a day of it, you can see the Greenwich Observatory and stand on Longitude 0 (marked in brass and stone in front of the observatory), visit the tall ship *Cutty Sark*, and shop till you drop.

Take the DLR to the *Cutty Sark*, right in the thick of it, or for more fun, ride the DLR through Canary Wharf, get off at Island Gardens, and walk through the ancient foot tunnel under the Thames.

🕑 Weekends 9–5 or 6 depending upon the market

✉ Greenwich High Rd., Greenwich

Ⓤ DLR: Cutty Sark for Maritime Greenwich

☞ Antiques, arts, crafts, books, toys, paraphernalia

Know-How

■ TWO MARKET TIPS TO REMEMBER→ In the end, if you like something and you can afford it, it's worth buying; you're the best judge of that. But it's annoying to buy an "English antique" only to find the Made in China label when you get home. To avoid disappointment:

Look for hallmarks. A lot of what passes for English silver is plate or outright fake. English gold and silver must, by law, be marked with hallmarks that indicate their material and the year in which they were made. Books of hallmarks are inexpensive to buy in London bookshops.

Buy crafts items directly from the makers. Ceramicists, jewelers, needleworkers and other artisans often sell their own work at markets. Besides buying the item, you may have a conversation worth remembering.

■ MARKET ETIQUETTE → You've probably heard that you're expected to bargain with the market traders to get the best price. That's true

to a degree, but London markets are not Middle Eastern souks, and most bargaining is modest. Unless you are an expert in the item you want to buy and really know how low you can go, don't offer a ridiculously low price. Instead ask the dealer, "Is that the best you can do?" If the dealer is willing to bargain, he or she will suggest a slightly lower price, maybe 10% less. You might try to get another 10% off and end up meeting in the middle.

like, don't wait—buy it. Prices are high, but some of the merchandise, especially jewelry, can be clever and original. The Jubilee Market, toward Southampton Street, is less classy, with printed T-shirts and the like, but on Monday has a worthwhile selection of vintage collectibles. This area is, frankly, more of a tourist magnet than others, and you won't find many locals shopping the stalls. Keep that in mind when judging what you spend in this popular place. ⊠ *The Piazza, Covent Garden, WC2* ⊗ *Daily 9–5* Ⓤ *Covent Garden.*

19

Side Trips
from London

WORD OF MOUTH

"You can do many day trips. Places like Windsor, Hampton Court, Greenwich, Warwick Castle, Canterbury, Cambridge, Bath, and Salisbury (and the list goes on) are very easy to get to via train from London."

–Lori

Updated by Robert Andrews, Christi Daugherty, and Julius Honnor

LONDON IS EXCITING AND ENTERTAINING, but it's not all Britain has to offer. If you have even one day to spare, head out of the city. A train ride past hills dotted with sheep, a stroll through a medieval town, or a visit to one of England's great castles could make you feel as though you've added another week to your vacation.

Londoners are undeniably lucky. Few urban populations enjoy such glorious—and easily accessible—options for day-tripping. England is extremely compact, and the train and bus networks, although somewhat inefficient and expensive compared to their European counterparts, are extensive and user-friendly. By train from London, it takes a mere 55 minutes to reach Oxford, an hour to reach Cambridge, and 90 minutes to reach Bath. Stratford takes a bit more planning, as direct trains from London take 2 hours, 20 minutes.

Although you could tackle any one of the towns in this chapter on a frenzied day trip—heavy summer crowds make it difficult to cover the sights in a relaxed manner—consider staying for a day or two. You'd then have time to explore a very different England—one blessed with quiet country pubs, fluffy sheep, and neatly trimmed farms. No matter where you go, lodging reservations are a good idea from June through September, when foreign visitors saturate the English countryside.

BATH

115 mi west of London.

"I really believe I shall always be talking of Bath . . . I do like it so very much. Oh! Who can ever be tired of Bath?" wrote Jane Austen in *Northanger Abbey.* Today thousands of visitors heartily concur. A remarkably unsullied Georgian city with remnants of its Roman occupation, Bath looks as if John Wood (circa 1705–54), its chief architect; "Beau" Nash (1674–1762), its principal dandy; and Jane Austen (1775–1817) might still be seen strolling on the promenade. Stepping out of the train station puts you right in the center, and Bath is compact enough to explore on foot. A single day is sufficient for you to take in the glorious yellow-stone buildings, tour the Roman baths, and stop for tea, though it will give you only a brief hint of the cultural life that thrives in this vibrant town.

Exploring Bath

Fodor'sChoice ★ The **Pump Room and Roman Baths** are among the most popular sights outside London. The Romans set about building the baths here around the healing spring of the English goddess Aquae Sulis in AD 60, after wars with the Brits had laid the city to waste. The site became famous as a temple to Minerva, the Roman goddess of wisdom. Legend has it the first taker of these sacred waters was King Lear's leprous father, Prince Bladud, in the 9th century BC. (Yes, it's claimed he was cured.) The British added the Pump Room—oft-described in Austen's works, and now beautifully restored—in the 18th century. You can drink the spa waters here, or have a more agreeable cup of tea. Below the Pump Room is a museum of quirky objects found during excavations. Last admission is an hour before closing, but allow at least 90 minutes for the museum. ⊠ *Abbey Churchyard* ☎ *01225/477784* ⊕ *www.romanbaths.co.uk* ☞ *£10, July and Aug. £11 combined ticket with Assembly Rooms £13* ⊙ *Mar.–June, Sept., and Oct., daily 9–6; July and Aug., daily 9 AM–10 PM; Nov.–Feb., daily 9:30–5:30.*

Bath Abbey was commissioned by God. Really. The design came to Bishop Oliver King in a dream, and was built during the 15th century. Look up at the fan-vaulted ceiling in the nave and the carved angels on the restored West Front. In the **Heritage Vaults** is a museum of archaeological finds, with a scale model of 13th-century Bath. ⊠ *Abbey Churchyard* ☎ *01225/422462* ⊕ *www.bathabbey.org* ☞ *Abbey free, suggested donation £3, Heritage Vaults free* ⊙ *Abbey Apr.–Oct., Mon.–Sat. 9–6, Sun. 1–2:30 and 4:30–5:30; Nov.–Mar., Mon.–Sat. 9–4:30, Sun. 1–2:30. Heritage Vaults Mon.–Sat. 10–4.*

NEED A BREAK?
Sally Lunn's Refreshment House & Museum (⊠ 4 N. Parade Passage ☎ 01225/461634), in Bath's oldest house (1482), may be the world's only tearoom-museum. You can see the old foundation of the house, plus the original kitchen. It's open 10 to 10 Monday through Saturday and 11 to 10 on Sunday.

One of the most famous landmarks of the city, **Pulteney Bridge** (⊠ Off Bridge St. at Grand Parade) was the great Georgian architect Robert Adam's sole contribution to Bath. In its way, the bridge is as fine as the only other bridge in the world with shops lining either side: the Ponte Vecchio in Florence.

20

★ Among Bath's remarkable architectural achievements is **The Circus** (⊠ Intersection of Brock, Gay, and Bennett Sts.), a perfectly circular ring of three-story stone houses designed by John Wood. The painter Thomas Gainsborough (1727–88) lived at No. 17 from 1760 to 1774.

On the east side of Bath's Circus are thrills for Austen readers: her much-mentioned **Assembly Rooms,** where the upper class would gather for concerts and dances. Within the rooms is the **Museum of Costume,** which displays fashions from the 17th through 20th centuries. Last admission is one hour before closing, and you do need at least an hour to tour the museum. ⊠ *Bennett St.* ☎ *01225/477789* ⊕ *www.museumofcostume.*

SIDE TRIPS PLANNER

Getting Around

Normally the towns covered in this chapter are best reached by train. Bus travel costs less, but can take twice as long. However, train routes throughout Britain are often subject to delays. Wherever you're going, be sure to plan ahead for any day trip: check the latest timetables before you set off, and try to get an early start.

Bus Travel

National Express runs buses from London's Victoria Coach Station to six of the towns in this chapter. Each day buses depart hourly for Bath (3 hours, 50 minutes), Brighton (2 hours), Cambridge (about 2 hours), and Canterbury (1 hour, 50 minutes); every half hour for Oxford (1 hour, 40 minutes); and about three times for Stratford-upon-Avon (3 hours).

The Green Line Bus 700, 701, or 702 can take you to Windsor in about 1½ hours. It leaves from Stop 1 in front of the Colonnades Shopping Centre on Buckingham Palace Road, *not* from Victoria Coach Station. (☎ 0870/608–7261 ⊕ www. greenline.co.uk.)(☎0870/580–8080 ⊕ www.nationalexpress.com.)

Train Travel

Trains run from Paddington Station to Bath (90 minutes, half-hourly departures), Oxford (55 minutes, half-hourly departures), and Windsor (40 minutes, departs hourly and requires one change). Direct trains leave Paddington for Stratford-upon-Avon (2 hours, 20 minutes) each morning; other routes depart from Marylebone (2½ hours) and Euston (2½ hours) stations and require a change at Leamington Spa. Direct trains for Windsor (1 hour, hourly departures) leave from Waterloo Station. Trains depart from King's Cross Station hourly for Cambridge (1 hour). Victoria Station is the point of departure for rail service to Brighton (1¼–1¾ hours, half-hourly departures) and Canterbury (85 minutes, hourly departures). There's also service to Brighton (95 minutes, departures every 15 minutes) and Canterbury (90 minutes, half-hourly departures) from London Bridge Station.

Contact **National Rail** (☎ 0845/748–4950 ⊕ www. nationalrail.co.uk), which oversees all the train stations, for more information. You can reach any train station by taking the Underground to the Tube station of the same name.

Visitor Information

🖪 **Bath Tourist Information Centre** ⊠ Abbey Church Yard ☎ 0906/711–2000 50p per minute ⊕ www.visitbath.co. uk. **Brighton Tourist Information Centre** ⊠ 10 Bartholomew Sq. ☎0906/711–2255 50p per minute ⊕www.visitbrighton. com. **Cambridge Tourist Information Centre** ⊠ The Old Library, Wheeler St. ☎ 0871/226–8006, 01223/464732 from outside U.K. ⊕ www.visitcambridge.org. **Canterbury Visitor Information Centre** ⊠ 12–13 Sun St. ☎01227/ 378100 ⊕ www.canterbury.co.uk. **Oxford Information Centre** ⊠ 15–16 Broad St. ☎01865/726871 ⊕ www. oxford.gov.uk/tourism. **Royal Windsor Information Centre** ⊠ 24 High St. ☎01753/743900 ⊕ www.windsor. gov.uk. **Stratford Tourist Information Centre** ⊠ Bridgefoot ☎ 0870/160–7930 ⊕ www.shakespeare-country.co.uk. **Warwick Tourist Information Centre** ⊠ Court House, Jury St. ☎ 01926/492212 ⊕ www.warwick-uk.co.uk.

co.uk ✉ *£6.50, combined ticket with Roman Baths £13* ⊙ *Mar.–Oct., daily 11–6; Nov.–Feb., daily 11–5.*

The 18th-century **Royal Crescent** is the most famous site in Bath, and you can't help but see why. Designed by John Wood the Younger, it's perfectly proportioned and beautifully sited, with sweeping views over parkland. A marvelous museum at **Number 1 Royal Crescent** shows life as Beau Nash would have lived it circa 1765. ✉ *1 Royal Crescent* ☎ *01225/428126* ⊕ *www.bath-preservation-trust.org.uk* ✉ *£5* ⊙ *Feb.–Oct., Tues.–Sun. 10:30–5; Nov., Tues.–Sun. 10:30–4; last admission 30 min before closing.*

Where to Eat

££–£££ ✕ **Number Five.** Just over the Pulteney Bridge from the center of town, this airy bistro, with its plants, framed posters, and cane-back chairs, is an ideal spot for a light lunch. The regularly changing continental menu includes tasty homemade soups, crostini of goat's cheese and cherry tomatoes, and grilled rib of beef with a red wine sauce. ✉ *5 Argyle St.* ☎ *01225/444499* ▤ *AE, MC, V.*

BRIGHTON

52 mi south of London.

Ever since the Prince Regent first visited in 1783, Brighton has been England's most exciting seaside city, and today it's as eccentric and cosmopolitan as ever. With its rich cultural mix—Regency architecture, an amusement pier, specialist shops, pavement cafés, lively arts, and, of course, the odd and exotic Royal Pavilion—Brighton is a truly extraordinary city by the sea. For most of the 20th century the city was known for its tarnished allure and faded glamour. Happily, a young, bustling spirit has given a face-lift to this ever-popular resort, which shares its city status with neighboring Hove, as genteel a retreat as Brighton is abuzz.

Exploring Brighton

★ In the 1850s, the county of Sussex featured the first examples of that peculiarly British institution, the amusement pier. **Brighton Pier**, which opened in 1899, followed in the great tradition, with a crowded maze of arcade games, amusement-park rides, and chip shops. The decaying ghost of a Victorian structure down the beach from Brighton Pier is **West Pier** (☎ *01273/321499* ⊕ *www.westpier.co.uk*). Built in 1866, it was the more upscale of Brighton's piers and was for many years the most recognizable landmark of the city. Storm damage and a partial collapse in 2002, followed by two fires in 2003, have left little more than the charred and distorted remnants of the original structure. Opinion in the city is split about a proposed £30 million renovation program. ✉ *Waterfront along Madeira Dr.* ☎ *01273/609361* ⊕ *www.brightonpier.co. uk* ✉ *Free, costs of rides vary* ⊙ *June–Aug., daily 9 AM–2 AM; Sept.–May, daily 10 AM–midnight.*

The heart of Brighton is the **Steine** (pronounced *steen*), a large open area close to the seafront. This was a river mouth until the Prince of Wales (later the Prince Regent) had it drained in 1793.

20

Fodor'sChoice
★
The most remarkable building on the Steine, perhaps in all Britain, is unquestionably the extravagant, fairytale **Royal Pavilion.** Built by architect Henry Holland in 1787 as a simple seaside villa, the Pavilion was transformed by John Nash between 1815 and 1823 for the Prince Regent (later George IV), who favored an exotic, Eastern design with opulent Chinese interiors. When Queen Victo-

ria came to the throne in 1837, she disapproved of the palace and planned to demolish it. Fortunately, the local council bought it from her, and after a lengthy process of restoration the Pavilion looks much as it did in its Regency heyday. Take particular note of the spectacular **Music Room,** styled as a Chinese pavilion, and the **Banqueting Room,** with its enormous flying-dragon gasolier, or gaslight chandelier, a revolutionary invention in the early 19th century. The gardens, too, have been restored to Regency splendor, following John Nash's naturalistic design of 1826. ⊠ *Old Steine* ☎ *01273/290900* ⊕ *www.royalpavilion.org.uk* ⌺ *£5.95* ☾ *Oct.–Mar., daily 10–5:15; Apr.–Sept., daily 9:30–5:45; last admission 45 min before closing.*

The grounds of the Royal Pavilion contain the **Brighton Museum and Art Gallery,** whose buildings were designed as a stable block for the Prince Regent's horses. The museum includes especially interesting art nouveau and art deco collections. Look out for Salvador Dalí's famous sofa in the shape of Mae West's lips, and pause at the Balcony Café for its bird's-eye view over the 20th-century Art and Design collection. ⊠ *Church St.* ☎ *01273/290900* ⊕ *www.brighton.virtualmuseum.info* ⌺ *Free* ☾ *Tues. 10–7, Wed.–Sat. 10–5, Sun. 2–5; closed Mon. except public holidays.*

The Lanes (⊠ Bordered by West, North, East, and Prince Albert Sts.), a maze of alleys and passageways, was once the home of fishermen and their families. Closed to vehicular traffic, the area's cobbled streets are filled with interesting restaurants, boutiques, and antiques shops. Fish and seafood restaurants line the heart of the Lanes, at Market Street and Market Square.

☉ **Volk's Electric Railway,** built by inventor Magnus Volk in 1883, was the first public electric railroad in Britain. In summer you can take the 1¼-mi trip along Marine Parade. ⊠ *Marine Parade* ☎ *01273/292718* ⌺ *£1.40 one-way, £2.40 round-trip* ☾ *Late Mar.–Sept., weekdays 10:30–5, weekends 10:30–6.*

Where to Eat

£££–££££   ✕ **Havana.** The mock Cuban building, high ceilings, rattan chairs, tan leather furnishings, and sophisticated food at Havana might make you think you're in London. Don't let that deter you, however—this place is a pleasure. Expect modern twists on British classics: the sautéed sea bream, for example, comes on a bed of braised fennel. The chic bar area is a perfect place to rest your feet at the end of the day. ☒ *32 Duke St.* ☎ *01273/773388* ▭ *AE, MC, V.*

ff–ffff ✕ **English's of Brighton.** One of the few old-fashioned seafood havens left in England is buried in the Lanes in three fisherfolk's cottages. It's been a restaurant for more than 150 years and a family business for more than 50. You can eat succulent oysters and other seafood dishes at the counter or take a table in the smart restaurant section. The restaurant's popularity means it's usually busy, and service can sometimes be slow. ☒ *29–31 East St.* ☎ *01273/327980* ▭ *AE, DC, MC, V.*

★ ff ✕ **Terre à Terre.** This inspiring vegetarian restaurant is popular, so come early for a light lunch, or book a table for an evening meal. The Jerusalem artichoke soufflé, tangy olive-cranberry couscous, and an eclectic choice of salads should satisfy most palates, and dishes have names to match their culinary inventiveness, such as Blackbean Cellophane Frisbee and Jabba Jabba Beefy Tea. ☒ *71 East St.* ☎ *01273/729051* ⌦ *Reservations essential* ▭ *AE, DC, MC, V* ◔ *No lunch Mon.; in winter, closed Mon., no lunch Tues. and Wed.*

f–ff ✕ **Nia Café.** In the interesting North Laine area, Nia has views down Trafalgar Street from its pavement tables. In addition to good coffees and leaf teas, excellent café food is available all day, from simple (but freshly made) sandwiches to fillets of cod stuffed with wild mushrooms. The dining room is simple, but large windows and fresh flowers add a friendly feel. It's also near the station, which is handy if you have time to kill before a train or you need to reenergize before a busy day's sightseeing. ☒ *87–88 Trafalgar St.* ☎ *01273/671371.*

CAMBRIDGE

60 mi north-northeast of London.

With the spires of its university buildings framed by towering trees and expansive meadows, its medieval streets and passages enhanced by gardens and riverbanks, the city of Cambridge is among the loveliest in England. The city predates the Roman occupation of Britain but the university was not founded until the 13th century. There's disagreement about the birth of the university: one story attributes its founding to impoverished students from Oxford, who came in search of eels—a cheap source of nourishment. Today a healthy rivalry persists between the two schools.

This university town may be beautiful, but it's no museum. Even when the students are on vacation there's a cultural and intellectual buzz here. It's a preserved medieval city of some 109,000 souls and growing, dominated culturally and architecturally by its famous university (whose students make up around one-fifth of the inhabitants), and beautified by parks, gardens, and the quietly flowing River Cam. Punting on the Cam (one occupant propels the narrow, square-end, flat-bottom boat with a long pole) is a quintessential Cambridge pursuit, followed by a stroll along the Backs, the left bank of the river fringed by St. John's, Trinity, Clare, King's, and Queens' colleges, and Trinity Hall.

VISITING THE COLLEGES College visits are certainly a highlight of a Cambridge tour, but remember that the colleges are private homes and workplaces, even when school isn't in session. Each is an independent entity within the university; some are closed to the public, but at others you can see the chapels, dining rooms (called halls), and sometimes the libraries, too. Some colleges charge a small fee for the privilege of nosing around. All are closed during exams, usually from mid-April to late June, and the opening hours often vary. For details about visiting specific colleges not listed here, contact **Cambridge University** (☎ 01223/337733 ⊕ www.cam.ac.uk).

By far the best way to gain access without annoying anyone is to join a walking tour led by an official Blue Badge guide—in fact, many areas are off-limits unless you do. The two-hour tours (£6.50–£8.50) leave daily from the **Tourist Information Centre** (⊠ The Old Library, Wheeler St. ☎ 0871/2268006, or 0044 1223 464732 from abroad ⊕ www. visitcambridge.org ⊗ Easter–Sept., weekdays 10–5:30, Sat. 10–5, Sun. 11–4; Oct.–Easter, weekdays 10–5:30, Sat. 10–5).

Exploring Cambridge

Emmanuel College (1584) is the alma mater of one John Harvard, who gave his books and his name to the American university. A number of the Pilgrims were Emmanuel alumni; they named Cambridge, Massachusetts, after their alma mater. ⊠ *Emmanuel and St. Andrew's Sts.* ☎ *01223/334200* ⊕ *www.emma.cam.ac.uk* ⊠ *Free* ⊗ *Daily 9–6.*

★ East Anglia's finest art gallery, the **Fitzwilliam Museum** houses outstanding collections of art, including several Constable paintings, oil sketches by Rubens, and antiquities from ancient Egypt, Greece, and Rome. ⊠ *Trumpington St.* ☎ *01223/332900* ⊕ *www.fitzmuseum.cam.ac.uk* ⊠ *Free* ⊗ *Tues.–Sat. 10–5, Sun. noon–5.*

Fodor'sChoice **King's College** (1441) is notable as the site of the world-famous Gothic-★ style **King's College Chapel** (built 1446–1547). Some deem its great fan-vaulted roof, supported by a delicate tracery of columns, the most glorious example of Perpendicular Gothic in Britain. It's the home of the famous choristers, and, to cap it all, Rubens's *Adoration of the Magi* is secreted behind the altar. The college's Back Lawn leads down to the river, from where the panorama of college and chapel is one of the university's most photographed views. ⊠ *Kings Parade* ☎ *01223/331100 college, 01223/331155 chapel* ⊕ *www.kings.cam.ac.uk* ⊠ *£3.50* ⊗ *Oct.–June, weekdays 9:30–3:30, Sat. 9:30–3:15, Sun. 1:15–2:15; July–Sept., Mon.–Sat. 9:30–4:30, Sun. 1:15–2:15 and 5–5:30; hrs vary with services, so call to confirm before visiting.*

Pembroke College (1347) has delightful gardens and bowling greens. Its chapel, completed in 1665, was the architect Christopher Wren's first commission. ⊠ *Trumpington St.* ☎ *01223/338100* ⊕ *www.pem.cam. ac.uk* ⊠ *Free* ⊗ *Daily 9–dusk.*

In 1284 the Bishop of Ely founded **Peterhouse College,** Cambridge's smallest and oldest college. Take a tranquil walk through its former deer park, by the river side of its ivy-clad buildings. ⊠ *Trumpington St.* ☎ *01223/338200* ⊕ *www.pet.cam.ac.uk* ⊠ *Free* ⊗ *Daily 9–5.*

★ **Queens' College**—built around 1448, and named after Margaret, queen of Henry VI, and Elizabeth, queen of Edward IV—enjoys a reputation

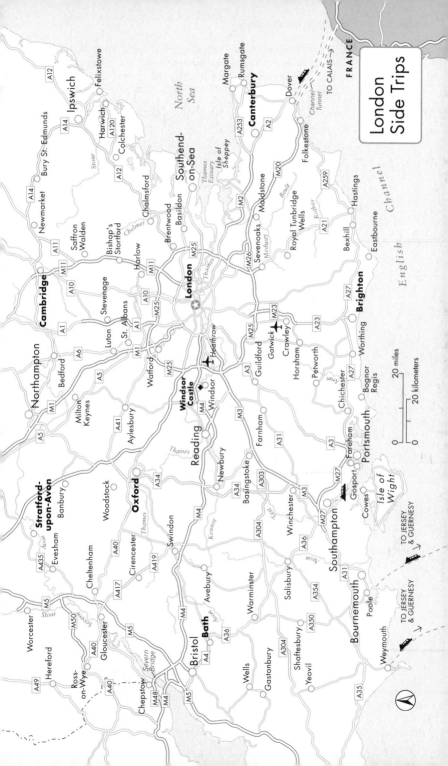

London Side Trips

as one of Cambridge's most eye-catching colleges. Enter over the **Mathematical Bridge,** the original version of which is said to have been built by Isaac Newton without any binding save gravity, then dismantled by curious scholars anxious to learn Sir Isaac's secret. The college maintains, however, that the bridge wasn't actually put together until 1749, 22 years after Newton's death, thus debunking the popular myth. ✉ *Queens' La.* ☎ *01223/335511* ⊕ *www.quns.cam.ac.uk* 🎫 *£1* ⊙ *Apr.–Oct., daily 10–4:30; Nov.–Mar., daily 10–4.*

Along King's Parade is **Corpus Christi College.** If you visit only one quadrangle, make it the beautiful, serene, 14th-century Old Court here; it's the oldest continuously inhabited college quadrangle in Cambridge. ✉ *King's Parade* ☎ *01223/338000* ⊕ *www.corpus.cam.ac.uk* 🎫 *Free* ⊙ *Daily dawn–dusk.*

St. John's College (1511), the university's second largest, has noted alumni (Wordsworth studied here), a series of beautiful courtyards, and two of the finest sights in town: the **School of Pythagoras,** the oldest house in Cambridge; and the 1831 **Bridge of Sighs,** whose only resemblance to its Venetian counterpart is its covering. The windowed, covered stone bridge reaches across the Cam to the mock-Gothic New Court (1825–31). The New Court's cupola's white crenellations have earned it the nickname "the wedding cake." ✉ *St. John's St.* ☎ *01223/338600* ⊕ *www.joh.cam.ac.uk* 🎫 *£2.50* ⊙ *Apr.–Oct., daily 10–5.30; Nov.–Mar. hrs vary.*

Fodor'sChoice **Trinity College** was founded by Henry VIII in 1546, and has the largest student population of all the colleges. It's also famous for having been attended by Byron, Thackeray, Tennyson, Bertrand Russell, Nabokov, Nehru, and 31 Nobel Prize winners. Many of Trinity's features reflect its status as Cambridge's largest college, not least its 17th-century "great court" and the massive gatehouse that contains Great Tom, a giant clock that strikes each hour with high and low notes. Don't miss the wonderful library by Christopher Wren, where you can see a letter written by alumnus Isaac Newton with early notes on gravity, and A. A. Milne's handwritten manuscript of *The House at Pooh Corner.* ✉ *St. John's St.* ☎ *01223/338400* ⊕ *www.trin.cam.ac.uk* 🎫 *£2.20 Mar.–Oct.* ⊙ *College daily 10–5; hall and chapel open to visitors but hrs vary.*

Where to Eat

★ **£££–££££** ✕ **Midsummer House.** In fine weather the gray-brick Midsummer House's conservatory, beside the River Cam, makes for a memorable lunchtime jaunt. Choose from a selection of traditional European and Mediterranean dishes. You might get tender local lamb or the best from the daily fish market, adorned with inventively presented vegetables. ✉ *Midsummer Common* ☎ *01223/369299* ⌕ *Reservations essential* 🖃 *AE, MC, V* ⊙ *Closed Mon. No lunch Sat., no dinner Sun.*

£ ✕ **Vaults.** Ochre and deep-red walls and metal chairs on slate floors lend a sleek, contemporary twist to the underground vaults. The zinc-topped bar with red sofas is the perfect place for lounging with a cocktail, and there's live music four nights a week. The evening menu is tapas style: lots of small portions of an eclectic mix of international cuisine. Lunchtime menus are more traditional. ✉ *14A Trinity St.* ☎ *01223/506090* 🖃 *AE, MC, V.*

[handwritten margin notes:] Hall 3:00–5:00 PM · 27–31 Dec. · college open 10:00–5:00 PM also 10 Jan '08 · 12:00–2:00 PM Mon.–Fri. · Saturday Am 10:30–12:30 during Term

CANTERBURY

60 mi north of London.

A bustling medieval Cathedral town, charming Canterbury has good shopping, plenty of history, and just enough to see in a day—making it an ideal day trip from London.

As you might remember from high school English classes spent studying Chaucer's *Canterbury Tales,* the height of Canterbury's popularity came in the 12th century, when thousands of pilgrims flocked here to see the shrine of Archbishop St. Thomas à Becket, murdered when King Henry II's complaints were misunderstood. The humble ancient buildings that served as pilgrims' inns still dominate the streets of Canterbury's pedestrian center.

Dig a little deeper and there's evidence of prosperous society in the Canterbury area as early as the Bronze Age (around 1000 BC). Canterbury was an important Roman city, as well as an Anglo-Saxon center in the Kingdom of Kent; it's currently headquarters of the Anglican Church. The town remains a lively place, a fact that has impressed visitors since 1388, when Chaucer wrote his stories.

Exploring Canterbury

You can easily cover Canterbury in a day. The 90-minute journey south from London's Victoria Station leaves plenty of time for a tour of the cathedral, a museum visit or two, and (if the weather's right) a walk around the perimeter of the old walled town. Canterbury is bisected by a road running northwest, along which the major tourist sites cluster. This road begins as St. George's Street, then becomes High Street, and finally turns into St. Peter's Street.

On St. George's Street a lone church tower marks the site of **St. George's Church**—the rest of the building was destroyed in World War II—where playwright Christopher Marlowe was baptized in 1564.

★ The **Canterbury Roman Museum** is below ground level, in the ruins of the original Roman town. There's a colorful restored Roman mosaic pavement and a hypocaust (the Roman version of central heating), as well as a display of excavated objects. Get a feel for what it once looked like via the computer-generated reconstructions of Roman buildings. ⊠ *Butchery La.* ☎ *01227/785575* ⊕ *www.canterbury-museums.co.uk* ☒ *£2.70* ☉ *June–Oct., Mon.–Sat. 10–5, Sun. 1:30–5; Nov.–May, Mon.–Sat. 10–5; last entry at 4. Closed last wk in Dec.*

Mercery Lane, with its medieval-style cottages and massive, overhanging timber roofs, runs right off High Street and ends in the tiny **Buttermarket,** a market square that was known in the 15th century as the Bullstake: animals were tied here for baiting before slaughter. Today it's a small market where you can buy books or homemade jam.

The immense **Christchurch Gate**, built in 1517, leads into the cathedral close. As you pass through, look up at the sculpted heads of two young figures: Prince Arthur, elder brother of Henry VIII, and the young

20

Catherine of Aragon, to whom he was betrothed. After Arthur's death, Catherine married Henry. Her inability to produce a male heir after 25 years of marriage led to Henry's decision to divorce her, creating an irrevocable breach with the Roman Catholic Church and altering the course of English history.

Fodor'sChoice   The massive heart of the town, towering **Canterbury Cathedral** was the
★   first of England's great Norman cathedrals. The nucleus of worldwide Anglicanism, the Cathedral Church of Christ Canterbury (its formal name) is a living textbook of medieval architecture.

The cathedral was only a century old, and still relatively small in size, when Thomas à Becket, the Archbishop of Canterbury, was murdered here in 1170. An uncompromising defender of ecclesiastical interests, Becket had angered his friend Henry II, who supposedly exclaimed, "Who will rid me of this troublesome priest?" Thinking they were carrying out the king's wishes, four knights burst in on Becket in one of the church's side chapels, chased him through the halls, and stabbed him to death. Two years later Becket was canonized, and Henry II's subsequent penitence helped establish the cathedral as the undisputed center of English Christianity.

Becket's tomb, destroyed by Henry VIII in 1538 as part of his campaign to reduce the power of the Church and confiscate its treasures, was one of the most extravagant shrines in Christendom. In **Trinity Chapel,** which held the shrine, you can still see a series of 13th-century stained-glass windows illustrating Becket's miracles. The actual site of Becket's murder is down a flight of steps just to the left of the nave, and marked with a simple sign that says only "Becket." If time permits, be sure to explore the **Cloisters** and other small monastic buildings north of the cathedral. ⊠ *Cathedral Precincts* ☎ *01227/762862* ⊕ *www.canterbury-cathedral.org* 🖼 *£4.50; free for services and for ½ hr before closing* ⊙ *Easter–Sept., Mon.–Sat. 9–6, Sun. 12:30–2:30 and 4:30–5:30; Oct.–Easter, Mon.–Sat. 9–4:30, Sun. 12:30–2:30 and 4:30–5:30. Restricted access during services.*

To vivify some of Canterbury's history, spend some time at an exhibition called **The Canterbury Tales,** an audiovisual (and occasionally olfactory) dramatization of 14th-century English life. You'll "meet" Chaucer's pilgrims at the Tabard Inn near London and view tableaux illustrating five tales. Actors clad in period costumes play out the town's history. ⊠ *St. Margaret's St.* ☎ *01227/479227* ⊕ *www.canterburytales.org.uk* 🖼 *£6.95* ⊙ *Nov.–Feb., daily 10–4:30; Mar.–June, Sept., and Oct, daily 10–5; July and Aug., daily 9:30–5.*

★   The medieval Poor Priests' Hospital is now the site of the **Museum of Canterbury** (previously the Canterbury Heritage Museum). The exhibits provide an excellent overview of the city's history and architecture from Roman times to World War II, although the displays are a strange mix of the serious (the Blitz) and the silly (cartoon characters Bagpuss and Rupert Bear). It even touches on the mysterious death of the 16th-century poet and playwright Christopher Marlowe. You can look at "medieval poo" under a microscope. Visit early in the day to avoid the crowds.

✉ *20 Stour St.* ☎ *01227/475202* ⊕ *www.canterbury-museums.co.uk* 🎟 *£3.20* ⏱ *Jan.–May and Oct.–Dec., Mon.–Sat. 10:30–5; June–Sept., Mon.–Sat. 10:30–5, Sun. 1:30–5; last admission at 4.*

Only one of the city's seven medieval gatehouses survives, complete with twin castellated towers; it now contains the **West Gate Museum.** Inside are medieval bric-a-brac and armaments used by the city guard, as well as more contemporary weaponry. The building became a jail in the 14th century, and you can view the prison cells. Climb to the roof for a panoramic view of the city spires. ☎ *01227/789576* ⊕ *www.canterbury-museums.co.uk* 🎟 *£1.15* ⏱ *Mon.–Sat. 11–12:30 and 1:30–3:30; last admission 1 hr before closing. Closed Christmas wk and Good Fri.*

Perhaps the best view of Canterbury's medieval past comes from following its 13th- and 14th-century **medieval city walls,** which were themselves built on the line of the original Roman walls. Those to the east have survived intact, towering some 20 feet high and offering a sweeping view of the town. You can access these from a number of places, including Castle and Broad streets.

Augustine, England's first Christian missionary, was buried in 597 at **St. Augustine's Abbey,** one of the oldest monastic sites in the country. When Henry VIII seized the abbey in the 16th century, he destroyed some of the buildings and converted others into a royal manor for his fourth wife, Anne of Cleves. A free interactive audio tour vividly puts events into context. The abbey is the base for Canterbury's biennial Sculpture Festival (held on odd-number years). Contemporary sculpture is placed on the grounds, and in other locations in the city, May through August. ✉ *Longport* ☎ *01227/767345* ⊕ *www.english-heritage.org.uk* 🎟 *£3.70* ⏱ *Apr.–Sept., daily 10–6; Oct.–Mar., Wed.–Sat. 10–4.*

There's not much left of the aptly named **Dane John Mound,** just opposite the Canterbury East train station, but it was originally a fortress and part of the city defenses. But among what does remain is a fantastic medieval maze.

Where to Eat

★ **££–£££** ✕ **Lloyds.** The magnificent beamed barn roof of this older building remains, but the interior—stripped wooden floors, and white walls enlivened by modern art—and the contemporary cooking are definitely up-to-the-minute. A crew of young chefs creates such dishes as roasted-pumpkin-and-amaretto ravioli with Parmesan, and pheasant with kumquats and juniper berries. The ice creams are homemade. ✉ *89–90 St. Dunstan's St.* ☎ *01227/768222* ▭ *AE, MC, V.*

££ ✕ **Duck Inn.** About 5 mi outside of Canterbury, this lovely, low-roof traditional pub is a great favorite among regular visitors to the city. Its pleasant rural location yields a bit of country charm, while dishes such as game pies are delightfully traditional. The name is said to come from the fact that the beams above the entrance are so low that you must duck as you enter or risk bashing your head. ✉ *Pett Bottom, near bridge* ☎ *01227/830354* ▭ *No credit cards.*

★ **£–££** ✕ **Weavers.** In one of the Weavers' Houses (the Weavers were Huguenots and Walloons who fled persecution in continental Europe in the 16th and 17th centuries) on the River Stour, this popular restaurant in the center of town is an ideal place to revel in the Tudor surroundings and feast on generous portions of British comfort food. Traditional pies, seafood, and pasta dishes are served along with a good selection of wines. Ask for a table in the more sedate ground-floor dining area. ⊠ *1 St. Peter's St.* ☏ *01227/464660* ▤ *AE, MC, V.*

£ ✕ **City Fish Bar.** Long lines and lots of satisfied finger-licking attest to the deserved popularity of this excellent fish-and-chips outlet in the center of town. Everything is freshly fried, the batter is crisp, and the fish is tasty; the fried mushrooms are also surprisingly good. It closes at 7. ⊠ *30 St. Margarets St.* ☏ *01227/760873* ▤ *No credit cards.*

OXFORD

62 mi north of London.

Oxford must be an extraordinary place to get an education. The university system that educated Prime Minister Tony Blair, former President Bill Clinton, and writers J. R. R. Tolkien, Percy Bysshe Shelley, Oscar Wilde, W. H. Auden, and C. S. Lewis is the heart and soul of the town. Its fabled "dreaming spires" can be seen for miles around, and it's not at all unusual to see robed students rushing to exams, or harried dons clutching mortar boards as they race to class on bicycles. It's a trip back in time, and a peek at what is arguably the kind of university we all wanted to go to.

Dating from the 12th century, Oxford University is older than Cambridge, and the city is bigger and more cosmopolitan than its competitor to the east. It's satisfyingly filled with hushed quadrangles, chapels, canals, rivers and vivid gardens. Bikes are inevitably propped against picturesque wrought-iron railings, and students propel flat-bottom boats down the little River Cherwell with long poles. (It's harder than it looks, but you can rent a punt yourself at the foot of Magdalen Bridge.)

In the end, though, central Oxford is also a bit of an illusion. Outside of the eminitely photographable university area, it's a major industrial center, with sprawling modern suburbs and large car and steel plants around its fringes.

VISITING THE COLLEGES The same concerns for people's work and privacy hold here as in Cambridge. Note that many of the colleges and university buildings are closed around Christmas (sometimes Easter, too) and on certain days from April to June for exams and degree ceremonies.

If you have limited time, get a detailed map from the tourist office and focus on selected sights. The Oxford University Web site (⊕ www.ox. ac.uk) is a great source of information if you're planning to go it alone. Guided city walking tours leave the **Oxford Information Centre** twice a day. ⊠ *15–16 Broad St.* ☏ *01865/726871* ⊕ *www.oxford.gov.uk/ tourism* 🖾 *£6.50 Sun.–Fri., £7.50 Sat.* ⊙ *Tours daily at 11 and 4.*

Exploring Oxford

Any Oxford visit should begin at its very center—a pleasant walk of 10 minutes or so east from the train station—with the splendid **University Church of St. Mary the Virgin** (1280). Climb 127 steps to the top of its 14th-century tower for a panoramic view of the city. ⊠ *High St.* ☏ *01865/ 279111* ⊕ *www.university-church. ox.ac.uk* ⌼ *Church free, tower £2* ☉ *Sept.–June, Mon.–Sat. 9–5, Sun. noon–5; July and Aug., Mon.–Sat. 9–6, Sun. noon–6.; last admission to tower 30 min before closing.*

FodorśChoice
★ Among Oxford's most famous sights, the gorgeous, round **Radcliffe Camera** (1737–49) is the most beautiful of the buildings housing the extensive contents of the august **Bodleian Library.** The baroque domed rotunda with an octagonal base sits in a lovely square where your photographic instincts can run riot. Not many of the 6-million-plus volumes are on view to those who aren't dons, but you can see part of the collection on a tour. Call ahead to prebook a tour. Note that children under 14 are not admitted. ⊠ *Broad St.* ☏ *01865/277224* ⊕ *www.bodley. ox.ac.uk* ⌼ *£4, extended tour £7* ☉ *Bodleian tours Mar.–Oct., weekdays at 10:30, 11:30, 2, and 3, and Sat. at 10:30 and 11:30; Nov.–Feb., weekdays at 2 and 3, and Sat. at 10:30 and 11:30. Divinity School weekdays 9–4:45, Sat. 9–12:30.*

★ The **Sheldonian Theatre,** built between 1664 and 1668, was Sir Christopher Wren's first major work (the chapel at Pembroke College was his first commission). The theater, which he modeled on a Roman amphitheater, made his reputation. It was built as a venue for the university's public ceremonies, and graduations are still held here—entirely in Latin, as befits the building's spirit. Outside is one of Oxford's most striking sights—a metal fence topped with stone busts of 18 Roman emperors (modern reproductions of the originals, which were eaten away by pollution). ⊠ *Broad St.* ☏ *01865/277299* ⊕ *www.sheldon.ox.ac.uk* ⌼ *£1.50* ☉ *Mar.–mid-Nov., Mon.–Sat. 10–12:30 and 2–4:30; mid-Nov.–Feb., Mon.–Sat. 10–12:30 and 2–3:30. Closed for 10 days at Christmas and Easter and for degree ceremonies and events.*

☾ Brush up on local history at the **Oxford Story.** Take your place at a medieval student's desk as it trundles, Disney-style, through 800 years of Oxford history. In 20 minutes you can see Edmund Halley discover his comet, and watch the Scholastica's Day Riot of 1355. There's commentary tailored for kids, too. ⊠ *6 Broad St.* ☏ *01865/728822* ⊕ *www. oxfordstory.co.uk* ⌼ *£7.25* ☉ *July and Aug., daily 9:30–5; Sept.–June, Mon.–Sat. 10–4:30, Sun. 11–4:30.*

Outside the "new" (they're actually Victorian) college gates of prestigious **Balliol College** (1263), a cobblestone cross in the sidewalk marks the spot where Archbishop Cranmer and Bishops Latimer and Ridley were burned in 1555 for their Protestant beliefs. The original college gates (rumored to have existed at the time of the scorching) hang in the library passage, between the inner and outer quadrangles. ⊠ *St. Giles St.* ☏ *01865/277777* ⊕ *www.balliol.ox.ac.uk* ⌼ *£1* ☉ *Daily 2–5, or dusk if earlier.*

20

★ The **chapel of Trinity College** (1555) is an architectural gem—a tiny place with a delicately painted ceiling, gorgeously tiled floor, and elaborate wood carvings on the pews, pulpit and walls. Some of the superb wood carvings were done by Grinling Gibbons, a 17th-century master carver whose work can also be seen in Hampton Court Palace and

> **HERE'S WHERE**
>
> The dining hall at Christ Church College should look familiar to fans of a certain young wizard–it appeared as the Hogwarts School dining hall in the Harry Potter movies.

St. Paul's Cathedral, and who inspired the 18th-century cabinetmaker Thomas Chippendale. ⊠ *Broad St.* ☎ *01865/279900* ⊕ *www.trinity. ox.ac.uk* ☞ *£2* ⊙ *Daily 10–noon and 2–4, or dusk if earlier.*

Fodor'sChoice
★ The **Ashmolean Museum,** founded in 1683, is Britain's oldest public museum. Some of the world's most precious art objects are stashed here—drawings by Michelangelo and Raphael, European silverware and ceramics, a world-class numismatic collection, and Egyptian, Greek, and Roman artifacts. The museum is currently being renovated one section at a time, so some galleries may be closed when you visit. Check the Web site in advance if you had a particular display in mind. ⊠ *Beaumont St.* ☎ *01865/278000* ⊕ *www.ashmol.ox.ac.uk* ☞ *Free* ⊙ *Tues.–Sat. 10–5, Sun. noon–5.*

St. John's College (1555), Prime Minister Tony Blair's alma mater, is worth a stop for its historic courtyards, neatly arrayed symmetrical gardens, and its library, where you can view some of Jane Austen's letters and an illustrated 1482 edition of *The Canterbury Tales* by the English printer William Caxton. ⊠ *St. Giles St.* ☎ *01865/277300* ⊕ *www.sjc. ox.ac.uk* ☞ *Free* ⊙ *Daily 1–dusk.*

Tom Tower, designed by Christopher Wren, marks the entrance to the
★ ☾ largest college of the southern half of Oxford: **Christ Church College.** Traditionally called "the House" by its students, Christ Church has the largest quadrangle in town. This is where Charles Dodgson, better known as Lewis Carroll, was a math don; a shop across from the parkland (known as "the meadows") on St. Aldate's was the inspiration for the shop in *Through the Looking Glass.* Don't miss the 800-year-old chapel or the medieval dining hall, with its portraits of former students—John Wesley, William Penn, and 14 prime ministers. ⊠ *St. Aldate's* ☎ *01865/276150* ⊕ *www.chch.ox.ac.uk* ☞ *£4* ⊙ *Mon.–Sat. 9–5:30, Sun. 1–5:30.*

Where to Eat

★ **££–£££** ✕ **Le Petit Blanc.** Raymond Blanc's Conran-designed brasserie is sophisticated even by London standards. The top British chef populates his menu with modern European and regional French dishes: you might see herb pancakes with Gruyère and ham, or a hake fillet panfried in hazelnut butter. At £12 for two courses or £14.50 for three, the prix-fixe lunch is an incredible value, and well worth the short walk north of the town center. ⊠ *71–72 Walton St.* ☎ *01865/510999* ☜ *Reservations essential* ▭ *AE, DC, MC, V.*

£ ✕ **Grand Café.** In a lovely 1920s building, this inexpensive café looks as if it should cost the world. Golden tiles, carved columns, and antique marble tables fill the place with charm, while the menu of tasty sandwiches, salads, and tarts, as well as perfect coffee drinks and desserts, make it a great place for lunch or an afternoon break. ✉ *84 High St.* ☎ *01865/204463* ▤ *AE, DC, MC, V.*

£ ✕ **Pizza Express.** Many people are surprised to discover that this unique restaurant in the former sitting room of the 15th-century Golden Cross— Shakespeare's stopover lodging on his frequent trips from Stratford to London—is part of a nationwide chain. Creativity is encouraged here, so vegetarians, vegans, and meat eaters alike can enjoy inventing their own dream pizzas. A terrace is open in summer, but be sure to check out the medieval paintings and friezes inside the restaurant before heading out. ✉ *8 The Golden Cross, Cornmarket St.* ☎ *01865/790442* ▤ *AE, DC, MC, V.*

STRATFORD-UPON-AVON

104 mi north of London.

Stratford-upon-Avon has become adept at accommodating the hordes of people who come for a glimpse of William Shakespeare's world. Filled with all the distinctive, Tudor, half-timber buildings your heart could desire, this is certainly a handsome town. But it can feel, at times, like a literary amusement park, so if you're not a fan of the Bard, you'd probably do better to explore some other quaint English village.

That said, how best to maximize your immersion in Shakespeare's works? It's difficult to avoid feeling like a herd animal as you board the Shakespeare bus, but tours like **Stratford and the Shakespeare Story** (✉ 14 Rother St. ☎ 01789/294466 ⊕ www.city-sightseeing.com ✆ £8), with a hop-on, hop-off route around the five Shakespeare Birthplace Trust properties (two of which are out of town), can make a visit infinitely easier if you don't have a car.

If you've never been here before, and you want to see everything, it's worth purchasing a combined ticket to the **Shakespeare's Birthplace Trust properties,** which include Shakespeare's Birthplace Museum, Nash's House, Hall's Croft, Anne Hathaway's Cottage, and the Shakespeare Countryside Museum. The ticket, which is valid for one year and is available at any of the properties, costs £14 for all the sites, or £11 for the three in-town properties (not including Anne Hathaway's Cottage and Mary Arden's House). ☎ *01789/204016* ⊕ *www.shakespeare.org.uk.*

20

Exploring Stratford-upon-Avon

Most visitors to Stratford start at **Shakespeare's Birthplace Museum.** The half-timber building in which Shakespeare was born in 1564 is a national treasure. It was owned by his descendants until the 19th century, and it became a national memorial in 1847. It's been furnished and decorated in bright colors that were popular in Shakespeare's time. All the fabrics

> **FAMILY TREES**
>
> Nash House belonged to Thomas Nash, first husband of Shakespeare's granddaughter Elizabeth Hall: you can see how tenuous the Shakespearean links can get around here.

have been hand-dyed using period methods. The visitor center tells the story of Shakespeare's life in great detail, which makes a good starting point for any tour of Stratford. ⊠ *Henley St.* ☎ *01789/204016* ⊕ *www. shakespeare.org.uk* ☞ *£7* ⊙ *Late Mar.–late Oct., Mon.–Sat. 9–5, Sun. 9:30–5; late Oct.–late Mar., Mon.–Sat. 9:30–4, Sun. 10–4.*

Nash's House contains an exhibit charting the history of Stratford, against a backdrop of period furniture and tapestries. The main attraction is really the vainglorious gardens around the adjacent remains of **New Place,** the home where Shakespeare spent his last years, and where he died in 1616. A gorgeous Elizabethan knot garden, based on drawings of gardens from Shakespeare's time, grows around the remaining foundation of the house, which was destroyed in 1759 by its last owner, Reverend Francis Gastrell, in an attempt to stop the tide of visitors. ⊠ *Chapel St.* ☎ *01789/204016* ⊕ *www.shakespeare.org.uk* ☞ *£3.75* ⊙ *Nov.–Mar., daily 11–4; Apr., May, Sept., and Oct., daily 11–5; June–Aug., Mon.–Sat. 9:30–5, Sun. 10–5; last entry 30 min before closing.*

★ **Hall's Croft** is Stratford's most beautiful Tudor town house. This was— almost definitely—the home of Shakespeare's daughter Susanna and her husband, Dr. John Hall. It's outfitted with furniture of the period and the doctor's dispensary. The walled garden is delightful. ⊠ *Old Town St.* ☎ *01789/204016* ⊕ *www.shakespeare.org.uk* ☞ *£3.75* ⊙ *Nov.–Mar., daily 11–4; Apr., May, Sept., and Oct., daily 11–5; June–Aug., Mon.–Sat. 9:30–5, Sun. 10–5; last entry 30 min before closing.*

"Shakespeare's church," the 13th-century **Holy Trinity,** is fronted by a beautiful avenue of lime trees. Shakespeare is buried here, in the chancel. The bust of the Bard is thought to be an authentic likeness, executed a few years after his death. ⊠ *Trinity St.* ☎ *01789/266316* ☞ *Church free, chancel £1* ⊙ *Mar., Mon.–Sat. 9–5, Sun. 12:30–5; Apr.–Oct., Mon.–Sat. 8:30–6, Sun. 12:30–5; Nov.–Feb., Mon.–Sat. 9–4, Sun. 12:30–5; last admission 20 min before closing.*

Fodor'sChoice ★ The **Royal Shakespeare Theatre** on the bank of the Avon is the home of the Royal Shakespeare Company in Stratford—it puts on several productions each season. The design of the smaller **Swan Theatre,** in the same building, is based on the original Elizabethan Globe theater. It's best to book in advance, but day-of-performance tickets are nearly always available. Backstage tours take place around performances, so call ahead. ⊠ *Waterside* ☎ *0870/6091110 ticket hotline, 01789/296655 information, 01789/403405 tours* ⊕ *www.rsc.org.uk* ☞ *Tours £5* ⊙ *Tours* *weekdays, except matinee days, at 1:30 and 5:30; tours matinee days at 5:30 and after show; tours Sun. at noon, 1, 2, and 3. No tours when shows are being prepared. Gallery Mon.–Sat. 9:30–6:30, Sun. noon–4:30.*

STRATFORD
ENVIRONS
★

The two remaining stops on the Shakespeare trail are just outside Stratford. **Anne Hathaway's Cottage,** the early home of the playwright's wife, is a picturesque thatched cottage restored to reflect the comfortable middle-class Hathaway life. You can walk here from town—it's just over a mile from central Stratford. ⊠ *Cottage La., Shottery* ☎ *01789/204016* ⊕ *www.shakespeare.org.uk* ▣ *£5.50* ⊙ *Apr., May, Sept., and Oct., Mon.–Sat. 9:30–5, Sun. 10–5; June–Aug., Mon.–Sat. 9–5, Sun. 9:30–5; Nov.–Mar., Mon.–Sat. 10–4, Sun. 10:30–4; last entry 30 min before closing.*

☼

The **Shakespeare Countryside Museum,** with displays that illustrate life in the English countryside from Shakespeare's time to the present day, is the main attraction at **Palmer's Farm,** the site of a recent and radical Shakespearean revelation. In late 2000, research findings based on newly discovered real-estate records revealed that the property, which had been referred to since the 18th century as Mary Arden's House, was not in fact the house in which Shakespeare's mother grew up. The real **Mary Arden's House,** hitherto known as Glebe Farm, was actually nearby and (thankfully) already owned by the Shakespeare Birthplace Trust. ⊠ *Wilmcote* ☎ *01789/204016, 01789/293455 for information on special events* ⊕ *www.shakespeare.org.uk* ▣ *£6* ⊙ *Nov.–Mar., Mon.–Sat. 10–4, Sun. 10:30–4; Sept., Oct., Apr., and May, Mon.–Sat. 10–5, Sun. 10:30–5; June–Aug., Mon.–Sat. 9:30–5, Sun. 10–5; last entry 30 min before closing.*

★ ☼

Some 8 mi north of Stratford in the medieval town of Warwick, **Warwick Castle** fulfills the most clichéd Camelot daydreams. This medieval, fortified, much-restored, castellated, moated, landscaped (by Capability Brown) castle, now managed by the experts at Madame Tussaud's, is a true period museum—complete with dungeons and a torture chamber, state rooms, and the occasional battle reenactment. ⊠ *Castle La. off Mill St., Warwick* ☎ *01926/495421, 08704/422000 24-hr information line* ⊕ *www.warwick-castle.co.uk* ▣ *Nov.–Feb. £13.95, Mar.–mid-July £15.95, mid-July–Oct. £17.95* ⊙ *Apr.–July and Sept., daily 10–6; Aug., weekdays 10–6, weekends 10–7; Oct.–Mar., daily 10–5.*

20

Where to Eat

£££££
✕ **Quarto's.** Views of the River Avon and its resident swans add to the appeal of this attractive spot in the Royal Shakespeare Theatre, where you can dine decently before or after a play. The lounge offers pretheater canapés and champagne. The menu is contemporary British, so expect such dishes as lamb with rosemary and goat-cheese salad. ⊠ *Royal Shakespeare Theatre, Waterside* ☎ *01789/403415* ⌖ *Reservations essential* ▤ *AE, MC, V* ⊙ *Closed when theater is closed.*

★ £££
✕ **Restaurant Margaux.** This chic French restaurant on two floors resembles a cozy bistro. The upscale menu highlights such dishes as quail and foie gras ravioli with baby leeks, chargrilled tuna with crab beignet and saffron dressing, and pistachio-and-strawberry parfait. It can be a bit

noisy upstairs—the spacious basement is the quieter alternative. ⊠ 6 *Union St.* ☎ *01789/269106* ⌕ *Reservations essential* ▭ *MC, V.*

££–£££ ✕ **Lambs of Sheep Street.** This friendly place is making a name for itself as one of the best restaurants in the region, with a menu that includes both traditional British favorites and interesting daily specials. You can try everything from fresh local sausages and mashed potatoes to creamy Thai green-curry chicken. Hardwood floors and oak beams make for a cozier ambience downstairs. The two- and three-course set menus (£11.50 and £14, respectively) are particularly good deals. ⊠ *12 Sheep St.* ☎ *01789/292554* ⌕ *Reservations essential* ▭ *AE, MC, V.*

£ ✕ **Black Swan.** Known locally as the Dirty Duck, this is one of Stratford's most celebrated pubs—it has attracted actors since the 18th-century thespian David Garrick's days. A little veranda overlooks the theaters and the river here. Along with a pint of bitter, it's a fine place to enjoy English grill specialties, as well as braised oxtail and honey-roasted duck. You can also choose from an assortment of bar meals. ⊠ *Waterside* ☎ *01789/297312* ▭ *AE, MC, V* ☉ *No dinner Sun.*

WINDSOR CASTLE

24 mi west of London.

The tall turrets of Windsor Castle, the largest inhabited castle in the world, can be seen for miles around. The grand stone castle is the star attraction in this quiet medieval town—though Eton College, England's most famous public school, is also just a lovely walk away across the Thames. The castle, the Queen's preferred home, is the only royal residence to have been in continuous royal use since the days of William the Conqueror, who chose this site to build a timber stockade soon after his conquest of Britain in 1066. It was Edward III in the 1300s who really founded the castle: he built the Norman gateway, the great Round Tower, and the State Apartments. Charles II restored the State Apartments during the 1600s, and, during the 1820s George IV—with his mania for building—converted what was still essentially a medieval castle into the palace you see today.

Exploring Windsor Castle

The massive citadel of **Windsor Castle** occupies 13 acres, but the first part you notice on entering is the **Round Tower,** on top of which the Standard is flown and at the base of which is the 11th-century Moat Garden. Passing under the portcullis at the Norman Gate, you reach the **Upper Ward,** the quadrangle containing the State Apartments—which you may tour when the queen is out—and the sovereign's Private Apartments. Processions for foreign heads of state and other ceremonies take place here, as does the Changing of the Guard when the queen is in. A short walk takes you to the Lower Ward, where the high point is the magnificent **St. George's Chapel,** symbolic and actual guardian of the Order of the Garter, the highest chivalric order in the land, founded in 1348 by Edward III. Ten sovereigns are buried in the chapel—a fantastic Perpendicular Gothic vision 230 feet long, complete with gargoyles, buttresses, banners, swords, and choir stalls. This is also where royal weddings usually take place.

The **State Apartments** are grander than Buckingham Palace's and have the added attraction of a few gems from the queen's vast art collection: choice canvases by Rubens, Rembrandt, Van Dyck, Gainsborough, Canaletto, and Holbein; da Vinci drawings; Gobelin tapestries; and lime-wood carvings by Grinling Gibbons. The entrance is through a grand hall holding cases crammed with precious china—some still used for royal banquets. Don't miss the outsize suit of armor, made for Henry VIII, in the armory. Make sure you take in the magnificent views across to Windsor Great Park, which are the remains of a former royal hunting forest.

> **DID YOU KNOW?**
>
> The queen uses Windsor often—it's said she likes it much more than Buckingham Palace—spending most weekends here, often joined by family and friends. You know she's in when the Royal Standard is flown above the Round Tower but not when you see the Union Jack. Arrive early at the main entrance, as lines can be long.

One unmissable treat—and not only for children—is **Queen Mary's Dolls' House,** a 12:1 scale, seven-story palace with electricity, running water, and working elevators, designed in 1924 by Sir Edwin Lutyens. The detail is incredible—some of the miniature books in the library are by Kipling, Conan Doyle, Thomas Hardy, and G. K. Chesterton, written by the great authors in their own hands. The diminutive wine bottles hold the real thing, too.

In 1992 a fire that started in the queen's private chapel gutted some of the State Apartments. A swift rescue effort meant that, miraculously, hardly any works of art were lost, and a £37 million effort has restored the Grand Reception Room, the Green and Crimson drawing rooms, and the State and Octagonal dining rooms to their former, if not greater, glory. ⊠ *Windsor Castle* ☎ *020/7766–7304 tickets, 01753/83118 recorded information* ⊕ *www.royalresidences.com* 🎫 *£13.50 for Precincts, State Apartments, Gallery, St. George's Chapel, Albert Memorial Chapel, and Queen Mary's Dolls' House; £7 when State Apartments are closed* ⊗ *Mar.–Oct., daily 9:45–5:15, last admission at 4; Nov.–Feb., daily 9:45–4:15, last admission at 3; St. George's Chapel closed Sun. except to worshippers.*

20

Where to Eat

£ ✕ **Two Brewers.** Two small, low-ceiling rooms make up this 17th-century pub where locals congregate. Children are not welcome, but adults will find a suitable collection of wine, espresso, and local beer, plus an excellent little menu with dishes from salmon fish cakes to chili and pasta. Reservations are essential on Sunday, when the pub serves a traditional roast. ⊠ *34 Park St.* ☎ *01753/855426* ⊟ *AE, MC, V* ⊗ *No dinner Fri. or Sat.*

UNDERSTANDING LONDON

LONDON AT A GLANCE

ENGLISH VOCABULARY

BOOKS & MOVIES

LONDON AT A GLANCE

Fast Facts

Type of government: Representative democracy. In 1999 the Greater London Authority Act reestablished a single local governing body for the Greater London area, consisting of an elected mayor and the 25-member London Assembly. Elections, first held in 2000, take place every 4 years.

Population: City 7.4 million, metro area 11.2 million

Population density: 11,841 people per square mi

Median age: 38.4

Infant mortality rate: 5.7 per 1,000 births

Language: English. More than 300 languages are spoken in London. All city government documents are translated into Arabic, Bengali, Chinese, Greek, Gujurati, Hindi, Punjabi, Turkish, Urdu, and Vietnamese.

Ethnic and racial groups: White 71%, Indian 6%, other 6%, black African 5%, black Caribbean 5%, Bangladeshi 2%, other Asian 2%, Pakistani 2%, Chinese 1%

Religion: Christian 58%, non-affiliated 24%, Muslim 8%, Hindu 4%, Jewish 2%, Sikh 1%, other religion 1%, Buddhist 0.8%

When a man is tired of London, he is tired of life; for there is in London all that life can afford.
—Samuel Johnson

Geography & Environment

Latitude: 51° N (same as Calgary, Canada; Kiev, Russia; Prague, Czech Republic)

Longitude: 0° (same as Accra, Ghana). A brass line in the ground in Greenwich marks the prime meridian (0° longitude).

Elevation: 49 feet

Land area: City, 67 square mi; metro area, 625 square mi

Terrain: River plain, rolling hills, and parkland

Natural hazards: Drought in warmer summers, flooding of the Thames due to surge tides from the North Atlantic

Environmental issues: Up to 1,600 people die each year from health problems related to London's polluted air. The city has been improving its air quality but is unlikely to meet goals it set for 2005. Only half of London's rivers and canals received passing grades for water quality from 1999 through 2001. Over £12 million ($22 million) is spent annually to ensure the city's food safety.

I'm leaving because the weather is too good. I hate London when it's not raining.
—Groucho Marx

Economy

Work force: 5.3 million; financial/real estate 28%, health care 10%, manufacturing 8%, education 7%, construction 5%, public administration 5%

Unemployment: 6.9%

Major industries: The arts, banking, government, insurance, tourism

London: a nation, not a city.
—Benjamin Disraeli, *Lothair*

Did You Know?

- With more than 7 million residents, London is the largest city in the European Union. It's among the most densely populated, too, following Copenhagen, Brussels, and Paris.

- London's ethnic mosaic includes communities of more than 10,000 people from 34 different countries.

- There are 481 foreign banks in the city, more than in any other world financial center. The London Stock Exchange deals with almost twice as many foreign companies as the New York Stock Exchange.

- Up to about £2,000 (about $3,680) of taxpayers' money can be used to purchase a wig for a London judge, who often still wears the antiquated accessory. Barristers and solicitors (lawyers) must pay for their own wigs and often buy them used.

- More than 100 species of fish, including smelt (which locals say has an odor resembling their beloved cucumber sandwiches), live in the Thames. In 1957 naturalists reported no signs of life in the river. The Thames looks brown because of sediment but is actually Europe's cleanest metropolitan estuary.

- Despite being surrounded by more than 5,000 pubs and bars, Londoners drink less than the average British resident. Twenty-three percent of men in London drank 22 or more units of alcohol per week from 2001 through 2002, compared with 27% in Great Britain as a whole.

- The Tube is the world's biggest subway system. With 253 mi of routes and 275 stations, it covers more ground than systems in New York, Paris, and Tokyo.

- City taxi drivers must pass a training test that requires between two and four years of preparation. Eight or nine of every ten applicants drop out before completion.

- The average home price in London is £210,100 ($386,580), about £75,000 ($138,000) higher than the average in the United Kingdom, and five times the average family income of first-time buyers. The average monthly rent for a one-bedroom apartment in private housing is £1,029 ($1,837).

ENGLISH VOCABULARY

You and a Londoner may speak the same language, but some phrases definitely get lost in translation once they cross the Atlantic. Here's a handy guide to help you avoid confusion.

British English	American English

Basic Terms and Everyday Items

British English	American English
bill	check
flat	apartment
holiday	vacation
lift	elevator
nappie	diaper
note	bill (currency)
plaster	band-aid
queue	line
row	argument
rubbish	trash
tin	can
toilet/ loo/ WC	bathroom

Clothing

British English	American English
braces	suspenders
bum bag	fanny pack
dressing gown	robe
handbag	purse
jumper	sweater
pants/ undies	underpants/ briefs
rucksack	backpack
suspender	garter
tights	pantyhose
trainers	sneakers
trousers	pants
vest	undershirt
waistcoat	vest

Transportation

British English	American English
bonnet	hood
boot	trunk
coach	long-distance bus

pavement	sidewalk
petrol	gas
pram	baby carriage
puncture	flat
windscreen	windshield

Food

afters	dessert
aubergine	eggplant
banger	sausage
biscuit	cookie
chips	fries
courgette	zucchini
crisps	potato chips
greasy spoon	café serving traditional English breakfasts, all day
jam	jelly
jelly	Jello
pips	seeds
rocket	arugula
spud	potato
starter	appetizer
sweet	candy
tea	early dinner

Slang

all right	hi there
bird	woman
bloke, chap	guy
cheers	thank you
chuffed	pleased
geezer	dude
guv'nor, gaffer	boss
hard	tough
mate	buddy
randy	horny
sound	good
ta	thank you
wicked	cool

BOOKS & MOVIES

London has been the focus of countless books and essays. For sonorous eloquence, you still must reach back more than half a century to Henry James's *English Hours* and Virginia Woolf's *The London Scene*. Today most suggested reading lists begin with V. S. Pritchett's *London Perceived* and H. V. Morton's *In Search of London*, both decades old. Three more up-to-date books with a general compass are: Peter Ackroyd's anecdotal *London: The Biography*, which traces the city's growth from the Druids to the 21st century, John Russell's *London*, a sumptuously illustrated art book, and Christopher Hibbert's *In London: The Biography of a City*. Stephen Inwood's *A History of London* explores the city from its Roman roots to its swinging '60s heyday. Piet Schreuders's *The Beatles' London* follows the footsteps of the Fab Four.

That noted, there are books galore on the various facets of the city. *The Art and Architecture of London* by Ann Saunders is fairly comprehensive. *Inside London: Discovering the Classic Interiors of London*, by Joe Friedman and Peter Aprahamian, has magnificent color photographs of hidden and overlooked shops, clubs, and town houses. For a wonderful take on the golden age of the city's regal mansions, see Christopher Simon Sykes's *Private Palaces: Life in the Great London Houses*. For various other aspects of the city, consult Mervyn Blatch's helpful *A Guide to London's Churches*, Andrew Crowe's *The Parks and Woodlands of London*, Sheila Fairfield's *The Streets of London*, Ann Saunders's *Regent's Park*, Ian Norrie's *Hampstead, Highgate Village, and Kenwood*, and Suzanne Ebel's *A Guide to London's Riverside: Hampton Court to Greenwich*. For keen walkers, there are two books by Andrew Duncan: *Secret London* and *Walking Village London*. *City Secrets: London*, edited by Robert Kahn, is a handsome little red-linen book of anecdotes from London writers, artists, and historians about their favorite places in the city. For the last word on just about every subject, see *The London Encyclopaedia*, edited by Ben Weinreb and Christopher Hibbert. HarperCollins's *London Photographic Atlas* has a plethora of bird's-eye images of the capital. For an alternative view of the city, it would be hard to better Ian Sinclair's witty and intelligent *London Orbital: A Walk Around the M25* in which he scrutinizes the history, mythology, and politics of London from the viewpoint of its ugly ringroad.

Of course, the history and spirit of the city are also to be found in celebrations of great authors, British heroes, and architects. Peter Ackroyd's massive *Dickens* elucidates how the great author shaped today's view of the city; Martin Gilbert's magisterial, multivolume *Churchill* traces the city through some of its greatest trials; J. Mansbridge's *John Nash* details the London buildings of this great architect. Liza Picard evokes mid-18th-century London in *Dr. Johnson's London*. For musical theater buffs, Mike Leigh's *Gilbert and Sullivan's London* takes a romantic look at the two artists' lives and times in the capital's grand theaters and wild nightspots. *Rodinsky's Room* by Rachel Lichtenstein and Iain Sinclair is a fascinating exploration of East End Jewish London and the mysterious disappearance of one of its occupants.

Nineteenth-century London—the city of Queen Victoria, Tennyson, and Dickens—comes alive through *Mayhew's London*, a massive study of the London poor, and Gustave Doré's *London*, an unforgettable series of engravings of the city (often reprinted in modern editions) that detail its horrifying slums and grand avenues. Maureen Waller's *1700: Scenes from London Life* is a fascinating look at the daily life of Londoners in the 18th century. When it comes to fiction, of course, Dickens's immortal works top the list. Stay-at-home detectives have long walked the streets of London, thanks to great mysteries by Sir Arthur Conan Doyle, Dorothy L. Sayers, Agatha Christie, Ngaio Marsh, and Antonia Fraser. Cops and bad guys wind their way around 1960s London in Jake Arnott's pulp fiction books, *The Long Firm* and *He Kills Coppers*. Martin Amis's *London Fields* tracks a murder mystery through West London. For so-called "tart noir," pick up any Stella Duffy book. Marie Belloc-Lowndes's *The Lodger* is a fictional account of London's most deadly villain, Jack the Ripper. Victorian London was never so salacious as in Sarah Waters' story of a young girl who travels the theaters as a singer, the Soho squares as a male prostitute, and the East End as a communist in *Tipping the Velvet*. Late-20th-century London, with its diverse ethnic makeup, is the star of Zadie Smith's famed novel *White Teeth*. The vibrancy and cultural diversity of London's East End come to life in Monica Ali's *Brick Lane*.

There are any number of films—from *Waterloo Bridge* and *Georgy Girl* to *Secrets and Lies* and *Notting Hill*—that have used London as their setting. But always near the top of anyone's list are four films that rank among the greatest musicals of all time: Walt Disney's *Mary Poppins* (complete with Dick Van Dyke's laughable Cockney accent), George Cukor's *My Fair Lady*, Sir Carol Reed's *Oliver!*, and The Beatles' *A Hard Day's Night*.

Children of all ages enjoy Stephen Herek's *101 Dalmatians*, with Glenn Close as fashion-savvy Cruella de Vil. King's Cross Station in London was shot to cinematic fame by the movie version of J. K. Rowling's *Harry Potter and the Philosopher's Stone*. Look for cameos by the city in all other *Harry Potter* films.

The swinging '60s is loosely portrayed in M. Jay Roach's *Austin Powers: International Man of Mystery*, full of references to British slang and some great opening scenes in London. For a truer picture of the '60s in London, Michaelangelo Antonioni weaves a mystery plot around the world of London fashion photographer in *Blow-Up*. British gangster films came into their own with Guy Ritchie's amusing tales of London thieves in *Lock, Stock, and Two Smoking Barrels,* filmed almost entirely in London, and the follow-up *Snatch,* with a comedic turn by Brad Pitt. Of course, the original tough guy is 007, and his best exploits in London are featured in the introductory chase scene in *The World Is Not Enough*.

Sir Arthur Conan Doyle knew the potential of London as a chilling setting, and John Landis's *An American Werewolf in London* and Hitchcock's *39 Steps* exploit the Gothic and sinister qualities of the city. St. Ermine's Hotel stands in for the 19th-century Savoy dining room in Oliver Parker's *The Importance of Being Earnest*. For a fascinating look at Renaissance London, watch John Madden's *Shakespeare in Love*.

Some modern-day romantic comedies that use London as a backdrop are Peter Howitt's *Sliding Doors* with Gwyneth Paltrow; Nick Hamm's sweet, romantic comedy about an American backpacker, *Martha Meet Frank, Daniel and Laurence (aka The Very Thought of You)*; the screen adaptations of Helen Fielding's *Bridget Jones's Diary* (and its sequel), starring Renée Zellweger, Hugh Grant, and Colin Firth; and Richard Curtis's holiday feel-good flick *Love Actually,* which included as many threaded-together romantic misadventures as it did A-list British actors. For a slice of Indian London, you can't do better than Gurinder Chadha's tale of a girl who wants to play soccer in *Bend It Like Beckham*.

SMART TRAVEL TIPS

Finding out about your destination before you leave home means you won't spend time organizing everyday minutiae once you've arrived. You'll be more streetwise when you hit the ground as well, better prepared to explore the aspects of London that drew you here in the first place. The organizations in this section can provide information to supplement this guide; contact them for up-to-the-minute details. Happy landings!

ADDRESSES

Central London and its surrounding districts are divided into 32 boroughs—33, counting the City of London. More useful for finding your way around, however, are the subdivisions of London into postal districts. Throughout the guide we've given the full postal code for most listings. The first one or two letters give the location: N means north, NW means northwest, and so on. Don't expect the numbering to be logical, however. You won't, for example, find W2 next to W3. The general rule is that the lower numbers, such as W1 or SW1, are closest to the city center.

AIR TRAVEL TO & FROM LONDON

BOOKING

When you book, look for nonstop flights and remember that "direct" flights stop at least once. Try to avoid connecting flights, which require a change of plane. Two airlines may operate a connecting flight jointly, so ask whether your airline operates every segment of the trip; you may find that the carrier you prefer flies you only part of the way. To find more booking tips and to check prices and make online flight reservations, log on to www.fodors.com.

CARRIERS

British Airways is the national flagship carrier and offers mostly nonstop flights from 18 U.S. cities to Heathrow and Gatwick airports, along with flights to Manchester, Birmingham, and Glasgow. As the leading British airline, it has a vast program of discount airfare-hotel packages.

🔏 **To & from London American Airlines** ☎ 800/433-7300, 020/7365-0777 in London 🌐 www.aa.

London
Postal Districts

com to Heathrow, Gatwick. **British Airways** ☎ 800/
247-9297, 0870/850-9850, in London ⊕ www.ba.
com to Heathrow, Gatwick. **Continental** ☎ 800/
231-0856 or 01293/776464, 0845/607-6760 in London ⊕ www.continental.com to Gatwick. **Delta**
☎ 800/241-4141, 0800/414767 in London ⊕ www.
Delta.com to Gatwick. **Northwest Airlines** ☎ 800/
447-4747, 0870/507-4074 in London ⊕ www.nwa.
com to Gatwick. **United** ☎ 800/538-2929, 0845/
844-4777 in London ⊕ www.united.com to
Heathrow. **US Airways** ☎ 800/622-1015, 0845/600-
3300 in London ⊕ www.usair.com to Gatwick. **Virgin Atlantic** ☎ 800/862-8621, 01293/450150 in London ⊕ www.virgin-atlantic.com to Heathrow,
Gatwick.

CHECK-IN & BOARDING

Always **find out your carrier's check-in
policy.** Plan to arrive at the airport about
two hours before your scheduled departure time for domestic flights and 2½ to 3
hours before international flights. You
may need to arrive earlier if you're flying
from one of the busier airports or during
peak air-traffic times. For flights out of
London, the general rule is that you arrive
one hour before your scheduled departure
time for domestic flights and two hours
before international flights for off-peak
travel. To avoid delays at airport-security
checkpoints, try not to wear any metal.
Jewelry, belt and other buckles, steel-toe
shoes, barrettes, and underwire bras are
among the items that can set off detectors.

Assuming that not everyone with a ticket
will show up, airlines routinely overbook
planes. When everyone does, airlines ask
for volunteers to give up their seats. In return, these volunteers usually get a several-
hundred-dollar flight voucher, which can
be used toward the purchase of another
ticket, and are rebooked on the next available flight out. If there are not enough volunteers, the airline must choose who will
be denied boarding. The first to get
bumped are passengers who checked in
late and those flying on discounted tickets,
so get to the gate and check in as early as
possible, especially during peak periods.

Always **bring a government-issued photo
ID** to the airport; even when it's not required, a passport is best.

CUTTING COSTS

The least expensive airfares to London
are often priced for round-trip travel and
must usually be purchased in advance.
Airlines generally allow you to change
your return date for a fee; most low-fare
tickets, however, are nonrefundable. It's
smart to call a number of airlines and
check the Internet; when you are quoted a
good price, book it on the spot—the same
fare may not be available the next day, or
even the next hour. Always check different
routings and look into using alternate airports. Also, price off-peak flights and red-
eye, which may be significantly less
expensive than others. Travel agents, especially low-fare specialists (⇨ Discounts &
Deals), are helpful.

Consolidators are another good source.
They buy tickets for scheduled flights at reduced rates from the airlines, then sell
them at prices that beat the best fare available directly from the airlines. (Many also
offer reduced car-rental and hotel rates.)
Sometimes you can even get your money
back if you need to return the ticket. Carefully read the fine print detailing penalties
for changes and cancellations, purchase the
ticket with a credit card, and confirm your
consolidator reservation with the airline.

When you fly as a courier, you trade your
checked-luggage space for a ticket deeply
subsidized by a courier service. There are
restrictions on when you can book and
how long you can stay. Some courier companies list with membership organizations,
such as the Air Courier Association and
the International Association of Air Travel
Couriers; these require you to become a
member before you can book a flight.
⁊ Consolidators **AirlineConsolidator.com** ☎ 888/
468-5385 ⊕ www.airlineconsolidator.com, for international tickets. **Best Fares** ☎ 800/880-1234
⊕ www.bestfares.com; $59.90 annual membership.
Cheap Tickets ☎ 800/377-1000 or 800/652-4327
⊕ www.cheaptickets.com. **Expedia** ☎ 800/397-
3342 or 404/728-8787 ⊕ www.expedia.com.
Hotwire ☎ 866/468-9473 or 920/330-9418
⊕ www.hotwire.com. **Onetravel.com** ⊕ www.
onetravel.com. **Orbitz** ☎ 888/656-4546 ⊕ www.
orbitz.com. **Priceline.com** ⊕ www.priceline.com.
Travelocity ☎ 888/709-5983, 877/282-2925 in

Canada, 0870/111–7061 in U.K. ⊕ www.travelocity.com.

🔳 Courier Resources **Air Courier Association/ Cheaptrips.com** ☎ 800/211–5119 ⊕ www.aircourier.org or www.cheaptrips.com; $20 annual membership. **Courier Travel** ☎ 303/570–7586 🖷 313/625–6106 ⊕ www.couriertravel.org; $50 annual membership. **International Association of Air Travel Couriers** ☎ 308/632–3273 🖷 308/632–8267 ⊕ www.courier.org; $45 annual membership.

ENJOYING THE FLIGHT

State your seat preference when purchasing your ticket, and then repeat it when you confirm and when you check in. For more legroom, you can request one of the few emergency-aisle seats at check-in, if you're capable of moving obstacles comparable in weight to an airplane exit door (usually between 35 pounds and 60 pounds)—a Federal Aviation Administration requirement of passengers in these seats. Seats behind a bulkhead also offer more legroom, but they don't have under-seat storage. Don't sit in the row in front of the emergency aisle or in front of a bulkhead, where seats may not recline. SeatGuru.com has more information about specific seat configurations, which vary by aircraft.

Ask the airline whether a snack or meal is served on the flight. If you have dietary concerns, request special meals when booking. These can be vegetarian, low-cholesterol, or kosher, for example. It's a good idea to pack some healthful snacks and a small (plastic) bottle of water in your carry-on bag. On long flights, try to maintain a normal routine, to help fight jet lag. At night, get some sleep. By day, eat light meals, drink water (not alcohol), and **move around the cabin** to stretch your legs. For additional jet-lag tips consult *Fodor's FYI: Travel Fit & Healthy* (available at bookstores everywhere).

Smoking policies vary from carrier to carrier. Most airlines prohibit smoking on all of their flights; others allow smoking only on certain routes or certain departures. Ask your carrier about its policy.

FLYING TIMES

Flying time to London is about 6½ hours from New York, 7½ hours from Chicago, 11 hours from San Francisco, and 21½ hours from Sydney.

HOW TO COMPLAIN

If your baggage goes astray or your flight goes awry, complain right away. Most carriers require that you **file a claim immediately.** The Aviation Consumer Protection Division of the Department of Transportation publishes *Fly-Rights,* which discusses airlines and consumer issues and is available online. You can also find articles and information on mytravelrights.com, the Web site of the nonprofit Consumer Travel Rights Center.

🔳 Airline Complaints **Aviation Consumer Protection Division** ⊠ U.S. Department of Transportation, Office of Aviation Enforcement and Proceedings, C-75, Room 4107, 400 7th St. SW, Washington, DC 20590 ☎ 202/366–2220 ⊕ airconsumer.ost.dot.gov. **Federal Aviation Administration Consumer Hotline** ⊠ For inquiries: FAA, 800 Independence Ave. SW, Washington, DC 20591 ☎ 800/322–7873 ⊕ www.faa.gov.

RECONFIRMING

Check the status of your flight before you leave for the airport. You can do this on your carrier's Web site, by linking to a flight-status checker (many Web booking services offer these), or by calling your carrier or travel agent. Always confirm international flights at least 72 hours ahead of the scheduled departure time.

AIRPORTS & TRANSFERS

International flights to London arrive at either Heathrow Airport (LHR), 15 mi west of London, or at Gatwick Airport (LGW), 27 mi south of the capital. Most flights from the United States go to Heathrow, which is the busiest and is divided into four terminals, with Terminals 3 and 4 handling transatlantic flights (British Airways uses Terminal 4). Gatwick is London's second gateway. It has grown from a European airport into an airport that serves 21 scheduled U.S. destinations. A third, state-of-the-art airport, Stansted (STN), is 35 mi east of the city. It handles mainly European and domestic traffic, although there's also scheduled service from New York. A fourth airport, Luton (LTN), 30 mi north of town, mainly handles flights from Europe. ⓘ Airport Information **Gatwick Airport** ☎ 0870/000-2468. **Heathrow Airport** ☎ 0870/000-0123. **Luton Airport** ☎ 01582/405100. **Stansted Airport** ☎ 0870/000-0303.

AIRPORT TRANSFERS

London has excellent bus and train connections between its airports and downtown. If you're arriving at Heathrow, you can pick up a map and fare schedule at a Transport for London (TfL) Information Centre (in Terminals 1 and 2). Train service can be quick, but the downside (for trains from all airports) is that you must get yourself and your luggage to the train via a series of escalators and connecting trams. Airport link buses (generally National Express Airport buses) may ease the luggage factor and drop you closer to central hotels, but they're subject to London traffic, which can be horrendous. Taxis can be more convenient than buses, but beware that prices can go through the roof. Airport Travel Line has additional transfer information and takes advance booking for transfers between airports and into London.

Heathrow by Bus: National Express takes 1½ hours and costs £8 one-way and £15 round-trip. It leaves for King's Cross, with stops at Notting Hill Gate, Bayswater, Marble Arch, Marylebone Road, Euston, and Russell Square, every 30 minutes 5:30 AM–9:45 PM, but there are around 14 stops along the route, so it can be tedious. The N9 night bus runs every half hour from midnight to 4:30 AM to Trafalgar Square; it takes an hour and costs £1. For the same price and a journey closer to an hour, National Express buses leave every hour for Victoria Coach Station from 5:40 AM to 9:30 PM.

Heathrow by Train: The cheap, direct route into London is via the Piccadilly line of the Underground (London's extensive subway system, or "Tube"). Trains normally run every four to eight minutes from all terminals from early morning until just before midnight. The 50-minute trip into central London costs £4.30 one-way and connects with other central Tube lines. The Heathrow Express train is comfortable and very convenient, speeding into London's Paddington Station in 15 minutes, but is more expensive than the Tube. Standard one-way tickets cost £14.50 (£26 round-trip) and £25 for first class (more space). There's daily service from 5:10 AM (5:50 AM on Sunday) to 11:40 PM (10:50 PM on Sunday), with departures every 15 minutes. At Paddington you can board the Hotel Express bus to get to a number of central London hotels for £2.50. There are also local trains that make multiple stops; these are cheaper, but slower, than the Heathrow Express.

Gatwick by Bus: Hourly bus service runs from Gatwick's south terminal to Victoria Station with stops at Hooley, Coulsdon, Mitcham, Streatham, Stockwell, and Pimlico. The journey takes 90 minutes and costs £11 one-way. Make sure you get on a direct bus that does not require you to change—otherwise the journey could take hours.

Gatwick by Train: The fast, nonstop Gatwick Express leaves for Victoria Station every 15 minutes 5:15 AM–midnight. The 30-minute trip costs £13 one-way, £24.50 round-trip. The Thameslink train runs regularly throughout the day until 11:30 PM to King's Cross, London Bridge, and Blackfriars stations; departures are every 15 to 30 minutes, and the journey takes almost one hour. Tickets are about £11 one-way.

Stansted by Bus: Hourly service on National Express Airport bus A6 (24 hours a day) to Victoria Coach Station costs £10 one-way, £15 round-trip, and takes about 1 hour and 40 minutes. Stops include Golders Green, Finchley Road, St. John's Wood, Baker Street, Marble Arch, and Hyde Park Corner.

Stansted by Train: The 45-minute journey on Stansted Express to Liverpool Street Station (with a stop at Tottenham Hale) runs every 15 minutes 8 AM–5 PM weekdays, and every 30 minutes 5 PM–midnight and 6 AM–8 AM weekdays, and all day on weekends. The trip costs £14.50 one-way, £24 round-trip.

Luton by Bus and Train: A free airport shuttle runs from Luton Airport to the nearby Luton Airport Parkway Station, from which you can take a train or bus into London. From there, the Thameslink train service runs to several London stations, terminating at King's Cross. The journey takes about 35 minutes. Trains leave every 10 minutes or so 24 hours a day and cost £10.70 one-way, £19 round-trip. For a cheaper journey, take the Green Line 757 bus service from Luton to Victoria Station. It runs three times an hour, takes about 90 minutes, and costs £7.50.

Heathrow, Gatwick, Stansted, and Luton by Taxi: Taxis can get caught in traffic; the trip from Heathrow, for example, can take more than an hour and costs anywhere from £35 to more than £50. From Gatwick, the taxi fare is at least £70, with a journey time of about an hour and a half. From Stansted, the £75 journey takes a little more than an hour. From Luton, the approximately one-hour journey should cost around £65. Your hotel may be able to recommend a car service for airport transfers. Charges are usually about £35 to any airport. Add a tip of 10% to 15% to the basic fare.

Transfers between airports: Allow at least 2–3 hours for an interairport transfer. The cheapest option is public transport: from Gatwick to Stansted, for instance, you can catch the nonexpress commuter train from Gatwick to Victoria Station, take the Tube to Liverpool Street station, then catch the train to Stansted from there. To get from Heathrow to Gatwick by public transport, take the Tube to King's Cross, then change to the Victoria Line, get to Victoria Station, and then take the commuter train to Gatwick. Both of these trips would take about two hours.

The National Express Airport bus is the most direct option between Gatwick and Heathrow. Buses pick up passengers every 15 minutes from 5 AM to 10 PM from both airports. The trip takes 1½–2 hours, and the fare is £17.50 one-way, £35 round-

trip. It's advisable to book tickets in advance via National Express, especially during peak travel seasons, but you can also buy tickets in the terminals. National Express also runs shuttles between all the other airports, except between Luton and Stansted. Finally, some airlines may offer shuttle services as well—check with your travel agent in advance of your journey.

🚩 Taxis & Shuttles **Gatwick Express** ☎ 0870/530-1530. **Green Line** ☎ 0870/608-7261 ⊕ www.greenline.co.uk. **Heathrow Express** ☎ 0845/600-1515. **National Express** ☎ 0870/580-8080 ⊕ www.nationalexpress.com. **Stansted Express and Thameslink** ☎ 0845/748-4950. **Taxi at Gatwick Airport** ☎ 0800/747737. **Taxi at Heathrow** ☎ 020/8745-7487. **Taxi at Luton** ☎ 01582/595555 or 01582/736666. **Taxi at Stansted Airport** ☎ 01279/662444.

🚩 Transfer Information **Airport Travel Line** ☎ 0870/574-7777.

DUTY-FREE SHOPPING

Heathrow, Gatwick, and Stansted have an overwhelming selection of duty-free shops, but the tax-free advantages are for travelers departing the United Kingdom for a country outside the European Union. For allowances, *see* Customs & Duties.

BIKE TRAVEL

Bicycling in London, as in any major metropolitan area, is not for the faint-hearted. Be prepared to battle double-decker buses for space in narrow lanes, motorists who decline to notice you at all, and even bicycle couriers' vicious habit of considering the road to be their own. For experienced cyclists, though, cycling through London is the fastest, cleanest, most pleasant way to travel.

BIKES IN FLIGHT

Most airlines accommodate bikes as luggage, provided they are dismantled and boxed; check with individual airlines about packing requirements. Some airlines sell bike boxes, which are often free at bike shops, for about $20 (bike bags can be considerably more expensive). International travelers often can substitute a bike for a piece of checked luggage at no charge; otherwise, the cost is about $100. Most U.S. and Canadian airlines charge $40–$80 each way.

BUS TRAVEL TO & FROM LONDON

National Express is the biggest British coach operator and the nearest equivalent to Greyhound. It's fast (particularly its Rapide services, which do not detour to make pickups and have steward service for refreshments) and comfortable (with washroom facilities on board). Services depart mainly from Victoria Coach Station, a well-signposted short walk behind the Victoria mainline rail station. The departures point is on the corner of Buckingham Palace Road; this is also the main information point. The arrivals point is opposite at Elizabeth Bridge. National Express buses travel to all large and midsize cities in southern England and the midlands. Scotland and the north are not as well served. The station is extremely busy around holidays and weekends. It's wise to **arrive at least 30 minutes before departure** so you can find the correct exit gate. Smoking is not permitted on board.

A newcomer on the bus travel scene, Megabus, has been packing in the budget travelers, since it offers cross-country fares for as little as £1 per person. The company's double-decker buses serve an extensive array of cities across Great Britain. Though it's relatively new, it has been giving National Express a run for its money, taking it on with rock-bottom fares, new buses, and a cheerful budget attitude. In London, buses for all destinations depart from the Green Line bus stand at Victoria Station.

Megabus does not accommodate wheelchairs, and the company strictly limits luggage to one piece per person checked, and one piece of hand luggage.

Green Line serves the counties surrounding London, as well as airports. Bus stops (there's no central bus station) are on Buckingham Palace Road, between the Victoria mainline station and Victoria Coach Station.

FARES & SCHEDULES

Apex tickets save money on standard fares, and traveling midweek is cheaper than over weekends and at holiday periods. Tourist Trail Passes, sold by British Travel International, offer great savings if you plan to tour Britain, and they can be bought in advance. Prices run from £49 for two days of unlimited travel within three days to £205 for 15 days of unlimited travel within months. The Discount Coachcard for students costs £10 and qualifies you for 20% to 30% off many standard fares over a one-year period.

PAYING

Tickets for National Express can be bought from the Victoria, Heathrow, or Gatwick coach stations by phone with a credit card, via the National Express Web site, or from travel agencies. Tickets for Megabus must be purchased online in advance, or by phone. Tickets bought online in advance rarely rise above £5.

🚌 Bus Information **British Travel International** ☎ 800/327-6097 within the U.S. **Green Line** ☎ 0870/608-7261 ⊕ www.greenline.co.uk. **Megabus** ☎ 0900/160-0900 ⊕ www.megabus. com. **National Express** ☎ 0870/580-8080 ⊕ www. nationalexpress.com. **Victoria Coach Station** ☎ 020/7730-3499.

BUS TRAVEL WITHIN LONDON

Red Transport for London (TfL) buses travel all over town, whereas buses in other colors cover the suburbs. Although London is famous for its double-decker buses, change is underway. The city has embraced long articulated buses (locally known as "bendy buses"), which have fully replaced the oldest buses—the beloved rattletrap "routemasters," which had the jump-on/off back platforms. Two routemaster "heritage" routes keep the old familiar rattletrap buses working, however. The No. 9 travels through Piccadilly, Trafalgar Square, and Knightsbridge, and the No. 15 rattles its way through Trafalgar Square down Fleet Street and on to St. Paul's Cathedral.

Bus stops are clearly indicated; the main stops have a red TfL symbol on a plain white background. When the word RE-QUEST is written across the sign, you must flag the bus down. When the sign simply says "bus stop," the bus must stop whether or not it's flagged. Each numbered route is listed on the main stop, and buses have a large number on the front with their end destination. Not all buses run the full route at all times; check with the driver or conductor. If you want to decipher the numbers, pick up a free bus guide at a TfL Travel Information Centre (at Euston, Liverpool Street, Piccadilly Circus, and Victoria Tube stations; at West Croydon bus station; and at Heathrow Airport).

Buses are a good way of seeing the town, particularly if you plan to hop on and off to cover many sights, but **don't take a bus if you're in a hurry.** To get off, pull the cord running above the windows on old buses, or press the button by the exit. Expect to get a little squashed during rush hour, from 8 AM to 9:30 AM and 4:30 PM to 6:30 PM.

Night buses, denoted by an N before their route numbers, run from midnight to 5 AM on a more restricted route than day buses. All night buses run by request stop, so flag them down if you're waiting or push the button or pull the cord if you want to alight.

FARES & SCHEDULES

All journeys cost £1.50. If you plan to make a number of journeys in one day, consider buying a bus pass (£3) or a Travelcard (⇨ Underground Tube Travel), good for both Tube and bus travel. Traveling without a valid ticket makes you liable for a fine (£10–£20). Buses are supposed to swing by most stops every five or six minutes, but, in reality, you can often expect to wait a bit longer, although those in the center of town are quite reliable.

🚍 Bus Information **Transport for London** ☎ 020/7222-1234 ⊕ www.tfl.gov.uk.

PAYING

In central London you must pay before you board the bus. Automated ticket kiosks are set up at these bus stops, which are clearly marked with a yellow sign BUY TICKETS BEFORE BOARDING. Otherwise, you can buy tickets at most central London Tube stations as well as at newsagents, and shops that display the sign BUY YOUR TRAVELCARDS & BUS PASSES HERE. Outside the central zone, payment may be made to the driver as you enter (exact change is

best so as to avoid incurring the driver's wrath). On some of the old buses, a conductor issues you a ticket.

BUSINESS HOURS

Generally, businesses are closed on Sunday and national (bank) holidays (⇨ Holidays). New Year's Day is a national holiday, but many major stores are open for the annual sales. Many restaurants are closed over the Christmas period.

BANKS & OFFICES

Banks are open weekdays 9:30–4:30; offices are generally open 9:30–5:30. *See* Mail & Shipping *for post office hours.*

GAS STATIONS

Most gas stations in central London are open seven days, 24 hours. As you get farther out of town, and off trunk and major roads, hours vary considerably depending on the gas company, but are usually 8 AM–8 PM.

MUSEUMS & SIGHTS

The major national museums and galleries are open daily, with shorter hours on weekends than weekdays. But there's a trend toward longer hours, such as one late-night opening a week.

PHARMACIES

Pharmacies, called chemists, are open, for the most part, Monday–Saturday 9:30 AM–5:30 PM. The leading chain drugstore, Boots, is open until 6 PM; the Oxford Street and Piccadilly Circus branches are also open Sunday and until 8 PM Thursday, and the Leicester Square branch stays open until 9 or later most nights. Bliss the Chemist at 5 Marble Arch has the longest opening hours, from 9 AM to midnight.

SHOPS

Shops and offices in central London tend to keep longer hours than those in the surrounding districts. The usual shop hours are Monday–Saturday 9 AM–5:30 PM. In the main shopping streets of Oxford Street, Kensington High Street, and Knightsbridge, hours are 9:30 AM–6 PM, with late-night opening hours in Oxford Street on Thursday until 7:30 or 8 PM, and in the latter areas on Wednesday. Many small general stores and newsagents stay open on Sunday; some chain and fashion stores in the tourist areas of Oxford Street and Piccadilly (and out-of-town shopping malls) also remain open.

CAMERAS & PHOTOGRAPHY

Don't be surprised if you're asked not to take pictures during theater, ballet, or opera productions, and in galleries, museums, and stately homes. Locals are generally happy to feature in your photos, but it's polite to ask if they mind before fixing the lens. There are many must-take sights in London, but guards on horseback in Whitehall and Big Ben top the list. The *Kodak Guide to Shooting Great Travel Pictures* (available at bookstores everywhere) is loaded with tips.

🖪 Photo Help **Kodak Information Center** ☎ 800/242-2424 ⊕ www.kodak.com.

EQUIPMENT PRECAUTIONS

Don't pack film or equipment in checked luggage, where it is much more susceptible to damage. X-ray machines used to view checked luggage are extremely powerful and therefore are likely to ruin your film. Try to ask for hand inspection of film, which becomes clouded after repeated exposure to airport X-ray machines, and keep videotapes and computer disks away from metal detectors. Always keep film, tape, and computer disks out of the sun. Carry an extra supply of batteries, and be prepared to turn on your camera, camcorder, or laptop to prove to airport security personnel that the device is real.

FILM & DEVELOPING

Film is available from pharmacies, newsagents, and supermarkets, as well as photographic stores. Kodak and Agfa are the most common brands, and prices range from £2 to £4 for a roll of 36-exposure color print film. Larger drugstore branches and photographic stores stock the Advantix line. These stores provide 24-hour film-developing services.

VIDEOS

Videos from the United States are not compatible with British and European models. If you're bringing your own camcorder, bring a supply of cassettes as well.

CAR RENTAL

Rental rates in London vary widely. Rates generally begin at £35 (about $65) a day and £160 (about $300) a week for a small economy car (such as a subcompact General Motors Vauxhall, Corsa, or Renault Clio), usually with manual transmission. Air-conditioning and unlimited mileage generally come with the larger-size automatic cars.

🖪 Major Agencies **Alamo** ☎ 800/522-9696 ⊕ www.alamo.com. **Avis** ☎ 800/331-1084, 800/879-2847 in Canada, 0870/606-0100 in U.K., 02/9353-9000 in Australia, 09/526-2847 in New Zealand ⊕ www.avis.com. **Budget** ☎ 800/472-3325, 800/268-8900 in Canada, 1300/794-344 in Australia, 0800/283-438 in New Zealand ⊕ www.budget.com. **Dollar** ☎ 800/800-6000, 0800/085-4578 in U.K. ⊕ www.dollar.com. **Hertz** ☎ 800/654-3001, 800/263-0600 in Canada, 0870/844-8844 in U.K., 02/9669-2444 in Australia, 09/256-8690 in New Zealand ⊕ www.hertz.com. **National Car Rental** ☎ 800/227-7368 ⊕ www.nationalcar.com.

CUTTING COSTS

Rates are generally cheapest at European rental agencies such as Europcar (⇨ Local Agencies). For a good deal, book through a travel agent who will shop around. Do look into wholesalers, companies that do not own fleets but rent in bulk from those that do and often offer better rates than traditional car-rental operations. Prices are best during off-peak periods. Rentals booked through wholesalers often must be paid for before you leave home.

🖪 Local Agencies **Easy Car** ☎ 0906/333-3333, 60p per minute within U.K. ⊕ www.easycar.com. **Enterprise** ✉ 466-480 Edgware Rd., Edgware, London W2 1EL ☎ 020/7723-4800. **Europcar** ✉ 245 Warwick Rd., Kensington, London W14 8PX ☎ 020/7751-1770 ⊕ www.europcar.com. **1car1** ✉ 82 Caledonian Rd., Islington, London N1 9DN ☎ 020/7427-2368 🖷 020/7237-6459 ⊕ www.1car1.com.

🖪 Wholesalers **Auto Europe** ☎ 207/842-2000 or 800/223-5555 🖷 207/842-2222 ⊕ www.autoeurope.com. **Destination Europe Resources** (DER) ✉ 9501 W. Devon Ave., Rosemont, IL 60018 ☎ 800/782-2424 🖷 800/282-7474. **Europe by Car** ☎ 212/581-3040 or 800/223-1516 🖷 212/246-1458 ⊕ www.europebycar.com. **Kemwel** ☎ 877/820-0668 or 800/678-0678 🖷 207/842-2124 or 866/726-6726 ⊕ www.kemwel.com.

INSURANCE

When driving a rented car you are generally responsible for any damage to or loss of the vehicle. Collision policies that car-rental companies sell for European rentals typically do not cover stolen vehicles. Before you rent—and purchase collision or theft coverage—see what coverage you already have under the terms of your personal auto-insurance policy and credit cards.

REQUIREMENTS & RESTRICTIONS

It varies by rental car agency, but most will not rent to drivers under 25 or over 70.

SURCHARGES

Before you pick up a car in one city and leave it in another, ask about drop-off charges or one-way service fees, which can be substantial. Also inquire about early-return policies; some rental agencies charge extra if you return the car before the time specified in your contract, while others give you a refund for the days not used. Most agencies note the tank's fuel level on your contract; to avoid a hefty refueling fee, return the car with the same tank level. If the tank was full, refill it just before you turn in the car, but be aware that gas stations near the rental outlet may overcharge. It's almost never a deal to buy a tank of gas with the car when you rent it; the understanding is that you'll return it empty, but some fuel usually remains. Some rental agencies will offer a car seat for babies for a small extra fee. Most agencies do not charge extra for additional drivers.

CAR TRAVEL

In London your U.S. driver's license is acceptable (as long as you are over 23 years old, with no endorsements or driving convictions). If you have a driver's license from a country other than the United States, it may not be recognized in the United Kingdom. An International Driver's Permit is a good idea no matter what; it's available from the American (AAA) or Canadian Automobile Association and, in the United Kingdom, from the Automobile Association (AA) or Royal Automobile Club (RAC). International permits are universally recognized, and having one may save you a problem with the local authorities.

The best advice on driving in London is: don't. London's streets are a winding mass of chaos, made worse by one-way roads. Parking is also restrictive and expensive, and traffic is tediously slow at most times of the day; during rush hours—from 8 AM to 9:30 AM and 4:30 PM to 6:30 PM—it often grinds to a standstill, particularly on Friday, when everyone wants to leave town. Avoid city-center shopping areas, including the roads feeding Oxford Street, Kensington, and Knightsbridge. Other main roads into the city center are also busy, such as King's Cross and Euston in the north. Watch out also for cyclists and motorcycle couriers who weave between cars and pedestrians and seem to come out of nowhere.

Remember that Britain drives on the left, and the rest of Europe on the right. Therefore, you may want to leave your rented car in Britain and pick up a left-side drive if you cross the Channel (⇨ The Channel Tunnel).

CONGESTION CHARGE

Designed to reduce traffic through central London, a congestion charge has been instituted. Vehicles (with some exemptions) entering central London on weekdays from 7 AM to 6:30 PM (excluding public holidays) have to pay a £8 per day fee; it can be paid up to 90 days in advance, or on the day you need it. Day-, week-, month-, and year-long passes are available on the Congestion Charge Customer Service Web site, at gas stations, parking lots (car parks), by mail, by phone, by SMS text message, and at BT Internet kiosks. Traffic signs designate the entrance to congestion areas, and cameras read car license plates and send the information to a database. Drivers who don't pay the congestion charge by midnight after the day of driving are penalized £80, which is reduced to £40 if paid within 14 days.

🔝 **Congestion Charge Customer Service** 📫 Box 2985, Coventry CV7 8ZR ☎ 0845/900-1234 ⊕ www.cclondon.com.

EMERGENCY SERVICES

The general procedure for a breakdown is the following: position the red hazard triangle (which should be in the trunk of the car) a few paces away from the rear of the car. Leave the hazard warning lights on. Along highways (motorways), emergency roadside telephone booths are positioned at intervals within walking distance. Contact the car-rental company or an auto club. The main auto clubs in the United Kingdom are the Automobile Association (AA) and the Royal Automobile Club (RAC). If you're a member of the American Automobile Association (AAA), check your membership details before you depart for Britain as, under a reciprocal agreement, roadside assistance in the United Kingdom should cost you nothing. You can join and receive roadside assistance from the AA on the spot, but the charge is higher—around £75—than a simple membership fee.

⚑ American Automobile Association ☎ 800/564-6222. **Australian Automobile Association** ☎ 02/6247-7311. **Automobile Association** ☎ 0870/550-0600, 0800/887766 for emergency roadside assistance. **Canadian Automobile Association** ☎ 613/247-0117. **New Zealand Automobile Association** ☎ 09/377-4660. **Royal Automobile Club** ☎ 0870/572-2722.

GASOLINE

Gasoline (petrol) is sold in liters and is increasingly expensive (about 91p per liter at this writing). Unleaded petrol, denoted by green pump lines, is predominant. Premium and Super Premium are the two varieties, and most cars run on regular Premium. Supermarket pumps usually offer the best value, although they are often on the edge of the central city. You won't find many service stations in the center of town; these are generally on main, multilane trunk roads out of the center. Service is self-serve, except in small villages, where gas stations are likely to be closed on Sunday and late evening. Most stations accept major credit cards.

PARKING

During the day—and probably at all times—it's safest to believe that you can park nowhere except at a meter, in a garage, or where you are sure there are no lines or signs; otherwise, you run the risk of a towing cost of about £100 or a wheel clamp, which costs about the same, since you pay to have the clamp removed plus the cost of the one or two tickets you'll have earned first. Restrictions are indicated by the NO WAITING parking signpost on the sidewalk (these restrictions vary from street to street), and restricted areas include single yellow lines or double yellow lines. Parking at a bus stop or in a red-line bus lane is also restricted. It's illegal to park on the sidewalk, across entrances, or on white zigzag lines approaching a pedestrian crossing.

Meters have an insatiable hunger in the inner city—a 20p piece buys just six minutes—and some will only permit a two-hour stay. Meters take 10p, 20p, 50p, and £1 coins. In the evening, after restrictions end, meter bays are free. In the daytime, take advantage of the many N.C.P. parking lots in the center of town, which are often a better value (about £2.50–£3 per hour, up to eight hours). A London street map should have the parking lots marked.

RULES OF THE ROAD

If you must risk life and limb and drive in London, note that the speed limit is 30 mph in the royal parks, as well as in all streets—unless you see the large 40 mph signs (and small repeater signs attached to lampposts) found only in the suburbs. Pedestrians have the right-of-way on "zebra" crossings (black-and-white stripes that stretch across the street between two Belisha beacons—orange flashing globe lights on posts), and it's illegal to pass another vehicle at a zebra crossing. At other crossings pedestrians must yield to traffic, but they do have the right-of-way over traffic turning left at controlled crossings—if they have the nerve.

Traffic lights sometimes have arrows directing left or right turns; try to catch a glimpse of the road markings in time, and don't get into the turn lane if you mean to go straight ahead. A right turn is not permitted on a red light. Signs at the beginning and end of designated bus lanes give the time restrictions for use (usually during peak hours); if you're caught driving on bus lanes during restricted hours, you could be fined. The use of horns is prohibited between 11:30 PM and 7 AM. By law, seat belts must be worn in the front and back seats. Drunk-driving laws are strictly enforced, and it's safest to avoid alcohol altogether if you'll be driving. The legal limit is 80 milligrams of alcohol, which roughly translated means two units of alcohol—two glasses of wine, one pint of beer, or one glass of whiskey.

THE CHANNEL TUNNEL

Short of flying, taking the Eurostar train is the fastest way to cross the English Channel. From London's Waterloo Station, the high-speed train travels through a tunnel underneath the Channel (to the Brits' amusement, only Americans still call it "the Chunnel"), arriving in approximately 2 hours and 40 minutes at Paris's Gare du Nord. It takes slightly longer to stations in Brussels and Lille. Even mild claustrophobes tend to find the journey acceptable, as you are only in the tunnel itself for approximately 20 minutes. The Eurostar's rates have been going up, so expect to pay around £100 ($190) for a round-trip ticket, but note that tickets cost slightly less with advance purchase, and can cost much more if purchased on or near the day of travel. Construction on a glossy new Eurostar station is underway at St. Pancras station, next to King's Cross station. If completed on time, the Eurostar will move from Waterloo in late 2007. Web site and phone numbers will remain the same.

🚗 Car Transport **Eurotunnel** ☎ 0870/535–3535 in U.K., 070/223210 in Belgium, 03–21–00–61–00 in France ⊕ www.eurotunnel.com.

🚗 Passenger Service **Eurostar** ☎ 1233/617575, 0870/518–6186 in U.K. ⊕ www.eurostar.co.uk. **Rail Europe** ☎ 800/942–4866 or 800/274–8724, 0870/ 837–1371 U.K. inquiries and credit-card bookings ⊕ www.raileurope.com.

CHILDREN IN LONDON

There's a kaleidoscope of activity for children to enjoy in London, and museums and major attractions have made great strides in special interactive features and exhibitions (particularly in summer and during Christmas holidays). At many museums children enjoy free admission, and between the great establishments there are masses of green spaces in the London parks. During school holidays, bookstores run story times; cinemas, concert halls, and theaters have plenty of programs to watch—and participate in.

Up-to-date information is available in the section devoted to children's listings in the weekly magazine *Time Out* (£2.30), available at newsagents and bookstores. *Fodor's Around London with Kids* (available in bookstores everywhere) can help you plan your days together. Contact Kids Out! or Londonline for tips on sightseeing with children in London.

When packing, include things to keep children busy en route. If you are renting a car, don't forget to arrange for a car seat when you reserve. For general advice about traveling with children, consult *Fodor's FYI: Travel with Your Baby* (available in bookstores everywhere).

📖 Local Information **Kids Out!** ☎ 020/7813–6018. **Londonline** ☎ 09068/663344 Children's London, calls cost 60p/min from a U.K. phone ⊕ www. kidslovelondon.com.

BABYSITTING

📖 Agencies **The Babysitting Co.** ✉ 130 Greyhound Rd., Hammersmith, London W6 8JU ☎ 020/ 7385–5111. **Nanny Connection** ✉ Collier House, 163–169 Brompton Rd., Kensington, London SW3 1PY ☎ 020/7591–4488. **The Nanny Service** ✉ 6 Nottingham St., Bloomsbury, London W1M 3RB ☎ 020/7935–3515. **Pippa Pop-ins** ✉ 430 Fulham Rd., Fulham, London SW6 ☎ 020/7385–2458. **Universal Aunts** 🖂 Box 304, London SW4 0NN ☎ 020/7738–8937.

FLYING

When booking, confirm carry-on allowances if you're traveling with infants. In general, for babies charged 10% to 50% of the adult fare you are allowed one carry-on bag and a collapsible stroller; if the flight is full, the stroller may have to be checked or you may be limited to less.

Experts agree that it's a good idea to use safety seats aloft for children weighing less than 40 pounds. Airlines set their own policies: if you use a safety seat, U.S. carriers usually require that the child be ticketed, even if he or she is young enough to ride free, because the seats must be strapped into regular seats. And even if you pay the full adult fare for the seat, it may be worth it, especially on longer trips. Do **check your airline's policy about using safety seats during takeoff and landing.** Safety seats are not allowed everywhere in the plane, so get your seat assignments as early as possible.

When reserving, request children's meals or a freestanding bassinet (not available at all airlines) if you need them. But note that bulkhead seats, where you must sit to use the bassinet, may lack an overhead bin or storage space on the floor.

LODGING

Most hotels in London allow children under a certain age to stay in their parents' room at no extra charge, but others charge for them as extra adults; be sure to find out the cutoff age for children's discounts.

The following hotels offer family rooms and/or cots, babysitting service, and children's portions and high chairs in the restaurants.

🚩 Best Choices **City Inn Westminster** ⊠ 30 John Islip St., Westminster, SW1P 4DD ☎ 020/7630–1000. **The Landmark** ⊠ 222 Marylebone Rd., Marylebone, NW1 6JQ ☎ 020/7631–8000. **22 Jermyn Street** ⊠ 22 Jermyn St., St. James's, SW1Y 6HL ☎ 020/7734–2353, 800/682–7808 in U.S.

SIGHTS & ATTRACTIONS

The Tower of London, Tower Bridge Experience, London Dungeon, Madame Tussaud's, and the Natural History Museum are just a handful of sights to excite children. Places that are especially appealing to children are indicated by a rubberduckie icon (🐥) in the margin.

TRANSPORTATION

On trains and buses, children pay half or reduced fares; children under five ride for free. Car-rental companies may have child seats available. By law, where there are seat belts in front and back, children must use them, but it's the responsibility of the driver to ensure that they do. Children do not need a child seat if they are over age

five and are 1.5 meters (4 feet 11 inches) tall, but they must wear an adult seat belt. Children must be at least three to sit in the front seat, and if less than 1.5 meters tall will need a child seat or adult strap, whichever is available.

COMPUTERS ON THE ROAD

If you're traveling with a laptop, carry a spare battery and adapter: new batteries and replacement adapters are expensive; if you do need to replace them, head to Tottenham Court Road (W1), which is lined with computer specialists. John Lewis department store and Selfridges, on Oxford Street (W1), also carry a limited range. Never plug your computer into any socket before asking about surge protection. Some hotels do not have built-in current stabilizers, and extreme electrical fluctuations and surges can short your adapter or even destroy your computer. IBM sells an invaluable pen-size modem tester that plugs into a telephone jack to check if the line is safe to use.

CONCIERGES

Concierges, found in many hotels, can help you with theater tickets and dinner reservations: a good one with connections may be able to get you seats for a hot show or prime-time dinner reservations at the restaurant of the moment. You can also turn to your hotel's concierge for help with travel arrangements, sightseeing plans, services ranging from aromatherapy to zipper repair, and emergencies. **Always tip** a concierge who has been of assistance (⇨ Tipping).

CONSUMER PROTECTION

Whether you're shopping for gifts or purchasing travel services, **pay with a major credit card** whenever possible, so you can cancel payment or get reimbursed if there's a problem (and you can provide documentation). If you're doing business with a particular company for the first time, contact your local Better Business Bureau and the attorney general's offices in your state and (for U.S. businesses) the company's home state as well. Have any complaints been filed? Finally, if you're buying a package or tour, always consider travel insurance that includes default coverage (⇨ Insurance).

⁊ BBBs Council of Better Business Bureaus ✉ 4200 Wilson Blvd., Suite 800, Arlington, VA 22203 ☎ 703/276-0100 🖷 703/525-8277 ⊕ www. bbb.org.

CUSTOMS & DUTIES

When shopping abroad, keep receipts for all purchases. Upon reentering the country, **be ready to show customs officials what you've bought.** Pack purchases together in an easily accessible place. If you think a duty is incorrect, appeal the assessment. If you object to the way your clearance was handled, note the inspector's badge number. In either case, first ask to see a supervisor. If the problem isn't resolved, write to the appropriate authorities, beginning with the port director at your point of entry.

IN THE U.K.

There are two levels of duty-free allowance for entering Britain: one for goods bought outside the European Union (EU) and the other for goods bought within the EU.

Of goods bought outside the EU you may import duty-free: 200 cigarettes or 100 cigarillos or 50 cigars or 250 grams of tobacco; two liters of table wine and, in addition, (a) one liter of alcohol over 22% by volume (most spirits), (b) two liters of alcohol under 22% by volume (fortified or sparkling wine or liqueurs), or (c) two more liters of table wine; 60 ml of perfume; ¼ liter (250 ml) of toilet water; and other goods up to a value of £145, but not more than 50 liters of beer or 25 cigarette lighters.

Of goods bought within the EU, you should not exceed (unless you can prove they are for personal use): 3,200 cigarettes, 400 cigarillos, 200 cigars, or 1 kilogram of tobacco, plus 10 liters of spirits, 20 liters of fortified wine, 90 liters of wine, or 110 liters of beer.

Pets (dogs and cats) can be brought into the United Kingdom from the United States without six months' quarantine, provided that the animal meets all the PETS (Pet Travel Scheme) requirements. The process takes about six months to complete and involves detailed steps. Other pets have to undergo a lengthy quarantine, and penalties for breaking this law are severe and strictly enforced.

Fresh meats, plants and vegetables, unpasteurized milk, controlled drugs, and firearms and ammunition may not be brought into the United Kingdom.

⁊ HM Customs and Excise ✉ Portcullis House, 21 Cowbridge Rd. E, Cardiff CF11 9SS ☎ 0845/010-9000 or 0208/929-0152 advice service, 0208/929-6731 or 0208/910-3602 complaints ⊕ www.hmce. gov.uk.

IN THE U.S.

U.S. residents who have been out of the country for at least 48 hours may bring home, for personal use, $800 worth of foreign goods duty-free, as long as they haven't used the $800 allowance or any part of it in the past 30 days. This exemption may include 1 liter of alcohol (for travelers 21 and older), 200 cigarettes, and 100 non-Cuban cigars. Family members from the same household who are traveling together may pool their $800 personal exemptions. For fewer than 48 hours, the duty-free allowance drops to $200, which may include 50 cigarettes, 10 non-Cuban cigars, and 150 ml of alcohol (or 150 ml of perfume containing alcohol). The $200 allowance cannot be combined with other individuals' exemptions, and if you exceed it, the full value of all the goods will be taxed. Antiques, which U.S. Customs and Border Protection defines as objects more than 100 years old, enter duty-free, as do original works of art done entirely by hand, including paintings, drawings, and sculptures. This doesn't apply to folk art or handicrafts, which are in general dutiable.

You may also send packages home duty-free, with a limit of one parcel per addressee per day (except alcohol or tobacco products or perfume worth more than $5). You can mail up to $200 worth of goods for personal use; label the package PERSONAL USE and attach a list of its contents and their retail value. If the package contains your used personal belongings, mark it AMERICAN GOODS RETURNED to avoid paying duties. You may send up to $100 worth of goods as a gift; mark the package UNSOLICITED GIFT. Mailed items do not affect your duty-free allowance on your return.

To avoid paying duty on foreign-made high-ticket items you already own and will take on your trip, register them with a local customs office before you leave the country. Consider filing a Certificate of Registration for laptops, cameras, watches, and other digital devices identified with serial numbers or other permanent markings; you can keep the certificate for other trips. Otherwise, bring a sales receipt or insurance form to show that you owned the item before you left the United States.

For more about duties, restricted items, and other information about international travel, check out U.S. Customs and Border Protection's online brochure, *Know Before You Go.* You can also file complaints on the U.S. Customs and Border Protection Web site, listed below.

U.S. Customs and Border Protection ✉ For inquiries and complaints, 1300 Pennsylvania Ave. NW, Washington, DC 20229 ⊕ www.cbp.gov ☎ 877/227-5551 or 202/354-1000.

DISABILITIES & ACCESSIBILITY

London has a way to go in helping people with disabilities, but it's moving toward making the city more accessible. Many of the tourist attractions and hotels are updating facilities, although traveling around is a problem.

The organizations listed below can provide advice for travelers with disabilities. It's also worth checking out the book *Access in London,* which lists everything from the best bus routes for people who use wheelchairs, to the most accessible restaurant bathrooms. It's available through the Access Project, which requests a £10 donation to cover the cost of producing the guide.

Local Resources Access Project ✉ 39 Bradley Gardens, Ealing, West Ealing W13 8HE ⊕ www.accessproject-phsp.org. **Artsline** ☎ 020/7388-2227 ⊕ www.artslineonline.com. **Can Be Done** ✉ 7-11 Kensington High St., Kensington, London W8 5NP ☎ 020/8907-2400 ⊕ www.canbedone.co.uk. **DIAL** ☎ 01302/310-123 ⊕ www.dialuk.org.uk. **Holiday**

Care ✉ 7th fl., Sunley House, 4 Bedford Pk., Croydon, Surrey CR0 2AP ☎ 0845/124 9971 ⊕ www.holidaycare.org.uk. **Royal Association for Disability and Rehabilitation** (RADAR) ✉ 12 City Forum, 250 City Rd., Farringdon, London EC1V 8AF ☎ 020/7250-3222. **Tripscope** ☎ 020/8580-7021.

LODGING

If you book directly through Holiday Care, you may be able to get discount rates at some hotels with special facilities.

Best Choices Copthorne Tara Hotel ✉ Scarsdale Pl., Kensington, W8 ☎ 020/7937-7211. **Novotel London Tower Bridge** ✉ 10 Pepys St., The City, EC3N 2NR ☎ 020/7265-6000.

RESERVATIONS

When discussing accessibility with an operator or reservations agent, ask hard questions. Are there any stairs, inside *or* out? Are there grab bars next to the toilet *and* in the shower/tub? How wide is the doorway to the room? To the bathroom? For the most extensive facilities meeting the latest legal specifications, opt for newer accommodations. If you reserve through a toll-free number, consider also calling the hotel's local number to confirm the information from the central reservations office. Get confirmation in writing when you can.

SIGHTS & ATTRACTIONS

Tour Guides Ltd. can tailor a tour for you. The London Tourist Information Centre has details of more easily accessible attractions. Suggested sights include the London Planetarium, London Zoo, National Portrait Gallery, and Natural History Museum.

Tour Guides Ltd. ☎ 020/7495-5504 ⊕ www.tourguides.co.uk.

TRANSPORTATION

London cabs have spacious interiors for wheelchair users. Many London buses have kneeling mechanisms and are wheelchair accessible. The free leaflet "Access to the Underground," available at some TfL Travel Information Centres and through the number listed below, provides information on traveling the Tube.

The U.S. Department of Transportation Aviation Consumer Protection Division's online publication *New Horizons: Information for the Air Traveler with a Disability* offers advice for travellers with a disability, and outlines basic rights. Visit DisabilityInfo.gov for general information.

�</mark> Information & Complaints Aviation Consumer Protection Division (⇨ Air Travel) for airline-related problems; ⊕ airconsumer.ost.dot.gov/publications/horizons.htm for airline travel advice and rights. **Departmental Office of Civil Rights** ⊠ For general inquiries, U.S. Department of Transportation, S-30, 400 7th St. SW, Room 10215, Washington, DC 20590 ☎ 202/366-4648, 202/366-8538 TTY 🖶 202/366-9371 ⊕ www.dotcr.ost.dot.gov. **Disability Rights Section** ⊠ NYAV, U.S. Department of Justice, Civil Rights Division, 950 Pennsylvania Ave. NW, Washington, DC 20530 ☎ ADA information line 202/514-0301, 800/514-0301, 202/514-0383 TTY, 800/514-0383 TTY ⊕ www.ada.gov. **U.S. Department of Transportation Hotline** ☎ For disability-related air-travel problems, 800/778-4838 or 800/455-9880 TTY.

🔲 Transportation Assistance "Access to the Underground" ☎ 020/7941-4600. **Transport for London's Unit for Disabled Passengers** ⊠ 172 Buckingham Palace Rd., London SW1W 9TN ☎ 020/7918-3312. **Wheelchair Travel & Access Mini Buses** ⊠ 1 Johnston Green, Guildford, Surrey GU2 6XS ☎ 01483/237668 ⊕ www.wheelchair-travel.co.uk.

TRAVEL AGENCIES

In the United States, the Americans with Disabilities Act requires that travel firms serve the needs of all travelers. Some agencies specialize in working with people with disabilities.

🔲 Travelers with Mobility Problems Access Adventures/B. Roberts Travel ⊠ 1876 East Ave., Rochester, NY 14610 ☎ 800/444-6540 ⊕ www.brobertstravel.com, run by a former physical-rehabilitation counselor. **CareVacations** ⊠ No. 5, 5110-50 Ave., Leduc, Alberta, Canada, T9E 6V4 ☎ 780/986-6404 or 877/478-7827 🖶 780/986-8332 ⊕ www.carevacations.com, for group tours and cruise vacations. **Flying Wheels Travel** ⊠ 143 W. Bridge St., Box 382, Owatonna, MN 55060 ☎ 507/451-5005 🖶 507/451-1685 ⊕ www.flyingwheelstravel.com.

DISCOUNTS & DEALS

Be a smart shopper and compare all your options before making decisions. A plane ticket bought with a promotional coupon from travel clubs, coupon books, and direct-mail offers or purchased on the Internet may not be cheaper than the least expensive fare from a discount ticket agency. And always keep in mind that what you get is just as important as what you save.

Discount passes, such as London Pass (⊕ www.londonpass.com), are available from the Britain and London Visitor Centre and London Tourist Information Centre branches (⇨ Visitor Information). Many of these passes offer savings on transportation, tours, and admission to museums and movie theaters.

For discount standby theater tickets, go to the TKTS booth in Leicester Square for that day's shows; it's open Monday–Saturday 10–7, Sunday noon–3:30. There's a service charge of £2.50 per ticket. Most tickets are half-price, but a few are only discounted 25%.

DISCOUNT RESERVATIONS

To save money, look into discount reservations services with Web sites and toll-free numbers, which use their buying power to get a better price on hotels, airline tickets (⇨ Air Travel), even car rentals. When booking a room, always **call the hotel's local toll-free number** (if one is available) rather than the central reservations number—you'll often get a better price. Always ask about special packages or corporate rates.

LondonTown.com operates the London Information Centre, adjacent to the TKTS booth, in Leicester Square; you can book discount hotel rooms in person at this kiosk, open 8 AM–11 PM weekdays, 10–6 weekends.

When shopping for the best deal on hotels and car rentals, look for guaranteed exchange rates, which protect you against a falling dollar. With your rate locked in, you won't pay more, even if the price goes up in the local currency.

🔲 Hotel Rooms Accommodations Express ☎ 800/444-7666 or 800/277-1064. **Hotels.com** ☎ 800/246-8357 ⊕ www.hotels.com. **LondonTown.com** ☎ 020/7437-4370 ⊕ www.londontown.com. **Steigenberger Reservation Service** ☎ 800/

223-5652 ⊕ www.srs-worldhotels.com. **Turbotrip. com** ☎ 800/473-7829 ⊕ w3.turbotrip.com.

PACKAGE DEALS

Don't confuse packages and guided tours. When you buy a package, you travel on your own, just as though you had planned the trip yourself. Fly/drive packages, which combine airfare and car rental, are often a good deal. In cities, ask the local visitor's bureau about hotel and local transportation packages that include tickets to major museum exhibits or other special events. If you **buy a rail/drive pass,** you may save on train tickets and car rentals. All Eurail-pass holders get a discount on Eurostar fares through the Channel Tunnel and often receive reduced rates for buses, hotels, ferries, sightseeing cruises, and car rentals.

ELECTRICITY

To use electric-powered equipment purchased in the U.S. or Canada, **bring a converter and adapter.** The electrical current in London is 220–240 volts (coming into line with the rest of Europe at 230 volts), 50 cycles alternating current (AC); wall outlets take three-pin plugs, and shaver sockets take two round, oversize prongs.

If your appliances are dual-voltage, you'll need only an adapter. Don't use 110-volt outlets marked FOR SHAVERS ONLY for high-wattage appliances such as blow-dryers. Most laptops operate equally well on 110 and 220 volts and so require only an adapter. For converters, adapters, and advice, stop in one of the many STA Travel shops around London or at Nomad Travel.

🔢 **Nomad Travel** ✉ 40 Bernard St., Bloomsbury, WC1N 1LJ ☎ 020/7833-4114 ✉ 52 Grosvenor Gardens, Victoria, SW1W 0AG ☎ 020/7823-5823. **STA Travel** ⊕ www.statravel.co.uk.

EMBASSIES & HIGH COMMISSIONS

🔢 **Australia** **Australia House** ✉ Strand, Covent Garden WC2 ☎ 020/7379-4334 ⊕ www.australia.org.uk.

🔢 **Canada** **MacDonald House** ✉ 1 Grosvenor Sq., Mayfair, W1 ☎ 020/7258-6600 ⊕ www.canada.org.uk.

🔢 **New Zealand** **New Zealand House** ✉ 80 Haymarket, Piccadilly, SW1 ☎ 020/7930-8422.

🔢 **United States** **U.S. Embassy** ✉ 24 Grosvenor Sq., Mayfair, W1 ☎ 020/7499-9000, 020/7894-0563 for Passport Unit ⊕ www.usembassy.org.uk.

EMERGENCIES

London is a relatively safe city, though crime does happen. If you need to report a theft or an attack, head to the nearest police station (listed in the Yellow Pages or the local directory) or dial 999 for police, fire, or ambulance (be prepared to give the telephone number you're calling from). National Health Service hospitals, several of which are listed below, give free, round-the-clock treatment in Accident and Emergency sections, where delays can be an hour or more. Prescriptions are valid only if made out by doctors registered in the United Kingdom.

🔢 **Doctors & Dentists** **Dental Emergency Care Service** ☎ 020/7955-2186. **Doctor's Call** ☎ 020/8900-1000. **Eastman Dental Hospital** ✉ 256 Gray's Inn Rd., WC1 ☎ 020/7915-1000. **Medical Express** ✉ 117A Harley St., W1 ☎ 020/7499-1991.

🔢 **Emergency Services** **Ambulance, fire, police** ☎ 999.

🔢 **Hospitals** **Charing Cross Hospital** ✉ Fulham Palace Rd., Fulham, W6 ☎ 020/8846-1234. **Royal Free Hospital** ✉ Pond St., Hampstead, NW3 ☎ 020/7794-0500. **St. Thomas' Hospital** ✉ Lambeth Palace Rd., Battersea, SE1 ☎ 020/7928-9292. **University College Hospital** ✉ Grafton Way, Bloomsbury, WC1 ☎ 020/7387-9300.

🔢 **Hotlines** **Samaritans** ☎ 020/7734-2800 for counseling. **Victim Support** ☎ 020/7735-9166, 020/7582-5712 after office hours.

🔢 **Late-Night Pharmacies** **Bliss the Chemist** ✉ 5 Marble Arch, Marble Arch, W1 ☎ 020/7723-6116.

ETIQUETTE & BEHAVIOR

The British stiff upper lip is more relaxed, but on social occasions the rule is to observe and then go with the flow. If you're visiting a family home, a gift of flowers is welcome; if you're eating at someone's home, you could bring a bottle of wine, perhaps, and maybe some candy for the children—but not necessarily all three. British people will shake hands on greeting old friends or acquaintances; female friends may greet each other with a kiss on the cheek. In Britain, you can never say please, thank you, or sorry too often; to thank your host, a phone call or thank-you card does nicely.

BUSINESS ETIQUETTE

In business, punctuality is of prime importance; if you anticipate a late arrival, call ahead. For business dinners, it's not assumed that spouses will attend unless prearranged, and if you proffered the invitation it's usually assumed that you will pick up the tab. If you're the visitor, however, it's good form for the host to pay the bill. Alternatively, play it safe and offer to split the check.

GAY & LESBIAN TRAVEL

The main gay communities are in the center of London (Soho, Old Compton Street, and west to Kensington and Earls Court). There's a thriving social scene of clubs and cafés, and the best notice board for gay life and services is Gay's the Word bookstore. The *Pink Paper* and *Gay Times* (both available at libraries, large bookstores, and gay cafés), and *Time Out* (available at newsagents) have comprehensive listings. Hotel front desks should serve any couple with courtesy, but using the travel agents listed below should send you in the right direction. The round-the-clock London Lesbian & Gay Switchboard has information on London's gay scene. The British Tourist Authority has a brochure and information on its Web site (www.visitbritain.com) for gay and lesbian travelers.

🔢 Gay- & Lesbian-Friendly Travel Agencies **Different Roads Travel** ✉ 1017 N. LaCienega Blvd., Suite 308, West Hollywood, CA 90069 ☎ 310/289-6000 or 800/429-8747 (Ext. 14 for both) 📠 310/855-0323 ✉ lgernert@tzell.com. **Kennedy Travel** ✉ 130 W. 42nd St., Suite 401, New York, NY 10036 ☎ 800/237-7433 or 212/840-8659 📠 212/730-2269 ⊕ www.kennedytravel.com. **Skylink Travel and Tour/Flying Dutchmen Travel** ✉ 1455 N. Dutton Ave., Suite A, Santa Rosa, CA 95401 ☎ 707/546-9888 or 800/225-5759 📠 707/636-0951; serving lesbian travelers.

🔢 Contacts in London **Gay Times** ⊕ www.gaytimes.co.uk. **Gay's the Word** ✉ 66 Marchmont St., WC1 ☎ 020/7278-7654. **London Lesbian & Gay**

Switchboard ☎ 020/7837-7324 ⊕ www.llgs.org.uk.

HEALTH

In the past, Great Britain had been plagued by concerns about bovine spongiform encephalopathy (BSE), or mad cow disease, but the scare is largely over. New rules regulate British meat, which is considered safe to eat. For the latest information, contact the National Centers for Disease Control and Prevention.

🔢 Health Warnings **National Centers for Disease Control and Prevention** (CDC) ✉ Office of Health Communication, National Center for Infectious Diseases, Division of Quarantine, Travelers' Health, 1600 Clifton Rd. NE, Atlanta, GA 30333 ☎ 877/394-8747 international travelers' health line, 800/311-3435 other inquiries, 404/498-1600 Division of Quarantine and international health information 📠 888/232-3299 ⊕ www.cdc.gov/travel. **Travel Health Online** ⊕ tripprep.com. **World Health Organization** (WHO) ⊕ www.who.int.

HOLIDAYS

Standard holidays include: New Year's Day, Good Friday, Easter Monday, May Day (1st Mon. in May), spring and summer bank holidays (last Mon. in May and Aug., respectively), Christmas, and Boxing Day (Dec. 26). On Christmas Eve and New Year's Eve, some shops, restaurants, and businesses close early. Some museums and tourist attractions are also closed then. If you want to book a hotel room during this period, make sure you do it well in advance, and check to see whether the hotel restaurant will be open.

INSURANCE

The most useful travel-insurance plan is a comprehensive policy that includes coverage for trip cancellation and interruption, default, trip delay, and medical expenses (with a waiver for preexisting conditions).

Without insurance you'll lose all or most of your money if you cancel your trip, regardless of the reason. Default insurance covers you if your tour operator, airline, or cruise line goes out of business—the chances of which have been increasing. Trip-delay covers expenses that arise because of bad weather or mechanical delays. Study the fine print when comparing policies.

If you're traveling internationally, a key component of travel insurance is coverage for medical bills incurred if you get sick on the road. Such expenses aren't generally covered by Medicare or private policies. Australian citizens need extra medical coverage when traveling abroad.

Always **buy travel policies directly from the insurance company**; if you buy them from a cruise line, airline, or tour operator that goes out of business you probably won't be covered for the agency or operator's default, a major risk. Before making any purchase, review your existing health and home-owner's policies to find what they cover away from home.

🚩 Travel Insurers **Access America** ✉ 2805 N. Parham Rd., Richmond, VA 23294 ☎ 800/284-8300 🖷 804/673-1469 or 800/346-9265 ⊕ www.accessamerica.com. **Travel Guard International** ✉ 1145 Clark St., Stevens Point, WI 54481 ☎ 800/826-1300 or 715/345-1041 🖷 800/955-8785 or 715/345-1990 ⊕ www.travelguard.com.

MAIL & SHIPPING

Stamps can be bought from post offices (generally open weekdays 9–5:30, Saturday 9–noon), from stamp machines outside post offices, and from newsagents' stores and newsstands. Mailboxes are known as post or letter boxes and are painted bright red; large tubular ones are set on the edge of sidewalks, whereas smaller boxes are set into post-office walls. Allow seven days for a letter to reach the United States. To contact the post office by phone, call the main office at ☎ 08457/740–740. Check the Yellow Pages for a complete list of branches, though you cannot reach individual offices by phone.

🚩 Post Offices ✉ 17 Euston Rd., NW1 ✉ 125–131 Westminster Bridge Rd., Westminster, SW1 ✉ 110 Victoria St., Victoria, SW1 ✉ 15 Broadwick St., Soho, W1 ✉ 54 Great Portland St., Soho, W1 ✉ 43 Seymour St., Marble Arch, W1 ✉ The Science Museum, South Kensington, SW7 ✉ 24 William IV St., Trafalgar Sq., WC2.

🚩 Major Services **DHL** ☎ 0845/710-0300. **Federal Express** ☎ 0800/123800. **Parcelforce** ☎ 0800/224466.

POSTAL RATES

Airmail letters up to 10 grams (0.35 ounce) to North America, Australia, and New Zealand cost 45p; postcards cost 40p. Letters within Britain are 28p for first class, 20p for second class (these rates are subject to change).

RECEIVING MAIL

If you're uncertain where you'll be staying, you can have mail sent to you at the London Main Post Office, c/o poste restante. The post office will hold international mail for one month.

🚩 **London Main Post Office** ✉ 24–28 William IV St., Covent Garden, WC2N 4DL ☎ 08457/740–740 ⊕ www.royalmail.com.

SHIPPING PARCELS

Most department stores and retail outlets can ship your goods home. You should check your insurance for coverage of possible damage.

MEDIA

NEWSPAPERS & MAGAZINES

For the latest information about shops, restaurants, and arts events, peruse Britain's glossy monthly magazines— *Tatler, Harpers & Queen, Vogue, Wallpaper, House & Garden*, the *Face*—and the weekly *Time Out* (⊕ www.timeout.co.uk). The *Times* (⊕ www.timesonline.co.uk), the *Evening Standard* (⊕ www.thisislondon.com), the *Independent* (⊕ www.independent.co.uk), and the *Guardian* (⊕ www.guardian.co.uk) have comprehensive arts sections including reviews and advance news of future events. The Web sites of these newspapers are full of tips on what's hot and happening.

RADIO & TELEVISION

The main channels are BBC1 and BBC2 from the British Broadcasting Corporation. BBC2 is considered the more eclectic and artsy channel, with a higher proportion of alternative humor, drama, and documentaries. The independent channels include ITV (Independent Television), which occasionally shows big-budget series and films, as well as occasional "reality" shows (*I'm a Celebrity Get Me out of Here*), and soaps, both homegrown (*Coro-

nation Street, which the Queen is rumored to watch) and international (the Australian *Neighbors*) and some U.S. series. Another independent channel, Channel 4 is a mixture of mainstream and off-the-wall, famous at the moment for its bi-annual series of *Big Brother,* while Channel 5 has a higher proportion of sports, U.S. cop shows, and B movies. Satellite and cable channels (many of which are beamed into hotel rooms) have increased the daily diet now available round the clock.

Radio has seen a similar explosion, with 24-hour classics on Classic FM (100–102 mhz), rock on Virgin (105.8 mhz), nostalgic on Heart (106.2 mhz), and talk on Talk Radio (MW1053 khz)—and that's just a sample of the independents. The BBC's Radio 1 (FM97.6) is for the young and hip; Radio 2 (FM88) is for middle-of-the-roadsters; Radio 3 (FM90.2) plays classics, jazz, and arts; Radio 4 (FM92.4) has news, current affairs, drama, and documentary; and Radio 5 Live (MW693 khz) has sports and news with phone-ins.

MONEY MATTERS

A movie in the West End costs £8–£12 (at some cinemas it's cheaper on Monday and at matinees); a theater seat costs anywhere from £10 to about £35, though you'll pay more for hit shows. Most museums are free, but the few that charge admission tend to ask for £5–£10. Coffee costs £1–£3; a pint of light beer (lager) in a pub costs £2.50 or more (glasses are bigger here than in the United States); whiskey, gin, vodka, and so forth, by the glass in a pub, cost £2.50 and up (the measure is smaller than in the United States); house wine by the glass costs around £2.50 in a pub or wine bar, £3.50 or more in a restaurant; a Coke goes for around £1 (although it can be double or even triple that in a pub); a ham sandwich from a sandwich bar in the West End costs about £3; a 1-mi taxi ride costs £4. Ticket prices on the Underground have gone up every year for the last five years, to the point where a single ticket within central London now costs £3.

Prices throughout this guide are given for adults. Substantially reduced fees—gener-

ally referred to as "concessions" throughout Great Britain—are almost always available for children, students, and senior citizens. For information on taxes, *see* Taxes.

ATMS

Credit cards or debit cards (also known as check cards) will get you cash advances at ATMs, which are widely available in London. To make sure that your Cirrus or Plus card (to cite just two of the leading names) works in European ATMs, have your bank reset it to use a four-digit PIN number before your departure.

CREDIT CARDS

Credit cards are accepted virtually everywhere in London.

Throughout this guide, the following abbreviations are used: **AE,** American Express; **DC,** Diners Club; **MC,** MasterCard; and **V,** Visa.

🔢 **Reporting Lost Cards American Express** ☎ 01273/696933. **Diners Club** ☎ 0800/460800. **MasterCard** ☎ 0800/964767. **Visa** ☎ 0800/891725.

CURRENCY

The units of currency in Great Britain are the pound sterling (£) and pence (p): £50, £20, £10, and £5 bills (called notes); £2, £1 (100p), 50p, 20p, 10p, 5p, 2p, and 1p coins. At this writing, the exchange rate was about Australian $2.42, Canadian $2.31, New Zealand $2.59, U.S. $1.92, and €1.44 to the pound (also known as quid).

CURRENCY EXCHANGE

For the most favorable rates, **change money through banks.** Although ATM transaction fees may be higher abroad than at home, ATM rates are excellent because they're based on wholesale rates offered only by major banks. You won't do as well at exchange booths in airports or rail and bus stations, in hotels, in restaurants, or in stores. To avoid lines at airport exchange booths, get a bit of local currency before you leave home.

🔢 **Exchange Services International Currency Express** ✉ 427 N. Camden Dr., Suite F, Beverly Hills, CA 90210 ☎ 888/278–6628 orders 🖷 310/278–6410 ⊕ www.foreignmoney.com. **Travel Ex Currency**

Services ☎ 800/287-7362 orders and retail locations ⊕ www.travelex.com.

TRAVELER'S CHECKS

Do you need traveler's checks? It depends on where you're headed. If you're going to rural areas and small towns, go with cash; traveler's checks are best used in cities. Lost or stolen checks can usually be replaced within 24 hours. To ensure a speedy refund, buy your own traveler's checks—don't let someone else pay for them: irregularities like this can cause delays. The person who bought the checks should make the call to request a refund.

PACKING

London can be cool, damp, and overcast, even in summer. You'll need a heavy coat for winter and a lightweight coat or warm jacket for summer. Always **bring a small umbrella and, if possible, a light raincoat.** Pack as you would for an American city: jackets and ties for expensive restaurants and nightspots, casual clothes elsewhere. Jeans are popular in London and are perfectly acceptable for sightseeing and informal dining. Blazers and sports jackets are popular here with men. For women, ordinary street dress is acceptable everywhere. If you plan to stay in budget hotels, bring your own soap.

In your carry-on luggage, pack an extra pair of eyeglasses or contact lenses and enough of any medication you take to last a few days longer than the entire trip. You may also ask your doctor to write a spare prescription using the drug's generic name, as brand names may vary from country to country. In luggage to be checked, **never pack prescription drugs, valuables, or undeveloped film.** And don't forget to carry with you the addresses of offices that handle refunds of lost traveler's checks. Check *Fodor's How to Pack* (available at online retailers and bookstores everywhere) for more tips.

To avoid customs and security delays, carry medications in their original packaging. Don't pack any sharp objects in your carry-on luggage, including knives of any size or material, scissors, nail clippers, and corkscrews, or anything else that might arouse suspicion.

To avoid having your checked luggage chosen for hand inspection, don't cram bags full. The U.S. Transportation Security Administration suggests packing shoes on top and placing personal items you don't want touched in clear plastic bags.

CHECKING LUGGAGE

You're allowed to carry aboard one bag and one personal article, such as a purse or a laptop computer. Make sure what you carry on fits under your seat or in the overhead bin. Get to the gate early, so you can board as soon as possible, before the overhead bins fill up.

Baggage allowances vary by carrier, destination, and ticket class. On international flights, you're usually allowed to check two bags weighing up to 70 pounds (32 kilograms) each, although a few airlines allow checked bags of up to 88 pounds (40 kilograms) in first class. Some international carriers don't allow more than 66 pounds (30 kilograms) per bag in business class and 44 pounds (20 kilograms) in economy. If you're flying to or through the United Kingdom, your luggage cannot exceed 70 pounds (32 kilograms) per bag. On domestic flights, the limit is usually 50 to 70 pounds (23 to 32 kilograms) per bag. In general, carry-on bags shouldn't exceed 40 pounds (18 kilograms). Most airlines won't accept bags that weigh more than 100 pounds (45 kilograms) on domestic or international flights. Expect to pay a fee for baggage that exceeds weight limits. Check baggage restrictions with your carrier before you pack.

Airline liability for baggage is limited to $2,500 per person on flights within the United States. On international flights it amounts to $9.07 per pound or $20 per kilogram for checked baggage (roughly $640 per 70-pound bag), with a maximum of $634.90 per piece, and $400 per passenger for unchecked baggage. You can buy additional coverage at check-in for about $10 per $1,000 of coverage, but it often excludes a rather extensive list of items, shown on your airline ticket.

Before departure, itemize your bags' contents and their worth, and label the bags with your name, address, and phone number. (If you use your home address, cover it so potential thieves can't see it readily.) Include a label inside each bag and **pack a copy of your itinerary.** At check-in, make sure each bag is correctly tagged with the destination airport's three-letter code. Because some checked bags will be opened for hand inspection, the U.S. Transportation Security Administration recommends that you leave luggage unlocked or use the plastic locks offered at check-in. TSA screeners place an inspection notice inside searched bags, which are re-sealed with a special lock.

If your bag has been searched and contents are missing or damaged, file a claim with the TSA Consumer Response Center as soon as possible. If your bags arrive damaged or fail to arrive at all, file a written report with the airline before leaving the airport.

🚩 Complaints **U.S. Transportation Security Administration Contact Center** ☎ 866/289-9673 ⊕ www.tsa.gov.

PASSPORTS & VISAS
When traveling internationally, carry your passport even if you don't need one. Not only is it the best form of ID, but it's also being required more and more. **Make two photocopies of the data page** (one for someone at home and another for you, carried separately from your passport). If you lose your passport, promptly call the nearest embassy or consulate and the local police.

U.S. passport applications for children under age 14 require consent from both parents or legal guardians; both parents must appear together to sign the application. If only one parent appears, he or she must submit a written statement from the other parent authorizing passport issuance for the child. A parent with sole authority must present evidence of it when applying; acceptable documentation includes the child's certified birth certificate listing only the applying parent, a court order specifically permitting this parent's travel with the child, or a death certificate for the nonapplying parent. Application forms and instructions are available on the Web site of the U.S. State Department's Bureau of Consular Affairs (⊕ travel.state.gov).

ENTERING GREAT BRITAIN
U.S., Canadian, Australian, and New Zealand citizens need only a valid passport to enter Great Britain for stays of up to six months.

PASSPORT OFFICES
The best time to apply for a passport or to renew is in fall and winter. Before any trip, check your passport's expiration date, and, if necessary, renew it as soon as possible.

🚩 Australian Citizens **Passports Australia** Australian Department of Foreign Affairs and Trade ☎ 131-232 ⊕ www.passports.gov.au.
🚩 Canadian Citizens **Passport Office** ✉ To mail in applications: 70 Cremazie St., Gatineau, Québec J8Y 3P2 ☎ 819/994-3500 or 800/567-6868 ⊕ www.ppt.gc.ca.
🚩 New Zealand Citizens **New Zealand Passports Office** ☎ 0800/22-5050 or 04/474-8100 ⊕ www.passports.govt.nz.
🚩 U.S. Citizens **National Passport Information Center** ☎ 877/487-2778, 888/874-7793 TDD/TTY ⊕ travel.state.gov.

SAFETY
The rules for safety in London are the same as in New York or any big city. If you're carrying a considerable amount of cash and do not have a safe in your hotel room, it's a good idea to keep it in something like a money belt or a neck pouch, but don't get cash out of it in public. Keep a small amount of cash for immediate purchases in your pocket or handbag.

Beyond that, use common sense. In central London, nobody will raise an eyebrow at tourists studying maps on street corners, and don't hesitate to ask directions. However, outside of the center, exercise general caution about the neighborhoods you walk in: if they don't look safe, take a cab. After midnight, outside of the center, take cabs rather than waiting for a night bus. Although London has plenty of so-called "mini-cabs"—normal cars driven by self-employed drivers in a cab service—don't ever get into an unmarked car that pulls up offering you "cab service." Only take a licensed minicab from a cab office, or, preferably, a normal London "black cab," which you flag down on the street. Unlicensed mini-cab drivers have been associated with a slate of violent crimes in recent years.

WOMEN IN LONDON
If you carry a purse, choose one with a zipper and a thick strap that you can drape across your body; adjust the length so that the purse sits in front of you at or above hip level. Store only enough money in the purse to cover casual spending. Distribute the rest of your cash and any valuables among deep front pockets, inside jacket or vest pockets, and a concealed money pouch.

SENIOR-CITIZEN TRAVEL
Many museums and galleries in Britain offer free admission to anyone over age 60, and stately homes and gardens may give discounts of up to 40%. When purchasing a ticket, ask if there are discounts for seniors or "pensioners," as they are, unfortunately, called here. To qualify for age-related discounts, mention your senior-citizen status up front when booking hotel reservations (not when checking out) and before you're seated in restaurants (not when paying the bill). Be sure to have identification on hand. When renting a car, ask about promotional car-rental discounts, which can be cheaper than senior-citizen rates.

🏫 Educational Programs **Elderhostel** ✉ 11 Ave. de Lafayette, Boston, MA 02111 ☎ 877/426-8056, 978/323-4141 international callers, 877/426-2167 TTY 🖷 877/426-2166 ⊕ www.elderhostel.org. **Interhostel** ✉ University of New Hampshire, 6 Garrison Ave., Durham, NH 03824 ☎ 603/862-1147 or 800/733-9753 🖷 603/862-1113 ⊕ www.learn.unh.edu.

SIGHTSEEING TOURS
BIKE TOURS
🏫 Tour Operator **Humdinger Bike Tours** ☎ 01689/827371. **London Bicycle Tour** ☎ 020/7928-6838 ⊕ www.londonbicycle.com.

BOAT TOURS
All year-round, but more frequently from April to October, boats cruise the Thames, offering a different view of the London skyline. Most leave from Westminster Pier,

Charing Cross Pier, and Tower Pier. Downstream routes go to the Tower of London, Greenwich, and the Thames Barrier via Canary Wharf. Upstream destinations include Kew, Richmond, and Hampton Court (mainly in summer). Most of the launches seat between 100 and 250 passengers, have a public-address system, and provide a running commentary on passing points of interest. Depending upon the destination, river trips may last from one to four hours.

A Sail and Rail ticket combines the modern wonders of Canary Wharf by Docklands Light Railway with a trip on the river. Tickets are available year-round from Westminster Pier or DLR stations; ticket holders also get discounted tickets to the London Aquarium in Westminster and the National Maritime Museum in Greenwich.

Details on all other river-cruise operators are available from London River Services.
🏫 River Cruise Operators **Catamaran Cruisers** ☎ 020/7987-1185. **London Duck Tours** ☎ 020/7928-3132. **London River Services** ☎ 020/7941-2400. **Sail and Rail** ☎ 020/7363-9700. **Thames Cruises** ☎ 020/7930-4097. **Westminster Passenger Boat Services** ☎ 020/7930-4097.

BUS TOURS
Guided sightseeing tours from the top of double-decker buses, which are open-top in summer, are a good introduction to the city, as they cover all the main central sights. Numerous companies run daily bus tours that depart (usually between 8:30 and 9 AM) from central points. You may board or alight at any of the numerous stops to view the sights, and reboard on the next bus. Tickets can be bought from the driver and are good all day. Prices vary according to the type of tour, although £15 is the benchmark.
🏫 Tour Operators **Big Bus Company** ☎ 020/7233-9533 ⊕ www.bigbus.co.uk. **Big Value Tours** ☎ 020/77233-7797. **Black Taxi Tour of London** ☎ 020/7289-4371 ⊕ www.blacktaxitours.co.uk. **Golden Tours** ☎ 020/77233-7030. **London Pride** ☎ 020/7520-2050. **London Spy Tours** ☎ 0870/060-0100. **Original London Sightseeing Tour** ☎ 020/8877-1722 ⊕ www.theoriginaltour.com. **Premium Tours** ☎ 020/7278-5300.

CANAL TOURS

The tranquil side of London can be found on narrow boats that cruise the city's two canals, the Grand Union and Regent's Canal; most vessels operate on the latter, which runs between Little Venice in the west (nearest Tube: Warwick Avenue on the Bakerloo Line) and Camden Lock (about 200 yards north of Camden Town Tube station). Fares are about £5 for 1½-hour cruises.

🚢 Cruise Operators **Canal Cruises** ☎ 020/8440-8962. **Jason's Trip** ☎ 020/7286-3428. **London Waterbus Company** ☎ 020/7482-2660.

EXCURSIONS

Evan Evans, Green Line, and National Express all offer day excursions by bus to places within easy reach of London, such as Hampton Court, Oxford, Stratford, and Bath.

🚢 Tour Operators **Evan Evans** ☎ 020/7950-1777. **Green Line** ☎ 0870/608-7261 ⊕ www.greenline. co.uk. **National Express** ☎ 0870/580-8080 ⊕ www.nationalexpress.com.

WALKING TOURS

One of the best ways to get to know London is on foot, and there are many guided and themed walking tours from which to choose. If you wish to tailor your own tour, you might consider hiring a Blue Badge accredited guide or using Great London Treasure Hunt self-guided tours. Pick up a copy of *Time Out* and check the weekly listings for upcoming special tours.

🚢 Tour Operators **Blood and Tears Walk** ☎ 020/8348-9022. **Blue Badge** ☎ 020/7495-5504. **Citisights** ☎ 020/8806-4325. **Great London Treasure Hunt** ☎ 020/7928-2627. **Historical Walks** ☎ 020/8668-4019. **Jack the Ripper Mystery Walks** ☎ 020/8558-9446 ⊕ www.jack-the-ripper-walk. co.uk. **Original London Walks** ☎ 020/7624-3978 ⊕ www.walks.com. **Shakespeare City Walk** ☎ 020/7625-5155 ⊕ www.shakespeareguide.com.

STUDENTS IN LONDON

Students get discounted rates on access to most sights in Great Britain. You need to have an International Student ID, available from a variety of sources including STA Travel. Whenever you purchase a ticket for admission to any sight, always ask if they offer a student rate.

Those under the age of 26 also receive steeply discounted rates on rail fare throughout the country, although not on London Transport. To receive the cheap fares you will need to get a Young Person's Railcard. To do that, you must go in person to a ticket office with your passport or International Student Card and a passport-size photo (there are photo machines in most large train stations). The youth railcard costs £20, but it can pay for itself in one train journey. Once you have it, show it at the ticket counter whenever you buy a train ticket in order to receive the discounted rates, and you'll also have to show it to the conductor on-board the train when he or she comes to check your ticket. Discount bus cards are also available for young people (⇨ Bus Travel to & from London).

📇 IDs & Services **STA Travel** ⊠ 10 Downing St., New York, NY 10014 ☎ 212/627-3111, 800/777-0112 24-hr service center ⬜ 212/627-3387 ⊕ www.sta. com. **Travel Cuts** ⊠ 187 College St., Toronto, Ontario M5T 1P7, Canada ☎ 800/592-2887 in U.S., 416/979-2406 or 866/246-9762 in Canada ⬜ 416/979-8167 ⊕ www.travelcuts.com.

TAXES

An airport departure tax of £20 (£10 for flights within the United Kingdom and other EU countries) per person is included in the price of your ticket. The fee is subject to government tax increases.

VALUE-ADDED TAX

The British sales tax (V.A.T., value-added tax) is 17½%. The tax is almost always included in quoted prices in shops, hotels, and restaurants.

Most travelers can get a V.A.T. refund by either the Retail Export or the more cumbersome Direct Export method. Many, but not all, large stores provide these services, but only if you request them; they will handle the paperwork. For the Retail Export method, you must ask the store for Form VAT 407 (you must have identification—passports are best), which you should give to customs at your last port of departure. (Lines at major airports can be long, so allow plenty of time.) Be ready to show customs officials what you've bought (pack purchases together, in your carry-on luggage). The refund will be forwarded to you in about eight weeks, minus a small service charge, either in the form of a credit to your charge card or as a British check, which American banks usually charge you to convert.

With the Direct Export method, the goods are shipped directly to your home. You must have a Form VAT 407 certified by customs, the police, or a notary public when you get home and then send it back to the store, which will refund your money. For inquiries, contact Her Majesty's Customs & Excise office.

A service processes refunds for most shops. You receive the total refund stated on the form. Global Refund is a Europe-wide service with 210,000 affiliated stores and more than 700 refund counters—located at major airports and border crossings. Its refund form is called a Tax Free Check. The service issues refunds in the form of cash, check, or credit-card adjustment. If you don't have time to wait at the refund counter, you can mail in the form instead.

🔳 **V.A.T. Refunds Global Refund Canada** ⬌ Box 2020, Station Main, Brampton, Ontario L6T 3S3 ☎ 800/993–4313 🖷 905/791–9078 ⊕ www. globalrefund.com. **Her Majesty's Customs & Excise office** ☎ 0845/010–9000 within U.K., or 208/929–0152 from outside U.K. ⊕ http://customs.hmrc.gov.uk.

TAXIS

Universally known as "black cabs," the traditional big black taxicabs are as much a part of the London streetscape as the red double-decker buses, and for good reason: the unique, spacious taxis easily hold five people, plus luggage. In order to earn a taxi license, drivers must undergo intensive training on the history and geography of London. The course, and all that the drivers have learned in it, is known simply as "the Knowledge." There's almost nothing your taxi driver won't know about the city.

Hotels and main tourist areas have cab stands (just take the first in line), but you can also flag one down from the roadside. If the yellow FOR HIRE sign on the top is lit, the taxi is available. Cab drivers often cruise at night with their signs unlit so that they can choose their passengers and avoid those they think might cause trouble. If you see an unlit, passengerless cab, hail it: you might be lucky.

Fares start at £2 and increase by about £1.80 for every mile or 30p per minute. Taxis cost about double after 10 PM, when they charge by the minute rather than by the mile. (This system was designed to convince more taxi drivers to work at night, but it has resulted in extortionate fares.) Surcharges are a tricky extra, ranging from 40p for additional passengers or bulky luggage to £2 for ordering by phone. At Christmas and New Year, the surcharge is £3. Fares are occasionally raised from year to year. Tip taxi drivers 10%–15% of the tab.

Minicabs, which operate out of small, curb-side offices throughout the city, are generally cheaper than black cabs, but are less reliable and trusted. These are usually unmarked passenger cars, and their drivers are often not native Londoners, and do not have to take or pass "the Knowledge" test. Still, Londoners use them in droves because they are plentiful and cheap. If you choose to use them, do not ever take an unlicensed cab: anyone who curb-crawls looking for customers is likely to be unlicensed. All those with proper dispatch offices are likely to be licensed. Look out for a yellow license disk on the front or rear window of the cab to be sure.

There are plenty of trustworthy and licensed minicab firms. For Londonwide service try Lady Cabs, which employs only women drivers, or Addison Lee. When using a minicab, always ask the price in advance when you phone for the car, then verify with the driver before the journey begins.

🔳 **Black Cabs Dial-a-Cab** ☎ 0207/253–5000. **Radio Taxis** ☎ 0207/272–0272.
🔳 **Minicabs Addison Lee** ☎ 0207/387–8888. **Lady Cabs** ☎ 0207/272–3300

TELEPHONES

All calls made within the United Kingdom are charged according to the time of day. The standard rate applies weekdays 8 AM–

6 PM; a cheaper rate is in effect weekdays 6 PM–8 AM and all day on weekends, when it's even cheaper. A local call before 6 PM costs 15p for three minutes; this doubles to 30p for the same from a pay phone. A daytime call to the United States will cost 24p a minute on a regular phone (weekends are cheaper), 80p on a pay phone.

Any cell phone can be used in Europe if it's tri-band/GSM. Travelers should ask their cell phone company if their phone is tri-band, and make sure it is activated for international calling before leaving their home country.

You can rent a cell phone from most car rental agencies in London. Some upscale hotels now provide loaner cell phones to their guests. You can also rent a mobile phone through www.rent-mobile-phone. com (☎ 0870/7500 770) for £1 per day plus usage.

AREA & COUNTRY CODES

The country code for Great Britain is 44. When dialing from abroad, drop the initial "0" from the local area code. The code for London is 020, followed by a 7 for numbers in central London, or an 8 for numbers in the Greater London area. Freephone (toll-free) numbers start with 0800 or 0808; national information numbers start with 0845.

A word of warning: 0870 numbers are *not* toll-free numbers; in fact, numbers beginning with this, 0871 or the 0900 prefix are "premium rate" numbers, and it costs extra to call them. The amount varies and is usually relatively small when dialed from within the country but can be excessive when dialed from outside the U.K.

The country code is 1 for the United States and Canada, 61 for Australia, and 64 for New Zealand.

DIRECTORY & OPERATOR ASSISTANCE

There are several different directory-assistance providers. For information anywhere in Britain, try dialing 118–888 or 118–118; you'll need to know the town and the street (or at least the neighborhood) of the person or organization for which you're requesting information. For the operator, dial 100. For assistance with international calls, dial 155.

INTERNATIONAL CALLS

To make an international call from London, dial 00, followed by the country code and the local number.

When calling from overseas to access a London telephone number, drop the first 0 from the prefix and dial only 20 (or any other British area code) and then the eight-digit phone number.

LOCAL CALLS

You don't have to dial London's central area code (020) if you are calling inside London itself—just the eight-digit telephone number.

LONG-DISTANCE CALLS

For long-distance calls within Britain, dial the area code (which begins with 01) followed by the number. The area-code prefix is only used when you are dialing from outside the city. In provincial areas, the dialing codes for nearby towns are often posted in the booth.

LONG-DISTANCE SERVICES

AT&T, MCI, and Sprint access codes make calling long-distance relatively convenient, but you may find the local access number blocked in many hotel rooms. First ask the hotel operator to connect you. If the hotel operator balks, ask for an international operator, or dial the international operator yourself. One way to improve your odds of getting connected to your long-distance carrier is to travel with more than one company's calling card (a hotel may block Sprint, for example, but not MCI). If all else fails, call from a pay phone. If you are travelling for a longer period of time, consider renting a cell-phone from a local company.

You can also pick up one of the many instant international phone cards from newsstands, which can be used from residential, hotel, and public pay phones. With these, you can call the United States for as little as 5p per minute.

🖪 Access Codes AT&T Direct ☎ 0500/890011. MCI WorldPhone ☎ 0800/279-5088 in U.K., 800/444–

4141 for U.S. and other areas. **Sprint International Access** ☎ 0800/890-877.

PHONE CARDS

Public card phones operate with special cards that you can buy from post offices or newsstands. Ideal for longer calls, they are composed of units of 10p, and come in values of £3, £5, £10, and more. To use a card phone, lift the receiver, insert your card, and dial the number. An indicator panel shows the number of units used. At the end of your call, the card will be returned. Where credit cards are taken, slide the card through, as indicated.

PUBLIC PHONES

There are three types of phones: those that accept (1) only coins, (2) only British Telecom (BT) phone cards, or (3) BT phone cards and credit cards.

The coin-operated phones are of the push-button variety; the workings of coin-operated telephones vary, but there are usually instructions on each unit. Most take 10p, 20p, 50p, and £1 coins. Insert the coins *before* dialing (the minimum charge is 10p). If you hear a repeated single tone after dialing, the line is busy; a continual tone means the number is unobtainable (or that you have dialed the wrong—or no—prefix). The indicator panel shows you how much money is left; add more whenever you like. If there is no answer, replace the receiver and your money will be returned.

TIME

London is five hours ahead of New York City. In other words, when it's 3 PM in New York (or noon in Los Angeles) it's 8 PM in London. Note that Great Britain and most European countries also move their clocks ahead for the one-hour differential when daylight saving time goes into effect (although they make the changeover several days after the United States).

TIPPING

Many restaurants and large hotels (particularly those belonging to chains) will automatically add a 10%–15% service charge to your bill, so **always check if tipping is necessary** before you hand out any extra money.

Do not tip movie or theater ushers, elevator operators, or bar staff in pubs—although you can always offer to buy them a drink. Washroom attendants may display a saucer, in which it's reasonable to leave 20p or so.

Here's a guide for other tipping situations. Restaurants: 10%–20% of the check for full meals if service is not already included (if paying by credit card, check that a tip has not already been included before you fill in the total on your credit slip), a small token if you're just having coffee or tea. Taxis: 10%–15%, or perhaps a little more for a short ride. Porters: 50p–£1 per bag. Doormen: £1 for hailing taxis or for carrying bags to check-in desk. Bellhops: £1 for carrying bags, £1 for room service. Hairdressers: 10%–15% of the bill, plus £1–£2 for the hair washer.

TOURS & PACKAGES

Because everything is prearranged on a prepackaged tour or independent vacation, you spend less time planning—and often get it all at a good price.

BOOKING WITH AN AGENT

Travel agents are excellent resources. But it's a good idea to collect brochures from several agencies, as some agents' suggestions may be influenced by relationships with tour and package firms that reward them for volume sales. If you have a special interest, find an agent with expertise in that area. The American Society of Travel Agents (ASTA) has a database of specialists worldwide; you can log on to the group's Web site to find one near you.

Make sure your travel agent knows the accommodations and other services of the place being recommended. Ask about the hotel's location, room size, beds, and whether it has a pool, room service, or programs for children, if you care about these. Has your agent been there in person or sent others whom you can contact?

Do some homework on your own, too: local tourism boards can provide information about lesser-known and small-niche operators, some of which may sell only direct.

BUYER BEWARE

Each year consumers are stranded or lose their money when tour operators—even large ones with excellent reputations—go out of business. So check out the operator. Ask several travel agents about its reputation, and try to **book with a company that has a consumer-protection program.** (Look for information in the company's brochure.) In the United States, members of the United States Tour Operators Association are required to set aside funds (up to $1 million) to help eligible customers cover payments and travel arrangements in the event that the company defaults. It's also a good idea to choose a company that participates in the American Society of Travel Agents' Tour Operator Program; ASTA will act as mediator in any disputes between you and your tour operator.

Remember that the more your package or tour includes, the better you can predict the ultimate cost of your vacation. Make sure you know exactly what is covered, and beware of hidden costs. Are taxes, tips, and transfers included? Entertainment and excursions? These can add up.

🚩 **Tour-Operator Recommendations American Society of Travel Agents** (⇨ Travel Agencies). **CrossSphere-The Global Association for Packaged Travel** ✉ 546 E. Main St., Lexington, KY 40508 ☎ 859/226-4444 or 800/682-8886 🖨 859/226-4414 ⊕ www.CrossSphere.com. **United States Tour Operators Association (USTOA)** ✉ 275 Madison Ave., Suite 2014, New York, NY 10016 ☎ 212/599-6599 🖨 212/599-6744 ⊕ www.ustoa.com.

TRAIN TRAVEL

London has eight major train stations that serve as arteries to the rest of the country (and to Europe). All are served by the Underground. As a general rule of thumb, the stations' location in the city matches the part of the country they serve.

Charing Cross serves southeast England, including Canterbury and Dover/Folkestone for Europe.

Euston serves the Midlands, north Wales, northwest England, and western Scotland.

King's Cross marks the end of the Great Northern Line, serving northeast England and Scotland.

Liverpool Street serves East Anglia, including Cambridge and Norwich.

Paddington mainly serves south Wales and the West Country, as well as Reading, Oxford, and Bristol.

St. Pancras serves Leicester, Nottingham, and Sheffield in south Yorkshire.

Victoria serves southern England, including Brighton, Dover/Folkestone, and the south coast.

Waterloo serves southeastern destinations, including Portsmouth and Southampton. The Eurostar service to France and Belgium departs from Waterloo International, within Waterloo Station.

Some trains have refreshment carriages, called buffet cars. Smoking is forbidden in rail carriages.

CLASSES

Some trains have first-class and reserved seats (for which there's a small charge, depending on the rail company). Check with National Rail Enquiries for details.

CUTTING COSTS

To save money, **look into rail passes.** But be aware that if you don't plan to cover many miles, you may come out ahead by buying individual tickets.

For the best rates, buy your tickets well in advance. Tickets bought two to three weeks in advance can cost a quarter of the price of tickets bought on the day of travel. You can purchase tickets online, by phone, or at any rail station in the United Kingdom. The best way to find out which train to catch, and where to catch it, is to call National Rail Enquiries. Operators there can put you in touch with the right train company, and give you a breakdown of available ticket prices. You cannot buy tickets from National Rail, but they'll put you in touch with the individual train company ticket offices.

Regardless of which train company is involved, many discount passes are available, such as the Young Person's Railcard (for which you must be under 26 and provide a passport-size photo) and the Family Travelcard, which can be bought from most mainline stations. But if you intend to make several long-distance rail journeys, it's far better to invest in a BritRail Pass (which you must buy in the United States).

BritRail passes come in two basic varieties. The Classic pass allows travel on consecutive days, and the FlexiPass allows a number of travel days within a set period of time. The cost (in U.S. dollars) of a BritRail Consecutive Pass adult ticket for 8 days is $269 standard and $405 first-class; for 15 days, $405 standard and $609 first-class; for 22 days, $515 and $769; and for a month, $609 and $915. The cost of a BritRail FlexiPass adult ticket for 4 days' travel in two months is $235 standard and $355 first-class; for 8 days' travel in two months, $349 standard and $519 first-class; and for 15 days' travel in two months, $525 standard and $779 first-class. Prices drop by about 25% for off-peak travel passes between October and March. Passes for students, seniors, and ages 16–25 are discounted, too.

FARES & SCHEDULES

Most of the time, first class on trains in England isn't particularly first-class. Some don't even have at-seat service, so you still have to get up and go to the buffet car for food. First class is generally booked by business travelers on expense accounts because crying babies and noisy families are quite rare in first class, and quite common in standard class.

Rail travel is expensive: for instance, a round-trip ticket to Bath can cost around £60 per person at peak times. The fee reduces to around £30 at other times, so it's best to travel before or after the frantic business commuter rush (before 4:30 PM and after 9:30 AM). Credit cards are accepted for train fares paid both in person and by phone.

Delays are the norm these days, but you almost always have to go to the station to find out if there's going to be one (because delays happen at the last minute). Luckily, most stations have coffee shops, restaurants, and pubs where you can cool your heels while you wait for the train to get

rolling. National Rail Enquiries provides an up-to-date state-of-the-railways schedule.

🎵 **Train Information BritRail Travel** ☎ 877/677-1066 in U.S. **Eurostar** ☎ 0990/186186. **National Rail Enquiries** ☎ 0845/748-4950, 0161/236-3522 outside U.K.

TRANSPORTATION AROUND LONDON

By far the easiest and most practical way to get around is on the Underground, or "Tube." This underground train system runs daily from early morning to night and provides a comprehensive service throughout the center with lines out to the suburbs. Tube fares can work out to be higher than bus fares, but if you're traveling a lot around town, you should buy a Travelcard pass (£4.50–£7 per day), which offers unlimited use of the Tube, buses, and the commuter rail (⇨ Underground Tube Travel).

All transport in London is priced according to zone. Central London, including most tourist sights, is Zone 1, which happens to be the cheapest option. There are six zones altogether, and the farther out you travel, the more your ticket or travelcard will cost. Kew Gardens, for example, are in Zone 4, so if you plan to visit Kew, remember to buy a Zone 1–4 travelcard for that day.

The overground rail system is a network that connects outlying districts and suburbs to the center. Prices are comparable to the Underground, and you can easily transfer between the Underground and other connecting rail lines at many Tube stations. Travelcards are also accepted on the overground commuter trains.

Buses crisscross all over town, and are a great way to see the city. Their routes are more complicated than the Tube, but by reading the route posted on the main bus stop and watching the route on the front of the bus, you won't go far wrong. Services are frequent. Bus-travel prices are cheaper than the Tube the farther you travel, but be prepared to get stuck in traffic, even though designated lanes for buses and taxis should speed up the journey. A taxi ride can clock up to three times the price of a similar bus fare for the same distance. If you're traveling with several people, however, riding in a taxi is relatively inexpensive and is more comfortable and convenient.

Finally, there's the River Thames, which makes a great way of getting around the city—no traffic, no claustrophobic tunnels, less pollution, and great views of Big Ben and the Houses of Parliament, the London Eye, and St. Paul's. There are several places where you can access boats, which operate under an agreement with the city's public-transportation agency, Transport for London. As many as 16 boats are in service in summer; seven boats ply the river in winter. You can purchase a Rivercard from kiosks at the boat piers near the South Bank, the London Eye, the Embankment Tube station, and elsewhere throughout the city. Rivercard prices vary from £4.20 to £16, depending on how many zones you wish to traverse. Rivercards are cheaper if you already have a regular Travelcard for that day.

🎵 **Transport for London** ☎ 020/7222-1234 ⊕ www.tfl.gov.uk.

TRAVEL AGENCIES

A good travel agent puts your needs first. Look for an agency that has been in business at least five years, emphasizes customer service, and has someone on staff who specializes in your destination. In addition, **make sure the agency belongs to a professional trade organization.** The American Society of Travel Agents (ASTA) has more than 10,000 members in some 140 countries, enforces a strict code of ethics, and will step in to mediate agent-client disputes involving ASTA members. ASTA also maintains a directory of agents on its Web site; ASTA's TravelSense.org, a trip planning and travel advice site, can also help to locate a travel agent who caters to your needs. (If a travel agency is also acting as your tour operator, *see* Buyer Beware *in* Tours & Packages.)

🎵 Local Agent Referrals **American Society of Travel Agents (ASTA)** ⊠ 1101 King St., Suite 200, Alexandria, VA 22314 ☎ 703/739-2782, 800/965-2782 24-hr hotline 🖷 703/684-8319 ⊕ www.astanet.com and www.travelsense.org. **Association**

of British Travel Agents ⊠ 68–71 Newman St., London W1T 3AH ☎ 020/7637-2444 🖷 020/7637-0713 ⊕ www.abta.com. **Association of Canadian Travel Agencies** ⊠ 130 Albert St., Suite 1705, Ottawa, Ontario K1P 5G4 ☎ 613/237-3657 🖷 613/237-7052 ⊕ www.acta.ca. **Australian Federation of Travel Agents** ⊠ Level 3, 309 Pitt St., Sydney, NSW 2000 ☎ 02/9264-3299 or 1300/363-416 🖷 02/9264-1085 ⊕ www.afta.com.au. **Travel Agents' Association of New Zealand** ⊠ Level 5, Tourism and Travel House, 79 Boulcott St., Box 1888, Wellington 6001 ☎ 04/499-0104 🖷 04/499-0786 ⊕ www.taanz.org.nz.

UNDERGROUND TUBE TRAVEL

London's extensive Underground train (Tube) system has color-coded routes, clear signage, and many connections. Trains run out into the suburbs, and all stations are marked with the London Underground circular symbol. (Do not be confused by similar looking signs reading "subway"—in Britain, the word "subway" means "pedestrian underpass.") Trains are all one class; smoking is *not* allowed on board or in the stations.

Some lines have multiple branches (Central, District, Northern, Metropolitan, and Piccadilly), so **be sure to note which branch is needed for your particular destination.** Do this by noting the end destination on the lighted sign on the platform, which also tells you how long you'll have to wait until the train arrives. Compare that with the end destination of the branch you want. When the two match, that's your train. Disruptions in service will be frequent on the Northern line in 2007; Regents Park station on the Bakerloo line will be closed through June 2007, and Shoreditch on the East London line will be closed through 2010. The zippy Docklands Light Railway runs through the modern Docklands with an extension to the *Cutty Sark* clipper and maritime Greenwich.

FARES & SCHEDULES

London is divided into six concentric zones (ask at Underground ticket booths for a map and booklet, which give details of the ticket options), so be sure to **buy a ticket for the correct zone** or you may be liable for an on-the-spot fine (£10 at this writing). Don't panic if you do forget to buy a ticket for the right zone: just tell a station attendant that you need to buy an "extension" to your ticket. Although you're meant to do that in advance, generally if you're an out-of-towner, they don't give you a hard time.

You can buy a single or return ticket, the equivalent of a one-way and a round-trip, for travel anytime on the day of issue. For single fares, a flat £3 price per journey now applies across all six zones. If you're planning several trips in one day, then consider a travelcard, which is good for unrestricted travel on the Tube, buses, and some overground railways. Bear in mind that travelcards cost much more if purchased before the 9:30 AM rush hour threshold. A one-day travelcard for zones 1–2 costs £6.20 if purchased before 9:30 AM, and £4.90 if bought after 9:30 AM. The more zones included in your travel (if, for example, you'll be traveling to Kew or Wimbledon), the more the travelcard will cost. If you're going to be in town for several days, buy a three-day travelcard. There are a variety of travelcard options: a seven-day travelcard (£19 for Zone 1–2) can offer significant savings, but only if you'll be traveling by public transport every day; family travelcards, which are one-day tickets for one or two adults with one to four children (£3–£3.40 with one child, additional children cost £1 each); and the Carnet, a book of 10 single tickets valid for central Zone 1 (£13.50) for use at any time over the course of one year.

The Visitor's Travelcard can be bought in the United States and Canada. Three ticket types for periods of two to seven days exist for zones 1–6, zones 1 and 2, or a round-trip Heathrow Express ticket. Prices start at about $20 for a zones 1 and 2 ticket valid for three days and go up to about $60 for a zones 1–6 ticket valid for one week. Apply to travel agents or, in the United States, to BritRail Travel.

The new Oyster cards are travel smartcards that can be charged with a cash value and then used for travel throughout the city. Each time you take the Tube or bus, you swipe the blue card across the yellow readers at the entrance and the amount of your fare is deducted. The London mayor is so eager to promote the cards that he set up a system in which those using Oyster cards pay discounted rates, making them the cheapest way to get around London. You can purchase an Oyster card for £3 at any London Underground station, and then prepay any amount you wish for your expected travel while in the city. Using an Oyster card, bus fares are £0.80 instead of £1.50, and underground singles within Zone 1 cost £1.50 instead of £3. If you make numerous journeys in a single day, your Oyster card deductions will always be capped at £0.50 less than than the standard price of a one-day travelcard. To get an Oyster card, pick up a form at any underground station, fill it out, and get back in the ticket line to pick up your card.

Trains begin running just after 5 AM Monday–Saturday; the last services leave central London between midnight and 12:30 AM. On Sunday, trains start two hours later and finish about an hour earlier. The frequency of trains depends on the route and the time of day, but normally you should not have to wait more than 10 minutes in central areas.

There are TfL Travel Information Centres at the following Tube stations: Euston, Liverpool Street, Piccadilly Circus, and Victoria, open 7:15 AM–10 PM; and at Heathrow Airport (in terminals 1, 2, and 4), open 6 AM–3 PM.

▮ Underground Information **Transport for London** ☎ 020/7222-1234 ⊕ www.tfl.gov.uk; for latest service changes, see www.tfl.gov.uk/tfl/realtime/planned.asp.

VISITOR INFORMATION

Learn more about foreign destinations by checking government-issued travel advisories and country information. For a broader picture, consider information from more than one country.

When you arrive in London, you can go in person to the London Visitor Centre at the Waterloo International Terminal arrivals hall at Waterloo train station for general information (daily 8:30 AM–10:30 PM) or to the Britain and London Visitor Centre for travel, hotel, and entertainment information. It's open June–October, weekdays 9:30–6:30, Saturday 9–5, Sunday 10–4; and November–May, weekdays 9:30–6:30, weekends 10–4. The London Tourist Information Centre has branches in Greenwich and in Southwark. The Londonline can provide tips on sightseeing.

The official Web site of VisitBritain, the British Tourist Authority is ⊕ www. visitbritain.com. Its "gateway" Web site, ⊕ www.visitbritain.com/usa, provides information most helpful to Britain-bound U.S. travelers.

🛅 In the U.S. **VisitBritain (BTA)** ✉ 551 5th Ave., 7th fl., New York, NY 10176 ☎ 212/986-2200 or 800/462-2748 ⊕ www.visitbritain.com/usa.

🛅 In Canada **VisitBritain** ✉ 5915 Airport Rd., Suite 120, Mississauga, Ontario L4V 1T1 ☎ 905/405-1840 or 800/847-4885 ⊕ www.visitbritain.com.

🛅 In the U.K. **VisitBritain** ✉ Thames Tower, Black's Rd., London W6 9EL ☎ 020/8846-9000 ⊕ www.visitbritain.com.

🛅 In London **Britain and London Visitor Centre** ✉ 1 Regent St., Piccadilly Circus, SW1Y 4NX. **London Tourist Information Centre** ✉ Pepys House, 2 Cutty Sark Gardens, Greenwich SE10 9LW ☎ 0870/608-2000 ⊕ www.visitlondon.com ✍ Vinopolis, 1 Bank End, Southwark SE1 9BU ☎ 020/7357-9168. **Londonline** ☎ 09068/663344.

🛅 Government Advisories **U.S. Department of State** ✉ Bureau of Consular Affairs, Overseas Citizens Services Office, 2201 C St. NW, Washington, DC 20520 ☎ 202/647-5225, 888/407-4747, 317/472-2328 interactive hotline ⊕ www.travel.state.gov. **Consular Affairs Bureau of Canada** ☎ 800/267-6788 or 613/944-6788 ⊕ www.voyage.gc.ca. **Australian Department of Foreign Affairs and Trade** ☎ 300/139-281 travel advisories, 02/6261-1299 Consular Travel Advice ⊕ www.smartraveller.gov.

au or www.dfat.gov.au. **New Zealand Ministry of Foreign Affairs and Trade** ☎ 04/439-8000 ⊕ www.mft.govt.nz.

WEB SITES

Do check out the World Wide Web when planning your trip. You'll find everything from weather forecasts to virtual tours of famous cities. Be sure to visit Fodors.com (⊕ www.fodors.com), a complete travel-planning site. You can research prices and book plane tickets, hotel rooms, rental cars, vacation packages, and more. In addition, you can post your pressing questions in the Travel Talk section. Other planning tools include a currency converter and weather reports, and there are loads of links to travel resources.

For more information specifically on London, visit one of the following:

The official London Web site is ⊕ www. visitlondon.com, which supplies event information and has accommodations booking with guaranteed lowest rates: if you book through its site and then find a lower price at the same hotel within 24 hours, they'll refund the difference.

Other sites of interest include ⊕ www. londontown.com, the *Evening Standard*'s online ⊕ www.thisislondon.com, Transport for London (⊕ www.tfl.gov.uk), No. 10 Downing Street (⊕ www.number-10. gov.uk), and the BBC (bbc.co.uk).

For London events and news months in advance, visit the following culture and entertainment Web sites: ⊕ www.timeout. co.uk, ⊕ www.officiallondontheatre.co. uk, and ⊕ www.kidslovelondon.com. At ⊕ www.londonfreelist.com you can find great listings of free and nearly free events and attractions.

INDEX

PHOTO CREDITS

Chelsea: 177, *Cahir Davitt/age fotostock*. 178, *Robert Harding Picture Library Ltd./Alamy*. 181, *Joe Viesti/viestiphoto.com*. **Chapter 10: Knightsbridge & Belgravia:** 189, *Doug Scott/age fotostock*. 190, *Atlantide S.N.C./age fotostock*. 193, *David Crausby/Alamy*. **Chapter 11: Notting Hill & Bayswater:** 197, *Dominic Burke/Alamy*. 198, *David H. Wells/age fotostock*. 201, *Doug Scott/age fotostock*. 203 (top left), *Guy Russell/age fotostock*. 203 (left center), *Peter Phipp/age fotostock*. 203 (bottom left), *Janine Wiedel Photolibrary/Alamy*. 203 (right), *Corbis*. 205, *Joe Viesti/viestiphoto.com*. 206, *TNT Magazine/Alamy*. 207 (left), *Andrew Holt/Alamy*. 207 (top right), *Dominic Burke/Alamy*. 207 (bottom right), *Salient Images/Alamy*. **Chapter 12: Regent's Park & Hampstead:** 209, *Earl Patrick Lichfield/British Tourist Authority*. 210, *Bildarchiv Monheim GmbH/Alamy*. 213, *British Tourist Authority*. **Chapter 13: Greenwich:** 223, *Michael Booth/Alamy*. 224, *Walter Bibikow/viestiphoto.com*. 227, *Walter Bibikow/viestiphoto.com*. **Chapter 14: The Thames Upstream:** 233, *British Tourist Authority*. 234, *Danilo Donadoni/Marka/age fotostock*. 237, *Danilo Donadoni/Marka/age fotostock*. **Chapter 15: Where to Eat:** 245, *John Angerson/Alamy*. 246, *Atlantide S.N.C./age fotostock*. **Chapter 16: Where to Stay:** 281, *Danita Delimont/Alamy*. 282, *City Inn Westminster*. **Chapter 17: Pubs & Nightlife:** 333, *Bo Zaunders/viestiphoto.com*. 334, *Everynight Images/Alamy*. **Chapter 18: Arts & Entertainment:** 355, *Lebrecht Music and Arts Photo Library/Alamy*. 356, *Grant Pritchard/British Tourist Authority*. 358, *Jerome Yeats/Alamy*. **Chapter 19: Shopping:** 379, *Ken Ross/viestiphoto.com*. 380, *Chris P. Batson/Alamy*. 382, *Helene Rogers/viestiphoto.com*. 429, *British Tourist Authority*. 430, *British Tourist Authority*. 431, *Ingrid Rasmussen/British Tourist Authority*. 432, *Ingrid Rasmussen/British Tourist Authority*. 433 (top), *Nigel Hicks/British Tourist Authority*. 433 (bottom), *British Tourist Authority*. 434 (top), *British Tourist Authority*. 434 (bottom), *British Tourist Authority*. **Chapter 20: Side Trips from London:** 437, *Andrew Holt/Alamy*. 438, *Mark Sunderland/Alamy*. **Color Section:** Big Ben and the Houses of Parliament at night: *Walter Bibikow/viestiphoto.com*. The boys of Westminster Choir perform at Westminster Abbey: *British Tourist Authority*. Horse-riding in Hyde Park: *The Hoberman/Alamy*. School children study the Parthenon sculptures in the British Museum: *Javier Larrea/age fotostock*. Crossing the Millennium Bridge to St. Paul's Cathedral: *Kathy deWitt/Alamy*. Raising a pint in a London pub: *Jiri Rezac/Alamy*. Skating on the ice rink in the courtyard of Somerset House: *Jasmine Teer/British Tourist Authority*. A waiter adjusts the confectionary delights at Yauatcha: *Herbert Ypma*. The Swiss Re Tower, in the City, at dusk: *Richard Osbourne/Blue Pearl Photographic/Alamy*. Design Museum: *PCL/Alamy*. Museum-goers ponder an installation at the Tate Modern: *Jack Sullivan/Alamy*. A view from a pod in the British Airways London Eye: *Roger Hutchings/Alamy*. A cricket match at Lord's: *Andrew Orchard/British Tourist Authority*. The Changing of the Guard takes place at Buckingham Palace: *Peter Adams/age fotostock*. The Great Court at the British Museum: *Nigel Young/British Museum*. The London Eye and South Bank at night: Eric Nathan/British Tourist Authority.

NOTES

NOTES

NOTES

ABOUT OUR WRITERS

Longtime contributor Robert Andrews loves warm beer and soggy moors, both of which he found in abundance while updating Bath for the Side Trips chapter.

A native New Yorker, Ferne Arfin has been living in London and writing about travel for more than 20 years. A frequent contributor to the *Sunday Telegraph* and Fodor's Travel Wire, Ferne updated the Soho & Covent Garden, Kensington & Chelsea, Knightsbridge & Belgravia, and Shopping chapters, and wrote the Street Markets feature—the perfect assignment, she said, for a dedicated Chelsea shophound.

Texan by birth, New Orleanian by nature, and Anglophile at heart, Christi Daugherty now lives miles from home in London, where she works as a freelance writer and editor. She has written and edited guidebooks for cities around the globe, and this year updated Smart Travel Tips, the Where to Stay chapter, and the Stratford side trip. Her mother wants her to move home.

When freelance journalist and editor Jessica Eveleigh first moved to London she avoided the Tube and walked wherever possible, allowing her to know the capital's backstreets and hidden secrets. Jessica also writes for national magazines and newspapers and, when she's not chasing new leads, can be found surfing. For this edition she updated the South Bank, East End, and Notting Hill & Bayswater chapters, and wrote the British Museum, Westminster Abbey, and Hyde Park & Kensington Garden features.

Julius Honnor has traveled widely but now lives in London. He has written or updated several guidebooks and is a contributor to *Fodor's Great Britain*. For this book he updated Arts & Entertainment as well as Cambridge in the Side Trips chapter.

An Essex boy by birth, James Knight has never quite managed to lose a wide-eyed sense of awe at London that comes only from being brought up just outside it. Stalking the streets of south London as a local correspondent for a doomed cable-television channel was the perfect excuse to start exploring the capital's nooks and crannies. James has written for Reuters, the BBC, the *Sunday Times,* the *Economist,* the *New Statesman,* and other publications.

Life-long London resident Katrina Manson has sailed the Thames in a wooden bathtub, danced on the stage of the London Palladium, and sold cheese at one of its smartest delis. She has written for Reuters, the BBC, the *Times,* the *Independent,* the *Guardian,* and several magazines. On the rare occasions that Katrina leaves the capital, you'll find her reporting from less-frequented countries in Africa.

James and Katrina co-wrote the Experience London, and Thames Upstream chapters, including the Tour of the Thames and Tower of London features.

Kristan Schiller has spent the last decade following her wanderlust through Africa, Asia, and the South Pacific, but she always relishes returning home to the comforts of London. Kristan updated the St. James's & Mayfair, Bloomsbury & Legal London, Regent's Park & Hampstead, and Pubs & Nightlife chapters for this edition.

Travel writer and editor Hilary Weston is one half of the South England–based writing team Apostrophe S, which has covered European cities from Dublin to Rome. Hilary wrote the St. Paul's Cathedral feature.

By day, Londoner Alex Wijeratna fights global hunger as an activist for ActionAid International; by night, he beats hunger by truffling out the best eateries in town for the Where to Eat chapter. With his mixed roots, Alex is well aware that London's restaurant boom is built on its ethnic diversity—and on a wall of money from the City's global finance center. He has written mainly for newspapers, including the *Daily Mail* and the *London Times.*